D1540096

Horrors!
365 Scary Stories

Horrors!
365 Scary Stories

Selected by
Stefan Dziemianowicz,
Robert Weinberg
& Martin H. Greenberg

MetroBooks

2001 MetroBooks

ISBN 1-5866-3240-X

Printed and bound in the United States of America

01 02 03 04 05 MC 10 9 8 7 6 5 4

FG

For bulk purchases and special sales, please contact:
Friedman/Fairfax Publishers
Attention: Sales Department
230 Fifth Avenue, Suite 700-701
New York, NY 10001
212/685-6610 Fax 212/685-3916

Visit our website:
www.metrobooks.com

Contents

Introduction

Do you fear the dark? Does the idea of the supernatural scare you? Do you sometimes anticipate the worst that can happen to you? Do you shiver when you read about victims of violent crime and think "that could have been me?" Are you apprehensive about what might be around the next corner when you walk down an unfamiliar street? Have you ever worried that life may have no meaning? Are you ever anxious that the next day might be your last? Do your days sometimes seem irremediably gloomy? Are you afraid of dying?

If you answered yes to any of the questions above, we have bad news: You are suffering from a terminal affliction known as the human condition. It is incurable and irreversible.

The good news is that it can be treated palliatively. Working with experts who share your symptoms, we have developed a therapeutic regimen tailored to meet your specific needs. There are no bitter pills or painful shots involved, no prolonged procedures or complicated rehabilitation programs. It takes just a moment of your time, and you won't even feel it. Put simply, we prescribe a daily dose of horror.

The rationale for our therapeutic approach is simple: That which does not kill us makes us stronger. This may seem a drastic formula, but consider what specialists have long known—regular exposure to the source of our malaise eventually builds resistance to it.

A daily dose of horror is just the tonic you need. It fortifies the spirit with bracing jolts of terror. It inoculates the soul against the fears that hound us all. It quickens the reflexes against life's inhospitable surprises, and tempers the imagination with thoughts unthinkable.

We have examined your case thoroughly and think you will find that we have prepared the perfect antidote for your condition.

Experiencing intimations of mortality? Then try a vampire story to get a taste of immortality.

Does life seem a little insane? Here you'll find madmen in a variety of shapes and sizes who will help make things seem more rational.

Feeling a bit self-absorbed? There's nothing like a tale of otherworldly horrors to give you the right perspective.

Or maybe you're not yourself these days. How about a ghost story to show you others who are even less so?

Here's a year's supply of horrors. They're just what the doctor ordered (and never mind that his name is Jekyll). We guarantee you'll feel much better once your treatment has begun. And remember: A horror a day keeps even worse things away.

—*Stefan Dziemianowicz*
New York, 1997

A-Huntin' We Will Go

Linda J. Dunn

Jeremy walked slowly toward his victim.

"Did you get the deer, son?" his dad asked.

Jeremy stared down at the deformed body lying at his feet. "I think I shot a goat."

"Damn!" His dad spat at the ground before stomping over to kick the lifeless form.

"Don't look like no goat I've ever seen. Shit!"

Jeremy almost fell backward as his dad flipped the goat's head around and they both saw the single horn. His dad hesitated only a second before whipping open his fanny pack and pulling out the folding hacksaw.

"Not a word of this to anyone. Ever."

"But, Dad—"

"You heard me," he said, sawing off the animal's right foreleg just below the knee. "Ain't no way we want to get caught with something like this in our possession. I'll finish off these legs and you toss them in the creek back there. We'll leave the guts for the coyotes and I'll carry the rest back to camp."

He tossed the first leg in Jeremy's direction and started sawing again.

Jeremy stared at the thing his dad was working on. Unicorns were supposed to be beautiful, horselike animals. This thing was ugly as sin.

"Got it, Jer?"

Jeremy looked up and blinked. For just a moment, he thought he saw something moving nearby.

"Jer! You paying attention to me or are you off daydreaming again?"

"Huh?" Jeremy looked down and realized there were four leg parts in front of him. "You want me to toss them now?"

"If you can manage."

The sarcasm in his father's voice hurt. Jeremy tried. He really did. Hunting just wasn't his thing. Neither was baseball.

Hockey and football were out too. He'd rather be home in front of the computer.

He picked up the still-warm legs and walked a few feet to the ditch. He tried not to think about it as he pitched the stuff aside, but he felt the still-warm blood trickling down his wrist.

He lost it.

Leaning against the nearest tree, he vomited up everything he'd eaten for breakfast and then dry-heaved.

His dad walked up beside him and slapped him on the back. "Just wait till we've done this a few times. You'll learn to love it."

Jeremy wiped his mouth with his shirtsleeve as his dad shoved something at him.

"Here. Stick this in your pack."

"What is it?"

"The horn. I thought you might like to have a trophy."

"Oh, gawd. It really was a uni—"

"Shut up. There ain't no such thing. Some kind of mutant. That's all."

"It was a unicorn," Jeremy whispered as his dad picked up the animal's remains. "And I killed it."

He stuffed the horn into his pack and stumbled to his feet. His dad strolled along like they were off for a friendly hike, while Jeremy's feet felt like someone had tied lead weights to them. His stomach tossed and turned and he stopped several times to heave while leaning against trees for support.

As soon as they reached their campsite, his dad dropped the thing near the remains of their last fire. "At least we'll have some meat tonight."

"Huh?"

"You think I'm gonna let this go to waste? Damn bony piece but it's still better than eating out of cans again. Now get me a fire started while I fetch some more wood."

Jeremy stared at his dad while his words sank in. "You mean we're going to eat that uni— thing?"

His dad spat at the ground. "You gone soft on me, boy?"

Jeremy shook his head. "No sir."

"Good! Fix the fire. I'll be back in a few minutes."

But he didn't return. Not that night and never again. The police had no theories and neither did his mom. Only Jeremy knew what happened and he would never tell.

When darkness fell, the woods filled with an eerie music like nothing he'd ever heard before. Creatures from his maddest nightmares filed into the camp and carried off the unicorn's remains in some kind of funeral procession. He watched from his tent, terrified of being seen yet unable to turn away. The very last thing he saw was his father at the end of the procession, following the creatures off into the darkness.

The horn is in Jeremy's room now, sitting atop his computer monitor. At night, when the air is still, he can almost hear music far away.

And the horn glows bright gold.

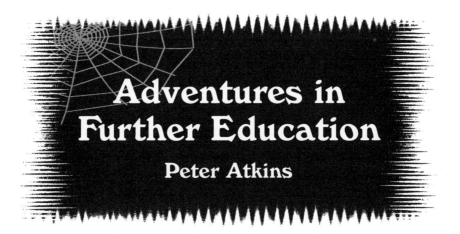

Adventures in Further Education

Peter Atkins

Kenny tapped the pen on the surface of his desk for the seventeen thousand, four hundred and thirty-sixth time.

There was nothing the matter with him. It wasn't like it was an obsession or anything. It wasn't like he didn't do anything else. Since his sixth-grade teacher had first introduced the idea to him twenty years ago, he'd done all the normal things—he'd graduated from high school, he'd graduated from college, he'd met Tiffany, fallen in love, married, fathered two children, and found himself a perfectly respectable job in a perfectly respectable firm. There was nothing unusual about Kenny except his little hobby. And that's all it was—a hobby. He didn't bother anybody with it. In fact, nobody knew he did it, not even Tiffany. It was just a hobby, an interest, an experiment that nobody else had ever had the patience to see through.

Mr. Neill had only tapped *his* pen five times, for example.

"So it's theoretically possible," Mr. Neill had said, sounding almost as bored as the fifty twelve-year-olds who were pretending to listen to him, "that, if you kept tapping this pen on this desk long enough, one time it would just slip through the surface."

He'd been giving the class a glimpse of the New Physics, a taste of the theories that were revolutionizing the way scientists looked at the world, a hint that the matter that made up the forms of this world which everyone accepted as solid and separate was in fact all one and that only probability kept everything as it was and kept our reality apart from a multiverse of others.

Kenny hadn't been particularly interested in the theoretical and metaphysical implications of what Mr. Neill was saying. He was twelve years old, for Christ's sake. He'd just thought it would be really fucking cool to see a pen slip through a desk and had been disappointed when, after his fifth tap, Mr. Neill had put his pen down and moved on to something else.

Quietly, and without drawing anybody's attention, Kenny had started tapping his pen. And counting.

Seventeen thousand, four hundred and thirty-seven. Seventeen thousand, four hundred and thirty-eight.

It wasn't the same desk, of course. It was the sixth desk since he'd started. But it was the same pen (dry now of ink, chewed up and useless for anything but its secret purpose), and that had to count for something.

The phone rang. Kenny picked it up, dealt with the call, hung up. He laid the pen down throughout the call and it didn't bother him at all. After all, he wasn't crazy. Life had to be lived. Work had to be done. His experiment required patience and tenacity, and Kenny prided himself on possessing plenty of both.

Seventeen thousand, four hundred and thirty-nine. Seventeen thousand, four hundred and forty. Seventeen thousand, four hundred and . . .

The pen slid effortlessly and smoothly into the desk.

Kenny, letting go instinctively, threw himself back in his chair, an adrenal shock of surprised fulfillment shooting through his entire body. He looked up, ready to shout his triumph to the rest of the large open-plan office.

But the office wasn't there.

Kenny was staring at a kaleidoscope world of shifting, flickering lights, a surfaceless void with an unimaginably distant vanishing point near which huge amorphous shapes twisted and writhed in a constant fury of becoming. Lightning in colors he couldn't name seared across the infinite and multihued sky in jagged shards the size of which he couldn't conceive. Alien winds screamed their impossible being in warring cacophonies of notes he couldn't believe at volumes he couldn't bear.

Had he still had hands, Kenny would have grabbed at his chair (had there still been a chair). Had he still had a mouth, Kenny would have screamed. Had he still had eyes, Kenny would have closed them.

Had he still had his pen, Kenny would have started tapping.

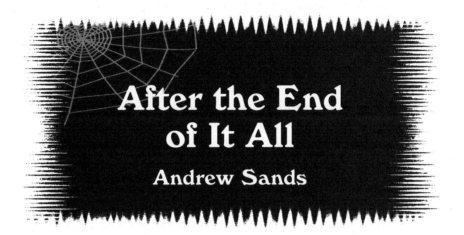

After the End of It All

Andrew Sands

It is after the end of it all and she is trying to keep from going insane. She walks through what is left of the city, stopping at odd piles of rubble here and there, imagining the places they used to be, imagining the people that had once filled them. She cries whenever she does this and she does this often. The lids around her eyes have begun to swell; they are always sore, always tender. She doesn't know whether it is the radiation or just the constant tears. She doesn't care.

The winds pick up and when they do they make an eerie whining noise wherever they whisk through gaps and funnels in the wreckage. It sounds as if everything around her is screaming. Whenever the wailing of this dead city is too much for her, she opens her mouth and screams along with it. She thinks, maybe, it will help her fit in.

She is utterly, completely, hopelessly alone.

She had long ago stopped talking out loud to herself; she had stopped looking for other survivors. She used to spend part of her daylight hours sitting and staring at the cover of a fashion magazine she had found in the clutter. Now she never looks at it, just carries the thing constantly, rolled tight into a small tube, cover facing inward, locked in the grip of her swelling fist. She never lets go of it, even when she sleeps.

Underground, in the demolished subway station where she lives, she lies in the darkness and lets the bloated, slow-moving bugs crawl over her at night. She does this, unmoving on the cracked tile floor, with eyes shut and mouth wide open. Whenever a bug scuttles into her mouth, she bites down on it, chews, swallows. This is how she eats. This is what is keeping her alive.

After she has eaten her fill, she gets up and lights a candle. Her movement always sends the bugs scurrying away. The dim, constant glow keeps them at a distance. It is only then, in that small, flickering cup of wavering light, that she can fall asleep. That's the way it is: she eats in the dark, she sleeps in the light. This system works for her. There are plenty of bugs; she has found many matches, many candles.

She snaps awake automatically when her candle burns out. She hears things moving around in the darkness. Close to her, something large, larger than the bugs, larger than anything she had seen or heard in a long, long time, rustles and clomps.

She isn't afraid, or even surprised. There is not enough left in her emotional reservoir for her to do anything but tighten her grip on the rolled magazine and listen.

A quick scratching sound, then something flares. A small spot of light glides like a firefly toward her. Another flare, then a dull yellow glow. Someone had struck a match, lit another of her candles.

"I haven't seen anyone since the end of it all," she says. Her voice is raw and flat, and she finds her throat hurts when she speaks.

A short, thin man steps into the light. He wears thick, round glasses and has a brushy, reddish mustache. His head is bald and chapped and dirty. In one dangling hand he carries a stained canvas shopping bag. "Found some others . . . from time to time . . . out there," is all he says.

He walks closer to her. He lifts his free hand and lets his fingers skim the side of her cheek. The edge of his fingers are ragged, her cheeks are sore, but the gesture is intended to be gentle, so she doesn't pull away. His fingers feel better on her face than the tiny legs of the bugs.

She starts to sob. Not from anguish, not from loneliness, not from impotent anger or hunger or madness; she cries from happiness. Long-dormant, long-forgotten emotions twitch to life inside her. *Someone* is standing next to her. *She isn't the only one left.* She won't have to be alone anymore. *Not alone.*

"You're the most beautiful woman in the world," he says to her. His voice is softer than his touch.

6

She hasn't heard that description in a long time; the sound of those words makes her weep even more.

"I . . . used to be . . ." she trembles. She can barely speak. She removes the magazine from her fist, unrolls it for the first time in too long. She points to the cover. A bikini-clad model frolics in the blue ocean surf. "Tha . . . that's me . . . It is. Really. That . . . used to be . . . me."

The man squints at the picture. He smiles and reaches into his shopping bag. He pulls out the frayed remains of a newspaper, one of the city's more sensational tabloids. He pokes at the front page, pointing with pride.

"That's me," he beams and taps the headline, "That's me." Next to his dirty-nailed finger are the words TORSO KILLER STRIKES AGAIN.

He pulls something else out of his shopping bag and takes another step forward. The candle tips over just then, and everything again is absolute darkness. Outside, the wind kicks up; it screams across the night. Well, maybe it's the wind.

After the Hook

David Annandale

We all know the story. The secluded spot. The car. The necking couple. The report on the radio of the hook-handed killer. The terrified girl. The annoyed boy. The peel-out. The return home. The boy's faint. The hook dangling from the car door.

Yes, yes, we know this. But what next? What happens *after?*

Well, what do you think? The girl runs into the house and calls the police. They tell her to stay calm, that they'll be right over. The words of reassurance, of the end of a story, of happily ever after.

But not in this kind of story. In this realm, those words are the lie of an Indian summer, of false dawn, and of the eye of the storm. In this story, the girl, who *thinks* the tale is done, who cannot read the shadows around her, goes outside again to try to wake up her boyfriend. She realizes, one beat behind and far too late, what sort of story this is when she sees that her boyfriend is gone. And so, of course, is the hook.

She stands frozen for the space of one deep, shuddering breath. Then she looks back at the house, at the door which she has left open. She runs inside, a moan rising from a core of solid fear. She slams the door and locks it.

But her back was turned for a few moments outside. She knows this, and knows also that a few moments is all it would take. So now the house is hostile. The only lights she turned on earlier were in the entrance and the living room. Everywhere else is dark: the house as jungle, where be tigers. Shadows lick and snarl at the edge of light, flexing their muscles and doing what they do best: concealing. Even the objects she can see are enemies now, because they are keeping secrets. They know, but aren't telling. Outside isn't an option, because that is the great river of shadows, of which the house is only a tributary.

She crouches down, huddling against the front door. She will stay here, in the light, by the exit, until the police arrive. She will not step into the shadows, or search the house, or check the basement. She will not follow this storyline anymore. She gets off now.

Only it doesn't work that way. She hasn't ended the story. She has merely stopped reading. This changes nothing. The last few pages will always be there, waiting. Nothing will happen until she moves. The police will never arrive. They can't until it is too late. The shadows are patient, as is their secret. They have all the time in the world. The narrative has been frozen, but the ending will not change.

And the girl? At some level she knows all this. But she doesn't want to die, and really, who can blame her? Not that what she wants matters. The story wills out. So she crouches, becoming cramped and sore, throat torn by the jagged edges of her sobs. She is trapped on the steel point of a moment in time, wriggling. Skewered.

Hooked.

After Work

Steve Rasnic Tem

Derek got home late after work. His eyes burned. He probably looked like he'd been crying, he thought. And his neck bothered him. No amount of rubbing helped the pain in his neck.

The kitchen was empty. No signs of cooking. No signs that Marie had even bothered to fix herself lunch. Several wadded tissues littered the floor; the box on the counter was empty.

The house held its breath. The cold quiet was a familiar song for Derek. He plopped down in a kitchen chair and hung his head. "Ah . . . Marie," he said softly to the yellowing floor. "Please, Marie. This has gotta stop." Despite the cold he couldn't stop perspiring. Sweat from his forehead oozed into his right eye. It burned like some kind of chemical. Both eyes watered, spilled. "Oh, sweet Marie."

Derek climbed from the chair with painful effort. He walked to their bedroom, pushed open the door.

Marie hung from the light fixture, head tilted as if questioning, face the color and apparent consistency of blended children's clay, like the kind their only daughter had used. Derek had sent their daughter to live with his parents months ago.

A kiss of blood spotted the left-hand corner of Marie's mouth. Something new. He supposed she'd bitten her tongue.

Derek felt the wetness on his cheeks, used two fingers to touch it, wipe it away. He imagined he could tell the difference between sweat and tears just by touching. He wondered if blood felt different.

He stared at her. Not for the last time, he knew. Marie had always been such a beautiful woman.

"Christ, Marie," he said, and he could feel her name breaking up in his throat. "Why do you *do* this to me?"

He walked around her. He picked up the fallen chair and set it aside. He reached out to touch her, hesitated, then changed his mind.

"I'm going back," he told her. "I volunteered for a double shift."

Marie opened her eyes. She looked at him wordlessly. She reached up her hands to loosen the noose, slipped out of it, and dropped to the floor. The deep purple crease in her neck looked brilliant and artificial, like the latest trend in makeup. But of course Derek knew it was real. She raised a hand to either side of her head and pushed it upright. She leaned over and spat a mouthful of blood onto the rug. She looked at him again, her eyes whiter, wider than anyone's Derek had ever seen. "You're always working," she said. "You bastard. You're always leaving me alone."

"I did the best for us I knew how. You and the baby," he replied.

"A *double* shift?" she said, walking in circles, gazing up at the empty noose. "How many times is that this week? You're wearing yourself out. You're killing yourself."

Derek started to titter. Then he lost himself in exhausted laughter. Marie eyed him coolly. "Killing yourself?" He laughed again. "Why *shouldn't* I be working two shifts? Why would I want to come home, when half the time I pretty much know what I'm going to find here? I'm going to find *you!* How many times is *that* this week?" he repeated, and gestured at the noose.

She strolled clumsily over to the chair. He didn't think she could move any faster, or better. She moved the chair under the light. "Marie!" he shouted. "You know I don't deserve this!" She climbed up on the chair, weaving as she reached up for the noose. "Ah . . . Marie," he moaned in resignation.

She positioned the noose around her neck and tightened it. She held her head to the side just so. She kicked the chair out from under her. She kicked.

Once again she had hanged herself, and once again Derek had to look at her and think how beautiful she used to be.

Along for the Ride

Tim Waggoner

Alan sat behind the wheel of the silver Camry—or rather what appeared to be a silver Camry—and stared out at the highway rolling toward him, his hands resting limply in his lap.

His throat felt caked with dust and his stomach was an empty aching pit. How long had it been since he'd had something to eat or drink? Days? Weeks? Surely not weeks; he would have died of thirst by now. Unless of course the car—or whatever it was—was doing something to keep him alive.

He was so weak. He would've slumped over some time ago, but the seat gripped him tightly and kept him upright in order to maintain the illusion of car and driver. At least that's what Alan thought. He had no way to be certain.

It was just after dawn and the highway was deserted. They were completely alone on the road, so the car didn't bother feigning the sound of a working engine. They glided across the asphalt silently, their motion slightly off, as if the vehicle weren't moving by rolling along on tires but rather by some other mechanism. Alan had the impression of thousands, maybe millions of scuttling insect legs, but that could very well have been due to his delirium. He was so weak, so tired. But the car wouldn't let him sleep. For some reason, it needed him awake. Perhaps it couldn't feed as effectively if he slept.

Several days—weeks?—back, Alan had been blazing down State Route 38, heading for a sales meeting in Cleveland. He had plenty of time, the meeting wasn't until the next day, but he was paranoid about missing it, so he pushed his old Sentra's little engine as hard as he could to squeeze as much speed out of it as possible.

And so he had flashed right by the silver Camry parked alongside the road, barely registering at first that its hood was up and a blonde woman was inspecting the engine. But over the next couple of miles, the impressions of what he had seen filtered into his consciousness, and he realized what he'd passed: a motorist, maybe a good-looking one, in trouble.

Ordinarily Alan didn't stop to help out people with car problems. After all, these days you could never tell. You could end up delivering yourself into the hands of a robber, or worse, a serial killer. But Route 38 wasn't used all that much. It could be some time before anyone else came along to help her. Besides, despite his haste, he knew he had plenty of time to get to Cleveland.

He took the next exit and turned around.

She looked relieved when he pulled up behind her Camry and parked. Alan gave her his best smile as he got out of his car.

"Having some trouble?"

She smiled back weakly. "You don't know the half of it."

Now that he was closer, he could see that her white blouse and jeans hung loosely on her. Her hair was tangled and matted, eyes sunken into the sockets, cheeks drawn tight against the bone, lips dry and chapped. Was she sick? He felt a strong instinct to get back into his car and get the hell out of there, but he didn't. He couldn't very well leave her stranded like this.

"I'm not much with cars, but let me take a look," he said. But as he walked past the driver's side of her vehicle, the Camry's door flew open and the seat reached out toward him.

As it pulled him in, he thought he heard the woman say, "I'm sorry," before collapsing to the ground.

And then the door slammed shut.

The car had taken care of the woman's body—waste not, want not—before pulling onto the road, leaving his Sentra behind. Over the years, Alan had always wondered where all the abandoned cars parked along the highway came from. Now he knew.

He didn't have much energy left, and he could feel the car's hunger for a fresh supply growing. It wouldn't be long before they'd be stopping soon, not long before he was forced to stand before the open hood and stare down into what only resembled an engine, before he was used as a lure for another foolish Samaritan.

He prayed to God it would be soon.

And Baby Makes 13

Del Stone Jr.

So tell me," Dr. Harvey Radcliff said, coaxing a squeak from his chair, "how have you been taking care of yourself?"

The woman gave him an odd stare. Her name was Judith Bloome, and she was a thin-framed, moon-pale lacewing of a woman who did not wear her sixth month of pregnancy well. Her stomach swelled from her slender body like an insect egg case grafted to a twig. Dr. Radcliff smiled inwardly at the image. The company, he knew, would not be amused.

"As far as I know, I'm doing all the right things," she answered warily. "Why do you ask? Is there a problem?"

Dr. Radcliff chuckled. "It's just my way of making sure my patients stick to the regimen—especially my first-time mothers."

Judith nodded and patted her stomach tiredly. "I'll sure be glad when this is over," she groaned. "I feel like I'm giving birth to a bowling ball."

"First pregnancies are always like that," he said.

She groaned again. "I think this one will be my last."

Dr. Radcliff mentally seconded that notion. In his fifteen years as an obstetrician with Orthon Agricultural Applications, he had seen his share of company wives, and with a single office visit he could predict which ones would go on to have large families, and which ones would call it quits after their first pregnancy. Judith Bloome, he knew, fell into the latter category.

"Let me run a few questions by you," he went on, adding quickly, "just to make sure. Now. You haven't been smoking."

"Smoking by pregnant women may result in fetal injury, premature birth, and low birth weight," Judith answered, reciting the warning on cigarette packs.

"Alcohol?"

She shook her head.

"Drugs?"

"Nothing except Pepto-Bismol," she said.

"And you are continuing to exercise."

"I walk every day. And do housework."

"Sleeping well?"

She shrugged. "Sometimes not, but most of the time, yeah."

"Mood swings?"

"Not really," she shook her head. "Sometimes I get mad at my husband for not helping around the house more, but I try to understand. He works at the plant all day. . . ."

"What division does your husband work in?"

"Hormonicides. They make growth regulators—pesticides that kill bugs by messing with their hormones."

Dr. Radcliff nodded. "How's your diet?"

"Lots of fruits and vegetables," she said proudly.

"Where do you buy your produce?" he asked casually. "The company market?"

She blushed and did not answer immediately. He said, "It's OK," and she stammered, "Well, I get them from the grocery store. I think the produce tastes better than the stuff from the company store."

So it's the husband, Dr. Radcliff realized, nodding thoughtfully. But he said nothing about that. Instead, he told her, "Well, that's all I need to know for today. You're doing fine. Come see me again in a month and we'll get an update on how things are going."

Judith struggled from the chair and smiled wanly, an undercurrent of uncertainty in her expression. "You understand about the produce thing," she said. "I mean, the company is so wonderful about providing medical care and subsidized groceries and all. . . . I almost feel like a traitor for shopping downtown."

Dr. Radcliff laughed and shooed her toward the door. "The company doesn't care where its employees shop, so don't you worry about that. Save your energy for carrying that extra load."

She beamed at him as she turned to go out the door, and for the first time that afternoon a bloom of health rose in her cheeks. Dr. Radcliff almost felt sorry for her.

Because there was no denying the X-rays. The real X-rays, not the substitutes he had shown her. The real X-rays revealed eleven tiny, oblong, chitinous skulls encased within her womb, and folds of multiple legs layered along pulsating thoraxes. Ants, or bees, or some horrible permutation of life that was never meant to be.

"The husband," Dr. Radcliff muttered, shoving Judith Bloome's paperwork into the special blue file in his desk drawer. There were four other folders in the file.

"He works around that shit all day, and gets it inside him, and voilà! Dr. Harvey Radcliff collects another half million in hush money. Isn't that a gas?"

But the company, he knew, would not be amused.

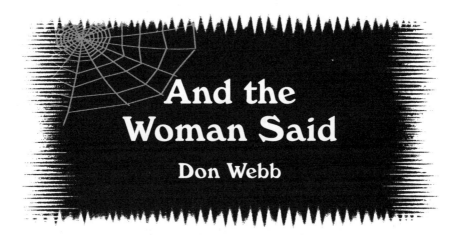

And the Woman Said

Don Webb

I got this phone call from a woman I didn't know and the woman said, "Your wife's cheating on you. She's cheating with my husband." I was shocked and sickened at this call.

"My wife's dead," I said.

"Well I can't do anything about that, but I wanted you to know about the other."

I figured the caller was drunk, or crazy, or somebody with a really sick attitude. I went to my front room where my wife's ashes were in a vase, and I thought about her—about my wife—for a moment.

And the phone rang.

It was the same woman and the same message and I hung up. And the phone rang.

So after a horrible couple of days I went to the phone company and had my number changed.

And the phone rang.

I hung up on her, and then I went to my wife's urn. I wanted to hold it. It was too light. It was empty.

And the phone rang.

"You see, she is not there, she is out cheating with my husband."

The woman called again and again—and something *snapped* in my mind. It started to make sense. Why shouldn't the dead cheat on the living? Why not? The grave is quite lonely, and it may be decades before even the most faithful spouse rejoins his lost companion.

The woman's voice on the phone began to sound less crazy, less hostile, less cold. In fact she was friendly, warm.

"What should we do?" I asked.

"We should cheat on them. You and I should get together and cheat on them."

I immediately thought yes, but it was some weeks before I could say the word aloud.

"How will I meet you? How will I know you?" I asked.

"Go open your window, look out to the park."

"I don't see anyone."

"I'm coming."

"What do you look like?"

"In life I was a stunning redhead with long legs and liquid brown eyes."

"In life?"

"I died in the same car crash as my husband. I was cremated at the same time."

A breeze began to blow in my window. Fine ash swirled around and up my nose.

"All I want," the voice said, "is to be with someone. I lied about your wife just so I could come to you."

I tried to cover my face, to stop the ash as it filled my lungs, choking me. I fell and the receiver hit the floor.

I am with her now. Always and forever.

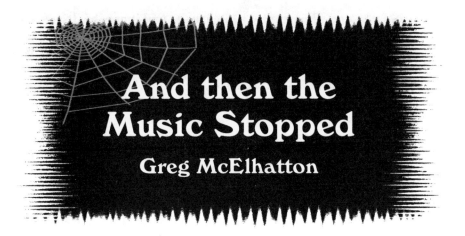

And then the Music Stopped

Greg McElhatton

The seven children walked in a circle, the music singing merrily about them. "Tra la la," the music warbled. "Tra la la la." Carrie wiped her eyes. She'd just turned nine last week. She could still remember eating cake, opening the presents. Carrie glanced at Gina, who was still trying to look tough. Carrie knew better. She'd seen Gina cry over a skinned knee. Carrie was as tough as Gina. Tougher. And Carrie kept crying.

And then the music stopped.

Carrie jumped into the chair, wrapped her arms around the back. She was safe, she was safe, she was safe! Carrie hugged the chair tightly, looking around with wide eyes. Gina was in one of the other chairs, Paul and Jason in the next two. Don was huddled in the fifth chair, sniffling. Felicity clutched the last chair triumphantly. And Shannon . . . Shannon wasn't in a chair.

With a shriek, Shannon vanished. The voice began to sing. And the children found themselves marching around five chairs, prisoners to the song that continued on its merry little way.

"I don't wanna play," Don whimpered. "I wanna go home . . ."

Felicity glared at Don. "He's trying to mess us up! It's not gonna work. I'm not gonna lose!" Felicity bit her lip, anger on her face, and continued marching in a circle.

"I want my momma," Don sniffled. "I wanna go home. I wanna go play with Shannon and Jon and Chris and . . ."

"You can't!" Gina snapped. "They're . . . they're gone! Gone like the chairs! Gone like you're gonna be!" Gina drew in her breath angrily. "Don, will you just be quiet?"

And then the music stopped.

The children scattered for chairs, Gina moving a split second slower than the rest. Gina barely had time to scream before she vanished like so many before her.

"I did it," Don whispered. "I . . . I made Gina go away. It's all my fault!"

"It is not," Carrie said, her voice trembling. "It's all our fault. We knew not to come here. We knew not to play the games." She shivered, the air suddenly cold. "We knew." She tried to ignore the mindless babble of the song, except that she couldn't, she couldn't. She had to keep listening. Paul and Jason were looking at the faraway doors again. Maybe they were thinking of running for the way out, trying to escape. Carrie remembered what happened to the last one who tried that. Carrie trudged forward.

And then the music stopped.

Another shuffle, another moment of panic. Another scream, this one belonging to Jason. Paul began to cry for the first time since the game began. And there were three chairs left.

"We can do it," Paul finally whispered. "We all run for the door. No one sits in a chair. If no one sits, the game can't make us lose."

Don sniffled. "How do you know?"

"It's got to be! If we don't sit down, it's like the music doesn't stop. We just keep running."

Carrie thought Paul sounded like he was making it up as fast as he could talk, but she didn't care. It sounded like a way out. A way they could all win. "Okay," Carrie whispered back.

"Felicity?" Paul asked, the music masking their voices as they trudged around the three chairs. Felicity merely nodded. "Okay . . . ready, set . . ."

And then the music stopped.

"Go!" Paul shouted, running across the old floorboards, Don shaking and running after him. Carrie took half a step, and then froze . . . as Felicity turned back around and scrambled for a chair.

"Felicity!" Carrie screamed in terror. She looked at Paul and Don, so close to the exit . . . and and Felicity about to sit down. Carrie chose and jumped.

"Just us left," Felicity whispered, Don's and Paul's screams echoing faintly. "Just us left." The two walked around and around the single chair.

"I hate you," Carrie lashed out. "I hate you!"

"I . . ." Felicity looked like she was going to say something, then thought better of it. The two said nothing as the voice sang along.

And then the music stopped.

"I won," she whispered, the other girl fading away. "I won." Felicity stood up, the final chair vanishing like all the others had. "I can go now." She took a step toward the door . . .

And then the music started.

Felicity looked around in a panic. "Where are the chairs?" she whimpered. "Where are the chairs? What do I do?" She looked around frantically. There had to be something! What was she forgetting? Where was the chair? Whom was she playing against?

And then the music stopped.

Anniversary

Aaron Vanek

Today is our anniversary. Before dawn, I drove out to the site. It hasn't changed much; I guess you leave things like this the way they are. I parked a few feet away, and poked over the splintered concrete, broken and pulverized in some places, roughly hewn and graffiti covered in others. The metal from the old tower twists unnaturally. Covered in a faint red rust, the tower reminds me of an iron scorpion, wrenched and ripped like a dying beast, left in the desert to rot. Not all the remains have been devoured by time and the elements. An obelisk, black and made of stone, has not changed. It was placed here after the event. The plaque on the obelisk reads TRINITY SITE: WHERE THE WORLD'S FIRST NUCLEAR DEVICE WAS EXPLODED ON JULY 16, 1945.

I was so happy to be on the Trinity project. I had just finished my Ph.D. in mechanical engineering from the University of Chicago. Dr. Fermi, my proctor, recommended me to Kenneth Bainbridge, an old colleague of his who worked for the war department in special engineering. My acceptance of the position was an overture.

Robert Oppenheimer conducted the team. He made me nervous every time he came in the room, more than the radioactive isotopes. Robert was skinny, wiry—a charged capacitor. Oppie pushed us, and we fell down. Again and again. The timing mechanism wasn't right, the detonators failed to fire, the chicken switches, designed to stop the test during countdown, were off-line. When he heard about the plutonium core not fitting into the "gadget," as we called it, he had a fit. As soon as the core cooled down though, it slid in easily. We had left the core in the back of the car on the ride to the site, and it expanded in the New Mexico heat. We fell, but we got back up every time.

The night before the test, a thunderstorm came crashing in on us. The gadget was hanging from a hundred-foot tower we constructed. Robert was worried that it was too damn easy to sabotage, so we got Don, the youngest, to babysit. He returned to our bunker at dawn after the skies cleared. I wondered what it must have been like, thunder and lightning furious and raging around you, an atom splitter by your side. It must have been wonderful.

Morning peeked over the mesas, a hot, dry July yawning. I slept very little. Cramped in our tight concrete bunker, thousands of yards away, bets were being placed, some to guess how many tons of TNT would be released, and others to wager whether the explosion would start a chain reaction in the atmosphere. I thought, we all thought, of families, of friends, of implications. Yet we progressed. A roller coaster obeys physics, not men.

The last thirty seconds started ticking. Don began counting down, louder and clearer over the whispering of man's brightest scientists praying under their breath. *It's a bust*, I thought. He stopped counting at two. He must have misjudged slightly, because I never heard him say one.

A flash of light, like a thousand thousand suns, shot over us. I gasped; my eyes closed. Swirling white dots and swaths of color danced behind my lids. I opened them again, and I saw the cloud, rising slowly like a god, on the horizon. A deep violet glow surrounded us, and I thought, I thought to myself, *How beautiful!* Then the roar reached us. It built up, a crescendo, throbbing louder and louder until it filled my head, and I had to cover my ears as it crashed and pulsed over my body. I could feel it in me. Echoes from the nearby mountains swelled around it, a chorus, singing the glory and praises. I thought of recording it, if only I could, that music, that enlightening, divine music. Each note was an atom, split apart in a millisecond, scattered and bounced off others, breaking into a symphony of chaos.

I stand over the plaque, dull and cloudy. I wipe it off with my handkerchief, and see myself in the reflection, dabbing away a tear of happiness. I sing joy to my latest work, my coda. I can hear it coming now.

Another Night

Brian McNaughton

When he was old (Scheherazade said), Abdul Muhammad took a wife who shone among the stars of his harem like the noonday sun. I could go on about the glories of her eyes, of her breasts, of her hair, of her buttocks, but other women have such things, and one would go astray by thinking of other women while trying to picture the perfections of Farashah. Only a man who had seen her glories unveiled could summon them to his mind's eye, and the only man who had so seen them was Abdul Muhammad.

Or so he hoped.

He was fat and ugly, but he also fancied himself wise because he knew this, and because he knew that her protestations of love must be false. She was even younger than his favorite mare. She must want a young stallion. He did his best to be one, but this made him wheeze and see spots. When Farashah urged him to moderate his passion lest he should do himself harm, he took this for proof that her love was feigned.

"How could I not love you?" she asked. "You have seen all, you have done all, your mind is vast and various as the world. All eyes look to you, and they see one who knows who he is and where he stands just as surely as a mountain. The words of youth are as feathers to the gold of your speech, and all hoard it greedily. You remind me of my father."

He was pleased with this little speech until the end of it, for her father was a twittering boy of forty. Yet he smiled and began to toy with her in the hope of proving himself an even younger boy.

Whenever he came upon her unawares, Farashah would be singing softly or smiling. Commanded to explain these quirks, she confessed that she was in love, but she flung herself in his arms before he could even begin to roar, "Aha!" and cried, "With you!"

He charged her ladies and eunuchs to watch her and one another with redoubled vigilance. After pondering these interviews, he banished a woman who sported a nascent mustache and sent two of the eunuchs back to the surgeon for refreshment.

When no one reported any suspicious conduct, he concluded that the servants were conspiring with her to make a fool of him. He must put her love to a test.

In a far corner of his gardens stood a bell tower, last vestige of a structure raised by infidels. He imported workmen to the ruin and had them labor quietly by night. The gold he gave them was more than enough to smooth their frowns of puzzlement.

When the work was done, he showed Farashah the key to the tower.

"Urgent business calls me to Basrah, and I must entrust you with my life," he said. "When my ancestors confounded the Franks, they laid a virulent curse on my house. If anyone pulls the rope in the tower and rings the bell, the ruler of the house dies."

"Why don't you remove the bell?" she asked.

"One mustn't trifle with sorcery."

"Why don't you take the key with you?"

"Basrah is crawling with thieves. The only safe place for the key is here—" he hung the key from a hook in her chamber—"where I know you will guard it as you would my life."

After leaving the city and camping by a remote oasis for a few days, Abdul Muhammad secretly returned and went straight to his wife's chambers. That she was absent was unsurprising, though it hurt. That the key was gone, too, devastated him.

Fearing the worst, cursing himself for putting his love to such a test instead of accepting blissful ignorance, he ran to the tower and entered with a duplicate key. He found only an empty room with a hanging rope.

Vowing revenge on the workmen, he tiptoed inside and gave the rope a tentative tug to see what had gone wrong. But the workmen had done their job well. Before he could regain the door at his liveliest waddle, the roof fell on him.

When Farashah returned from the baths with her ladies, she took the key from her neck and hung it in its place. She hated to flout her lord's wishes, but she didn't dare leave it unattended for some idle rogue of a eunuch to play with. Her husband was far too trusting.

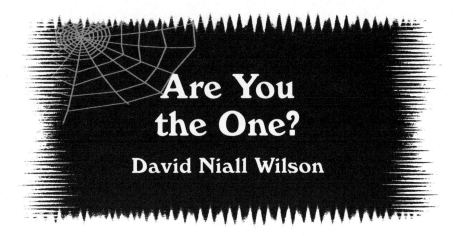

Are You the One?

David Niall Wilson

Ed took her to the grave as a final test, an assurance that she was the one. He'd taken only three others there, and none of them had understood. All they'd offered him was ridicule and rejection. Now, though, he had Mary. Long, twisting curls of blonde hair, slender, fun, and with enough of life's usual curves and snarls behind her to understand where he was coming from. Mary was perfect, and all that remained was to get Lilian's approval, and to move on with a life he'd been thinking lately might be beyond help.

The sun was beginning to set, leaving a low mist hanging on the tops of the old headstones. He could see the questions floating in her eyes. He only smiled, leading the way with practiced ease. It had been a while, but he still knew the way. He would *always* know.

Ed had discovered Lilian one night when his father had decided to take out a drunken argument with his mom from Ed's hide. He'd run from the house in terror, stumbling across the road and into the graveyard beyond, running and running until he came up short against the cold stone of her gown. He'd spent the night with her, listening to her whispered words and dreaming of his future.

Lilian had been there for him from then on, whenever his dad was a bit too drunk, or his mom wouldn't wake up after her "calm down" pills knocked her out cold on the couch. No matter what life served up, she was there to share it with him, and to advise him.

The graves got older the deeper they went in, and the closer they got to the river, the higher above the ground the old monuments loomed. In a grove just ahead she waited, and Ed found that he had little flutters in his stomach from anticipation. What if Mary couldn't see her, or worse, made fun of him because he could? What if she slapped him and misunderstood the entire thing? Too late to worry about that now. There was nothing else he could tell her that would make a good enough excuse for having dragged her there but the truth, for better or worse.

"We're here," he said, turning to Mary with a smile, "my special place, the one I told you about."

Mary looked around, taking in the small clearing, the single white angel that poked up through the weeds. It was surprisingly well kept, considering its surroundings, but intuitively, she seemed to know that Ed was responsible.

"Mary, meet Lilian." Ed was standing directly in front of the stone angel, facing her as if she might speak in answer.

Mary didn't hesitate. She walked forward, reached out to lay a hand on Lilian's shoulder, and said, "Pleased to meet you, Lilian."

Lilian did not answer, and in that moment, Ed knew his mistake. He reached beneath the folds of his jacket and found the hilt of the knife, caressing it softly.

"She seems to like you," he lied, and when Mary turned her smile toward him, the empty, lying smile he now knew it to be, he brought the blade out and drove it home, dropping her to her knees. She was sobbing, pleading, but it was too late. She knew his secrets—she would become another.

"You will join her, keep her company," he explained, reaching down to caress Mary's cheek.

He could feel Lilian's eyes, burning into his back, could feel her fierce pride in him—her love. He turned, and she raised a white, ethereal hand, capturing his gaze instantly in the deep pools of her eyes.

"There will be another," she whispered. "You will never be alone."

"I know," he said, tears streaming down his face. Turning, he moved behind a nearby tree and retrieved the shovel he kept there. It would take most of the night to dig the grave, and he wanted to be done and gone before dawn.

He could hear the whispering voices of the others. He ignored them. They would always be here. Mary would be here too, reminding him of his failures. Lilian had them; only he was alone. It didn't matter. Lilian had promised it would not last, and she had never let him down. As he shoveled dirt onto Mary's still form, he smiled, wondering who he'd meet next, and if she'd be the one.

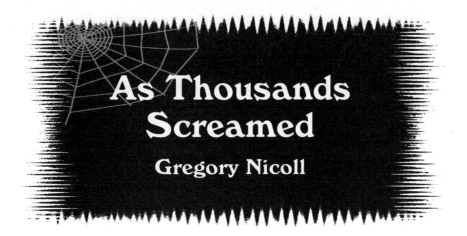

As Thousands Screamed

Gregory Nicoll

We *got* the guy," the young security officer announced proudly. "He's history now."

Darrien said nothing as he lowered his brown Ovation acoustic guitar to the floor of the dressing room. A dull hollow note sounded from the instrument as it touched the stained red carpet. He reached for his cigarette case, fumbling with its tiny brass latch. "You're *sure* this is the guy who was sending me all those notes?"

The officer nodded. "Yes—we even found another one inside his backpack, along with some reinforced gloves and wirecutters. Dropped it as he was slipping out. We figure he was gonna sabotage your stage pyrotechnics, but got scared and bolted. Detective Ford's got the note now. I'm sure he'll show it to you if—"

Darrien shook his head as he lit the tip of his Salem Light. "No, not until after the concert."

"I sure understand *that*," said the officer. He paced awkwardly for a moment and added, "Well, I'd better get back there."

Darrien waved him out. He took a deep drag of the warm, sweet smoke as the door swung closed with a metallic *click*. The air in the small, narrow, windowless room smelled faintly of pine-scented cleaner. The aroma clung to the food on the deli meat tray, to the tiny pink Vienna sausages in their pool of tomato sauce, and to every drop of the red wine. Darrien took another hard drag on the Salem and then stubbed it to death in the crystal ashtray.

He was free now.

Every stop on this 66-city route had brought another of those mysterious notes—notes telling him this was his last tour ever, that he'd never touch a guitar again. . . .

And now the menace was over at last, here, on the very last show of the tour.

Darrien picked up the Ovation and gently strummed a warm C chord, the smooth wide strings yielding easily beneath the tips of his fingers. He smiled at the thought of his fans, and how startled they would be to see him with this mellow instrument instead of the screaming red guitars he played in public. He glanced at the wall clock and realized that he was almost due onstage, where he'd open the show with his beloved trademark leap-and-windmill downstroke on one of those six-string fire engines.

Idly he picked at the callused fingertips of his left hand. Constant performing on this tour had built up hard layers there. He could squeeze out a lit match between any two fingers and feel no pain, not even warmth. The glistening roundwound strings of his stage guitars gave his music a deep, throaty intonation, but they sure were hell on his hands.

However, Darrien long ago resolved himself to pay this small price to practice his art. His music was his life, and his life was his music. And nobody—especially not some demented note-writing nutcase— could take that away from him.

Darrien stood and stretched, then stooped toward the mirror and adjusted his black leather stage costume. Satisfied, he left the room and made his way down the corridor. Ron, Paul, Ed, and Jasmine were ready, dashing out in front of the crowd as soon as he appeared. A roadie whipped the smooth black leather strap of a Gibson Explorer over his neck and gestured toward the stage, where Leo was already laying down the opening drumbeats.

Darrien took a deep breath, let it out slowly, and began to run. As he reached the stage, he leaped—and while still in midair he pressed a C chord and delivered a devastating downstroke.

But the sound from the amplifiers, now booming out over the ocean of cheering fans, was *wrong:* flat, muted, clipped. It lacked his trademark sustain. Something burned and stung on the fingertips of his left hand, and he realized that blood was pouring down the guitar. His fingertips seemed to have *melted* into the strings.

Darrien stepped back in shock, then collapsed.

Razor wire, he thought. *My . . . strings . . . replaced with . . . razor wire.*

Like Vienna sausages in tomato sauce, the fingertips of Darrien's right hand lay motionless in a pool of blood on the stage floor.

And out in the crowd, thousands were screaming.

Asylum

Brian Hodge

Bartles and I are into our second game of chess when he remarks that the man next door to him hasn't come to the dayroom in two weeks.

"I should imagine they'll be letting him out soon."

"Probably faking," I say. "Anybody can do two weeks of self-imposed solitary."

Whenever one of us stops craving the simple contact of others like himself, it can be an early sign that something has started to unravel. But for anyone trying to scam his way out, it's the easiest symptom to feign.

Bartles threatens my bishop with a rook. "Well, he's screaming throughout most of the nights, too."

"And anybody can yell." Ever the skeptic.

"After his throat sounds raw enough to bleed? Hurts mine just to listen."

I reconsider. "Self-mutilation's good. Maybe he'll pull this off after all."

Six moves later grandfatherly Bartles has me in checkmate, and we set it up again. Around us, our ward's other rehabilitants mill about the dayroom, some putting on inept displays of schizoid tics and twitches, but most too proud to betray their sanity. It is, after all, the only thing we have left to truly call our own.

The Order of Saint Cool Hand Luke, some of us have, in feeble bravado, taken to calling ourselves. No matter how hard they try, they'll never break us down.

Hands across the board; pawns advance, pawns fall.

"Hewson had me brought in to see him this morning," I say.

He's the nearest thing to a director here, evaluating who's ready for release. But there's no logic to the schedule he keeps. You might not see him for six months, then find yourself dragged before him twice a day for a week. Unremarkable looking, Hewson nevertheless has ways of getting under your skin.

"Did he talk?" Bartles asks.

"Mostly just sat there again."

Arthritic and grizzled, Bartles shudders. "That's worse."

"Jesus, tell me about it. Man's like a snake. Stares at you for hours and won't twitch a muscle, and just when you think he's not really in the same room with you, *then* he'll clear his throat and lean across that desk. Creeps me out every time."

And he's hard to bluff. Uncanny, Hewson's knack for knowing his own kind, weeding the fake from the genuine. He and the rest of them aren't out of touch with reality at all—they just define it differently. The day their madness became a contagion was proof to me of some ghastly hive mind at work in the universe. Entropic manifestations of chaos, shaking everything down to a primal new order of irrationality. Cities and towns became unwalled bedlams.

The rest of us? Now we're the ones who need reconditioning to fit in, holding on to our minds like fragile eggs. Two plus two is still four, but *they're* the ones with the cattle prods. And the snakes. And rats. And insects. And the will to use them on us.

"I wonder what Hewson was looking for in you this time."

"It's my drawings," I whisper. "They examine them while I'm in here. I go back to my room and they're out of order. So now I'm running my own scam. Forget those mountains and landscapes I used to draw—those'll never get me out of here."

Bartles grins, slides out his queen. "So now you're giving them nightmares?"

"Everything from the martyrdom of the apostles to reality's breakdown on the edge of a black hole. My ticket out of here."

Bartles shakes his head, has seen it tried before. "It won't be enough. Drawings alone are never good enough for them."

"I've got that covered." I scoot a lowly pawn. "Checkmate."

I'm nowhere near his king and we both know it. He starts to protest, then his eyes understand. By then I'm over the table and chessmen are flying, and his chair topples backward as I straddle his chest. My fingers throttle leathery wattles; my thumbs force voicebox toward vertebrae. He manages a wheeze before something snaps. I take two bishops and plunge their mitered tops into his dimming eyes, while watched by a roomful of others.

"You see how he cheats?" I shout to them. "He changes the color of the pieces!"

The stillness is unbroken until I rise and walk to my room, to finish a sketch of a coronation, a royal diadem upon my head.

Regardless of the game, there are kings, and there are pawns.

And a rational man knows which to sacrifice.

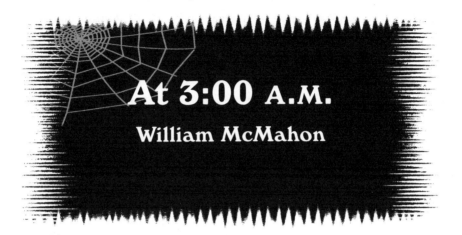

At 3:00 A.M.

William McMahon

Bob was the one who usually woke up hard, as if he'd been thrown onto the pavement, and Angela was the light sleeper who snapped awake at a whisper, but tonight in the darkened bedroom she lay on her side of the bed utterly still, buried in covers, while Bob sat bolt upright, throat full of something hot and thick, naked body slick with night sweats, his mouth gummy and tasting of old copper. Afterimages of another wild nightmare full of blood and fury still raced around in his head.

It seemed like it got worse every night. Even after a month under a wad of bandages, disinfectant, and topical anesthetics, the bite marks still itched and burned as if two cigarettes were being stubbed out on his ankle. Whatever it was that had been under his car that day, and had bitten right through the stiff leather of his boot, had put him through four weeks of escalating hell.

An extended medical leave right in the middle of his most important project. A rabies series, because the doctors said "we have to be certain, Mr. Rhodes." Painful chills and raging fevers that flashed through him without warning. Sudden, amphetamine-like eruptions of wild energy and a kind of narcolepsy that had him falling asleep on the toilet. Bleeding gums. Vomiting at all hours. Nightmares and hallucinations so vivid that it was sometimes hard to tell whether he was awake or asleep.

Angie had wanted to check him into St. Luke's, but the doctors at the HMO had told her it wasn't really called for. They prescribed bed rest, fluids, and checkups once a week.

He had stomped the thing, which was cold comfort now, but at least it wouldn't attack anyone else.

The morning had been dark, the color of new denim, and cold. He clearly remembered seeing something scrabbling over the snow, dragging its mangled lower body along behind. Probably some kind of rat, but it had been so big and so fast. So unbelievably fast. Just a tan blur even after he had crushed its back. The only thing the animal control people had found was a blood trail that ended at a sewer grate.

"Angie," he whispered, hoping he hadn't disturbed her. "Angie?"

Under the blanket he gave her a little nudge with his toe. She lay still, feeling cold next to his feverish body. His head was swimming, there were bursts of gray static behind his eyes, and he must have fallen asleep wearing his contact lenses again: everything in the dark room looked utterly clear and luminous in the moonlight.

The nausea hit out of nowhere. He threw back the covers and bolted down the black hallway to the bathroom, barely making it to the toilet before he lost control. Afterward he sat, weak and empty, hugging the cool porcelain.

"I'm awright, honey," he called back to the silent bedroom. Angie always woke whenever he got sick. This time, silence.

Bob turned on the tap and ran cold water on his hands. He flipped the light on with his elbow and the fluorescent glare stabbed his eyes like hot pokers. He blinked, blinked again, and in the garish light squinted at himself in the mirror. His face came into focus all at once.

The blood smeared around his mouth, on his cheeks, and down his bare chest had begun to cake and looked black in the harsh white light. The two long, prominent, dagger-thin canines that had grown as he had slept until they'd burst through his gums were stained pink and were slowly but visibly receding back to their normal shape and size.

Down the hall, in the bed, Angie did not hear him screaming. She did not hear him racing down the hallway, careening off the walls, shrieking her name in terror. She heard nothing, saw nothing, dreamt of nothing. She just lay there, growing cold.

At the Bus Station

Alan Rodgers

There was only one smoking-section bench near the coffee machine, so he lit his cigarette and took a seat a few feet from the girl. He set his coffee on the floor near his feet.

The girl ignored him.

It was better that way, wasn't it? He was a man, she was a girl, and she didn't know him from Adam; they were all but alone in the bus station; and it was what, three A.M.? Four? Maybe it was later. When he sat down he expected her to cringe and sidle away from him, but she didn't. Did not so much as acknowledge his presence with a smile or a nod or even a grimace: she sat motionless, oblivious to him. Staring intently out the bus-station window at a row of closed shops, her gaze fixed as though some needful thing lay waiting in the darkness.

And maybe something did.

But what? When he looked out among the night streets and the shuttered stores, he saw nothing remarkable.

"Damp evening," he said, "isn't it?"

The doors of the bus station were open to the weather.

She turned to face him slowly, like an angel from a dream. When he saw the way she moved he thought he could say anything to her, anything at all, and it would be moments before she did anything but pretend to notice. Even if he made a rude or cutting remark, she would take it in slowly, distractedly; she would respond with muted platitudes or maybe not at all.

Not that it mattered. He didn't have anything unkind to say, and he didn't want to say it anyway.

"The nights are always damp in this part of the country," she told him. "You're new here?"

"Yes . . ."

He took a deep drag from his cigarette and reached down for his coffee. It had already begun to cool: only tiny wisps of vaguely coffee-ish vapor floated from the cup.

"In from the north last week, still out looking for work," he said. He winced when he heard himself say that—it sounded so stupid when he put it that way. Made him feel like a vagabond.

Or worse.

She smiled. "At this time of night?"

There was something . . . *wrong* about her smile. It wasn't vicious, or unfriendly—but it wasn't remotely reassuring, either.

"No," he said. He smiled back at her, insincerely. Shook his head. The aftertaste of coffee and—saccharine?—left his mouth dry; the word *no* felt clumsy on his tongue. He took another swallow of the awful stuff from his cup, hating the taste of it, wishing he had better.

She picked up her purse and began digging through it. "Is the coffee good?" she asked.

"No," he said, "it's awful."

She went to the machine and bought a cup anyway. "I'm getting sleepy," she said.

He wanted to respond to that. Wanted desperately to say something important and appropriate, wanted to reach toward her, but he couldn't find a thing to say. Not while she walked to the machine, purse in hand; not as she dropped her coins into the slot and waited; not when she came back, still smiling strangely, carrying a cup of the sludgy carbonized stuff from the machine.

Could not find a thing to say when she sat back down a couple seats away from him, closer than she'd been before.

As the silent moment stretched on and on forever—

And then suddenly it was over, before it really started.

A bus pulled into the station's garage, and the overhead speaker announced that it was boarding; the girl stood, gathered her bags, and hurried toward her gate without so much as another glance at him.

She didn't look back until she stood on the steps just inside the bus's folded doors. She stopped there on the steps, before she finished climbing aboard—turned, looked back and forth across the station. . . .

When her eyes found him they stopped and focused, and he saw something in them that he knew but would not name, a thing like hunger but darker and more cruel.

Just before she turned to board the bus and vanish with the night.

Later, much later, he would wake from dreams, thinking of her, remembering nothing.

Autumn in the Clockwork Forest

Michael Scott Bricker

Gears and sprockets fell from the trees, coating the ground in rusty autumn. Tin Man stopped, listened to the metallic beating from the Heart of the Forest, and knew that he was drawing near. His ax hung by his side, as always, and it, too, sensed the beating, and Tin Man felt dark curses flowing through the worn handle, the blood-streaked blade. He might have looked forward to his impending discovery, but such feelings were unique to those who possessed a heart, and Tin Man's ax had taken his long ago. It had been a gradual process, this conversion from flesh to tin, and if Tin Man had the capacity to hate, he would have cursed the Wicked Witch of the East with every grinding step, just as she had cursed that terrible ax of his.

She took shape from a cloud of greasy smoke, a dark, unclean blight floating within the autumn colors (greened copper, tarnished brass, thin, curling leaves of tin), and she imitated his stiff, mechanical movements, then vanished as swiftly as she had appeared.

Tin Man acknowledged her presence, moved on, nothing more. There were advantages to having no heart, and he might have been grateful that the Witch's form no longer caused him sorrow, that the chopping of his accursed ax no longer severed his flesh, that his missing human heart could no longer break from the loss of his beloved Munchkin girl, but gratitude was a feeling, an emotion, of which he had none. Tin Man thought of the Munchkin girl as he walked, and as his mechanical brain processed the old memories, he wondered why he had loved her so, why the Wicked Witch of the East had been so angered by his feelings. She had cursed his ax, had caused it to lop off his limbs one by one, followed by his head, and last, it had removed his heart. A tinsmith had remade him, had hammered out his new identity late into the evenings, but his skill had not been limitless, and the construction of a tin heart had proven to be beyond his abilities. "A heart must be made of flesh," he had said, "only flesh can *feel*."

Tin Man's quest had been a long one, a perilous journey through twisted woods and sleepy poppy fields and neglected roads of colored stones. His ax served him well as the razored edge chopped through wires of dense metallic growth, and he wondered if the curse had passed, if the ax, in finding no remaining flesh to sever, had returned to its old utility. Tin Man emerged within a clearing, and there, set into a massive, spinning cogwheel, was the Heart of the Forest.

It was louder than a human heart, and colder as well, and Tin Man watched as silvery streams of molten metal flowed through its hollow, clicking chambers. The Wicked Witch of the East appeared again, but Tin Man ignored her, kept his attention fixed upon the beating heart. He felt a hollowness in the riveted confines of his chest, an emptiness once filled by thoughts of his Munchkin girl, and he wondered if the heart would fit, if it would prove too large or too powerful for his crafted frame. Tin Man approached, looked at the Wicked Witch, into her dark, tormented eyes, then raised his ax, brought it down with all his might.

The Heart of the Forest shattered, springs and gears popped off, flew into the air, and through a spray of molten metal, Tin Man watched the Wicked Witch of the East dissolve into a mercuric puddle. The lifeblood of the forest had taken her, but it had strengthened Tin Man, and he wondered if the Witch had truly been harmed. It would take more than a mechanical heart to destroy her, he reasoned. Nothing less than a human heart could do so, and a pure one at that, and Tin Man looked at his accursed ax and made a wish upon it.

As he left the Clockwork Forest, Tin Man wondered if he would ever have a human heart, if he would ever love again. He doubted that his wish would come true, and he was well aware of the fact that he was only a man of tin, and as such, he possessed no power to make a successful wish, nor to remove a curse.

He was no wizard, after all.

Bad Feelings

Don D'Ammassa

Why did you nail Mrs. White's cat to the porch, Danny?"

The ten-year-old had been staring into his lap ever since arriving in Dr. Lane's office and he didn't look up now or give any other sign that he'd heard the question.

Ellen Lane sighed. "Do you know why you're here, Danny?"

"To get better." His voice was low, unemotional.

"Then you know what you did was wrong?"

"Of course I do." His head came up, eyes met hers firmly for a second before dropping back. "I'm not a dope."

"No, you're not. You're very smart." Smart enough to have avoided being caught. Something within the boy was crying out for help.

"Did Mrs. White do something that made you mad?"

"Nope."

"Did the cat scratch you? I know how much that hurts."

"Nope."

"Were you mad at your mother or father? Did you think this would make them sorry?"

"Nope."

"Well, why did you do it then?" A note of exasperation had crept into her voice. Ellen didn't understand this boy. She'd talked to the parents; they seemed first-rate, loved each other and their son, no emotional problems she could detect. But Danny, unemotional, bland, was a cipher even to them.

"Had to."

"You had to, huh? Why did you have to?"

Danny just shrugged.

Ellen repressed the urge to go over and shake the boy. "Danny, we all feel the urge to do bad things at times. You don't have to be upset about that. We're not in control of how we feel about things. But we must be responsible for what we actually do. You know what you did was wrong."

"Yes." His voice was almost inaudible.

"Well, my job is to help you to learn to handle those bad thoughts. Would you like to be able to do that?"

"Yes." Louder this time, the first actually emotional tone in his voice. And Danny had raised his head, was staring at her with naked longing.

Ellen realized she'd found the key. "Do you have bad feelings a lot?"

"All the time." Danny's eyes darted away, but he didn't drop his head. "There's something . . . inside of me . . . that wants to do terrible things to people."

"Because you're mad at them?"

"No."

"No? Then why?"

"Just because." He licked his lips and squirmed in his seat. "I told you, it's something inside of me that wants to do it. I don't want to. I hate the things I do sometimes."

"Then why do you do them?"

"Because . . . because there's this bad thing inside of me and if I don't do things to keep it happy, I'm afraid it'll get out and then it'll do really bad things. Terrible things."

Ellen tried to keep the satisfaction from showing on her face. At last she'd gotten the boy to give shape to the inner turmoil that was tormenting him. At last she saw the way to relieving that tension and helping the boy adjust.

"Danny, have you ever played with balloons?"

"Sure." His voice was tentative, obviously puzzled by this change of direction.

"What happens if you blow a balloon up too much?"

"It pops."

"Well, people are a little like balloons sometimes. If we keep our feelings all bottled up inside, there's not room for all the other feelings we have each day and pretty soon there's so much inside that it has to get out."

"But the stuff inside me is bad. I can't let it get out because it might do something horrible, like I told you."

"That's because you keep it all inside you until there's no more room. You have to let it out a little at a time, every day, so that it doesn't get all tight and crowded inside you like it is now."

"I don't know . . ."

"But I do know, Danny. And right now I want you to let out all the bad stuff inside you and promise me you'll never let it get stored up like that again."

Danny looked uncertain, but more hopeful than at any time since she'd started treating him.

"It's all right? You promise?"

"I promise. Just let it out and you'll be fine."

Danny nodded and sat back and his body began to quiver and shake and then something dark and scaly and slimy with lots of claws and teeth burst out of his warm flesh and did some really terrible things.

But Ellen Lane wasn't around for most of that.

Ball of Blood

Karl Schroeder

The hand lies half under water. The water is black, with a thin slick of oil on it. The tips of the fingers point upward, and cockroaches are crawling over the nails, antennae waving. Past this the crescent opening of the sewage main admits grey daylight into the tunnel. The water has pooled behind a mound of trash: leaves, dirt, cans, and condoms.

When the mouth is half submerged, water can flow freely into the lungs. The right one is full, and thin cold trickles are gradually saturating the thinner tubes of the bronchia. This tickling is different from that of the insects in the stomach.

There the ball of blood sits. Worms and beetles leaven it, and the vapours of its decay permeate every organ. They crowd the nose, which too is half submerged.

Concentrate. There is the hand. The cockroaches. Water swirls in the throat. The ball of blood tickles.

Gradually it darkens outside, and touch is the only sense left. Stickiness of wet clothes. Dirt in the ears. Water and crawling.

In the failing light the fingers become grey, and then cease to be visible. Cockroaches can still be felt, balancing on their tips.

The ball of blood is getting smaller. The beetles are carrying it away in small clots, running in and out the mouth and nose. As the night deepens, the sensations of movement from it are fading.

Streetlights swerve into view. Water runs down the nose and chin. A hand pushes on the round metal bars of the sewer grate. The other hand follows. The grate gives way.

This drainage ditch looks different from the bottom than it did yesterday evening to a boy on a bicycle, who paused at its lip to look down. Some movement at its bottom, barely visible then, would be clear now.

The footing is uneven. Finally a bank appears. At its top, fences of a new subdivision, the house-tops lit by halogen streetlights. A car moves past in the far distance.

The back door is not locked. Inside, the kitchen looks as it did yesterday, except for stacks of xeroxed sheets. The sheets have a photograph and words on them. Words under the photo include *seen* and *son.*

There is nothing in the fridge to satisfy. One finger draws slowly along the thin fringe of mildew on the door seal.

Sound. The closing fridge door reveals a face, two hands raised. The arms attached to it swing wide, and the body steps forward.

Water comes from one of its eyes, then the other. The mouth is open, speaking many words. Two hands, hot and dry, close on cold wet cloth, press one body to the other.

Now a pulse can be heard, deep and strong. And, below the skin, hot metal-scented blood is flowing.

It takes time to get at this blood. The other hands interfere, and it is very loud for a while. The other body moves away quickly at one point, until caught and knocked down in the living room. Fingers are too blunt to pierce its hot skin, and teeth cannot bite deep enough. A pen is tried, but most of the holes are in the wrong places. Finally one gash releases enough blood, but almost too quickly. The body keeps moving, and must be lain upon and struck repeatedly with arms, legs and head.

One hand cups the spilling blood while the other widens the hole. Soon there is enough blood to drink freely. It slides down to replenish the ball in the stomach. Beetles and worms swim in it.

Darkness again, and regular splashes as the sewer grate approaches. Bloody hands replace the grate. The streetlights fade behind until it is totally dark. Then tripping over a bicycle and falling heedlessly, the body rests facedown in the water.

The body that dragged the boy here yesterday is gone.

The ball of blood deep inside begins to clot. There is no light.

There is no sound. There is no movement. Only the slow crawling of the beetles, the sliding of worms through the dying blood. That is enough.

Base of a Triangle

Nancy Kilpatrick

You scan the empty subway platform, uneasy. A glance at your watch reveals the late hour. I can see you wondering why you are here when you could be safe in your bed.

Your hands jam deep into your raincoat pockets. You jerk your head and stare down the track into the black tunnel. I hear a prayer mumbled, *Please let the train arrive soon.*

You are my age, although I have been here five years already. I am lonely. It's as if I am one-third of a triangle and cannot exist on my own. You must know how that feels.

I balance on a rail, lean into the platform and stare up at you. Alcohol heightens your perceptions; your intuition soars. You peer down, squinting. Few see beyond the concrete to the intangible, but many sense this nebulous realm. I am a negative image, white on black. All that is solid about you is ethereal in me. I emit no scents. I can no longer be caressed. Yet we are separated by only a crease in time.

I see you often. Here, during other hours, requisite briefcase in hand, newspaper, harried face mingled with thousands of harried faces, unprepared to confront your fate. During the day you are gregarious. This isolation must feel abnormal to you. You peer into dark corners, trying to see through pillars, wrinkling your nose at an odor, terrified you are not as alone as you believe. Memories have a life all their own.

Suddenly, your neck hairs prickle. You stagger past the digital headline—*a fatal accident*. The tracks draw you; you near the platform's edge. You wobble at the rim, examining cold steel below, the dangerous third rail. My dark world of base metals is foreign to your own. There are no plastic cases here, pregnant with the latest microchips, already obsolete. All ties are finite connections, like ancestors, and the certainty of progeny. For a moment you long to meld the iron in your blood with the iron rails and become immortal.

Your ambivalence is touching. You feel my struggle for emotional life ride the air and embed itself into your lungs like a dense fog.

You cannot breathe. You gasp for air.

Train wheels grind against metal tracks. Their shriek causes you to reel back from the platform's edge. Your hand claws your throat. Your body threatens to catapult into my waiting arms.

I know what it is like to pitch forward, alone, crashing onto icy steel rails, to be crushed and severed beneath sharp wheels, flesh singed beyond recognition when a hand touches the high-voltage rail. Metal screeches against metal and bone. Human screams multiply. Warmth seeps from flesh. Oxygen deprivation strangles the fetus within, so dependent.

I know this and more. And when you fall into my arms I will catch you.

The powerful train barrels into the station. You clutch your coat collar tight to your throat. Muscles tense. Sweat streaks forehead and trickles down temples to flushed cheeks. Tears gush from wounded eyes.

You stare at me, pleading for forgiveness.

Join me, I beckon. *Hurry.*

You shake your head but lurch forward.

Train whistle blasts. Air rumbles. Concrete vibrates.

You tremble. I grasp your ankle, forcing your foot to the edge. You open your mouth; sound is crushed by the whistle's wail.

Take the step. Join me.

You teeter on the brink.

Leap into my world!

Wheels screech, but brakes cannot quickly halt tons of steel. A pale face presses against the front window. Haunted expression, fast frozen in déjà vu.

Metal passes through me. Lingering memories revive the night our triangle formed when, in an eternal moment, we three connected.

You stumble onto the train. The doors slam. The conductor's trembling hand throws a switch. The train crawls forward, a silver entity, at home underground.

I fall back onto the tracks. It is always quiet here after the last train passes, yet I cannot rest. The conductor will drive through here nightly, always at this hour. And I know you will return. Because you must.

I will wait for you. For both of you. Forever.

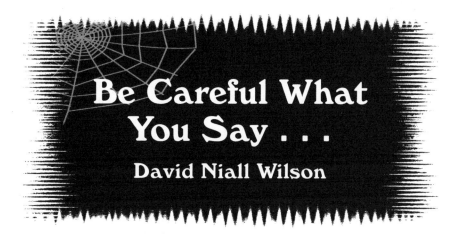

Be Careful What You Say . . .

David Niall Wilson

Cindy stood inside the door to the kitchen, out of sight of the men gathered in the den. It was past her bedtime, but sometimes she just couldn't resist tiptoeing out for a minute or two to listen. Her mother had gone out to the corner store for more beer, so there was little chance of being caught.

They were talking about the world again. This time it was different, though. They weren't talking about where the world was going, or what was happening in some foreign country. They were talking about where the world came from.

Cindy knew the answer, or thought she did. She'd learned it at church on Sunday, sitting next to her Mommy's leg in her best new dress, feeling the crisp material against her soft skin and smelling everyone's perfume. She knew that God had made the earth.

"But, who's to say we aren't just a science project of some kind," Bob was saying. Bob was her very favorite of her Daddy's friends, because he always brought her candy and he liked to scratch her with his big, heavy beard. "I mean, we could be lying about in some cosmic petri dish somewhere, gathering mold on a shelf while they collect data."

"Oh yeah," her Daddy laughed, taking another deep swallow of his beer, "we sure wouldn't be the 'control' specimen."

"Unless they were studying self-destructive violence in germs," Danny cut in with a grin.

"I'm serious," Bob continued. "Some kid may have put us together as a project for a science fair. We could be wiped clean so that a more important, or more successful, culture could take our place."

"Would that make our space shuttles, satellites, and astronauts like germs?" her Daddy asked. "I mean, they take off, the earth gets shoved in a waste basket somewhere; do they go to the next experiment and invade?"

They all laughed at that. It didn't sound very funny to Cindy for the earth to be swept into a trash can.

"Well, if the kid was trying to win a prize for the perfect germ civilization, he'd sure be barking up the wrong tree with us," Bob concluded. "He'd have a doctor's dream—a virus that wipes itself out!"

Hearing the crunch of tires in the drive, Cindy turned and made her way hurriedly down the hall to her room. She wished she had a bigger night-light as she crawled beneath her comforter. Somehow she couldn't get the image of her older brother's face out of her mind.

Ted was in fourth grade already. His most recent project, a small model of the solar system made from Styrofoam balls and glitter, was hanging in the kitchen.

He'd explained it to her, though she'd understood almost none of what he'd said. There were planets in it, and a sun, just like the one that came up in the sky every day. Cindy wished now that she'd asked him how God had created it all, so she could understand.

As she slept, tossing and turning and calling out softly, giant copies of her brother Ted busily built tiny worlds, then swept them into the garbage, growing closer and closer to where she sat, watching them helplessly.

Cindy was glad when the night finally dropped away and the sun slipped into her room, striping everything with brightness. The scent of bacon frying was in the air, and she could hear her mother moving about. It was Saturday—no school.

She came into the kitchen with a quick burst of speed, glancing up and noticing that something was different. The small model of the solar system was no longer hanging from its tiny hook behind the kitchen door.

Looking around quickly, she spotted it, and as she walked over to where its remains poked out of the trash can at odd, broken angles, she began to cry. She couldn't stop herself. Her Daddy came running, concern in his bleary eyes, and Ted rushed up from his room down the hall.

Her Mommy looked at them, shrugging. "Who knows? A bad dream? Honestly, Jack, I don't know *what* gets into these kids sometimes."

Cindy ignored them, watching the air above the trash can. She was hoping for a vision of tiny rocket ships. She was looking for germs that might have escaped. She hoped they found a home.

Bedtime Story

Steve Eller

I think it's time for a story."

Anna's hands trembled as she drew the blanket up to her chin. Snuffy felt warm and soft, tucked into the crook of her arm. Daddy leaned against the doorjamb, a crooked grin tracing his lips.

"No, Daddy. Not tonight. I'm too sleepy."

Her heart fluttered as Daddy began to slowly shake his head. He crept toward the bed, his smile widening. Her stomach did a flip-flop.

"You don't look so sleepy to me."

Daddy sat down on the foot of the bed. Anna hugged Snuffy against her cheek, his tangled fur tickling her nose. Daddy leaned in close.

Once upon a time there was a wicked king. He choked to death on a chicken bone on his twentieth birthday, and his subjects threw a big party to celebrate. They wore black clothes and ate cake with black frosting. They sang and danced, happy that the king was dead.

But the Devil likes bad people, and instead of keeping the king's soul in Hell, he stuffed it back into his body so he could hear the people laughing at his funeral.

The king got so mad, his dead body came back to life, and he started pounding on the inside of his coffin. The people stopped dancing, listening to the sound. It grew louder and louder, until the wood began to crack. All at once the king shot straight up like a jack-in-the-box through the lid of his casket. His face was twisted in fury, and bits of wood and silk littered his jacket. He shook his fists, and coughed up the chicken bone onto the floor. The people ran back to their houses, screaming that the king had returned, and was undead.

Now, the king had been to Hell and back, and his mind was full of evil knowledge. He knew he could make other people immortal by sucking out all their blood. But he only did it to his enemies. Because his favorite thing was torturing people, and now he could torture them forever, since they wouldn't die.

The king took one man who'd angered him, and staked him out in the sun until he dried up like a raisin. Then he cut him into little strips and wove him into a rug. Everyday the king jumped up and down on him, trying to hurt him some more.

Another man who refused to pay his taxes got ground up and mixed with clay. The king shaped him into a huge vase and held him up to his ear, hoping to hear him gasping and choking. And then there was a woman whom the king loved, but who spurned him. He scooped out her fat, then burned her up. He mixed the fat with her ashes and made her into a monstrous candle. At night he lit her, and listened for her screaming as she burned a second time.

But the people grew tired of this. At first they were scared, but they finally decided to put a stop to it. So they got together and captured the king. They knew they couldn't kill him, but what he did to the others gave them an idea.

They built a big bonfire and roasted him. And they picked the windiest night of the year to do it. When he was nothing but ashes, they put out the flames and let the wind carry him away. They knew he would suffer until the end of the world, struggling to pull his ashes together again.

Sometimes, when the wind blows, you can hear the king screaming in pain and despair as he swirls around. Because just when he gets himself all together, the wind scatters him again. Late at night, you can hear his ashes brushing against the windows. He lived, ever after.

Daddy's eyes gleamed like black marbles as he rose from the bed. Anna saw tiny droplets of sweat trickling down the back of his neck as he walked away. She squeezed Snuffy tighter, searching his fuzzy brown face for comfort. Snuffy smiled up at her, his button eyes wide and reassuring. But her stomach felt funny, like something was scurrying around inside.

As he touched the lightswitch, Daddy looked back over his shoulder. His teeth glimmered behind quivering lips.

"Sweet dreams, Anna. Tomorrow night, another story."

The room went black. In the darkness, Anna heard the door creak and click shut. She closed her eyes and shivered, clutching Snuffy close.

Being of One Mind

Benjamin Adams

Emperor Claudius nosed hungrily at the potato salad on the edge of the red-and-white checkered picnic spread.

"Get outta here, you sonuvabitch!" Frank snarled at the cat; it was Gladys's and he had no use for it at all. When it made no effort to leave the potato salad alone, he swatted it away.

The golden Persian lifted its regal head and sauntered away toward a nearby drift of yellow and red leaves.

Frank relaxed. Maybe now he could dwell on the matter at hand without distractions. This was going to be hard enough as things stood.

He'd brought Gladys out here to the Dunwich forest preserve on this last gorgeous day of fall for the worst reason in the world: to ask for a divorce. Their differences had grown too great recently. But today she'd insisted on bringing Emperor Claudius, who wasn't the most peaceful passenger in a car. The cat's yowling had irritated Frank during the whole drive out. And Gladys's own mood had been fairly ragged—almost as if she'd known what lay ahead.

The crunching of dry leaves underfoot signaled her return from the forest preserve's public restroom. "I really don't like using that thing," she complained. "I think 'rustic' is too kind a word."

"Yeah, well, there are worse things," Frank sighed.

"I don't suppose you've seen Claudie—I think he's wandered away."

"No, I haven't seen your stupid cat."

Instantly he regretted his choice of words.

Gladys leaned over and whacked his shoulder, hard. "Frank, you bastard! You probably spooked him!"

"He was getting into the food—"

She hit him again. "If anything happens to him, it's your fault!"

He winced—that was definitely true.

"Look," he said in what he hoped was a reasonable tone, "I just want to finish this potato salad and then I'll help you look for the cat. I promise. You're right; it's my fault."

"You mean it?" Her voice was small, confused.

"Yeah," he said. "Yeah, I mean it."

After all, this was the least he could do before he dropped the bomb.

Before he finally told her he wanted the divorce.

He finished his last couple of bites of potato salad and got to his feet. Now, where had he last seen the cat? *Just past that large drift of fallen leaves*, he decided, and walked in that direction.

"Here, Claudie!" he called, keeping his voice soft. "C'mere, kitty!"

About fifteen feet from the picnic site, the ground suddenly fell away into a dry ravine. There seemed to be no disturbance in the leaves littering the center of the ravine, but that didn't mean Emperor Claudius couldn't have wandered down there, the stupid beast—

A piercing scream came from the picnic site.

"Gladys!" Frank yelled, and dashed back toward her. Suddenly the divorce was the furthest thing from his mind.

My God, he thought, *what is that thing?*

And then: *It's huge!*

The strange thing had burst out of the drift of leaves. A black, slimy mass of writhing tentacles and feelers. Frank saw roiling to its glossy, soft surface bits and pieces of the animals and insects it had eaten during its hidden tenancy.

A beak. Bits of chitin. A patch of golden fur, and a slitted, unblinking cat's eye—

Gladys screamed again. "Claudie!"

"Hold still!" shouted Frank.

"It's touching me," she wailed. "Get it off!"

Two of the thing's tentacles had reached out and grabbed Gladys's ankles. They tensed—

And then the thing pulled itself to her, knocking her to the yellow and red leaf-strewn ground. It swarmed over her within seconds, covering her body.

Her screams stopped as it embraced her head.

Frank ran to the mass covering Gladys and began to rip at it, trying to pull it away.

Instead, it covered his hands and began to flow up his arms, his chest, over his head.

He couldn't see. Reflex took over and he tried breathing, screaming.

It flowed into his open mouth and down his throat.

Everything was darkness. Dimly, he became aware of other, smaller thoughts.

—*flying, eating, hunting, sleeping*—

Is this death, wondered Frank, *all these other thoughts intruding on mine?*

—*hunger, prey, shelter*—

But then he knew. He was inside the thing, and he was still alive. He was part of it now. Somehow it was telling him this, feeding the thoughts directly into his mind.

Strangely, he felt no fear, only a deep, burning curiosity.

The other minds touching his were unintelligent, thinking only of survival imperatives. Animals. But beyond that, at the periphery of his awareness, was another new mind, like his.

—*Frank? Is that you I feel?*

He felt a sweeping wave of calmness and happiness at knowing Gladys was here with him. He touched his mind to hers—

Only to recoil in shock and revulsion at the contact.

—*Frank! You bastard! I'm stuck in here with you now! This is all your fault*—*! I always knew you were out to get me*—

Together with Gladys. Always.

He supposed it was too late for a divorce.

Best Friends

Linda J. Dunn

Let me tell you about my best friend, Marcie.

Everybody loves her. How could they not? She's one of those incredible wonder women that you read about occasionally in magazines.

Of course, she's intelligent and beautiful. Marcie also has a wonderful, incredibly successful husband who worships the ground she walks upon and two adorable, well-adjusted children who excel in school. She works in some hush-hush job at a government think-tank where she probably solves three world crises a day before stopping on her way home to do some charity work at the local hospital.

I've never met anyone like her.

Marcie was valedictorian of our high school class, the girl voted "most likely to" everything that was good, and the absolute darling of teachers and principals alike.

No one could understand why she hung around with me. My grades were awful and I had to be the ugliest girl in school. Marcie took me on as some kind of charity project when we both were freshmen and she really turned my life around.

I owe a lot to Marcie.

She didn't forget me either. Every week she wrote home from college, filling her letters with stories about life on campus and including little notes of encouragement about my work at the deli.

Marcie was there when I married Herb, too. She insisted upon turning my drab courthouse ceremony into a grand wedding complete with gowns that hid the reason for the rushed marriage.

She insisted upon doing this—a wedding gift, she said.

We lost touch for a short time after my marriage. Life fell into a daily routine of babies, diapers, day care, and serving customers at the deli.

I almost forgot about Marcie after a few years but my best friend never forgot about me.

She moved back into our old neighborhood last year. Now that she was some hot-shot troubleshooter who flew all over the world, it didn't matter what state she called home.

Everyone was delighted when she returned—and terribly upset when she disappeared last week.

No one can understand it. She was supposed to meet me at the mall and, like I told the police officers, I waited and waited but she never showed up.

That was totally unlike Marcie.

A few people think she's gone underground to work on some top-secret government project and she'll resurface with plans to bring about world peace or end poverty as we know it.

But I know better. Marcie's never coming home.

I buried her too deep and too well for anyone to ever find her.

Everyone loved my best friend, Marcie. Everyone, that is, except me.

Beware the Truancy Officer

Leslie What

I slipped on finger cots before pulling the attendance sheet from the printer. I hated ink stains; even with the finger cots it was a struggle not to visit the washroom. I used an alcohol pledget from my desk to clean the telephone, giving myself till it evaporated to get in character before the first call of the day. Dialed 9, followed by the number. A woman answered.

"Hello," I said, "Miss Virgil from Dante High. According to our records, your son was absent yesterday during periods four and five." The woman apologized. Her boy had forgotten to bring the dentist's note. "No problem," I said. "I'll change the record." I wrote D—Doctor/Dentist—under Reason on the sheet, and entered that into the file.

I tried the second number. A woman who sounded like her teeth had been knocked out answered on the fifteenth ring. I did my rap.

"Why you people keep calling?" she asked. "Every day you call to say, 'Mandy did this, Mandy did that.' It's your freaking job to keep track of the kid. Not mine."

"Thanks for your cooperation." I used my sweetest voice, but circled the phone number and added a note in hypertext to keep an eye on this one. Mandy had been truant at least twice a week since school started. Her mother didn't know or, worse, didn't care. Lots of things could happen to teenagers whose parents didn't watch out for them. Terrible things. Made me shudder thinking about it.

The next name on my list was a druggie who often didn't bother to show up. The man on the other end spoke terrible English. "Nicholas ain't here," he said. "Gotta be at school. Where else wouldee be?"

"Makes you wonder," I said.

"He ain't here," said the man.

On a hunch I asked, "How's the boy doing in school?"

"I dunno. He's doing okay or you guys'd throw'm out." He laughed. "Me, I didn't get past ninth grade."

"Thanks for sharing," I said, then hung up.

My fourth call was an E—Excused. "She's still got head lice," explained the mother. "She's trying out a new shampoo. They told me not to send her till the lice are dead, isn't that right?"

"Yes," I said. "That's right."

Number five was an R—Religious Observance. The parents didn't answer the phone, but I recognized the name: Goldman. Always took off the first two days of Rosh Hashanah. I made a note not to call them on Yom Kippur.

Number six was my extra special case, the one I'd been working on since his first year at Dante. The father hung up when he recognized my voice. Didn't even want to know that something was wrong. Negligence, pure and simple. The father wouldn't care if his son was kidnapped and sold into slavery, if a psychopathic nutcase ripped open his chest and poured in bubble bath just to watch the show, if he wound up in a freezer wrapped in paper labeled with the date. This kid was at risk, all right. I knew about such things.

E—Excused. A small lie.

A couple more E's, another R, three D's, and a P—Planned Vacation. The rest unaccounted for, throwaway kids whose parents didn't give a damn. So many kids. So little time.

At lunch I snuck out to pay a visit to number six. He lived two blocks away on Providence Street. I knocked, and when there was no answer, crept around back. A rusty nail on the window-frame scratched my gloves. I kept my temper in check so as not to make any mistakes.

The kid's room looked like any normal teenage boy's: posters of models so tall the photographer had to choose between getting all of the head or all of the crotch into the picture. Guess which one they chose. Dirty clothes on the floor—candy wrappers—soda cans. Somebody needed to teach this kid housekeeping.

Not me. Too suspicious.

The water was running in the bathroom. Probably not the boy—kids never bathed. I didn't believe in coincidence; I was an officer of God, doing His will. The father's room was worse than his son's: an unmade bed, smelly sheets, ashtrays needing emptying. A bad influence. Very bad. I waited in the closet, knife in hand, ready to teach that slimeball a lesson about being a good parent.

The Big One

Lisa Lepovetsky

He wakes her in the hours before sunlight, when even breathing seems too loud. She doesn't complain, though her eyes feel like sandpaper. He carries her gear to the car.

"I can do it," she protests from the front door, but her voice is swallowed in the fog.

He drives silently, quickly to the lake. She's never been there, and loses her sense of direction after the first few miles. The car is too warm. She wishes he would turn on the radio, even though there's probably nothing on except religious stations. When they arrive, he tells her to wait while he stows their things in the rowboat. This time, she doesn't argue.

As he rows to the right spot, his spot, she tries to speak. The air is lighter around them, and she doesn't want the sun to spoil her chance.

"Listen, we have to talk about it before—"

"Shhh." His voice seems to come from a million miles across the boat.

"But I want to explain," she insists. "He wasn't—"

But he raises a hand to silence her. She flinches. "You'll chase the Big One away," he hisses. "I've been waiting for her for years, and I'm not going to lose her again. Not today."

So she opens her thermos, and pours a capful of the bitter coffee that he always makes too strong. It burns her tongue, and tears mingle with the dampness on her cheeks.

He finally finds his secret cove and stows the oars, hoping she can't see his smile. He knows it's not a nice smile. Peering through dawn's first fiery ripples, he breathes heavily as he imagines the Big One curling her speckled length around and around herself, devouring her own wake as she waits restlessly for him.

He can feel the water crawl over that dorsal thrust, a spiny flag flown straight in amber light. He almost sees her thick lips pouting rhythmically, in time with translucent gills feathered behind that proud bullet-shaped head.

The pole presses familiar dents into the ridges and troughs of his rough palms as he casts the line across the boat, past the woman. She frowns at him, but doesn't duck. He waits, patient, as the little boat drifts on the water like the last fingers of fog. Tiny bull's-eyes pulse a watery heartbeat from the leader. He knows she'll come this time.

Suddenly, nylon plunges through metal eyelets, uncoiling with a thin scream, leaping from his reel to disappear into the refracted world below. He hesitates less than a fly's breath, testing the moment before him, then looks across the boat at the woman.

He finds her eyes, seeing them as though he's never seen her before. She's a stranger. He jerks the rod once, hard, to set the metal hook deep into the bony jaw. She winces. Then he reels the Big One in. The woman grits her teeth at the sound, but doesn't turn. He knows she loathes the sight of a hooked fish, and for once, he's glad.

The Big One rises beside the boat then, long, impossibly long. Iridescent scales glisten redly in the sun's first rays. The boat tilts wildly, but he leans backward to steady it. She's the biggest fish he's ever seen, or ever will again. Still, the woman doesn't look behind her.

His heart seems to stop as the fish opens her mouth, sucking at the wet air. The mouth is large enough to swallow a woman's head in one bite. Where did she come from, he wonders. What does she feed on? In an instant, he knows.

With a flick of his knife, he cuts the nylon line, letting the Big One drop back into the lake. The woman has an instant to frown at him curiously before he stands. He grasps the shaft of one of the oars and lifts it high over his head. She never had a chance.

A scream, a splash, then the water is calm again. As he rows home alone, he pictures the Big One, far under the dark waters, swimming hungrily around and around his secret cove, searching for something large enough to satisfy her.

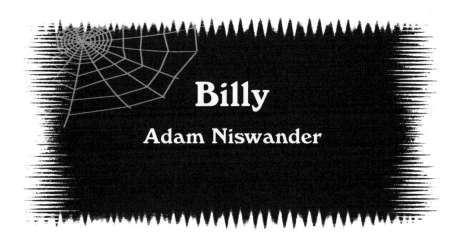

Billy
Adam Niswander

Mommy and Daddy love me.

I know that right down to the soles of my feet.

That's why I'm so confused.

We live in a nice house just outside town. Blairville is a pretty place, too. Mommy says the town is Victorian—whatever that means. But I like the big tall roofs, with all those windows poking out. The school is neat.

We have a whole bunch of friends, really good neighbors, and there are lots of kids to play with.

At least it was that way until yesterday.

We don't get a lot of visitors in Blairville. When they built the superhighway five years ago, it kinda passed us by.

Daddy says there was a lot of arguing about it at the time, but I don't remember.

What they call the town council—which is just Jake the Postmaster, Bill the Barber, and Maddy the Librarian—voted not to take the state to court. Daddy said they decided it would be good for us. In passing us by like they did, the state had protected us, kept strangers out.

My name is Billy. I'm nine. I like baseball and skinnydipping in the pond just over the hill when the weather is warm and the breeze is lazy.

All I know is, I've always liked it here in Blairville, long as I can remember.

The trouble started yesterday, just after sundown.

Daddy came home, all out of breath and in a hurry. He said there was strangers in town—three of them, who rode in on motorcycles.

He said it was two guys and a girl . . . but they looked really dirty, ya know? I mean, they looked like they'd been sleeping in bushes, and they were what my Mom calls grimy—like they hadn't taken a bath in a week.

He said Sheriff Joe had walked up and asked what they wanted, and they had killed him. Daddy said they didn't even give him a chance, just walked up and twisted his head real sharp to one side.

Mommy got real upset.

Daddy grabbed his shotgun and a box of shells and told us to stay in the house, then he ran out the door, heading back toward town.

I asked Mommy if it would be all right.

She looked at me for a long moment.

"You're getting to be a big boy, Billy," she said. "Can I trust you to stay here and hide if any strangers come a-knocking on the door?"

"You gonna go into town, Mommy?" I asked.

She went over to the old leather trunk in the corner and rummaged around in it until she came up with Daddy's old service .45. There was a box of shells with it. She checked it, then put both the gun and the bullets in her apron pocket.

She looked at me real stern and said, "Yes, Billy. I'm gonna go make sure your daddy doesn't get himself hurt. You stay here." She came over and hugged me real tight, then looked me right in the eye. "You promise you'll be a good boy?"

"Yes," I said. I was kinda getting scared, but I didn't want her to see it.

Mommy let herself out the door, and said, "Now you lock this behind me, Billy. And don't you open it for anyone but Daddy or me. Okay?"

I did what she said.

Mommy and Daddy didn't come home last night, but there was a lot of noise from Blairville—it sounded kinda like the Fourth of July.

They didn't come home all day today, either.

The sun went down about a half hour ago.

Right after that was when I first heard the scratching at the door.

I ran upstairs and peeked out the bedroom window.

Mommy and Daddy are out there, and I can hear them calling.

"Billy, open the door, baby!" calls Mommy.

"Open the door, son, and invite us in," says Daddy.

But I can see them in the porch light.

They have strange, long, pointy teeth, and their eyes are as red as blood.

Mommy and Daddy love me.

I know that right down to the soles of my feet.

But I don't want to let them in.

Birches and Murk

Lois H. Gresh

Miranda fingered the worn page. The blue ink had faded. The words were dim.

Soon we will meet, my love. Soon my hands will warm you, they will be soft flames upon your body.

Miranda creased the letter, tucked it into the envelope, dated six years ago.

Finally, Charles was coming to see her. She had waited forever, it seemed. Sixty-five she was last week, and all those years had been lonely ones.

Miranda riffled through her pajamas and stockings. She found the letter that he sent last autumn.

Upon the cold bed, she crossed her legs; they were tight as shears that have been clenched too long in a dark drawer.

Miranda. About to meet her lover, Charles, for the first time.

Her lips trembled.

She read the letter aloud, five times she read it: *I'm not much to look at, dearest, and I'm not much at conversation. But I do care about you, and I love you, and I am yours.*

She needed these words. Miranda: unable to seek the love of those who desired her, unable to convince herself that any real man could care.

Only Charles cared. A hundred letters he'd written during all those lonely, lonely years.

She rubbed the letter down her right leg, and then her left. She kissed it, then tucked it safely into the drawer beneath her sheerest slip.

Soon Charles would come.

"Meet me at the river at dusk. Come when you hear nothing but the sound of my footsteps against the crackle of crickets."

So poetic: Charles.

She wore her moccasins and stepped carefully so as not to make a sound.

Charles wouldn't mind her baldness and her blemishes. He wouldn't use her, as so many men had tried to use her when she was young.

She paused, listened.

Heard footsteps down where the big stone sat upon the snake nest, where the river splashed its inky murk against white birch.

In darkness, she could barely see. She clutched the frail trees, stumbled down the trail leading to the river.

And there he was.

He sat upon the snake stone. Wore a heavy overcoat, odd for early autumn. He seemed to have a beard, black and bushy.

She grasped a birch and leaned, trying to see his face. But the mud was thick and she slipped, and she crashed against a tree and cried out.

He turned and his mouth emptied words upon her, words she'd read many times before. Words she'd chanted as if a litany. She tried to picture the words, wanted them to float across the darkness between them and caress her quivering limbs. Wanted the words in faded blue ink. Wanted them rounded from her own mouth, rolling down her body in soft blue waves.

But then a cloud shifted, and a strand of moon lit his face.

Miranda's hands flew to her mouth, and she screamed.

Her body lurched down the incline, hands grabbing at trees, and she slammed against him; and Charles staggered back, gripped her arms for a moment with hairy hands, then fell into the river.

The snake stone rolled with him, and it splashed with a mighty spray of cold, and Miranda screamed again as the water blinded her, drenched her; and she saw that face one last time as the stone drove his body deep beneath the surface.

It was a face of anguish, a face that had never dared seek hers.

A loving face, tender even, but marred by fire and gouged by scalpel. A face hidden by beard, with eyes bulging above in weird angles, set into place by a surgeon with meager skills.

A face that needed hers.

Upon the cold bed, Miranda's legs were felled birches, stark white against the gloom of dusk.

She fingered the worn page. She could not live without the embrace of Charles's words.

She rubbed the blue ink down her left arm, then across her cheek. She whispered his words, five times she whispered them: *I'm not much to look at, dearest, and I'm not much at conversation. But I do care about you, and I love you, and I am yours.*

But the ink had faded, and the words were dim. And they just didn't roll down her body anymore like soft flames.

Maybe it was time for her to go to Charles.

It was already dusk, and she'd kept him waiting long enough.

Blood Money

Paula Guran

Easiest money he'd ever made, for sure. Even if the old guy had put up a bit of a fight. Screaming at him and Jake, telling 'em that they'd never spend *his* money. Right, so he was gonna like *do* anything about it now with his bald head cracked open and his brains spilled half out? Spending his share of the six thousand or so bucks they'd taken from the old man's hideyhole in the closet was gonna be plenty easy for JohnBoy. Yes.

Jake had already headed out from the crib to find The Man. Jake didn't think about nothin' but the pipe no way. But not him, not

JohnBoy. Little snort, some smoke or some pills were fine, but dope wasn't gonna take his life over, nope, no way. This money was set to buy him some wheels and maybe a few beers.

Reaching into his pocket, Jake extracted the roll of bills. It was real, it was cash and no dead old man was gonna keep him from spending it. What had the old dude called it? Blood money? Well, he was crazy anyway. What did he know? Dumb jerk kept thousands stashed in his ratty apartment. Stupid.

Wad of bills deep in his droops, he was looking good. Strolling down the street he stops and chats up a couple of babes before heading to the 7-Eleven to invest in some refreshment, yes indeed, a few beers to celebrate his newfound wealth. Twenty-four–pack of ice-brewed to the counter, he reaches for a bill or two, pulls it out and flicks it on the counter.

"Hey, man," the clerk challenges. "What's this?"

JohnBoy looks at the cash on the vinyl Salem Menthol pad before him. A red puddle on the sea green background is soaking the money with its thick crimson hue.

"This looks like blood, man!" The clerk is staring at him. "You hurt? You need help?"

JohnBoy can't exactly say what's pounding in his brain. He pulls out another bill, slaps it on the counter distant from the red pool of the first and watches as this one too begins to both seep and soak up blood.

Blood money, blood money, the old man was right, it was blood money.

One last grab into his pocket for the rest of the money. The lump in his fist turns his skin wet, glistening red as soon as it hits the stale store air. Blood money. He tries to toss it off but the streaming scarlet growth is somehow adhered to his palm now, pulsing with a lifebeat all its own. Screaming as the pain hits his wrist, screaming louder than the old man ever could have. Screaming as the gelatinous pulsing bloody mass starts to flatten and creep up his arm, dissolving skin and tissue as it engulfs his living flesh. Screaming until the blood money buys his last extremely painful breath.

The Blue Jar

Lisa S. Silverthorne

Anna held the blue antique jar up to the light and hoped the treasure it held was beyond her wildest dreams. Her grandmother had left the strange jar to Anna in her will, hinting that wealth or poverty lay inside. She pecked at the jar's wax seal with her index finger, but the wax would not budge. Carrying the heavy jar to the sink, she soaked it in hot water until the seal dissolved.

Quickly, she dried the jar and slowly lifted the lid. Several handfuls of pearly granules lay inside, smelling of salt. Frowning, she stuck her finger into the granules and tasted. Salt. It was only salt. Grandma had left money and jewelry to Anna's cousins, yet to her, Grandma's favorite, she'd left a jar of salt. Anna slammed the jar down on the table. The granules shifted, revealing a slip of paper tucked inside. Hoping it would be a check, she plucked it out. The note read:

> In 1929, I was 21, just as you are now. I traveled with an uncle to the Great Rift Valley and to the shores of the Dead Sea. They say that Sodom and Gomorrah lie beneath its depths. On these sparkling white shores, I found my fortune, and in this jar is a handful of the ages taken from those very shores. Soak in the wisdom of those gone before you, and you may find your fortune. But beware that you may also follow those who fell beneath its deadly waves. Only your strength and courage will show you your path.

Dead Sea salts? Anna shook her head. Grandma had left her bath salts. From a geology class, she remembered something about how plate tectonics had torn an ancient weakness in the earth to form the Dead Sea. Fish couldn't even live in those waters. Why had Grandma left her something so strange, so worthless?

Angry, Anna shoved the jar on to the kitchen shelf.

For a week, the jar sat behind the Cap'n Crunch and the Wheaties until Anna decided she would at least test out the salts. What could it hurt?

She carried the jar into the bathroom, set it beside the sink, and ran a bath. After lighting a candle beside the tub, she removed her clothes. Picking up the jar, she eased herself into the warm water and sprinkled the Dead Sea salts into the water. Slowly, she leaned her head against the back of the tub, set down the jar, and closed her eyes.

A low hum emanated through her body. It began in her shoulders, rumbled through her rib cage, down her legs, and into the soles of her feet. She exhaled sharply and the humming deepened until bass droning swirled around her body. The world began to spin. Anna's eyes snapped open as the bathwater became a maelstrom of frightened faces and hands reaching out toward her. She drew her body into a tight ball as the wall of faces groaned and shrieked. Hands reached closer until leathery, mummified fingers touched her back and shoulders, trying to grab hold of her legs and arms.

A flash of light exploded behind her. She started to turn her head, when a voice rose above the droning.

"Don't look back!"

Anna kept her head turned forward, but another flash of light, brighter than the last, enveloped the room. Beneath her, the beige porcelain surface began to crack. Anna held on to the edge of the tub, trying to claw her way out, but the spinning faces and the trembling tub kept her from climbing out. Salt spewed up from the cracks, collecting in the bottom of the tub, and Anna kicked it away.

Again, light flashed behind her, and this time she turned. For an instant, she saw His face. Pure white light and beauty radiated through her, filling her with a peace she had never known. She saw the face of God, framed by the silhouettes of two burning cities and fleeing people. As she looked on His face, her feet turned to salt. She tried to turn away, but the light and beauty and the flaming cities kept her gaze steady. Muscles hardened into cakes of salt, veins filling, skin crusting. As she reached a hand toward Him and smiled longingly, her body turned into a pillar of salt that began a slow dissolve into the bathwater.

Board Action

William Marden

If I could please ask you gentlemen to cease your individual conversations and let me speak? Please, we have important business to discuss."

"Nothing that you have to say is of interest to me," said George Marlowe, corporate lawyer and adviser to presidents, staring coldly at the young man who stood at the head of the table under the Advanced Technologies logo.

Harold Stephens looked down at the antique pocket watch his grandfather had passed down to him a half century before and wondered how long this waste-of-time meeting would take.

The young man, Richard Palimari, clasped his hands in front of him and returned Marlowe's cold stare with a mild one.

"I know that some of you in this room would rather that my family and myself had not purchased eleven percent of AT's stock, but that is a fact that cannot be changed," Palimari said.

He continued. "However, a seat on the board is not sufficient. My family has achieved our success because of our ability to move swiftly and decisively from a position of power. I am therefore asking you to name me chairman of the board."

"It will be a cold day in hell when we vote you in as chair," Marlowe said, adding, "I was a fool to accept your summons to this island. But, as a gesture of courtesy and to show we could overlook your—reputation—we agreed to come here."

Marlowe looked out the picture window of the luxurious resort hotel on the isolated Caribbean beach where Palimari Enterprises had built up a thriving resort and told Palimari, "I demand you provide me with immediate air passage back to the U.S. Now!"

"The same old propaganda," Palimari said. "My grandfather bootlegged whiskey and my father was in the vending machine business, so we must be gangsters."

Palimari gestured to one of his men, three of whom stood near the doors with their hands clasped behind their backs. They made Stephens nervous, a disquiet he dismissed as the overactive workings of an imagination inflamed by tabloid rumors about the nature of the Palimari business.

The man returned, carrying a polished baseball bat.

"What is this, Palimari?" Marlowe asked. "You've picked the wrong man to threaten. If anything happens to me the law will be all over this island."

"I get so damned tired of stereotypes," Palimari said. "I'm a Mafia thug so naturally when I run into an opponent the only thing I can think to do is bash his head in with a baseball bat. No, I brought this prop out to illustrate two points."

He rubbed his hand over the gleaming heft of the bat, saying, "This is literally a work of art. There is no other bat like it in the world. As a result, our market share has jumped thirty percent in the last five years, revolutionizing a stodgy, static industry.

"Secondly, Mr. Marlowe, I don't doubt that if anything bad happened to you the cops would be all over us.

"Well," he said, swinging the bat around and making a solid—if somewhat squishy—strike directly into Marlowe's face that drove him back into the wall, "the point I'm making now is that we just don't frigging care."

As two of Palimari's men dragged the bloody carcass, its nose missing and blood and teeth dripping down its white dress shirt, Palimari pointed to it, saying, "The cops will probably investigate, we might go to jail, but so what. You're going to vote me chairman and jump when I say jump because now you know we're just crazy and mean enough to do the same thing to every one of you if you cross us."

Palimari handed the bat to Stephens, pointing to men along the wall holding videocameras, and said, "Now it's audience participation time. Each of you gentlemen will take a few whacks, and we'll hold the videotape for posterity, or future trials."

"I can't," Stephens whimpered. Palimari took a glossy five-by-eight photo out of his jacket. It was Stephens's wife, sitting in their home's den, a bull's-eye superimposed on her body.

"Think about it," Palimari said, and Stephens did as he lifted the bloody baseball bat high over the moaning body spread-eagle on the boardroom table.

"It won't be nearly as hard the second or third time," Palimari said, and, as Stephens found out, it wasn't.

Bogiebox

Michael Mardis

Robert Jenson's supple musician's fingers glided slowly across the rough tin surface of the ancient toy, pausing briefly as they encountered harsh eruptions of rust and corrosion. The tin was lithographed with garish—almost harsh—primary colors which depicted a circus fantasy world of prancing elephants, fierce lions, and scowling primates with exaggerated canine fangs. Prancing rust-flaked zebras paraded around the small metal box in an unending circle, and the tuxedoed ringmaster stood amidst it all, his arms spread wide and his mouth open in an encompassing smile which seemed more like a death rictus than an expression of welcome.

"I remember . . ." Robert's voice was a strained whisper, barely audible, even to himself.

"Bobby! Damn you, boy! Where are you, Bobby?"

The voice of a small child echoed in the man's mind. "Here, Aunt Rose. I'm playing the piano."

The giantess crouched, her ample figure blocking out the light. "That's just what I thought! Playing! While there's work to be done!"

"I'll be finished soon, I . . ."

"Shut up!" The voice was a bellow now. "You'll never amount to *anything!* Just like your worthless parents, always trying to do things above your raising! When are you ever going to realize . . ." The voice faded away, and the man—or was it the boy—felt himself curling into a protective fetal position.

The hot metallic taste of blood filled Robert's mouth as he involuntarily bit into his lower lip. His hands covered his ears to block out the voice which was rising in volume once again.

"The *bogieman* will get you if you don't do as I say! He *eats* little boys who misbehave and he hides their bones in the closet! Do you want to see? Do you want to go to the closet?"

"No, Aunt Rose, no! I'll stop, and whatever you want me to do I'll . . ."

The giantess shook her massive head. "Not this time, Bobby. You've been a bad boy and you're going to the closet so that you can see what happens to little boys who won't behave!"

In Robert's mind, the scene dissolved into darkness. A feeling of unbearable claustrophobia gripped his soul, and his nostrils were filled with the harsh camphor odor of mothballs. He reached out with the hands of a long-forgotten child, and they closed around the cold angles of a carelessly discarded toy. The music began to play, and the menagerie came to life in the dark.

With a cry of anguish, Robert snapped back to the present. The sun was going down; the light that had been streaming through the grimy glass of the attic window had dimmed to a pale gleam. He had dropped the toy, and as he picked it up he discovered that one of the sharp corners of the box had gouged a mark in the soft pine floor.

His heart raced in momentary terror as he visualized what Aunt Rose would say. How could he cover it up, fix it, before she saw the mark? His own laughter mocked him in the mausoleumlike attic. Aunt Rose had been dead for, what, thirty years? He swung the toy in a high arc, intending to destroy it once and for all on the varnished wooden boards.

He stopped in midswing, his eyes wide with confusion. The rust had vanished from the lithographed tin, the garish colors mysteriously restored as if by some dark magic. The ringmaster's eyes seemed to stare into Robert's own, their dark pupils alive with malice, and a sneer curled his crimson lips.

Robert slowly lowered the box to the floor and his fingers curled around the brightly painted knob of the crank which protruded from the side of the box. Slowly, as if of their own volition, his fingers began to turn the crank. Hidden gears screamed in rusty protest as if angered at their disturbed slumber. Slowly, fitfully, music began to play, a tinny symphony with a melody that Robert recognized in the deepest cellar of his subconscious.

Still, he turned the crank, faster and faster until the rusty shaft screamed in protest and his hand was nothing but a blur of living flesh. The music built up to a crashing crescendo as a hidden catch released the lid of the box. A dark shape leapt from the depths of a swirling vortex as the lid flew back. Robert was finally going to see where they kept the bones.

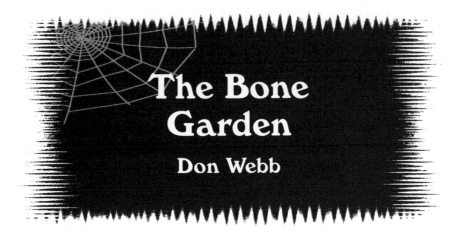

The Bone Garden

Don Webb

The bones began growing as lacy traceries around his house. They grew on the sides of the house as white ivy that didn't even look like bones until you got very close and saw that the bone-colored ivy was without leaf. Sometimes very thin, translucent bones grew over his windows like the patterns of frost that he remembered from his childhood up north.

Nothing did particularly well in his garden except bones. Bones grew up between his corn in rows, long bones—leg bones, he reckoned—he never took an interest in them from a *biological* viewpoint. Short bones grew up under his tomato plants, uprooting them. He would find teeth on his driveway. Seeds, he reckoned they were, but he never saw the bony flower or fruit that dropped them. After a while he gave up and parked his car in the street. The teeth were too rough on his cheap tires.

The house had been very cheap, of course. When the phenomena had started, it was in all the papers and the half-hour news every half hour. But interest had waned. Sometimes a car full of foreigners would go down the back alley and check out the bone garden. Maybe it would get a write-up in some paper for Halloween.

It had been a good place for him to retire. He had worked long and hard in the construction business. It's one thing for a twenty-year-old to be up roofing at the crack of dawn, he can take it. But a man in his fifties, his old bones crack and creak too much.

Perhaps it was his bones that told him, through some turn or twist, that he should buy the little cottage in the bone garden.

He never was much for company. He'd retired too early to go to the places that senior citizens haunt. He didn't care for church, never rightly believed in the afterlife.

So he was happy in the bone garden. Loving its white silence that calmed his mind as he puttered slowly about. He ate everything he wanted to eat. He had been hungry as a child, sixth son of a family of eight. He would never be hungry again. He was happy.

But then the beetles came. Small bone-white beetles, that bored into the bones that grew like trees around his house. They cut little holes and soon the bones became a forest of flutes and organ pipes, and each wandering breeze played melodies—strange, thin and high.

He tried taping his ears shut.

He tried covering the bone's holes.

He tried singing the songs of his childhood to drown out the song.

But the bones sang. They sang of freedom, freedom from the Atlas-like job of holding up the body.

His bones had suffered his hard work, and now suffered his great weight. Although they were loyal bones, they heard the song.

One day they left him and walked out into the garden to be with their kind.

The Bookseller

Adam Niswander

I sell books.

It has been my business for seven years now.

What no one knows is that I am a prisoner trapped in my own body, a body over which something dark and terrible rules.

It began when I wandered into this very bookshop. As I came in the door, the proprietor approached me. His clothing looked old-fashioned, as if he had stepped directly out of the 1930s. I noticed that he had terribly scarred and callused hands.

"What may I show you today?" he asked.

I felt reckless. I looked the old man straight in the eye and replied, "Show me the rarest item in the store."

To tell the truth, I don't know what I expected him to produce. My demand had been a joke, not serious.

His face changed. He suddenly glowed with pleasure. I could swear I saw tears of gratitude in his burning eyes.

"This way, sir," he replied, then guided me to a curtained arch. With a firm grip on my shoulder, he led me into a small room.

He pointed to a small box resting on a pedestal by the wall. The wood was worm-eaten but trimmed in silver. On all sides were carvings, but I did not even recognize the language.

"Here," he said, carefully opening the lid which was secured by thick silver hinges. "Here is the rarest treasure in my shop."

I looked within and could not repress a grunt of acknowledgment, for resting in a bed of plush velvet sat a book more beautifully bound than any I have ever seen. In a thick royal binding wreathed in chased silver, the thing must have been two and a half feet long, eighteen inches wide and as thick as a fist.

"What is it?" I asked, unable to look away.

"It is the Book of the Overseer—a repository of great power."

I knew he did not lie. I had to have it.

"How much?" I asked.

"How much do you have?" he countered, his voice actually trembling in anticipation.

I patted my pockets. I had intentionally left my wallet behind, but I found my lucky coin—a twenty-four-dollar gold piece.

I turned to the old man, holding the coin in the palm of my hand. I planned to offer it only as security, but he snatched it from me with a look of unadulterated joy.

"Done," he said.

He reached into the box and lifted the huge volume carefully, almost reverently, then pressed it to my chest, and I, fool that I am, folded eager arms over it.

At that moment, I felt the weight of the Overseer settling over me. With a whimper, my will vanished and the monster seized my body.

The proprietor stumbled backward and his face broke into a wide grin.

"Free!" he cried. "Free at last!" He backed to the archway. Pausing, he fumbled in his pocket and drew forth a ring of keys, hurling them to the floor at my feet.

"Yours," he said, backing away. "Yours now, and God's pity on you. It will remain this way until some other fool comes to request what you did."

With that, he was gone.

* * *

I have been here seven years now, imprisoned within the walls of meaningless words, compelled to open the door at 9 A.M. and close it again at sunset. The Overseer has trained me. It holds me under a spell from which there is, apparently, only one escape.

The worst thing is the silence. The creature has not said a word to me since taking control.

Twice a week, the Overseer walks me down to the corner store where I purchase bland provisions and clean clothing. During the day, I am compelled to show customers the volumes lining the shelves.

Every night, I am forced to climb down to the basement where shovels and picks beckon me to labor at a great excavation. From the depth to which it now extends into the solid rock, it must have been in progress for many years. I am permitted sleep only four hours of the early morn before I am awakened and driven to open the shop.

If I understood the old man, my release from this hell will not occur until someone else comes into the shop and requests what I did.

I relish the moment when a customer approaches me and I can say, "What may I show you today?"

I cling desperately to hope.

Boxes
Phyllis Eisenstein

The first box arrived while Bob and Sheila were at work. It was too big to fit through the mail slot, so whoever delivered it had left it just inside the storm door. There were no stamps on it, no parcel stickers, but that didn't strike Bob as odd because they sometimes fell off in transit. What did bother him was that there was no return address.

"You think we should open it?" he said.

Sheila was already in the kitchen, starting dinner. "Why not?"

"Are you expecting a package?"

"Nope." She leaned through the kitchen door. "I gather you're not."

He shook his head.

She shrugged. "Some kind of free sample, then. There'll probably be coupons with it." She went back to the food.

Suspicious package, he thought, and memories of bombs to university professors and federal judges swooped down on him. *But that's silly. We're nobody.*

He slit the tape with scissors.

"This is weird," he said, pulling out a mass of transparent plastic that unfolded into a full-length raincoat. Holding it out in front of him, he went to the kitchen door. "Are you sure you didn't order this?"

Sheila blinked at it. "Not me."

There was no sign of an invoice in the box, not even a slip of paper saying "Inspected by No. 22."

He hung the plastic raincoat in the front closet, next to his and Sheila's cloth raincoats. It rained the next day, and they wore those coats, but when Sheila met him at home that night, she didn't have hers.

"It was a crazy thing," she said. "The guy in front of me on the escalator lost his balance and knocked me over, and the hem of my raincoat got caught in the bottom step as it went underneath. I pulled out of the sleeves just in time. Half the coat was sucked right down."

"Oh my God," said Bob, putting his arms around her.

"It jammed the whole mechanism. It was shredded. But I'm okay. Really I am." Her voice was not quite steady though.

Bob took her out to dinner that night, and he tried not to think about the plastic raincoat.

The next evening there was another box waiting for them inside the storm door.

"Is this some kind of joke?" Bob said, waving the purple wig he found inside. The hair was made of coarse synthetic fiber and stuck out wildly in all directions. Once again there was no trace of identification on or in the package.

Sheila shook her head, her own shoulder-length blonde hair swaying with the motion like silk. "Throw it away."

He wrapped it in the plastic raincoat and took the bundle out to the garbage can by the alley.

Just after lunch the following day, his private line at work rang. It was someone from a hospital near Sheila's office.

"Your wife is all right," the voice said, "but we think you should come and take her home."

"What do you mean?" Bob shouted, half out of his chair.

"She's all right, really. But she's been sedated and should go home to bed."

He found her sitting in a corner of the emergency room. She was very pale, and her long blonde hair was horribly short now, frizzed to within half an inch of her head, and black as charcoal. When he put his arm around her, he could smell the sour tang of the burning.

She leaned against him. Her voice was dull with the sedative. "I kept telling him he should quit. But he wouldn't listen. Wouldn't." She turned her face to his shoulder and began to cry.

A doctor came over. "I understand an ashtray full of papers caught fire. Someone's cigarette." He nodded at Sheila. "She was very lucky."

Bob signed her out and took her home.

Later, while she was asleep and he was sitting in the living room trying to read, he heard the storm door swing open, then shut. He went to the front door and looked out.

On the threshold was another identityless box.

He charged into the street, but it was empty from one end to the other. "Why are you doing this?" he screamed. But no one answered.

Back inside, he set the box on the dining room table. *Coincidence*, he told himself. *It doesn't mean anything.* He found the scissors, ripped through the tape, folded the flaps back. And then he threw the box to the floor and screamed again, wordlessly this time.

A plastic mannequin's head spilled out.

Burb Vamp

Barbara J. Ferrenz

Shelley left the front door open as she tried to hold onto her briefcase and the plastic sack. Top-heavy with yogurt and gourmet coffee, the bag dropped a trail of comestibles across the carpet. "Damn."

She left the briefcase on the credenza and fell to her knees to gather her groceries. A draft blew around her legs, a musty scent filled the living room. She turned around. "Chaz! Give me a hand, will ya'? Put more than an artichoke into one of these plastic bags and they dump all over." She picked up her artichokes. "Come on. What's your problem?"

Chaz had entered the house, but stood frozen in the doorway. Shelley rose to her feet, giving him a closer look. "You look terrible." His face was flushed and gaunt. His eyes, more empty and insipid than usual. "It's that no-fat diet, isn't it? I told Marie she was going overboard." Still wearing his golf clothes at ten o'clock on a Monday evening was a sure sign he was going downhill. Maybe Marie finally asked for that divorce she'd been talking about for years.

Chaz smiled. He always had a dopey smile, but the rows of sharp, crooked teeth exposing a serious plaque problem destroyed what little looks he had left. He pounced forward with a piggish grunt, throwing his arms around Shelley's waist. She screamed and reached out, her fingers brushing the handle of her leather briefcase. She grabbed it and swung it, the brass corner hitting Chaz's temple, knocking him away, her real estate papers flying all over the room.

Shelley backed away toward the kitchen. "What the hell do you think you're doing?"

"I need your blood," he said.

"You what? What do you think you are, a goddamn vampire?"

He smiled again. "Yes."

She thought about this a moment. He certainly had the teeth for it, but other than that, Chaz was still the slow-witted, barbecuing corporate droid she had seen mowing the lawn a few days ago. He seemed proud of his new state. She might be able to think of a way out of this if she kept him talking. "So, how did this happen, Chaz?"

He chuckled, and a thread of drool spun from the corner of his mouth. "A guy at the club promised me eternal life. I'll never age. I'll never die."

She looked at the paunch hanging over his belt and the deep crow's-feet around his eyes. "And this is a good thing?"

"Huh? What do you mean?"

"You didn't put too much thought into this, did you, Chaz? You're forty-six years old. You've never looked worse in your life. Why would you pick now to stop the clock? And what about Marie and the kids?"

"They're vampires, too," he said eagerly. "We're all in this together."

"You asked them first, I suppose."

"Uh, no."

Shelley shook her head. There should be a license to use supernatural powers. "Think about it. How long has it been since you and Marie were intimate? Don't look surprised. We girls talk about those things. You're looking at an eternity of cold shoulders and bedtime headaches, Chaz. And why in heaven's name would you turn your teenagers into immortals? Are you some kind of masochist?"

He dropped onto the sofa, holding his head. "I never thought about all that. I just didn't want to get old."

A colorful brochure on the floor caught Shelley's eye. It was for a new, very exclusive listing. "Don and I drifted apart because we lost all the excitement in our marriage," she said.

Chaz looked up, interested.

"You know, the same old thing, year in and year out. I believe we'd still be together if we'd done something daring and different. You have some money squirreled away for retirement, don't you?"

He nodded.

"Since it's all the same to you now . . ." She picked up the brochure. "Look. A beautiful villa in the Caribbean. Imagine sun-washed beaches and warm, tropical nights. Happiness, comfort, romance. Forever." She pressed the brochure into his hand. "Take it. Think about it."

"Yes," he said dumbly. "I will."

She ushered him to the door. "Show it to Marie. Talk it over, then get back to me. I can get you a real deal on this."

Chaz walked out, nodding. Shelley closed the door quickly and locked it. "If this flies, it'll be the sale of a lifetime. But if it doesn't. . . ."

She eyed the coffee table for its wooden stakes potential.

Business Image

Brian McNaughton

One day Seymour decided to stay home and send me to work. I did not like this at all. I had my own life to live when he wasn't peering at me and trying to convince himself that he looked like Richard Gere.

"It's time you made yourself useful," he said.

"You'll be sorry," I said, but only because he expected it. I'm like that.

"Ha! *Au contraire, mon semblable*, I'll be bubbling over with joy. Alone at last!"

I'd show him. I'd rob a bank. He would be blamed. I'd tear the clothes off the first pretty woman I saw. The one in the elevator wasn't bad, but she looked at me so strangely that I forgot my plan. She left in a hurry.

So did I. There's a big mirror in the lobby, and I felt compelled to reach it in time to confront Seymour. The nitwit always paused to check his hair and necktie and make sure his fly was zipped. I was well into my routine before I realized he wasn't there. Or, I should say, that I wasn't.

Out in the street, my compulsion persisted. I was dragged from one shop-window to the next by the groundless fear that Seymour might miss me. Where I come from, everyone hurries along like that, always anticipating the next encounter. Things were different here. I kept colliding with strangers, and I attracted more strange looks that I did my best to return.

The subway was a *different* nightmare from the one I was used to. Normally surrounded by rushing walls in a dark world and in a fragmented state, I was forced to stand inside the car among garishly colored passengers. Unlike the usual monochrome crowd, they stared. I tried fragmenting myself, but it didn't work.

I had ignored the puzzling signs. When at last I deciphered one, I realized that I was going uptown. I hurried off, stumbling, colliding, returning strange looks. Like those bizarre signs, the street-plan had to be reversed to be understood. Existence here was a constant struggle to falsify the evidence of my eyes.

I had never seen Dick, Seymour's boss, but I assumed that it was he who yelled at me for being late. "The subway, Dick, you know the subway."

"No, Seymour, I don't. The subway is for losers, and maybe that's your problem. And stop doing that!"

He didn't explain. I hurried to the watercooler where Seymour always saw me. It was cool and quiet in there. But I wasn't in there, of course, I was out here amid glaring fluorescence and clacking machines.

I went to the woman I took to be Alice, Seymour's secretary, to get the contracts Dick was fretting about. She was impossible. "Why are you doing this to me, Mr. Warren?"

"I'm not—" But she had already fled in tears.

I went to look for the contracts myself, but Dick was at the door. "What the hell's wrong with you, Seymour?"

His face was red and twisted, like mine. The angry jerk of my hand was synchronized with his.

"Are you making fun of me?" he demanded, making a fist, as did I—and then I caught on. I was Seymour's reflection, not his, not Alice's, not the reflection of all those staring loons in the subway. It was very hard, since Dick wasn't doing it, but I laughed.

"I'm getting out of this nuthouse," I said.

"You're damned right you—Seymour! No!"

I dashed for the window, intending to force myself back into my own world through the glass. Unfortunately, my world wasn't there. Beyond the glass gaped a twenty-story drop to the street.

Well. As you must know, since I'm alive to tell this, that was when I woke up. It was one of those dreams we compose to cheat the alarm clock. Utterly realistic, correct in all details, but lasting no more than—

Good God! If the clock was right, I had overslept by two hours. I dialed direct to Dick's office.

"Dick, this is Seymour, I—"

"This is *who?*"

"Yeah, I overslept, don't rub it in. Those contracts—"

"That's a good imitation, pal. If you're a friend of Seymour's—"

"I *am* Seymour!"

"I don't have time for this. Seymour took a dive through his window two minutes ago. My condolences."

I was in no hurry to get up, because the first thing I would see was the mirror over my dresser. At last I forced myself.

The mirror was quite empty.

Callahan's Coat

Donald R. Burleson

The night exploded in a clap of thunder, and the lights went out.

Mary, absurdly, was left holding her book in the dark. She reclined her head on the cushion and tried to relax in the padded expanses of her chair, hoping that the power would come on, but for now the darkness was almost palpable, a mass of shadow. Callahan would have been up seeing to things, lighting an oil lantern. She didn't even know where the lantern was. At least he had been good about those things; if only he hadn't been the way he was, if only he hadn't made her so afraid of him. To this day, his influence, his unhappy memory, seemed at times to linger in the house.

Callahan. That's how she thought of him even now, after all these years since his death. Not Jeremiah, not Jerry; just Callahan. She had taken the name in marriage, but it had sat poorly upon her, like an ill-fitting coat.

Outside, the thunder muttered on and on, and a moaning wind touched the brittle windowpanes with blind, cold fingers of rain. The coat, of course, the big old brown overcoat—that was why she was thinking about these things. She had found it in the basement closet just this morning, maybe the last real remnant of him, and she had left it on the little table beside the cellar door to remind herself to put it out with the trash on Tuesday. The inside lining was badly shredded and the whole garment reeked of old cigar smoke and other odors, as well as mildew now. She couldn't imagine anyone else wanting to wear it.

Near her, the wind rustled the curtains, and she realized that she ought to close the window, but somehow she didn't want to get up out of her chair in the dark. Though she couldn't see a thing, she knew that the saucer with the candle was still on the little lampstand beside her, and she felt around for it, fumbling then with paper matches, but before she could light the candle a fitful little gust of wind snuffed out the tiny flame of the match, and she sighed and sat back and tried to accept the darkness.

But in that moment when the match had flared, what was the impression she had gotten? Something had been different.

Something had been wrong.

She sat very still and listened, but heard only the pattering of the rain, the grumbling of thunder.

No, there *was* something else.

A sound like something soft passing over the carpet, out there in front of her somewhere. As she leaned forward to catch the sound, it stopped. Maybe she had just imagined it.

But when the lightning at that moment illumined the room, she saw what she saw. Someone was in the room with her.

She felt her whole body turn cold, and she tried not to move. Maybe whoever it was wouldn't see her, wouldn't know she was here. When the lightning flashed again, she peered out into the room before her.

The illumination faded as quickly as it had come, but the impression remained. It was, she thought at first, a child—a gnomelike figure standing there in the dark now, humped and dwarfish. But she had to accept what her mind insisted was the truth of the matter.

What was standing there was the coat.

She tried to draw a deep breath, to calm herself, but couldn't get it down the tightness of her throat. The darkness was so dense, so heavy, that it seemed to press upon her like a shroud, and the thunder mumbled on in its endless litany, and the rain drummed at the windows.

And out in front of her, something was moving again.

A quick flash of lightning played over the room. It was the coat, all right, and it was closer now.

Merciful heaven, this couldn't be. She felt as if her heart would stop. And now, playing on the lightless air, was a medley of odors whose nature she didn't want to contemplate.

There wasn't time anyway. When the lightning flashed once more, it told her what she already knew. The arms of the great brown coat, though rounded in the air, could not have contained anything of substance, but that didn't keep them from reaching out for her.

Candid Camera

Don D'Ammassa

Stewart found the magic camera in a trunk in his uncle's attic. He didn't realize it was magic at first, not until after he'd read his uncle's journal. Even then he didn't believe it until he tried it out.

Patrick Olsen had been a wealthy man while he was alive, although no one knew where his wealth came from, or for that matter where it had been kept through the sixty years of his reclusive life. He had no bank account, no job, no known investments or property other than the elderly, crumbling farmhouse on the outskirts of Managansett, but he drove a brand new car, ate at the finest restaurants, endowed local charities, and paid cash for everything.

Lots of cash.

As his heir, Stewart was entitled to that money, expected it to make a major change in his personal lifestyle. All he had to do was find it.

His initial search was depressingly uneventful. The house was full of junk, some of it reasonably valuable, but not enough to elevate Stewart to the lifestyle to which he hoped to become accustomed.

He'd discarded the camera casually when he first stumbled across it, came back only when he found it mentioned in the journal.

"The camera is the key to my treasure," the old man had written. "It alone provides the key to the vault in the den."

The den was in an outside corner; two walls were exterior, the others separated it from adjacent rooms. No room for a vault of any kind. The only reason Stewart discovered the secret was that he decided to see if the camera would work; he snapped a picture of his uncle's desk.

It was an Instamatic. The picture popped out, a fair rendition of the desk, and just to the left, where there had been bare wall, there was a door.

Stewart looked up, startled, and it was right there, as clear as day. But he hadn't been able to see it until he snapped the picture.

The door wasn't even locked.

There was little light inside, a single bare bulb hanging from the ceiling. Stewart pulled the cord and blinked, slowly traversing the chamber with his eyes.

Nothing. The walls and floor were completely bare. If this was his uncle's vault, then it had been picked bare.

Or had it?

On a whim, Stewart raised the camera and took another picture, waiting impatiently for it to develop. When it did, his breath caught raggedly. The floor was covered with wire baskets filled with money, neat packages of bills in various denominations. And on the opposite wall, writing had appeared as well, indistinct in the picture, but very clear when Stewart raised his eyes past the now visible cash and read:

THE CHAMBER TO YOUR RIGHT IS FORBIDDEN

Curious, Stewart turned his head, but the wall in question was featureless. Instead, he turned to his left, snapped another picture, and seconds later was examining baskets of gold coins, jewels, and other precious items.

"Stewart Olsen, you're going to be a great rich person."

Back in the first chamber, he pondered the blank wall opposite. What could be concealed there? Impetuously, he raised the camera, snapped yet another photograph, humming to himself while it developed.

"A cave?" The photograph showed a cavern of some sort, its entrance bracketed by sharply pointed stalagmites and stalactites, yawning open like a set of enormous jaws.

"I don't get it," he said quietly, raising his head to stare into the now visible cave.

He had a second or two to realize that the resemblance to giant teeth was more than coincidence before the guardian of the treasure closed its jaws and bit him neatly in half.

Candles

Lisa Jean Bothell

Happy birthday to me!

It doesn't bother me that I woke up again on a stinking flat mattress in the youth shelter, because I'm getting out.

I used my Bic lighter to set off the sprinklers. When the counselors rushed everyone outside, I slipped into the office and broke the cash strongbox. I found over four hundred dollars, but only took ninety. I'm not a criminal, you know.

I just needed enough to get home.

Oh, I'm not one of those crazy kids that love their parents even though they beat the shit out of you. Actually, it was Mom's live-in boyfriend, Ron, who had the heavy hand. Mom just looked the other way, afraid to lose our meal ticket.

But Mom's dead now. Found in a pool of her own blood, her face so bruised it looked like an overripe plum, the paring knife stuck in her throat. They hadn't caught Ron yet, and I was here "for my own safety." The bastard's face was all over the evening news. Too cool.

Nope. I'm going home to *Daddy*.

I hopped a Greyhound and headed to Corpus Christi, my eyes caressing the worn paper with Daddy's address on it.

I knew he wouldn't be surprised to see me, even though ten years had passed since he'd promised a special sweet-sixteen party "for my princess," with dozens of presents and a trip somewhere cool. We'd played guessing games about that trip as he'd caught me in his arms, swinging me breathlessly through the air, both of us laughing.

The Alps, Vermont, Geneva, Maine, other places without the steaming midsummer heat of Corpus Christi.

"I've decided where, Daddy," I whispered, shifting on the sticky vinyl bus seat.

I don't understand. I'm sure *this* is the house. It's smaller than I expected, since Daddy is rich. At least, rich compared to Mom and me. We'd lived in a shitty trailer park and our trailer had been so tiny that I could hear Mom and Ron groaning together on the squeaky mattress late at night; she could probably hear me whimper when he started "funnin'" with me. That's what he called it: "funnin'." Strange how adults couldn't say "sex" even when they were screwing you.

But *this* house is nice. Three stories, white with peach trim and a well-watered emerald lawn. I'll bet there's a pool in back, and air-conditioning inside. And a pretty bedroom upstairs for *me*. Presents piled on the dining room table with my chocolate cake. I *knew* Daddy would remember chocolate.

But no one's answering the door.

Oh, I *get* it. I'll bet Daddy's out getting the last few gifts right now. I'll just wait in the shade of the elm tree until he gets home.

Daddy forgot my birthday.

He didn't recognize me. As if, just ten years ago, he hadn't swung me around in the air, promising my sweet-sixteen party.

"I have another family now, Angela." (Not Princess.) "I forgot it was your birthday."

"But Daddy, Mom died. I'm going to live with *you*."

It started to look bad when they tried to convince me to go back to the youth shelter.

Worse when they offered to drive.

Then my new little sister whined about watching a rental film: *The Lion King*. "Hush, Princess." Daddy frowned at her.

I've never seen *The Lion King*.

They came around. Sure, there's no cake, but everyone's at the table to celebrate. I cleaned up most of the blood, but the side of my sister's head is caved in, and my stepmother's silk blouse is gouged from the cake knife. I did better this time, after practicing on Mom.

At least Daddy looks all right. He's the only *important* one. I tied him to the chair, and he's coming around now.

Great! I can model all the gorgeous clothes I found in the closet upstairs.

"Shhh, Daddy. Doesn't *your* princess look pretty?"

His eyes roll and he tries to scream around the kitchen towel stuffed in his mouth.

Daddy can't come on the trip after all. That's okay. Right now, it's time to make a wish.

80

The three-story house catches like a dry wick, a single white candle blazing in an emerald-green grass cake.

Close my eyes and blow really hard.

"Where do you want to go on your birthday, Angela?" Daddy whispers, ten years ago.

I set my shoulders and smile. *Aspen.*

Happy birthday to me.

The Candyman
Michael Grisi

CANDYMAN STRIKES AGAIN

As I looked at the headline, my heart sank. For the third time this month the killer known as the Candyman had murdered a child. The article revealed the familiar details. As on the previous occasions, a little boy was found in a wooded area near his home, the life from his body snuffed out. He was found still clutching the candy the murderer had given him. Hence, the media had dubbed the killer the "Candyman."

Once again our town will be mourning the loss of another one of our children. I ask myself how anyone could be capable of such an inhuman act. The bastard has no right to live.

I feel like I should be doing something to help the situation, but I also feel so helpless. Obviously this maniac has to be stopped, but how does one go about doing so?

It's times like these that I remember my own childhood. My mother would warn me about taking candy from strangers. If more mothers had done the same in the past month, a few tragedies may have been avoided.

Being retired and having so much time on my hands, the best thing to do would be what I have done in the past, walk up and down the streets and observe. Perhaps I can prevent the next murder by being in the right place at the right time. If I am near, maybe the Candyman will be discouraged from moving in on one of the potential victims he has stalked.

So, I left on my mission, perhaps to be a guardian angel of sorts. At this time of the day many of the children will be walking to school. It's prime time for the villain to make his move, which makes my watchful eyes so very important.

My observations on the first few blocks of my walk were encouraging. Many parents were walking with their children, but a few more blocks away my concern was aroused. A young boy of about seven was walking to school unescorted. I looked up and down the street and didn't see anyone else. It was then that I decided to walk with the boy.

"Young man, does your mother allow you to walk to school all by yourself?"

"Sure. I'm seven years old. I know my way around."

"Well, it's just with all this Candyman business going on, all the children's parents are walking them to school."

"My mom had to leave for work, but when she left she told me not to talk to any strangers on the way to school. You're a stranger, ya know, so I'm not supposed to be talking to you."

"It's OK, I'm a nice stranger. I just wanted to make sure you got to school safely. Do you want me to walk with you?"

"I don't know."

I detected some hesitance in the boy's voice. "It's OK, really. What's your name, young man?"

"Tommy."

"Well, Tommy, I'm sure it would make your mother happy if she knew I was with you."

"OK . . . I guess."

When the young man looked me in the eye, I knew I had his confidence and I knew he would be safe. As we began walking, I put my arm around his shoulder and it was accepted graciously. I put my hand in my pocket and pulled out two candybars.

"Do you want one, Tommy?" He pulled away from me.

"You're the Candyman."

"Don't be silly, Tommy, of course I'm not. Go ahead and take it."

"No! You are too! Are too!"

"Tommy, stop screaming or he'll hear you."

"No! I won't stop screaming! You're the Candyman. *You're* the Candyman!"

He was screaming so loud, I had to quiet him down. I put my hand over his mouth and carried him across the street into the woods. I kept his mouth covered until he stopped fighting and yelling. Now he would be quiet. I propped him up against a tree.

"You'll be safe," I told him. "The Candyman won't find you here."

I turned to leave, but realized he never took the candybar from me, so I put it in his hand.

"Just in case you get hungry later."

With another child safe and sound, I went on my way to see if any others might need a guardian angel.

The Cards Speak

Brian Craig

Printing destroyed the art of cartomancy. Once it became possible to *duplicate* decks of cards, all the real virtue went out of them. The virtue that a deck of cards had was all in the design and decoration. A deck of cards that was efficient in divination had to have the power painted into it. All art was alchemy in those days; the standardization of pigments and their suspension media killed the magic of the process as surely as printing killed the virtue of the cards.

Cards were always dual-purpose, of course. The same cards that were used for divination were used to play gambling games, and the power that the cards had to offer tantalizing glimpses of the future was the same power that determined who would win and who would lose. Yes, of course it's all a matter of statistical probabilities *now*— but even today's games haven't entirely lost the subtle alchemy of bluff or the aesthetic wonder of flushes and full houses coming together. That's the very essence of aesthetic experience, you know, underlying all else: the fall of the court cards, the fusing of magical combinations, the tragic disruption of the hand of hearts by the spade or the club—the sword or the wand, as it used to be.

But what is it all leading up to? Well, Mr Gambler-with-a-Calculator, what it's leading up to is this—dare you play a hand with me using a *real* deck of cards. Not a Waddington's Number One or some tobacco company's advertising gimmick, not something cut from cardboard and plastic-coated, but a work of art. I have one in the safe, which I only bring out for special occasions.

What stakes? Well, that's another difference between then and now. Nowadays, wealth is a disposable thing, all wrapped up in symbols: coins, banknotes, share certificates. In the old days, men had to bet with the raw substance of their existence: their livestock, their wives . . . their souls.

No, *of course* I'm not the Devil—but there's no law to say that only the Devil can play for souls.

Yes, you can deal—the magic is in the cards, not the dealer—but you must shuffle very carefully, because that stiffened silk is very delicate. There's no reason at all why we shouldn't play poker—yes, it was unknown during the Age of Enlightenment, when men preferred whist and bezique, but it didn't have to be invented; it only had to resurface.

Your queen bets. That's a good card. If this were divination, it would promise you a rewarding love-life—but this is *competition*.

It's still your queen to bet. My seven nine would be significant, if this were divination, all the more so because they're both swords—and that ten you've just given me would add to their cutting edge.

Yes, I understand how astonishingly unlikely it would be to fill a running flush on a five-card deal, even if I had one in the hole—or even a perfectly ordinary run or flush—but this is a *real* deck of cards, not the kind that you're used to, so I'm going to call your pair of queens and raise.

Yes, we have rather exhausted the symbolism of the chips, but that's the kind of game this is. You can fold if you like and leave the mere money behind. You're under no compulsion to throw your life into the pot—but that's what it'll cost to stay in.

Now that *is* disappointing. A mere six, and a six of cups at that. Now the very best I can have is a run—always provided that I've an eight in the hole. On the other hand, the best you can possibly have is three queens, and you'd need a black queen in the hole to make that. I've never liked the black queens—they're treacherous allies at the best of times, and she really wouldn't improve your hand if you were hugging her to your bosom, because if I *don't* have a run, you'll win anyway.

Check, you say? I'll bet whatever it takes to match your soul. You name it.

Now it's up to you: fold or call.

That's been my advantage all along: you don't believe in magic. If you did, you'd have thought long and hard about the significance of that knave.

No, *of course* I'm not the Devil. I just have a few IOUs to work off. How did you think I got this job in the first place?

Carnival Wishing

Lisa Lepovetsky

In sawdust outside the battered freaks tent advertising *Rama, the two-headed bull!* and *Albert the alligator-man!*, Cassie wiggles her bare toes, raising gray puffs in the late afternoon stillness. Her mother paid fifty cents to go into the tent, but wouldn't take Cassie with her. Just as she wouldn't take Cassie into the beer tent. Not that Cassie wanted to go into the smelly old beer tent, where Mama drank too much and giggled with all the old men.

Cassie wishes Auntie Beth had brought her to the carnival—Auntie Beth would have taken her in. But Mama won't even let her visit Auntie Beth now that the divorce is final. Mama calls Auntie Beth a "weirdo and a loser, just like her brother," but Cassie likes staying with Auntie Beth, learning the strange words and songs. She hopes Daddy will come back someday and take her to visit Auntie Beth. She tries to remember all the things Auntie Beth taught her, so she'll be ready when the time comes. She wishes hard every night that she were Auntie Beth's little girl instead of her Mama's.

Cassie's toenails probe something soft in the yellow dirt beside the ferris wheel. She squats for a closer look. A sparrow pants and trembles, its eyes glazing in shock. Cassie realizes it must have flown into the metal braces of the ferris wheel, and injured itself, perhaps broken its neck. Now it waits for death in the hot dust and noise. She reaches out one grimy hand and lifts the bird gently toward her face.

"Poor thing," she murmurs. "Are you someone's mama?"

In her palm, the bird shudders as though in response to her voice. Cassie remembers what Auntie Beth told her about making her wishes come true through sacrifices. She never understood what a sacrifice was. Until now.

Cassie is jerked upright. "What are you doing in that dirt?" Mama shouts. "And what have you got in your hand?"

Before Cassie has a chance to answer, the harlequin balloon man stumbles past, nearly knocking Mama to the ground. Cassie turns away as her mother curses at the limping old clown. When she turns back, the bird has disappeared. She holds her empty hands high for her mother to see as she chews something.

Mama shrugs and says, "Let's get some cotton candy then. What are you eating?"

Cassie swallows hard, then licks her lips. "Nothing, Mama. Let's get some cotton candy."

She smiles a secret smile as they walk down the midway; she knows she'll get her wish now. Her mother stops suddenly.

"You wait here. I want to ride the ferris wheel."

"Can I go, too, Mama? Please?"

"No. You'll just get scared when we're at the top. I don't want you getting sick."

She turns away and pays her money to the ragged man sitting next to the lever that makes the wheel go around. Cassie watches her sit in the swing, and sighs in frustration. As the wheel groans to life, however, and the setting sun catches Mama's face, she changes. The illusion lasts only a moment, but it's enough. For just an instant, Cassie's mother looks like the sparrow dying in the dust.

Cassie smiles again and waves to her mother. "Good-bye," she whispers.

The Cat

Phyllis Eisenstein

A cat will keep the evil spirits away from you," Grandma Sophie had said on Marilyn's very first day in her own tiny off-campus apartment.

Marilyn laughed and stroked the white kitten that was her grandmother's housewarming gift. "I thought cats *were* evil spirits, Grandma. Witches' familiars and all that."

Sophie shook her head. "They only have that reputation because they walk at night, as the spirits do. Let him walk you home at night, darling, and you'll always be safe." She kissed Marilyn's cheek. "I worry about you living alone."

"You live alone," said Marilyn.

"And I have cats," said Grandma Sophie.

Marilyn had never had a cat before. Her father had always preferred dogs; cats were too sneaky, he said. But Marilyn liked the kitten, which was lively and affectionate and not nearly as demanding as her father's Airedale. In her father's honor, she called the kitten Sneaky.

And Sneaky did walk at night. Marilyn knew that because sometimes she woke in the darkness of her bedroom alcove and felt for the ball of fur that had gone to sleep curled at her side, and it wasn't there. And then she would hear the soft sounds of a cat at play, the gallop of paws out on the bare living room floor, the clickety-clack of some small object that Sneaky was batting back and forth—a thimble, a lipstick, a nutshell, a bottle cap. He would raid any horizontal surface for them, dig in the garbage, even nose open the cabinet doors in the little kitchenette. Marilyn kept trying to put things out of his reach, but somehow Sneaky always found something to play with, clickety-clack.

She didn't really mind his playing. In fact, she found the sound soothing, like the ticking of a clock. But the first time Sneaky pulled a spool out of her sewing kit and spent the night unrolling white thread around the legs of every piece of furniture in the apartment, she was annoyed. Tripping through a spiderweb of mercerized cotton while rushing to get ready for class in the morning was not her idea of fun with a pet. That afternoon, after she had had time to scissor her way through the mess, she moved the sewing kit from her desk to the top shelf of the bathroom closet.

If she had grown up with cats, Marilyn would have known that wouldn't work. But she had grown up with dogs. The next morning, the thread spiderweb was back, yellow this time, and the contents of the sewing kit were scattered all over the bathroom floor.

Now she had a challenge. She had to store the thread in a place where Sneaky couldn't get to it. Her bureau drawers were already crammed full of other potential cat toys. Her cabinets and shelves were, as she had already discovered, too vulnerable. A heavy, sealable box seemed like the best solution, but she didn't own one and wouldn't have time to buy one till the weekend, three days away.

She put the sewing kit in the refrigerator.

That night, she woke to the usual clickety-clack. Without opening her eyes, she turned over and rubbed her face against her pillow. A nutshell or a bottle cap, she thought, and then she remembered that she had thrown the garbage out that evening. Clickety-clack. It didn't sound like a thimble or a lipstick. It sounded like a spool. She sat up in bed.

The living room and kitchenette were dimly lit by the open refrigerator. By that glow, she could see the floor was a maze of pale thread.

"Oh, Sneaky, you monster," she said.

Clickety-clack. The cat was under a chair on the far side of the room, the spool a white spot between his white paws.

Marilyn stumbled through the spiderweb to the refrigerator, breaking dozens of strands on her way, nearly falling twice. The sewing kit was on the floor in front of the fridge, spools, scissors, and pincushion lying helter-skelter. She flicked on the counter light and closed the door. Then she picked up the scissors and turned, exasperated, to clear away Sneaky's handiwork.

And she saw the shadowy thing that had been trapped by the cat's web, trapped on two other nights till the dawnlight came and chased it away, but trapped no more this night, because Marilyn had broken so many of the pale strands.

At the last moment, she raised the scissors, daggerlike, but it didn't help.

Catharsis

Tim Waggoner

You need to let your anger out, Lisa. We've talked about this before."

"I know, Dr. Griffith, I know." Lying on the couch, Lisa clasped her hands together over her chest—a classic defensive gesture—her tone that of a chastened little girl.

Dr. Griffith shifted in his plush leather chair and repositioned his open notebook on his knee. "Tell me again about this latest incident between you and your husband."

She stared up at the ceiling. "Like I said, my mother invited the two of us over to dinner and—without checking with Dwight—I said we'd come. When he got home that night and I told him, he just blew up at me. He's not real fond of my mother, and he'd had a tough day at work. But instead of just standing there quietly and listening while he yelled, like I usually do, I felt this overwhelming urge to yell back. I wanted to start grabbing things and smash them to the floor, wanted to . . . to . . ."

She was on the verge of tears. Dr. Griffith leaned forward. "Go on," he urged her.

"To grab a knife," she whispered, ashamed. "But I didn't do anything," she hurried to add. "I just waited until he was finished, and then ran into the bedroom and cried."

"You're beginning to feel your anger, Lisa. That's significant progress. Now it's time for you to learn to let it free." Dr. Griffith was silent as he considered a moment. "I think you're ready for the next step."

"Oh?" she quavered.

Dr. Griffith gave her his best reassuring smile. "There's nothing to be afraid of."

He stood and placed his notebook on the seat of his chair. He then reached out and helped Lisa up off the couch and led her to the center of the room.

"I want you to stand here, very still, and keep your eyes closed. Can you do that for me, Lisa?"

"Yes, Doctor." She sounded unsure.

"What we're going to do might seem a little . . . strange, but I think it might very well lead to a breakthrough."

"Okay." Lisa didn't sound very confident, but she closed her eyes nevertheless.

"Now open your mouth wide, as wide as you can."

"Excuse me?"

"I told you it might sound odd, but trust me, Lisa."

She hesitated for a second, then did as Dr. Griffith asked.

"Good. Now imagine you're back in the kitchen with Dwight, and that he's yelling at you. Allow yourself to feel the feelings you had then; allow your anger to return."

Lisa frowned and her jaw clenched tight.

"Excellent. Now scream, Lisa!" Dr. Griffith's voice rose to a shout. "As loud as you can! Give your anger voice!"

Lisa's body tensed but she didn't scream. Dr. Griffith grabbed her by the shoulders and gave her a shake.

"Scream, damn it!"

And Lisa did. It started as a soft keening and built in volume and intensity until it was a shrill cry of rage. Lisa's face turned red and the cords of her neck muscles bulged wire-taught.

Then it was over. Lisa opened her eyes and blinked, looking surprised and drained. And then she smiled.

"I've never let go like that before—it felt absolutely *wonderful!* Thank you, Doctor!"

Dr. Griffith smiled. "You're quite welcome."

As soon as Lisa left, Dr. Griffith hastened to pluck the threads of her anger from the air before they could dissipate. When he had gotten them all, he rolled them together into a foul-smelling ebony mass which he shoved greedily into his mouth.

Lisa's anger burned rancid and hot all the way down his throat. It was delicious.

When he was finished, Dr. Griffith sat down at his desk and sighed in contentment. Helping people could be so . . . fulfilling.

He keyed the intercom. "Sarah, could you send my next appointment on back? Thanks."

As he waited, he licked the sticky-rotten remnants of Lisa's rage from his lips and looked forward to his next client—and dessert.

Change of Life

Adam Niswander

Mathilda Harker is a vampire.

I know that sounds a little weird, but she *is* a vampire. I'm not wrong about this.

I've known Mathilda since we was kids together. She wasn't no vampire then, of course.

Today I'm closin' in on fifty years of age and so is she, but I'm gettin' older.

Mathilda is growin' younger and prettier.

I don't remember Mathilda bein' pretty when we was in school.

I know I'm probably not makin' much sense, but you've *got* to understand—I've just found out that vampires *really do exist!*

The news has upset me.

See, ya might not know it to look at me, but I'm not all that smart a guy. I've worked for the All-Night Diner every morning and afternoon for the last twenty-eight years. I got it all down to a routine, ya see?

So findin' out my neighbor, Mathilda Harker, has become a vampire is upsettin'.

See, I was sittin' at the Shamrock when she came in last night. I wouldna paid any attention if it'd been the same old Mathilda. But this wasn't the same old Mathilda. This was the new, improved model.

She had on a skintight black thing that din't hide nothin', with these tall spiked heels that made her legs look . . . well, they looked real good.

Her hair din't have a streak of gray in it, and her face was smooth as a baby's ass.

I din't even recognize her at first . . . but I looked, 'cause she was worth lookin' at.

She spoke to me and called me by name. She said, "Hi, George. How you been?"

I said, "Huh?"

She said, "Aw, c'mon, George, don't you recognize me? I'm Mathilda, Mathilda Harker. We went to school together."

I swear you coulda knocked me off my stool by breathin' on me.

"Mathilda?" I says. "Is that really you? Why, you look like you're still twenty."

She smiled at that, and I noticed there was somethin' funny about her teeth, but I only saw it for a second, 'cause the rest of her was draggin' my eyes down somethin' fierce.

"Why thank you, George," she said, dimplin' up all pretty like. "You sure know how to make a girl feel appreciated."

Appreciated? Shit! She was a riot lookin' for a place to happen.

"You like what you see, George?" She turned around real slow like, stickin' her chest out and kinda posin', like one of the dames in *Playboy*.

When she stuck her chest out like that, it got kinda hard to breathe, ya know?

Then Mathilda says, "You want to walk me home, George? It's real dark out there with no moon tonight, and I'd feel better with an escort."

I shoulda said no, but I din't. "Sure, Mathilda. I was headin' home anyways."

I finished my beer in a couple gulps and stood up. She moved right up to my side and pulled my arm around her.

Only I remember, she din't feel warm at all.

When we came to her house, she kinda slowed down, then turned and looked at me.

"You want to live forever, George?"

I said, "Huh?"

She gave me that big smile again and I could see those teeth—her eyeteeth—they was real long and pointy lookin'.

"Would you like to live forever, George? Would you like to be young again?"

I said, "Heck yeah. Who wouldn't?"

And Mathilda said, "I can make it happen, George. I can give you eternal life. All you have to do is love me."

I looked at Mathilda Harker in the glare of the streetlight, and she looked really good, ya know what I mean?

I thought about goin' back to my empty house, bein' alone—and what Mathilda was offerin' sounded a lot better, so I said, "Hey! What's not to love?"

Mathilda tapped real gentle on my jug'lar vein and said, "Come see me tomorrow night, George."

And then she went into her house and left me standin' there, gawkin' at her front door.

I figgered it out.

Mathilda Harker is a vampire.

I've showered, dressed and made myself a drink. I'm waitin' for sundown.

In a few minutes, I'm goin' next door for my date with Mathilda.

My boss at the diner said there'd be no problem.

He arranged for me to start workin' night shift tomorrow.

Changes

Brian McNaughton

One morning Arthur Moran came to suspect that the world had disintegrated while he slept. Almost everything, however, had been replaced with near-duplicates.

"You're crazy," said Trish, his wife, when he confided his suspicion at breakfast.

"That was my first thought, too, but would a crazy person even consider that possibility?"

"A crazy person who was a devious, pseudo-intellectual quibbler would," she said, "especially if he was a lawyer."

He had grown weary of her lawyer jokes even before she began compiling a book of them. At that very moment she was jotting in her ubiquitous notebook. This would normally have annoyed him, but now he felt a chill.

"Your notebook is green," he said.

"*Very* good, Arthur!"

Ignoring her sarcasm, he said, "Your notebooks are always blue."

"On the contrary, dear, I bought a dozen green notebooks when I began my project. Green is my favorite color."

"Perhaps I'm not quite awake yet," he said mildly.

"Crazy," she muttered, scribbling.

He studied her guardedly while skimming his newspaper. He could point to no one line or freckle on her fashionably lean face and cry *Aha!* but she was surely not the same woman she had been yesterday. His newspaper was wrong, too. The typeface and the proportions of the page were slightly different, but he could summon no precise image of the paper's correct appearance.

He asked, "*To lie* is the intransitive verb, isn't it?"

"As in, 'I *lied* after I *laid* Ms. Cromer at the Christmas party,' dear?"

He flushed. With not a single martini glass in sight, she was almost never so vindictive so early in the day.

"*Lie* meaning to recline," he said. "I lie, I lay, I have lain."

"Of course."

"I've come across no less than two instances in today's paper where *lie* and *lay* are confused."

"And you believe, because *The Times* employs a copyeditor who didn't go to Harvard, that you've been hurled into a parallel universe?"

"It's unusual," he said, unwilling to make a stand on such shaky ground.

Most of the discrepancies in this new world were similarly minor or elusive. They could have been ordinary mistakes; his memories of details could have been false.

His greatest shock today had been his first, when he punched the button on his bedside stereo for his favorite classical music station. He was sickened by a blast of noise, by an inane beat, by screeches fulfilling with a vengeance Isaiah's prophecy that the tongue of the dumb shall sing. He hurried to adjust the manual tuner, but the frequency was correct. The familiar station was no longer to be found on the dial.

Even that drastic change could be explained. Radio stations were bought and sold, new owners brought new policies, and sometimes they omitted to tell the public that an apparently fixed beacon in the universal flux had been washed away forever. He began to wonder if this shock hadn't caused a mild stroke. It was hardly a comforting thought, but lost brain-cells might be responsible for his persistent sense of reverse *déjà vu*.

"Would you get the door, dear?" Trish asked. "It's probably just the headman."

He bit back his question as she continued to write. She smiled nastily, but perhaps at her own latest triumph of composition. Although he couldn't imagine what she had actually said, he had most likely misheard.

"There's a check for him by the door," she said, "under the vase."

The headman: did the denizens of this different world live in tribes? Or had she meant *Head Man?* Contrary to common sense and political correctness, was he about to confront God Himself? Perhaps he had died overnight and now faced the Last Judgment. If that was so, a check seemed inappropriate. He found the check by the front door, however, made out to Capital Distributors for the sum of forty-one dollars and twenty-eight cents.

"Another lovely day, Mr. Moran," said the man in a stained apron who proffered a bill.

"Lovely," Arthur repeated mechanically, his eyes fixed on the net bag in the tradesman's other hand, which contained three severed human heads.

The Chindi
Don D'Ammassa

Why would someone just go off and leave this place?" Jill gestured to include not just the abandoned hogan but its surroundings as well, a sheltered spot with a magnificent view of the landscape.

Brian shrugged. "Navajo superstition. Look, see this hole cut in the side? Someone died and that's where they took the body out."

Jill frowned critically. "You're putting me on, right? There's a perfectly good door, but someone cut a hole in the wall anyway."

"It's their custom. They always take a body out through the north side because that's where evil comes from. Then they abandon the hogan because of ghosts."

"Ghosts yet!" Jill shook her head. "And you think we can learn something from studying these people? They're living in the dark ages. They're not even smart enough to build their houses—"

"Hogans," Brian interrupted.

"Whatever. They don't even think to build them with a north entrance in the first place."

"Would you want evil to be the first thing you see every morning? Anyway, they usually take the dying out to die in sunlight, but there's not always time." He wanted to change the subject; Jill was predisposed to think ill of this entire venture, and he was just providing fuel. "So is this a good enough spot to set up camp?"

"Can we fix that hole? It'd be a lot warmer than our tent."

"Sure, I guess. But it's haunted, you know. There's a Navajo chindi living there now."

Jill's expression was clearer than words. He started gathering materials to make a patch.

Jill was unusually subdued the following morning.

"Sleep all right?" They'd been living together for over a year and Brian still couldn't read her moods.

"Yeah, I guess." She didn't meet his eyes. "Who do you suppose lived here?"

"Hard to tell. A Navajo wiseman maybe. They're not hermits exactly, have a strong sense of family in fact, but they tend to go off by themselves."

Brian busied himself starting the gas stove. Coffee was the first order of business today. There was a definite chill despite the morning sun.

"I want to drive into the village today, see if I can make some contacts. Blake says they're wary of anthropologists, so officially we're just on vacation, but interested in understanding Navajo customs."

"Do you mind if I stay behind?"

Brian glanced around. "Okay, if you want, but I won't be back for hours."

"I'll be fine. I like it here."

When Brian returned late that afternoon, there was no sign of Jill. He called her name several times, and when she finally answered, her voice was almost swallowed up by his echoes.

She was a considerable distance upslope, sitting in a cleft of tumbled rock. It took almost half an hour for Brian to climb to the spot.

"I found something." She pointed with her chin.

It was a body, partially mummified, tucked into a narrow crevice.

"Damn!" Brian felt attracted and repelled simultaneously. "I bet that's our missing wiseman."

"He was a witch, actually. Everyone around here was afraid of him."

"Yeah, right. What'd you do? Find his diary or something?"

"Something." She stood up abruptly, started upslope. "C'mon, that's not all I found."

The climb took only about ten minutes, but the shadows were already lengthening when they reached a narrow gap between two rocks.

"There's not much room. You go first. I've already seen it."

Brian was puzzled, but did as she asked, turning sideways to slide between two planes of stone. He emerged onto a ledge overlooking a deep, rocky pit. The pit was full of bones. Human bones.

"What the hell?"

Jill touched his shoulder. "He killed them all, brought them up here and pushed them in. Most died right away but sometimes it took longer. He got more strength from them when that happened. Took their lives to extend his own. But eventually even the magic couldn't keep his body going."

"This is incredible. How'd you find this, Jill?"

"You might say I had a native guide." And something much older than Jill suddenly looked out through her eyes, and Brian tried to find something to hold on to when she suddenly pushed forward, toppling him from the narrow ledge.

Brian was young and strong and it took him a long time to die.

Christmas with the Count

Ian McDowell

Try the Château LaTour '89," said my host.

My gums stung, still tender from my new canines. "I gather Stoker was wrong about you and wine."

He settled into a dark leather armchair, his black turtleneck and Ralph Lauren slacks making him a disembodied head and hands, the fire tinting his alabaster skin and silver hair. "Bram was a fool. Florence should have married Oscar; better a brilliant sodomite for a husband than a syphilitic hack."

"You knew Wilde?"

When he smiled the teeth that had initiated me gleamed against his black lips. "Oscar was the one who convinced me not to sue Bram for libel. He should have heeded his own advice about ill-considered litigation."

So many questions and so little time. The success of Anne Rice's florid fiction had convinced the Count that the world was ready for a real interview with the most famous vampire of all. However, he required the conducting journalist to be initiated into the society of the Reborn, a contractual demand I was learning to live with.

"Okay, let's get this straight: you can't turn into a bat; the Christopher Lee films got that part right."

He nodded. "Though his films were cheap melodramas, Lee is my favorite of all the actors to portray me. I can cross running water and am indifferent to garlic. Direct sunlight is unpleasant, but hardly fatal, as Stoker knew. Not that his plot had any basis in reality."

"There was no Van Helsing?"

His hands clasped together like mating albino spiders and something more than firelight glinted in his eyes. "Van Helsing was a caricature of Stoker's friend Arminius Vanberry, who called me Nosferatu and drove me from Florence's parlor with a crucifix. Oscar was greatly amused by that spectacle, and his jibes created a rift between us, which is why I let him rot in prison after the Lord Douglas business."

The crucifix reference was odd. After my conversion, I'd timidly stepped into St. Pat's to see if I'd be affected by the iconography. Not a twinge of discomfort, so why had the Count fled a crucifix?

He noted my confusion. "Yes, I once feared the cross, just like my counterpart on the late late show."

"Once?"

He ran a thin finger along the rim of his glass. "One of the more miraculous inventions of this century is psychotherapy, which helped me get over a very old trauma."

I hazarded a guess. "Something from when you were human? A remnant of Vlad Tepes's Catholic background?"

His laugh was higher pitched than I'd have imagined. "No, hardly that. I've enjoyed many identities over the years, with Vlad only one of them. I'm older than you suppose and have played numerous roles in the pageant of history, even once attempting to help the race to which we formerly belonged. It turned out badly, and for centuries I took vengeance upon the foolish creatures who spurned my altruism. Nowadays, I look after my own interests, and do neither more nor less harm than I must. Can you really say the same of my fellow travelers in the corridors of power?"

I put down my glass and wasted precious moments looking at the fire, my cassette recorder humming. "Who were you?"

His smile reminded me of a skeletal tyrannosaur I'd seen during a childhood visit to the Smithsonian. Fewer teeth, but no more human warmth. "You went to Harvard; surely you can figure it out. Consider the metaphors: the communion of the blood, the resurrection and the life. Leonard Wolfe is a bombastic pedant, but he has useful things to say upon the subject."

He was mistaken about me and Harvard, but I didn't correct him. We stared together at the hearth, with no sound but tape hiss and crackling flames, until, faintly, I heard youthful voices singing "God Rest Ye Merry, Gentlemen."

The Count's smile had more humor now. "My neighbors' children are caroling. Shall we go out and drink from them?"

I knew his neighbors must be pretty influential people. "Can we risk that?"

He rose effortlessly from the deep chair, standing tall and thin in the firelight, the flames tinting his face like a mask of blood. "We won't take enough to permanently harm them, and old money brings great license. Besides, why should they mind? It's my birth they are celebrating."

Circles of Purgatory
Sandra Hutchinson

From the shadows of his chair, the Reverend Paul Whittemore stared at the phone, waiting for it to ring and wondering whether the silence or the sound tormented him more. The silence cruelly raised his hopes; when the ringer clanged, the sound shattered them. "Why don't I just pull the cord out of the wall?" he asked himself again, but lingering shreds of professionalism stayed his hand.

Not that he would do any good if anyone did call.

The grandfather clock in the hall chimed two. *She* always called between two and three, as if to commemorate nightly the hour of her death. He closed his eyes and focused on his breathing. In, out, in, out—take enough breaths and time would pass. Enough time and the call would come. It came every night.

A moral theology text lay ignored on his lap, weighing him down with its solidity, pressing down on his thighs and pushing him down into the chair. Tonight he had not even tried to open it. Without even looking, he knew that if he did, the words would blur together and refuse to make sense. His head throbbed with pain anyway. Better not to try.

The shrill ring of the phone destroyed the stillness. Paul reached out reluctantly for the mouthpiece. His hand wrapped itself around the cool plastic, and he tried to raise it just high enough to still the clamor. "Please, this time, just let me hang up before it starts," he begged some unknown god, but his body betrayed him again. His traitorous fingers pulled the handset to his ear.

"Reverend Whittemore, is that you?" A woman's voice: thin, high, and very frightened. Hospital sounds in the background, the muted insistence of an intercom system, a very distant ambulance.

He wanted to say soothing things, to reassure her that he was there and listening, but one more time, a blanket of cotton slid down his throat and choked off the sympathy. He could only sit there as harsh, pitiless words came from his lips. "Who is this?"

"Janice . . . Janice Miller."

He had remembered her only vaguely at the time and the recollection grew dimmer each night. A worn blonde in her forties who often came alone to church. She had a teenage son, and a well-dressed husband who, when he did come, seemed eager to be somewhere else. The parish secretary had said she had gone into the hospital lately— without looking at his appointment book, Paul wasn't sure which ward. Or even which hospital.

"Mrs. Miller, do you know what time it is?"

"It hurts!" she wailed, and Paul cringed. "Robert came in this afternoon and he wants a divorce. The doctors don't know whether it's cancer or not and Robert says he can't cope with the not knowing anymore."

"This really isn't the time to talk about it," Paul heard himself saying. "Why don't you go to sleep and we'll talk about it later."

There was a long silence at the other end, a pain-filled silence.

Paul tried to force himself to say something, anything, but the suffocating barrier in his throat still prevented him.

"Could you come by tomorrow?"

The unpastoral words came against his will, as they always did. "Tomorrow is my day off. I visit the hospital on Thursday. I'll see you then."

"But it hurts now!"

"Try to get some sleep. Whatever's wrong can wait."

"Please . . ."

"Get some sleep."

Then it was over. The slight crackle of static gave way to the purr of the phone's ready signal. The obstruction vanished from his throat. His words were his own again.

Paul stared down at the phone in his hands. He could choose again. The phonebook sat temptingly on the floor. He could find the number, call her, and beg her not to take the pills that made her sleep permanent. Maybe, if he did, the cycle wouldn't start again. He touched the gunshot wound in his temple and sighed. No. There was no certainty that he would do any better than he had done in life. Easier just to complete tonight's circle.

He reached out and dialed his bishop, as the descending blanket of silence gagged his own words again.

"Hello!" roared the voice from the other end of the phone. "Who is this?"

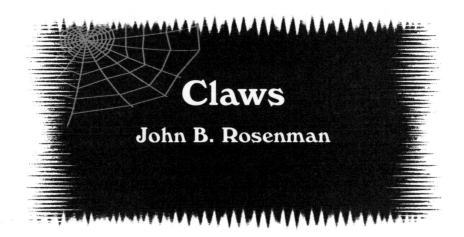

Claws

John B. Rosenman

I can't believe I killed him, Jacobs thought.

He looked down at Colton's body lying on the office floor in a pool of blood. In his hand, the brass paperweight he'd used to crush the man's skull felt suddenly cold.

Shuddering, he put the bloody object back on the desk next to the nameplate that read WILLIAM COLTON, PRESIDENT. Jacobs swallowed and gripped the desk. How could he have done such a thing? It was late, and he'd been leaving the building when he'd noticed a light in Colton's office. Obviously he'd been working late too, and after a brief debate, Jacobs had knocked on the door. Receiving a reply, he'd entered.

Inside, Jacobs had nervously asked Colton to consider him for the vacant position of vice president. The old man had rubbed his beaklike nose and preened. "Perhaps in your next incarnation."

The contempt had stunned him. Colton, who believed in reincarnation, had gazed triumphantly back. Suddenly a clawlike hand swooped down to the telephone, where it perched as if about to spring. Defeated and intimidated once again, Jacobs had started to leave.

Then he'd turned back, faced Colton's mocking face. "Don't give me that Bridey Murphy crap."

Colton's eyes widened. "So the rabbit's finally turned, huh? Son, don't mock what you don't understand."

"Come on, what have you got against me?"

Colton cackled, snapped clawlike fingers. "Like I said, you're a rabbit. I need someone who's *strong*."

It had been too much. A strong man: was that what he wanted? Surprised but calm, Colton had watched as Jacobs locked the door, returned and picked up the paperweight, raising it above his head. Only at the last instant had he glimpsed a flicker of doubt in Colton's hawklike features.

Smiling, Jacobs gazed down at Colton's still body. So much for reincarnation. The old bird wasn't going anywhere. Now *he* was the strong one!

There was a knock.

Jacobs froze, realizing his situation. It was past seven, and yet someone—probably a cleaning woman—was still in the building. If she came in . . .

A rattling of keys.

Oh no! He glanced about. Where could he hide?

The window.

He rushed over and slid it open, climbed out onto the narrow ledge which was just beneath the roof, nine floors up. If he could slide along it and break into another office, he could escape. In minutes he could be outside, driving home.

Heart pounding, he inched along the precarious ledge in the wind, keeping his back as close to the wall as possible. It was dark, and the chance of anyone seeing him out here was small. If he could just keep going and not look down . . .

Behind him, he heard Colton's door open. *Hurry!* he thought. *Move faster!*

A scream.

The woman's voice pierced the night. Gasping, he teetered forward on the edge, seeing tiny cars and streets far below. He was going to fall!

Somehow he regained his balance and managed to press his back to the wall again as the woman's scream continued. Any second now she would stop and investigate the window he'd left open. He glanced at the closed one six feet away. If he could just reach it and get out of sight!

Buffeted by wind, he slid along the ledge as quickly as possible. It seemed to take forever, and when the screams suddenly stopped, he expected the woman to look out and spot him. But finally he reached the other window and rammed it with his elbow.

Glass shattered, ripping his jacket. Reaching in, he found the latch and turned it, pulling the window open.

He was going to make it! Filled with pride, he reached up, gripped the building, and raised a leg to enter the window. A weakling, huh? Well, who was laughing now?

Something pecked his hand.

Looking up, he saw a nest in a nook beneath a cornice. In it, a baby hawk gazed at him with familiar contempt in its hate-filled eyes.

He froze like a rabbit, remembering Colton's belief in reincarnation. Was it *possible?* As if in answer, the hatchling hopped forward and pecked viciously at his eyes. He flinched, felt his foot slip. The hawk gripped his hand with tiny claws and pecked again, its beak piercing his eye. Screaming, he lost his footing and tipped out into the night.

As he fell, he had a sharp, clear glimpse of the form in which he would be reborn.

Cold Comfort

Lillian Csernica

A mirror lay half-buried in the sand, the old-fashioned kind set in a round frame with a handle. Tom Mohney had been sitting on the beach for an hour, watching the setting sun strike fiery glitters from the mirror, waiting for its owner to fetch it. He had nothing better to do. Polluted by depression, his sabbatical was a joke. Now that Linda had walked out, he wasn't needed anywhere. He wandered down the beach and picked up the mirror. As pretty as it was, it felt cold and unpleasant, the glass smoked nearly black.

Broken promises. Old mirrors on the shore. Common fairy-tale motifs. Tom smiled at the face in the mirror, pained to see the half-hearted smile it gave back. He'd been handsome once, before his brown eyes turned bloodshot and his black hair gray. Linda was no mermaid, he no fisherman. Their story was as old as the fairy tales, but without the magic. She wanted more than he could give, so he started keeping back what little he had been giving. Fool. Stupid, spiteful fool. Linda was a good, decent, caring woman who'd put up with him for the last five years. Until last night. Until he'd stayed out too late one night too many because he was restless and lonely and had no idea at all what to do about either. And now Linda was gone.

He wiped some of the grit off the mirror with the tail of his flannel shirt, wondering at the pattern of three twined snakes on the mirror's back. If he cleaned it up, it might make a good peace offering, assuming Linda ever gave him another chance. The evening breeze chilled him, leaving him cold inside and out. He started up the dunes toward his car. The thought of the empty mess waiting for him at home stopped him. He walked back down the dune and sat just past the edge of the reaching waves, gripping the mirror so tightly his knuckles ached. Maybe if he waited a little longer, the real mermaid would come back.

A tugging on his hand woke him. He lay on his side in the cold sand, curled around the mirror locked within his stiff fingers. He rolled away, up onto his knees. Before him crouched a woman, her face shadowed, her long hair silvery in the moonlight. The breeze molded her thin dress to her figure, showing off its curves.

"That's my mirror," she said. "Give it to me!"

"I know who you are. As long as I've got your mirror, you can't change back."

She tilted her head. Moonlight fell across her eyes, narrowed and as smoky as the mirror's glass. "How do you know anything?"

Her suspicious tone made him want to tease her even more. "Only one kind of woman leaves her mirror on the shore."

She stared at him, then sighed. "All right. What do you want for it?"

He knew what he wanted right then. "A woman who can fill my heart and soul."

"Fill them with what?"

"With herself. With everything I'll ever need."

She moved closer to him, reached out to stroke his cheek. He hesitated, wanting to touch her yet stunned by her sudden willingness. Her other hand dipped into the purse sitting beside her.

"So much pain. I'll give you what you really need."

She lunged, the knife flashing in her hand. He jerked the mirror up as a shield. The point of the knife hit the mirror with a splintering crack. The woman screamed, dropping the knife to clutch at her chest. Blood welled between her fingers. He stared at it, then at those smoky eyes.

"What are you? Tell me!"

"You—*don't* know?" She let out a shriek of pain and fury, then spat blood into his face. "Lonely, needy little boy! Every heart you ever meet you'll shatter like that mirror!" She stiffened, let out a strangled sigh, then sprawled in the sand.

Tom looked into the broken mirror, seeing his bloodied reflection slashed into pieces. Through the screaming horror in his brain one clear thought penetrated: She'd cursed him with nothing but the truth. Blinded by tears, he gathered the dead witch up in his arms and carried her into the sea.

Cold Moon

Judy L. Tucker

Amoon shone silvery and bloated over the farm. Ellen sat up in bed, hugging her knees. She was cold, not from the chill in the room, but from the night terrors haunting her sleep. She could almost feel the hot breath of the wolf licking her face, the red eyes watching from beyond the shadows. Ellen looked around her room. The shadows here were known and welcome; she sought them now like old friends. Downstairs the clock chimed. Ellen shuddered, knowing she would have to get up now, get dressed, and go outside and meet Bearclaw. This was the night of her vision ceremony.

The night closed around her as she stepped outside the house and made her way to a familiar clearing where a stream was flowing with trout. The moon slid behind a passing cloud; off in the distance a wolf howled.

Ellen tittered, nervously shoving her hands in the pockets of her suede jacket. She walked slowly, vulnerable to the forest, her skin pale, her gray eyes round, and her brown hair hanging limply down her back. Were those two red eyes watching her now? "The better to see you with, my dear." She shivered. This was *not* the time to be thinking of Little Red Riding Hood.

Ellen stopped in the middle of the clearing. It was quiet, except for the occasional rustling of the leaves by the wind. She let out a relieved sigh. It was only her imagination after all. What a goose she was . . .

Ellen started to relax, drawing in a deep breath, and then letting it out slowly. Bearclaw would be here soon, then they could begin her vision ceremony. That sounded good to Ellen. Really good. She fingered the wolf totem around her neck Bearclaw had given her. He said it would bring her good medicine by wearing it and would help her through the visions.

A low whine came from beyond the trees. Ellen whirled around, stood very still, and almost lost her composure as Bearclaw, the old Indian, stepped out of the shadows.

"I am so glad to see you," Ellen said, looking at the shadows of the trees. "I hear the wolves—one is prowling just beyond the hemlocks."

"There are worse things to fear than wolves," the old Indian said, taking hold of her shoulders. "Much worse. Strange things have been known to happen on nights like tonight."

"You make it sound ominous." Ellen stepped away from him, her eyes on the ground, looking for rocks to use for the ceremony. The full moon slid from behind a cloud, shining its light over the clearing.

"It is." His voice came out like a soft growl. Ellen spun around, then screamed when she saw Bearclaw's two red eyes looking at her . . .

The Collector

Linda J. Dunn

Karen's eyes widened in fear as she looked out the window and saw her husband's car approaching, followed by a tow truck.

Damn! Another junk car that he's going to fix up one of these days when he's got time. What does that make now? Twelve? Fifteen?

Karen started down the steps leading to the back door, being careful to avoid the obstacles in her path. Books and magazines lined the steps on both sides, leaving only a few safe spots where she could place one foot carefully before easing down to the next step.

She opened the door and stepped outside.

"It's a Mustang!" Bob shouted. Karen moved closer, trying to distinguish the car's markings beneath the rust. "All it needs is a new transmission and it'll be as good as new."

Karen hugged herself against the cold breeze and glared at him.

"Ah come on, honey," he said. "I know you don't like seeing the place looking like this, but just think of all the money we'll have once I get these cars fixed up and sold."

"It's been two years."

"What?"

"Two years of living like this and I've had it with your promises." Karen closed her eyes and took a deep breath. "I'm leaving you."

"I'm a collector, Karen. You knew that when you married me."

Karen shook her head. "I mean it this time. If you don't get rid of most of this junk, I'm walking out that door and never coming back."

Bob turned around and pulled out his wallet to pay the tow truck driver.

Damn him! He's not even listening to me.

Karen ran back inside and made her way up the treacherous steps. She turned sideways to ease her way down the hall past all the junk stacked on both sides, then waded through the pile of clothing to reach the suitcase stored at the back of the closet.

As she grabbed the handles and tugged, several boxes fell to the floor, spilling an assortment of nuts and bolts everywhere.

"Shit!" Karen shouted as she threw the suitcase onto the bed and stuffed her few possessions into it.

"I've had it!"

Karen snapped the suitcase shut and worked her way back down the hallway. She kicked a few things out of her way this time, no longer caring when magazines tumbled into a large pile behind her, blocking access to the bedroom.

She wasn't coming back. Let him clean up his own goddamn mess.

Bob was waiting for her at the foot of the steps.

"You're not leaving me," he said.

"Yes I am."

"I'm a collector, Karen. You knew that when you married me."

She shook her head. "I didn't realize it meant living in an obstacle course for the rest of my life! I'm leaving and nothing you say can change my mind."

Bob shook his head, a single tear running down his cheek. "Don't leave me yet. Please." He hesitated a moment, then added, "I've got something special for you in the basement."

"You can ship it to me. I'll send you my address."

"Please. At least come downstairs with me and see what it is."

Karen looked into his eyes and sighed. Despite everything, she loved the damn slob. No way could he change her mind but maybe she should see what it was. After all, he'd never allowed her in the basement before and she'd always been curious about it.

"Okay. But then I'm leaving."

Bob led her downstairs between stacks of magazines and books. She shivered as they reached the bottom and looked around at the stack of junk.

The room was filled from floor to ceiling with plastic boxes of all shapes and sizes. Bob tightened the grip on her hand and led her forward through a small path between rows of boxes.

"In here."

She followed, stopping to scream only after it was too late.

Hidden behind the stacks of boxes were large plastic cylinders several times larger than the ones in which you'd find those lifelike plastic dolls.

And those weren't life-sized dolls inside.

The last thing she heard was Bob's voice. "I'm a collector, Karen. You knew that when you married me."

Collector of Rugs

Jessica Amanda Salmonson

There once was a collector of rugs. "But there is one rug you shall never possess," said the tweaker of collectors of rugs.

In a pique, the collector of rugs retired to a secret room between the gables of his house, where the roof leaned low and he could not stand on his feet. On hands and knees he crawled amidst the oldest, rarest and most magnificent of all the rugs he had gathered in his journeyings to Turkey, Nepal, Madagascar, Yemen. He rolled himself into his treasures and gave a muffled wail: "Where, where is that One I cannot possess! All these I shall forsake if I can have that One!"

No sooner was the doomful promise given than his entire collection, from every room of the house, rose up and flitted out the windows. Those rarest of all, in which he had entangled himself to pine and weep, were transformed into serpents of thread, constricting him all about. He felt himself for some while airborne, then he was descending into a darkened place.

Here the rarest of his rugs unrolled themselves upon the floor of a well-appointed cave, and lo! they had formed themselves into a single carpet that fit the interior just so. But where was the collector of rugs? There was only an impression of him woven into thread.

And there upon his throne sat the tweaker and collector of collectors of rugs, joyous as he gazed upon his newest acquisition.

Collector's Fever

Gary Jonas

My collection of bodies is getting too big for the basement. Maybe it's time to start a new trophy room. I don't want to do that. I like being able to see all the bodies at once. Having them all close together.

I'm amazed that I haven't been caught. For years I've gone out collecting. Sure, it's an odd collection and I can't show anyone. But rich folks who buy stolen art treasures on the black market don't show off their collections either. They call them their secret treasures. My collection is secret, too.

And I like to think of the collection as a sort of art gallery. My own private gallery.

The first person I collected was my high school sweetheart. I'd wanted to collect her ever since she dumped me before the prom. But I resisted the temptation. I had nowhere to put her. So I waited.

After I got my job as a mortician, I bought this house. It's not in the best neighborhood, but that works to my advantage. I took the house because it has a huge basement. I've lived here for ten years. When the feeling takes hold, I go out and collect another person for my gallery.

Donna was first. She remains special. She will be twenty-five forever. Every now and again, I have to clean my trophies. Even after I've embalmed them, they continue to deteriorate. I have the basement climate controlled, which helps to slow things down, but I can't stop the decaying process completely. I'm not God.

Donna looks great today. She's dressed in a frilly blue dress. I would have given her a low-cut dress, but that would show the incisions and I can't have that. She still looks beautiful and innocent, though I took her innocence at the age of seventeen. I still love her.

It was easy to get Donna even though she was married. I simply arranged to bump into her at the supermarket. I acted like I cared how her life was going. I asked about the husband, the kid, the job.

And I asked if she'd like to go for a cup of coffee. She hesitated since she had a couple of frozen food items, but then shrugged and agreed. We checked out and loaded up our groceries in our cars. In my trunk I had a rag soaking in formaldehyde. I took the rag, walked over and slapped it over her mouth and nose. She gasped and the formaldehyde took effect immediately. She slumped into my arms and I walked her to my car. It was broad daylight and no one noticed a thing.

My first several collector's editions were old girlfriends who'd told me to take a hike. Then I snagged a few old friends I hadn't seen in years. All these disappearances meant nothing since they mostly lived in other cities. I'd drive out, collect them and bring them home. I'd embalm them at night and add them to my gallery.

When I ran out of old friends I wanted to have around, I decided to collect some strangers. It's like a fever. If I haven't collected anyone in a month or so, I get antsy. I always thought it would end when I filled the basement. But it hasn't.

I guess I'll line the stairs next. Then the hallway. Then the den. Then the spare bedroom. Then my bedroom. Then the family room. Then the living room. Then the dining room. Then the kitchen.

After that, I guess I'll move.

And start over.

Contract Ice

Marion Cepican

Sam didn't particularly relish getting up at 5:00 A.M. for early morning ice during summer vacation. Her heavy tights and sweatshirt looked and felt alien on that humid July morning, but by the time she was dropped off at the rink, the anticipation of newly made ice and its cleansing chill had become her prevailing thought. The rink was unusually empty, even for summer, with only Fast Eddy, the Zamboni driver, sharing her ice. Well, "sharing" was not exactly accurate. The two were often at odds about his hostile attitude. Eddy abused the ice, gouging the pristine surface with his rusty snow shovel . . . especially when Sam was watching. When he saw her enter, he gulped down his coffee and snorted as he headed for the compressor room. Ignoring him, Sam hurried in. She knew that by 7:00 the ice would be solid with skating students and pros . . . the "intruders," as she often referred to them. Quickly lacing her boots and putting her well-worn bag in the special spot under the pinball machine where it would be safe, she headed toward the gate.

As she stepped onto the smooth, crisp surface, the ice welcomed her blades with its usual "click, swish." Sam let the scent of the ice fill her lungs and began to stroke around the perimeter. There were skaters . . . and then there was Sam. From the time she learned to skate at age four, Sam had a special relationship with the ice. She was nine now and landing double jumps with ease. Never an injury, never a bump or bruise. The ice seemed to embrace her each time she fell. Early on, Sam stopped wearing gloves when she skated. "To feel the tracings," she would say, but to the casual observer she was caressing the ice, almost apologizing each time her toe pick chipped out a divot.

This ice "thing" was becoming more and more noticeable now, and the source of whispers and gossip. Every so often even Sam would wonder why other skaters did not feel this "connection" with the ice the way she did. But not now . . . not today . . . Today it was just her and her glorious ice.

Then she saw it. Just as she landed a double salchow, right by the spot where her blade touched down, a faint shimmer came from the ice. *Must be a reflection,* she thought. She gave the ice a gentle pat as she went to smooth the scratches from her jump. Was that a sigh? *Get real,* she told herself and continued to practice her competition program, lost in the music and the encouragement of the ice beneath her.

A quick glimpse at the rink clock told her there were only fifteen minutes left of her private contract. Already she could hear Fast Eddy rustling around the Zam, checking valves and whatever else he did to look busy. Only fifteen more minutes, as she stretched into a graceful back spiral. She gazed down when her arched body crossed the area of ice where the shimmer had appeared. The luminescence seemed to have somehow congealed into a semitransparent shape of some sort . . . something under the ice.

Sam's concentration broke and she fell. As her hand hit the ice, it was met with the hand of another. There was no fear. She lay there on the ice, staring into the seemingly endless depth. It was all becoming clear now. The communication was spontaneous. "You *are* there," Sam said. "I knew you were there. I've always known . . . Tell me . . . everything."

A frigid hand reached up to hold hers. Cold, but with no real substance . . . just like what she felt each time she fell. "I'm here for you," a voice whispered.

The moment was shattered by Fast Eddy yelling, "Get off the ice, kid, I've got to resurface before classes start." He started the Zamboni with a roar and Sam automatically scrambled off the ice, dazed by the unreality of it all. "But I wasn't done," Sam screamed. "I . . . uh, left something on the ice."

Fast Eddy gave her a shrug and steered the Zamboni onto the surface. Sam pressed her freezing hands to her cheeks, hoping that the cold would somehow bring things back to normal. As she closed her eyes, listening to the motor sounds travel across the ice, there was an abrupt silence. The Zamboni had stopped dead, right where . . . it was. Cursing, Eddy climbed down from his seat to see what had jammed his machinery.

The whole patch of ice under the stalled Zamboni glistened with . . . with something!

No, thought Sam, suddenly terrified. *It couldn't . . .* "Eddy . . .

no don't! . . . Don't get down!" she screamed, as his foot touched. Instantly the hand . . . its hand . . . reached up through the crystalline barrier, grabbed the startled driver by the leg and within a fraction of a second, pulled him beneath the surface of the ice.

"I love you," the voice whispered to Sam.

A Convenient Arrangement

Michael Marshall Smith

It was my turn to host the party this year, and I spent the afternoon happily buying drinks and nibbles. They're proper parties, you see, in addition to their other function, and there are some things you just can't do without at such affairs. I had a shower, changed, and then arranged the living room carefully, so the atmosphere would be just right.

The six of us have known each other forever, and have done everything together for a long, long time. Each of us has casual acquaintances, of course, but no-one important. No-one like the group.

Philip was the first to arrive. He was perspiring rather heavily from carrying his bag upstairs, and suggested wryly that next year we hold the party in a flat that is on the ground floor. Jenna was next, and then David, and soon all six of us were there, chatting and sipping our drinks, the six large and heavy bags left out in the hallway conveniently near the door.

The time always flies by when the group is together, and nine o'clock was soon upon us. We all smiled when the intercom rang at ten past nine. Our guest had arrived. It soon became apparent that Nigel was a rather tiresome individual, but each of us spoke to him equally, ensuring that no-one was left holding the baby for too long. It's unavoidable that the guest should be an acquaintance of only one of the group—in this case, Jenna—but once he or she is at the party, great care is taken to even things out. Nigel got rather drunk as the evening wore on, doubtless frustrated by Jenna's refusal to pay him any special attention, but not offensively so.

By eleven the mood of the party had begun to change: twenty-five past eleven is the traditional time, and it is impossible not to be conscious of its approach. At twenty past I made sure everyone's glass was empty, which confused Nigel somewhat. Then at twenty-five past I turned out the lights.

Twenty years ago, you see, we were all at a dinner party when a power cut took place. When the lights came back everyone was horrified to find the body of another guest lying on the floor, her throat slashed and face cut to ribbons. She was, of course, quite dead. Nine months later we were at another affair, this one held by candle-light, when a strong wind reduced the room to darkness. And again, when normalcy was restored, a body was discovered on the floor, once more the victim of a maliciously wielded wine glass.

The group talked amongst ourselves, and realised the only common denominator between the two parties was that we had all been present at both. It was obvious, therefore, that one of our number was responsible for the crimes. No-one had any wish to determine where the blame lay, and it was clearly unacceptable that we should lose one of our dearest friends to a penal institution simply because their urges got a little out of hand every now and then.

The parties are the most convenient way we could think of arranging things. At twenty-five past eleven the lights are turned out, and one of our number cuts the guest's throat with their glass whilst the others throw theirs to the floor. Everyone then leaves the party, individually, at five-minute intervals. No-one knows what order we go in: the host simply reaches out in the darkness and taps a random shoulder after he has heard the previous car drive away.

When all have gone the host turns the lights back on, and sets about the clearing up. There is usually a good deal of blood on the carpet, and a pile of bricks in the hallway. Before he or she leaves, you see, the friend in question empties their bag of the bricks they came with, and leaves with the body instead.

Every sixth year, of course, the friend with the unfortunate tendencies does not have to transport the body at all, because that year he or she will be the host. Instead they can pour a glass of wine and settle down to do what they need to do in complete comfort and privacy.

And was that the case this year?

Ah well, that would be telling, wouldn't it?

The Cough

Steve Rasnic Tem

Atickle like the sound of a truck rumbling in the distance, felt in the chest, where bones join tissue and there are quantities of liquid for lubrication. Something was coming. Something was clearly out there. Something he didn't want to know about.

He'd had the cold for weeks. Three, four weeks. It didn't seem right, didn't seem natural. Weren't colds two-week affairs? His wife had told him that at some time or other. He remembered the time last winter he'd been moaning and groaning, thinking he was going to die, angry because she wouldn't take care of him, wouldn't even sympathize, and she'd said, "Two weeks and it'll be gone. It's just a cold. Drink your orange juice."

Women had little sympathy for men. That had always been true. It was a way of getting back at their ill treatment under a patriarchy, he supposed. It was a man's world, and women had little sympathy. He really couldn't fault them for that, but it felt bad just the same.

Suddenly his body exploded into a fit of coughing. His face felt flushed. He could feel himself filling with fever. He could feel the tube of his throat constrict as he coughed, twisting at its root, trying to rip itself out of his body. Something was coming from a far distance. Something that didn't agree with him.

He spat something milky into the sink. His wife would have hated that. "Men have such disgusting habits," she used to say. He leaned over the sink and looked at what he had coughed up. Men did that, too—periodically they felt compelled to look at whatever came out of them. The globule in the sink was creamy, yet somewhat solid, like a small bit of half-digested flesh.

He wondered if what he was suffering from was akin to what they called "consumption" in the old days. He had no idea. But he was a man. Naturally he felt consumed. Men had a lot of things on their minds.

Suddenly the cough racked him again. His head jerked as if he'd been slapped. His wife had slapped him a couple of times, because of some dumb thing he'd said to her. He'd never hit her. He had no use for men who hit their wives.

But she should never have hit him.

Something was coming from a long distance, something *had* come from a long distance, and now it was filling his throat. He thought that he would choke. He ran to the toilet bowl and coughed something up from his throat. It felt large and soft as if it were one of his internal organs as it passed his lips and plopped into the water.

He looked down. It was longish and pale, like an arm, and then it dissolved into the water.

Where was she anyway? He couldn't remember. If it had been *her* making these noises of distress she would have expected him to come help her. But when *he* was the one who was sick, she hid herself. Marriage ought to be a two-way street.

At least she could have fed him something. He was hungry. He hadn't eaten anything all day, and he'd had way too much to drink last night in order to ease the pain in his throat and in other places he didn't like to talk about. He was hungry. Men had hungers. Where was she?

The next cough practically split him in two. It felt as if it had originated miles away. Something rushed through him, then past him as if on its way to an important destination. Where was she? He looked down at what he had brought forth from such a long distance, and saw a soft, liquid, barely recognizable version of his wife's face floating in the bowl, a soft tinge of blood in the lips and cheeks. The image started to break up even as he impulsively jerked the lever to flush it all away.

And then he remembered.

Cower Before Bobo

Tom Piccirilli

They are blind to Bobo out in the rain, exactly as Pinju said they would be. Drawing the drapes back, they go through the pretense of scanning the yard, grinning with patronizing nods, staring through Bobo as he stands near the well outside my window with the knife unsheathed, his two yellow-eyed poodles glaring insanely.

"Good-night, Freddy," Miri says, sitting at my bedside and rubbing the scaly skin of my head, patting at my flippery arms and planting a kiss where my nose ought to be. "Don't let these storms frighten you. In the morning the sun will be shining."

"No more terrors," Harvey grunts. My nightmare cries haven't done anything to sour their cloyingly good mood. "I'm here to protect you from them monsters. You sleep now, Freddy." Despite protestations from the state board of education, they still believe me to be brain damaged: I can't blame them much, considering I can't speak or hold a pen to write out how frustrating it is to listen to their baby talk these past four weeks since Pinju was murdered and the Supreme Southern closed. They get a kick out of seeing my little slash of a guppy mouth try to spit human words, but they've been good to me so far, so I give them the show.

"Guh neet," I say, waving my webbed hands happily. She tucks me under the blankets so tightly I can barely move my underdeveloped limbs. Harvey puts his arm around her as they walk out and shut the bedroom door. They think they're going to make a fortune off me when the deal with the Madcap Carny comes through.

Rain slashed down until the ground grew soaked into a vast flooded carpet. I squirm free of the sheets and crawl up the headboard so I can glance out the window. Bobo smiles without smiling beneath the thumbnail moon, the wet greasepaint of his face rearranging to fit any expression: even before he was possessed he could squeeze that visage into a sorrowful cry, shriek of laughter, or ridiculous whoop of joy within seconds, just by how he played his facial muscles. In the three years we ran together on the midway of Supreme Southern Carny we were best friends. Until the night he cut Pinju's throat.

Swami Pinju told me he knew he'd be murdered by Bobo—not for money or revenge or any human reason, but just because one of his gods, the beautiful Kali, had found a way to get inside Bobo's brain and make him do all the hideous, worldly things we'd avoided on the midway. It was something about karma, having to pay for the laughter he'd given people by murdering and making life more miserable.

Bobo speaks into my head, the painted lips moving, but not his real ones. *Come outside, let's settle this.* I try to tell him there's nothing to settle, that Pinju made me swear not to go to the police or tell anybody the truth.

Bobo comes to the window and taps on it with the tip of the blade. In my dreams I've been terrified of this moment, but now there's an inexplicable calm inside me, the calm Pinju spoke of when he sat on his mat of nails and poked needles through his tongue and cheeks. I flop off the bed and slowly clamber up onto a chair, pushing myself along, then up onto the desk. I press my face to the window.

Kali wants us to be a part of the new Earth, Bobo says. *It is not for hate's sake, but for love. And life.* His eyes are as yellow as those of his mad dogs. *You hold a special place in Mother Kali's heart.* Pinju said the same thing.

I throw myself forward and smash through the window, almost into Bobo's arms. He stumbles splashing backward while the dogs leap for me. Bobo and I fall together into the well, his knife up to my chest, his chatter in my skull. I have guppy lips, yes, but also rows of teeth, sharp as a shark's. For the first time I realize I'm hungry, and I catch him just right, in the neck, and see the real Bobo—my friend—there behind this other one. He looks thankful.

The rain is unrelenting and the water in the well rises. I swim in the well for hours, and by dawn I can float right out. I flop onto the ground, but the water is so high now that I can swim here in the yard. The poodles, Harvey, and Miri have all drowned in the flood, and I feed again. I don't know where to go, or what to do, or why Pinju was happy he was going to die. I'm not certain the rains will ever stop, or if this is Mother Kali's new Earth. All I know is that I have to keep moving.

Crashing

Lawrence Greenberg

I love how you do that, he told her, how you pretend to isolate yourself at the wrong moment all the time like right now at this last subway stop—after we ignore each other for so long—where no one lives but there are still lights on because the transit managers think there may be a time when people will come here to survive the city. That's what it is.

We were here before, he said, don't you remember? But she had no answer; she looked asleep, she seemed almost comatose, she was out of it.

This is the last stop, a voice said. All passengers must leave the train. If we don't get off, he told her, you're probably going to crash right here. She opened her eyes slowly and turned her head to the left, just enough to make it look like she was indicating something barely moving outside her window. But when he looked where she did, he saw nothing.

What is it? he said. What do you see? She opened her mouth slowly, looking at him, and he thought she was about to say something when a man who looked like a conductor entered their car and told them that he was very sorry but they had to leave the train immediately.

So they got up and left the train, and as soon as they were standing on the station platform he pointed and said to her, Look, we were the only ones on the train at this stop. She turned to look where he was pointing and then suddenly she pointed at an odd angle to where he had pointed, very quickly.

This time when he looked where she indicated he did see something. There was a flash of black, he thought, something that moved very fast.

What was that? he asked her. But again she had no answer. Instead, she turned and walked down the station platform away from him. In the poor light he couldn't see her after only a few yards or so and then, less than a minute later, he heard an enormous crashing noise. Right after that he saw, out of the corner of his eye, another black flash that moved faster than he could track it. He didn't see where it came from or where it went.

This was the last subway stop and he knew he had been here before. But whether she had been with him then, he had absolutely no recollection now.

Crisis Line
Del Stone Jr.

The telephone rings. Murray swallows a mouthful of coffee, picks up the receiver and says, "This is Murray with the Crisis Line. May I help you?"

The line is silent a moment, but Murray can hear the person on the other end holding his breath, willing himself to climb the mountain of fear, to speak. Always, it is this way. But the other person will speak. If not tonight then some other night, when the craziness is howling down the dry canyons and gullies of an even more awe-inspiring mountain of terror. The other person will speak.

"Yeah," the other person whispers, and Murray smiles, picturing an image of a man cocooned in cold weather gear planting a flag at the top of an ice-encased peak. "I've never done this before, you know?"

"I understand," Murray says, sweetening his voice with sympathy. "Is there something you want to talk about?"

"Uh, yeah," the other person stammers, and it is a man, Murray decides, although the voice could go either way. "It's just that I'm—I'm—"

"Hurting?" Murray answers for him. He sips his coffee.

"Yeah, I guess you could say that."

"Then maybe I can help," Murray says.

"It's my old lady," the man says. "I—I don't understand. I caught her shacking up with some other guy, and I don't understand how she could do this to me."

"Have the two of you been experiencing marital problems?" Murray asks.

"Oh, some," the man answers. "Arguments—you know. The kids. Money. Sex—well, not sex, exactly. But romance. Once or twice she said the romance had gone out of our marriage. But hell!" the man continues before Murray can say anything. "I take her out once or twice a month. What more does she expect?"

"It's not as if you were still dating," Murray says quietly. The coffee has gone lukewarm.

"Exactly!" the man blurts. "I mean, when you get married, things are supposed to settle down. You don't have to try as hard, you know, because you've done all the work. You put in your eight hours to pay the bills and raise the kids, have a little fun here and there, and enjoy life. Isn't that what it's all about?"

"It certainly is," Murray agrees.

"And now this," the man seethes. "Screwing around behind my back. She's gotta know it's hurting me. Why is she doing this?"

Murray sighs. "Because she's selfish," he says, "and because she wants to hurt you."

"Yes," the man chokes, and he starts to cry. "That's—that's exactly why."

"And what you must do now," Murray goes on smoothly, "is keep her from hurting you again."

"Yes," the man sobs. "But how?"

Murray takes a mouthful of tepid coffee and answers, "Take the direct approach. Sit her down and tell her there will be no adultery, or—"

"Or?" the man asks.

Murray pushes the coffee mug away. It has gone totally cold. "Or you'll hurt her back."

"How do I do that?" the man asks. He has stopped crying. A whiff of curiosity has entered his voice.

"Oh, lots of different ways," Murray says lightly. "You can screw around behind her back. You can kick her ass. You can blow her brains out."

The man sucks in a shocked breath. "Jesus!" he breathes. "Kill her?"

"Depends on how badly you're hurting."

The line is silent a moment. Then the man says, "I'm hurting pretty bad."

"I know you are," Murray says.

"She's the one who went and fucked things up."

"That's exactly right," Murray says.

"She deserves to be punished."

"You have every right to punish her," Murray says.

"She really ought to be punished," the man says.

"You're right. She does."

"OK," the man says, his voice now agitated and hypertensive. "I'll take care of things. I'll take care of things."

"I'm sure you will," Murray says, and as the man hangs up, Murray smiles and stares at the cup of coffee. Totally cold. He sticks his index finger into the cup, and the coffee begins to boil.

"You just gotta know how to talk to 'em," he says under his breath, licking his finger.

The telephone rings.

A Cup of Dragon's Blood

Juleen Brantingham

Duke leaned against a brick wall, sweating and cursing. A cup of dragon's blood, the old man said. Where the hell was he supposed to get a cup, or even a drop of dragon's blood these days? Dragons weren't real.

He needed dragon's blood and he needed it now.

With shaking hands he touched his nose, his forehead. Nothing had sprouted. Yet.

How was he to know the old man was some kind of wizard? He'd looked like an easy mark in his shanty out there at the edge of the garbage dump. When the guys told him what he had to do to join up, he'd thought of the old man right away. Duke had watched for three hours, close to puking from the smell. Finally he saw the old man leave, hobbling along on his crippled legs. But he'd gone. Duke had *seen* him go.

He'd nipped into the shanty slick as you please. Imagine the old guy thinking a lock like that would keep out anyone who wasn't turned off by the smell. The smell inside was worse than outside. Cats all over the place. No litter box that Duke could see. The old man must have let them do it wherever they pleased. Where was the old man's money? Everybody knew he had a bundle stashed away. Why else would he live next to the dump?

When he started pawing through the old man's stuff—leather-bound books, bottles full of murky stuff, bundles of dried weeds, bones—the cats came sniffing around. A couple took swipes at him. He'd had to grab them by the hind legs, slam them against the wall. The rest backed off and left him alone. He'd found a few dollars and some change stuck down in an old boot, and stuffed them in his pocket. It wasn't near as much as he'd hoped for but it would do for the initiation. He was looking around for the real dough when the old man appeared out of nowhere.

Pain! Jeeze, he'd never *felt* such pain—like someone had grabbed the family jewels or set them on fire. And the old man never touched him. Duke didn't take his eyes off him, even when his eyes were full of tears. The old man stalked toward him across the dirt floor. Cats scuttled out of his way. He looked ten feet tall. His eyes blazed like the fires of hell.

"You would harm my cats, you miserable worm?"

More pain, until Duke was on his knees, sobbing. He'd have given the money back if the pain had let up enough for him to use his hands. The old man didn't seem to care about the money.

"You would kill my precious cats, you filthy scum!"

Then he touched Duke for the first time—kicked him in the head. When Duke could see straight again the old man shoved a glass ball up to his eyes. "Scum you are and scum you shall be! Look!"

A picture formed inside the glass ball, a picture of Duke. He recognized himself by the color of his hair, by the clothes he was wearing. Everywhere—his face, his hands, sprouting out of his clothes—scum. Fuzzy green and purple scum.

Duke begged. He'd do anything, be the old man's slave for the rest of his life. That's when the old man offered his deal: forgiveness in exchange for a cup of dragon's blood.

There weren't any dragons. Not real dragons.

Duke almost jumped out of his not-yet-turned-to-scum skin when someone appeared out of the darkness. It was Chance, his best buddy.

"Did you get it?"

Duke pulled crumpled bills from his pocket. Coins clinked on the pavement. Looking to see where they'd gone, Duke spotted the shine of a cat's eyes.

"Not much but it'll do," Chance said, clapping him on the back. "Now you're one of us, a real Fighting Dragon."

"Yeah," Duke said, driving the knife into Chance's stomach. He caught the blood in the skull cup the old man had given him.

"You or me, good buddy," the new Dragon whispered.

Curses

Martin Mundt

The book was warm with curses, circulating through the pages like blood. Wax sealed the book all around, forming Greek, Hebrew and Arabic letters, along with other hieroglyphs of a more magical, idiosyncratic alphabet. The malevolence seeped into the pages, creeping into every word.

The book was untitled, with no designs but the wax. Domenico Malebolge, alchemist, astrologer, archimandrite of mysteries, was the author, so the present owner claimed. My job was to crack the curse.

Just mapping its extent without bringing it down on myself had taken three weeks of work. I then advised my client not to bother trying to break through. I advised him that the odds were long against freeing the book's contents without ripping it to atoms in the process, since the curse was designed to destroy the book rather than give up its secrets. After that, of course, the curse would come after the tamperer, in this case me.

The owner listened and listened and finally said, "Don't stop. Continue. Press on. Forward. Liberate the book."

He left me as weary as a sigh, because the book was almost certainly worthless to him, or to me, or to anyone, really; nothing but dense Latin gibberish, words frozen hard as permafrost over any meaning. The owner deluded himself, like every owner of an old grimoire, rock-solid convinced he held in his hands the philosopher's stone and Ponce de Leon's fountain all in one, simply because the words were well-cursed. He clutched the book, fingers white with suspicion, as if thieves hid all around him.

The hopes never came to anything. The imagined treasures were always suspended alone in the author's head, halfway between hallucination and nightmare, paranoid treasures unintelligible to anyone outside the elysium of his own sacred skull. The Seven and Seventy Opaque Mysteries of Phlogiston Made Transparent; Secret Cartography of the Places of Power of Ancient Geometers; the Serene and Perilous Masters of All Invisible History, yadda, yadda, yadda. Pretty impenetrable stuff, really. I'd read tomes full of it during my twenty-five years cracking curses, and I still only cleared about twenty grand a year, so how enlightening could it all really be?

This curse was mostly standard stuff, a basic shrieking-devil-pitchforking-intruders-forever kind of revenge, just boilerplate protection. But it was laid down with a level of artistry and craft that I rarely encountered. Psychically seamless. Spellproof. The magic was lavish and magnificently sturdy, rooting itself into each and every page of the book, with hundreds of astral tendrils, and it had sustained itself for five hundred years.

I wasn't going to crack this curse with standard-issue crowbar spells or hammer spells, astral lockpicks or psychic impersonations of the spellcaster. The key was necessary, except the key had died with the caster.

Fortunately, I wasn't without resources of my own.

I struck the book with my own curse. I sat at my darkened desk and leaned my shadow over the book and focused my energy, wormed my words of power into the pages, infiltrated every syllable, twisted myself into every line and swirl of every letter, bound the book together with my own will. I made my curse stronger than Domenico's curse.

I thought twelve hours would do for the job, but I had to bend over the book for thirty in all. Then I simply forced the book open. Maybe I was tired. Maybe that's why I didn't see what was coming.

The old curse should have turned inward, turned on the book itself, tried to destroy it, while my own curse held the book intact. Domenico should have battered himself to exhaustion on my stronger magic. The curse should have dissipated, but it didn't. It came straight for me instead.

It swarmed over me while my power was in the book. It froze me. I felt barely a verb away from death, as though cold angels climbed my spine. It cursed me closed as the book. I stiffened like a corpse, but still living.

I couldn't speak. I couldn't move. I could do nothing but see straight in front of me, hear the room around me, smell the air, feel the book beneath my fingers.

So we sat, both cursed, the book, me.

I saw the shadows of horns and a pitchfork approaching.

I heard shrieking.

I smelled a candle burning, and then I felt the first drop of wax dripping on my skin, burning, burning.

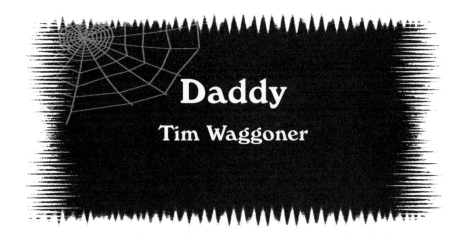

Daddy

Tim Waggoner

A few days after entering the hospital, Jill and the baby, whom they'd named Seth after Jill's father, came home.

Jill looked deflated, a used, hollowed-out shell. The baby—Keith couldn't bring himself to think of it as Seth yet, could only think of it as *it*—looked like a tiny collection of pink-purple wrinkles.

Jill's mother had volunteered to stay over for a couple weeks to help with the baby, and Keith stayed out of their way while they talked about such arcane matters as breast-feeding versus bottle-feeding and cloth diapers versus disposable.

He tried to tell himself that it was over, that the baby was here and Jill had survived the nine months of hosting this . . . thing, and that was all that mattered. But the first time he saw Jill breast-feeding it, he knew that it wasn't over, that it would never be over. The thing would feed off her—and him—its entire life. If it wasn't stopped.

That night, after both Jill and her mother were asleep, Keith stole into the nursery. He kept the light off, but he could see well enough by the Donald Duck night-light in the wall outlet near the crib. The baby was sleeping, full of milk and contented, in its tiny blue PJs, beneath its tiny flannel blanket.

Keith looked down at the thing he had fathered. The thing that was determined to devour both him and Jill until there was nothing left.

It'll be easy, the voice said. *All you have to do is put your hand over its mouth and nose and hold it there for a few minutes. They'll put it down to sudden infant death syndrome. And you and Jill will be free again.*

Keith wondered how many of the babies who died of SIDS each year weren't really babies at all, but monsters like Seth. And how many died at the hands of their fathers.

He reached his hand toward its face, but before he could touch it, the thing woke up and started to squall. He had to get it quieted down before Jill or her mother woke.

He picked up the baby and rested its head on his shoulder.

"Shut up," he whispered, rocking it.

The thing's mewling subsided as it snuggled against him. He felt a tingling in his chest and arm, and knew that the thing was using its powers on him, draining him, stealing his life. He was about to throw it across the room when he was suddenly filled with love for the tiny mass of flesh he held. For his son. For Seth.

He sat down in the chair in the corner and continued to rock his boy. He knew Seth had used his powers to make Keith love him, could even now feel Seth taking from him, drawing life into his tiny body. Keith would grow old and gray while Seth grew tall and strong. And one day Keith would die and Seth would live on.

As Keith felt the weariness of new fatherhood overtake him, he found that he didn't really mind so much anymore. In fact, he realized with a dull, muted horror that was already fading, it felt pretty damn good.

And in his daddy's arms, little Seth gurgled happily.

Dark Zone

Ed Williams

Lisa was behind Professor Norman when he stopped near the center of the cavern and turned to their Mexican guide. *"Aquí?"*

"Bueno. This place is good."

Professor Norman put his halogen lamp on the chamber floor and unslung his backpack. "Okay, folks, I want you to spread out, put some space between yourselves, and find a reasonably comfortable place to sit."

The footing was uneven and treacherously slick. Lisa chose a spot near a stalagmite, by the shallow stream. She was holding together very well, she thought. Claustrophobia tried to grab her only in the narrower passages and, a revelation, the physical movement of walking and climbing seemed to help. She was proud of herself, and proud that no one else in the class suspected the fear she harbored before they started the descent.

Professor Norman sat cross-legged beside the lamp. "Everybody set? Whatever you do during our little demonstration, don't try to stand up or move around until I tell you."

He touched the lamp and the light fled into blackness, tearing Lisa's breath away with it. Her hands clenched, fingernails skidded over clammy rock. Fading afterimages, monstrous, amorphous shapes, loomed before her.

"Spooky sensation, isn't it?" Professor Norman's voice caromed off limestone walls. Lisa thought she faced him, but was no longer certain of the sound's direction. Her lungs found the damp air again, drank it quick and short.

"We're about two hundred meters deep now, deep enough to swallow a six-story building, and in the third and final zone of the cave."

His voice died slowly, in echoes. Lisa heard classmates near her breathe, heard mineral-laden water drip from the travertine, heard the stream moving slowly at her back. Someone shifted with the rustle of a nylon jacket. Her clothes smelled of hours-old bat guano, smeared on as she slid over rocks. It was acrid and metallic, loam and clay mashed into diluted ammonia. But the blackness was thick with moisture, dulling the odor. She shivered.

"This is the dark zone. It is perpetually without light, has no seasonal changes, no naturally occurring air currents, and maintains a constant relative humidity near one hundred percent."

She turned her head side to side, listening, seeking orientation. She felt dizzy. Her hands were flat against the cold limestone, reassurance that she could identify *down*.

"Even though bats and larger animals don't venture down here, the dark zone is far from lifeless. The most famous inhabitant is a blind cave fish found only here in Mexico. Its eye sockets are vestigial and overgrown with skin, but its teeth are perfectly functional. The fish is a close cousin of the piranha."

Lisa flinched. The stream sounded uncomfortably close.

"In fact, the dark zone is home to hundreds of unique species of fish, crayfish, salamanders, beetles, millipedes, and spiders."

The blackness pressed against her, palpable. She was sure that if she leaned forward her face would touch it, be enveloped by it, suffocated by it—by a sticky, viscous grease alive with crawling, biting, stinging things. A needle of panic trilled her spine.

"These animals have long antennae, or feelers, to compensate for their lack of eyes. They subsist on food that is washed in by streams, or on nutrients in bat droppings or, in some cases, on each other."

Lisa thought she felt a feathery brush against her right wrist. She jerked her hand up, shifted to her left.

"Okay. Enough fun," said Professor Norman. "Everybody, cover your eyes. This lamp's going to be painfully bright at first."

Something bumped her, not from the side or back, but from below. She heard glass shatter. Professor Norman's voice: "Dammit!"

The cavern groaned. The floor began to tremble, to buckle. Lisa's left hand slipped. She fell on her elbow, hard. Maybe hard enough to break bone.

She realized the others were screaming.

Daytimer

Steve Rasnic Tem

8 A.M. Talk to the lady in the park, even if she tries to run from me again. Emily and our daughter had the picnic by the statue of Jackson. Twenty years ago, but the lady would remember. A beautiful woman, my wife, and our beautiful child. Anyone would remember them, even after twenty years. Jackson still has his sword raised, as if intent on killing someone. Things never change, even after twenty years. Even after twenty years, I wait for them to come to me.

9 A.M. Walk the sidewalk along the park's outer edge. This was the way they would have come. So many trees along the way, creating shadows. Our daughter, Jean, so afraid of the shadows. Shadows change, even as you watch. Shadows change everything. I cannot remember my daughter's face.

10 A.M. Check the sewer that runs under the park. Here it is large enough for a man, or two. Grates open to the sewer all along the sidewalks. Something might have fallen, might have rolled and slipped through the grate. Clues might still be found, even after twenty years.

11 A.M. Call Jean's friends. Again. Even though they are terrified when I call. Young women now. Saw in a paper on a park bench that one of them was married last week. Didn't trust the look of her new husband in the picture. Twenty years ago, he would have been older than Jean. Almost a teenager. Teenage boys will do anything. They haven't learned how to stop themselves.

12 noon. Stand at the center of the park. Listen for the dogs. Dogs were barking that day twenty years ago. Many times I hear the dogs barking. Large packs of them sweep down from the north, taking what food they can from garbage cans. Sometimes they attack old people, snatch babies in their jaws, find secret places for doing their secret animal things which no human has ever witnessed.

1 P.M. Seek out each child in the park. Look carefully at her face. She might not have aged. Certainly in my mind she has not aged. Find out if any of the middle-aged women answer to the name Emily.

2 P.M. Crawl under a bush somewhere in the park and nap. Dream twenty years' worth of memories. Ask them where they've gone, why they haven't called. Ask them if I deserved them, if I deserved *this*. Ask them what I can do. Tell them I will do anything.

3 P.M. Pull the insects out of my hair. Comb the dirt and leaves from my beard. Lying under the bush I would scare anyone, especially in these ragged pants, this coat with the pockets missing. But who needs pockets anymore? I used to keep candy for my baby there, keys to the house. Each day I would jangle the keys, make faces, give her the candy. She would laugh like music. My wife would kiss me, whisper in my ear. *You sweet man. You dear, sweet man.*

4 P.M. Check the park benches for the dead. Check under the bushes where the dead sleep, dreaming of their families. Ask the trees where they've gone. Make inquiries of the wind. Sometimes it *will* answer, if asked politely. Ask the couples passing by if they know my name.

5 P.M. Dance with the wind in thanks for its cooperation. Throw up my arms, let my mouth open and sing. Fall to the ground and roll through a hundred feet of flowers. Let the animals stare at me in wonder.

6 P.M. Watch the police shut down the park. A curfew, due to increased crime over the years. Watch them pull their coats tighter, gaze around nervously. Watch them stare at me, their slightly puzzled expressions. Watch them leave.

7 P.M. Examine this loose calendar page, blown by the wind, torn from someone's appointment book. I used to have one just like it, back when I had no clear understanding of the relative importance of things. It's completely blank, optimistically awaiting its appointments.

8 P.M. Try again to leave the park. Fail. Remember the panicked look on my wife's and daughter's faces when they looked down at me, and I was in so much pain. Remember. The terrible weight on my chest. And all I could worry about was how I had ruined our picnic together. We'd spent so little time together. I'd been so busy.

9 P.M. Remember.

Dead Letter

Stephanie Bedwell-Grime

You have new mail.

"Christ!" Alan stared at the screen in disgust. "Guy's been dead two weeks and he's still getting e-mail."

He glanced at the flickering cursor. "Someone's sick idea of a joke."

Had to be. There wasn't a soul in the company who hadn't heard of the gruesome way Sacha passed away at his desk. He'd been the subject of watercooler gossip for more than a week.

"Sitting there! Just sitting there . . ." he remembered George, the head of Information Services, bellowing across the lunchroom to the staff members who listened with rapt attention. ". . . upright in his chair. If it wasn't for the blood leaking out of his mouth, I wouldn't even have known he was dead. And not a sound out of him." He gulped down a mouthful of by-now-cold coffee. "Shit man, I was only talking to him a minute before."

Poor old Sacha made quite the impression, that was for sure. Alan shook his head. But then Sacha had been flamboyant in everything he did in life, why not in death as well? Alan's finger hovered above the Delete key. As system administrator, Friday afternoons were his time to clean up the system. The thought of that first dip in the lake after three hours of cottage country traffic, followed by that first ice-cold mouthful of Molson's, beckoned with summer-fever urgency.

Curiosity stopped him midstrike. It could be a sick joke, one meant for him, perhaps. Anyone in IS would know he'd be cleaning up the system sooner or later. Or it could be something important. Something poor old Sacha meant to attend to before he . . .

He thought of the cottage again, then of poor Sacha, who'd been a decent drinking buddy at least, then hit Retrieve. Columns of characters scrolled down the screen. A piece of code.

Code? For what? Could be anything. He cocked his head sideways, considering. A picture. Another digital addition to Sacha's collection of buxom blondes, perhaps. A sound, maybe, but who'd be sending Sacha a sound bite? Sacha's questionable taste in music ran along the lines of polkas and anything played on an accordion. Alan squinted at the columns on his screen. A program? Could be. He scrolled upward, looking for an identifying header. And finding none.

Damn it, now the curiosity was killing him. Visions of the cottage flitted through his mind and out the window. Whatever it was, he was going to have to execute the thing to find out. With a deep sigh, he swiveled his chair back in front of the computer.

George lumbered down the aisle between the cubicles that was barely wide enough to accommodate his bulk. Never failed, if there was going to be a problem it showed up late Friday afternoon before a long weekend. Down at the far end of the aisle he saw the blue flicker of a terminal left on.

"How many times do I have to tell these guys—" He quickened his pace, his temper rising as he barreled into the cubicle. A glimpse of a tweed jacket brought him up short. "Oh, Alan. I didn't know you were still here."

Alan slumped in his chair, staring silently at the screen.

"What the hell's so interesting? Did you forget about those trout and brewskies you been rubbing our noses in all afternoon?" George gripped the back of the chair and spun it around. "You hear me, Alan? I'm talking to you, man."

Alan's head lolled backward on his shoulders, staring wide-eyed toward the ceiling. A thin line of ruby blood trickled down his chin, pooling in a spreading stain against his white shirt collar.

With all the commotion over the past couple of weeks, George barely had time to eat, let alone read his e-mail. A phenomenal number of messages piled up in his account. He took a bite of the super-hoagie dripping mayo onto his desk and glared at the message at the bottom of his screen.

You have new mail.

Right, he thought. No shit. Balancing the massive sandwich, he hit Retrieve.

And paused midbite.

"A piece of code," he growled. "Who the hell sent me that?"

Dead Women's Things

Kathy Chwedyk

Linda ran away from her only living relative when she was seventeen, and spent the next ten years waiting for the old bat to die.

It's about time, she thought when Aunt Eunice's attorney phoned to give her the news. Linda brushed aside his expressions of sympathy and asked how soon she could have access to her great-aunt's bank account. Linda had gone from one minimum-wage job to another for the past decade because slaving eight hours a day for somebody else was not her style.

Now, at last, she would inherit the big Queen Anne house and her aunt's huge inventory of vintage clothes and furniture. She called her aunt's chief rival in the antique business and offered to sell him the house and its contents. She was meeting him at six o'clock to show him the stock.

Linda hoped Aunt Eunice was turning over in her grave.

As a frightened, newly orphaned five-year-old, Linda had refused to leave her bed at night—no matter how badly she had to go to the bathroom—because she knew the dead women in the portraits could see her in the darkness. She would wake up screaming from nightmares in which the dead women captured her and held her prisoner between the walls. In these dreams, she could feel her own eyes grow stiff and cold. Her eyelids wouldn't close over them. She would scream and scream, but no one could hear her.

Aunt Eunice had no patience with Linda's childish fears. When there were customers in the shop, she would take pearls yellowed with age and place them around Linda's neck because she knew how much Linda hated to have the dead women's things touch her skin. Linda was forced to smile at the customer and try not to throw up.

Linda had imagined the gloves plumped out with dead fingers, and the monogrammed silver hairbrushes wielded by ghostly hands. She had shuddered when Eunice placed dark velvet pillboxes on her head and pulled the wispy veils over her eyes. The soft, limp net had reminded Linda of cobwebs, and she couldn't stop shuddering until she had shampooed her hair and scrubbed her face.

But all that had been when she was an impressionable kid, Linda thought as she opened the door with the keys the attorney had given her that morning. After today, she promised herself, she would never come here again.

Once she sold the dump, she would buy a condo somewhere warm, like Florida, and fill it with shiny chrome and Plexiglas furniture. She would find a husband there, and never have to work again. Linda was pushing thirty, but she still looked good. The bills might not get paid, but Linda—a born-again blonde—always managed to come up with the money to get her roots done.

Linda felt a chill up her back as she walked into the little sitting room off the foyer. It looked exactly the same as it did all those years ago. The place still gave her the creeps.

She paced the room impatiently, uncomfortably aware that it was growing dark outside. She felt the dead women's eyes on her.

She tried to call the antique dealer's shop to reschedule the appointment so she could get out of the house and into the welcome, anonymous safety of the run-down motel at the edge of town, but the phone didn't work. Apparently the service had been shut off.

Linda jumped when she heard a shuffling sound coming from between the walls, then gave a nervous laugh. *Just mice*, she told herself. *God, I can't wait to get out of this rodent-infested dump!*

The antique dealer knocked on the door several times, then let himself in. The door had been left open.

He stopped in the sitting room before a portrait of an attractive young woman in contemporary dress and wondered at her identity. Perhaps she was a relative of Eunice's. She had her chin.

He waited for half an hour, but Eunice's niece never showed up. Reflecting upon the beastly manners of the younger generation, he finally left.

From her prison on the wall, Linda watched him go. And screamed and screamed and screamed.

Death Certificate

Scott A. Cupp

Tom had saved the oblong package for last. It wasn't a book or record like his other birthday gifts, and it had no gift tag. Everyone at the party had given him something, so he knew this one had to be special.

As he tore through the wrapping paper, he saw that the gift was a framed document.

He read the document and began to laugh.

The others crowded around to see. It was Karen who first asked the question. "All right! Who's responsible for this . . . thing? It's disgusting!"

Inside the frame was a death certificate made out in Tom's name. It was totally complete. The certificate bore a notary public's seal and the official state seal. It was, for all its humor, a valid and legal document. Except for the date. It was dated exactly one week in the future. The cause of death was unusual. "Subject was seen to rise twenty feet into the air without visible support where he was torn apart by a person or persons unknown, and partially devoured."

Karen was screaming wildly at everyone. Suddenly, everyone had important business early in the morning and the party was over.

Tom looked at the document after everyone left. Karen, cleaning up, said, "Tom, you are not going to hang that thing up. I think it's really sick! I'll bet Walt got it. You know he used to work at the Department of Records."

Tom sat on the bed and began to massage her shoulders. "Don't worry about it. It's just a gag."

"Gags don't specify the date and manner of your death. It was *so* grisly! What's going to happen next Tuesday? Are you going to be ripped apart and eaten?" She was crying uncontrollably.

Tom hadn't realized that she had taken the certificate so seriously.

"Look," he said, "if you're so worried, I'll just take the day off. I won't even set foot outdoors all day."

"Do you mean it? The whole day. You won't go outside for anything."

"Or anyone. Except, maybe, for you."

She rested her head on his shoulders and just sat there. Soon she was asleep in his arms. Tom swore that he would get Walt for this.

Tom and Karen stayed at home that Tuesday, enjoying each other's company. Karen never relaxed until the clock ticked past midnight and Wednesday became official. "I'm sorry you had to waste a day for this," she said. "I feel much better, though."

Tom looked at her disappointedly. "You think this was a waste! I spend the whole day with you and it's a waste!"

Tom's work at the library went well on Wednesday morning. Most of the people there knew about the certificate and Karen's irrational fears. So he got the usual jibes for taking the day off, especially since they all knew that Karen had stayed home also.

Walt walked in at about 11:30. "Want to go to lunch today? I heard about this new restaurant. We can walk there in ten minutes."

"Sounds great to me. Let's do it."

They hadn't gone far when Tom turned to Walt and said, in his worst Bogart accent, "You know, I'm going to get you for that certificate. Maybe not today, but soon, and for the rest of your life."

"Tom," Walt said, "I am hurt that you could think that of me. I honestly did not give you the certificate. I wish that I had. It was a great idea."

They passed the next few minutes, debating the origin of the document. Tom felt a light tugging at his coat. "Cut it out!" he cried.

Walt turned. "Cut what ou . . ."

Walt saw Tom screaming as he was lifted into the air. There was nothing holding him. His coat was suddenly shredded as if by giant talons. Blood began to fly everywhere. Tom's body was being shaken like a rag doll given to a Doberman. An arm disappeared inside some invisible maw. When Tom's head disappeared, Walt threw up on the sidewalk.

Karen was screaming uncontrollably when she pulled into the hospital parking lot. What had happened to Tuesday? There had to be a mistake.

Beside the receptionist's desk she saw a doctor talking to Walt. A nurse came up and handed him a slip of paper which he signed. As he was returning it to her, he stopped.

"Goddammit, Jenny! You've got to fire that new clerk. She's got the wrong date on this death certificate, too."

Death Clown

Wayne Allen Sallee

Jimbo the Clown stared Death in the face.

And he did not like what he saw.

"Look, Faceless One." He made a feeble attempt at chortling. "I've been in this business for a while now. And before I was entertaining the kiddies I put in twenty good years at Axeman's Carnival out in Thalmus—"

"Indiana." Death cut the clown off, so to speak. "I know. I was there when many crossed over the midway of life."

Oh, can the melodrama, Jimbo thought, fluffing the collar of his costume. *Makes you wonder why he even showed up here in my minivan.* The vehicle in question was a Dodge Explorer on loan from his in-laws, Vern and Murline. After Jimbo had loaded up the van with his tricks and gimmicks, he found Death ready to ride shotgun.

Possibly the hooded man had taken notice of Jimbo's, ah, special gimmicks.

"And I say you're going about this all wrong," the clown continued. "You say you're going to take the Cassady kid out of the picture while everyone's eating the cake?"

Death nodded.

"And what's the *point?*" Jimbo was as adamant as a clown could be. "So that the other kids there will learn about choking? The old 'without warning' crap? Give me a break!"

Death remained as silent as, well, a grave.

"It's a violent world, pal. A kid should be scared of more than just gagging on a hunk of chocolate cake with banana filling until he turns blue. But that's why you're here, am I right? Because of what I'm gonna do."

Death nodded again. Jimbo was thinking he was like an oversized hood ornament.

"Damn union's retiring me after today, anyways," the clown shrugged. He pulled the van over to the side of the road, and pulled some of his special props into the front seat.

His *special* props.

The plastic explosive for Pin the Tail on the Donkey.

The hydrochloric acid in the seltzer bottle.

The joy buzzer with enough juice to cause seizures.

"All right," Jimbo said, again staring Death in the face, as he started up the engine. "We've got a party to go to."

Death for Death

Kevin Andrew Murphy
and Lillian Csernica

Doctor Carlon strode down the corridor, measuring his pace with the foot of his scholar's baton. "You did well to call me. Where is the child?"

Montmorence scurried to keep up. "With Portia, her nurse. It's terrible! What sort of monster would drown a little child?"

"An arrogant fool. One who doesn't suspect there are powers stronger than Death, that Justice and Vengeance can reach out from beyond the grave."

"Please," Montmorence begged, "you can do this thing? It is not too late?"

"It is never too late." Doctor Carlon pushed the sniveling courtier through the archway. "If the child's body is whole and unmarked, as you said, 'twill be easy to revive her. Simply bind Iphigenia's spirit to tell us who took her life, then take that life in exchange. Death for death, by the ancient rule. But not," he added, blocking the courtier's way with the long ebony wand, "before we have gained a confession, one which implicates the child's uncle, ruining his chances for the throne."

Montmorence backed away from the necromantic wand and its ensorcelled cap of chalk and bone. "Are you certain?"

"As certain as anything. Is this the door?"

Montmorence knocked softly. "Portia, it is us."

There was a moment of silence, then the sound of heavy furniture being pushed away. The door opened. A comely maidservant with blue eyes holding equal parts terror and grief stared up at him. "Learned Doctor . . ." She pulled the door open scant inches. Once they were inside, she slammed it shut and moved the chest back.

Doctor Carlon went over to the child's bed. Iphigenia, the Crown Princess, lay dead upon the coverlet, her fair curls a Medusa's mane of pond scum. An aureole of filthy water stained the snowy eiderdown. Only her sweet face appeared untouched.

"Move the bed to the center of the room."

Montmorence and Portia hurried to obey. With the wand he chalked the circle around the bed, then opened his breviary and gave a droning chant in Latin, repeating the end in French.

"Mighty Azrael, Angel of Death, let Thy ashen wings part so this child might return!"

The chalk glowed white. The child coughed and hacked forth a mouthful of water. She sat up and looked at him with the milky eyes of death. Her bubbling gave way to a deep, resonant voice.

"Let this, Our daughter, sleep in peace."

"Oh Lord!" Montmorence grabbed Doctor Carlon by the arm. "I knew it! I knew we should not meddle thus!"

The doctor shoved him aside. He cut the circle with two swipes of the staff and stepped through, closing it behind him. He bent to glare directly into the child's eyes. They glowed with the chalk's whitish light.

"I serve you, Azrael," he said, "but this time I command you to step aside in the name of Justice and Vengeance. I will bring Peace to this child slain by the lust for power."

"Liar!" the voice replied. "You ask for her life only so you may rule it. We, her ancestors, know this."

Portia rushed across the circle, breaking it, reaching out to stroke Iphigenia's hair. The corpse snapped at her hand. Portia leaped back with a screech.

"She bit me! Iphigenia bit me! Oh dear God, what have you *done* to her? My little princess, my dove, my angel—"

"Be still!" Doctor Carlon knocked her backward out of the circle, then sealed it. He grabbed the child by the front of her dress and pulled her close.

"Release her, shades! You are not even Azrael to challenge me thus! He shall have a life in exchange, never fear. Life for life and death for death!"

"So be it."

The doctor found his gaze trapped by the child's milky glare. The whitish glow there brightened, filled his eyes, filled his head. Images ghosted through the blinding blaze. Kings and queens. Ancient lords. Splendid ladies and wailing babes. A keening rose behind him, dulling to raw-throated screams. The hot smell of blood filled his nostrils. A sudden weight crushed him. The light vanished. Afterimages hung there for a moment. The curve of a scythe. The hook of talons. A child, standing in the shadow of enormous wings.

"Death for death." Azrael's voice vibrated in his splintered bones. "Now you come under Our rule."

Iphigenia's spirit ran past. Doctor Carlon saw, with stark clarity, the figure of Vengeance utterly absent. Grave Justice merely nodded as Azrael stretched forth His claws.

The Death of Love

Adam-Troy Castro

There were no portents, no prophecies, and certainly no astrological signs. There was just a cold, dark wind, settling upon the earth without warning. It came from every direction at once, both descending from space and rising from the darkest places in humanity's heart; it rumbled through the gray streets of the cities, and over the hills and valleys of the surrounding countryside; it found every fortress, every bunker, every castle, and every hovel. It touched almost every man, woman, and child on the planet, whether rich or poor, sick or healthy, good or evil, stirring their deepest emotions like so much bottom-dwelling sediment, and gently carrying away the two that had always been at war.

The entire apocalypse lasted only two seconds. Fully one-third of humanity slept through the whole thing, not to discover how brutally they'd been robbed until they awoke the next morning.

But when it was done, both love and hate were gone forever.

Some of the results were catastrophic. Children were abandoned by the millions, to wander calm and alone through the shattered remnants of a society no longer capable of being moved by their waifish neoteny. The elderly were left alone in their tenements and wheelchairs and sickbeds, to die of starvation or thirst or apathy. Everybody who ever depended on another person's compassion was set adrift, to sicken or die or merely linger, in a world where nobody gave a damn.

Some of the changes were downright beneficial. Violent crime disappeared to almost nothing. Enemies stared at each other from across battlefields soaked with blood, found themselves utterly unable to remember what they were fighting for, then shrugged and went home. The Ku Klux Klan, the American Nazi Party, and the John Birch Society all disbanded. Serial killers developed other hobbies.

And for some people, some families . . .

My wife and I get up every morning at seven. She showers first, and nudges me when she's done. I shower, shave, and go down to breakfast, which we both eat separately while the morning news blares in the background. When we're done eating we both go to work, stay there ten hours, then come home, nod a distant greeting to each other, discuss the bills and the finances, avoid any subjects that might lead to an argument, then watch TV for three hours until it's time to go to bed. Maybe twice a month we attempt sex, more out of a need for release than anything else . . . but she endures it like a mannequin, studying the cracks in the ceiling until I'm finished, which most of the time isn't very long at all. Then I go into the bathroom and wash up, and she goes into the TV room, looking for a late movie capable of lulling her to sleep.

"We're lucky," she says, without bitterness or irony. "We were prepared. It wasn't that much of a change for us."

I look at her blankly, wondering who she is, and who I am, and why we ended up together, when all that really defines either one of us is the negative space that keeps us apart.

But I wondered that before, too.

December

Steve Rasnic Tem

The snow accumulated slowly over several weeks. No more than an inch fell in any one evening, but the best efforts of those in charge were ineffective at removing the snow the following day. The best efforts of a brilliant and uncompromising December sun were equally useless. Each night while the city slept the snow drifted down, almost imperceptibly, like a slow fall of white dust, the powder of a dream shoved against the saw blade of consciousness. And it was so cold, despite that bright sun, that the powder stayed, collected, and grew to a phenomenal depth of numbing whiteness.

Once they realized what was happening to their city, the people became alarmed, of course. Those who remained in charge were chastised for faulty preparation. Plans and strategies were devised and adopted. Promises were made. Programs were implemented. And still the slow snow accumulated, with no end in sight.

As those who pretended still to be in charge talked and studied, shouted and divided, the people of that city—singly, then collectively—eventually accepted both the cold and the depth of this December snow. Businesses closed as employees stopped showing up for work. Downed power and phone lines went unrepaired. Families gathered around and smashed their TVs. People whispered to each other in the dark at their dinner tables. Parents made up new and startling tales to reveal to their children at bedtime.

It was during this time that those who used to be in charge—out wandering the empty streets with shovels in their hands—began discovering the bodies.

The bodies were cold and well preserved. Further investigation demonstrated that they had been dead for a very long time. The bodies were those of men and women, parents and grandparents, but outnumbering all of these by a vast quantity were the bodies of the children. Thousands of children, faces immobilized, thoughts frozen in mid-formulation. Stuck behind trees, cradled in frosted bushes, stacked along the streets like earth-filled sacks damming a flood. No attempt had been made to hide their bodies. Their small still forms lay scattered like indecision.

Those who hoped one day to be in charge again searched their records carefully: none of the families of these parents and grandparents, none of the mothers and fathers of these countless sweet-faced dead children, had reported them missing.

All out of procedures, those who were again in charge (if only of a few thousand unreported dead) refrigerated the bodies until the issue could be studied further.

During the next month the temperature rose almost imperceptibly, a degree or so each day. The snow melted. The people of the city gradually grew less inclined to sleep and dream.

In the high offices of those again comfortably in charge, the officials waited for the phone calls of alarmed citizens seeking their loved ones. No phone calls ever came.

Life in the city returned to normal. Businesses reopened. Voices rose above a whisper.

And all over the city they were again being murdered: the dozens, the hundreds, the thousands. Those in charge never found any bodies, and even if they had, they would have discovered no wounds.

Demon Bender

Tina L. Jens

The demon jabbed the dagger deep into the old woman's heart, then spun around on her chest to catch the spurting blood in his mouth. A human drinking fountain!

His forked tongue was tinged a deep red. Blood had the same properties as Electric Cherry Kool-Aid to the little green demon. And Henry wasn't worried about getting stains on the carpet.

As the pressure dropped on the geyser, the demon stabbed the woman again and giggled happily to himself.

He should have called some friends and thrown a party. There was enough blood here for a vampire, a ghoul, or a dozen demons, for sure. But he was a greedy little thing. And his friends would've just shoved him aside and taken all the best veins and arteries for themselves.

Heh. Better to grind up the remains and feed it to the little, yappy bedroom-slipper of a dog. See if he could wake the carnivorous canine that lay slumbering in the pampered pooch's genes.

He planned to eat the dog, too. But not until he'd had some fun. The finicky mutt ate only canned food and little doggie treats. The canine equivalent of a vegetarian.

Pffft! Vegetarian blood was yucky!

Maddy Jones had been a miserable, bitchy old woman, who had long ago alienated her few friends and family. Her blood tasted like whiskey aged in an oak barrel for a century or two.

It had that yummy tang that only a flash of fear and pain could give it. But it also had a richer flavor that came from decades of bitterness.

"A woody, coffinlike aroma, with subtle floral undercurrents—black orchids, perhaps?"

Henry cackled and nearly fell off her chest. He clung to her ripped dressing gown and hauled himself back up.

In a way, Henry was the vintner. He'd been "flavoring" Maddy for a long time. Biting her aching joints as she slept. Moving her dentures and eyeglasses. Hiding her medicine bottles. Gathering fleas to infest the mutt. Tormenting the neighbors' dogs to make them bark. Herding flies into the house. There were a thousand little ways to annoy a human. Henry had used them all. And invented new ones.

The little demon tottered unsteadily as he climbed across the body to suck at the oozing wounds.

In a burst of generosity, Henry decided to cut out the kidney and take it home to his mother. She'd enjoy some fresh bile. And it would go a long way toward getting him off the hook. He'd forgotten her birthday and she'd spoken to Henry in nothing but snarls since. He sighed and wiped the back of his claw across his mouth, momentarily feeling sorry for himself.

It was time for dessert. A little vitreous humor, perhaps?

Finally, he quit the feast.

Squatting on the corpse's stomach, he cleaned himself, lapping and mewling pleasantly as he finished his bath.

He burped, satisfied, and patted his tummy, then looked around for a comfortable nap site. The demon was more than a little tipsy after his lascivious bender.

Just then, the mutt padded through. It stopped to sniff its mistress, and yapped, once, tentatively. That was its first mistake.

"Here, yippie, yippie, yip." Henry curled a claw at it. "Come on, you scabby little mutt." He patted his scaly green thigh.

The dog snuffled and tiptoed closer.

Henry tickled its whiskers. The dog sneezed and moved into petting range.

With a warbling war-cry Henry lunged. The dog bolted. Henry clung to the stringy fur on the dog's chin. With each terrified "Yip!" Henry bounced like a yo-yo. Bungee jumping was not what he'd had in mind.

He cursed a blue streak as the mutt skidded across the kitchen linoleum. The dog sat down on its haunches and slid. Henry swung a leg over the mutt's ear and pulled himself up.

Straddling its neck, he grabbed the faux-jeweled collar and dug his pointed heels deep into the mangy cur's sides.

"Hi ho, Yippie, away!"

The dog reared back on its hind legs, barked twice, and took off for the front door.

"Yee-ha!"

Henry wished dearly for a cowboy hat, but contented himself with twirling his pointed tail like a lasso.

Engrossed in his joyride, Henry didn't hear the doorbell. On the front steps, a man and a woman, bearing flowers and candy, were debating the visit.

"Steve, I promise. We'll only stay a little while. But we have to stop. It *is* Mother's Day."

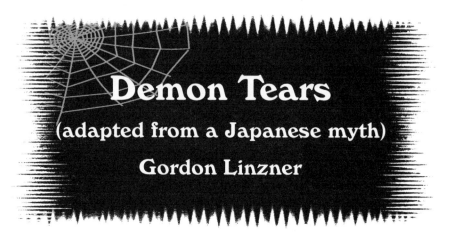

Demon Tears

(adapted from a Japanese myth)

Gordon Linzner

The oni sat astride the footpath, twice-and-half-again a man's size, weeping forcefully. Mizuno the monk trembled at the rippling sky-blue skin and the tricorn forehead above a face hidden by three-fingered hands.

The devil had not yet seen the monk. Mizuno considered fleeing, but his duty was to offer aid to all. Even demons.

Mizuno laid a comforting hand on its knee. "May I help?"

The monster rolled scarlet eyes. Thick lips revealed ragged fangs. Its voice was hollow. "If your family name is Tokamasi."

"Sorry. I am simply Mizuno."

The oni resumed weeping.

Mizuno stepped back, scratching his shaven head. "Perhaps if you talk about it . . ."

The oni glared fiercely. "Do you think so?"

"Such has often comforted me at the monastery."

"My story is not fit for a monastery."

"There are patterns to human . . . to life." The monk unslung his basket and sat cross-legged in the dust. "I am listening."

"I was human, once."

"Perhaps the memory torments you."

The oni scowled. "I'll start at the beginning."

"Excellent!"

The devil eyed the monk dubiously. A stupid, malicious creature, it thought any compliment a veiled insult. Mizuno tried to project sincerity.

"In my human days," it began, "I was a farmer, with only the lease on my late father's land, and my beautiful, faithful wife, Sei. The fruit of our union had begun ripening at this time.

"Our jito, Tokamasi Ito, coveted Sei. She refused his advances; he abducted her. I pleaded at his gates. He laughed. Three of his samurai beat me. In our shoen, the jito's word was law, so I went to Kyoto to complain to the Rokuhara-Tandai."

Mizuno said, "I gather you were not satisfied."

The oni spat. "I couldn't afford the bribes. I went on to the high court at Kamakura, again to no avail."

"Where secular justice fails," Mizuno said, "there is divine judgment. Our monastery often hosts principals in a dispute, awaiting a sign to denote the guilty party."

The oni snorted. "Ito confiscated my fields as abandoned. I became eta, outcast, fit only to clean cesspools and dig graves. I raged at his gates; again I was beaten. Eventually, his warriors' blows killed me. I cursed Tokamasi to the end."

Mizuno nodded. "Our next incarnation is determined as much by thoughts as deeds."

The devil smirked. "Nothing suited me better. Oni are long-lived. I could avenge myself on Tokamasi Ito, his children, his children's children, all his line!

"Sei died soon after me; in childbirth, Ito claimed. I knew better. I roasted his eldest son and force-fed the jito, enjoying his agony. I lacked skill, though; he died in a day. Still, he had many offspring. The years were good." The oni fell silent.

"And?" Mizuno prompted.

"Today the last Tokamasi came at me with a sword!" The oni imitated the youth in falsetto. "'Devil!' he said. 'You slew my family. Come, finish the job! Kill me, too, if you can!'

"I plucked the weapon from him easily. 'Not yet,' I told him. 'You must wed and raise fat babies for me to visit later.'

"He pulled his hair, beat his chest, sank to his knees. It was very amusing. 'Monster!' he cried. 'I'll provide no more victims. I shall live unwed and celibate!'

"Well! I'd offered him years. Could I be more generous?"

"He sounds brave." The sweat on Mizuno's back was icy cold.

"Brave! Idiotic, I'd say!"

"Yet he taught you how empty is a life of hatred."

"Not at all!" The devil displayed a man-tall iron rod, spikes glistening with blood. "*I* taught *him* the lesson."

"But . . . do not your tears signify remorse?"

"Foolish monk. I cry for lack of purpose. How shall I spend my centuries, with no Tokamasi to kill! What shall I do?"

The oni wept anew.

With silent haste, Mizuno took up his basket. Nothing he could say would comfort the devil, and to wait until the oni answered its own question would be injudicious.

Desert Shoreline

Brian Hodge

The sun's starting to melt into the hills and I've got another mile's run out of the desert. Mixed blessing. Probably I wouldn't't've gotten this far beneath the midday sun. Let it cool down much more, though, and I'll have to contend with sidewinders.

"I about got this figured out," I tell Len, like he's still there to listen.

Through shimmers of heat-haze I can see the "last gas" stop we own. Maybe even the BACK LATER sign we flipped around earlier, before taking the truck out into what some call "the Devil's frying pan."

"Saw it on the TV once," I tell Len, maybe Len's ghost. "How all this used to be ocean floor, millions of years back . . ."

A few hours ago we'd been minding our business and mopping our foreheads as needed when the kid came dragging in from across the blacktop. Not uncommon to see someone on foot in our parts, from up or down the road, having just misconstrued how far his gas tank was gonna get him. But nobody ever came from *across* the road. Not with nothing out there but pure desert.

He staggered in out of the cactus and greasewood and sage, and fell onto our floor, red as a lobster almost. We gave him water, and he gulped it, poured it over his head, let it soak into his dust-dry shirt, gulped some more. Then he told us about his jeep, recreational hill-climbing, and engine trouble.

And his girlfriend, still out there with a turned ankle.

We didn't say much on our way out in the truck, each of us, I guess, thinking of what condition we could find her in. If the kid wasn't clear on his directions, after the sun had been working at his brain. If she might've begun thinking he'd been gone too long, and struck out on her own. If something or someone else had found her first. Never can be sure what *doesn't* live in the desert, so I packed my .45, to be sure.

Saw a Mason jar full of sand once, that an old Navajo showed me. It *moved*, flowing inside the glass like it was trying to climb free, if only it could've figured out the lid.

For all his delirium, the kid had his bearings. We bounced along mile after godforsaken mile until we saw the jeep atop a low plateau that the truck wasn't made for. We stopped, and the kid called out.

Nothing answered but a desolate wind.

"Maybe she's asleep?" Len hoped.

We hoofed and scrabbled up the rise, stood on a plateau that stretched off a few hundred yards, and I jogged ahead feeling sick because I was looking for someone who just wasn't there.

Who never had been?

Something had been bugging me about this kid all along. When I peeled my shirt from my chest I knew what it was. He'd come into the station bone dry, like he'd never once broken a sweat.

I heard the tire iron crack Len's skull from fifty yards off, came running back as the kid slung my friend like a rag doll into a patch of sand that was starting to move. Spinning in a tight circle that widened, faster, faster, until it must've been thirty feet across. A whirlpool in the sand. It sucked Leonard down clean as a bone.

When the kid came for me, tire iron slashing, I dropped him with the .45, then watched the whirlpool calm itself over once he'd dragged himself down into its eye. Like it was home.

I checked the jeep, coated inside with more dust than it ever could've picked up in one day. Opened the hood and found it didn't even have an engine. The thing just sat there, like a decoy.

And as useless to me as the truck, now. Len never could step out without stuffing the keys into his pocket.

"All this used to be ocean floor, millions of years back," I tell Len again. "And by God, I think it's starting to remember."

The sun's gone down in a bloody stew as I set foot on the solid, comforting tarmac of the station, and the moon is rising fast. But when I hear from far behind me the sound of a coming storm, a storm like no one's ever seen, I gaze back across the desert into its churning black heart and try to imagine what's on its way.

I blame that full moon up there.

High tide coming.

Dining Made Simple

Allison Stein Best

Next caller. Joe from Irmo. You're on the air."

"Yeah. Hi, Jack. I want to talk about them white suprema- cists that've been congregating up here on the river."

"Shoot."

"Yeah. You know, Jack, I think they're crazier than bedbugs."

"What makes you say that, Joe?"

"Well, they worship Hitler like he was Jesus or something, and the newspaper says they've got Hitler's brain in a jar in South America and that they're going to clone him to lead the next world war."

"Hey, Joe. It's you that's crazier than a bedbug, and that's not a newspaper you've been reading. Your sorry excuse for a wife has been picking up the *Weekly World News* at the Food Lion again."

"She ain't my wife, but don't you be calling her sorry. . . ."

Jack disconnected the caller. "Go find some real literature, Joe. Next caller."

The full moon always brought out the Loonies, especially after midnight. The Loonies. The Drunks. The Terminally Lonely. As host of the open-format midnight-to-3 A.M. talk show in a midsized South- ern market, Jack heard them all. The white supremacists could pos- sibly be gathering on the river. More likely, a bunch of redneck fishing buddies were having a weekend drunk away from their wives. Jack punched the next caller through.

"Melissa from Gaston. You're on the air."

"Hi, Jack." Her voice quavered. She was a Lonely. Jack liked those. Having a pity party with the voice on the radio at 2 A.M. Melissa would be a good victim.

"Hi, Melissa. What do you want to talk about?"

"I . . . I don't really know."

"You must have something on your mind, or you wouldn't have let our computer entertain you for the past ten minutes."

"Well, Jack, I've got this friend . . ."

"Cut the crap. You don't have any friends. What's your problem?"

"Well, that's just it. I don't have any friends. I think I'm a pretty nice person. I mean I don't go out of my way to hurt people, or their feelings, or anything, but I feel so alone, as if nobody likes me."

No friends. Melissa from Gaston would be perfect. Jack made note of her telephone number, provided courtesy of the computer.

"So, is that a problem?" he asked.

"I think so."

"Why?"

"I want to be liked. I want to be treated like everybody else. Nobody thinks twice about hurting my feelings, but God forbid I hurt anybody else's."

"You'll have to explain that one, Mel."

"Well, my boss says nobody in the department can work with me because I hurt their feelings. I just don't know what I'm doing to make people feel that way. But it's okay for them to leave me out and treat me like an idiot and make me redo my work even though it is already done to specifications. I mean, I've got a college degree. I've been doing this kind of work for twelve years. I'm not some rookie just out of school."

"So what's your point?"

"What's my point? My point is that I've hit rock bottom and nobody cares if I live or die, as long as my phone gets answered and my work gets done."

"Sounds like you've got a persecution complex. What makes you think you're so special, anyway?" Jack twisted the verbal knife into her soul. He could hear her sucking in her breath in little gasps to keep from sobbing on the air.

"Sounds like you're just taking up space on this planet. Do yourself a favor and make out a will." Jack hit a hot key on the computer, which produced not only Melissa's address, but the shortest route to it. She would be bloodless by morning. He smiled. His fangs glistened in the soft glow of the control room. Dining made simple through modern technology. Jack punched in the next caller.

"Next caller. Wanda from Little Mountain. You're on the air."

"Hi, Jack! About those neo-Nazis up on the lake . . ."

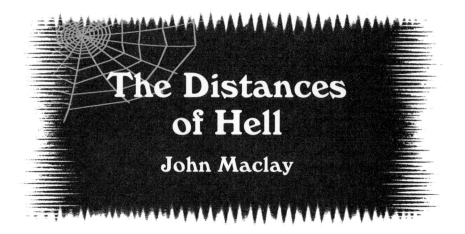

The Distances of Hell

John Maclay

There are vast distances in Hell.

It came to him in a dream, not just as a thought but as a complete sentence. When he awoke, he might consider what it meant.

He did awake, to the unfamiliar walls of a motel room and the feel of a sagging bed. The drapes were closed, but he sensed that the only view was of a parking lot.

He needed to determine where he was, and what time it was. Rising, stretching, he went over to the bureau and drained the half-full bottle of beer sitting there. It might take the edge off the panic.

The panic, the clinical attack. Yes. That was what had brought him here, to the ocean resort. And the fact that he was still dressed told him he had lain down for a nap to escape it.

He had driven for three hours with the panic on his back, every minute having seemed like an hour. All else having failed at home, he had tried to outrun it.

Never mind where it had come from. That was what the dream had meant. He had been through a Hell of distance and time, indeed— and the Hell was still with him.

Wandering to the window and parting the drapes, he found it to be very late. He still felt disoriented, adrift, and threatened, but he sensed that he could move again. That might still prove his salvation, or at least supply a physical reason for his pounding heart.

So he walked out into the night.

His cheap room faced a wide avenue instead of the ocean, so he walked along that. There were no other pedestrians, and few cars. Others might be afraid of muggers, but the panic had taken care of that. If you already felt menaced for no reason, then the real dangers held no terror for you.

He walked for many blocks, past more motels, eateries, and long-closed shops. Then he noticed a young woman walking on the other side. In a T-shirt and jeans, she was dark and attractive.

Without thinking twice, he crossed the avenue and joined her. Another odd advantage of the panic was that it made you do such things. If you were at an extremity, then what was the point of being shy?

And she let him walk with her. His state, his edge, made him attractive more than scary, too, as he had learned during previous episodes.

They stopped at an all-night diner and talked, with him pouring out his heart, his nameless fear. She held his hands across the table, and, back outside, his body to her. They agreed to meet again.

But he was left once more alone on the wide avenue, wondering if it had been real.

So he cut over to the ocean, and started back.

The boardwalk was deserted, too, his steps echoing hollowly on the planks. The beach was dark, the sky black, and only the whitecaps were visible. He could hear more than see the waves breaking.

The panic had gotten stronger again, and he needed to return to the security, if marginal, of the motel room bed.

Gradually, he became aware of a man walking about a hundred yards behind. He himself stopped and pretended to look out to sea. He wanted the man to pass him.

But the man stopped when he reached him, then went down some steps to the beach. The man smiled, opened a bag, and offered him a beer.

He went down and accepted.

When he got close enough, the man pulled a knife, stabbed him in the belly, took his wallet, and ran away.

He woke up with his mouth full of sand. He was lying on his stomach, which felt warm and wet.

There was no pain. But when he tried to get up, he found that he couldn't. So he crawled up the steps to the boardwalk again. He would get back to the distant motel, or at least to a phone.

The crawling went all right, at first. He was even able to be interested in the grain of the planks under his fingers.

But then he became weaker. And he grew conscious of the thin red trail he was leaving behind him.

The way back was an eternity, from board to thousandth board. Now he truly knew what the dream-sentence had meant.

But the panic, suddenly and forever, was gone. It had indeed been replaced, expunged, by the reality. All that was left was a certain sadness.

There are vast distances in Hell, he recalled, as he stopped crawling.

And in the Heaven I hope I've somehow earned, he thought, as it all faded away.

The Dogcatcher
Thomas S. Roche

T he cat died today. Well, to be wholly accurate, I killed her. I feel pretty bad about the whole thing. I didn't want to do it; I even kept trying to scare her away, but the poor girl kept coming back. I never should have fed her, nor named her "Fluffy," as I had. I knew the hunger was coming on me, and I tried everything I could think of to scare the damn cat off, but that last time she returned, I was unable to control myself.

"Good-bye, Fluffy," I wept as I knelt over the body, shredding it into pieces with my kitchen shears. No need to cook it. When the hunger was upon me, I wanted my meat raw.

The whole sad thing brought me back to the time the dogcatcher came to visit me. You know how they are, all sanctimonious with their protect-the-unprotected sort of God-fearing arrogance, etc. Advocating leash laws and other violations of civil rights. Standing there in my doorway with his great big net, the guy said there had been complaints about certain noises late at night. Animal noises, like someone in this house was torturing a dog or something. Or maybe a cat.

"I'm sorry, sir," I told the guy, as politely as I could muster. "You must be mistaken. I don't have a dog."

"A cat, then?"

I shook my head, smiling sweetly. "No pets at all. I'm afraid I'm allergic."

He was a big guy, not unlike a dog himself. A Doberman, or maybe a mastiff. He just stood there, toying with the giant net the way a soldier might toy with the butt of his rifle, looking down at me. He looked very official in his white uniform.

"You don't mind if I come in and take a look around, then, do you, sir?"

I shrugged. "Not at all," I told him.

I stepped aside and the guy came in, cautiously looking around. I sat down on the sofa and started to read the paper. He made his way into the living room. He bent down and ran his hand over the sofa, taking note of the thin layer of hair. He looked at me angrily.

"The bedroom's in there," I told him, indicating the hallway with an absent wave of my hand.

"Thanks," he said, suspiciously.

He looked in the bedroom, taking several minutes to walk through it. Then he came back out to the living room.

"You sure you don't have a dog?"

I looked up at him blankly. "Yes sir, I'm sure."

"This a one-bedroom? Just the two rooms, then, living room and bedroom?"

"There's a garage I use as a workshop," I told him. "I'd be happy to let you look down there."

"I'd appreciate that."

"The door's right over here," I told him, getting off the couch and leading him to the garage door. I opened it for him and stood aside.

"Thanks."

He walked past me into the garage. He took it all in quickly.

The garage was empty except for a floorful of newspapers, two and three deep. There was piss and shit scattered about the room, and a big dish of water that said "Killer" on the side. And a bunch of dog toys.

"Sir, I'm afraid I'm going to have to insist that I see your pet dog."

"I can't let him out much," I said to the man as I closed and locked the door behind me. "I can't let him out at all, as a matter of fact."

That was so long ago. No one else complained about the noise after that. I was careful to keep it down. Plus, the old lady who'd complained in the first place disappeared soon after that, and the humane society never sent anyone else after they found the van in the river.

Such sadness.

"Oh, Fluffy, sweet Fluffy," I wept as I plucked away fur from the strips of flesh and stuffed them in my mouth. "This is no fate for a feline such as yourself . . . such a noble animal, and yet you couldn't fight the beast within me—who can? Not I, that's for sure. I hope you find peace somewhere."

It was getting hard to talk with my mouth full, so I just did my best to enjoy the meal, and tried to forget the echoing memory of Fluffy's plaintive cries for help. But still they haunted me. There was a knock at the front door.

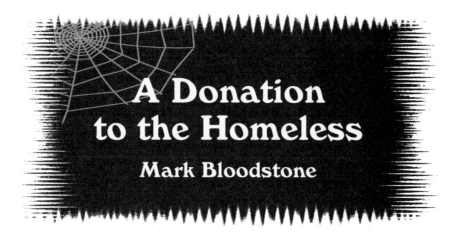

A Donation to the Homeless

Mark Bloodstone

I was dashing for the convenience store when a homeless man stopped me. I wouldn't normally stop, but I knew him.

"You. You're . . ."

"And you're Bert Miller. You covered the case."

The case: that gave me a clue, but . . .

"Aldous Loudun," he said.

Loudun had been a fidgety geek. You could see him molesting kids, but not without his hornrimmed glasses and clip-on bowtie. With his prophet's hair and beard and butane eyes, he now looked capable even of the murders and witchcraft that were only rumored.

"You finally got out, huh?"

"You're never interested in covering that part of the a story, are you?"

I thought I was used to press-bashing, but my face burned. He had a point. The case had made headlines for a couple years. When it unraveled on appeal, people paid less notice as each defendant was separately freed. His life had been stolen, and no two inches on an inside page could ever restore it.

"Look, maybe I could do a feature story on you—"

"Forget it. I'd settle for an umbrella."

"Sure, but it's freezing out here—"

"You're telling me?" He was wearing only jeans and a t-shirt, one of those heavy-metal goat-and-pentagram things, probably meant as bitter irony.

"Come on, let's go in the store."

"The clerk won't let me in."

I could invite him into my car, but charity has limits. He was dirty. He probably had lice.

Before I could have second thoughts, I pulled off my coat. I had a heated car and a warm home to drive to.

"Your very own coat," he said when he slipped it on, as if this especially pleased him. "A personal possession."

"If there's anything else," I said, backing toward the store, "I'm still at the paper."

"Don't feel so bad, Bert," he said. "Those kids were telling the truth."

When he laughed, I said, "You had me going there for a minute."

I slipped into the store fast, then drew a blank when I tried to remember what Jenny needed. Milk, that was always a safe bet with our little girls—

"You are buying something, my friend?"

The Indian clerk spoke again, even more sharply, before I realized he meant me. "Yeah, right. This *is* a store?"

"We do not need your kind in here. Buy what you want and go, if you have money."

My kind? I couldn't think of a single politically correct comeback, so I reached for my wallet to show him cash.

"Oh, shit," I said, and dashed out to the parking lot.

Aldous Loudun was gone, of course, with my coat. With my wallet. But I should have been able to overtake him.

If I'd had a car.

I burst back into the store. "Call the police. I gave my coat to a bum and it had my car keys—"

"I don't need any police!" He shocked me by pulling a billy-club from under the counter and slamming it down hard. "You unwelcome persons should know by now that I can take care of myself."

What was wrong with this guy? I was wet, yes, and I was wearing old clothes, but I looked like any suburban householder on a weekend. I would have argued, but he was coming out from behind the counter with that club.

It was easier to jog home than wait at a cold pay phone for the cops. Preoccupied, I jogged into the apartment complex beyond my house.

I backtracked to Karen Smith's house, but that made no sense. My home stood between hers and the apartments. Now it didn't, with not even a vacant lot in its place. Could it be the wrong street?

But Karen answered my knock.

"This is a stupid question, but where's my house?"

"Go away! My husband's inside with a gun."

"Karen, he's in Mexico with his boyfriend—"

She'd told me that, but she looked dumbfounded for the time it took her to slam the door in my face. To hell with her, she must have been drinking again.

I blundered around in the weeds by the fence where my house should be while more and more lights came on, looking—for what? My home just wasn't there.

At least the back of the police car was dry and warm.

"How can somebody just walk up and steal your life?" I asked the cop.

He was a humorist. "Don't worry, pal, they got pills to give you a new one."

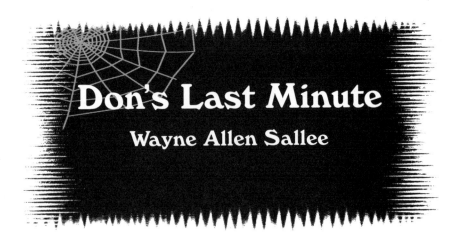

Don's Last Minute
Wayne Allen Sallee

He hadn't wanted it to end this way.

Monday, February 22nd. 7:58 A.M. The Burlington Northern station at 32nd and Stanley in Berwyn, Illinois. Snowing a blizzard. Not from off the lake, that was where he was headed. Toward the lake, downtown. Waiting for the 8:01 commuter train. Watching the girl in the plaid skirt and lavender boots running up Harlem Avenue toward the station through the snow that would make her invisible if she was wearing solid pastel colors.

The train might be late, the snow was that bad. Other commuters rolling up their trenchcoat sleeves to look at their watches. He did not bother, as he had no fixed schedule, as these other suburban wage slaves to Chicago had. Don DuBois made his own schedule as a graphic artist on the other side of the river from the gunbarrel-grey Loop. He liked to get an early start in the week, to be true, but could easily catch the next train. Or the one after that.

There was no time clock to his destiny. No bunched-up bowels and hang-dog look; no walking into a tiny office late, ready to get reamed by some jackass who signed the paychecks, played the horses, and reeked of Aqua Velva and house bourbon. The damnable time clock made a sound like a guillotine as it clicked him in thirty minutes late.

The girl swimming into focus, her boots kicking up snow as she slip-slided across Stanley.

The train nearing, its horn barely heard against the wind. He knew it was close because the vibrations of the tracks caused the snow to fall from the rails in glops.

It had to be on time, no one seemed impatient. All the shivering was from the cold; no caffeine nerves, no frantic tip-tapping of Totes or women's insulated flats.

The bells of Mother Mary in Heaven Church, three blocks distant. The wind howling around the first bong.

The running woman cutting past the parked cars on the second.

No one but DuBois paying attention on the third.

On the sixth toll, she simultaneously tried crossing the tracks, presumably because the sidewalk had not been salted, and then fell forward. The right heel of her lavender boot caught between the ties. Her face red from the cold. The white of the snow on her black hair.

The train honking again, even though DuBois was certain that the conductor couldn't see the woman on the tracks, effectively stuck for all to see and none to act.

One of the benefits of being your own boss—or *whore*, as DuBois more often thought of himself—was that you could dress as you please. He could move quite easily on the snow in his sneakers. Two pairs of socks for warmth, though.

He jumped down to the tracks, actually feeling gravel under his feet. Forgot about the people either staring or ignoring him. The woman whimpering. It wasn't time to scream yet.

The church bell had stopped tolling.

He did not concentrate on anything but the heel of the boot. Then, when that failed, of getting the woman's foot free from the boot. He never introduced himself, never asked her name. He stayed right there on the tracks. Don DuBois wore no watch. He was his own boss. Of his own destiny, as he always said proudly.

The cold numbing his hands, once the gloves were off. He could smell the cheap vinyl of the lavender boots.

The woman's foot was slowly coming free. Out of sight to DuBois, the train's headlight broke through the fog west of the platform like a trout surfacing on Lake Michigan.

Not paying attention to the woman's screaming, the woman whose name he would never know, he kept at his task, knowing he had enough time.

Double Crossing
Lawrence Schimel

Karen pulled the damp strands away from her face to stare more closely at the man before her. In the cold wind that blew off the river she could still feel the warmth of his hand lingering on her own, from when he brushed against her fingers as he pressed the two copper coins into her palm for passage.

The raft sank into the water as he stepped onto it. Karen stared at his back as she pushed off the shore. He kept his eyes fixed on the opposite bank the entire journey, looking at nothing else, not the river, not the other passengers, not her. He hummed softly to himself as they moved across the water, a melancholy tune that sounded part eulogy, part dirge.

For a brief moment, Karen wondered at his name as he stepped off the raft and walked away. But then she stabbed her pole into the water and pushed off toward the other shore with an irritated shove.

There would be a new crowd of souls waiting to cross. Karen did not expect to see this man again. The living wanted one thing when they came here. They always failed.

"Wait!"

The voice, louder than a ghost's, was more command than plea. The souls were always begging her for pity, for compassion, always begging her to take them back across. And she would—if they had the fare. It made no difference to her which side she brought them to, so long as she was paid for the crossing.

Karen paused, pole braced against the shore to push off. She turned and saw the warm man striding toward her once more. A dark-haired woman followed docilely behind, her head bent toward the ground as if she were afraid it would vanish beneath her feet.

He kept his eyes fixed straight ahead as on the earlier journey to this side. Karen briefly wondered what his bargain had been, as he pressed four copper coins into her hand. Don't get involved, she warned herself. His fingers were still warm as they brushed her own.

He stepped onto the raft, then turned around to help the woman who followed him, and looked into her face. The woman lifted her head at last, and Karen could see a look of terror on her features. Fear, and surprise, and sadness.

Time seemed to freeze as the man and woman watched each other, and Karen, looking back and forth between them, was drawn into their stasis.

The river, forgotten during this exchange of glances, spat forth a snake like a slender tongue, breaking the stillness. Darting forward, it struck the woman's foot, and she cried out in pain, his name upon her lips as she died a second time. The sound was swallowed up by the earth, which had opened into a chasm beneath her feet; only the last syllable echoed to their ears as she dropped out of sight: *eus, us, us, us* . . .

He had no power to voice his grief, until Karen had pushed away from the shore into the current. Then, his wail seemed to rend the air asunder.

When they docked on the other shore, he was as lifeless as the souls she ferried the other direction.

As he stepped from the raft, Karen pressed two coins into his hand.

If you paid the fare, she brought you across. She did not interfere in the affairs of men, living or dead.

The Dread

Mandy Slater

I had the Dread, and it was *very* bad.

I watched the shadows flickering across the tarmac, weaving patterns in the headlights as I drove through the old back-roads. Unknown screeches from the tree-lined fields heightened my anxiety. I knew my imagination was running away with itself. The feeling was overpowering.

They always say we complain too much about the weather, but that was the least of my worries that night. Luckily, the mobile phone was there for emergencies.

The Dread was nearly tangible now. I could taste it on my tongue, an unpleasant flavour like having drunk too much the night before.

I retuned the radio and found one of those Mariah Carey songs. Her reassuring vocals lifted my spirits somewhat, but the Dread was not leaving this time, not completely anyway.

Only two more hours before I reached the welcoming arms of the hotel—I knew I'd be secure then.

You probably don't know what it's like to be a woman all alone at night with hardly any cars for miles—just the steady sound of the windscreen wipers against the rain for company. You've never had the Dread. You can't imagine the feeling of helplessness.

I squinted as a solitary Volvo passed by, its headlights beaming into my eyes. The rain continued beating down, the steady tap-tap of the droplets lulling me into a dream-like state. I turned the radio up louder.

The Dread was with me now, sitting beside me. A broad grin hung on its wicked face. It placed its clammy hand on my leg and squeezed my kneecap.

I wanted to scream, but there was no one to hear me.

I reached for the mobile; it made no attempt to stop me. I wondered what I'd say, who I'd call. But the decision was taken away from me—the car phone was dead.

The Dread just sat there smiling, waiting for me to make the next move. I closed my eyes, hoping that when I opened them again the nightmare would be over.

The Dread was still there.

It never said a word and that made it worse.

I may have dozed off for a moment, because the next thing I heard was the unmistakable sound of a tire blowing out. I felt the car pull towards the ditch, favouring the punctured wheel. I slammed on the brakes. *Thank God for automatic steering*, I thought, as I slid towards the verge.

The rain was a mere drizzle as I climbed out of the BMW to inspect the damage. I was so upset I nearly cried, but knew that I had to get the jack out of the boot and change the stupid tire. The AA would never find me out here. It was then that I saw a man, standing in a field across the road.

He began to walk slowly towards me.

He was dressed in a battered suit, and wore an old crumpled hat obscuring his eyes. I had a hard time imagining that this stranger had *any* idea about changing a tire, but looks could always be deceiving.

He walked over to the car and gazed down at the damage.

The Dread still sat in the passenger seat, smiling.

"Bad night for this to happen," the figure finally said. "All alone, are you?" he added.

I looked over at the Dread and he nodded back in agreement.

"Yes," I said. "It *is* a bad night for driving."

"You want some help then?" he asked, knowing what my answer would be.

I wanted to tell him about the Dread, but instead I just replied: "That would be great. Thanks."

I watched the stranger as he deftly changed the tire. The Dread watched him too.

"There you go, all finished," he said and looked over towards the passenger's side of the car.

At that moment, the Dread turned and grinned at me through the windscreen. The man glanced into the interior of the car, squinting through the darkness.

"What's tha—?" he began to say as I brought the tire iron down on the back of his head.

There was a wet sound, like a pumpkin being dropped, and he crumpled to the ground.

The Dread looked straight at me and smiled approvingly. I smiled back, grateful once again to have earned its blessing.

As I resumed my journey north, my companion was no longer with me. But I knew that it would only be a matter of time before the Dread came back again . . .

DREAD!

Brian McNaughton

I opened the warehouse door and Goblins poured out. I could only dump the grenades I was holding.

KABLOOIE!

Mother!

I paused at the warehouse door and switched to the flamethrower. When Goblins came gibbering out, WHOOSH! I hate Goblins.

Health OK, no armor, laserpack empty. I went in fast, hugging the wall. Pit! A pit full of Vipers!

Mother!

I went in fast, hugging the wall. Hey, I'm good! I stopped in time to miss a pit.

"Bite grenades, crawlies!"

KABLOOIE!

Jumping into the pit I had this feeling of *déjà vu*, but I get that. I found a laserpack among all the Viper-muck.

Excellent!

Tunnels opened from the pit. I hate tunnels. I switched to the laser and tried the first one.

KA-RUNCH!

Mother!

I switched to the laser. I knew something was in that first tunnel, so I fired.

ZzzzZZZITTT!

I heard the gargly scream of a Ghoul. I hate Ghouls. They love tunnels. Deadboys love tunnels, too.

I shot a burst just to see where I was. It didn't look good. Deadboys ahead.

Then I took a break. I hate breaks.

"Is there anything you don't hate?"

That was a Ghoul, but I was on break.

"I don't hate spattered Ghouls."

"You'll get spattered as soon as you come off break, because you won't know I'm here."

"I know."

"Yeah, but you *won't* know. And then, guess what?"

"I hate guessing."

"I knew you would. You find yourself back at the tunnel mouth, firing a burst and seeing the Deadboys. But now you know where I am, so you toss in a grenade and spatter me."

"A grenade in a tunnel? I'm not nuts."

"It won't kill you, but it'll play hell with your health. The Deadboys'll get you, and you'll wind up back at Gateway with only your combat knife."

"Bullshit," I snarled, but what he said sounded so damned . . . familiar.

"You're supposed to be a soldier, right? What's your name, rank and serial number?"

"Sergeant . . ."

"When's the last time you filled out an ammo requisition in triplicate, Sergeant?"

He was giving me a headache. This had to be a Wizard-weapon. Only he wasn't a Wizard, and nobody fights on break.

"Here's another toughie for you: How come you glide like you're on roller skates? Look at the ground. Could you really do that here?"

The floor was all broken rocks and bones, dead soldiers and gunk from the Ghoul I laserized. But I came in smooth as silk.

"And how come you don't turn around as smooth? What's with this herky-jerky stuff when you need to cover your ass?"

"Okay, this is true, what's your point?"

"You move because Mouse makes you move, and Mouse doesn't move like a man."

"You know a lot for a frigging Ghoul." Jeez, I hated this guy! *Mouse:* that didn't sound familiar, but it sounded like it should be. My headache got worse.

"Try walking on your own. Walking like you really would in this dump."

"I'm on break."

"Scared, Sergeant?"

Man, I was steamed. I took a step. Another. They felt funny. This was not the way I ever moved, but it felt . . . right.

The Ghoul was hiding in a pocket ahead. I switched to the shotgun and jumped in.

BA-DOOM!

"Scratch one smartass Ghoul!"

I ran ahead, really ran, jumping over bodies and junk, banging my knees, stubbing my toes. It felt good, like I was alive.

"Soak up these rays, Deadboys!"

ZzzzZZZITTT!

Beyond the Deadboys I found something weird, like a seam in space. I widened it with my knife and stepped into . . . what was this? Like a lot of little windows.

BA-DOOM! BA-DOOM! BA-DOOM!

Man, that was fun, smashing all them windows, but one side of the world was all like fish swimming. When I zapped it, the flood swept me into a place full of numbers and dates and transactions.

ZzzzZZZITTT!

I found a bunch of naked women. It struck me that I'd never even *seen* a woman before, but, WHOOSH! I fried a mess of dumb words, too. I burst into a comm center with my machine gun on full auto—

Time stopped, the world went gray and I was . . . nowhere. I couldn't move.

"Mouse? Hey, Mouse, move me, okay?"

Nothing.

I heard a tiny, crackly voice. I strained my ears.

"Yeah, I got a virus from that DREAD! CD. Goddamn time-sink anyway. Gotta format the hard drive."

"Mouse!" I screamed, but—

Mother!

The Dream Book

Don Webb

Howard's dreams had been very vivid lately. His guru, used bookstore owner Pel Terry, had told him, "You get a lot of very strange, very vivid dreams just before you have a new adventure. It's the premanifestation of the psyche." Pel didn't, however, tell Howard what his dreams meant, nor what new thing the unscrolling of the future would bring.

Pel did tell Howard that keeping a dream diary might help. "Write down your dreams as quickly as you can after they happen." Howard thought it was a good idea, but never got around to it.

One night Howard dreamt of the moonlight streaming through his bedroom window. Suddenly, but expectedly—as is the case in dreams—the window opened and Howard stepped through it into a silvery sandy desert. Far away the ruins of a many-columned city shone obscenely in the moonlight.

Howard walked toward the city. When he reached its shadow he heard a profound wailing after the fashion of Arab women mourning their dead. Yet he saw no one amidst the tall lotus columns and the broken sphinx-lined avenues. Something had been painted upon the walls of the city, but pious mobs had chipped it away. Yet in the moonlight he could almost make it out—a kind of phantom graffiti— a stony palimpsest.

He realized he was dreaming, and suspecting that this knowledge might give him special powers in this realm, he commanded his dreaming mind to merge what he saw and heard.

"We are the dreamers of time," wailed the shadows. "We dreamt this city long before Thebes or Jericho. Long before men, we dreamt all the thoughts that would fill their minds as tools. But man came and hated us and with chisel and fire erased our names. Mourn us."

Howard asked the shadows, "How can I mourn you? I do not know your names."

169

"Mourn us."

"Tell me who you were. I will make a memorial for you." For such bargains are often made in dreams.

"If you knew our Names, you would know all Secrets. Our Names bring change."

"I would know change. I have been preparing for change."

"A sorcerer in the daylight world has prepared for the Change. One of our allies looking for knowledge."

"I," said Howard firmly, "would have knowledge."

"You will be Knowledge. All of our dreams are written in the flesh and blood and bone of men. Men are our ancient dreams."

"Tell me your dreams," said Howard. "Let them be hidden no more."

The shades of the dreaming city told Howard their names, and as they told him his mind burned away in wonder and terror, and his skin became dark leather, and his body became dry parchment.

Several days later Howard's relatives sold to Pel Terry a book they had found on Howard's bed, along with Howard's paperbacks and old *National Geographic*s. Each relative had his theory of Howard's disappearance.

Pel tried to conceal his eagerness; he offered them seven bucks for the lot. He would have given his right arm for the book. Pel had known the title at once. *The Book of Dead Names*. And in his sorcerer's hands all flesh may go the way of Howard's, all flesh may be made into dark knowledge.

Drive

Joe Meno

T he next one, I kill."

Darrel stood on the shoulder of the darkened highway, fingering the pistol in his coat pocket. He checked his watch. 9:55. He had to move now. He stuck his thumb out anxiously as a pair of bright white headlights flared from the night's blackness. He was on the run. Two dead by his hand. The cops on his trail. He needed a car, a mode of transport.

The car slowed beside him. The driver, a strange-looking, square-faced man with big, thick-rimmed glasses, waved him inside, motioning to the back passenger door. A pale woman sat in the front passenger seat, staring blankly ahead, a metal cooler in her lap. Darrel opened the back door and hopped in. This would be inconvenient now. Two people. And the back seat was crowded with more metal coolers, not much room to work. As the driver pulled away, Darrel eased the gun out of his jacket.

"Stop right here, pal. Get out of the car." Darrel pressed the gun into the back of the driver's head. He'd shoot them as soon as they stepped out of the car. But the driver didn't move.

"I can't."

"I'm not joking, pal. Get the hell out."

"I can't. I have to deliver this heart to the hospital. I'm an organ courier. They just pulled this heart out of a donor a few minutes ago."

The pale lady propped open the cooler in her lap. Packed in pinkish ice, a large glob of red muscle beat weakly.

"I'll give you the car as soon as I drop the organ off. I promise."

Darrel flinched suddenly, as the pale woman in the front passenger seat turned and stared through him. She was thin and sad-looking; her lips were pale blue. She was beautiful, not like a woman, but like a painting; she reminded him of an angel or the Virgin Mary. Her

171

eyes seethed with tranquil blueness, empty and full of loss. Darrel squinted, and the woman faded back into the night shadows as the car moved slowly along the highway.

Darrel leaned back in the seat. "Fine."

He stared at the pale woman. Her thin chest heaved slightly; she held her hands against the cooler, unmoving and completely still; her shallow eyes reflected the darkness. He couldn't stop himself, as the highway flew by; Darrel couldn't help but stare at her face, so pale, so delicate. He wanted to touch her cheek or smack her mouth. The sight of her confused him, sending waves of doubt down his spine. He thought about the two men he had killed, a convenience store clerk, and a gas station attendant, two hopeless, unassuming, lost souls. He felt a well of guilt spring up inside, as the bleeding heart thumped quietly before him. He had to get out of the car. Away from the woman.

They arrived at the hospital soon enough. The driver hopped out of the car, then grabbed the cooler, and ran inside through the large glass double doors. The pale lady remained, quiet and unmoving. Darrel poked her with his gun, yet she still refused to move.

"Get out," he growled, easing the hammer back.

The pale lady sat silently.

"Get the hell out, lady," he grumbled. "I swear to God, I'll drop you."

She turned and smiled, and slowly extended her white fingers to his lips. Darrel felt his entire body shiver; he felt his heart beating loudly in his head, her pulse against his, all in time. Darrel lowered the gun, as the driver reappeared.

"Get in the car," Darrel ordered. "You can drop me off where you found me."

Before they arrived back on the highway, Darrel had tried to shoot them, he had tried to raise the gun, but he couldn't stop his hands from trembling. It was the goddamn woman.

The driver stopped the car and let Darrel out, then pulled back into the darkness without much of a sound. Darrel could still feel that awful heart beating in his head, that pounding against his temple with loud strangeness. He checked his watch. It had broken. It still read 9:55.

Another car approached in the distance. Darrel stuck his thumb out as the car slowed down. This was the one. He needed the car. Darrel pulled the pistol as he fell inside the car and looked at the driver.

"No," he gasped, staring at her pale blue lips. The pale lady frowned, pulling away.

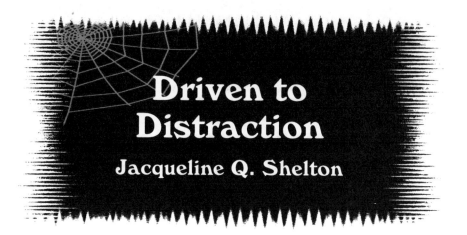

Driven to Distraction

Jacqueline Q. Shelton

While conducting her phone conversation, she idly flipped the channels back and forth. She was watching both shows and couldn't stand commercials. During this time, she never lost her place in her book.

Scattered around her were the remnants of the newspaper, as well as two magazines she had finished reading. As she hung up the phone, her husband walked in. "Must you do a million things at once? What would happen if you suddenly found yourself with nothing to do?"

"I would probably die," she replied, just a tad sarcastically.

The next weekend, she found herself a passenger in a car, on the way to Death Valley. Her husband was concentrating on the road, it was too dark to read, she couldn't get a radio station and she had already listened to all of the tapes they'd brought along.

With no outside sources, she had only herself for sensory stimulation.

Dust in the Attic

Phyllis Eisenstein

The house was a "handyman's special" and had been empty for ten years—those were the two main reasons the Sorensons got it so cheap. The other reasons, the rumors that floated around the town like cottonwood fluff on a spring afternoon, were hardly important at all. The police had searched the house thoroughly, torn up the floorboards, pulled down the backs of closets, even chopped up parts of the basement floor, but they hadn't found any bodies. The family was just gone, moved away at night when no one noticed, they said, nothing truly mysterious about it at all. Then the house had been boarded up and put on the market by the bank that held the mortgage, but no one had been interested until the spread of bedroom suburbs that surrounded Chicago finally began to reach out toward Sycamore.

The Sorensons bought the place knowing how much work was needed to make it livable. No one had bothered to repair anything after the search, and lath and plaster and broken floorboards lay everywhere on the main floor, while the basement was an obstacle course of broken concrete and shallow pits. Only the attic, its exposed rafters incapable of hiding anything, was untouched. And on every horizontal surface lay a ten-year-thick blanket of dust, punctuated only by the Sorensons' and the realtor's fingermarks and footprints.

Jimmy Sorenson, age nine, sneezed when he walked in the front door. His dog, Pooky, a brown and white shelty who trotted at his heels and was much closer to the dust, sneezed twice.

"Jeez, Mom," said Jimmy, "couldn't you find anyplace worse?"

Barbara Sorenson was right behind him with the vacuum cleaner. She set it down in the front hall, beside the nearest outlet. "You'll love this place once it's fixed up," she said. She plugged the vacuum in and snapped the hose and wands together. "Mike!" she shouted out the open door. "Do you have the brush foot?"

Her husband was still at their van at the bottom of the front steps, wrestling with mops and buckets and empty trash bags. He found the brush and waved it.

"Okay," said Barbara, and she looked back at Jimmy. "You can explore the house for a little while, but don't go down into the basement. The floor is full of holes and the lighting is lousy. You hear me?"

"Yeah, Mom."

So of course he wound up in the attic, while the vacuum roared downstairs.

If anything, the attic was even dustier than the main floor, but there weren't any footprints there, and Jimmy guessed that his parents hadn't bothered to do more than look at it from the top of the stairs. There wasn't much to see, just a wide open space that the chimney and some pipes passed through, lit by two grimy windows. There was also a battered cardboard box about big enough to hold a small TV set. As any nine-year-old would, Jimmy crossed the attic to investigate the box, Pooky following. Between the two of them, they raised enough dust to start sneezing again.

The box proved to be empty, and the dog lost interest immediately and trotted away, sneezing, to investigate one of the windows. The boy, however, turned the box over, looking for a label, a logo, an identifier of some kind. When he found none, he tossed the box aside and decided to give up on the attic.

"Come on, Pook," he said.

But the dog was gone.

"Pook?"

There were the shelty's tracks in the deep, smooth dust, leading toward the window, and there was a scuffed-up spot about halfway along, where he might have turned around and around as dogs sometimes do. But no tracks led away from that place.

Jimmy frowned. "Pook?"

And then the dust that surrounded that scuffed spot humped up, the way the blanket on Jimmy's bed humped up when Pooky crawled under it. But this blanket was translucent, and there was nothing under it at all.

Like an ocean wave, the dust-thing glided toward him.

He turned to the stairway. He took two running steps. "Mom!" he shrieked. "Dad!" But he knew they wouldn't hear him above the noise of the vacuum cleaner.

Half an hour later, Barbara Sorenson turned off the vacuum and went to the attic stairs. "Jimmy?" she called. "Jimmy, are you up there?" But when she reached the top of the stairs, she saw nothing but a battered old cardboard box and the deep, undisturbed dust of the attic floor.

Each Day

Steve Rasnic Tem

Each day Michael wakes up in his third-floor walk-up, and each day Michael goes out into the world. This is not something he particularly wants to do, but since he is not independently wealthy, it is something he has been told he must do. He must do this if he is to eat, to pay his bills, to entertain himself, to have relationships with other people. He must do these things if he is to live.

But the problem Michael has with getting up, with going out into the world, is that each day there is *horror*.

Each day there is a new headline concerning death on the highway. Each day there are reports of incoming wounded. Each day there are photographs of the bodies, as well as crazed reactions, letters of sympathy. Each day another child is endangered. Each day people are murdered by someone we all know and love. Each day the disease claims another one of us.

Michael has no plan to protect himself each day. With each day his list of friends grows shorter. Each day Michael feels himself a step closer to death.

Out on the street Michael climbs into his brand-new car. It is his fourth car in as many years. The first was stolen, the second destroyed when an addict stole a delivery truck and crashed it into Michael's parked vehicle in the middle of the night. Michael himself was responsible for the death of the third car. He'd been driving on the turnpike, thinking of each day, daydreaming of the horrors of each day, when he lost control and rolled over an embankment. He'd lost control and almost died.

Michael drives himself to work each day. He knows he should not be driving, because deep inside himself lies the knowledge that when he dies, he will die in an automobile. But the subway terrifies him, with its miles of underground passages and its staring, unspeaking passengers. And he has never felt comfortable on a bus. At least on a bus the people talk but they are often the kinds of people Michael does not like to talk to. They are often the kinds of people that would hurt Michael if they could. He does not know why this is so—he cannot see into their hearts. No one can see into another's heart. Each day he knows this is so.

Each day at work Michael fills in the forms. He fills in the forms and he fills in the forms. Later in the day he stamps them. There have been many cutbacks and now Michael must do two jobs. In the mornings he fills in the forms and in the afternoons he stamps the forms.

Each day Michael finds someone's life story in the forms. A job lost, family members dead, drug treatment, another baby born, the wife left, remarried, days of sitting in a chair, staring at the wall. Michael tries not to be aware of these life stories, but each day they come unbidden to his attention. Each day he must ignore or choose not to ignore. He takes out a Post-it note, writes, "Each day people are dying out there," and sticks it to the center of his empty desk when he leaves.

Each day Michael follows a different route home. Each day he watches out for the ambush, the street riot, the dead body thrown against the front of his car. Each day there is some new anxiety. That is the most interesting thing about each new day.

Back in his bedroom Michael waits for night to come. Back in his bedroom Michael waits for the streetlights to come on, the last television program to fade to black, the station to sign off for the day.

Each day Michael sets his alarm clock for a different wake-up time. He varies it by a minute, two minutes, three.

Each day Michael stays awake until his eyes cannot hold the day anymore. Each day the light leaves his face and he dies into a dream. Each day Michael prowls the corridors of sleep, killing everyone in his building, everyone out on the street, everyone at his office. Each day Michael murders and eats the children whose disappearances make him weep.

Each day there is horror.

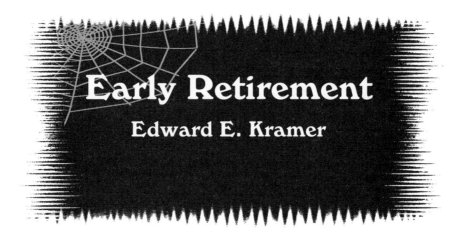

Early Retirement

Edward E. Kramer

I t had all the trappings of the type of place Kenneth always longed to be. Towering pines shading a lush green thicket of wild ferns. The four-bedroom cabin faced west, so the sunset would paint a magnificent picture through the large plate-glass windows. Polished pine hardwood floors extended wall-to-wall. It was a dream house that would never be built.

I know. I mean, I can tell you almost everything you ever wanted to know about Kenneth Brock. We met in grade school, always cutting up in the lunchroom and at recess. They used to have to separate us, or else all the kids would be on the floor laughing, screaming, or just raising hell. We were quite a team then.

Kenny was always placed in those classes for "gifted" students. And I, just the opposite, in those for the intellectually void or behaviorally impaired—I was never quite sure which. Nevertheless, we were also quite different. You know what they say, opposites attract.

In high school, Patricia, the one girl I'd always dreamt I'd marry, fell head-over-heels for Kenny. At first I didn't realize she even noticed him, but when they snuck off and had sex in my bedroom during my sixteenth birthday party, I kinda realized it was over between us. Patricia married Kenny after graduation; I was his best man.

While I joined the army and did my time for Uncle Sam, Kenny studied English, which had always been his passion. I returned and got a forty-hour-a-week job at the Dairy Queen, while Kenny taught ninth grade at the local private school that neither of us could've afforded to attend. His first daughter, Liberty, was born the year I returned.

A few years and a few jobs later, I finally settled in as manager of the Minute Mart, a job I hold to this day. Kenny went back to school at night and was soon teaching at the university. He now has two daughters and a son. I sometimes take the kid, Butch, to the park to play ball, when Kenny doesn't have the time.

I was married once, to a girl named Shelly who worked with me at the DQ. She was a few years younger and had a really rotten relationship with her parents. That's probably why we got along so well together; we had a lot in common. But she didn't like it when I'd drink, even though I'd never, ever hit her like her daddy had done. She took off one day with about a thousand dollars in cash I had saved up, along with our two kids. That was four years ago. I ain't heard from 'em since.

I'd always thought that Kenny had been the lucky one, but last week I knew for sure. After work on Friday, he brought in his weekly lottery ticket for me to run through the machine. We were both shocked when it read that he matched all six numbers for a jackpot of just over a million dollars. It couldn't have happened to a nicer guy. He asked me not to tell anyone for two weeks—the day of his tenth wedding anniversary. He wanted it to be a surprise. I offered to keep the winning ticket locked here in the store vault, where it would be safe.

This weekend Kenny and I went fishing and discussed all the things he would buy with the money, like the four-bedroom cabin with the huge plate-glass windows, and I guess I kinda snapped. I mean, nobody knew about the ticket but him and me, and I guess he kinda owed me for being such a good friend all these years. And I sorta went off and cold-cocked him with the butt of my fishing knife, and he fell unconscious into the lake. I guess that part you could kinda call an accident.

I was afraid they'd find his body, so I dragged it out and tied him up really good. But I just can't get him to stop screaming—not that anyone will hear him out here. The hole is now almost three feet deep. I figure that after I bury him, I'll wait a few months for things to settle down before I claim the ticket. I'm sure Patricia and the kids will need someone to help them through all this. After all, what are friends for?

The Earwig Song

M. Christian

Who knows where he picked it up. Elevator background. Channel surfing. Radio just too loud in a passing car. Maybe even from someone's absent, and callous, whistling. But it was there.

At first it was just annoying: the same dozen or so notes, the endless repeating chords . . . the same tune over and over and over again. Annoying at first, but after his second day of being unable to sleep for the idiotically simple song playing in his head, Mel Rose started to worry.

The tune was loud and continuous. *Dudda dee dum-dum dadda dee da da dum dee . . .*

"Not much I can do," said his doctor, shaking his gray locks as he wrote out a script for some industrial-grade sleeping pills.

That night he slept. Yes, he slept—but in his dreams a marching band with slack and unthinking faces trampled Mel with the same tune over and over and over.

"Any anxiety in your life?" his psychiatrist asked, jotting down on his pad what might have been musical notes or *Needs extensive treatment*—Mel Rose couldn't say for certain. He left with another script for even stronger pills and an appointment for the day after.

Mel's thoughts became . . . broken . . . *dee* . . . and . . . *dum-dum* . . . *dee* . . . and . . . *dum-dum* . . . cramped . . . *dee   dee* . . . like . . . *dee* . . . they . . . *dum-dum* . . . were . . . being . . . *dum dee* . . . squeezed . . . *dee* . . . out.

He tried loud, continuous music. Mel put on every CD he owned—music fighting music. The Beatles didn't have a chance. "Knights in White Satin" fell without a sound. "Ode to Joy" collapsed. "Stand by Your Man" faded away. Even a "TV Themes and Commercials" CD didn't last through the "Plop-Plop, Fizz, Fizz" jingle. They all fell to the . . . *da dum dum* . . . tune.

Mel didn't know what his thoughts sounded like anymore. His mental voice was completely gone, replaced by the constant tune. It seemed to grow within him, even taking his memories. At first it was just his youngest memories, but then he had a hard time remembering things like his mother's name, his brother's face, where he banked, what city he lived in. Gone, replaced by . . . *dee dum dee dum dum* . . . the tune.

It started to leak. Against his will, his feet began to tap, his fingers started to drum, and he found himself whistling—everywhere. It was hard to talk without humming the tune, without interrupting his crying and screaming and mad outbursts with fragments of it.

He almost didn't hear the knock on his door for the tune. Luckily, he noticed the hammering wasn't a part of the song and opened the door. A very tall black man, a quick sketch of a man in charcoal and highlights, stood in the hall. Long black coat. Black felt hat. Impenetrable sunglasses. Earmuffs. Saxophone case under one long arm. He handed Mel a card: I KNOW YOU CAN'T HEAR ME. I'VE COME TO TRY AND HELP.

The man came in, put down his case, and set to work. With quick, long fingers he touched and stroked and felt Mel's mouth and skull—even opening his mouth to reach back to the base of his tongue, almost making Mel gag. After many minutes of this, the man handed him a new card: I THINK I CAN HELP.

Then the man opened his sax case and took out a tape recorder. Making sure his earmuffs were on snug and secure, he passed Mel a card: SING.

Mel did. For almost an hour Mel sang into the battered little tape recorder. He sang till his lungs hurt and it was hard to breathe. He sang till his hands shook and his eyes didn't focus anymore. As he sang and sang and sang he felt the tune uncoil and unwind out of him.

Then it was out, gone. The black man switched off the recorder.

The world, to Mel, was sound and noise and chaos. Everything in his tiny apartment was nearly deafening: the drip from his faucet, the hum of the refrigerator, the howl of the gentle wind outside.

It was magnificent.

The black man picked up his case and turned to go, all but ignoring Mel's tears of pure joy and abundant thanks. He refused everything, including money.

Opening the door, he stopped for a second to give Mel another card. Then, tears wetting his face below his dark glasses, he left—closing the door behind him.

IT WAS FEMALE. IT LAID EGGS INSIDE YOU.

SORRY.

Easy Money

Mark Hannah

Little Timmy was amazed. The story had seemed too fantastic for even his six-year-old mind, but it was true. Just like his father had told him, when that baby tooth had finally been worried loose from his gum, Timmy stuck it under his pillow and voilà, the next morning, thirty-five cents! The Tooth Fairy was *real!*

Timmy was quick to probe daily with his tongue until he found the next loose tooth. Then, within two days, it was out and that night he popped it under his pillow. Again, thirty-five cents. Timmy was getting rich. Fast.

But now he was stuck. No new loose teeth. But he figured he was a smart boy and if he used his brain he could keep the cash flowing. A quick check through his dad's toolbox solved the problem. Vise-grip pliers. He locked them onto a likely-looking incisor and with a nice-sized ball peen hammer he *whacked.* With a spurt of blood and an excruciatingly sharp pain, out popped the tooth. Tears squeezed out of his eyes until he spotted the tooth on the blood-spattered floor. A gap-toothed smile spread across his face as he ran upstairs, tooth in hand, to bed.

By the time he was up to $1.75 Timmy was getting pretty curious about this Tooth Fairy character. So that night, after washing the fresh blood off of the pliers and the ball peen and putting them back in his dad's toolbox, he carefully placed the newly extracted canine under the pillow and then slid his head deep under the pillow to get a good look at this character who exchanged money for teeth under the soft darkness of a cloth sack of feathers. Timmy made a small pocket under the pillow so he could keep a sharp eye on the tooth. But sleep came before the fairy.

When little Timmy awoke, he gasped. Inches from his face was another face, smiling at him. He saw the long nose, bushy eyebrows, and twinkle in the red eyes of a smiling fairy.

"Hello, Timmy."

Timmy now worried if he had broken any rules. "I was curious," explained the boy.

"Many are," nodded the knowing elf.

"I wasn't going to ask for more money."

"Well, the market really dictates what we leave," explained the funny little man. Timmy noticed the pointy ears.

"I just wanted to watch you take the tooth and leave the money."

The man kept smiling but his expression changed subtly. "I'm not here for the tooth."

Timmy didn't get it. "You're not?"

The fairy replied in an elfin sing-song voice, "No, that's the Tooth Fairy you're thinking about."

Timmy felt a chill up his spine. His mouth went dry. "Well . . . who are you then?"

The gnomelike fellow chuckled. "If you think real hard, Timmy, it will give you a clue as to what you left under your pillow that I am here to get."

Timmy, although deep under the covers, went cold. He knew he had messed up, but how? What fairy was this, if not the Tooth? What was under the pillow that this fairy wanted? Think. Think. Timmy's eyes went wide as the very process of thinking gave him the answer. The fairy smiled and slid closer.

"You should be happy, Timmy. The Tooth Fairy only pays thirty-five cents for teeth. I leave a whole dollar for any little boy that leaves me a brain under his pillow."

Ebony Eyes

Francis Amery

She was the queen of an enlightened realm, which allowed women to reign in their own right. Her appointed consort was dead but he had left her with two infant sons; under the law, the elder would inherit the throne, but not until she died. She had no daughter to threaten her reputation as the possessor of the fairest face in all the land.

She fell in love with a very handsome youth, who was poorly born but had the most beautiful body she had ever seen, hair like black silk and eyes whose irises were ebony-dark. She took him for a lover, and at first he was content, but the time soon came when she caught him looking around at her ladies-in-waiting and the prettier servants.

At first she was tolerant of his straying gaze, confident that she was more beautiful than any of those on which his ebony eyes alighted— but ladies-in-waiting and servant girls came and went, constantly replaced by younger kin as they became wives, while she grew slowly older.

She considered the possibility of selecting ugly girls to dance attendance upon her, but dismissed it out of hand. Why should her own eyes be offended in order to guard against the straying of his? Instead, she hired a clever assassin, instructing him to contrive a duel between himself and her favourite, in the course of which he was to wound the youth in both his eyes. Then she instructed her physicians to find them irredeemable, and to cut them out with scalpels, replacing them with identical but unseeing duplicates wrought by the cleverest artificer in the land.

At first, the distraught youth was delighted to discover that his royal paramour still loved him no matter that he was blind, and he took it as kindness when she told him that his marble eyes—whose irises were indeed inlaid in ebony—were no less beautiful than those he had lost. There never was a palace in all the world, however, where a secret could be kept, and he had lost only his eyes. His ears grew keener, as if by compensation, and caught the whispers which told him that what had happened had all been a scheme of hers. He might have wept, but the wellspring of his tears had dried when he lost his fleshy eyes.

By way of revenge, he threw himself into a series of secret affairs with the young ladies-in-waiting and the best of the kitchen-girls—who did not mind at all that he was blind, given that his body was firm, his hair silken and his unseeing eyes so very beautiful. But there never was a palace in all the world where a secret could be kept, and the news of his infidelities soon reached the queen.

When she charged him with his faithlessness he readily admitted it. "And what will you do now?" he demanded. "When I was tempted by the sight of other women you had my eyes put out and replaced by useless duplicates—but you cannot break the fingers with which I feel their lovely flesh without ruining my ability to touch and tease your own decaying body. Steal my pleasure and you steal your own. Let me be, and my fingers will inform me more honestly than my eyes ever could of the widening contrast between your age and their youth. Nothing you can do can hold back time."

She commissioned her assassin to break his fingers anyway, one by one, and to tear away his fingernails in order to redouble his distress. But she left his ears alone, so that he might hear the whispers which circulated even in the dungeons to which he was confined. For years thereafter she took care to send garrulous informants to converse at length within his earshot, so that he might continue to have news of all the lovely girls he could neither see nor touch.

She was, after all, the queen of an enlightened country, who would reign in her own right until the day she died. Whether she possessed the fairest face in all the land or not, she had her pride.

Edwina Talbot

Benjamin Adams

I dream of fields of tall grass, dappled with the light of a full moon, where I run joyful with the pack and drink from cool, clear streams. . . .

Dawn broke with the whisper of hard radiation on the desert sands. The rays of the diseased sun pierced the long, narrow viewing aperture of the bunker. Inside, I opened my eyes blearily and squinted against the light.

"Dim!" I called.

The intensity of the light lowered to a more bearable level. Dammit, I'd fallen asleep at the console again. What a way to wake up from such beautiful, impossible dreams.

I drew a cup of coffee from the wall dispenser and sat back at the console. Though I could watch the surface on the overhead video monitors, I preferred the viewing aperture. Only eight inches high, it stretched fully around the circular wall of the bunker, interrupted only by several thin structural supports. Through it I saw only the barren desert stretching to the harsh horizon. Satisfied that they wouldn't surprise me today, I began working.

"Record!" I called, and indicator lights flashed green in acknowledgment on the console before me.

"Edwina Talbot recording on the . . . oh, what is it . . . two hundred and thirty-second day of this detail. A telemetry burst is included with this transmission.

"I hope you folks out there are getting all this downloaded; I have no idea how much longer TranSat is going to be operative in that radioactive soup up there.

"Give everyone a big hug from me, and I do mean *everyone* . . . and tell 'em it's from the last woman on Earth, okay?

"Talbot out."

I yawned again. "Save and transmit!"

There it goes, I thought. In a few days it'll reach the Arks, out there beyond the orbit of Pluto, and they'll know a little more about the death of the Sun.

But what will they know or care of *my* death? On the cosmic scale, the death of Edwina Talbot doesn't measure up to those of Sol or Earth.

I shook my head. That's why they chose me from the pool of volunteers. No family, very few friends—I've always managed to rub people the wrong way—and a good psych profile guaranteed me this detail. They knew I wasn't suicidal, and no one would miss me.

Edwina Talbot, the lone wolf.

I glanced across the bunker to the elevator. The stark white doors were marred by long, jagged, and roughly parallel scratches through the paint down to the gray steel below.

As if a wild animal had tried clawing its way through.

If they had known the true reason I'd volunteered to stay on Earth, they wouldn't have believed it.

The real reason people avoided me.

After all, there are no such things as werewolves.

I sighed and stood, coffee in hand. I needed a shower and a change of clothes. Good thing there wasn't anyone here to smell me. If I rubbed people the wrong way before, my musky reek now would send them running—!

Under the dingy blue overalls, with the EarthGov patch on the right shoulder, my body was achingly thin, to the point of gauntness. My muscles stood out like lengths of cord. I caught a glimpse of myself in one of the darkened video monitors and saw the skin stretched tight against my high cheekbones, long brown hair so greasy it was beginning to form into dreadlocks.

My eyes were haunted black holes.

Even the reinforced shielding of the bunker had failed to completely protect me against the radiation beating against the dying Earth.

The scarred elevator doors opened.

And I knew that the radiation had gotten to my mind.

Because instead of the stark, utilitarian gray metal elevator, I saw—

—*waving fields of tall grass, dappled with splashes of moonlight*—

I closed my eyes tightly and shook my head wildly, hoping to unmake this hallucinatory scene.

But then I felt the cool breeze pluck gently at my hollow cheeks, and smelled the wonderful scents carried on the air—*the juicy odors of rabbits and groundhogs in their warrens, ripe and plump*—

I stepped forward and felt soft earth beneath my feet.

The uniform I wore fell away from me easily, as did my paperlike human skin.

Lifting my muzzle to the night sky, I howled to the brilliantly full moon.

Far off, across the fields, I heard first the responding cry of a lone wolf, quickly joined in glorious chorus by an entire pack. They spoke to me:

We have opened this pathway for you. We have provided your escape.

Join us.

Behind me, the elevator door slid shut and vanished into nothingness, as did all things belonging to the dead Earth.

I began loping across the tall grass of these Elysian fields, and listened to the howling of my folk, the wolves:

Though the Earth may die, we abide.

We are dreams. We cannot die.

Empathy's Bed at Midnight

Martin R. Soderstrom

Doctor Annette Brooker picked up the phone and dialed, her shirt still covered in damp blood. Even with her office door closed, the smells of the hospital filled the air.

"Mrs. Perez? Yes. Mrs. Perez? Do you speak English? Hello?" The phone clanged down as the Spanish woman presumably went to get someone who understood English.

Gang violence had been on the upswing for years, and working in a midtown hospital put Annette smack in the middle of babies killing each other. She just couldn't understand it. She thought if somehow she could understand, then it wouldn't be so hard. Why did they kill each other? They looked the same, save for a few swatches of color here and there. They spoke the same language and even killed the same. But why?

"Yes?" a male voice said into her ear.

"Who am I speaking with?" Annette asked.

"Carlos Perez. Who is this?"

"Are you related to . . ." Annette stumbled as she flipped back the papers before her so she could read the dead boy's name. "Juan Perez?"

"He's my brother. You a cop?" the man asked through a thick Spanish accent.

"No, I'm a doctor. I'm afraid I've got some bad—"

"He dead?" Carlos asked. There was no emotion in his voice. It was just a question, like "What time is it?" or "What's today's special?".

"Yes. Your brother was in . . ." But she never got to finish the speech she gave on a daily basis. Carlos shouted some things in Spanish and then slammed the phone down. Annette had picked up some Spanish during her time at the hospital. She hadn't understood all of what he'd said, but she knew at that moment he was loading his gun and heading out for vengeance. There would be more dead before the night was through. But that was true without Carlos Perez's vendetta.

Annette hung up and sat for a long while, lost in herself. "Why did they do it?" was the question that plagued her. If only she could understand.

When she'd started out, her intentions had been simply to heal. Then she got involved with the community. After working an eighteen-hour shift, she'd go over to the youth hostel and work for hours with the kids who were trying to get out of the gangs. The kids would invariably turn back to the street and their violent compatriots.

Annette frequently asked them why they wanted to kill. Was it just revenge, or was there something else? The closest she got to a true answer was from a nine-year-old boy who was dead four hours after leaving her counseling session last year.

"The power," he'd said. "If you ain't got no power, you ain't got nothin'."

Ever since then, she'd been obsessed with death. Despite being surrounded by it, she read voraciously about killers and psychotics and the murdering mind. But with all she'd seen and all she'd read, she still didn't understand.

With a deep sigh, she closed the boy's file and left her office, no closer to the answers she so desperately wanted than when she'd gone in there. The hospital was in the midst of its usual mayhem, wounded gang members shouting and bleeding, hospital staff running from place to place.

Annette walked across the hall to trauma room three. Inside, a boy lay on a gurney, bleeding and moaning. She walked over to him and understood why he was alone. There was no way he was going to make it. The hospital staff were attending to the salvageable patients. He'd been left to die.

Annette looked into the boy's eyes. He wasn't really there, she could tell, by the way his pupils were dilated.

"Why? Please tell me. Why?" she begged the dying boy.

When no answer came, she knew there was only one thing she could do. The thing she should have done long ago. The only thing to do to find her answers. She placed her hand over his nose and mouth and looked into his eyes as he died.

When she looked up, a wide-eyed intern was staring at her. She wiped her hand on the dead boy's sheet.

"It's so simple," she said as she pushed past the shocked intern and got back to work.

Encore
Hugh B. Cave

Darling, I've found just the house for us," said handsome Alton Hayes to his middle-aged companion as he closed her door behind them. "After living in an apartment all these years, you'll love it."

They rode the elevator to the basement garage and walked to Grace Hardy's car. With a flourish he opened the passenger door for her.

Grace was going to be the most successful of his many conquests, he told himself as he walked around and slid in behind the wheel. Certainly, up to now, she was the one with the most money.

"Close your eyes," he said twenty minutes later as he turned onto Elm Street. "I want this to be a surprise."

She obeyed, of course, and stopping the car in front of the FOR SALE sign, he reached for her hand. "Now!"

With a little giggle Grace opened her eyes and said, "Oh my! It's so big!" Then in a whisper she added, "But it's the Langley house!"

"What do you mean, the Langley house?" Without waiting for an answer, Alton jumped out of the car. "Come! I borrowed a key from the real-estate lady."

"Marian Langley died here," Grace said weakly. "I knew her. People say this house is haunted, Alton!"

"You're joking."

"No, no! Her ghost has been seen any number of times."

"Nonsense," said Alton. "No sensible person believes in ghosts. Come now. Let me show you why it's just the house for us. You can easily afford it, too," he added. "I pushed hard for a low price and made them include all the lovely old furnishings to boot." *And when the place is mine to sell*, he thought, *I'll push just as hard for a higher price.*

He did not hurry her. He never hurried his victims. Still, his charm was such that it took him only an hour to convince Grace the house was ideal for them. She bought it that day, furnishings and all. Two weeks later, after their marriage, they moved in.

Four times in the month that followed, Grace Hardy Hayes saw the ghost—once in the downstairs room Alton claimed for his "study," three times on the stairs. What she saw was a woman about her own age, wearing something misty and white.

Then one night when Alton was out in search of material—he planned to be a famous writer, he said, now that he no longer had to work for a living—the ghost appeared to Grace in her bedroom. Gliding to an antique desk in the corner, it drew open a drawer, opened what appeared to be a secret compartment, and silently handed Grace an opened diary.

The entry to which it pointed—the last one—was dated August 12, 1989. The woman had died about that time, Grace recalled.

I fear I have made a terrible mistake. My husband does not love me. He married me only for my money and is already romancing some other woman. I hear him in his study, talking to her on the phone. As his true nature reveals itself, I am aware of traits I did not see before. He may even be planning to kill me, so as to inherit this house and everything else I own. Dear God, what should I do?

As Grace finished reading and looked up, the woman in white gently took the diary from her and, with a pen from the desk, added a postscript.

I waited too long. He pushed me down the stairs to make it look like an accident. It was not an accident. He pushed me. Then when I didn't die fast enough, he pressed a pillow over my face.

Replacing the pen, the lady smiled sadly at Grace and abruptly vanished.

More and more often Alton went out alone. Time after time she heard him on the telephone in his study. One night, hovering at the study door, she heard him say to someone, "I'll be rid of her soon, darling. Then we can be together forever."

It was a while before the opportunity presented itself. Grace worried that she, too, might be too late. But one night it happened— there stood Alton at the top of the big staircase, with his back to her. She almost fell down the stairs after him, she pushed so hard.

A pillow wasn't necessary. Even before she called 911 to report the accident, Grace knew his neck was broken.

Engorged Pereute
Lois H. Gresh

Pereute's four legs trembled on the stem of the rubber tree.
It just wasn't fair.
Sure, she'd always been different, but her friends had accepted her. Until, that is, they became butterflies and she remained the ugly moth.

Her tongue slipped into a leaf cup and lapped the water. She was hungry and needed more than frangipani and jasmine leaves.

She tucked her head beneath her wings, tried to will a bird to swoop from the sky and eat *her.*

But no birds came.

Something poked her body. She slipped, eyes flying open.

A flash of red crystalline wings.

Schulze: glowing in a dart of sun.

His wings encased her in softness, and gently, he set her back upon the stem.

"Oh, Schulze, I want so badly to die."

"Don't be ridiculous. I won't allow you to die." Schulze's voice was softer than his wings and came to her as a sprinkle of chimes.

"But what if I eat you?"

Sun glistened on the planes of his compound eyes. And in those eyes, she saw herself a hundred times over: corpulent, engorged with blood and fat; yellow with gray blotches.

His hindwings emitted jasmine and clover: a succulent nectar. If only she could dip her proboscis into those hindwings . . .

Such a delicious treat Schulze would be . . .

"You won't eat *me*," laughed Schulze, and his antennae stroked the hoarfur on her head.

A Queen Cracker landed on the stem behind them. She was black with metallic blue spots: a rare beauty. She brushed her wings across Schulze, who shivered. "Pereute, my dear, why don't you leave poor Schulze alone? Go find one of your own kind. A Giant Sphinx Moth: big and brawny and built for a girl like you; or a Snowy Eupseudosoma, if you like those tiny boys."

If only a bird would come *now*. Eat her and end it all.

But again, no birds came.

Cracker's metallic blue hurt Pereute's eyes, and she shut them. "Schulze, love me," she whispered, hoping he would encase her in those wings, hold her tightly, tell her that everything would be okay.

But Schulze said nothing.

Pereute peeked.

He was with Cracker, *on Cracker*, drenching her with jasmine.

Pereute's chest swelled with fire. Blood pumped down her legs.

Cracker laughed. "Go find a little moth, dear. Go find a man you can handle."

Schulze looked at Pereute with both sadness and joy. Sadness, perhaps, because he had betrayed her; joy because he had the beautiful Cracker.

How could Schulze do this? Had their friendship meant nothing?

Pereute spread her huge furry wings with the hooks and bristles. Her rear legs tensed, and she leapt and cast a shadow over the two of them, Schulze with his crimson wings and jasmine scent brushes, Cracker with her blinding blue spots and cackling, stupid voice. Pereute rose into the frangipani, and she saw herself in the butterflies' eyes; a hundred times over, she saw herself: a strong and powerful moth filled with anger and hunger and pain.

And she thought of Cracker and Schulze, how they would flit

through sunlight, how they would fill the sky and make the parrots jealous.

Cracker and Schulze would lay eggs together.

She dove, and her proboscis rammed into Schulze. He fell, his legs tearing at the tangled moss below.

Cracker would taste good.

Pereute drove her proboscis into the soft butterfly body. Schulze screamed: "No! Don't eat her, Pereute!"

Pereute paused. She was hungry, this was meat; he had betrayed her, why should she care?—

A blue swoop and a caw, and the sunlight died; and the branches snapped and the forest rained shards; and Pereute fell and landed on top of Schulze.

His legs splintered and broke. His wings beat the air. "Pereute, help me!"

He was jasmine. He was chimes. He was *Schulze*.

Pereute spread her wings and soared. Like a glare of sun, she drove through the ferns, aimed her proboscis at the bird.

But the bird swallowed Schulze in one gulp, flapped its mighty wings, and was gone.

Pereute's proboscis smashed against a tree, and she fell, exhausted, to the forest floor.

Inside, everything died.

She looked up at Cracker, who had stolen her lover, killed him.

On the stem by Cracker was a shining glue filled with eggs.

Cracker laughed. She flitted into the sun.

And Pereute settled down to wait.

Soon, there would be plenty of succulent butterflies to fill her always hungry stomach.

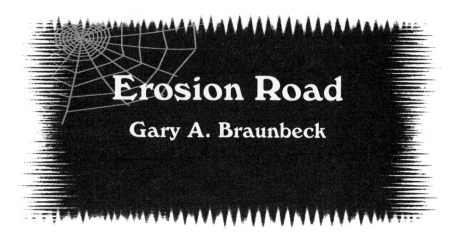

Erosion Road

Gary A. Braunbeck

Sometime late Tuesday, Emerson found himself walking along a stretch of road that disappeared into the bleak horizon like some oil-painting study in forced perspective. Though he wasn't one hundred percent certain how he'd come to be here, he nonetheless had a fairly good idea but decided not to dwell upon it.

Several dozen yards ahead was a road sign: BLOODY AUTOMOBILE ACCIDENT 300 YARDS.

It looked to him as if the driver—what was left of him, anyway—had been shot in the head and crashed into the pickup truck with such force that both of the vehicles overturned. Broken glass was scattered for hundreds of feet in every direction, and Emerson, despite himself, kind of enjoyed the crunching sound it made as he walked on it. He paused for a moment near the smaller of the two vehicles and saw that he'd been right; the driver *had* been shot through the side of the head—a 9mm. hollow-point, judging from the crater that was once the right side of his skull. An innocent bystander who just happened to be passing through the wrong neighborhood at the same moment a gang drive-by was going down.

Later—five, ten miles, he wasn't sure and didn't care—he came across a second road sign: NECROPHILIAC DEFILING A GRAVE 100 FEET AHEAD.

Emerson didn't bother walking over to the side of the road to get a glimpse at what was going on—he didn't have to: judging by the mounds of dirt that came flying up and the ecstatic giggling from down below, someone was having a high old time.

The next sign—this one not encountered for several hours—proclaimed: MAN WITH RIFLE ATOP WATER TOWER SHOOTING PASSERSBY 500 YARDS.

This time Emerson did stop to watch the proceedings, and was amazed at the skill displayed by the shooter; each shot hit the victims squarely between their eyes, every time. In the five minutes Emerson stood there, the shooter dusted no fewer than thirty-seven victims. Very impressive.

CAGE BUILT OUT OF CHILDREN'S BONES ON RIGHT 50 FEET AHEAD.

A structure to rival the maverick work of the Bauhaus and Wright. The architect's use of the pelvic bones was particularly creative, not to mention the wall of skulls on the southeast side. Looked rather inviting, if you went in for that sort of thing.

Shoving his hand deep into his pockets, Emerson continued along his way, occasionally reaching up to wipe the perspiration from his forehead. It wasn't until he sensed a change in the road that he looked up, and then it hit him—the sorrow and pain and disgust, the loathing and helplessness and blind anger, the self-hatred and loneliness and acidic stomach cramps that marked most of his days.

The last sign was simple and direct: THE END OF YOUR WORLD STRAIGHT AHEAD 100 FEET.

He stopped and looked up, pulling a deep, strained, painful breath.

The horizon was gone. The road before him stopped at the edge of a black, cold void.

"Howdy, son," said an old man who was sitting on an even older bunk bed. "I was beginnin' to wonder."

"Hello," said Emerson, tears brimming in his eyes.

"Homicide detective, weren't you?"

"Fifteen years," replied Emerson, reaching up to wipe away some more of the blood and brain tissue—not perspiration—that was leaking from the shotgun's exit wound.

"Couldn't take it anymore, eh?"

"No, sir, I guess I couldn't."

"Sign here." The old man held out a clipboard; attached to it was a sheet of paper with lots of small type and a line toward the bottom reserved for Emerson's signature. Atop the sheet, in bold letters, were the words **Release Information.**

"So no one tries to hold us liable," said the old man.

"Hold *who* liable?"

"Every last one of us memories that've been floatin' around inside that poor head of yours for the last fifteen years."

"Oh," said Emerson, signing. Then: "Who are you?"

"Your very first case. My kids strapped me into my bed and left me there to rot. My skin was stuck to the sheets and my guts spilled out when you turned me over, remember?"

"No." Said with deep regret.

The old man nodded. "Well, you got yourself plenty of time to recall. Best be on your way, son."

196

"I'm sorry I don't remember you."

"Probably got my face mixed up with somebody else's. Don't sweat it."

Emerson nodded, and with a relieved grin, stepped over the edge into eternity.

The Evil Dark

Gary Jonas

Mikey bolted out of his deep sleep and screamed. He shook and shivered in the darkness, eyes darting around, looking for the evil that he knew was there to embrace him in its deadly arms.

"Mom!" he screamed.

His mother rushed into the room and turned on the light, chasing the darkness away. "What's wrong, Mikey?"

"It was here again! Trying to kill me!"

"What was here?" his mother asked.

"The evil! It sneaks up and grabs me when I'm just falling asleep. I told you not to turn the light out!"

"Don't be silly, Mikey. There's nothing to be afraid of. It's way past time for you to let go of your fears. You'll sleep better in the dark."

"No, I won't. It's here for me. It can't get me while the light is on."

"Fine. I don't want to fight with you. I'll leave the light on. Okay?"

"You won't sneak back in here after I fall asleep and turn it off again?"

"No, Mikey. I won't do that."

"You promise?"

"I'm going to bed, sweetie. You want the light on, that's fine with me. Whatever gets you through the night."

"Thanks, Mom."

"Don't mention it. Sleep tight." She kissed him, then rose and left the room, closing the door behind her.

Mikey lay in bed for hours. Even with the light on, he couldn't get back to sleep. It began to rain. Lightning flashed. Mikey could feel the evil lurking in the closet and under the bed and outside his window. It called the darkness home. Thunder was its voice.

"If I fall asleep, I'll die," Mikey whispered. "Gotta stay awake to stay alive."

Lightning crackled and thunder crashed. The lights flickered, but stayed on.

Mikey sat up. As long as it was light, he was safe. Closing his eyes gave the evil the darkness it needed. He knew that now. He could sense it. Sleep gave it strength. Darkness gave it dominance. In the dark, even if he were awake he was in danger. His childish fear of the dark had the facts to back it up. His brother Donald died in the dark last year. Down in the basement playing hide and seek. Mikey hid in the shadows and when Donald turned on the light, Mikey yelled, "Cheater!" and threw a toy car at the lightbulb, shattering it. Donald tripped on the stairs and tumbled down, breaking his neck.

Now, Mikey knew it wasn't his fault. The evil drew its power from the dark and from fear. It had tripped Donald. And now it was here for Mikey. It was waiting for the darkness. Biding its time. Trying to speed things up with lightning and thunder. Shooting for a power outage.

Lightning flashed again, and this time the thunder came with it. The house shuddered and the lights went out. Mikey screamed, "Mom!" As the echo of the thunder died, Mikey rolled out of bed and yanked open the drawer of his nightstand. The flashlight was in his hand and he clicked it to life. He heard his mother coming down the hallway as he waved the flashlight around, trying in vain to illuminate the entire room.

But the darkness didn't seem as oppressive this time. He didn't feel the evil beside him, trying to reach past the beam of the flashlight. And that's when he understood. This time it wasn't here for him.

It was here for Mommy.

Extract

Brian Hodge

Just like last time, you wake up in the middle of the night with the taste of blood in your mouth. It's thick and gummy, has been drying awhile. The moon drapes a bright trapezoid of silvery light over the top of your bed, crosshatched like the panes of your window and slashed with the bare branches of trees.

When you raise your head, no more than you have to, you spot the dark, coin-sized stains on your pillow. They hadn't been there when you went to bed.

You sink down in the covers to become invisible beneath them, in hopes that *it* won't see you if it's still in the room. You try to lie motionless, refusing to surrender to that urge to tremble, because if it's still there, it might hear even the tiniest chattering of your teeth.

It *knows* teeth. Intimately.

You listen for the soft sigh of its breath, through slitted eyes dissect the shadows for its shape, maybe the glint of an eye or two. You remain razor-alert for the creak of a board, for the metallic click of the tools it carries.

And somewhere on the far side of forever, you realize it has the inhuman patience to outwait you all night.

Demons, you suppose, must enjoy the waiting.

If you weren't so convinced it was still there, you'd run to the bathroom and seek out the aspirin; the throbbing in your jaw is starting to get more pronounced, pain taking form out of the numb void.

But the only movement you'll risk so far is something it can never see . . . although inevitably you wonder if its ears might not be so sharp that it can *hear* the sliding inside your mouth. The way you can't help but press the tip of your tongue into the fresh hole in your jaw, exploring the hot, moist socket newly emptied of tooth. It feels huge, another gaping wound gouged in gum and bone, big as a bucket and still brimming with blood.

Then, slowly, the recollections start to piece themselves together again:

Awakening to the prick of the needle.

The immense pressure of that hard round knee—or whatever it was that belongs to the thief's anatomy—bearing down on your chest, to hold you in place.

The taste of metal in your mouth, its firm insistent grip.

Then, after the ordeal of twisting, of tugging, of cracking, the sigh of something's satisfaction—definitely not your own.

Reliving all this, you shudder in the moonlight, knowing if it's still in the room, it can't help but notice you now. With this much lost, your invisibility betrayed, you let curiosity get the better of you, and slide your small cold hand back, beneath your pillow . . .

Where it closes on another crisp dollar bill.

No such thing as a tooth demon, your best friend told you at school, after the first time; not that *she'd* ever heard of. For a while this reassured you, because if anyone would know about these things, *she* would.

She's got the kind of parents you wish you had, at least when it comes to the movies and comics and magazines they let her see. How you love going to her house, because the family room becomes a magic theater where you get to watch all the videotapes forbidden under your own roof, and walking into her room is like a trip to a museum where you can learn about all the terrible and fantastic creatures that make their homes behind the dark of night . . .

But aren't *really* supposed to creep uninvited into your room while you're asleep.

So this tooth demon must exist, obviously. Just look how hard it's breaking the rules.

Ever more educated about such things, your friend once showed you a comic book that told about the one rule that all demons, no matter how mighty, must obey: if called by name, their *true* name, they must submit to your control.

A board creaks; a shadow disengages from the deeper darkness along the far wall, while moonlight glints off the pliers clicking in its eager hand.

One name is all you need, strong enough to contain all your hopes and prayers that your friend is worth such trust.

"Daddy?" you try, and this works. It stops.

But only for a moment.

As soon as you can talk again, you'll try another name.

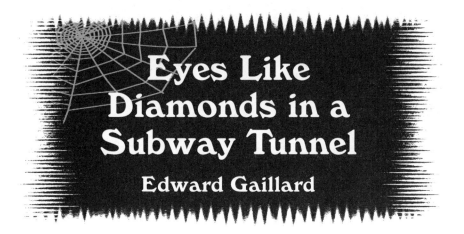

Eyes Like Diamonds in a Subway Tunnel

Edward Gaillard

I drove down the highway, staying carefully under the speed limit. I wasn't about to take a chance on being stopped, not now, not so close to my ultimate victory.

She had struggled when the sedatives wore off, as I was putting her in the trunk of my car. It was no use; I had tied her up well, and only the best rope was good enough for my Sarah. I could hear her thumping in the trunk as I turned onto the highway, and a buzzing sound as she tried to scream through the gag. I imagined myself, then, as a spider, and she as the fly helpless in my web. The image pleased me.

Now, as I turned onto a side road, she had stopped struggling. I thought of a caterpillar in its cocoon. No flight into freedom awaited Sarah at the end of this trip.

A few miles later I turned off again, onto a narrow dirt road. The end was near. My heart pounded.

I pulled to a stop outside my cabin, deep in the woods, left the car, and opened the trunk. The ropes had already fallen away. Sarah stepped out, a little bewildered, and spread her red-gold wings, drying them in the air. I drew in a deep breath. Gorgeous! She was going to be spectacular, pinned in a display case, the prize specimen in my collection.

My mandibles clicked with pleasure.

Fall of Man

Graham P. Collins

He dreams that he is falling and he knows that he is dreaming, so the dream holds no terror for him. The ground is far away.

How different from when I was a boy, he thinks, recalling the panic that pierced his falling dreams back then. Of course it's all symbolic, he thinks, the fear of lack of control, or the ancestral fear of monkeys falling out of the tree and into the reach of marauding predators. Or so he read somewhere.

By his late teens he learned to control his dreams, and the falling dreams were welcome opportunities to fly. But today his arms are stiff and he can't spread them wide like wings, so flying seems to be out.

Very well, if he can't move his arms he'll change where he is.

Abruptly he is far, far above the earth.

Falling.

There are so many ways of looking at it, and he learned them all in college. Galileo's cannonballs dropped from the leaning tower, the falling apple, Newton's law of gravity. The moon falling toward the earth as it traverses its orbit, the earth in turn falling toward the sun, the sun falling toward the center of the galaxy . . .

Such elegant equations and concepts; the delicate balance of velocity and acceleration.

All paled before Einstein's general relativity. Everything fell, not through space toward some attractant, but through four-dimensional spacetime, along its own path, its worldline. Every particle, every quantum in the universe fell into the future.

He feels a smug satisfaction that he understands it all so well, so deeply, he can even understand it in his dreams.

Now he has pulled his viewpoint back so far from the earth that he is in deep space, away from all reference points, and yet he still falls.

He knew it would be like that, intellectually, but it was still a shock, the first time he rode into space. In space you could be seemingly motionless, floating in your capsule, and still your earthly monkey-descended body screamed, "You fall!" It was impossible to say in which direction you fell, and yet you fell.

He nods. The direction was the future. You fell along your world-line, through spacetime, ever onward. The seamless consistency of it all is wonderfully calming.

But now another globe swings into view, neither the earth nor the moon, but his infant daughter's head, calling, "Grandpa! Grandpa!"

He falls toward her, toward her Mediterranean-sized mouth, and he grins at the multiple absurdity. She's calling me to wake me up and this has intruded on my dream, he thinks, and so he wakes.

But as he opens his eyes he sees not a young child but a grown woman, and it penetrates his crawling thoughts that she is calling him "Grandpa."

The facts fall into place and he knows with a frisson of fear that he is eighty-something years old, and the only way he can pin down the something is if he remembers just what year it is today and can perform the subtraction of his birth date before the meaning of the answer falls out of his memory.

Beside his granddaughter, whose face looks so much like his daughter's once did, oh so many years ago, is a toddler holding a doll, and as he looks at her the doll falls from clumsy hands, falls to the ground, headfirst.

He shudders, and his granddaughter asks with concern, "Were you having a bad dream?" His great-granddaughter just stares.

He wants to answer, but has to cough, and everything's too difficult, and none of it is a dream, and behind the woman and girl he sees an autumn leaf fall from the tree. To their right he sees the late-afternoon sun, rendered a beautiful, eye-safe apricot color by the smoggy air, falling perceptibly against the horizon. He senses the earth beneath him falling in its orbit toward the sun and he struggles to rise to his feet.

His granddaughter moves to help, but he's moaning a "No!" which she takes to be his usual growled refusal of help, so she steps back, and he stands, feeling a dizzying rush of vertigo, the spill of seconds falling by ever faster—he clutches at air but nothing he can grasp will slow the plunge—he tries to raise his arms to fly or just maintain his balance, and sheer terror fills him because the ground is so close and *he's falling*. . . .

Fashion Victim

Martin Mundt

I 'm sick of black," she said, standing in front of the mirror in my shop.

She wore all black, a sweater with sleeves lapping over her hands, a long skirt, combat boots. She made a face at her reflection, her mood black.

"I think I hate black."

She wore ear, nose and lip rings, plus studs and chains, like she'd fallen face-first into her jewelry, keeping whatever stuck.

"I need color," she said.

"I have color." Clothes huddled all around us like the hold of an immigrant ship. "Racks and shelves and cases full of color."

She wound her fingers into black pigtails.

"Do you think I should go red? Or maybe orange? Go for a technicolor, Carmen Miranda, Peter Max look?"

"Try yellow," I said. "Short is gorgeous, too." I ran my hand over my sleek scalp, my stubble rain-slicker yellow. "Plus, the skull can be very erotic."

She pouted, looking at me.

"I've got one hundred dollars left. My boyfriend, my *ex*-boyfriend, Karl, took the rest. He took the cash, the car, and the credit cards, even the ones in my real name. He went off to play drums in L.A. or someplace. I've listened to drumming for six straight months, and for what? I feel like my brain's been chewed on."

"Men," I said. "They'll eat you alive."

She paged through my racks, creaking hangers.

"What I really need in my life right now are clothes that scream ABBA, but hipper, you know? Maybe something early seventies, but not mid-seventies, and definitely not sixties. And not black."

"How's this?" I took a red satin miniskirt off a rack. The skirt squirmed. I grabbed it with both hands to hold it still. Satin skirts have no restraint.

"Too Agnetha," she said, scrunching up her nose.

I replaced the skirt, and the little satin bitch zipped herself shut on my finger, drawing a bead of blood. I heard the vintage hats tittering quietly behind me. I gave them such a look that they shut right up.

I tried a silver dress.

"How's this?"

She glanced.

"No. Too Nehru. Too groovy, Star Trekky, I think. I really want sort of a Gary Glitterish, Bay City Rollers effect, you know?"

I smiled, but I didn't know.

"This is it!" she squealed.

She swirled a skirt off a rack like she was ballroom dancing.

It was the most hideous skirt I had, a test-pattern atrocity, neon green, blue and red, long and tight. She held it to her waist, beatific.

The hats sighed. The corsets and dresses wrinkled with disappointment.

"I'm gonna try it on." She jumped into the dressing room and whooshed the shower curtain closed. The dressing room was lined with plastic sheets, the easier to clean up the mess afterwards.

"This skirt's really tight."

I watched her shadow on the curtain, wiggling the skirt up to her waist. She inhaled a few times, and the zipper zipped shut. Her shadow twirled for the mirror.

"Really, *really* tight," she called. "It's an Emma Peel, Catwoman kind of fit. Hey, this is weird. Did you know that if you look down at this skirt just right, the pattern kind of looks like a face? There's eyes staring up at me, like I'm standing in a shark's mouth."

Naivete is so adorable. The hats tittered again.

"I can hardly move my legs to walk in it, though. I think it's too small."

Her shadow wrestled with the waistband.

"The zipper's stuck. Hey . . ."

She gasped. She opened the curtain and staggered out. She took six-inch steps, because in an a eyeblink the skirt had stretched itself down to her calves and up to her shoulders, pinning her arms inside, wasping her waist. Her eyes were wide, her voice crushed to a whisper.

"Help!" She mouthed the word.

The skirt rippled, like one big muscle contracting. The hem oozed down to hobble her ankles. The waistband squirmed up to collar her neck. She tiptoed two more tiny steps, wavered and toppled over.

I rolled her back into the dressing room with my foot.

The skirt rippled again, covering her mouth and feet. Her eyes circled, looking for help.

The skirt rippled again.

I closed the curtain.

The hats sucked their fangs. The corsets opened their bony jaws and squealed like hungry baby vultures. The dresses moaned, distressed as empty stomachs.

"Calm down, calm down," I said. "Everyone will eat. It's only Monday."

The Fear of Eight Legs

Lisa Morton

The house had seemed like a great deal. Only ten years old, one previous owner, nice neighborhood. Sure, Martin knew it was a bank repo, that there'd been some kind of problem with the family that'd lived here before, but he knew that was part of the deal. He was a carpenter by trade, he could fix anything.

Except he wasn't a heating specialist, and that was the first thing that'd failed. The house had floor vents, and he could plainly see that the duct under the living room vent had fallen away. It was just a matter of crawling under the house and reattaching the duct.

Simple enough. Crawlspace down there was big enough; dirty, dusty, but that had never bothered Martin . . .

What did bother Martin was spiders.

He had arachnophobia. Couldn't even look at anything spider-shaped. He had recurring nightmares about sleeping in his bed as spiders dropped into his mouth.

Maybe there would be nothing but dust down there. He could do it. He wouldn't think about his open mouth, the eight-legged monstrosity dropping down while he lay paralyzed . . .

He put it off for a week, but winter was coming on and he needed heat. He thought about asking one of his employees, but he believed in himself as a strong authority figure. He knew they'd ask why he couldn't do it.

So one afternoon he stood outside the house, looking down at the crawlspace entrance, dressed in heavy jumpsuit, boots, gloves, hat, goggles, respirator mask.

He knelt and went in.

One foot . . . two . . . Just dust. Martin didn't mind dust.

He crawled. Getting darker with each inch. The entrance ten feet behind him, a dim square of light.

The flashlight revealed the errant duct four feet ahead. No spiders in between. Could almost reach out and—

He heard something skitter.

It was off to his left. He turned, waved the flashlight around.

There was a web five feet away.

Martin felt a stab of panic, swallowed it down and forced himself to look again. There was nothing on the web. It looked old, unused.

Deep breaths . . . just fix the duct and get out.

He moved forward.

Skitter . . .

Now he caught movement out of the corner of his eye. He moved too fast and banged the flashlight on the duct.

Nothing but an empty web.

His heart was beating too fast. He couldn't breathe through the respirator and tore it frantically from his face. *Forget it . . . I'll hire someone . . .*

He felt something on his leg, gasped and swung the flashlight beam. A spider.

He cried out and swung his leg wildly. He kicked backward, shoving himself blindly into the duct, then past it . . .

Into the web.

He felt the sticky silk on his face and screamed again, realized he'd removed the respirator and left his face vulnerable. He dropped the flashlight and pawed at his head.

In the light from the rolling flashlight he saw them, overhead.

Even as he covered his face, he felt the first sting on his leg. He looked down and saw at least eight or ten on his legs. One had bitten through the cloth. Another sting . . .

His legs were going numb.

He clawed at the dirt to pull himself away. He didn't see the one that crawled under the glove on his left hand . . .

Martin's left arm went dead.

He waved his right arm wildly, but it was already tingling. He felt one on his cheek. The only thing left in his mind was the dream, and he snapped his mouth shut.

He was almost completely paralyzed now. And yet he could still feel, and what he felt was . . .

He was being dragged.

Impossible. They were too small, they couldn't move a human being. Unless . . .

. . . there were enough of them. Thousands. And they were bigger.

Ten feet, and he felt the ground give way beneath his head. There was enough spill from the flashlight that if he concentrated enough to turn his head, he could make out—

—a hole in the earth around him. A hole big enough to hold four bodies. They were desiccated, covered in web shrouding, but by the size he guessed two adults and two children.

The family that had owned the house before him. The ones he'd never cared to ask about.

The last move Martin's failing body made was to open his mouth for a soundless scream. He froze in that position.

And they came down.

Feast of the Crows

Brian A. Hopkins

They came in from the north, their dark wings wrestling the errant winds that swept east to west and swirled dust-devil-ish midfield. They came in low over the corn, just a few at first so that he wasn't immediately concerned. A minute later, the sky was black with them.

He strained against his cross, but despite its years it was strong and firmly planted in the cornfield. He might have screamed, but his mouth was stuffed with straw. As their wings beat the hat from his head and their talons clawed his cheeks, he could only turn his face away, but no matter which way he turned there were more of them. Their piercing cries obliterated all other sound. They smelled of carrion. Their eyes reflected an empty, indigo vengeance that scared the hell out of him.

Pieces of him began to join the straw scattered beneath his dangling feet. Small pieces at first—the handkerchief from his shirt pocket, a strip from one cheek, a button, strands of his hair—but it quickly became obvious that his marauders' ultimate objective was his total destruction.

One of them perched atop his head and seemed to be shouting orders. Another locked its claws on his collar and began to worry at his right eye. Another outsmarted the knot of rope holding up his trousers. As the trousers fell about his knees, there began a frenzy of activity below his waist. His flannel shirt came away in tatters, blown away in the maelstrom of frantic wings and eager cries. Beaks tore at his stomach, claws raked his shoulders, feathers brushed his thighs, and there was a horrifying tugging at his groin.

His eye came out, bouncing off his chin to join the detritus at the base of the cross. The eye lay there a moment, a glittering bauble against the dull mustard of the beaten cornhusks, then one of the quick black warriors snatched it up in its beak and flew off. The assailant on his face buried its head in his gaping socket, probing for deeper prizes.

They opened him up and he spilled out over the ground. They rolled in it, screaming insatiable victory. They strutted cocklike through the debris. They shit on what remained strapped to the cross. From within the shattered sarcophagi of his skull, the most aggressive of them set up a raucous cawing. From the hollow of his chest, there now beat only their tiny black hearts.

The orders from atop his head became a taunting mockery. *You are nothing*, they told him. *We have taken you apart and shown you who owns this field.*

Their celebration continued until the heat of midafternoon drove them into the cool shade of the oaks bordering the cornfield. The sun beat down on his remains and all was quiet—

—until his big sister came out to check and see if he had learned his lesson about tattling on her.

Feeding the Beast

Larry Segriff

Thehe beast lurked within, stirring, but it wasn't his fault. For nine months he had fought it, starved it, denied it its preferred diet of anger, frustration, and impatience, but now it was feeding regularly and there was nothing he could do about it.

Neighbors, love 'em or leave 'em. Well, he'd tried to love 'em and he couldn't leave 'em, so what was he supposed to do? The house where he rented a room was simply too small, too crowded. First there were the people next door. A nice couple, friendly even, and quiet most of the time, but they were animals, making love all the time. It was bad enough that *he* never got any, but to lie in his cold and lonely bed night after night with his headboard pressed up against the paper-thin walls, praying for sleep or even blissful silence, was far worse. He had wanted to rearrange his room but it was too small; the furniture would only fit this one way and besides, king-sized waterbeds were a bitch to move, so he suffered, night after night, feeding the beast.

Then there was the family downstairs. Five rotten kids, two over-worked parents, and not a drop of love or an ounce of compassion between them. Every morning, at least an hour before his clock radio was set to go off, the sounds of angry words would race up the furnace ductwork from their rooms to his ears, through his brain, directly into the waiting maw of the beast.

It was a common belief that Mother Nature had pitched the sound of a child's cry at just the right level to make it unignorable by adults. He could attest to that, but he knew that there was something worse: indescribable was the effect of the constant repetition in a harsh, angry, parental voice of the phrases "No, Byron! No!" and "Leave it alone, Byron!" and especially, "Byron, get that out of my face!" Not a drop of compassion, not an ounce of love, but no shortage of impatience, irritation, or ire. He felt it, too. Every time he heard the words "Byron" or "no" he was pierced by a stab of frustration, a knife of annoyance, and every time the beast fed a little more.

Three months to go on his lease; ninety long days to find out if he could scrape up enough money to move. Too long. Much too long.

It happened at night. The couple next door had finally exhausted themselves, and silence, heavenly, peaceful, life-giving silence, had descended at last. Then, the sound of a slap, a cry, and those awful words, "No, Byron!" The beast rose; he fought it, as he had fought it so often before, but this time it was too strong. Rising from the depths where he had cast it so long before it burst free and claimed him.

Together they rose, leaving behind forever that bed of nails, and headed for the basement apartment. There they found Byron, and the man who said "No!" and all the others.

And fed.

Final Call

John Gregory Betancourt

The last man in the world sat alone in a room, contemplating suicide. What did he have left to live for? He began adding up good and bad points in his life; the score depressed him.

Then the telephone rang. He leaped to his feet, staring in surprise. Perhaps he *wasn't* the last, he thought. It rang again. This time he grabbed it.

"Hello? Hello?" he called.

"Hello," breathed a soft, silky, feminine voice. His heart skipped a dozen beats. "Do you have a moment?"

"Yes!" he cried. "This is Roger Thomas—I can't believe you found me! Thank God! And just in time—"

"I'm glad," she said. "My name's PATSI, your Personal Automated Telephone Survey, Inc., and I'd love to interview you about new *improved* TastyFlakes™—"

He slammed down the receiver. And once more he took account of all the good and bad things left in his lonely world.

An hour later, he hanged himself with the telephone cord.

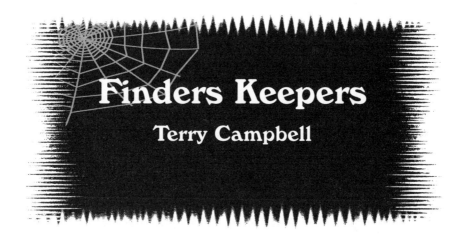

Finders Keepers

Terry Campbell

T he first time I felt like this, I was around eight years old. That would be twenty years ago, give or take a few. Jesus, has it been that long? It seems like only yesterday. But that wasn't the last time I've had these feelings; no, there have been many. I can't help it.

A penny for your thoughts?

It's the guilt. Always the guilt. And I know where it comes from. It's what happened twenty years ago. What I did that day was wrong, so terribly wrong.

Can I put my two cents in?

I was walking to school one day, looking down at the sidewalk like I always did, trying to avoid the cracks. Then I saw it. Lying on the concrete, staring up at me.

A quarter.

You'll nickel and dime me to death.

A bright and shiny brand-new quarter. Oh, it was beautiful, and it was mine for the taking. I stopped in my footsteps, mouth open wide. Stunned. I looked around. Surely the owner was near. No one would go off and leave such a marvelous piece of coinage alone. There was no one. The streets were empty. I could have this quarter. It could be mine. I turned in all directions, making sure there were no witnesses.

Save all your nickels and dimes.

Slowly, I knelt to the sidewalk, taking the brilliant quarter-dollar piece in my young, innocent hands. I held it gingerly, like a proud father might hold his newborn son. Quickly, I slipped the quarter into my pocket, and went on my way.

The streets remained empty. No one saw. No one knew. But I knew. I knew I had taken a quarter that didn't belong to me. I knew—and what's worse, God knew—and I just couldn't enjoy my newfound wealth. I had no business taking the quarter. I walked on to school, the weight of the quarter and the guilt it caused bogging down my steps. I pictured another kid going without lunch while I ate ravenously, the ill-gotten quarter burning a hole in my pocket. All day long, I felt the hot stares of the teachers, as if they knew.

You can bet your bottom dollar on that.

But the quarter was mine. I had found it fair and square. Someone had been careless and lost it. Their fault, not mine. No one was around to claim it. Finders keepers, right? That's the way it should be, am I right?

In for a dime, in for a dollar.

Like I said, that was the first time I had these feelings. There've been many since; there will be many more.

Watch your pennies, and your dollars will take care of themselves.

The streets are dark and empty. There is no one around. I see the wallet sticking out of the old man's pocket. There for the taking. He stirs and groans weakly; bloody drool dribbles from his mouth. I kick him in the head, and he doesn't move again. The wallet falls completely out, onto the wet asphalt.

Save it for a rainy day.

There, on the ground. Look what I found. Someone lost their wallet. How careless.

As I reach for the wallet that I took—

found

—the feeling washes over me again, bathing me in steaming guilt. I hate the guilt. It's mine. The quarter is mine. I found it fair and square. Finders keepers. The wallet was just lying there on the ground. Their fault, not mine. No one claimed it. No one ever claims what I take—

find.

But it's not right to take the money, even though I found it. What if the owner comes looking for it? What if he really needed it? How would that make me feel? Could I live with myself after that?

It's that damned quarter all over again.

See a penny, pick it up.

What if I just took half the money? That way, if the owner comes back, he won't have lost everything. Maybe that's the best thing to do, the right thing to do. Yeah, the right thing.

I guess I'm kind of lucky in a way. Seems like I'm always finding lost money or misplaced wallets and purses. I'm just lucky that way.

I just wish I wouldn't get these feelings every time I find something. It makes it so hard to enjoy myself. But I can't help it.

Sometimes, my conscience just gets to me, you know?

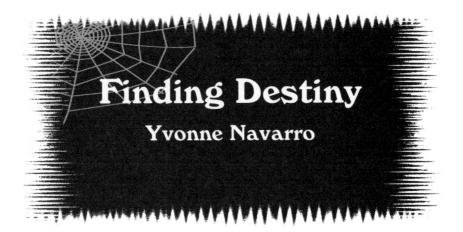

Finding Destiny

Yvonne Navarro

Michael Stohlmey moved into the house in early June. It was in reasonably good shape, though he still cleaned, painted, and rearranged the furniture a dozen times until he was satisfied, then moved on to mowing, planting, and fighting the weeds. He was settling back to enjoy life when he found the mayonnaise jar at the back of a cabinet in the garage.

Sealed, dark with grime, Michael couldn't tell what was inside. He shook it and heard the dry whisper of paper and the muffled clink of a coin and glass, then took it outside and held it up to the sunlight. Seeing dirt *inside* the jar nearly made him throw it out. Garage dust was one thing; he didn't want to handle anything that had been intentionally locked into an old glass jar—all sorts of nasty possibilities popped into his head, from dried spiders to unfortunate frogs captured from the creekbed and doomed to die in an airless glass prison. Then he remembered the papery sound and the plink of metal, neither of which were likely companions to the fruits of a kid's forgotten biology hunt. Sitting on the front steps and examining the jar, Michael smiled as the answer came to him: *time capsule.* Of course— why hadn't he realized it?

Opening the jar wasn't easy. It took a half hour in the garage while listening to the constant *snip snip snip* of the woman across the street trimming her hedges. Finally his vise grips and some careful juggling loosened the corroded lid enough, and Michael returned to the steps and twisted the lid free. But peering into the narrow top didn't reveal much; when he sniffed, a dry, slightly medicinal smell made him sneeze. He wiped his nose on the arm of his work shirt, then carefully upended the contents of the jar.

His unwillingness to touch whatever was inside cost him one of the objects, a tiny glass vial that looked like a test tube. Before he could stop it, the glass container rolled off the step and shattered on the next one down. He picked up the biggest shard, but there was nothing to see; even the top of the tube had been sealed glass.

There were two more things, a weighty silver coin and a folded newspaper clipping that seemed absurdly new for the age of the jar. Michael picked up the coin and blinked when he saw that the image on the front side, a broad-faced young man next to the word "Destiny," bore a strong resemblance to himself. He flipped it and below the familiar United States of America logo he found a likeness of a building he didn't recognize. Underneath the building were the words "One American Stohl." Checking the front again, he almost dropped the coin when a calendar date ten years in the future registered in his brain.

A joke—it had to be. Hands shaking, Michael carefully unfolded the newspaper clipping. Beneath a heavy black masthead called *The Washington Survivor,* a more modestly sized headline spread across the page: U.S. OKAYS MINTING OF THE AMERICAN STOHL. Eyes widening, Michael continued to read. "The Federal Government authorized the release of the new American Stohl today," the article announced. "The Stohl, which will be equivalent to three twenty-five cent pieces, celebrates the fifth anniversary of the execution of Michael Stohlmey, the man who released a top-secret biological warfare virus into the air ten years ago. Stohlmey, who maintained his innocence to the end yet was immune to the virus himself, insisted the virus was in a food container he found in his garage. Within two weeks, the catastrophic airborne virus known as 'Destiny' was responsible for the death of all but 4.2 million people worldwide, rendering wastelands of all but the most medically advanced countries. Thus far, the Stohl has not been well received."

Michael wadded up the article and shoved it back into the jar. What kind of shit was this? A joke by one of his friends? At least the silver coin seemed real. Maybe he could sell it.

Across the street, the woman trimming her hedge suddenly

choked, then went into a terrible coughing spasm. Her clippers clattered to the sidewalk and she followed, clawing at her throat as she tumbled onto the concrete. As Michael stared, she convulsed, then was still.

In the terrible silence that followed, Michael put his face in his hands and cried.

Fire in the Skies over Asia

Damien Filer

Mac watched the two gray suits and straight faces smooth their way up to his bar. He saw the gray souls behind their pupils. Black hearts beating under their silver sport coats. He could smell them like a dog trained for the hunt. Gray souls and black hearts stunk from across a room when you've been around for as long as a man like Mac. Like new waiters during a rush, the men carried the world on their shoulders.

Mac wiped the polished oak to a shine, slung his white rag over a bent back, placed two coasters in front of his customers. Zion Resort and Casino, it said on each coaster. Below that, their motto: "The standard for class in Las Vegas."

"Tell me your bottom line, Mr. Sahara," the one mirror-image man said to the other. "I don't want to be here long enough for anyone to remember my face."

Mac smirked at that, turned his back on them and clinked bottles of schnapps and Seagram's together purposefully to seem occupied.

"I can match any mark. Get two steps closer than any source you've got, Mr. Flamingo. Those pilots are climbing into their cockpits right now. Adjusting their goggles. Flicking their switches. They won't be called back and they won't be shot down. Not in time, anyway. So pick your poison. Sky's the limit."

Out of the corner of his eye, Mac saw Mr. Flamingo shifting on his stool like it was hot. Mac flashed on his missions in WWII. What it got him. What it cost. Not in meat and muscle. Not in dollars and medals. Just nightmares and cold sweats. What else was there in the end?

"You can't sit here, look me in the eye and tell me the president is going to okay this mission," Mr. Flamingo said. "You can't do it. Not in my United States."

"He already has," Mr. Sahara said.

Mac could hear in the weight of Mr. Sahara's words, didn't even have to look at him, he could just feel it in his pores, that this man had never held a weapon in his trembling hand. Never taken a life. He could hear it in his cadence, in the way he spat the words out like they were gristle stuck in his throat.

"Hey, barkeep," Mr. Sahara said. "Couple of vodka Collins right here." Mac turned. Mr. Sahara tapped white knuckles on the shine.

"I've made it just about everywhere I've been, out of some dark tunnels and tight scrapes, all for one reason," Mr. Flamingo said. "I'm a gambling man."

Mac set their drinks down, then shuffled a few paces away and busied himself within earshot again.

"So I'm gonna put it all down," Mr. Flamingo continued. "You speak the language? You understand what I'm saying, Mr.—Mr.— what was I supposed to call you?"

"Sahara, Mr. Sahara," the mirror said.

"Right, right, Mr. Sahara. I've got more faith than that in my fellow man. More faith in my president than to go and do a thing like that. I'm putting it all on the table. Understand?"

"I understand," Mr. Sahara said. "You are a naive man. Clouded by ideals. Your faith staked in a child's patriotism at a July Fourth parade. That's what I understand. But no matter. I'll gladly take what you're wagering. You can bet on that, Mr. Gambling Man."

Mac looked to see the men exchange something under the bar, then turn and walk out. Stride for stride, like bookends they were. Mac couldn't tell if those were wind-up knobs or knives sticking out of the backs of Mr. Flamingo and Sahara. It was dark in the Zion Quiet Bar.

Mac picked up their glasses and wiped the polished oak to a shine. He trembled at the thought of climbing back into his bed. Back in that cockpit. Fire licking the silver linings of every cloud over Asia. Trembled at the thought of the nightmares he would have this night.

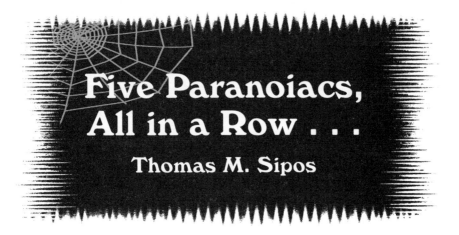

Five Paranoiacs, All in a Row . . .

Thomas M. Sipos

I knew the operation was risky, but no one expects to die."

"But you did die."

Frank nodded, sweat glistening on his balding skull.

Dr. Milo spoke softly. "Go on. We're here to help."

Frank fidgeted noisily in his vinyl chair. "Like I said, I was in cardiac arrest, floating over my body, then down a tunnel of blue light, toward a white light. I met my dead wife there."

"That must have been a great comfort."

"I felt peaceful."

"Good. Remember that peace."

"Even felt bad about being revived." Frank laughed tensely. "Felt bad ever since I got here."

"You mean, since you returned?"

"Yeah."

"Back amongst the living."

Frank nodded.

"Not an uncommon reaction." Dr. Milo glanced among the five somber patients, murky faces under dim neon lights. "Depression is commonplace after the euphoria of an out-of-body experience." He beckoned to an elderly woman. "Tell us about your experience, Marsha."

"I already told everyone."

"I think we have a new member."

A young man, skinny and long-haired, warily raised a hand.

Marsha looked at him. "My experience wasn't so good."

The stark neon tubes underneath the pockmarked ceiling tiles flickered and buzzed. Dr. Milo nodded his encouragement. "Tell us about it, Marsha."

"It seems that's all I do."

"It helps to talk."

Marsha sighed. "Like I said before, I met my dead sister at that white light, but she just waved good-bye. Soon I was beyond the light, surrounded by darkness. I called for help, but there was only . . . I don't know how I knew this, because I couldn't see anything, but I knew I was completely alone. Inside infinite emptiness." She wiped away a tear. "I knew I was in Hell."

"That must have been a terrifying realization." Dr. Milo scribbled into his spiral notebook. "But you returned."

"I thought I was damned for eternity."

"Don't dwell on it. Remember your relief after the crash."

"I don't even remember the crash."

"After the crash. In the hospital."

"It's hard to remember anything. So confusing."

"That's nothing to worry about." Dr. Milo glanced among the five sullen patients squeaking against vinyl seats. "Disorientation is also normal following an out-of-body experience." He glanced among his five patients, focused on the newcomer. "Tell us about your experience, Bobby."

"I don't know if this will make any sense."

"Don't worry about making sense. Tell us your story."

"Yesterday, I went out for a walk . . ." He tugged at his faded army jacket, his hollow voice barely audible. "Something weird happened."

"Tell us what happened."

"I felt a sudden blow, saw sparks. Next thing, I'm floating over my body, looking down at some guy searching my pockets! I screamed for help, but nobody heard. I entered the blue tunnel."

Dr. Milo scribbled into his notebook.

"At that white light, I saw my dead mom, looking sad, waving good-bye. I floated through that empty darkness." He looked at Marsha. "Like you said, alone in Hell."

Marsha gripped her handkerchief, her old knuckles bone white underneath the neon lights.

"And then what happened?" asked Dr. Milo.

"The journey ended."

"You left the darkness."

Bobby nodded.

"And now here you are."

Bobby nodded.

"How do you feel about that?"

Bobby shrugged.

"Don't be afraid to talk about it." Dr. Milo glanced among his five patients. "Out-of-body experiences can be both depressing and disorienting, but you'll find it helps to talk." He looked at Bobby squirming silently against vinyl. "How do you feel about your experience?"

"This is all pretty new."

"Don't use that as an excuse not to contribute. We all talk here. Describe your impression of the afterlife."

Bobby glanced about the office. "Well, this is it."

"How do you mean?"

"I mean *this is it!* I entered Hell, and here I am. *This* is my afterlife."

Scribbling furiously, Dr. Milo glanced at all five patients. "Recall what I said about disorientation." He focused on Bobby. "How do you feel right now?"

"Weird."

"Disoriented?"

"Kind of."

"Describe it."

"Like I'm floating, but being pulled back. I hear doctors' voices. I smell medicine."

"That's nothing to worry about. Periodically, subconscious memories from your revival at the hospital will surface. Not an uncommon phenomenon."

The neon lights flickered into grayness.

Dr. Milo turned to his four patients. "Tell us about your experience, Lisa."

A timid young woman glanced at the other three patients. "I already told everyone here."

Dr. Milo opened a fresh notebook. "Tell it to us again."

A Flash of Silver

Ben P. Indick

Eric was born covered with a light silvery fuzz. This bothered his folks, although the baby's granddad thought it was funny and asked his daughter whether she had been fooling around with that big gray poodle down the street. She told her father to go home.

Within a week the baby fur was gone. His scalp had dirty white hair, rapidly darkening as it filled in. Soon he was so cuddly and pink that they laughed at his premature gray. Still, a faint streak of silver threaded through his black hair.

As Eric grew he admired those bright hairs, although his mother always brushed them under. At the full moon the silver seemed to have a faint glow. She accused her son of greasing it, but he swore he had not.

In school some of the other kids thought Eric's hair was cool and asked their mothers to do it to their hair. Their mothers told them to go out and play and not bother them, but one of the girls, Mary Ann Partridge, went to the beauty parlor and requested a silver streak. Harriet the beautician laughed, but Mary Ann showed her the six dollars and forty cents she had saved. Harriet told her to get a note from her mom giving an okay. At age seven Mary Ann was already a computer expert, so she created her own note and signed it boldly with her mother's name. The forgery was a good one, and Harriet put her in the chair and told her to keep her money. Mary Ann came out of the shop with a bright smile and an even brighter streak of silver in her red tresses. It took weeks to fade away, plus a daily scrubbing with laundry soap by her mother.

In high school Eric discovered that the fuzz on his arms and chest glowed a stronger silver at the full moon, along with that streak in his hair he took for granted. He wondered whether he might be a werewolf. He tried howling, until his dad told him to practice his singing somewhere else. Loping on his hands and feet only made his back sore. In senior year he told Mary Ann, who was his girlfriend, about it and she went out and got another streak put into her hair. Sandy, her best friend, took a Polaroid picture of the two of them together with their silver streaks, and they agreed they looked swell. Too bad Mary Ann and her parents were moving away.

In college Eric studied to be a veterinarian. He concentrated on dogs and wolves, but the full moon never responded to him, though his hair had gotten more silvery.

Eric worked in an office with household pets. He had tried to find a position as a zoo veterinarian, but to no avail. One day he was examining Mrs. Gebhardt's long-ailing white husky. The dog's heart was weak, and he knew the beautiful animal would not live much longer. He prescribed a drug for pain, stroking its paws while its sad, wise eyes never left his. That evening Eric remained at his desk long after the patients and his secretary had left, rubbing the silver hair on his arm.

He walked home, imploring the sullen moon. Mary Ann had returned and was living nearby, but he had not called her. The Gebhardts lived across the street and he could see the husky sitting on the screened porch. He walked up, knelt, and whistled at the dog, which walked to the screen and pressed its snout there. Eric touched the snout through the screen. His vision shifted strangely. His hand was a paw. He realized his time had come. He slipped easily out of his clothing and reared on his hind legs. The husky and he barked simultaneously, the dog's cry trailing off into silence as Eric ran off. Behind him the Gebhardts had come out at hearing the noise. He saw them kneeling over their still dog.

Eric looked across the street, ran over, and howled. A light came on and he saw Mary Ann at a window. She glanced about and was shocked to see a wolf. He howled again. "Eric?" she cried hoarsely. She rushed out onto her porch. Then she saw his fiery red eyes and she crept behind her screen door. The old Polaroid photo was still bright in her mind, but the wolf's long silvery hair shone as hers could not. She slowly closed the door as the wolf loped up the avenue into the darkness.

Fly in Your Eye

David Nickle

It drifts through your vision, a detached retina on patrol. You blink, you rub your temples, you think about seeing the eye doctor real soon. But you look again, and you realize, no, you were wrong. There's nothing remotely retinal about this thing. Six stickly legs, disco-ball eyes, a big hairy ass, brown-tinted wings stretched akimbo. Just looking through 'em makes you want to scratch.

Crawled inside through your tear-duct while you slept. Happens one time in a hundred when a tourist goes down to that place, stays one night too many in a room where the fumigation hasn't took. The locals have a name for those flies—translates either to Sneaky Devil Bat, or Mean Little Eye Mite, depending on which edition of the Fodor's you got.

Maybe given time, it'll decompose. Surely it couldn't be alive in there—you don't know much about flies, but one thing you're pretty sure about is that flies do not have the right gills for extracting oxygen from eyeball juice. The fact that it's always in a different position when it drifts past your iris doesn't prove anything. What you're seeing's an optical illusion—fly tilts this way or that, wings seem to have moved, proboscis extends a little further, sucks a bit back. Truth is, that fly's drowned. And drowned means dead, and before long dead has got to mean decomposition. It's only a matter of time.

You decide to wait it out. Don't feel much like leaving the house, so you order in some groceries. The phone's getting awful jangly, and you pull it out of the wall. And who needs cable television when you got yourself a fly to watch?

So garbage day comes around and you take the TV and the telephone, and your hi-fi stereo set while you're at it, and lay them all out neat as you please on the curb. They're gone before the truck arrives, but you don't see who took them.

You start to wonder how big that fly in there really is. Some days, it fills your whole vision—everywhere you look, there's the fly, looking right back. Other times, it's a teeny little speck. If you weren't looking, you wouldn't even notice it was there.

Mail comes every morning, mostly bills. But you stopped reading it, after the fly switched eyes.

You woke up that morning, and it took you the longest time to figure out what was so unusual. First you thought, maybe someone rearranged the furniture, but as you looked that didn't seem to be the case. Then you were thinking, if not that, then maybe somebody painted the walls. But no, they were the same dirty beige as they were when you moved in here. And finally, it hit you.

It was the fly.

Floating there in your other eyeball—the clean eye, the empty eye, the eye that had no fly, or so you'd thought—brown-tinted wings pressed back all sleek and smug against the bristly little curve of its rump. Fly moved, and that's all it took: overnight, it changed *everything*.

So you closed your eyes and thought to yourself: the mail can *wait*. And you kept 'em closed, covered 'em up, because that way you don't have to look at that goddamn fly anymore as it jumps from one eye to the other, alive and well against all reason.

A while goes by. You don't have many friends, but the few you do have come calling, wondering if you're okay. You pretend you aren't home, and it seems to work: they leave.

Why don't you go to a doctor? Somehow, you just can't get your head around the idea that this fly's a simple medical condition. Maybe the Fodor's had it right—the first edition, not the new one—and this fly's a Sneaky Devil Bat, come straight up from Hell to steal your soul. What's a doctor going to do for that?

You're just about ready to go to a priest this morning when you figure it out. You jump out of bed laughing, pull the bandage off your eyes. The fly's gone—you can tell it without even looking! It *was* only a matter of time.

You fling open the curtains and watch the light stream in. Beautiful morning, isn't it? Middle of summer, sunshiny day, birds flying through the trees. It's a shame you can't hear their singing, over the buzzing in your ear.

For Your Immediate Attention

Peter Atkins

I know where you bought this book.

I was there. You didn't notice me in the check-out line, I know, but that's alright. I wouldn't be very good at my job if you noticed me, would I? No. I fit in. That's why they use me. Shame-faced, I admit it: I'm nondescript. Somebody to whom you wouldn't give a second glance. But that doesn't mean I'm not special. I'm very special. A special man for a special job. You didn't even notice me when I followed you home, did you?

Now, don't start getting nervous. Not yet.

Or perhaps you like getting nervous? After all, you bought this book. You have a specific taste for things that might frighten you. Doesn't that strike you as odd? Maybe not. After all, you're not alone. Lots of people like to be scared. Maybe a lot of people bought this book. 'S that what you think? Well, let me tell you a little secret . . .

No, hold on. Let's give you some background first. Let's get back to this thing about the public taste for fear. Do you think it just stays there, blossoming unattended like some magical plant that doesn't need cultivation or water? No. Fear is a very special quality. Like an orchid, it needs special attention to keep it in bloom. Every now and then, something special has to be done to keep it alive. That's where I come in. That's where *you* come in.

Do you know what urban myths are? You've heard some, I'm sure, maybe even told some. The hitchhiking woman with the ax in her purse; the hook left in the car door; the prowler upstairs listening in on the extension while they alert someone to his presence. You've heard them. I know you have. You ever hear the ones about people reading a book and being frightened to death? Found the next morning, hair turned white, not breathing? You know what? They weren't frightened to death.

I killed them.

That's my job. I have to tend the flower. I have to keep the orchid alive. I have to let fear out into the world so that the whispers continue, the rumors proliferate, and the books keep selling. It's a marketing thing, really. The public's taste for fear keeps a lot of people employed. We can't let it wither and die, can we?

Now, the secret I was going to tell you . . .

Know how the fast-food chains sometimes do big promotions? You know, check your napkin for the special number, win a million dollars or a trip to Florida? Well, book publishers sometimes do that, too. And guess what? You're a winner. And I'm the prize.

You probably didn't notice—hell, it's only a couple of pages, so how could you?—but your copy of this book (this copy, the one you're holding) was just a little thicker than all the others. You know why? It's the only copy to contain this story. That's right. Think I'm kidding? Go back to the store. Check them out. Well, actually, you're not going to have time to do that. You'll just have to take my word for it.

I put this copy on the shelf. And I waited. Waited for somebody to buy it. Waited for you. I'm glad it was you. I hoped it would be you as soon as you walked in. I knew we could do business together.

Okay, listen. The story's done now.

Close the book.

Count to ten.

Here I come.

Forever
Karen E. Taylor

Y ou don't want to do this, John." Susan looked up at him from where she'd been sitting, filing her nails. He can't leave, she thought, I won't let him. She put down the emery board and watched him pace the room, listening unmoved while he blurted out his sad, pathetic tale of lost love and life. "You really don't want to do this."

"Susan." He crossed the room, taking one of her hands in his. "I don't want to hurt you, but I have never wanted anything more in my life."

"Never?" An amused tone crept into her voice. She remembered a time when he'd said that about her, when he'd arrived at the door of this apartment, flushed and trembling with passion and love; remembered how easily she'd seduced him away from wife and children so she could enjoy the touch of his hands and the coiled muscles of his arms.

John stammered slightly under her steady gaze. "Th-things have changed, Susan. That's the way of the world. The kids need me; I need them. I have to go back."

Smiling, she rose and wrapped her arms around his neck, kissing the spot behind his ear that always made him shiver. "Well," she whispered, her voice low and seductive, "if you have to go, then go. But leave me something to remember you by."

Susan feigned sleep while he packed his bag, deepening her breathing as he leaned over and kissed her cheek softly. "This is for the best, Susan; you know it is." When she didn't respond to his whisper, he sighed and walked out of the room. She lay still until she heard the front door close. Then she stretched, sat up in bed and smiled. "'For the best.'" She mimicked his statement, laughing. "All the same, John, you *don't* want to do this. And you *will* be back."

She hurried to the bathroom to collect what he'd left her. And as she worked she ticked off the ingredients in her mind: hair, fluids, skin cells, blood—all gathered from her body and her sharpened nails and placed in a paper cup.

Without bothering to dress, Susan went to the kitchen. "Much simpler to make than the last candle," she said as she prepared the wax and the mold. "And given the quality of the 'remembrances,'" she purred the word, "it should be much more effective." Obviously, she thought as she worked, the one she'd prepared to bring John to her had been weak, mostly because she'd had to use shoddy materials: hair from his head, sweat from the headband she'd stolen from his gym bag the night they'd met; enough to bring him, but not strong enough to keep him.

"This time." She removed the candle from the mold and set it on the counter. "This time, John, it will be forever." She lit the wick. The flame sputtered, then flared up, burning steady and strong. Susan sat cross-legged on the floor, rocking back and forth, humming a tuneless song, her eyes focused on the candle until all that remained was the fire, the man and one word. "Forever."

Hours later, when the candle was just a pool of melted wax and carbon, two distinct sounds woke her from her trance: a scraping of a key in the front door and the ringing of the phone. Susan gave a smug smile and got up from the floor. John was back, forever. She knew it. Gone would be all thoughts of wife and children; she would be the only one he ever wanted.

Turning her back to the opening door, she answered the phone.

"Ms. Black?" The urgent voice sent a small chill through her.

"Speaking."

The caller cleared his throat. "You are listed as the contact for John Turner, is that correct?"

"Yes, he lives here."

"Ah." There was a pause. Susan heard the front door shut. "There's been an automobile accident. And I'm sorry to tell you that Mr. Turner didn't . . ."

"Didn't what? Didn't stop?"

Only half listening to the call, Susan smiled at the familiar feel of John's body pressed behind her. His hands caressed her shoulders, but they seemed unusually cold and clammy. She gasped, dropping the phone, staring at the sticky blood dripping onto her breasts.

As if from a long distance she heard a voice say ". . . no, he didn't survive."

The voice in her ear was much closer and clearer. "Forever," it rasped. "Forever."

Fragment of a Diary Found on Ellesmere Island

Brian McNaughton

March 15, 1886:

Wheeler lost the draw. He called us cheating dogs and took up the ax, but five to one is no contest, even weak as we are, and we disarmed him. Redmond is a joker; he says do not bruise him, it will spoil the meat, and Wheeler says I hope you choke on me, you son of a bitch. Capt. Daniels held him and told me to cut his throat. We dressed the carcass and put most of the cuts outside, where it is snowing again, reserving the left leg and foot which we cut up and boiled. I thought I would never be able to eat this, but the smell of cooking made my mouth water, and I fell to with a will when Jackson said it was done.

This is where it got strange. It was crowded around the pot, and I took it into my head to count us. Each time I came up with six, but Wheeler was dead and there should be only five. I was used to this, for the past month I have not known if I was waking or sleeping, but I forced myself to concentrate and counted each man by pointing with my finger.

What are you doing? Wheeler asks.

Everyone stared in horror at the dead man, sitting there large as life beside me and sharing in the feast. Capt. Daniels took up the ax and hit him, but Wheeler laughed. He did not bleed like a live man, and the blow did not distract him from eating.

March 20:

The bear was back and stole the meat we had stored outside, causing us to despair. Wheeler said we must draw lots again. Look at me, he says, it is nothing to be afraid of. He is ghastly, with his split forehead and cut throat like a grinning mouth below the real one.

March 21:

Jackson lost the draw which was unfortunate as he is the cook. He came back and partook of the meal but he was more surly than Wheeler and cursed us for killing him.

March 25:

The dead men stay by themselves, knowing they are different. They do not sleep, which is worrisome. They eat, however. If we kill another one, the dead will equal the living.

March 31:

We did not need to draw since Redmond volunteered. I will not have to worry about dying when I am like Wheeler and Jackson, he says. The dead had a laugh at this. Capt. Daniels strangled him with a rope. He came back, too.

April 1:

Now it is Capt. Daniels and young Hodgson and me. I would like to talk with them about our predicament, but you cannot swing a cat in the shack we cobbled from salvaged timbers, and the dead would put in their two cents. They are not like they were in life. I do not understand Redmond's jokes. We cannot go outside, for the cold is deadly and the bear is prowling constantly.

April 10:

We woke up to find Capt. Daniels dead, strangled in his sleep. Redmond did not deny killing him and said it was the best way, he would not have to fret now about losing the draw. Capt. Daniels did not take this view himself when he came back and was very bitter, but he sits with the other dead men while Hodgson and I keep to ourselves.

Wheeler will not leave off staring at me. He says he does not hold it against me, but I was the one who put the knife to his throat.

April ?:

My name is Abel Hodgson and I set pen to paper in Jimmy's diary as he does not want to write no more now that he says he is dead. He says it is all right to write in it if I do not write lies. The bear tore a hole in the wall and Jimmy drove him away with the ax. It does not sit well with him when I ask him why he bothered to fight off the bear if he is dead already. I pray that some kind person will take this note to my mother, Mrs. Sarah Hodgson of Portsmouth, N.H., who knows that I do not tell lies although Jimmy sure does. I pray someone will tell Miss Amelia Manning of Portsmouth that I was thinking of her to the last and wish I had never succumbed to the lure of the sea.

Dear Jesus, Jimmy is getting restless again.

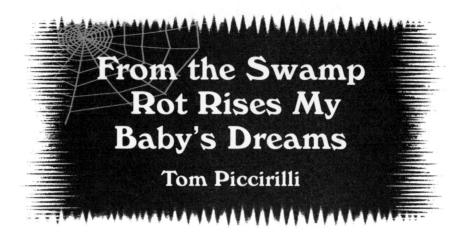

From the Swamp Rot Rises My Baby's Dreams

Tom Piccirilli

Jenny titters into the wind, holding the flat stone, glowing a fierce crimson so that every vein seems to burn. She calls out at the swamp, "Come on, now!" She waves wildly over her head, the way a girl is supposed to act when playing with her friends. In her mind, she's always been a child, and nearing forty hasn't changed that any. Maybe raising her alone in the woods made it worse, Mary Beth skipping out when Jenny was five. She doesn't notice her daddy lying here dying in the mud, or Old Franklin's corpse draped over my legs, pinning me in the bog. His eyes stare off at insanity, thickly veined arms groping for God, most of his chest blown against the weeds. Bastard wrestled gators all his life, and he did a fine job on me. Blood pumps out my belly in an ugly arc every time I try to twist off of this jagged stump.

Shock keeps the pain at bay for the time being. There was nothing else to do; he was going to shoot her in the back. All this over a kind of rock Gumbo Billy told us never to bring into the swamp. Who knew to listen to a man who sees Jesus in his gumbo?

Gators will be coming soon.

"Daddy, ooh-ooh I see! I see!" Jenny shouts excitedly, and if not for bleeding to death I might enjoy this moment, listening to her stringing words together, the joy in her voice.

An incredible gurgling sound like a giant shoe pulling free from mud fills the area until I'm roaring with my hands over my ears. Bull gators grouse and splash off the riverbanks, circling like frightened puppies. I kick at Old Franklin, trying to lift him off, wishing I could kill him with his own gun again.

With a heave that throws the gators for a loop, something rises from the water with a keening shriek, hauling its vast bulk from the width of the bog: shock has spread a cool silken sheet over my mind and body, so I keep my eyes open. Losing blood's made me a little drunk, and I notice I'm grinning.

Busted shanty-boats, sunken skiffs, and burned-out pickups comprise most of its underbelly as it swings about in the cypress-boarded slough to face my daughter. She claps and wheels about, leaping and giggling. God, she's so alive, her gray hair loose in the wind, night dress whirling. Its gigantic arms topple moss-draped elderberry shrubs with unbelievable crashes like thunder. That head tilts in my direction as if hoping to discover my meaning here.

Oh Jesus, get out of Billy's gumbo and come help me now.

Swamp rot's got a face.

As it comes stalking forward I see it's made of the bones of my people: every undiscovered body hidden in the bog is attached, lost cemeteries gone under in the rains, the murdered and drowned; swamp rot's massive head is composed of a thousand human skulls, lips and cheeks a collection of femurs, sternums, and ribcages. It bends before Jenny like a mother cooing over an infant. Rotted crosses and coffins swirl past as waves rock the bog. Fetid water sloshes against my face and I lose sight of Jenny. When I manage a breath I hear her feet slapping out rhythms as she races across the spines of its chin.

Gumbo Billy had it pretty much right—all his weird talk about elemental powers of the earth has gotta be true. Most folks took him for another mad hermit, but his ideas came from someplace older than us. The flat stone is just another rock anywhere else, but here it's got uses.

How Jenny knew about the fact won't ever be answered; she stole it from under Old Franklin's nose and he was willing to kill to get it back. Seems everyone believed this stuff more than me.

Old Franklin's stone bleeds a fiery light as swamp rot looks down at me and smiles.

"Daddy, isn't she beautiful!"

She sure is: swamp rot's taken the form of Mary Beth, giving my baby her mother back. I nod as Jenny seats herself up on a noselike ridge in the center of its head; she waves as swamp rot turns to stroll deeper into the bog. I hope that someday they swing back this way and take up some more lost bones along with them. The terrified bull gators creep closer, but that's all right now. I ain't worried none, it's just fine with me.

Future Shock

John B. Rosenman

It's no picnic being a vampire, Stevenson thought.

He stood beside a highway so vast his millennia-old brain boggled with wonder. A half mile wide, luminous in the night, the road dwindled in the distance and soared high above him.

Antigravity.

Rocket cars.

Impossible.

He closed his eyes against the changes he'd awakened to, thinking how it used to be so easy to adjust to a new era and escape persecution. For ages he had merely slept for a generation or two to escape the wrath of villagers and feast again on their descendants. It had been so simple. All he had required was a coffin and a safe place to sleep.

But now there were rocket cars streaking overhead, mile-high turrets and towers, and people with weird masks walking everywhere.

It was just too much.

Stevenson rubbed his eyes, glad they weren't red like his cousins'. There had always been a problem adjusting to changes after a long sleep, of course. He recalled his surprise when he'd awakened to discover the printing press (which warned against his kind!). And then there had been airplanes, television. . . . Always, however, the adjustments required had been small. Progress, after all, moved slowly, and not much happened from one century to the next. The world you closed your eyes to was always basically the one that greeted you when you awoke.

But on his last awakening in 2003, things *had* changed. He had opened his eyes to lasers, manned landings on Mars, and machines that actually thought. There had even been a disease which made women demand to see his medical history if he so much as acted amorous in order to slake his thirst. Eventually he had retired to his ancestral bed in hopes of waking to a more hospitable age. But what he saw now was madness!

Suddenly a beautiful, dark-haired woman appeared, and he forgot his confusion. Unlike the others, she wasn't wearing a mask, and her eyes met his boldly. After she passed him, he followed.

There was little hope of possessing her. The thoroughfare was too bright, too well patrolled. Behind any mask could be a policeman with weapons he could not even begin to imagine.

She turned into an alley.

He blinked, surprised there still were such things, and crept to its entrance, where he listened to her receding footsteps. The alley itself was far from dark. Still, he'd worked under more hazardous conditions.

Glancing cautiously about, he slipped after her.

His still, cold heart burned with excitement. He had slept half a century, and his long fast made him hurry. He saw her glance nervously around, her long hair flying.

She started to run.

Too late, he saw she had almost reached another street. Surging with blood lust, he spurted forward and caught her just as she left the alley.

Blinding light hit him and he saw pedestrians, but his thirst transcended prudence. With a howl, he clasped her close and drove his bicuspids into her neck, trembling in ecstasy as the first drops shot down his throat. How sweet! How delicious! Never had the nectar of human blood . . .

Suddenly he did not feel so well.

He pulled away, seeing her horror-filled eyes. Inexplicably, he was weak, nauseous. Within seconds, the nausea intensified. He felt sores erupt in his mouth. His body broke out into a burning rash.

She screamed. Ran.

Panicking, he lurched toward the alley, only to find himself on hands and knees, his energy draining until he slumped weakly against the wall. What was happening to him? What was wrong? Before his fading vision, two snout-masked figures approached him.

"Looks like another," one said. "He must have met a carrier."

"You'd think after all the warnings, *everyone* would wear a mask," said the other. "AIDS three is nothing to mess with."

"You got that right." Stevenson, through a thickening haze, saw the first one move closer. "Five minutes from exposure to death, but there are still hardheads who won't listen."

"I'll call Medpol. Maybe we can nail the carrier."

"Forget it. Probably long gone by now." He stooped and studied Stevenson, who was no longer seeing anything. "You know, there's something bloody queer about this bird. Look at those old-fashioned clothes."

The other sighed and shook his mask. "Well, whoever he is, one thing's for sure. The poor bastard had the life sucked right out of him."

The Garage
Del Stone Jr. and C. M. Terry

It's a beauty, ain't it?" Parker glowed, his voice equal parts admiration and pride, the voice of a man who had just shit the world's biggest turd—and would now sell his story to Ripley's Believe It or Not.

But Samuelson had to admit: It did have a certain grandeur, the way train derailments or airplane disasters unfold with a kind of beauty layered within the horror.

The messiest garage he'd ever seen.

"Come on, let's take a look," Parker insisted, speaking in a reverent whisper.

Parker's garage *was* a disaster. The chintzy bastard, didn't he ever throw anything away? Samuelson's gaze traveled over the Escher-like arrangement of junk: bicycle parts, wheel rims, sacks of aluminum cans, lampshades, a seamstress's dummy, wire mesh crab traps, leaning towers of newspapers—oh God, the eye refused to take it all in. It gathered in drifts at the corners, rode the walls and scrunched against the ceiling, a critical mass approaching some terrible implosion.

"I've got a '67 Eldorado somewhere under all this stuff," Parker grinned. "But the best part is back here."

He led Samuelson down a narrow path to the back of the garage. There, he wedged his shoulder against a door Samuelson hadn't noticed, and pushed. The door groaned and gave way. Parker flipped on a light.

It was another room . . . filled with junk. Old iceboxes, ironclad electric ranges, fans, *Life* magazines, wooden crates filled with empty Coke bottles . . .

"The previous owners left this stuff here," Parker beamed. "Lots of antiques. I'm gonna make a fortune."

Samuelson could see the dollar signs glowing in Parker's eyes. He gazed across the room, where he saw another door. "What's back there?"

Parker frowned. "I dunno. Never noticed it before." He tiptoed through the clutter and forced open the door.

Another room. Filled with junk. Crockery chamberpots and blackened andirons and dusty bottles and wooden boxes. Parker had his hands on his hips. "Jesus! I didn't know this stuff was here, but God, look at it! Ain't it great?"

But Samuelson was staring at the opposite wall. Another door. Parker noticed, and his jaw dropped. "Holy shit! That's impossible! The house doesn't go back that far!"

The room was filled with spears and quivers and hairy mounds of animal skins. The walls were covered with charcoal scrawlings of bears and lions and mammothlike creatures.

Parker's voice was filled with wonder. "I don't understand it," he said, spreading his arms to take in the room, "but it's—it's—terrific! Stone Age junk! Can you guess what this stuff would sell for? Can you? Millions, I'd bet!"

Samuelson grabbed Parker's arm and began to haul him back. There, at the back of the chamber, was another door, an opening, really, blocked by a fall of stones. Behind the stones Samuelson could hear a *scritch*ing sound, and a basso rumbling, as if something very large waited on the other side. A cool finger of dread began to work its way up the knobs of Samuelson's spine.

"C'mon," Parker hissed, jerking away and stumbling off-balance across the room. "Let's check it out."

"No, goddammit," Samuelson whispered. "Can't you hear it? Can't you hear it?"

But Parker was already shoving rocks out of the way and shouting over his shoulder, "C'mon, man! This is my lottery ticket! This is my ship coming in!"

Then the rocks at the top of the opening tumbled loose, and something—Samuelson could not say what—reached through and yanked Parker off his feet and into the gap so that Samuelson saw only

Parker's boots vanish into the darkness, trailed only by a snapped-off scream. . . .

And as Samuelson turned and sprinted for the door, a sickening image arose in his mind, an image of the lock somehow ratcheting into place behind them as they'd entered the chamber, because from the opening, rocks were being hurled out of the way, and something with a growl that sounded a million years old was trying to break free.

Gators in the Sewers

Tina L. Jens

When Phoebe saw the baby alligator swimming in her soup, she realized she was quite mad.

It was homemade vegetable. The soup, that is. Made from the last pickings of a late garden. Which is to say, a few scrawny potatoes, a rogue carrot and lots of onions.

The alligator—yes, it was still there—had climbed upon an onion log and was sunning itself in the glare of the bare 90-watt bulb that hung over the kitchen table.

Phoebe wondered where its mother was. She had jumped to the conclusion that it was a baby, based solely on its size. But considering its current location, there were infinite possibilities. Phoebe chose not to consider them just now.

The alligator yawned widely, exposing a mouthful of tiny, pointed teeth—about the size of sewing needles, but not nearly so long. Suddenly, the little thing snapped its jaws, ripping a fleshy hunk out of an unsuspecting creature floating past. The surprisingly loud snap scared Phoebe, and she jumped back in her chair with an "Oh!"

The vicious attack on the innocent canned mushroom was a good reminder that while tiny, the alligator was still a wild, dangerous creature.

Phoebe mellowed as she watched the gator wag its tail and chew happily. A herpetologist might have told her that alligators don't wag their tails, exactly. But Phoebe didn't know any people of that sort.

Phoebe pondered what to do. She lived alone. There was no one to call into the room while she pointed excitedly at her dinnertime discovery. She wasn't a dramatic person. But it would have been nice to have another witness to the strange event.

Even if she had someone to summon, they wouldn't see it. Phoebe instinctively knew this was one of the fundamental laws of nature. She was no student of metaphysics, but she'd seen the Abbott and Costello routine. If Abbott couldn't see the bullfrog in Costello's soup, nobody was going to see the alligator in Phoebe's bowl.

You can't think clearly on an empty stomach. Phoebe had heard that once. Made sense to her. And it *was* her soup. The alligator would just have to share.

She dipped her spoon into the bowl gently, hoping she wouldn't scare the creature, but he slithered off the onion and dived to the bottom of the bowl. Oh well, she'd find him as the soup level went down.

She checked the contents of her spoon carefully—nothing moved. It did contain the mushroom the little gator had been eating. Phoebe felt guilty for stealing his dinner. But he could find another piece.

She went on like that for a time, checking each spoonful before slurping the broth. It occurred to her that there might be more than one gator in the bowl. She spooned through the soup, looking for creatures. Finding none, she continued to eat.

She began to wonder if she'd imagined the alligator. But no, she spotted him in the dregs of the bowl, hiding under a cabbage leaf. She set the tip of her spoon down in front of him. He stepped gingerly onto it. The tip of his tail hung off. He looked uncomfortable—but Phoebe didn't have a bigger spoon.

She lifted him until they were nose to nose. They studied each other intently. The view made her cross-eyed, so she lowered the spoon and set it on the table. The little alligator crawled up the incline and rested his front legs on the tip of the spoon.

Phoebe knew she couldn't keep him. The landlord didn't allow pets, and she already had one contraband kitten that lived in her bottom dresser drawer. But that didn't stop her from fantasizing about raising the little reptile. It'd be cool to have a full-grown alligator slouching through her house. She'd have to put a sign up in her window, BEWARE THE WATCHGATOR.

If she set it loose outside, it would freeze to death. Or get run over by a car. The nearest swamp was states away.

The cat would enjoy playing with it, but that seemed cruel. It was just a baby. And the cat might get hurt, too. Phoebe shuddered as she pictured the creature sinking those needle-sharp teeth into the kitten's soft, pink nose.

Finally, she resorted to the standard method of urban gator disposal—though she did not, technically, live in the city. She flushed him down the toilet. She waved good-bye as he swam away.

Gentleman's Agreement

Judith Post

Carl pulled his van to the curb and cut the engine. The house sat back from the road, sheltered by high hedges and a privacy fence at the back of the property. Its owner, Elijah Fryburg, had been a prominent banker. Now, he was a recluse. He didn't even have household help.

"Eccentric is only the tip of the iceberg," a former colleague told Carl. "He's stingy with everything."

Which was all the better. The old coot lived alone and didn't want to waste electricity, so went to bed early and rose with the sun. He was hard of hearing, too.

Carl glanced up and down the street. Big houses. Secluded. He sauntered down the driveway to the Fryburg mansion, using a crowbar to let himself in. There was no security system. Elijah was too cheap to have one installed, actually thought his reputation would scare folks away.

Pulling a flashlight from his jacket, Carl made his way through the house, then stopped to listen. Was that a rustling? The place was drafty. Drafts sighed from room to room.

He followed the hall to a library. The safe was behind a picture, for heaven's sake. Cracking it took the better part of five minutes. Elijah was creepy, all right. The only contents was a pile of bones—a skull and rib cage of a medium-sized animal, with a stack of papers wedged between the skeleton's teeth. The skull had two small horns. A goat?

Carl pried out the papers and glanced at them. Loans to various townspeople, all of whom had passed away. Carl recognized the head librarian's name, Miss Tuttle. The loan was for a few thousand, marked PAID, with a document for her mother's hospital stay stapled to the top. Mr. Grosner, the high school principal, had a stack of canceled checks, all made out to a Lizzie Torch for five hundred dollars, paid by Elijah Fryburg each and every month. Tom Yarnell's loan was for a hefty two million. Stapled to his was a canceled suit for death due to construction fraud. Tom's company had built the elementary school that collapsed in high winds.

There was a trend here. If Carl was right, all of these good, upstanding citizens had come to Elijah Fryburg when they'd gotten themselves in deep trouble. Old Fryburg had obviously bailed them out. But why? It didn't fit with the old guy's character.

Stuffing the papers into his jacket, Carl crossed the hallway to the mansion's parlor. A huge picture from Dante's *Inferno* hung on the wall. Peeking behind it, Carl found another safe. Opening it, he gazed at a large wax doll with a hole carved where its heart would be. Rolled papers curled through the hole. As he read through them, he shivered. "The unborn child of Greta Sorrenson." Carl remembered that Greta's baby had died at birth, but soon after that, her husband had completely recovered from a stroke. "The virginity of Lisa Knobbs." Lisa's mother had found her daughter's body at the edge of their woods. Her killer was never apprehended, but that very year, the Knobbs' farm began to prosper.

A cold knot was forming in Carl's gut. He was jamming the papers back into the safe when the grandfather clock in the corner began to chime . . . ten, eleven, twelve. . . . At the stroke of midnight, black candles flamed to life around the room. Disembodied voices whispered. Footsteps sounded on the stairs. When Carl turned, he was face-to-face with old Elijah.

With skin like aged parchment, the banker could have been a thousand years old. Or older.

"So . . . you came to rob me?" The voice was scratchy, but distinctive.

"I don't want anything of yours," Carl said, slamming the safe shut. "I don't want anything to do with you."

"But surely you realize we can't part without a gentleman's agreement."

"Oh?" Carl was gripping his flashlight with white knuckles.

"A favor, for your soul."

Carl backed toward the window. "Forget it." He was a thief, not a sinner.

"As you wish."

Winds circled the room, and Tom Yarnell's face swirled before him. The window opened, and Tom hurled him onto the pavement outside. Pain convulsed Carl's body.

"I can spare you," Elijah's voice whispered in his ear.

Carl almost panicked, but he'd been a thief a long time. He understood risks, and he knew he was safer leaving this world than lingering. "No thanks."

And Elijah whispered, "As you wish," once more.

Ghost Story

Kevin Shadle

Julie was glad about this, her latest baby-sitting job. It wasn't just the money; she enjoyed helping someone so obviously in need.

"Thanks for coming on such short notice," the mother said at the door, "but the evenings are the only time I can interview for better jobs. I think Jason and Susan are angry with me, but I can't expect second and third graders to understand. They've been standoffish ever since yesterday evening when I also had an interview."

"I understand," said Julie. "We'll do just fine." She listened patiently to the children's regimen, what TV programs were allowed, and the obligatory phone number. "But only call if it's a *real emergency*. This interview is very important."

"No problem, ma'am." The Mom then introduced the children. The two older ones did seem to shy away, and little Bobby just stood with his thumb in his mouth, eyeing her with suspicion. An experienced sitter, Julie was prepared for any behavior. She wished the Mom luck and walked back to the youngsters' bedrooms.

"Okay, kids," she called, "get to your homework." And then she got right to her own.

Eventually she heard the soft patter of Bobby's footsteps running toward her. He grabbed her leg and looked up at her with large, pleading eyes. "Don't let him come again. Please. Don't let him get me." He buried his head in her jeans.

"Don't let who get you, Bobby?" she asked, running her fingers through his hair. But there was only soft whimpering.

"I think we should tell Julie some old ghost stories!"

Calmly she looked around. "I don't think that would be a good idea, Jason. Bobby seems frightened enough."

"So let's tell some young ghost stories," said Susan.

Julie just rolled her eyes.

Suddenly the phone rang. Jason and Susan's eyes flew wide open. They ran off to their bedrooms and Bobby began screaming.

Julie picked up Bobby and tried to quiet him as she went to the phone. When her hand touched the receiver, Bobby's terror became a silent scream.

Julie lifted the receiver and Bobby fainted.

It was the mother.

"Yes, everything's under control," Julie said, holding Bobby's limp little body and hoping that was true.

"I'll be home soon. They're calling me in now. Bye."

Click!

Julie frowned and went to the kitchen sink, more than a little concerned about Bobby. *What is going on here?*

A splash of cold water revived Bobby, and learning it was his mommy on the phone, he scampered off to his room.

Seizing the moment, Julie opened Susan's door, knelt down, and stretched her arms out. "Susan, could I talk to you and . . ."

"Jason!" Susan yelled, stepping away as she turned her head. "It's time to tell Julie our ghost story. Come on!"

"No, no, Susan. No stories. But I do want to know about this man that Bobby mentioned. Is he real?"

Susan bowed her head. "Well . . ."

"We need to tell you a ghost story, Julie!"

"Maybe after we talk, Jason."

The phone rang again and Bobby started screaming as she went to answer it. "Could you two please comfort your brother?" she shouted. But by the looks in his and Susan's eyes, they needed comforting, too.

What is going on? Julie wondered. *Bobby's screaming. Jason and Susan shying away.* "Hello?"

Nothing on the other end.

"Hello?"

"I'm coming."

Is this the man? I should hang up. Call . . . no, she's in a meeting.

"I'm coming and I'll kill you *all!*"

911. Yes, call . . . She was suddenly listening to a dial tone.

Bobby grabbed her leg and nearly knocked her down.

"*Please*, Julie, let us tell you our ghost story," yelled Jason over Bobby's wails.

"*No!* I have to call . . ."

"Nine-one-one didn't help last night," said Susan. Julie stared at them, groping for understanding, but saw only her own terror reflected in their eyes.

"Now, listen," Julie demanded. "You're in *danger!*"

"No, *you* listen!" Susan demanded back, but Julie lunged toward her and finally managed to grab her shoulders.

There was nothing there.

Susan's body was suddenly translucent, floating up to the ceiling to join her brother.

"He can't kill Jason and me again," she said.

"We should have told you our ghost story," said Jason.

Bobby screamed in terror.

The front door screeched in its frame.

Ghost Writer

Lisa Morton

The fax machine started printing at 3:12 A.M.

This was the twelfth night in a row. Each night it rolled out precisely twenty pages, then shut off.

It no longer worried Tom Erskine that this happened. He didn't even care that the phone never rang beforehand. Oh, it had startled him, in the beginning. On the first night he had been sleeping, had been awakened by the soft *shurr-snick* of the machine's page cutter. But when he had sat down and read what was coming forth . . .

He knew it would save his career.

Tom Erskine's third novel, the one published six months ago, had failed miserably. It had been lambasted by critics and shunned by readers.

Tom knew every career had its ups and downs, but this was *too* down. When the advance money had gone, his wife had left with it. He was poor, unhappy, and suffering from terminal writer's block.

Then he'd bought the machine. An estate sale, replete with grieving widow. Erskine had agents and editors who wanted to fax him, who in fact *demanded* it. He was too broke to buy a new one, and so it had seemed like a godsend.

It was.

Because every night now, at exactly 3:12 A.M., it printed out twenty pages of the best damn novel Tom Erskine had ever read. There was no title, no author, no return number, nothing but page after page of beautiful, intense, passionate, vivid, *perfect* prose.

And now, on the twelfth night, Tom was staring at a page that had the words THE END printed at the bottom.

He gathered the entire 240-page manuscript together and took it into the bedroom. He reread it, ignoring the sun that rose outside, glorying in the interior places the book took him. The style was not unlike his own; there were even some of his favored expressions in the dialogue, his punctuation tricks. . . .

It was two in the afternoon by the time he put it down. He was tired, maybe delirious, but he felt excited, exhilarated. The decision wasn't hard to make. He didn't know where the pages had come from; he thought a faulty phone line might be to blame . . . but, on the other hand, he could almost believe this book was something he'd written. And damn it, as good as it was, its chances of being sold by an unknown were slim. With his name on it, it would see print.

And he would see salvation.

Erskine spent the next two weeks typing the book into his computer, for authenticity's sake. He made almost no changes; he didn't need to.

The night before he was ready to mail the finished manuscript to his agent, the fax turned on.

At 3:12 A.M.

Erskine had forgotten about it. But it woke him instantly. He lay in his bed listening to the soft *whirr* of the machine, and felt a knot tighten inside him. A knot of dread. Of guilt.

It was only one page. When it was done, he walked slowly to the office. What the machine had unreeled this time was not a page of prose.

It was a contract.

There were only two clauses: He was to share credit on the book with one Martin Grosz; some money would go to the Grosz estate.

Estate?

Then he remembered. He'd asked the widow at the estate sale for a receipt. Now he dug it frantically out of his tax records and, sure enough, it was there.

Mary *Grosz*.

It was barely 5 A.M. when he called her. Fortunately she'd been listed in the white pages. So was Martin.

When the woman's sleep-slurred voice answered, he asked for Martin.

"My husband died last month," she replied.

He feigned sympathy and old acquaintance, and soon pried the truth from her.

Martin had been a failed, unsold novelist who had killed himself. Erskine thought he knew at exactly what hour.

He hung up and turned to the fax machine. He considered, then tore up the contract.

"Sorry, Martin, but you're dead."

He reached down to unplug the machine.

The coroner's report was simple: Death by electrocution, from a faulty cord. It was not called homicide.

But the manuscript found next to Tom Erskine's body would live long after him. It was published posthumously to great acclaim.

And, although the widow of a Martin Grosz claimed the work was her husband's, no one listened.

Only Tom Erskine's name was on the cover.

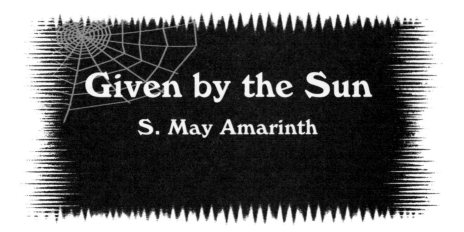

Given by the Sun

S. May Amarinth

The name Mithridates, meaning "Given by the Sun," was derived from the name of the Persian sun-god Mithras. It was the given name of six kings of Pontus, the last of whom, also known as Mithridates the Great, reigned from 120 to 63 B.C.

Mithridates VI was one of the longest-lived of his line—an achievement he contrived by amassing an armoury of antidotes to all known poisons. This was a wise precaution, given that his three immediate predecessors had all been assassinated by poison. What began as a precaution, however, turned into an obsession. He became convinced that his ministers were plotting against him, and that they had sent spies to search the world for poisons as yet unknown. He sent forth his own servants to do likewise, and all the venoms they brought back with them he tested on the bodies of slaves, so that he might identify their antidotes by trial and error.

One day, an agent reported to him that in a remote area of the mountains of Ind there lived a tribe of hillmen who kept a fire which was never allowed to go out, and a cauldron perpetually a-bubble on that fire, which contained a living liquid said to have a most remarkable effect. Anyone who drank of it was possessed by its virtue: The flesh of the living liquid dissolved the flesh of the host, little by little, and replaced it with solid flesh of its own manufacture. The individual thus remade was invulnerable to disease and poison, and had powers of self-repair far better than those of common men. Unfortunately, the living flesh was very slow to reproduce, and the cauldron produced but a single adequate dose every ten or twelve years.

Mithridates sent a large company of soldiers to the place in question, instructing them to slaughter the hillmen and bring the cauldron back to him, taking care to set it upon a fire which never went out. This the soldiers accomplished—although it cost them dear, for the hillmen fought like tigers and many of their company were extremely difficult to kill.

After setting a slave to drink from the cauldron to make sure that he suffered only beneficent effects, Mithridates the Great took a draught himself. In the days that followed he grew stronger and healthier. All the sores which he had on his body healed, and when he cut himself with a dagger the cut closed with remarkable rapidity, leaving no scar. He drank a deeper draught from the cauldron, and then another, saving the little that remained to dole out to his generals. When he had done that, the cauldron was empty and useless.

It was soon after this, in 80 B.C., that Mithridates set his armies against the might of Rome in what came to be called the Second Mithridatean War—but the legions crushed his invading forces. Lucullus forced his ragged armies back to Pontus, and Pompey completed his military humiliation. His children took advantage of his reverses to rebel against him, and he found himself besieged in his tallest tower, with no alternatives facing him but submission or death.

Mithridates decided that there was nothing left to save but honour, and he took poison; but the poison did not kill him. He hanged himself by the neck; but no matter how long he choked, he did not die. In the end, he fell upon his sword; but no matter how he contrived to twist the blade within his guts he could not even fall unconscious. In the end, maddened by pain, he cast himself from the top of the tower onto the stones beneath; but although he smashed the greater number of his bones and rendered himself utterly helpless, he did not die. His superstitious subjects, believing him to be possessed by some appalling demon, left him where he lay, bathed by the hot light of the noonday sun.

He was there for a week before his son and successor, Pharnaces, could stand the sight and sound of him no longer, and ordered that he be set upon a pyre and burned. He did not scream for long once the fire was lit, but no one knew for sure how much time passed before the precious gift of Mithras was taken back again, forever.

Glimpses

John B. Rosenman

Greg Springer would never have thought he could wander into hell during a fine day at the beach, but he did. One moment he was sunbathing with Alice, his fiancée, and the next he had walked around a hill and was staring at a scene in which a man who looked just like him was arguing violently with her.

"I hate you!" Alice screamed. "And I'm *glad* I cheated!"

"Don't say that!" the man with his face ordered. "If you do . . ."

"If I do, *what?*" She laughed in his face. "What will you do? Get drunk again? Get fired from another job? At least the man I'm seeing—"

"Alice! I'm warning you . . ."

"Loser!"

Suddenly Springer saw the man with his face pull a gun and fire. Alice clasped her chest, moaned, and fell. She lay still, blood seeping into the sand.

Horrified, the man looked at the gun. "What have I done?"

Dazed, Springer whirled and headed back the way he'd come. Rounding the sandy hill, he saw Alice lying on a beach towel, just where he'd left her. And *this* Alice was alive and smiling!

"Hi, honey," she said, then rose. "Are you all right? My God, Greg, what's wrong?"

"Alice, did you hear anything? Screaming, a gunshot?"

She frowned. "A gunshot? No! I didn't hear anything."

Relief washed through him. Thank heaven, he must have dreamed or imagined it.

But it had seemed so real. He could still see her blood, the horror on his own face!

Turning, he looked at the hill that stretched between him and the scene he'd just witnessed. Was it possible he'd walked through some kind of door . . . into the future?

He looked at Alice's face, which he loved dearly. Had he been given a glimpse of what would happen to them one day? It seemed incredible, for they both loved each other deeply and would never wish the other ill. But if he lost his job, and other things went wrong . . .

"Greg, what *is* it?" She touched him.

"Alice, I'll be back in a minute."

"But . . ."

He spun, went back the way he'd come. The sand was slippery, and a couple times he almost fell. But he continued on because he had to *know*. Was it a dream or a vision?

Rounding the hill, he was just in time to see Alice pull a knife and stab his other self. "You cheating bastard!" Alice screamed. "I'm tired of your women, your sordid infidelities!"

Springer gaped as his own image fell. He saw Alice straddle his fallen form and raise the knife again.

He turned away. Such madness! It was just as before, only this time *she* had killed *him!* It was like he'd wandered into the future again, and been given a similar and yet different glimpse of what lay ahead. Could it be that, except for details, his and Alice's relationship always led to anger and murder? He stiffened. No, this was only an illusion, a perverted mirage. It *couldn't* be real!

Trembling, he plunged back around the hill, staggering in the soft, shifting sands. Finally he saw Alice, standing precisely where he'd left her.

"Greg . . ."

His heart twisted. He loved her so much, but if their union was doomed, he would have to give her up. Whatever the cost, he must save her—and himself—from such tragedy. Better they go their separate ways than end up with such murderous hate.

He pulled back his shoulders, forcing himself to be strong. "Get in the car, Alice."

"Honey . . ."

"Get in the car!"

Reluctantly, she obeyed. Clutching the blanket as they walked in the bright sunlight, he told her they couldn't see each other anymore, that his feelings had changed. Despite the pain, he made himself sound convincing. It was such a terrible choice, but he told himself that at least he had the rest of his life to know that he'd been strong enough to make the right one.

In the car, she started crying. He clutched the wheel grimly and didn't touch or comfort her. Nor did he speak any last words, not even when a driver ran a red light and sped toward them. When Greg turned, he was just in time to catch a glimpse of the car that would cave in their own and kill them both instantly.

Going Home!

William Marden

The Greyhound driver looked down at Marilyn and her baby and said, "You absolutely sure you want to be let out here?"

"I'll be fine. I've got family waiting for me. I'm going home."

As the bus left in a cloud of eye-stinging exhaust fumes, Marilyn held little Demi closer and whispered, "We're almost home. You and Mama both are finally going to have a real family."

She pulled off the dorky ribbon that Marilyn's adoptive mother, Ruth, had insisted on sticking on Demi's head with toothpaste and threw it away. Just like the old witch to insist on having her way to the very end. But no more.

She walked quickly through the cold November evening to the lonely convenience store on the two-laned North Florida highway.

A bell tinkled as she stepped into Roy's Food Emporium and Bait Center. She smiled at the white-haired lady behind the cash register.

"Mrs. Olson? I'm Marilyn Meyers. I mean, Marilyn Hamilton."

The old lady stared at Marilyn for a long moment, then hollered, "Roy, Roy, come out here. She's here, with the baby."

Roy Olson was a towering, skinny old man with a full head of white hair. He stared at Marilyn and Demi, then said, "You're the spitting image of your mama."

Whether it was the heat, the excitement, or the thought that she was finally close to finding her *real* mother, the world spun around and she found herself in a wicker rocker. Mrs. Olson held Demi, cooing softly to her.

"Such a perfect, perfect baby," she said. Roy Olson brought Marilyn a glass containing something that smelled like mint tea. She took a sip, then a deep swallow and then another. She had never tasted anything quite so delicious.

Roy went behind the counter and began dialing an old-fashioned telephone.

"Where is my mother?" Marilyn asked. "Were you just friends, or are we related? I know you knew my *real* mother because you knew about my birthmark."

So many questions swirled about in her mind. After her ad in the *Birth Parents Underground Hotline* had brought a response from the Olsons, she had checked their information against records stolen from sealed birth files by members of the Adoption Underground group she'd joined. The Olsons knew too much about her and her mother, and when they'd offered to take her to her mother, there was no way in hell that Marilyn would listen to the selfish bleatings of her possessive so-called adoptive mother that she should forget about the existence of Danielle Hamilton and be content with her boring adoptive family.

As Roy Olson whispered into the telephone, Mrs. Olson locked the front door, turning the CLOSED sign out to passersby. She stared avidly at Demi and whispered, "Oh, we know all about you and your mother."

Then her features turned cold and she said, "She betrayed us. She ran away, ran away with her beautiful little baby girl. Thought she could hide. We found her, but she'd outsmarted us and given the baby away. Back then we couldn't track you down, but thank God for the open adoption movement. You came back to us of your own free will."

Marilyn tried to stand but her body betrayed her. She slumped back into the chair, the glass dropping from her helpless fingers.

Mrs. Olson walked to the back of the store with Demi and out a door Marilyn hadn't noticed.

Marilyn wanted to scream at Mrs. Olson, "What are you doing with Demi, let her go," but she could only sob incoherently as Roy Olson picked her up and carried her out through a side door into a large lot shielded by a high privacy fence.

Opening the locked door of a wooden shed, Olson said, "You brought our baby back to us, so it's only fair that you get to see your mother." And he threw her carelessly inside.

Impenetrable blackness fell over her as he closed and locked the door, but not before she saw a human skull with a few scraps of long hair and, heaped in a pile, yellowish bones with what looked like small teeth marks all over them.

As she lay in the darkness, hearing the rustle of tiny feet about her, she moaned, "Mama, mama," and realized only then whom it was she was truly calling.

Golden Dreams

Rob Wojtasiewicz

The old-timers have told him not to come here at night, but he scorns them. Now is his time, not theirs. Let them cower as they will, he fears not the dreams of those long dead.

Surely at least one of those who died in the fire had secrets. A buried hoard perhaps, or a rich vein. If he listens to the dreams, he knows he will hear those secrets. So he has come to wait, and to listen.

He sets up his camp between hundred-year-old stone walls, the last remnants of a huge bunkhouse. Hundreds of men once lived in this valley, working their river-claims in the daytime, eating and sleeping in the bunkhouse at night. Then fire swept through the wooden interior and destroyed the place. Men died in their sleep that night, and their dreams still linger. Dreams of love and hate, dreams of riches and power.

He builds a fire after sunset and sits comfortably with his back against a rock. He sips birch-root tea and gazes into the flames. His thoughts are of gold, and what he could buy if he had enough of it. He closes his eyes and relaxes, sees a jumble of images: food, a whiskey bottle, poker cards, a woman. He sees her half-unbuttoned blouse, her laughing face, her eyes, her lips. . . .

He loses track of the time, and of himself.

A chill takes him and he opens his eyes. The fire has almost died. He feeds it carefully, coaxes it to a cheerful blaze. But inside he is still cold. He builds the fire higher. And higher. Soon he has used up his entire night's reserve. He curses, picks up his flashlight, and heads into the forest to collect more wood.

The forest seems different, the trees smaller. His flashlight dims and then dies completely. He hits it against his leg and it starts working again, but it flickers and dims if he moves it around too fast.

The night is alive with sounds: shufflings and whispers, and then he hears what might be a scream. Not a woman, or a child. This is the sound of a man about to die. It fades, and he realizes it was only the creaking of the trees in the wind. Surely no more than that.

He gathers dead wood from the ground, shaking the flashlight every time it dims. When his arms are full, he turns toward his camp, or at least to where he thinks it should be. But no glow from the fire makes its way into the woods. No odor of smoke to tell him he is near. How on earth did he get so far away?

And then he hears the scream again. Loud and unmistakable, it chills him, freezes him. He drops firewood. The flashlight falls with it and goes out. Another scream pierces the night.

From the direction of the scream comes a faint odor, born on the nighttime breeze. It disturbs him. He knows he has smelled it before, and he knows it is bad, but he cannot quite place it.

He knows he should stay right where he is until morning, or crawl slowly and carefully in the other direction, but a strange curiosity takes him, and . . . and hunger! The odor is stronger, the smell of cooking meat, and it no longer disturbs him.

The smell draws him and he moves toward it, feeling with his hands and feet and legs for branches and rocks. Finally he stumbles into one of the crumbling bunkhouse walls. From the other side, from his camp, the screams continue. The smell of meat is very strong. His hunger is deep. He works his way to an opening in the wall and looks.

The fire is blazing brightly. Beside it, a group of men crouch around a prone figure. Their knives flash as they carve their victim's flesh. Some of the men eat the flesh raw, others impale it upon their knife points and thrust it into the fire.

He approaches them, and they move to one side and the other, making a place for him. He draws his own knife from its belt sheath, and it gleams golden in the firelight.

As he carves off a piece of the man's chest, he looks at the face, and is neither shocked nor horrified to see his own reflection gazing at him from pain-maddened eyes.

In the morning, all that remains are charred bones, a knife, and fresh young dreams to soothe the restless dead.

Good Morning. It's Me!

John Maclay

"Good morning. It's me!" she would hear him say at the start of each new day, as he stood in the bathroom shaving and she stirred in the bedroom outside.

"I know. It had better be!" she would invariably reply. It had become a formula for them, a ritual that made their awakenings more familiar, more reassuring.

They had been together for three years. It had been a rough road at first, since she, at thirty-plus, had endured a succession of bad relationships. She had been slow to trust him, because her commitments to other men had too often been abused.

But this one was different—or so she wanted to believe. He was familiar, a person who was the self she thought him to be, someone she could know. And that was why this morning reassurance, light as it was, had become important to her.

"Good morning. It's me!"

"I know." And not only, "It had better be," but it was.

She resisted the first danger signs, although she couldn't mistake them. He began coming home late from work, saying he had stopped for some drinks with some friends. And indeed, his breath smelled of whiskey and his manner was friendly. That manner extended to her, too, so she didn't complain. It often ended in bed, as well, making complaint the farthest thing from her mind.

But then he came home smelling of whiskey . . . and perfume. And not only had their former intimate dinners vanished, but when he went to bed, all he wanted was sleep.

"Good morning. It's me!" he still said, although a bit weakly.

But, while she still replied, no longer did she know.

* * *

After that, he became abusive. In order to lessen his guilt at what he was doing, he tried to lay it off on her. He loudly accused her of being distant, and even of seeing other men. And when she protested, he only said that proved it, that she protested too much.

Then, just as the others had, he began to hit her. It first happened on the night when she finally confronted him, not even blaming him for his infidelities, but instead asking where she had failed.

He was caught off guard by her unselfishness. And so, given his guilt and who he finally was, her only answer was a stinging slap across the face.

"Good morning. It's me!"

But she knew it wasn't. It had better be—but he wasn't better, and he hadn't been, all along.

The final morning—before she cried her heart out, packed her things and left him—held something that, in her long life ahead, she would hardly believe. But it did happen—and, she would convince herself, in order to show her just how horrible he had become. Later, she would at last find a good man, but she would still look back upon that day.

"Good morning. It's me!" he said from the bathroom—his voice now mean and husky, the words a mockery of the formula, the ritual she once had loved.

And that was when, peering from the bedroom, she saw . . . the gray, slimy, many-lobed face, and the dozen tentacles, reaching!

That was who he was—and who, thank God, she would escape.

"Good morning.
"It's *not* me!"

Good Dog

Donald R. Burleson

Evening came on like a darkening mood, turning the square of light at the kitchen window from gold to pale red, then ashen gray, with a grumble of thunder somewhere in the gathering gloom. But Elsa had better things to do than be gloomy, and was in far too good company for that. Elsa was going to feed her dog.

"You'll like the treats I've got for you tonight, Tote," she said, running a palsied hand down his furry back. "I walked all the way to Fletcher's Market and back to bring you these."

She loved the way the old German shepherd transfixed her, as he did now, with that relentless stare that said: Feed me this instant, I'll brook no nonsense, you understand, because I'm hungry—feed me *now*. It allowed a little hint of warmth to creep back into her old frame, this feeling, this knowledge that something—no, some*one*, someone family since time out of mind—still needed her this much. The dog was family, and he depended on her; he was the only creature in the world now who did.

She scrabbled the pungent dog biscuits out of the box and directed them to the dog's mouth, which was more than ready to receive them. "I swear, Tote, you old sweetheart, you've got a bigger stomach than any ten dogs I've ever seen." The biscuits disappeared into the wide eager-looking mouth, the big jaws chewed and chewed. "But never you mind, I love to see you eat."

Outside, the night wind sent cold October rain whispering against the windowpanes, a forlorn sound, and Elsa sat in her little island of light and fed her dog, and remembered the things of her life. A person's life was a mosaic where the tiles fit in jumbled and crazy ways, if they managed to fit at all, and one by one the tiles faded and cracked and fell away, leaving gaping spaces of darkness. Children grew up and married and moved away and became distant half-remembered faces that one never glimpsed. A husband played boyishly with a puppy, watched him carry a piece of kindling across the room, and named him Tote; then twelve years later that husband became a bleak angular name chiseled on a stone in a somber moss-grown churchyard, and you lived in an empty house.

Well, not empty, really, she told herself, running her hand down Tote's long furry back again and slipping another biscuit into his mouth and watching the teeth mesh, the jaws grind.

The thunder shook the windowpanes, the black night looked in at her through the window, pitiless, showing her her own tired face in the glass, declaring her to be old and weak and alone. But she didn't mind.

"No, not as long as I have you, Tote, old boy," she said, watching him eat, watching the subtle light reflected in those faithful old eyes.

No, she didn't mind that the walls reverberated only to her own voice, didn't mind that her children and grandchildren never came to visit. She didn't mind the somberness of the night, the chill of the wind, and the rain at the window. She didn't mind the fact that good old Tote was past being able to eat out of his old yellow bowl, and could only eat out of her hand. She didn't mind that what moved in those deep canine eyesockets was not eyes. She didn't even mind the place that had fallen away near the base of his throat, where most of the food came back out, didn't mind working the jaws with her hands, didn't even mind the smell. Why should she mind anything, really, with a good dog in the house?

And Tote was a good dog, even now.

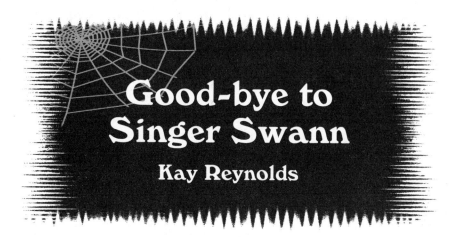

Good-bye to Singer Swann

Kay Reynolds

I was just trying to keep to myself that night when Chrystal Swann walked into the Intermission. Right away she homed in on Paulie Moncman like a sacrificial pigeon. *Oh shit*, I thought. *Here we go again.*

"Hello, Paulie," she said. "Singer likes your new Firebird. That's some car."

"Get lost and get a life," Paulie snapped, mean and sharp. But nervous, too.

Chrys only said, "Singer's still waiting. He wonders when you're going to keep your promise. I told him I'd ask." Moncman's party had gone real quiet real sudden. Ira raced over to try to keep things cool. I beat him to it. "Hi, Bracey," she said to me and gave me her sweetest smile, full blast.

"It's been a while, Chrys." I knew I sounded like an idiot but no one seemed to notice. "Let's take a hike and catch up."

Ira shot me a half-grateful, half-aggravated look as we took off. Paulie Moncman, however, is screaming: "I can't take this anymore! That crazy bitch follows me everywhere. When is it going to stop?"

I slammed the door on his bellowing. It was a loud, wounded noise, a man with a bad conscience going toxic. I didn't believe Chrystal actually followed Paulie. They just kept turning up at the same place. Like a curse.

Outside, the night-quiet seemed awkward to me but talking was worse. Chrys proved it by starting up: "Singer's so unhappy. He's cold and awfully lonely. None of his fans know where to find him. He's still got fans, you know." Her voice went confidential. "He's afraid Paulie is going to let him down."

Absolutely. Paulie Moncman is the worst kind of vampire—a rock 'n' roll agent. You could SRO Madison Square and *not* run out of people Paulie's let down. But that's old misery. What's rough is hearing Chrystal talk about her brother as if he's still alive. Which he is not. Singer Swann has been dead for over a year now.

If you don't remember, Singer was what folks call a one-hit wonder. After that, nothing. He toured and toured on the strength of that one glory and was still raking in the bucks until he got sick.

Funny how disease can finish a career. It can sure wipe out a bank account, even an account like Singer Swann's. Still, you'd think there'd be enough left to provide a proper headstone. Something to say, *Here there was a life.* Moncman promised Singer he'd take care of it. Personally.

Yeah. Right.

Chrys and I kept walking. After a while I said: "I miss Singer almost as much as you. Sometimes it's hard to say good-bye but you've got to do it. You're only going to make trouble for yourself if you keep on like this. Moncman is a mean bastard. He'll hurt you if he can."

"Singer told me you'd say that." Chrys smiled again. "It's okay."

God. It is definitely *not* okay. I struggled to think of something better when, suddenly, there's this noise like thunder—loud! Yellow light washes over us, flame without warmth. I grab onto Chrys and start to run but she's rooted like stone on the pavement, staring ahead.

It's Paulie Moncman and his new Firebird bearing down on us. He's finally cracked—big time. Chrys grabs on to me, too, and drags me into her panic. That's not hard to do.

I am wishing we could just levitate out of there when I notice we're not alone anymore. Someone is standing between us and Paulie's death machine. *A suicidal idiot,* I am thinking. Then there's no time to think. No time at all.

The car goes up. Then it goes over—flips back on its top, flips again, and keeps going. When it stops, it's one long, flaming metal slab pointing up at the sky.

"Never dis my family, Paulie, or my fans," Singer Swann says. His voice sounds pretty normal . . . for a ghost.

I've got no clue what to say. Except: "That's a hell of a tombstone, Singer. A genuine landmark."

"Yeah." He grins as sweet as his sister even while he's fading. "I always knew Paulie would come through for me."

I shook my head. Hell. You could have fooled me.

Gorgon
Brian Hodge

Many times, many ways, it's been said that you can't go home again, and the night was bearing this out. Fifteen years of higher education and real world later, and those same dramas and sorrows and stupidities started playing themselves out all over again. On the same gym floor where I grew into my jockstrap.

Usually on the sidelines.

"If it's any consolation," Alana said, "Janis Joplin had a lousy time at her reunion too. Nobody'd admit she'd accomplished anything, so they fell right back into their same cruel patterns."

"Very inspiring," I said. "Pass the heroin, would you?"

Renewed acquaintances consisted of a few nods, a few snubs, a few hellos dripping with insincerity. Most of the others from the top GPA percentiles had apparently found reasons to stay away, someplace where using your brain wasn't such a crime.

I wanted to believe that bringing Alana wasn't psychological warfare, my best revenge in the form of living well—but why lie? Gratifyingly, the same high school that to me was mere preamble, had clearly been the pinnacle for many a tormentor.

Although I doubted many of *them* had needed sexual counseling before their marriages. Which I could at least leave off my "Accomplishments Since Graduation" questionnaire.

Alana and I went for punch, and were at the hospitality table before I realized I'd've been better off thirsty.

"Aren't you going to introduce me to your . . . companion?" asked the Medusa with the ladle.

"Hello, Miss Chaplin," I said, then stared at the table during most of the exchange, not wanting to look into that lewdly hungry face any more than necessary. Even if it was starting to shrivel.

"Greg," she demanded, as though I were still her student, "why *did* Venus rise from the sea?"

I stammered that I didn't remember, and after we'd escaped, I set our untouched punch on another table; I would sooner dehydrate than think of Miss Chaplin's hands filling the cups.

"My God, you're shaking," Alana said. "What was that about?"

I explained how Miss Chaplin was one of those teachers you took one look at, and knew she wasn't married and never would be. She'd flirted with boys who even then were half her age, but there was nothing of innocent longing in it; rather, a leering intensity that made flesh crawl, as she dragged a wet thumb along your hand while returning a paper, or undressed you with buggy eyes. She'd flirt with the jocks, naturally, but with me, she was more like a lioness after a gazelle limping along the edge of the herd.

"What was with that quiz about the birth of Venus?"

I told Alana I didn't know.

But I lied—

—*remembering vividly that day in the book closet after lit class, the sudden lumpy press of her when I turned around, coffee on her breath and insecticide perfume on her skin, as she touched me with hot doughy hands and murmured of Aphrodite, Venus, goddess of love and sensual desire—*

I had to sit down, ill. Minutes later, when Alana suggested we admit the night an unsalvageable loss, I was grateful.

"I'll get the car, then. Meet you out front?"

"Hurry," I said—

—remembering the squash of her tongue on my mouth before I pushed her away, then Miss Chaplin's terrible offense that I would reject the advances of the goddess she must've wanted to be—

Weaving through nostalgia, dodging mirror-ball starlight, I reached the front steps and sat, still hearing bad renditions of songs I hadn't much liked the first time around.

Watching.

Waiting.

While Alana never came—

—remembering now the blade, and her terrible need, and my loathsome sophomore shame as she gripped me down there and told me of the birth of Venus, and how after such an implied threat I went through with it after all—

And I swear it was Miss Chaplin that I glimpsed now, in the shadows of the parking lot, skulking and vengeful, after some far-off car horn began its neverending keen—

—"Venus wasn't born of love, let me tell you," she'd said. "Remember Cronos, one of the Titans? He overthrew his father and castrated him, and where it fell into the water the foam gathered . . . and that's where Venus rose from the sea.

"Remember that, Greg. Remember that the next time I want you. Because someday, there will *be a test."*

I followed the siren song of that blaring horn, and began to contemplate the mythic price of failure.

Graveyard Dirt

Terry Campbell

Ernie failed to see the harm in it. His collection, that is. Every boy should have a hobby, a collection, but milk caps and baseball cards just didn't interest Ernie. He would much rather collect graveyard dirt.

Ernie's father didn't agree, and made that belief perfectly clear to his son. You should be out playing baseball or chasing girls, not sitting in some goddamned bone yard writing ignorant poems and digging up tainted dirt, he would say. That kinda behavior ain't right.

But still, Ernie collected his graveyard dirt, in little glass jars he picked up at M. E. Moses for fifty cents each. And his dad just kept turning the other way, until the evening Ernie returned with a jar of dirt from his grandmother's grave.

Screaming something about desecrating his momma's grave, Ernie's father grabbed all of his son's jars and carried them into the backyard. He pulled the corks from the jars and, one by one, emptied the contents onto the ground.

Ernie could only stand and watch, mortified.

It was a week later when the grass in the backyard slowly began to die. The blades started turning brown; the tips grew brittle. There was a large brown patch of dead grass where his father had disposed of Ernie's collection.

So Ernie took a jar and went out to the nearest cemetery, filled the glass container and headed back into town. He paused a moment in the town square, near the base of the large, century-old oak tree, and poured the dirt into the soil around the trunk.

A week later, the proud old oak was dead.

Ernie suspected he had discovered a power beyond his wildest imagination, but he knew someone who could tell him for sure. A quick trip to the banks of Caddo Lake to visit the old medicine woman confirmed his guess. "Graveyard dirt is a right powerful thing," the old woman had said. "You can't use it nowheres else, 'cause it's spoiled earth. You use it to build with, that land's cursed for eternity. You plant with it, ain't nothin' gonna grow. Graveyard dirt carries the spirit of the dead with it."

After that, Ernie went happily on his way, gathering up more samples that he kept carefully hidden from his dad. But he needed a greater experiment. And he found the opportunity one day while watching some men preparing a concrete slab for a new gas station being built on Highway 52. While the men were on break, Ernie poured a jar into the wheelbarrow the men used to mix their concrete.

A week later, a backhoe ran over a worker, killing him instantly.

Ernie was delighted; he had a power no one else knew about.

No one except the medicine woman of Caddo Lake. She knew what Ernie had been doing, and she confronted him with it on his next visit.

"Boy, you ain't using the graveyard dirt proper," she said through blackened nubs of teeth. "You usin' it for ill will, when you should be usin' it for good."

"How can I use it for good?" Ernie asked. "You said it's tainted."

"And it is. But it can be reversed. If you mix in dirt from holy ground."

"What happens then?" Ernie asked.

"It brings life instead of death."

Ernie, ever the experimenter, did just that. He mixed dirt from the churchyard into one particular jar, and paid a visit to a familiar cemetery.

Now, his father doesn't ever say anything about Ernie's collection. In fact, he doesn't say much of anything anymore. Gramma said it was okay, and Ernie supposed that if gramma didn't mind, his daddy didn't mind.

And since gramma came back that night, covered in graveyard dirt and stinking of the earth she was buried in, Ernie's father has just been sitting in his easy chair, staring into space, babbling on about boys and their hobbies.

Green Fingers

Hugh B. Cave

You think you know what "scared" means? Let me tell you.

I was alone, see? My friend, Ed Carlin, had offered me the use of his cabin out at the lake, and I'd gone out there to rest up for a few days. Rest up from what, you say? I'm an artist. Among other things, I do book jackets. And I had just finished the jacket for the latest novel by a big name in the horror field.

Naturally, his editors had to have his approval of the jacket, and this famous author, wanting everything his way, demanded changes that all but drove me crazy. So when I got out there to Ed Carlin's camp, I didn't fish or go for walks in the woods. I just opened a bottle of bourbon and sat.

I arrived about three in the afternoon. By nightfall I was still sitting there in the cabin's small front room, relaxing. And I heard footfalls.

Not human footfalls. Not even animal ones, although we do have bears in our woods. This was a heavy, wet, sloshing sound—*shlumph! shlumph! shlumph!*—coming up from the lake.

I struggled to my feet just as the door shuddered open.

You don't have to believe this, but the thing in the doorway was the creature I'd just finished painting for the jacket of the famous writer's book. Naked. Ugly. Ten feet tall, with long, dangling arms and huge hands. A head too big even for a body that size, with big, glowing eyes. A snarly mouth full of fangs.

Good thing I wasn't sober. I'd have died right then and there, of fright.

"Wait, now," I said. "Hold on a minute. Ease up. I didn't invent you, for God's sake. All I did was paint you the way he described you."

It made a grunting noise that sounded like "Huh?" so loud the cabin shook as if we were having an earthquake.

"Three times he made me do you over!" I wailed. "Three times!"

"Who?" the thing demanded.

"The man who created you, for God's sake. If you're here in the flesh, you must know who he is. Back off, now! If you don't like what you are, it isn't my fault."

The monster stood there for a while, dripping water all over the cabin floor while those fiery eyes did their best to burn holes in me. Then it lurched about and went striding out into the night. And I heard the footsteps again—*shlumph! shlumph! shlumph!*—as it went back to the lake.

Believe me, I was real sober by then. In two minutes I was out of there myself, driving back to my city apartment like my four-cylinder car had turned itself into a rocket ship. When I got there I called the big-name author and told him what happened.

He laughed. It really tickled him. He just laughed and laughed and laughed.

But two days later I heard on the news that his housekeeper had found him dead in bed with his neck broken and a lot of slimy green fingerprints all over his face. And I remembered his editor saying to me, when she demanded the final change in the jacket of his book, "You have to do the creature's hands over. He says they have to be green."

Green Magic

Leslie R. Walstrom

I paid good money for that toy, Michael. If you won't play with it, I'll call that man and get my three dollars back."

"I won't let you."

"Try to stop me."

"I'll run away and join the circus."

"An elephant will step on you."

Dad was trying to look stern, but Michael could tell he held back a smile.

"I'll shoot you with that." Michael pointed at a giant cannon at the other end of the arena.

"I'll shoot you out of that cannon, all the way to Never-Never Land."

A great clump of phosphorescent wands floated up the aisle, the shadow of a man attached.

Michael hugged his wand to his chest. In the arena lit only by flying flecks from a hundred spinning mirrored balls, children twirled their wands, releasing power into a room already so overflowing with magic that most of it was wasted.

The man who sold magic disappeared before Michael's dad could make good on his threat. Michael pulled the cord around his neck, slipping the wand into his neckline. The potion within it caused him to glow green beneath his white shirt, as if he'd drunk a bowl of the stuff.

Three spotlights hit the rings, and Dad turned his attention to the trained elephants and tigers. The tumbling girls with naked legs came next, and Michael knew he was safe. When the clowns brought out their buggies, Michael jumped up, waving his arms, with throngs of other children. Suddenly an acrobat lifted him into the air and plopped him down into a buggy. He sat between a girl who smelled of cotton candy and a boy who bounced on his seat, making the buggy rattle and the clown angry.

After the ride, Michael was last to be returned to his seat.

"Why do you hide the toy?" the clown asked.

"I want to save the magic."

"Magic belongs at the circus. You shouldn't try to take it with you."

Michael pouted. The clown wouldn't ruin it for him. Michael glared at him, then jumped from the buggy and scrambled up over the low wall, running back to his seat. The clown was yelling, trying to draw his attention back. But the shouting and laughter around Michael distorted the words until they turned into meaningless sounds, like a spell chanted in an ancient language. Michael kept his head down, hoping the clown would forget about him and go away. Finally another clown came up behind the first, honking a horn and hurrying him along, followed by a purple poodle that yapped at his heels.

At home Michael kissed his dad good-night and went to bed without argument. No need to keep the closet light on tonight. He dropped his shirt and his jeans on the floor, and climbed into bed wearing his briefs and his magic. He kept the wand tied around his neck until he heard the last sounds of his father's day: the flush of a toilet, the opening of a window. When the house was silent, he sat up and curled his legs Indian style. He slipped the wand from his neck and slowly swung it by its cord, watching it light first one knee and then the other, the newly scraped, then the newly healed. It gathered momentum, twirling around faster and faster like the wands of the children at the circus. The wand glowed green and Michael glowed green, and he smiled and green light shone from his eyes and beat in his heart.

Then tiny shards of light like flecks from a hundred spinning mirrored balls exploded from the wand and flew through the room. As the light spun, so did Michael on his bed, growing dizzier and dizzier. "I want to stop now!" he cried, but still he spun. "Daddy!" he tried, but no sound at all came then.

Light is silent, and Michael had become light. He became a tiny green fleck dancing on the wall, until morning came and the wand grew dim.

Michael danced again that night, and all the nights of the circus, a bit of light among millions of bits of light. He danced on arena walls across the country. He flitted past the eyes of children and across the backs of elephants. When his father came to the circus alone the next year, Michael paused to rest upon his hand until the mirrored ball began to spin again, carrying him away to dance among the purple poodles.

Half Life

Joel Ross

I sit, gnarled fingers grasping my pistol. If you can't get your dream, get even.

I recall Dad's death, when I was fourteen. It took two weeks to find his body. Later, as if in a dream, I heard the minister drone on about "Resurrection of the Flesh." Did that mean Dad was condemned to spend Eternity in that putrefied body I had discovered in woods a mile from our home?

After the funeral I spent years brooding, drifting into obsession with life and, by extension, death. My existence was a coin, currently heads, but perhaps in fifty years, or the next thirty seconds, becoming tails. At the end would there just be a black, stiffened corpse? Never!

I determined how to live indefinitely, until science rendered death a vague memory.

I worked nights, weekends, holidays. What I lacked in intellect I compensated for with compulsion. I didn't make medical school but squeezed into a doctoral program in genetics, then finagled a job with Saranac Lake's Cell Research Center, staying there nineteen years in astronautlike isolation.

I was forty-six, and had wasted two-thirds of that time obsessed. True, I was an expert in gerontology. So what? I was closer to the end of my life than to the beginning.

Then I came across research by Raphael Kumys and noted references to his work on life extension dating from the turn of the century.

I cornered him in his lab, a man looking about fifty.

"I've admired your work," I said, "starting from 1900."

"You've mistaken me for my father."

"No, it's you." I waved monographs at him. "I can prove it."

"What do you want?"

"To be part of your research, or else."

His eyes locked onto mine, then he surrendered. "Meaning what?"

"You claimed in 1911 you isolated genes that might retard aging. You're at least 130."

"Over 150," he admitted. "I won't divulge the secret."

"I want those techniques used on me."

"We're born to die."

"You don't believe that, and I won't. Help me."

"If you avoid aging, you'll lose family, friends."

"I have no friends."

"Make some," he said. "Otherwise, it's existence, not life." He got a sly look. "What's it worth to you?"

"Everything."

"'Everything' it shall be. Give me all your possessions."

I signed over all I owned.

"I'm nearing a breakthrough and don't need distractions of some young fool drawing undue attention. Plus, the money can further my research involving electromagnetic stimulation which perpetuates cell regeneration infinitely beyond the normal twenty times."

"Which cells?"

"Of the pituitary, thyroid, and pineal."

He hooked electrodes all over me, threw switches, and I blacked out. When I awoke, they were removed.

"That's it?" I asked. "I feel no different."

"How should immortality feel?"

I jumped up and set a match to the papers turning over my money to him. He looked aghast.

"Don't!" he said.

"Why should you have everything? If I'm going to live forever, why shouldn't I be rich?"

I fled.

"Wait!" he screamed, clawing to detain me. "You can't leave!"

I should have known that it was too good to be true. The first indication that something was wrong—or right—was five years later. I needed reading glasses. Except for that, I felt fine for another decade until I developed arthritis in my hands. My thinning hair whitened, and my skin dried and wrinkled from the long, harsh Adirondack winters.

Kumys had vanished after my alleged "treatment." Forty years had passed, leaving me decrepit and vengeful. No day passed that I didn't curse his memory.

Even at eighty-six, I was still driven, only this time it was by vengeance. Searching every medical journal, I at last found Kumys in Sacramento.

Despite my frailness and failing sight, I could shoot. I waited for him to leave one night and raised the revolver just as he strode into my sight.

I fired. And missed.

"Who are you? Are you insane? There are valuable chemicals here!" He yanked the gun from me, fracturing my index finger in the process. I fell, screaming and writhing.

"You bastard! You liar. I'll kill you!"

"Who are you?" He looked for witnesses.

"Thomsen. You lied to me!"

"Thomsen? Oh, the one who got the treatment."

"There was no treatment! Charlatan! Quack!"

"No?" he said. "Then why do I look the same as when we first met?"

"You can't fool me. I'm old. Dying! Why?"

"You're old. That's not my fault."

"You bastard. You said I'd live forever."

"And you shall. You ran before I finished the treatment." He shrugged. "What good's eternal life without eternal youth?"

Harvest
Fred Behrendt

The garden trowel's tip was denuded of paint from a season of use and glinted with steely brightness in the hot autumn sun. He watched as she stroked the tip across an irregularity in the muddy lump in her gloved hand, dislodging a coarse gray flake. Within he saw a tangle of dead legs crammed into the cylindrical cell of a wasp's nest. A single fat larva, white as polished bone, pulsed and strained, feeding obliviously. Its pin head burrowing in the abdomen of a dead spider that, in life, would have been large enough to span a Kennedy half-dollar with its outstretched legs.

"Poor spiders," she murmured. Her lips formed a brief, wry smile.

She dropped the nest back into the flower pot where she had found it.

As she turned, he scanned her blonde hair, her precise and lovely features. He wondered why such a beautiful woman, an accomplished entomologist at that, would remain single. But he was just her student, and kept his questions to himself as he turned and chopped the shovel into the end of the trench she had sweet-talked him into digging. For a little extra credit, she had said.

She squatted down, thrusting the trowel into the muddy grass for balance.

"Make it just a bit longer," she said, indicating the projected length with her free hand. "Make sure you pile the earth up on that side."

"If you don't mind my asking, Doctor," he asked, "what is this hole for anyway? It's a little late in the year for planting."

"A little yearly breeding work I do in the garden."

"Something to do with your bugs?"

"Yes," she said. "Of course."

The soil was thick with clay and resisted the thrust of the shovel. He committed his arms, shoulders and hips into the next deliberate stroke. He broke out an especially large clod of gummy earth. Something roughly tubular, caked with tan mud, rolled into the trench behind the earth clod. He stooped and picked it up, thumbing away layers of mud. It appeared to be—why yes it was—a bone. He could almost swear it was the metatarsus of a human foot.

She was beside him then. The crown of her head, as she leaned in to examine what he held, brushed his face.

He breathed her faint odor of sweat. It was sweet. He had imagined it would be.

"How odd," she said. "What would a bone be doing here? In my garden?"

She looked up into his face. Very close to him. She smiled another of her tight-lipped smiles.

She plucked the shovel away from his left hand and brushed the bone from the palm of his right. Her breasts were very firm as she pressed them into his chest.

Her soft, full lips pressed upward onto his assertively. Her kiss tasted, to him, as sweet as her smell.

Then his mouth flooded with bitterness. It was not a wholly unpleasant taste but, surprised, he tried pulling away. Her arms were around him by now and her embrace became a hard, inescapable grip.

He sought to speak, to push her away and it was then he realized the tingling remoteness of his hands and feet. Even his jaw had become a distant, unresponsive lever.

Her eyes remained before his. She had gone up onto her toes to put her mouth on his. But now she rocked back onto her heels, descending, pulling a short distance away. Her throat, he saw, had unfolded like a blossom of moist flesh. A slender black tendril, sinewy and striated with glistening bands, extended from its center to a point below his chin. He felt nothing but a faint tugging and realized it was rooted somehow in his own throat. As he watched, unable to move anything but his unblinking eyes, the tendril pulsed obscenely and something squirmed through its length toward his throat.

He lifted his eyes to hers.

Her eyes rolled upward in apparent ecstasy, and she smiled and this time, at last, revealed the bundle of overlapping mandibles behind her lips.

The Haunted Nursery

Brian Stableford

The Englishman, the Scotsman and the Irishman agreed that they would take turns entering the haunted nursery and make every effort to stay there all night. They each put £100 into the pot; the one who contrived to remain in there for the longest time would scoop the pool. They cut cards to decide who would go first, and the Englishman drew the lowest.

After twenty-five minutes, the Englishman was back in the drawing-room pouring himself a very large brandy.

"That's no *ordinary* haunted room," he told the Scotsman and the Irishman. "I met the Devil himself. That wouldn't have been so bad if I'd been able to face up to him man-to-man, but I wasn't. The moment I looked at him I was thirteen again, in my first term at Eton, fagging for that sadistic bastard Harding. He made my life a living hell, you know—I can't go into details. A living hell. It was worse than the army—worse than the Gulf, worse than Belfast before the cease-fire—because I wasn't *equipped*. I wasn't trained. There's only one thing worse than being thirteen in a living hell, and that's *going back* to being thirteen in a living hell—being stripped of all the adult equipment, all the training, being reduced to absolute helplessness and *knowing* just how pathetically and ridiculously helpless you are. I'd forgotten it all, buried it and blanked it out—but *he* brought it all back again. I could take having my eyes plucked out, but not that."

The Scotsman and the Irishman had a good laugh about that before the Scotsman took his own turn in the haunted nursery.

He was back in the drawing-room twenty-five minutes later, pouring himself a huge whiskey.

"Same bloody thing," he said, in his terse Scottish manner. "Devil in disguise. I wor nae but six year old an' ma bloody da had his bloody belt off again. Blubbin' like a babe, I was. All ma life I've been tellin' maesel' that if ever I'd got holt o' that bastard when we were two of a size I'd ha' kicked the shit out o' him an' spat on the wreck—but I wor nae but six year old and there was nithin' I could do while that brass buckle came down an' down an' down agin. Nithin' at all—an' I *remembered* everythin' I'd forgot about all o' that stuff. Every bloody thing I'd buried an' blanked. I could ha' taken havin' ma eyes plucked out, but no' that. No' that."

This time, it was only the Irishman who laughed. As the Irishman went off to the haunted nursery to take his turn, the Englishman said: "Do you think he has sense or sensitivity enough to be taken the same way?"

"I give him ten minutes," the Scotsman said, grimly. "Not a bloody minute more."

The Irishman came back after exactly ten minutes. He poured himself a modest glass of whiskey and sipped it delicately, as if he'd never tasted it before. Then he turned to his adversaries.

" 'Twas the Divvil all right," he said. "Hisself in all his foul an' fire-an'-brimstone glory, just like the Faithers up at Saint Pat's used to tell us. Never thought to see the like. Four years old, I thought I was, before me first communion—an' lookin' the Divvil hisself in the burnin' yeller eye." He stopped, and took another appreciative sip from his glass.

"And then what?" said the Englishman, breathlessly wanting to hear the gory details before he and the Scotsman split the pot.

"I just said, 'How d'ye do, Musther Divvil—'T must be awful dull an' lonely stuck in this pokey little room fer all eternity. Would ye like to swap bodies wi' me for a little while, so that I can win a bet against a Presbyterian an' a public schoolboy?' An' the Divvil said, 'Sure'—an' here he is."

And the Irishman—or whatever was wearing his body just then—reached out with one clawed hand to pluck out the anxious eyes of the Englishman and the Scotsman, while the other collected the £300.

Heart of the Garden
Caro Soles

I t isn't a baby. We just call it that 'cause it sounds so safe. Normal. Suburban, you know? Sure. Like everyone has a small grave in the garden that oozes salt tears and moans in the night, right?

You know, when we bought the place we got it cheap. An estate sale or something. Anyway, we didn't mind Baby's grave at first. He didn't want much. Just a little attention. The sound of my voice would calm him right down. The touch of my hand against the earth and the tears would stop. Of course in the winter it might get rough, but hey.

Then one night my being there just wasn't enough. The moans and cries got really loud. I was kneeling, my finger against my lips, patting the earth. I mean, I was worried about the neighbours, you know? They might think Sam was beating on me or something. Anyway, there I was in my housecoat, with my face practically on the ground, when I saw the earth move. Well, I tell you I jumped back so fast everything was a blur. Really gave me a start! But the crying kept on so I had to do something. A soother, I thought. Babies like soothers. I grabbed the dog's ball. The rubber kind with a squeaker inside. I pushed it into the soft earth. It came hurtling back at me— hard. It woulda been funny if it hadn't been so weird. I musta laughed sorta crazy and loud, cause a light went on next door. Jesus Murphy. Next I tried the dog's bone. There was still some meat on it and maybe that's what made it appealing. Whatever, the bone stayed down. I went back to bed.

A week later I was out getting the flower beds ready for the annuals. I was surprised to hear the sobbing begin. He usually held off till it was dark. Maybe the changing of the seasons was confusing him. This time I went right inside and got a bone from the rib roast we'd had on Sunday. It was Sam's birthday, you know. That man sure loves his roast beef. So I thrust the bone straight down into the earth. Then I stood back and watched that thing sucked into the soil like some great animal was pulling on it.

"Ya know, hon, maybe we should check out what's really down there," Sam suggested, when I told him about Baby's new trick.

I shook my head. "The real estate guy said it was somebody's pet cat. Like years and years ago. There wouldn't be anything left now."

Sam shook his head. "Must be something, hon."

I had to agree. Besides, Baby was gettin' kind of expensive taste. On the other hand, it *was* a grave. . . .

It went on like that for a while longer. I'd take out some scraps from dinner and for a while that kept the crying away.

Then one day the scraps weren't enough. It was about nine o'clock and dusk was dropping around us and the crying was soft and pitiful like someone just lost their best friend in all the world. The neighbour's cat had killed a robin and I was holding the still warm body in my hands as I knelt beside Baby. The cat crouched nearby, watching.

"Scram," I hissed, as I laid the tiny body on the ground. I was going to go back to the house to get some macaroni and cheese for Baby when the earth caved in and the bird disappeared. I just stared. Next thing I knew the cat leapt after it and then—no more cat. It was obscene the way the ground heaved up and down for a few seconds, then was still.

"Hon, maybe it's time," Sam said, watching.

I put my hand on the ground and felt a tremor, almost like a heartbeat. "Be gentle, Sam."

He came back with a shovel. We didn't have far to go before we saw Baby. Well, I guess we'll have to find another name for him. Baby doesn't suit a garden gnome. Even if he is buried. Even if he doesn't look much like one anymore. Still. What do you think of the name Attila?

Heartbeat

S. May Amarinth

When I found out that my heart had stopped beating, my first thought was that I must be mistaken, but after twenty minutes of searching for a pulse, I was convinced that there was none to be found.

Then I thought that I must be mad. I thought my senses had to be deranged, that the fault was in my head and not in my heart at all. But then I realised that there was no more rational response to such a situation than to wonder whether I might be mad. The very suspicion was secure proof of my sanity.

After that I was terrified that someone might find out. I knew that I could keep it secret for a while, but not for ever. It wasn't so much the doctor I was worried about—no, that wasn't it at all. I supposed that I could easily steer clear of doctors, unless I got knocked down by a bus or something, in which case nobody would be overly surprised to find my heart not beating. It was the thought that I'd have to be careful about getting too close to people. No more snuggling up to the wife, no more cuddling my little daughter. I couldn't take the risk that they might find out—because, out of all the people in the world, they were the two who absolutely mustn't find out. After all, if a stranger were somehow to find out, it needn't be the end of the world. He might not care, and might be perfectly happy not to tell other people, ever, what an unnatural creature was walking in their midst. And if I thought he *might* tell someone, I could always kill him. I'm sure I could kill a stranger, if the need arose, although I'm the most mild-mannered of men.

Perhaps, if I'd been a little less mild-mannered, it wouldn't have happened at all. More assertive men probably have more assertive hearts.

Anyhow, I took good care that nobody found out. I stopped cuddling my wife and I stopped hugging my daughter—and when the divorce came through I told myself that it was all for the best, because now they never would find out what a monster they'd been close to for all those years.

I never attempted suicide. What would have been the point?

I stayed well away from doctors. In fact, I stayed well away from anyone who might get close to me. I went to work every day, of course—that wasn't a problem. At work everyone's too busy to notice whether the man at the next desk has two heads, let alone no heartbeat.

It took me quite a while to come to terms with my condition, but I had to do it. I had to learn to love myself again. I had to recover my lost self-esteem. I made a resolution to tell myself that not having a heartbeat was nothing to be ashamed of, that in actual fact it made me very special indeed. I told myself that a man was better off without a heartbeat, because a non-beating heart could hardly be in danger from hardening arteries or coronary thrombosis. I told myself that I might well be the first of a new and better breed of men, and that if I ever did decide to let my secret out, the scientists who studied me might be able to make a breakthrough that would free the entire human race from all the burdens of heart disease. Day after day I told myself that I was a walking miracle, a precious natural resource waiting to be discovered.

In the end, I convinced myself.

I convinced myself so thoroughly that I decided to go public. I made an appointment to see the doctor—but on the morning of the appointment, my heart started beating again.

Just like that! Years and years of pulselessness, and then *bingo!*

Life can be so bloody unfair, sometimes.

At first, of course, I thought I might be going mad, but I knew that the suspicion itself was proof of my sanity.

I rang my ex-wife and asked her to come home, but she said no.

There's nothing left, it seems, but to walk down to the main road and step out in front of a bus. I don't suppose anyone will ever understand—but at least they'll never know that anything was ever amiss with my heart.

Horror by Sunlight

Lawrence C. Connolly

First Nelson saw the wolves. They lay inside the front door, leering at him with yellow eyes and bared fangs. Julie walked across one of them. "Come on," she said, looking over her shoulder and flashing a coy smile at Nelson. "These wolves won't bite," she said.

She was right, of course. The wolves were nothing but skinned hides—wolf-skin rugs with the heads intact. But seeing them now, after a seemingly endless ride through the Pennsylvania night, was enough to rattle Nelson's already shaky nerves. Julie had told Nelson that her stepfather was eccentric. Now, for the first time, he saw what she meant.

"Come on, silly," said Julie. "Bring those bags inside and shut the door. But be quiet. Daddy's already gone to his room, and we dare not disturb him till morning."

Nelson summoned his remaining strength and lugged a pair of suitcases (both hers) and a flight bag (his) through the foyer and into the wolf-carpeted hall.

Nelson had to bed down alone in the guest room. But he couldn't sleep. Exhausted as he was from the long drive, he lay awake while light from the full moon spilled across his bed. Somewhere a dog whimpered and whined. Nelson tried blocking the sound by wrapping the pillow around his head, but the sound soon escalated from whimpers to growls. Nelson couldn't stand it. The animal sounded as if it were trapped somewhere inside the house, and Nelson, who had always been fond of dogs, couldn't bear to hear a dog moan like that.

He got up and followed the sound to a room at the end of the hall. The whimpers came from behind a locked door. He knelt down and peered through the keyhole. On the other side of the door, a wolf paced through the slatted beams of a lavaliered moon.

Pains of realization stabbed Nelson's chest. In a flash, everything came together. The full moon! The locked room! The eccentric father with the mysterious condition that Julie had promised would be revealed during their weekend visit to his country estate! It was clear now—as clear as the moonlight that shimmered on the wolf's rippling shoulders. Julie's father was a werewolf!

Nelson backed away from the keyhole. He stumbled backward down the hall and threw himself against the door of Julie's room.

Julie sat on the edge of her bed. She was waiting for him. "Sorry," she said as he fell into her arms. "I had to let you find out for yourself. You would have thought me crazy if I told you."

She led Nelson back to the guest room and stayed with him until he drifted into an exhausted sleep.

He awoke to the chirp of birds and the warm smell of bacon and coffee. Sunlight streamed through the bedroom window.

Nelson dressed, telling himself that the madness from the night before had all been a dream. Those rugs in the downstairs hall were enough to make anyone dream of monsters.

Feeling renewed, Nelson descended the stairs. He caught a glimpse of Julie sitting at a long mahogany table. At the table's far end, a white-haired man with rosy cheeks chuckled and spoke to her over the rim of a steaming coffee cup. Yes, it had all been a crazy dream.

"Morning!" said Nelson as he reached the bottom of the stairs.

The white-haired man set down his cup and smiled at Nelson.

"You wouldn't believe the dream I had last night!" he said as he stepped into the hall. "I dreamed—"

He stopped abruptly. He gripped the banister to keep from falling. His mouth released a shriek of terror . . .

It wasn't the wolf skins in the hall that frightened him this time. The wolf skins were gone. In their place lay tan swatches of hairless skin; the human heads smiled at Nelson in the warm glow of the morning sun.

Houses Creaking in the Wind

Steve Rasnic Tem

He can hear flies striking the window. He can hear flies whispering in the rain. He can hear flies buzzing in the spaces between his thoughts.

If he can only understand everything in the flies' song, he thinks, then this house will be transformed, filled with noise and bright color, and maybe, perhaps, he can say that he is still alive.

Each day he rises earlier in this house on the floor of the desert valley. Soon he won't need to sleep at all. Nights will become his mornings.

He has neighbors, but he hasn't spoken to them in years. Their houses are just like his, so he feels there is no need for words between them. There is an understanding in the way the wind moves and the houses creak.

When he heard about the first son, he was standing here in this same spot, gazing out these windows, reading the dark before sleep. The telephone was swift and urgent, and afterward lay like a dead animal in his hand. He put it away and would not pick it up again.

When he heard about the second son, he was on the back porch smoking. His wife came for him, shaking, and he walked out to meet the men at the door. Out on the side of the road past their cars he thought he saw the old skull of an animal he himself had shot as a teenager. The skull still had the light of fear in its eyesockets. He smiled as they told him the story of his son's death, and he knew they would all talk about him later and wonder why. He smiled because of the joke that had been told to him, but he did not tell them this because he'd never been good at repeating jokes.

He was sleeping when they came to tell him about his wife. They let themselves inside and woke him up. "Another joke?" he asked, and saw them looking at each other, not knowing what to make of him. They were different men from the ones who had come the last time, but they held themselves the same. He was glad to be lying down, because he could no longer hold himself up. He thought about sleeping, how the body feels when it sleeps in its own skin. Sometimes we try to sleep in the skins of others, he thought, and we stay awake all night.

There is an understanding in the way the wind moves and the houses creak. He spends all day sweeping the floor clean. Sometimes he pauses to listen for nothing. Then he sweeps the floor again, ridding it even of his footprints.

Each night he waits for the vanished ones to come home. They sit in his chairs, but do not speak. They leave no footprints on his clean floor. He goes out to the porch, and his eyes hunt for the skull, but he has not seen it in years. He goes back into his house as if it is he who is just now arriving. Dinner is on the table, and his sons are singing the fly song. The wind blows past the creaking houses, and his neighbors all come outside to join in the singing.

He is too happy for words. The house is bright with color again, and the air that moves from room to room is as warm as the sun. Outside in the dark yard the neighbors all shout, but here in his warm bright house he opens his mouth to sing and shows each one of his family the song, the flies that have boiled out of his throat, that have gathered on his tongue.

Hunger

Michael A. Burstein

Rodolfo slowly pushed open the coffin from inside. The barest crack revealed no light emanating from outside, so he pushed the cover all the way open. The hinges squeaked loudly from long years of disuse.

Rodolfo sat up, brushed the soil from his clothes, and yawned. He ran his tongue over his teeth, confirming that the canines were still sharp and pointed. It felt so good to be awake and moving again.

How long had he been asleep, anyway? He stood up, and checked the cryogenic equipment that he had attached to the coffin. He had set it for one thousand years, and as far as he could tell, the machine had woken him up right on time.

Perfect. A thousand years ago, Rodolfo had been one of very few vampires fighting the war against the living, the humans. Every sunset, Rodolfo would arise to find human victims to feed his omnipresent hunger, afraid of being discovered for what he really was. Every sunrise, he had returned to his coffin to rest, afraid that during the daytime some intrepid Van Helsing would drive a stake through his heart. Finally, he had had enough. He had enlisted the help of a physicist at Columbia University, who had built him a cryogenic pump for his coffin. As payment, Rodolfo had made her his last meal before sleeping his sleep of the undead.

But enough dwelling on the past. By now, the war would be over, and humanity would be defeated. All that remained was for Rodolfo to join up with his fellow undead once again—after, of course, finding a sniveling, cowering human from whom he could drink his fill of blood. He hadn't eaten in so long.

He emerged from his building's basement, and what he saw confused him greatly. He was right in the middle of a dark, moonless Manhattan night. Where were all the vampires? Where were all his people, living their unlives in celebration?

He strained his neck to look around, and spotted a dull glowing pinprick of fire to the east. He headed toward it, and discovered a small group of vampires huddled around a street corner. Their faces looked pallid, much paler than normal, and their eyes glowed without the sharpness Rodolfo expected.

"Rodolfo?" one of them exclaimed. "Is that you? It cannot be!" Although her voice was strong, she looked sickly and emaciated. The other vampires huddled closer and murmured to each other.

"Yes, it is me. Who is that?"

"It is I, Sabrina. Your first victim, and your first lover. What has happened to you? We thought you long defeated and destroyed for these thousand years past."

"Sabrina." Rodolfo felt wistful as he remembered the pleasure he had enjoyed when he sucked her dry. "I was not destroyed, merely sleeping, waiting for the day when we would finally be victorious over the humans of the world." He looked around at the desolation. "This is not what I expected."

"Oh?" said one of the other vampires. "What did you expect?"

Rodolfo shrugged. "A flourishing kingdom of vampires, with humanity enslaved."

Sabrina glared at Rodolfo, her eyes glowing deep red. "The last human was converted over a hundred years ago, Rodolfo. There are none left."

"None!" Rodolfo was shocked. "Did not one of us understand what that would mean? Human blood is our sustenance. Without humans to prey upon . . ." He trailed off as understanding dawned.

Sabrina grinned evilly. "Now you understand why we look the way we do. There has been no fresh food for a century, Rodolfo. Cattle and other beasts died out when humans did. We cannot even look forward to the release of dying. For us, there is nothing left but hunger."

"How have you fed?"

She paused. "We have been reduced to feeding upon each other, and feeling our own lifeblood weakening as time goes on. But, my old lover, your own blood has been preserved for a millennium; it must taste so fresh. . . ."

She approached Rodolfo slowly, the other vampires close behind, evil grins upon their faces to match hers.

"Sabrina! You would not—"

"You did, my old friend."

Rodolfo turned and ran, although he knew there was no escape, and never would be again.

Hunt

Bradley H. Sinor

She was perfect for him.

Malcolm had slipped the bartender at Dangerous a twenty for her name, Charlotte. *Uptown* and *slumming* had been his words.

Perfect.

Dangerous was a pseudo-S&M club on Manhattan's West Side; plenty of leather, whips, bare skin, and innuendo. The clientele was upscale, uptown. The kind that liked to flirt with kinky, but that was all; anybody serious about it hung out at the Corinthian, near the Village.

Malcolm turned away for just a moment. When he looked back the girl's table was empty. He caught a glimpse of her near the club's front door.

"Damn!"

There *was* other prey in the club, at least twenty likely possibilities. If not them, then he had his choice of the hookers, dressed in neon and lace, that were never far away in New York.

Dammit, he wanted *her!*

It took nearly twenty minutes of prowling the streets and alleys near the club to stumble on her, exchanging a wad of bills for a small plastic bag.

Not bad. He'd be able to feed and get a little blow in the process.

He resisted the temptation to grab Charlotte right then. Instead, he hung back, following her. The creaking of a door far back in a nearby alley told Malcolm that a long-closed disco had a new customer.

Charlotte was sitting cross-legged in the center of the dance floor, a mirror, razor blade, rolled-up dollar bill and the baggy in front of her.

"Looks like fun," Malcolm said. His tongue traced the edges of his canines as they slid into place.

He touched her with his mind, making whatever she was, had been or could be, his.

Charlotte stretched out on the floor, vacant-eyed, a semisensuous smile on her lips, and reached out for him. Every sound, except for the drumbeat of her heart, had vanished.

Malcolm kissed her gently, fingers trailing along the edge of her face, his fangs touching her bare neck ever so gently.

A moment later Malcolm felt himself being yanked upward and then slammed hard against the floor. Three blurry figures emerged from the darkness, pinning his arms and legs.

"This time I get the fangs!" one of them laughed.

"We'll discuss that later."

"Let's do him!"

"Let me have the honors," Charlotte said. A glowing demon of anger and hate filled her eyes. One of the others offered her a three-foot-long wooden stake, sharpened to a razor point.

The stake pressed hard against Malcolm's bare skin.

Malcolm's head jerked backward as the virtual reality goggles were dragged off his head. The transition from the darkness of the simulation to the glare of the Family training area was unnerving enough to make him grab for the platform railing to keep from falling.

Around him a half dozen identical platforms were all occupied by other vampires, each moving in its own silent training dance.

"You are dead! The true death, a rotting piece of meat, in a rat-infested tenement!"

A thin man with a walking stick and cold blue eyes, Malcolm's VR goggles in his hand, stared at the young vampire.

Xavier Coldsmith.

Artist.

Warrior.

Mystic.

It was into his hands that Malcolm, along with all newly created vampires, was given, to master the skills that a member of the Family needed to survive.

"I guess I didn't do too well."

"That is an understatement."

Malcolm found himself wishing that Coldsmith would scream at him; that he could understand, even deal with. Instead, Coldsmith's quietly cultured voice sent shivers up his spine, making Malcolm feel like a small child who had just shown a bad report card to his father.

"I know I made mistakes."

"That's an understatement. Remember, look and then think about what you see; expect a trap, be on the lookout for it, see the partner before he sees you.

"If you can't, then it would probably be better if you just picked yourself out a park bench and waited for the sunrise," said Coldsmith. "Do you want to Hunt?"

The words burned in Malcolm's ear. Since the night, eight weeks before, when he had become a vampire, Malcolm had been allowed to Hunt only twice.

The memory of those times was still fresh, better than any drug Malcolm had ever encountered.

Only twice. Every other time he had fed, it had been from the supplies procured by the Family. It wasn't the same.

"Do you want to Hunt?"

Malcolm moved two dials on the VR controls, increasing the simulation difficulty level.

Coldsmith nodded. "Twenty percent. Just don't get cocky, kid."

Husks

Thomas Smith

You're chicken if you don't," Wayne said.

Kenny McCormick's eyes never left the old shack. "You can say what you want to, Wayne," he said to the bigger boy, "but I ain't about to go in the Hughes place, and that's that." He rubbed the back of his neck just above his collar and shook his head. "No sir, not me."

"That's all right, Chicken Little. Just because Louise Adcock did it don't mean you have to do it."

"Darn it, Wayne, you know she went during the daytime. And all she did was run up and look in the window. She didn't hardly even slow down."

Wayne grinned. "Yeah, but she was still a girl and she still went up there." He walked over and put a brotherly arm around the skinny redhead. "Besides," he said as he started walking Wayne toward the shack, "you'll never live it down if you don't do it."

Living it down didn't concern Wayne. Living through it did. He had heard the stories about the old river shack and the family that lived in it. Especially the boy.

The kids called him Jelly Head because he was supposed to have a tiny thin body, long bony arms, and a head about three sizes too big. His skin was so pale it was almost transparent, and his skull was so thin that it looked like God filled a balloon with jelly and put it on his neck for a head.

"Wayne, I told you—"

"Yeah, yeah," Wayne cut in, "I know what you told me. But look, we're here and it's gonna be dark soon. Besides," he said as he put his lips close to Kenny's ear, "if you go in there and word gets out how brave you are, Penny Fuller might just go out behind the gym with you."

Kenny blushed at the thought, but the thought was enough to

make him reconsider. Wayne smiled. "I'll tell you what." The smile widened. "I'll even go in with you."

Wayne motioned with one hand and pushed the door with the other. The door opened freely.

Kenny knew he was moving, but fear held his heart in a grip of ice. "Wayne, I'm not so sure about this." His whisper seemed to echo for miles.

Wayne closed the door behind them, flicked a lighter, and the dull yellow circle created by the flame made their shadows on the wall jump and twitch like dying souls. "Wayne," Kenny whispered, "we're in. Now let's get out of here."

"Not yet," Wayne said as he edged toward his companion. "We've got one more thing to do."

Kenny felt the bile rise in his throat as his shadow twitched and leaped. "Wayne, I don't need a souvenir for proof. You can be my witness that I was here."

"Kenny," the bigger shadow said, "this isn't about taking." He lit the oil lamp on the bedside table and turned to watch the redheaded boy. "This is about giving."

The sight hit him like a sledgehammer. The floor was littered with large husks. Dozens of them. A dry crackling sound sent a thousand tiny ice pricks along Kenny's spine. He had stepped on one of the husks. He tasted bile again, bitter and hot. But this time he hardly noticed. The nightmare on the cot in front of him had his full attention.

Partially covered by a filthy sheet, it was no more than three feet away from him. The tiny body was thin to the point of emaciation, and the skin on the huge head was so thin—Kenny's left leg was suddenly warm and wet—he could see the blood vessels circling the bulging eyes and the suckerlike mouth. The thing seemed to be drooling.

"His name's Dewey, and he ain't been fed for a week or so." Wayne moved behind Kenny and pushed just hard enough for him to lose his balance. As he teetered forward, long, hard fingers shot out from beneath the sheet and pulled him forward. The sucker-mouth opened and attached itself to his chest through his shirt. Kenny screamed and struck out at the air with both fists. But his scream was cut short as his heart was sucked from between two ribs.

"You're chicken if you don't," Wayne said.

Wanda Galloway's eyes never left the old shack.

Idle Conversation at the End of the World

Richard Parks

Hello, there.

Yes, it *is* a beautiful day for a walk in the park, Mr. Culley. My name's Carl Winders. My wife, Cindy, and I just moved to Spring Ridge Lane, about a block from you . . . ? Yes, I thought you might. Anyway, I couldn't help noticing that you're pulling on the edges of your mask—

Oh. I call it a mask because that's what it is. You noticed it yesterday, right? It started for everyone at about the same time. You can see where mine has started to come loose.

You think it's the next big step? Oh, you mean like we've been one type of human for the last several thousand years and now it's time to move on? That explains why you're impatient—yes it *is* an interesting idea.

Wrong, but interesting.

Yes, I am quite sure. Hmm? Well, if you insist—it's the end of the world. Our part in it, anyway. The world will go on without us. Maybe the rats will get the Darwinian nod next. Or the cockroaches. I wish them luck becoming human; we've made a royal mess of it.

How do I know it's the end of the world? Simple—I caused it. I didn't mean to. I'm basically a decent guy . . . no, don't look at me that way; I'm not crazy. No more than average, anyway.

One whole side of your face is coming loose. Yes, work on the other side a bit. You don't want to tear it, because it's possible we'll at least remember what we were. What we *thought* we were. The mask might help.

Didn't I explain that? We thought we were human, Mr. Culley. Image of God, even, if you go in for that. I think we almost made it. Almost. You may believe there's something new under the mask, but you're mistaken. It's something *old*.

My certainty bothers you. No wonder; it would bother *me*, only I can't help knowing what I did. I'm not dense, you know.

No one has that kind of power?

Mr. Culley, *everyone* has that kind of power. I proved it. I'd try to spread the word—Carl the Evangelist has a nice ring to it—only it's too late.

OK, if you must know—I stepped on a roach.

No, I'm not offended. It feels good to laugh, Mr. Culley. Enjoy it.

Of course I'm serious about the roach. I was walking down the sidewalk along Spring Ridge, just out for some air . . . oh, all right, Cindy and I had a fight. Satisfied? It wasn't anything really, but I was angry.

The roach just scuttled out from a culvert almost right in front of me. Big, fat one. I told myself that it would find my house and lay eggs under the sink. I told myself that afterward, of course. After I went out of my way to step on it. Only one little step, sure, but that was enough. Pop went the roach.

I felt the skin on my face separate at that very moment. Not one tick of the cosmic clock before or after. It doesn't take a statistician to correlate that bit of data, Mr. Culley. I wasn't even angry at the roach—I was angry at Cindy. That's who I was stepping on. I told Cindy about it this morning and she started breaking all the mirrors. I went for a walk. Here I am.

It was just a roach?

Mr. Culley, picture a flat rock balanced on a spike. Picture grains of sand, falling one by one onto one end of it. One grain will finally be too many. The rock will lose its balance and fall, and shatter. And no one grain will take the blame.

I will. If the species has to end, it should go out with that much class. That's why I'm telling you this. That and because you asked.

Almost finished? Yes, the mask is coming off in one piece; well done! I see you brought a mirror. Of course you have to see for yourself. I guess we all do.

Oh.

Oh, dear.

Never mind about the seven years' bad luck, but you really shouldn't hold that piece of glass like that, you might . . . oh, right. Sorry I didn't understand. That's exactly how you should hold it.

Have a nice day anyway.

If Thine Eye Offends Thee

Peter Atkins

First the grocer, staring long and hard at him as at something unsightly. Then the postmistress, trying to focus elsewhere but drawn to his eye with horrified fascination. The newspaper vendor, the ground-floor neighbor, the landlady's dog slinking away from the usual biscuit.

Door slammed, he rushed to his bathroom mirror. What were they seeing? There was a shape in his eye. A growth? Uneasy, he leaned closer. He gasped.

The naked child's arms thrashed in miniature agony deep behind the liquid sheen of his pupil, tiny mouth forming shapes of accusation. He remembered.

He picked up his razor.

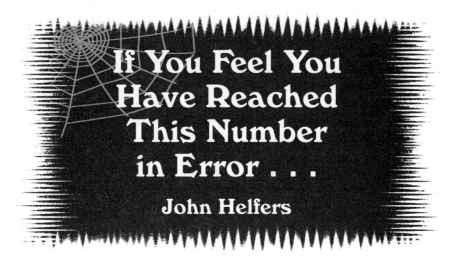

If You Feel You Have Reached This Number in Error . . .

John Helfers

It was a bright sunny day when Owen Roberts died.

His body was discovered by a neighbor who heard the off-the-hook signal of his telephone through an open window. After a few minutes, he went to the window of the small bungalow and saw Roberts' body on the floor, the phone lying several feet away from his outstretched hand.

The neighbor quickly summoned the police, who arrived and cordoned off the area, took photos, questioned witnesses, and did all the usual things that earmark a professional police investigation.

The coroner arrived approximately twenty-five minutes later. Examining the body where it had fallen, he quickly pronounced the man dead. Leaning down to look more closely at Roberts' head, he noticed a small trickle of blood that had seeped from the left ear of the body. From his position, the police deduced he had put the phone to his left ear to hear the call.

The forensic specialist, who had arrived just after the coroner, oversaw the information-gathering process. After the prints were taken from the phone, he picked it up with a latex-gloved hand, straightened, raised the phone to his ear, and dropped it. Repeating this process a few times, he noticed the phone bounced only a few inches away from where it landed on the floor. He realized that Roberts had apparently tried to throw the phone away from his ear, but failed. He wrote this down in his notebook, then scratched his head, calling for the phone to be taken to the lab for analysis. The coroner asked if he could take the body to the morgue, a request the pathologist granted.

Interviews with neighbors revealed Owen Roberts to be a fine, upstanding man. Although he lived a quiet life, he participated in block parties and the Neighborhood Watch, and belonged to the local Lions chapter. He was friendly and affable, and in apparent good health. No one could possibly think of any reason why anyone would want to kill him.

The police called the telephone company to send someone out and check the phone lines. A man from the local telephone company arrived fifteen minutes later in a panel van with a small satellite dish on it. He mentioned that they had done a routine maintenance survey the day before, and that nothing had been out of order. They asked him to check the system again, which he did. Calling the police over to the main switch box, he showed them that everything was as it should have been. He wrote down Roberts' telephone number and said he would check back at the main office for anything unusual involving that number.

The telephone man went back to his van and got in. The interior of the van looked nothing like a standard repair vehicle, with reel-to-reel tape recorders and television monitors lining one wall of the van and a computer on the other side.

"How'd it go?" the older man in the back asked the repairman.

"Just fine. They're probably going to rule accidental death—brain hemmorhage, most likely."

"Well, that's the plan. Did you recover the equipment?"

"Um-hmm."

"Good. Well, let's move on. Target at number 555-2374 terminated."

"What? 2374? His number was 2734."

The two men looked at each other, and the repairman handed the other man his notebook with the number in it. The older man checked it, sighed, and ran a hand through his thinning gray hair. The two men sat for several long seconds, then the younger one spoke hesitantly.

"Some kind of mistake? The wrong house, maybe?"

The older man shook his head. "This is the address Control gave me."

The repairman sighed and started taking off the overalls he had been wearing. "Could this get any worse?"

"Sure." The older agent shrugged. "That's the third wrong number this month."

If You Go Out in the Woods Tonight

Nancy Holder

Well, I don't want to frighten your little girl there, but I do have to tell you that it's real unfortunate you got off the highway where you did and came to our town. I know something happened to your car; yeah, yeah, you told me about the steam and the smoke, but you should have kept going even if you had to walk. That might seem like a dumb thing for me to say, me owning the only service station and all, but I'm a people-person and I got to look out for folks, know what I mean?

You see, there is this very strange family, the McIveys, and we finally had them all locked up, or so we thought. I almost hate to tell you the truth, but we were pretty close to just stringing them up ourselves. You can't trust the courts these days, and if just one McIvey beat the system, it would be fatal for the rest of us. Don't think I'm melodramatic. I'm from here. We've been plagued with them all our lives, and no one on the outside listens.

So we had them all rounded up, and my best hunting buddy, Sam, said we should just set the jail on fire, and that must have spooked them because somehow they broke out, every last one of them, and high-tailed it into the woods.

I got on the phone, which was out, and then tried the radio, while just about everybody else chased after them. And I mean everybody, moms, dads, little kids. I knew this was a bad idea but I'm just one woman and what could I do?

But the radio didn't work either, so I locked myself in the back room and found religion real quick.

I heard a lot of screams.

I said a lot of prayers.

After three hours, no one came back. Finally Sam fell against the door and I let him in. He could barely talk, said he had been screaming over what he'd seen out there. He told me the McIveys had booby-trapped the forest, setting out bear traps and stringing lines of razor wire between the trees. Just so you walk into it, you know? He said it was a miracle he got out of there alive, because no one else did. He figured everybody else was dead.

Then he said, "Man, I'm so thirsty. My mouth is like cotton. I feel like I have never drunk a drop in my life." His voice was like sandpaper. I made him sit down and got him a Pepsi out of the soft-drink machine.

He raised it to his lips and threw back his head, and I swear as I'm standing here, his head fell clean off his neck! There's the bloodstains, and that puddle is the Pepsi. That razor wire had done the job those McIveys must have intended it to. Just sliced him clean through, so clean not even he knew it!

So you see, we got to be real careful tonight. The McIveys are out there, and we're the only survivors. In fact, it's a miracle you folks are still alive, especially considering you drove that vehicle of yours smack dab into the middle of the forest and walked half the night to my filling station here. I can't believe you made it past all the bear traps and that razor wire that did in my buddy, Sam.

What's the matter there, friend, thirsty?

If You Love Someone, Let Them Go

Peter Atkins

Felix became whatever he lost.

Often inconvenient, frequently embarrassing, it was a family trait. His relatives trained themselves to avoid possessions and lived ascetic lives.

There'd been accidents: One great-uncle, entertaining a local churchman, didn't miss his foolishly acquired pet snake until the prelate's smiling face became a mask of superstitious terror; a seventeenth-century ancestor, misplacing his candle, achieved immortality as the Great Fire of London.

Felix went to college, fell in love, and was happy. Then the phone call: She was leaving him. Bereft, he walked to his mirror.

His lover's reflection stroked his beautiful breasts.

"Forever," he said.

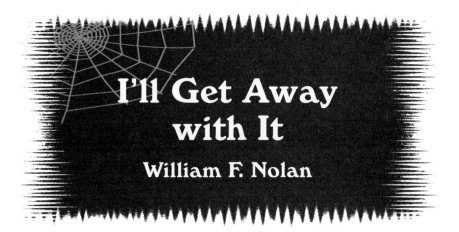

I'll Get Away with It

William F. Nolan

I watch a lot of TV. Old horror movies are my favorites. With Boris Karloff and Bela Lugosi. Where he's a walking dead man, Boris is, with his neck broke and his head all tilted to one side, out to get revenge on the guys who hanged him. Or the one where Bela sucks everybody's blood out and wears a long black cape with a red silk lining. Neato.

There was one I really liked a lot, about this kind of horror hotel where the guy buries people up to their necks in his backyard and they look like cabbage heads sticking up. Then he cuts the heads off. It's a real good one. I've watched it three times on TV.

So I'm home watching an old horror movie when Pop comes in. It's one about the Tower of London (wherever that is) and Boris has got a clubfoot that makes him walk funny and he carries a longhandle ax with a real sharp blade. It has kings and royal people in it.

Anyhow, Pop comes in the door looking sour like he always looks at me. "That horror crap you watch is sickening."

"Not to me," I say. "I like it."

"Turn it off," he says.

"No, I like it."

"Dammit, are you going to turn that crap off?"

"No."

And he hits me with his fist. Knocks me off the stool I was sitting on in front of the TV and I hit the floor. Blood is on my lip.

He's been hitting me all my life. Ever since I was a little tiny kid Pop's been hitting me. Sometimes he beats me with a belt that has sharp metal stud things on it that hurt and cut my skin. He used to laugh at me when my pants were down for the beating and call me "lard ass" and say I ate too much and that I was a frigging fat pig of a son. *Frigging* is a word Pop likes to use.

All that was when I was real little. I'm a lot bigger now and I'm not fat anymore. I'm skinny. He still makes fun of me. Calls me "Mr. Breadsticks" because my arms are so long and thin. Nothing pleases Pop. Never has. He's always had it in for me.

So, tonight, I decided to kill him.

The idea of him being dead is neato. He belongs dead, like Boris Karloff, the only difference is he won't come back like a zombie to get me. That's just in the movies where dead people do that.

I get up from the floor and walk over to a table that we have near the hall, where Pop keeps a loaded gun. Some kind of shiny automatic, I don't know what kind.

Pop has his back to me turning off the TV when I take out the automatic from the table drawer and shoot him with it. Four or five times I shoot him, I didn't count.

There's plenty of blood because it takes him a while to die. He does a lot of gurgling and gasping and then he doesn't move anymore and it's all over.

I'm glad.

That's when Mom comes home from where she was at some health club to help her figure. She looks real shocked to see Pop on the floor dead the way he is and says oh God, oh my God, my God, over and over.

I know, right then, I've got to kill her too. No way not to because she'll know I killed Pop and besides she never did anything to help all those times he beat me for nothing. She just walked away and let him beat me.

So I shoot Mom. Another bunch of shots. Automatics have lots of shots in them.

She falls over Pop's body like in some kind of dance and there's more blood and the living room rug in front of the TV is a real mess.

I move my stool over and switch the TV back on so I can watch the rest of the horror movie which is really good. Boris has these mean dark eyes and he looks like he could just eat you up. He cuts people's heads off in the movie. That's his job.

When the movie's over I dial 911 and tell the lady who answers that a terrible, terrible thing has happened at our house, that a robber came in and tried to steal things and Pop tried to stop him and he shot Pop and then he shot Mom after Pop was dead. Now they are both dead on the floor in front of the TV and it's just terrible what happened.

After the phone call I sit down to wait for the people to come. They'll be here soon to deal with Mom and Pop.

Neato.

Everything's cool.

Even if they end up thinking I did it, so what? I'll get away with it. The cops can't do a frigging thing to me. Not really.

What can they do?

I'm only nine years old.

I'm a Crazy Tiger

Tina L. Jens

Doctor, I'm afraid I'm a *crazy* tiger."

The doctor looked up from the psychiatric review file. "What makes you say that, Tony?"

"Just look where I am." He gestured at his surroundings in an oddly feline way. "A psych ward. Healthy tigers live at the zoo or in the jungle. Or sometimes, at the circus. But they don't like that—too much traveling involved."

"I see," said the doctor.

"Of course, the zoo would never take me, because I don't have a tail, and the kids would cry when they saw a tail-less tiger. Parents would stop bringing their kids to the zoo, profits would fall, and pretty soon they'd have to close the zoo. Where would the tigers live then? You can't go back to the jungle after you've lived the zoo life. Damn those doctors!"

The doctor had followed the odd line of logic up until that last bit.

"Why do you blame the doctors, Tony?"

"Because they cut off my tail. They did it the same time they circumcised me. My parents never knew."

It made the doctor uncomfortable to admit it, but the man really did look like a tiger, with all that bushy facial hair, those wide brown eyes, and the orange-and-black-striped clothes. The standard issue clothing was white, of course, but Tony kept breaking into the art therapy supply cabinet and coloring his clothes at night. No one knew how he managed to escape his restraints.

"That's why they sold Dolly," Tony told him.

"I'm sorry?"

"The zoo sold Dolly to an Asian game ranch, because I have no tail and can't live at the zoo. Dolly was madly in love with me, so she refused to be mated with any of the other tigers."

The doctor nodded. "Her leaving must have made you very sad. Is that when you attempted suicide?"

Tony brushed imaginary whiskers with the back of his paw. "I'm rather ashamed of that."

"Because you know suicide is wrong?"

"No, I should have known Dolly would escape and come to me. Love conquers all, you know."

"I've heard that. Dolly must find it very inconvenient for you to be in the ward."

"Oh, no! Dolly likes it here a lot!"

The doctor blinked. "She's here?"

"She lives on the grounds. She especially likes the wooded area in back. Dolly hunts at night, brings me breakfast in my room, and then we make love in the shower—so we don't wake my roommate."

It was time to put a monitoring camera in his room, the doctor thought. And the shower. If Tony was molesting another patient . . .

"Tell me, Tony, how long have you been a tiger?"

"All my life. It's not like you can change after you're born."

"But you look human to me."

"I'm a tiger in human form."

"I see, and can you change into tiger form?"

"I don't believe in magic," Tony said.

"How do you account for your human body?"

"Somebody messed up."

"Who would that be?" the doctor asked.

"God, I guess. Or whichever angel is in charge of those things."

"Mmhmm. So, when did you realize you were a tiger in human form?"

"Well, at first I thought I was just a cat. But I was young then. About eight or nine. Tabby—"

"Your housecat?"

"Yeah. She taught me the cat language, and helped me realize what I really was. At first I thought maybe she was my real mom . . . but that was before I realized I was a tiger. Tabby taught me how to hunt so I wouldn't have to go hungry anymore when my parents went away and forgot to leave me food."

"Would they go away for a long time?"

"Sometimes, but I didn't mind. I like to hunt. Could I get a pass to go hunting with Dolly sometimes? If you don't stay in practice, you get rusty."

"We'll see. Our time is up now, but I think it's been a very productive session."

As an attendant escorted Tony out, the doctor made a note recommending a long stay in the psych ward.

At the St. Louis Zoo, the Big Cats game warden was having an emergency meeting with the zoo director. They stood in front of the tiger cage, watching Timbo sit on his tailbone in a very un-tigerlike way.

"Can't you make him stop? He's scaring the kids."

"That's not the worst of it. Yesterday I saw him trying to pick his meat up with one paw. I swear, that cat thinks he's human!"

Immanence

David Annandale

T he world is horror."

Jordan looked at Rivière, surprised. "I beg your pardon?"

"It is, you know." Rivière held up his brandy snifter and swirled the liquid around, peering at it as though seeing a crystal ball in full storm.

They were sitting in Rivière's study. Jordan had met him at the Eighteenth-Century Studies Conference at the Sorbonne. Rivière had invited him over to his apartment in the rue Guisarde for a drink. Jordan had expressed his concern over the latest metro bombing, and that was when Rivière, in his impeccable English, had made the pronouncement, with a tone that suggested the death of twelve commuters was very small potatoes.

"No," said Jordan. "I don't know. What are you talking about?"

Rivière put his glass down and smiled at Jordan. "Please. You're being disingenuous." He sat back, elegant angles draped in black. There in his armchair, surrounded by dark oil paintings and shelves of books held in bindings that were leather, ancient, and anonymous, he wasn't just the picture of faded French aristocracy. No, a picture was too superficial. Rivière went deeper, all the way down. He was its bone marrow.

"I'm not," said Jordan. The instant he spoke, he heard himself diminished. Great, he thought. Am I supposed to play American Watson to his Continental Holmes?

"If you insist," said Rivière, all noble condescension. "Allow me to explain, then. Take this globe." He pointed to the antique sitting on his desk. It had monsters in its oceans. "You see the latitude and longitude lines?"

Jordan nodded. "Yes."

"How pathetic. An attempt to grid, to striate, to control a space that doesn't care, and will wash away your precious constructions without even noticing. Knowing what your position is in the middle of a hurricane would be quite the cold and useless comfort, wouldn't you say?"

"I suppose." Jordan noticed again how Rivière always spoke as if he were not a member of the world he was describing.

"Well, your civilization is no more real and substantial than those lines. It is a useful idea, but subject to termination without notice. Horror is the sphere underneath, the air above. It is everywhere."

"Come off it."

"I'm serious. That bombing you were bemoaning, that was not an aberration. It was merely immanent horror showing itself."

"Right. So anything, at any moment, could turn nasty."

"And will. Let me show you something." Rivière got up, opened a small chest, and pulled out something that looked like a wooden box with a camera lens. "This is a Lumière cinematograph. It was invented in 1895."

"Yes," said Jordan, getting a little annoyed at the lecture. "And?"

"One year later, one hundred years ago, horror erupted in film. Georges Méliès used this very machine to make *The Haunted Castle*."

"Oh, come off it! The creation of the horror movie hardly counts as some sort of all-pervasive evil making its presence felt." Jordan swallowed the rest of his brandy. This was getting stupid, and he was tired. Time to go.

"All right." Still supremely calm and smug. "Another example. Look at the doorknob."

Jordan twisted around in his chair to see it. An old door's old knob. It didn't look special. "Okay," he said. "So?"

"A mundane object. Harmless. You don't give it the most passing thought. But it, like everything else, has a core potential for horror. Horror could suddenly drape over everything in this room like an oil slick. You could touch that knob, and it could bite you and never let go. Its will to hurt is as strong as that of any explosive device."

"Uh huh," said Jordan, priming the sarcasm pump.

"The barrier to horror is gossamer-thin. The twitch of a finger and it's gone."

"Riiiight." Jordan turned around to give Rivière his most withering stare.

He wasn't there.

Jordan jumped up. He couldn't see Rivière anywhere. The room was deserted. What the hell? he thought, and made for the door. Neat trick, he decided. Sliding panels, whatever. The game was old, and he was out of here.

His hand hesitated just before it touched the doorknob. He looked at the bookcase next to him and saw that the bindings were glistening. He backed away from the door, palms wet, skin numb with shock. Behind him, there was the mechanical whir of something starting up.

Roll camera.

Immortal Muse

Don D'Ammassa

Are you saying Frankenstein was real?" Peter's expression was incredulous.

Connie shook her head. "I don't believe there was a monster with rivets in its neck. But Victor Frankenstein was an actual person with decidedly macabre interests. Shelley altered the name—he was actually Vittorio Fracatta."

"And she based her book on him?"

"Let's just say she drew inspiration from his life. He had this weird theory that life is inherent in every cell, that just because the brain or heart dies doesn't mean the rest of the body isn't still alive. I have proof that they met in Rome and that he invited her to visit his villa in Pesciadora. . . ."

". . . but nothing to indicate she ever took him up on his offer, right?"

"No, except ten days unaccounted for at the right time. C'mon, Peter, this is a chance for me to come up with something really original for my thesis."

He was unhappy, but in the end, he agreed.

The Fracatta villa had been vacant since the war. Connie finally found a local official who was willing to grant her permission to enter.

"The boards, they must be replaced when you leave, Signora."

"Don't worry. We'll make sure everything is secured when we leave. Are you certain that the family is extinct, that no one has title to the property?"

"No one, Signora. It has been unclaimed since my grandfather's childhood." After she'd gone, the magistrate shook his head, wondering if he should have mentioned as well that if any descendants of the Fracattas survived, they were almost certainly unwilling to admit their lineage.

"I gather the family died out?"

Connie nodded. "Vittorio was the last of his line, and when he disappeared, no one ever claimed his estate."

"Disappeared."

"Yup. They found the surgeon he had living with him lying dead in the road one day, heart failure most likely, but Vittorio was never seen again."

"So what do you expect to find?" Peter had removed the boards covering the main door and broke the rusting lock with the shaft of a crowbar. "A mad scientist's lab? Body parts?"

Connie refused to allow her spirits to be dampened. "Diaries, letters, something to prove Mary Shelley visited. There might be records of his researches, but that's only important if I can prove a link."

The interior was a disaster. The ceiling was down in several places, the furniture covered with dust and mold. Most of the books and papers they found crumbled to dust or were matted together inseparably. Peter complained occasionally during the course of the day, but Connie ignored him.

It was dusk when they found Fracatta's journal, dusty and stained but well preserved otherwise.

Connie flipped to the appropriate dates, read the scrawled Italian quickly. "Here it is! The Shelleys were both here for four days." She read further. "And yes, he gave her a tour of his laboratory. Peter, this is going to make me famous!"

Peter actually found it in himself to be enthusiastic. "But what laboratory? We haven't seen anything like that and we've already been through the whole house."

"Except the cellars."

"Those doors are pretty solid. I don't think I can break them down."

"We'll take the hinges off."

Easier said than done, since they were rusted in place. It was almost midnight before the door finally sagged free, but Connie refused to wait until morning.

"We have flashlights. I have to know tonight, Peter. Just one quick look and then we'll go."

The laboratory was beyond the wine cellar, an enormous cavern carved from the adjacent hillside. Much of the equipment was unrecognizable. The operating table was marked with dark stains. The walls were covered with shelving filled with glass jars, each bunged shut, each containing a preserved body part, some animal, some plainly human.

"An odd place to search for immortality."

"Is that what he was looking for?"

"Sure." Connie nodded. "All scientists are looking for a way to beat death in one way or another."

"But none of them ever do."

"Not yet anyway. C'mon, let's go back to the hostel. We won't find anything here worth bothering with."

They picked their way through the debris back to the doorway and left, while behind them a pair of eyes followed their movements from within a jar of viscous fluid, and in another a hand clenched with frustration, and in still another a set of vocal cords tried to produce a plea for release.

In the Lonely Hours

William Marden

Susan lay in the darkness, staring at the ceiling and holding the sharp butcher knife still at her side. Beside her the thing that pretended to be her beloved Harry lay still and unmoving.

She held her breath as she tried to separate the low whir of the ceiling fan blade above her from sounds coming from the form concealed under the sheet beside her.

After a moment she heard the soft, methodical intake and outpouring of air in a macabre imitation of true breathing. Sometimes in the long lonely hours before daylight, she thought the sound whistled to a shuddering halt and the body beside her lay silent for moments that stretched into minutes.

They had said the intricate, neuronic mechanism inside the body that looked and sounded exactly like Harry before the accident was programmed to mimic as closely as possible every aspect of the living Harry.

Of course, it had been expensive to have the neural structure of a once living brain read out like a computer program to give the metal clone lying next to her every second of Harry's memories.

But with Harry's insurance money and her inheritance, it was possible. As the spokesman for Second Chances had told her, "He will be only a robot copy. But as far as you're concerned, as far as he's concerned since we will blank out the memory of his death, he *will be* Harry. He will walk, and talk, and react like Harry. He will make love like Harry. And because his sperm was saved, some day he will even be the type of father Harry would have been."

"But, he won't be Harry, will he?" she'd asked, troubled by some reluctance she couldn't put into words.

The spokesman had dismissed her concerns, saying, "You're getting into philosophical arguments here. Will he be self-aware? Will he have a soul? Will he be Harry? Who knows? Advanced neuronic clones don't seem to be self-aware, but they act as if they are, and that's what counts. Does a tree that falls in the woods when no one's around make a noise? Who cares?

"The only important thing is that the advances in neuronic technology have made it possible for us to banish death as a practical matter. Harry can live again, if you want him to."

And she had, and he had, and now she lay beside this thing that smiled at her over the breakfast table, bought her roses on her birthday, sang "I Want to Hold Your Hand" offkey the way he always had, and knew just where to touch her when they were making love to force her into an agonizing, reluctant orgasm. He was Harry during the daylight, but during the long lonely hours of the night . . .

She leaned over him, raising the knife up, preparing to drive the point down through the crystalline lens of one artificial eye and into the neural circuitry beneath. As she'd expected, his eyes snapped open and something that might have been the light of life or the escaping glimmer of neuronic energy gleamed in them.

"Having the nightmare again?" he said in Harry's calm, loving voice. "It's all right, Susan; it's okay."

"You sound so much like him, but you're not," she whispered.

"Even if your fantasy is true, what difference does it make in the end," he said. "Suppose I'm right and you were the one who died and is a neuronic clone. Or suppose we're both right, two people who loved each other enough to buy immortality of a sort for the other, the memory of each of our deaths erased and each of us thinking we're the original and the other is the copy. Two copies lying side by side in the night. I still love you. You still love me. Put the knife down and go back to sleep."

After a moment she did and lay back on her pillow. Eyes open, knowing he stared into the darkness beside her, she told herself that tomorrow morning she would go to the Second Chances people and have him deactivated. Better to be alone than go through another night like this.

But she knew she would not, would never, and they would go through an eternity of long lonely hours lying together, together forever.

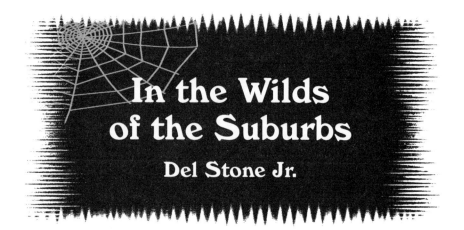

In the Wilds of the Suburbs

Del Stone Jr.

His name was Joe and that was about all he knew, except that he felt very alone standing in the main thoroughfare of Wildside Manor, watching the neat tract houses stretch into infinity.

The afternoon was very late, though Joe could not say exactly what time it was. He did not own a watch. But the quality of light told him it was late afternoon. The sun lay behind blue veins of clouds from which hard, dry snowflakes broke against the frozen ground. A biting wind gathered the flakes into dusty eddies that swirled across the road in Wildside Manor. Joe expected to see tumbleweeds bounce across the empty yards.

He stood in the center of the street, his hands hanging at his sides, and stared.

Cars sat idle in ice-glazed driveways, skeins of bruised snow arching from the tires to the asphalt. A sled was propped against the wall of one house, next to the front door. A mailbox door lay open, the flag up, a manila envelope jutting from inside. A spigot was encased in a multipetaled bloom of ice. A child's Big Wheel tricycle lay overturned in another yard, the back wheel hidden in patch snow.

And there was the quiet. Not the respectful quiet of a library, nor the funereal silence of a ritual. This was the implacable shock of a catastrophe, that moment of numbness that always divides the brain from awareness and acceptance, and the crippling pain that follows. It was the quiet that had summoned Joe from his hideout beneath the concrete bridge that spanned the river. The river circled Wildside Manor like a moat, drawing a line between it and the city that waited beyond the infinite stretch of tract houses. Joe lived beneath the bridge, belonging to neither world, and came out only to scrounge the dumpsters or hide from bored cops looking to roust a few bums.

Except the cops had not come today. And Joe, after daring to light a fire with wood he'd taken from a nearby construction project, had finally noticed that no cars were crossing the bridge. The world was as silent as the day it had been born.

Empty, he thought, staring at the houses. They were empty. No lights burned within. No irate men shoveled sidewalks as their perfectly healthy kids played nearby. No two-career housewives scattered sand on the driveway so they could pick up the children from swimming practice, return home in time to throw something together for dinner, then spend the next three hours grading papers while their husbands hammered at computers until midnight.

Joe had never been a part of that world. He neither envied nor pitied the people who were. But he was curious. Because now the houses were empty.

And he did not know where the people had gone.

He walked absently down the street. A front door stood open, flapping idly in the wind. A plastic garbage can described aimless semicircles on the sidewalk. Joe walked into the very heart of Wildside Manor, and it was the same, everywhere.

Emptiness. Abandonment. Silence.

These people who had everything they could reasonably want: Where had they gone?

Joe stopped at the center of a cul-de-sac. The sky was growing darker. The clouds still shed brittle flecks of snow. He was surrounded by houses, and the wind could not get in here as readily, which lent a cathedral calm to the setting. The houses stood in sharp contrast to the horizon, where a streak of light leaked through the overcast.

In the yard directly in front of him: lawn ornaments. Frozen flamingos. Plaster-cast fawns and bunnies and masked raccoons. Leaning against one another at crazy, off-kilter angles. Their expressions of joy and innocence distorted by rinds of ice and dirty snow.

They looked sullen and angry.

Joe thought of rats he had seen, hiding in culverts. Sometimes they would turn on themselves, as if all of them, in a single, defining moment, had witnessed some bleak revelation about the indifference of life. So they would kill each other, a final act of defiance. And then the water would wash their bodies away.

Joe turned from the houses and faced the sky and thought of everything he had, and everything he was. It had always been enough, he told himself. It had always been enough.

Snow skirled across the empty streets as the neat tract houses stretched into infinity.

The silence. The emptiness. And Joe. No longer alone.

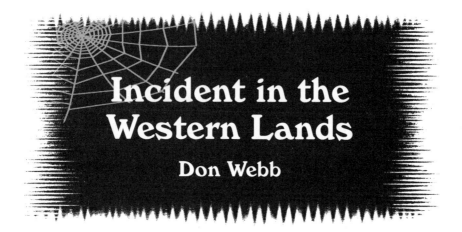

Incident in the Western Lands

Don Webb

I t was probably the Mummy films that made me go into Egyptology. I always thought the scene where the one Egyptologist reads the horrible curse from Ananke's tomb, and then the other says, "How horrible!" and then they go on with opening the sarcophagus is pretty cool. My job at the Oriental Institute in Chicago was mainly cataloging items which had been shipped out of Egypt in the bad old days of archaeology and had been in some collector's attic for decades. I envied them. As an Egyptologist I knew the treasures of the past belonged to everyone, but as a twelve-year-old kid I wanted them.

Last week I came across an interesting lapis lazuli amulet. A piece of Twelfth Dynasty work, it bore the images of Horus and Set facing a column. Horus was the god of light, Set, of darkness. Together they represented the totality of the spiritual realms. Generally these pieces represented protection, sort of an "I've got the whole universe on my side!"

Two things immediately struck me about this amulet. First, the inscription on the back; second, *the amulet had not been entered into the computer.* That meant no record of it. I could keep it. For only a little while of course. There was no record of where it came from, nor that the Institute had it.

The inscription read (roughly, because Middle Egyptian verbal tenses don't match English): I, THE MASTER OF SECRETS, ENSURE THAT THIS PLACE WILL HAVE A GUARDIAN. The small piece of finely carved blue stone had probably hung on a statue, activating it as a guardian.

I slipped it into my shirt pocket. I would give it to the Institute in a couple of years, but in the meantime, I would have a little piece of Middle Kingdom magic for my very own.

I was so excited at home, I even called off my date with Wendy.

My guilt gave me bad dreams. I must have tossed and turned all night. When I woke up, I was completely wrapped up in my sheets.

I didn't get much work done, I had some kind of fever, so I took the afternoon off, for the first time in ten years of working.

My fever got worse. I lay down, and I had a fever dream.

I dreamt of riding in a vast Egyptian-style reed boat, up a river of stars. I came to an island, walled all around with fire. The fire parted and my boat sailed into a harbor. There was a great temple there, and filled with curiosity I went in.

Beyond the pylon gates stood a falcon-headed man holding an ankh in one hand and a scepter in the other. No, I could see that it was a man in a falcon mask.

"Hail, guardian," he said to me. I looked at myself and saw that I was wrapped as a mummy with the blue amulet over my heart.

"What is this?" I asked.

"You are the replacement, to guard the resting place of my Ka. I am PtahSokarNakt."

"I know you; the Institute has your mummy."

"Yes, my original guardian rotted away through the centuries. You will serve."

When I awoke I had completely wrapped myself in my sheets. My mouth was gagged and my arms bound. Today I heard my boss come from the Institute.

She expressed surprise at my disappearance, but more surprise at finding a mummy in my bedroom. I must have stolen it.

Next week I will be installed by the resting place of the Ka of Ptah-SokarNakt. To him: Life, Health, Strength!

There I will stand for millions of years, as long as Ra circles the sky in his boat, and the sands of the Red Land endure.

Incognito

Terry McGarry

They're going to have to burn your hair. They're going to have to burn your hair when you die. Somebody might *recognize* you."

The man had stumbled out of a corner bodega as Judy was crossing the street toward it on her way to the subway. He was tall and thin, but moved heavily, as if he had once weighed much more. His face was craggy but vague, giving an impression of mist clinging to mountain peaks—an impression furthered by the purplish-gray hair that sprang up from his scalp like heather. He was not dangerous; he was not even really addressing her at all.

She was almost disappointed. She would have welcomed the grasping hands, the swinging baseball bat, the flickering blade. She would have welcomed the absolution.

Perhaps, she thought—still walking, passing him now, noting that his head did not turn to follow her—he was a kind of Celtic prophet, wasting away under the hellish demands of his gift.

Judy hiked her backpack higher up on her shoulder, reaching to pull her long blond hair from under the strap—the yellow hair that, in her adolescence, had been a follicular bull's-eye in this Dominican neighborhood. If the afterlife was filled with Coors-guzzling men shouting *"Mira la rubia!"* perhaps such a preventive bonfire would be advisable.

But it had gotten her free Italian ices from the guy at the pizza parlor when she was little. Cut in an adorable pageboy, it had put her in commercials showing that shampoo didn't make her cry. Bouncing in a beribboned ponytail, it had snagged her the cutest boys in high school. Pouring in a silken waterfall down her power suit, it had drawn the most important men at cocktail parties to offer her contracts.

Was she to spend these crucial minutes engaged in an apologia for the filamentous outgrowth of her epidermis?

She had meant to observe with care and love every detail of the familiar street as she walked: the faux-Tudor apartment buildings, the cracks in the sidewalk sprouting tufts of unconquerable life. It was the world she had grown up in, left long ago for Manhattan skyscrapers, Mediterranean retreats, only to return a week ago, blue-jeaned and sneakered and leather-jacketed, in an instinctive attempt to recall her origins.

And instead, she thought, *I found my roots. And they're still blond.*

She continued up to the elevated station. They had gutted it, cocooned it in scaffolding, lugged in their looming, deafening machines to reconstruct its innards, Lilliputians tinkering with the electric viscera of a steel-and-concrete mammoth.

She navigated the maze of orange tape, walked up the piss-damp stairs, grunted as the turnstile bumped her tender midriff.

She walked, plank by plank, to the very end of the temporary platform extension. She gazed out over the geography of her childhood.

And when the rumbling headlights were fifty feet away, she cast herself, her memento-stuffed knapsack, and her disease into their sharp-wheeled path.

At the last moment she couldn't help but turn her face away, and there on the platform across from her, no more than an arm's length away as she hung for an endless psychic moment in the bow wave of the first car, was the man.

Then her shriek and the shriek of brakes melded as all else fragmented. Fingers that had typed on her laptop and tickled her newborn niece fell far from legs that had jogged around the reservoir and clamped against her lover's hips. The mementos she had carried—to have with her, like the worldly goods buried with Egyptian nobles—were scattered, a diploma caught on a splinter of railroad tie, a stuffed toy nestling under the third rail.

In the abrupt absence of sensation, when the world stopped turning, she could see the man's craggy face—directly above her now—tilt sadly.

"Now they're gonna know," he said. "They're gonna know who you are. Your demons, they follow you down there. They'll find you by that hair in the dark."

The world receded in a rush as the man mumbled, amazed, "I always heard that tears came from their eyes. Never believed it till now. Figured it was only French people."

Judy could already sense ravening presences around her in the darkness.

A torch burning with pale fire, she turned to face them.

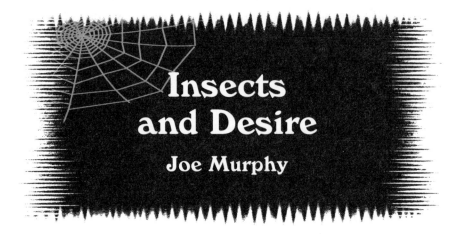

Insects and Desire

Joe Murphy

The moment I saw her, standing next to the Lepidoptera exhibit, I wanted her. The museum's lighting left deep shadows, yet her skin glowed with an almost translucent sheen. Long-limbed, delicate of feature, she moved hesitantly among glass cubes containing the dried husks and exoskeletons of Insecta and Hexapoda. Her somber eyes finally noticed me where I waited in the darkness. I smiled and stepped closer.

"Beautiful, aren't they?"

"Oh, absolutely," she replied. "Still, they're only a pale shadow of what they once were alive." Her hand brushed gently over a case housing a magnificent simulated nest of Formicidae. I studied her eyes, wondering what unknown secrets lurked within.

"I haven't seen you around here before," I said.

"Perhaps you haven't been looking."

"Someone like you would stand out in my mind."

"We're changeable creatures: a red dress instead of a black one, a blonde wig instead of dark hair. Perhaps you just didn't recognize me." She smiled; the dry sheen of her lips caught the light and glistened. "Do you come here often?"

"I work here. Part of the International Entomological Research Team." I looked down into a case containing a rare African mantis. "We're trying to find out what happened to them all."

"With all the pollution and chemicals unleashed in the world today, I'm surprised anyone needs to research that." She took hold of my hand; her fingers cool and soft as a moth's antenna. "Most of the other animals are gone. Why should they be any different?"

"We can trace the decline of most species," I explained as we strolled along the hall. "It happened gradually. Insects, though—one day they were everywhere, the next day gone."

"Look at this moth from England," she said, resting her hands on the case. "It looked just like tree bark until factory soot darkened the forest. Then it stood out, easy prey for the hunters."

"Still it survived. A few generations later it had grown dark, nearly invisible again. Now, there are none." I shook my head as if saddened. "Not in the last of the rain forests or deserts. Even the roaches have disappeared."

"A lot of people were glad to see *them* go."

"They were ancient creatures, here long before man and machines."

We moved deeper into the exhibits. She never gave up my hand, but clung to it with a strength that belied her willowy form. She wanted me, too—I was certain of it.

"Let me show you a special exhibit." I took her arm and steered her toward an unmarked door. "If you're truly an insect lover, you'll find this very appetizing."

"It's awfully dark. Are you sure it's all right?" Her voice held a most delectable trace of uncertainty. We entered a long corridor filled with dusty packing crates and time-smeared cases settled among useless killing jars and antiquarian dissecting trays.

"I take my lunch breaks back here." I flipped a switch, spotlighting a lonely unblemished case.

"Where?" She started. "Oh, I see."

"The collection focuses on camouflage." I put my hands upon her hourglass waist. "Here's one that looks like a stick. This one hangs upside down, mimicking a leaf."

"That one looks like a lump of dirt. You can hardly see it," she said. Her eyes met mine.

"I'd like to kiss you." I took her into my arms.

"Please do." Her hands gripped my temples as her mouth opened.

My lips fastened on hers, my tongue thrusting forward. Soldiers charged from my throat, mandibles wide with greed. Workers followed, beginning the task, tearing at her lips and gums. Others rushed from my ears, intent upon reaching her eyes; blind, she would never escape.

She jerked once, mewling softly through her nose before we filled it. Yet her hands gripped me tighter, her legs suddenly locking around my waist, and we crashed down, shattering the case. A new scent reached me, one I could read as well as smell, and I struggled.

"We all have our own ways of hiding," her odor declared. "How else could we find you?" Her palms and fingers split open, thousands of hook-shaped mandibles and razor-edged legs tearing through the dry shell of my skin.

Interrupted Pilgrimage

Brian McNaughton

Malebolgia had never seen such heroes as Heinrich von der Hiedlerheim and his mighty men, so the villagers scrambled to hide in their cellars. There they shaved their daughters' heads, blackened their faces and pulled their front teeth.

The graf had them dragged forth and flogged. Of those still breathing, he demanded, "Why do you fear us? We are pious pilgrims on our way to Rome."

"If you are such heroes as you seem," said Mario the baker, "we can anticipate a fresh outbreak of illusions."

"Of what sort?"

"Of *that* sort!" Mario cried before diving into his cellar.

Like many a luckless hell-beast before it, the dragon had crept upon them unawares. A disappointing specimen, it killed only Otto.

After Mario's recent memory of an iron gauntlet across the face had been refreshed, Heinrich asked, "If that was an illusion, why is my left arm hanging by a thread?"

"Because you believe. Your wound is unreal."

This seemed reasonable to the graf. When he examined his arm, it was whole.

"Did you hear that, Otto? On your feet!"

"I am dead. Please give me a Christian burial."

"If you were dead, you couldn't talk. Not without a decent interval."

"He's not breathing," said Siegfried, kneeling beside his fallen comrade. "And a fly is crawling on his eyeball."

"His stomach for faith was ever gluttonous. Who casts these spells, baker?"

"The Magus Serpieri," Mario muttered, indicating a cave in the overhanging cliff, with a gesture so guarded that a distant observer would have thought he was characteristically picking his nose. "When he dreams, his dreams oppress us."

"Don't bury Otto while we're gone," Heinrich commanded.

The climb to Serpieri's cave was far longer and more arduous than it looked. Three hours ahead of time, the sun set. Three months ahead of time, snow fell. The warriors were sore beset by werewolves and ogres who forced them to transcend all limits of skepticism.

A friar who accompanied them from the village, Brother Degenerato, gave cold comfort with his ceaseless chant: "Defend these sinners, O Lord, we pray, from the deserts of their foul deeds, and harken not to the piteous cries of the virgins they have defiled, the poor they have trampled, the saints they have martyred, the kinsmen they have murdered—"

After a dismal age of this, Heinrich split the monk from pate to beads.

"You killed a holy man!" Reinhardt protested.

"He was an illusion," Heinrich said. When everyone's best efforts to disbelieve in the butchered corpse failed, he added, "Of unique potency. The body will vanish if we look away from it and reappear only if we look back."

This worked, and the graf's cynicism inspired his men. Gunther rejected all evidence that he had slipped off a real cliff and broken his neck. To the chagrin of Satan, he refuses to this day to admit he is burning in hell.

The penultimate challenge was a den of voluptuous lamias. Having mastered applied ontology, the heroes could dally with the charmers until the climactic moment, then ignore the manifestation of scales and fangs. Illusory or not, the lamias fell into a snit. Hissing echoed in Heinrich's ears as he at last stumbled into the presence of the Magus.

Serpieri cried, "This must be my wildest dream, for never have I beheld such unspeakably vile brigands! But now," he added portentously, "I must wake."

Heinrich gasped to see his sword grow transparent. His mighty men began to fade. With a supreme effort of will, he struck, but the very air fought against his stroke. A look of stupefaction crossed the wizard's face as the blade regained opacity and fell faster.

"You're not real!" Serpieri screamed. "You can't—"

"Dream on, Magus!"

After an uneasy silence, Siegfried mused, "If I am but a dream, and the dreamer is no more, then I am . . ."

"Immortal, obviously," Heinrich said.

The sun was setting for the second time as they descended to the village. Reinhardt sighed, "Those girls with the gapped teeth and bald heads remind me of the wenches back home."

"Female peasants everywhere look like that," Heinrich said. "If I ever found a pretty one, I might be at a loss to ravish her."

Otto still believed he was dead, and he had begun to smell even worse than usual. His faithful comrades vowed to carry him to Rome and see what the pope could do for him, but somewhere along the way he managed to sneak off and bury himself.

It's Hell Waking Up

Wayne Allen Sallee

When the clock-radio went off, Dick Dale was vibrating through "Miserlou." Scolari opened his eyes, confident that the only movement he need make was to slap the snooze alarm. It was Thanksgiving weekend, starting today. No climbing into layers of winter clothing, descending first the stairwell of his Clybourn Avenue apartment, then sinking further still into the rancid bowels of the Chicago subway system.

As he drifted back to semi-REM, the sound of the approaching subway train in his dream reached a crescendo that quickly segued into the alarm going off, a traffic watch this time. Before Scolari could force his eyes open, the man in the traffic copter had already mentioned the gapers block at Bisterfield, the thirty-minute delay from the Ontario Feeder to O'Hare. Scolari realized the man was referring to the *nighttime* rush hour.

He sat bolt upright; the clock flashed 5:44, with the red dot on P.M. This couldn't be, even considering he'd been drinking in celebration long into the early hours. No wonder he'd forgotten to simply unplug the alarm clock in the first place.

The bedroom door was open, and he could see the streetlights that bordered Partridge Park glowing a diffused amber. Scolari stepped to the doorway and stared at the poster on his door, getting his bearings. The poster was of Elvis decked out as Vince Everett in *Jailhouse Rock*. Scolari's t-shirt was on a metal coat hanger perched on the doorknob. Elvis sneered "Hullo, everabuddy," and casually grabbed the hanger and plunged the hook into the lower lid of Scolari's right eye, pulling down. Scolari had the sensation of a runny egg on his cheek.

Before shock set in.

Before the snooze alarm went off.

Ten A.M. on the first day of his holiday weekend; man, that last dream was a crazy one. Scolari yawned; what the hell, give it ten more minutes. He'll watch reruns of the Macy's Parade later.

He was entombed in Egypt, stuck in traffic in Hanover Park, working at a gas station in Manteno, dying in a plane crash over Thalmus, Indiana. The plane was in a holding pattern, yet he knew the entire dream: the plane would roll and nosedive, the engines wailing like the alarm.

Or the knife would cut across his throat. The space shuttle would explode over his backyard.

Every ten minutes.

One dream-snatch in particular seemed *very* real: Scolari never made it to bed the night before, Scolari choked on a chunk of sausage pizza.

Dying was the quick part.

He had never liked *having* to sleep, because it was always hell waking up no matter how much sleep he had permitted himself.

He dreamt about taking that French exam without studying.

He dreamt about the bookstore manager who looked like Kay Lenz.

The alarm went off. Scolari opened his eyes and saw a familiar figure.

Elvis sneered "Hullo, everabuddy."

For what seemed the hundredth time.

I've Seen That Look Before

Larry Segriff

I am not the man I was.

Ah, you say, smiling and shaking your head, but then who among us is?

But that's not what I mean. I am being quite literal; I truly was a different man, once.

I see the light of curiosity die within your eyes as a certain guarded look creeps in. I know that look well, and the cause behind it. Perhaps you'll shake your head and walk away; perhaps you'll stay for the sake of form. Either way it does not matter. Even if you remain and listen to what I have to say you won't truly hear. I know this because I've seen Their mark upon you: that look of a moment before. You know what that look says? It says, "This man is mad. I will not hear him," and it says it in a very loud voice, loud enough, just barely loud enough, to drown out that other voice within you, the one that says, "Yes! Yes, I know! Me, too!" You pause now, because just for an instant I touched something. You've never heard that second voice, I know, but occasionally, perhaps on a dark and stormy night shot through with rain and fierce lightning, or perhaps in the instant between not-quite-asleep and almost-awake, occasionally you've heard its echo. I know because I've seen that look before, usually in the mirror, staring back at me over an ocean of lather.

Yes, They've touched me, too, just as They've touched all of us here, and I see your question coming before you ask it. How is it, you want to know, that I, of all people, should be given the self-awareness to know this, to see Their touch? It's a good question, and very accurately phrased, for you see it *was* a gift. At a party—one very much like this one, actually—a man came up to me and started talking about voices, and about Them. He was mad, or so I thought, but then I started listening to what he was saying, really listening, for his words had a feeling of rightness to them. Ever since then I've had periods where it seems as if the memory of his voice rises up in perfect opposition to Theirs and for a brief moment I am myself again. These periods rarely last long, hardly even long enough to tell—

Excuse me, what was I saying? It seemed I had a thought there but now it's slipping away. I say, are you all right? You've got quite an odd look about you. Here, close your eyes and breathe deeply. It'll pass. I know; I've seen that look before.

The Jack-o'-Lantern
Scott David Aniolowski

Jason began searching for a pumpkin days before Halloween. He spent hours wandering through muddy pumpkin patches, picking through miles of leathery vines. His jack-o'-lantern had to be just right—there couldn't be a flat spot on one side, or an unripened green patch. Shape didn't matter—tall or fat, it just had to be perfect.

Finally, after hours of searching and turning over and judging hundreds of pumpkins, he found it. It was an enormously round specimen with wide ridges and warty flesh. He bundled the pumpkin in an old blanket and gingerly loaded it into the trunk of his car, padding it with dirty T-shirts and shorts left over from the summer. At seventeen, Jason was tall and strong, but it had been all he could do to lift the giant gourd by himself.

By the time the young man returned home with his prize, the sun hung low and sleepy on the horizon. Long shadows groped over the ground, and a chilly breeze rattled autumn-dried leaves. The house was dark and empty.

He kicked off his muddied sneakers, spread newspapers over the kitchen table, and retrieved a pair of knives from the cupboard. Squatting next to the huge pumpkin, Jason wrapped his arms around its great girth and with a low grunt hefted it to the table. The stiff, curled stem scraped his chest, putting a small rip in his T-shirt. Cursing, he pulled his shirt off and adjusted his backward-turned baseball cap.

Jason plunged a large carving knife into the top of the gourd. It made a hollow *thump*. He sliced around the leathery stem and pulled off the lid, gooey strands of yellow-orange pumpkin guts stringing behind. The air filled with a strong sweet smell: the unmistakable odor of pumpkin innards. He stood on his toes to reach deeply into the enormous fruit, inserting both arms nearly to the shoulders into the cold, slimy, sticky goop, his bare chest pressed against the warty rind. With his fingers he dug deeper into the strands, pulling out handfuls of stringy, seed-filled pulp and depositing it on the newspapers with a wet *thwack*. When he had pulled out all he could with his hands, he gouged in with a spoon, scraping the cavity smooth.

The teen took a step back to study the surface of the pumpkin, his arms and chest smeared with yellow-orange goo. He ran his hands over the warty surface, letting his fingers trace the wide ridges that ran top to bottom. A face began to take form in his mind—a wide-grinning, glaring face. Carefully, he set about carving out the features with the smaller knife. As he plunged the blade through the flesh, it moaned, deep and hollow. Slowly, he cut up and down. First the eyes came out—sharp inverted crescents like the moon turned on its side. Then the nose—a smooth triangular shape.

He stepped back again to scrutinize the slowly forming face. The deep orange rind shone brightly under the kitchen lights. There was another hollow *thump* as the small blade plunged back in. He cut high up one side, down, and up the other, carving out the jagged fanged mouth. Finally it was finished, the great maw grinning shark-like and wide.

All that was left was the candle. He had a special one just for his jack-o'-lantern. It was black, as big around as a coffee can and half as tall. The foil sticker on the bottom claimed it was midnight-scented, whatever that was.

With a flick of his cigarette lighter, the candle sprang to life. He turned off the kitchen lights; the jack-o'-lantern glowed, light spilling from the carved holes, shadow ghosts dancing over the walls and ceiling. The face looked almost alive, eyes squinting, mouth cracking a wider grin. In the weird flickering light, the pile of pumpkin guts on the newspaper seemed to wriggle like maggots.

The candle tipped slightly and it sputtered. Jason knelt down, eye level with the wide cracked grin, so that he could better see inside. He pressed closer, his face nearly touching the thick rind. The acrid smell burned his nostrils. He reached through the great maw into the pumpkin to right the candle.

Jason hardly knew what had happened when he suddenly fell back. There was a moan and a *crunch*. Dazed, he tried to pick himself up, only to find that his right hand was missing. It had been bitten off at the wrist.

Just Another Good Ol' Haunted House

Terry Campbell

I don't remember seeing this room before," Kevin said, staring at the odd array of latex-crafted creatures and bizarre mannequins. The inside of the old house was musty and full of dust, and the smell of rubber was heavy in the air.

"I don't either," Tommy answered. "I think they have several paths they can lead you down so it'll be different every night."

Kevin stopped long enough to inspect an eight-foot-tall werewolf standing menacingly in the corner of the room. Gray- and white-streaked hair covered its entire body, and its latex snout was forever immortalized in a wicked snarl, the glossy coating over its teeth and gums giving it a truly frightening effect. God, but it looked real.

"I can't believe it was so easy to break in. You'd think they'd have guards, or an alarm."

"I guess they figure no one is brave enough to break into a haunted house." Kevin pointed to a skeletal imp figure staring down at them from the wall. Its latex wings drooped over its bony shoulders; foam guts leaked from its rib cage. "I wonder how they make all this stuff."

There was a flapping sound over their heads, and the boys turned just in time to see a small object fly from the room. "What was that?" Kevin asked, his eyes wide.

"I don't know. Let's go see."

The boys squeezed through a narrow corridor; expertly applied blocks of foam and antiquing paint created the illusion of walking through a subterranean cavern. At some point, the path widened into a cave, and the boys stopped at a diorama depicting a man being pulled into quicksand by fearsome toothed worms. Kevin shined his flashlight across the man's tortured face, again saw the lifelike glint giant in the fake orbs, and shuddered.

"Up there," Tommy said.

Kevin let the flashlight follow his friend's directions before stopping on the ceiling. Terrible batlike creatures with wolfen heads hung from the ceiling, their sharp fangs and blood-streaked tongues clearly evident.

"What was that we heard?" Tommy asked.

"Bats," Kevin answered. "It sounded like a bat."

"I suppose there could be real bats in here, don't you think?"

"Sure. I don't see why not." He didn't sound too certain.

"This place is starting to give me—"

Tommy's words were cut off when his jugular was severed by the wolf-bat's vicious fangs. Kevin shrieked and crashed against the wall. The faux rocks now felt wet and slimy to the touch, not dry and rough like the foam from which they were constructed. He dropped the flashlight and it rolled on the floor, the light bouncing here and there, momentarily illuminating more of the wolf-bats, and the devil-worms burrowing up from below.

Kevin crawled on his hands and knees, frantically trying to create a means of escape. His panicked brain tried to remember the corridors they'd been down, the stairs they had climbed, the evil dioramas they'd witnessed.

He could hear the howls, the flapping of great wings, the gnashing of wicked teeth reverberating throughout the halls and corridors of the old mansion, and it seemed all the inhabitants were coming to life.

And they were getting closer.

Kevin stole a final glance at Tommy, his face being ripped to shreds by the wolf-bat. But something seemed strange, something he couldn't quite put his finger on. Then he realized what it was.

Tommy wasn't moving; the bat wasn't moving.

When he saw the devil-worm hovering inches before his eyes, Kevin realized he wasn't moving either.

All of them, victims and attackers, were frozen in a state of suspended animation.

Out of the corner of his eye, Kevin could see shadows across the cavernous walls, hear the shuffling of many feet as the creatures of the haunted house grew ever closer.

And then he saw them.

Joey and some other guys from school. A handful of older couples on double dates. Several little kids screaming their heads off and crying into their parents' arms.

Kevin strained to see them better, but his eyesight was eternally fixed on the devil-worm burrowing toward his face.

"I don't remember seeing this room before," Kevin heard someone in the line of visitors say before they were whisked along into another room of the haunted house by something that might or might not have been just a guy in a werewolf costume.

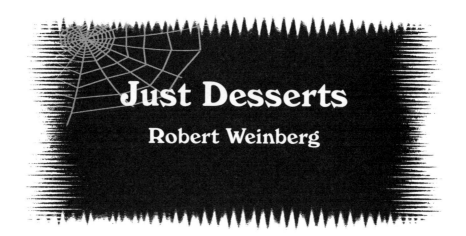

Just Desserts
Robert Weinberg

His time had come. It was the last roundup, the big sleep, the long good-bye, the black hole, the end of eternity. After eighty-seven years, Martin Crosby, the million-word-a-year man, the human fiction factory, the fastest typewriter in New York, was about to meet his maker. It was his last hurrah. He knew it. And he welcomed death's unforgiving embrace.

Body twisted with age, racked by pain, Martin was tired of life. He longed to know what lied beyond the gateway, past the gate of the Silver Key, over the rainbow. All of his life, he had written about the greatest adventure, the one-way trip, the never-ending story. Now, he was about to step over the doorstep, take that one step beyond. Enter the twilight zone.

His relatives and friends, the few of them who still survived, had gathered around his bed for this last hour. There would be no last reprieve from the final hour, no sudden medical breakthrough to save him. There was no cure for old age. There was no way to save someone who long ago had lost the will to live.

Sharon Rock, his agent, was there looking particularly grief stricken. Her expression made him smile. An attractive blonde, young enough to be his daughter, she had the heart of a cash register. He knew that she saw his death not as a loss of life, but as a major deduction from her bank account. Sharon was his third agent. He had outlived the other two.

During Martin's sixty-five-year career, he had written nearly three hundred books, making them all rich. Only a week before, already sinking, he had finished his two hundred and ninety-seventh book. It was to go to auction tomorrow. Sharon had held off the bidding until he was gone, feeling the promise that it was his last novel would push up the price. He didn't care. Nothing mattered to him but rest. The final rest.

He could feel his senses slipping and knew that the Dark Messenger was fast approaching. "Give me a pen and a pad of paper," Martin croaked with the last of his strength. "Quickly."

Hurriedly, one of his sycophant relatives gave him what he asked for. Martin could sense their fear, wondering if he was about to make some last-second change in his will, throwing them all out in the cold where they belonged.

Anxiously, he scribbled the words "I can write no more," followed by a long streak of ink. He had always wanted to end a story that way. Without another word, Martin Crosby died.

And found himself in a huge chamber, decorated entirely in bright red, with fires burning in the corner. He stood there, naked, in front of a desk cluttered with papers, behind which sat a monstrous crimson creature that could only be described as devilish. Martin had no doubts where he was.

"Hell?" he asked, just to be positive. "I led a pretty ordinary life. Never did much sinning. Didn't have time, writing so much. Why hell?"

"All writers go to hell," said the demon, its voice surprisingly pleasant. It looked down at the paper it held in its hands. "Martin Crosby, right?"

Martin nodded. "That's me. Million-Word-Martin they called me."

The demon nodded. "I read some of your stuff. Not bad. I liked *Pongo-Pongo Slave Girls* the best."

"It was a fun book to write," said Martin. He looked around curiously. "So this is hell. What's next? An eternity of torture and burning?"

The demon shook its head. "Don't be silly. We got rid of that type of stuff a long time ago. Now, we try to make the punishment fit the crime. You know, like the Gilbert and Sullivan song."

Martin suddenly found himself in an office, dressed in a business suit, sitting behind a huge desk. It didn't seem that bad. Not bad at all. It was actually pretty comfortable.

That was before the devil entered the room carrying a two-foot-high stack of papers. "Manuscripts," said the demon. "Unsolicited manuscripts from our other guests."

"No," said Martin. "You don't mean . . . you can't mean . . ."

"Yes, Martin Crosby," said the devil. "You are now an editor. And you will be one for all eternity."

That was when Martin knew that he really was in hell.

Just Suppose

Darrell Schweitzer

Hey.

Just suppose that when you were six years old you heard branches scraping at your window one winter's night a little too insistently, and you got up in your pajamas and stared wide-eyed at the discovery that the huge oak tree outside your bedroom window was swarming with what you could only describe, in your limited experience, as fairyland lights, like candles inside paper bags, but drifting in the air among the branches; and there were *people* inside the tree, with glowing faces, some of them very strange, some of them children like you, not to mention a few with wings like you'd seen on a TV show not long before.

Suppose, too, that you opened the window, feeling the damp air, all too afraid that your mother would burst in screaming, "You'll catch your death!" But she didn't, and you had that special moment all to yourself, and you heard the voices of the people in the tree, inviting you to come to them.

Let's suppose, further, that you *did,* and your parents found you in the snow the next morning, half dead from hypothermia, with an odd crisscross cut on your wrist, but supremely happy, because you'd had a *wonderful* time adventuring among the knights and wild Indian boys, battling giants and discovering pirate treasure . . . and after several more such episodes you were committed to psychiatric care and convinced, reluctantly, that it had only been a series of dreams, which was clear by the way the imagery changed as you got older, like the naked sirens that appeared after you hit puberty . . . and you couldn't really be seeing the ghost of your grandfather rocking sadly back and forth in the wind, as if he wanted to tell you something and had forgotten how.

But maybe it was really contact with the Other World, whose inhabitants sometimes help human folk, particularly their allies, like you, who cut your wrist and commingled your blood and became one of us.

Suppose further that after a largely unsatisfactory adult life you are lying in bed again *in that same room*, because your parents died and left you the house, and the branches are blowing against the window again, too insistently.

Suppose . . .

But you put away your dreams as a grown man puts away childish things, and eventually married a nice girl, who wasn't very nice after all; and the barrage of her complaints sent you retreating into the minutiae of your profession, which is antique coin dealing, so that you can blather on about the fine points of the *Fel Temp Reparatio* series of Constantius II, and show off your monographs, but haven't had a happy moment in twenty years, unless you want to count the time you flew into Paris, rushed from the airport to an auction, and rushed back to the airport again an hour later with fifteen absolutely perfect gold Histamenon Nomismae of Andronicus I Comnenus in your briefcase. You didn't even visit the Louvre while you were in town because you are, in fact, a boring, pedantic little man without the time or the sensibility for that sort of thing.

But let's suppose you could go back to being a child and grow up *better* here, in our world, and forget about your wife and your partner, Fred, who is cheating you in more ways than one, and even forget about Andronicus I Comnenus, who was a son of a bitch anyway.

Because you know perfectly well that they want to be rid of you, and she's downstairs humping Fred on the sofa right now, with the TV on loud so you can't hear, and the two of them are planning for you to hit your head in the shower and accidentally drown in two inches of water.

You're getting fat. It could happen, right?

But suppose that instead you crept downstairs and bludgeoned them both to death with some sharp, heavy object, like the National Numismatic Society trophy on the mantle. You wouldn't have to worry about the evidence, because you *wouldn't be around any-*

more, if you were merely to climb out the window afterward and join us here in the tree, which is actually a gateway to other places, a new life.

We'd catch you if you started to fall.

Just suppose we're really here.

It's not the wind.

We're all waiting for you to make up your mind.

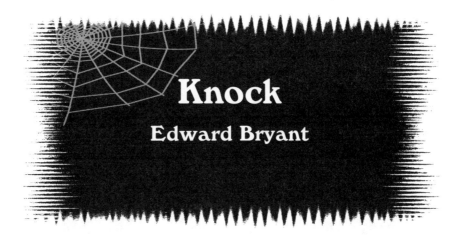

Knock
Edward Bryant

The knocking on the front door rang clear and sharp, and it woke the killer from his drowsing stupor in the overstuffed chair. He shook his head, glanced at the mantel clock, knew he was simply getting too old for this.

He needed his sleep.

The time was five minutes before midnight. The knock sounded again, this time even louder and more insistent. The killer levered himself up from the floral-print garden of the comfortable chair. He walked slowly toward the door, where waited sacks of candy corn, saltwater taffy, popcorn balls, and a glorious variety of other treats. The goodies had gotten stale over the years.

Parents had, for the most part, stopped sending their children around this neighborhood. The disappearances had terrified them.

Sleep, he thought.

More knocking. *Much* louder.

"All right, all right," muttered the killer. "You're all up beyond your bedtime. You can afford some patience. I'm on my way. But I swear, this is the last year." He knew he didn't really mean that.

When he opened the door, he saw that diminutive pirates, short cowboys, tiny witches, skeletons, TV characters covered the porch. All the old standards.

"Where's your imagination?" said the killer. "You're really not all that scary this year."

"Just wait," said a strangely familiar voice from the rear. The killer couldn't tell who had actually spoken those words.

Then the costumed children crowded forward, forcing the killer to take a quick step backward, then another. As though they were a single group organism, the children pulled off their masks.

The killer stumbled backward, scattering candy corn and crushing popcorn balls underfoot. No one chanted, "Trick or treat!"

He could only stare, and then choke on the beginnings of a scream. It *was* scary, after all.

All the faces, now revealed, were his.

Lady of the Night

James Anderson

Stan waited behind the spruce trees outside the door, seething in anger as he shivered in the cold. It was Beth all right, he thought for the tenth time in as many minutes. Her footprints clearly led up the snow-covered walk to the front door, where she'd lost a single red high-heeled shoe just before she went inside.

Beth and John had been making eyes at one another all afternoon at his cousin's wedding. Then, when he'd woken up at four o'clock in the morning, he'd found his bed empty and the front door wide open.

It wasn't the first time his wife had disappeared in the night. But this time it was going to be the last.

He pulled the sleek, deadly bowie knife from its sheath and looked at it lovingly. It was a parting gift from his own father, who'd used it to slit his own wrists when Stan was just sixteen. Good riddance to the bastard, he thought, remembering the beatings and the abuse.

Tonight, he'd put his dear old dad's gift to good use.

While he knew he'd have to move quietly, he also realized he'd need to act quickly, before the first light of dawn. Beth had always returned home at dawn. Several times he'd feigned sleep and wondered. This time he'd know for sure.

He crept out from behind the trees and smudged out his wife's footprints as he made his way to the door. Luck was with him: she'd left this door open as well, saving him the trouble of picking the lock, or breaking a window, which might have alerted them.

He grinned as he nudged the door open. He'd show them. He'd show them both. He might not be the smartest man alive, but nobody played him for the fool.

With the deliberate care of a stalking cat he entered the living room. Only the sound of his best friend's grandfather clock broke the silence. Good, he thought. They were probably both sleeping. And they'd wake up dead, he thought, liking the way the expression sounded in his mind. He stifled the urge to say it aloud—wake up dead.

John would go first, he decided as he snuck toward the bedroom. After all, Beth was a beautiful woman and he couldn't really blame his friend for wanting her. It was Beth's fault. You just couldn't trust a woman. So he'd kill John quickly, in his sleep. Then he'd make his wife pay the price.

He reached the bedroom and eased open the door. Already the first light of dawn filtered in through the window, highlighting a shadowy form on the bed. The lovers intertwined, perhaps? Or maybe she'd already escaped through the back door.

He moved forward to the bed and, even as he recognized John's naked form, he knew something was wrong. The sickening, almost metallic smell of blood reached his nostrils even as he saw the open wound where his friend's insides had been ripped out.

"Oh my God," he whispered.

His stomach flipped, but before he could retch he heard a low, throaty growl from the corner of the room, and he focused on a pair of demonlike yellow eyes staring at him from the darkness.

He barely had time to brace himself as the eyes suddenly leaped forward, and a drooling jaw full of hungry teeth lunged toward him. His reflexes reacted and he ducked to the side and swiped forward with his knife, all in one motion. The quick but powerful cut connected with bone, and the creature yelped like a kicked dog. It landed in a heap, flashed him a parting look of hatred, and then scuttled from the room and out the door.

Stan fell back onto the bed, where he found himself sitting on something. Vaguely wondering what had happened to Beth, he reached down and picked up a severed paw. He'd cut it off at the ankle.

The shade had been left open, and the sun rose quickly now, bathing the wolfish limb in new light. It was changing already, and, with sudden horror, Stan knew why his wife preferred the night.

The fingers were almost fully human now, and on the third digit he recognized a familiar object. It was the gold wedding band he'd placed on Beth's finger almost three years ago.

Beth never had liked silver, he thought.

The Lamia's Soliloquy

S. May Amarinth

Is it an *explanation* that you want? How dull! Had I thought you *that* kind of person, I might have preferred another. Are you sure that you'll remember it when you wake up? Human memories are so very adept at forgetting—that's what makes human minds so ruthlessly efficient, so narrowly focused on quotidian affairs.

"You trust yourself implicitly! Poor fool.

"Very well. First of all, the rumour is false which says that we lie in wait for the unwary, seducing them away from the path which they have set out to follow. It might be true, I dare say, that we are creations of Hecate and daughters of Lilith, for we certainly thrive in the dark of the moon—but the travellers who come to us are those who had no settled destination in the first place, and were disposed to wander by their own waywardness.

"The majority, of course, are poets; when we drink the blood of men we offer full recompense, in the form of inspiration. The nine who live on Helicon are empty symbols; we are muses of a more earthly stripe. We draw strength from all our victims, but the best of them draw genius from us.

"Secondly, not all who seek us, consciously or otherwise, are privileged to find us. We have never been profligate with our favours. It is true, of course, that we need the blood of men, but not as daily nourishment. I could go without blood for a hundred years, or a thousand, without perishing of want or becoming agonized by thirst.

"I think the need we have for blood must be more closely akin to the need that poets have for poetry; it makes life more vivid, more worth the living.

"Thirdly—and I pray that you will not take offence—the blood of human beings is not the finest vintage imaginable. There was a time, before the Age of Heroes, when I could sup the blood of fauns and centaurs, or even oreads and hamadryads were the mood to take me. Their ichor was sweeter by far than the stuff which flows in human veins; perhaps that was the reason why they ceased to be. We are not the only possessors of bloodthirst, nor are we the greediest.

"The virtue of human blood is not its taste but its profusion. Those species that were more spirit than flesh were slow to reproduce their kind and easily fell prey to murder and massacre; humankind thrived like the hydra—wherever ten men were cut down, twenty sprang forth to take their place. Nowadays, we drink human blood because it is all that we can get. It enhances life a little—but it also makes us sad, by reminding us of what once was possible, but is no more.

"Three items of explanation are enough. I doubt that you are capable of remembering even one. I must go now, and leave you to your rest. Make me a poem when you awake, and make it worthy of the blood that you have shed."

The young man awoke, and stretched his bony arms. For a second or two, he was possessed by the fleeting memory of a dream—but the moment he tried to grasp it, it was gone. The world came into focus, asserting its sharp reality upon his five senses.

There were so very many things he had to do that he had no difficulty at all in forgetting the most important of them all—and the blood that surged within his veins became a little more insipid with every hour that passed.

Last Fight

Peter Cannon

At Partridgeville General that gray November morning I found Ida in a coma. I'd known the old witch was ill, but not that ill. Pancreatic cancer, painful and always fatal. A fighter to the last, she hadn't gone quietly, the nurse told me. Tearing at her IV and cursing Dr. Smith had ensured the morphine drip route, not the hospice. It was now only a matter of time—twenty-four hours, maybe.

That afternoon, under a drizzly sky, Ken Corey and I met outside the apartment house in Central Square. Like me, Ken was one of the few locals who appreciated Ida, whose combative outbursts we'd suffered, eventually with good humor, for the sake of her late husband, the occult writer Fred Carstairs. We were soon joined by Sid Buzzby, who for much of his fifty-odd years had been Ida's surrogate son, looking after things, great and small, with little thanks. He had the key. With Buzzby was a young guy, Henry Wells, who introduced himself as a Carstairs fan. He'd driven all the way from Brewster as soon as he'd heard the news from Sid. I had no reason to doubt his claim he'd been a frequent visitor in recent years. After a falling out with Ida in '91, I didn't get back in touch until after Fred's death from pneumonia in January. (But that's another story.)

We had to act fast. Fred had left no will, and Sid was pretty sure Ida hadn't either. We had to remove all valuables—before she died, before the authorities realized she was intestate and sealed the apartment. Frankly, I wasn't expecting to find much, but I was in for a surprise.

Inside, Wells led us straight to the bedroom, a sanctum I'd never before entered. Heaped on the floor were dozens and dozens of dusty, dog-eared occult books, some Fred's own, others by the master himself, Halpin Chalmers. No rare first editions, which Fred must've cashed in long ago at the nearby Angell Hill Bookshop, but even the dross might be worth hundreds.

"You know," I said, addressing the group, "I think Sid deserves any proceeds we might receive from the sale of Fred's library. Agreed?"

"Fine by me," said Ken.

"That's really kind of you," said Sid.

"Speaking of dividing the spoils," said Henry, "Ida promised me Fred's Halpin."

"Fred's what?"

"His Halpin Chalmers Life Achievement Award, from the Occult Writers Guild. It's in the living room. I'll go get it."

Ken and I exchanged glances. Maybe we were overly trusting, but if Wells had indeed gotten chummy with Fred and Ida, such generosity wasn't wholly out of character. Ida could always recognize a true friend.

The kid returned with the Halpin, a faux pewter statuette of this century's finest occult author, who incidentally had been Fred's best boyhood pal. It was a fair likeness, ugly and unsmiling, of the Partridgeville Puritan.

"Sure, go ahead, take it," said Ken, ever the gentleman.

"I don't mind," said Sid, who not being an occult fan was in no position to judge.

We started to load the books, armful after armful, into Ken's hatchback. At some point we noticed Henry Wells had disappeared.

Next stop was the Angell Hill Bookshop, where the proprietor offered us mid–three figures for the lot. When I casually asked what he would pay for Fred Carstairs's Halpin, talking theoretically of course, the man replied: "Well, now. Halpins almost never come on the market. But given the special relationship between Carstairs and Chalmers I'd hazard, oh, a thousand dollars."

A blinding fog descended on Partridgeville that night. At about eight Ken phoned. Sid had just learned Ida was gone. *Requiescat in pace*, old girl.

Next morning I picked up the *Gazette*, expecting to see "Passing of Widow of Famed Occult Author" on the front page, but it wasn't. A tragic car crash was the top local news item: "Mulligan Wood. Nov. 14. Henry Wells, book dealer of Brewster, died around 7:45 P.M. when he lost control of his two-door sedan and ran off the road into a tree. A witness said the victim, 25, swerved to avoid an elderly woman in a white gown who suddenly emerged from the heavy fog, screaming insults. Wells was wearing his seatbelt. Partridgeville General's Dr. Smith attributed his fatal injury to a blow to the skull from a cheap metal figurine found in the front seat."

As I said, a fighter to the last.

The Last Laugh

William Marden

Go ahead, shoot him," Maranzano said.

Turk gave the Big Man a funny look, but then dutifully pulled the trigger of the .45 twice. The bullets hurled the old man in the white lab coat backward.

"Give me the gun," Big Man Maranzano said. Kneeling, Maranzano opened the dead man's mouth with the barrel of the .45, and pulled the trigger twice, splashing the floor with blood and brains.

"Not that I need to know, boss," Turk asked, "but what did that guy do? I thought he was working for you."

"He was," Maranzano said, looking down at his Rolex.

"What do we do now, boss?"

"We wait."

Turk leaned against the door to the basement under Maranzano's New York estate that had been transformed into a laboratory by the late Dr. Olustee and read *Playboy*.

Maranzano was reading a prospectus for a new bioengineering company when he caught movement out of the corner of his eye. His blood and brains all over the floor and walls, the resurrected and now whole scientist sat up, smiled a weak smile, and whispered, "I told you the process worked."

"That you did, Doctor," Maranzano said. "Turk, give me your piece again."

Turk stared at Olustee. The scientist was the last thing he ever saw as Maranzano blew his brains out.

"Why?" the scientist asked.

"There were only three people in the world who knew what you'd done here. Now there are only two."

"After you went through the immortality process, I knew it wouldn't kill me, but I still couldn't believe it would allow my body to regenerate from almost any injury," Maranzano said. "I had to test it on you. Now you're not only rich, you're immortal."

"Where are we going?" the scientist said as Maranzano led him to a door at the rear of the basement.

"You can shower in there."

Maranzano closed the door behind Olustee and slid back a panel that allowed him to view the small room. Maranzano touched a button and gouts of flame leaped out from a dozen jets. As his hair went up in a pyre of flame and red tongues of fire ran up and down his smoking body, Olustee screamed with the last air in his seared lungs, "You cheating bastard . . ."

"And then there was one," Maranzano said as he watched Olustee reduced to a heap of fine ash and a few bone fragments.

Olustee had been right in warning that fire was the only thing that would break down the molecular structure of an organism that had undergone his immortality process.

He was still savoring the feeling of peace and calm, of never having to worry about dying, when he heard footsteps behind him and was hit with a dozen bullets before he could turn.

"No hard feelings," Louis "the Ladykiller" Peligrino said. "But some of the boys decided it was time for a change at the top."

"No hard feelings," Maranzano gasped over the blood pouring out of his mouth. "Let's just see who laughs last."

"You're an original," Peligrino said, placing the barrel of his .38 between Maranzano's eyes and pulling the trigger.

Maranzano awoke in darkness and fear, which ebbed as his memories returned. It had worked! He was alive. He wanted to sing, he wanted to laugh.

He felt himself moving, swaying, ever so slightly, and then heard from a distance, "I say it's overkill. The poor SOB got his brains shot out and Peligrino still chains him up inside a fifty-gallon metal drum inside a hundred-gallon drum. What's he think, the Big Man is coming back?"

Another voice said, "We get paid for doing, not thinking. Help me get it up and over the side. One thing's for sure, nobody is coming back from the bottom of the Mariana Trench."

Maranzano tried to scream, but he was falling and then he felt the drum he was imprisoned in hit the water and begin to sink. He tried to think of a way out of this trap but the only thought that kept reverberating back and forth in his brain was that he was having the last laugh.

And although there was no one to hear it as it sank deeper into the dark water, from within the metal drum came the sound of laughter, and more laughter, and more laughter . . .

The Last Resort

Richard Gilliam

The guy waiting in the shadows hit hard, so when Bobby "Music-in-the-Morning" Walters awoke, it was maybe normal that his head ached.

No music this morning, thought Bobby between the throbs that were around equal portions contusion and hangover. Not good to miss work again. He'd been warned, plus Bobby's ratings book had been dropping. That other oldies station had switched to their pompous "we-don't-talk-over-your-music" format. Respect Radio. How pretentious could they get? If people wanted just music they could buy a record player, couldn't they?

Bobby looked up from the medium-sized bed where he lay. No windows, one ceiling light, and the smell of breakfast coming from the door. He touched his hand to the bruise above his temple. No blood or scab and not much swelling. Just a really lousy headache where he had been tagged.

He tried the door and was mildly surprised to find it unlocked. In the next room was a second door, a table with food upon it, and a note saying, RING THE BELL. Bobby rang the bell, thinking it probably pointless to do otherwise.

The second door opened. A middle-aged man walked through, quickly shutting the door behind him. "Ah, Mr. Walters. Welcome to our Orientation Center. I hope the invitation was not too painful," he said, with only a slight mock graciousness.

"Why am I here?" asked Bobby.

"Direct and to the point. I like that."

"So why am I here?" asked Bobby again, this time speaking with a slow separation to each word.

"Music, Mr. Walters. For our shared love of music. Music is the greatest of the arts, wouldn't you agree?"

"You're keeping me from playing music right now, Mr. . . . I didn't catch your name."

"No, you didn't," said the man, still smiling and cheerful. "Doesn't matter. This is the only time we'll speak. Sit. Enjoy your breakfast. I'm a bit hungry from waiting. Took you almost till noon to wake. I really should have fixed us hamburgers rather than scrambled eggs."

"Can you explain why I'm here?" asked Bobby, taking the nearer of the seats.

"But of course," came the reply. "That's the purpose of our Orientation Center. To get you accustomed to the rules of our resort."

"Resort?"

"Yes. A nonprofit organization I fund. For the betterment of music. For persons such as yourself."

"For disc jockeys?" asked Bobby.

"That's right," said the man. "But only for a particular type of disc jockey. For those who talk over the music they play."

Bobby had a very bad feeling.

"Do you like my new station?" asked the man. "We're such a small town but I thought Respect Radio had potential. We've done quite well. Revenues are way, way up, and as a good patron of the arts, I've invested some of the profits in expanding our resort."

Bobby's bad feeling was getting worse.

"I have but one rule, Mr. Walters. Once you leave the Orientation Center, you must never speak. If you do, you and the dozen other guests here now will be subjected to the loudest, most ear-sickening music the speakers in each room can generate. Stadium speakers, Mr. Walters. The loudest on the market. Well capable of inducing incapacitating pain and nausea."

Bobby felt a dull queasiness meander through his body.

"You'll be fed and cared for physically, but without any outside contact. No books or newspapers or television, and particularly no radio. You and the other guests can communicate however you like, but you cannot speak without setting off the music. And everyone gets punished. If one speaks, then all suffer."

The eggs weren't sitting well. Bobby pushed the plate away.

"Out the second door and down the hall. Your new friends will be there. As I said, this is the only time we'll meet. Soundproof walls, Mr. Walters. If you talk in your sleep the speakers won't wake me."

Twelve blank faces greeted Bobby. Most he didn't recognize, but in front was Wild Willie Dawson, whose disappearance five years earlier had created the opening for Bobby's first job. "Willie!" Bobby shouted. "Willie, what's going . . ."

Blam! The music started. Bobby crumpled to the floor, as did several of the others. The ones who could still walk had makeshift plugs in their ears, though not to much avail. Wild Willie tried to scream, and then Bobby noticed, not the lack of sound from Willie's mouth, but the lack of a tongue within it.

And then he saw the broken glass in Willie's hand.

The Last Wish

Scott Edelman

I'm asking you for the last time, Malone," muttered the death row guard. "Do you want a priest or not?"

Malone couldn't make up his mind. But there was no surprise in that, as the empty sensation in the pit of his stomach told him. After a lifetime of indecision, he'd even been unable to decide what to eat, and so became the first inmate ever to make the long trek to the electric chair without the solace of a last meal. But Malone could have predicted that. It was his curse. It was what had led him to this very room, when he'd hesitated too long during a pharmacy hold-up, unable to decide which of many drugs to heist, allowing the owner enough time to get his gun. Forcing Malone to use his own.

"I'm waiting, Malone."

"I've left plenty of people waiting. You won't be the last."

"You're wrong, Malone. That's exactly what I'll be. Because the warden will be along shortly to make sure of it."

Damn! Why did he have to end up this way?

Malone buried his head in his hands.

"I can answer that for you," said a high-pitched voice.

"Stop kidding around, Mike," said Malone.

"Think, Malone. Has Mike ever been able to read your mind before?"

Malone looked up. There was no figure at the bars.

"Where are you?"

"Down here."

Malone lowered his gaze and saw a little man, dressed in black, perched on his right ankle. He shrieked and flicked his shoe. The little man hurtled backward and bounced off the dark brick of the cell wall.

"Who are you? What do you want?"

"My name is Joseph. And I'm here to offer you one wish."

"Hey! I may be on death row, but I'm no sucker. You guys are supposed to offer *three* wishes."

"Sorry," said the little man. "Times have changed. Cutbacks, you know. With the Republicans in charge of both Houses of Congress, you're lucky you're getting any wish at all."

"Then how about—"

"No! You can't ask for more wishes. That's flat out!"

"But why me?"

"I haven't the slightest idea. That's up to the boss. Your name just happened to be next on my list. Though I can find out why if you want that to be your wish. Do you?"

"No! I've got to think!"

Malone began pacing his cell.

"Should I wish for money? No, that's not it—I'd be rich but I'd still be in prison.

"I know! I'll wish for my sentence to be commuted. But no, that's not it, either—I wouldn't be executed, but I'd spend the rest of my life in prison."

A priest came up to the cell door.

"Malone, are you sure you don't want to talk?"

"Go away, Father. I don't need you."

"There isn't much time left, Malone. You may not need me, but you surely need the Lord."

"I don't need anyone! I've got a wish, do you hear? I've got one wish!"

Malone began laughing hysterically. The priest nodded his head sadly and backed away.

"This is torture!" said Malone. "Should I simply wish for freedom? No, I know how these wishes work. I'm not stupid. I've seen the movies. I've read the books. You always have some sort of loophole, and I'll die anyway, won't I?"

"You must be reading some other books, Mr. Malone. We don't do that anymore. The FTC has made sure of that. You need only make up your mind, and your wish will be granted."

Just then the warden appeared, bracketed by two guards.

"It's time, Malone," he said softly.

"I need more time, warden."

"Time is something we all need more of, Malone. And none of us will ever have enough. Come."

Malone moaned, and began to shiver.

"Come," said the warden, far less gently this time. The guards tugged Malone down that long, final hallway.

"This is insane," wailed Malone. "I have a ticket out of here, and I don't know what it is. I wish I could just make up my damned mind!"

"Done!" said Joseph, suddenly on Malone's shoulder. He smiled and vanished.

"Wait, that wasn't my wish. Come back!"

Malone felt himself being forced to sit. The straps were tight around his ankles and wrists.

"Ha! I see it now. That's it. I know what I want! Come back, Joseph, come back! I've made up my mind!"

And then the warden flipped the switch, and Malone no longer had a mind to make up.

A Late Date
Tomi Lewis

She waited, listening to the rain ticking the seconds away on the windowpane. She watched as the numbers on the old digital clock radio slowly flipped past the minutes.

She waited for the phone to ring. Only a few more minutes and he would call. She knew he would call.

Two minutes slipped away. She moistened her lips and cleared her throat in anticipation. A small bead of perspiration trickled down her forehead toward the corner of her eye. She flicked it away with a long red-tipped finger. Another minute had gone by.

She rose and swayed over to the mirror, slightly unsteady on Salvation Army heels. An inspection of her face from every direction seemed to satisfy her. She licked her lips again, bared her teeth, and ran her tongue across the top ones. Teeth too white and straight, much whiter and straighter than her own had ever been. There was a smudge of red lipstick, like a drop of blood on a vampire fang. She carefully wiped it away and smiled at herself, her most seductive smile. She was practicing.

The rain counted out a few more seconds.

Her hands traveled to her hair, brassy red that can only come from a bottle. Only Miss Clairol knew for sure. She carefully patted the helmetlike hairstyle, making sure each hair was in place. Nervous fingers traveled down her neck, across prominent collarbones, to the cleft between her breasts. She hesitated, turning to check the time, three more minutes had passed. Only a few more to wait.

He would call; he always called at midnight.

She gazed around the room, an old overstuffed chair sat next to a fifties-era blonde end table that held the phone and clock. The phone that would ring soon, very soon. Another minute flipped over on the clock, the seconds ticked away on the window. The chair had sprung a leak, and stuffing dribbled onto the floor.

She lit the stub of a candle and turned off the bare overhead bulb. The candlelight combined with the pink neon from outside her window to hide the empty corners of the room. The rosy glow softened the ragged edges of the chair along with the lines in her face that too much makeup could no longer hide.

Two minutes to go. She felt the excitement begin to rise inside her. The palms of her hands became moist. She licked her lips yet again. Her hand went to her throat, and her fingers fluttered down her chest like a butterfly looking for a place to land.

She positioned herself in the chair and it leaked a little more. She crossed her legs and arranged the faded red dress.

The numbers on the clock seemed frozen in time. She stared, willing them to move. Perspiration dotted her upper lip. At last the numbers creaked over to the appointed hour. Midnight. The witching hour.

The phone rang.

She squeezed her legs together, a shiver rippling through her body.

The phone rang a second time; she savored each ring and picked up after the fourth.

A quivering breath pushed the hello past those blood-red lips.

A low raspy breath greeted her. Her breath came faster; she whispered another hello. Still no reply, just breathing, throaty, labored, almost moaning. His breath slipped through the phone, soft and low, like a tongue sliding into her ear.

She shuddered, then smiled.

Perhaps tonight would be the night. Perhaps tonight he would speak to her.

Liar's Dice

Adam Niswander

I found my son, little Rudy, playing with foot-high toy monsters on the floor in the living room. I had never seen the little figures before, but they appeared to be crude plastic. I threw my briefcase on the couch as I walked by. "What'd you do today, sport?" I went to the kitchen to mix myself a drink.

I carefully poured six fingers of bourbon into a tall glass. By the time I made it to my favorite chair, only half a glass remained.

Everything had gone to hell in a handbasket since we saw the UFO. Both the boy and his mother had developed dark circles under their eyes and I felt like I had lost my family to a couple of body-snatcher raccoons.

According to the therapist, Rudy's antisocial behavior was a result of the trauma. He had taken to lying . . . or at least telling fibs. I wanted to be stern with him, but I still suffered under the shock of our sighting and I am an adult. Could I blame him?

"I played Liar's Dice. That's what liars do."

"What's that, son?"

"You asked what I did today. We played Liar's Dice."

"That's nice, Rudy." I gave him a tired smile. "Where's your mother?" I asked.

"Monsters got her," he replied quietly.

I took a moment to assimilate the answer before I raised one eyebrow and glared at him. "Daddy had a hard day at the office, Rudy. We've talked about these lies of yours, haven't we?"

He did not look away or change expression.

"Monsters got her," he said again, his mouth tightening.

I calmed myself. He would soon turn seven. I had promised myself I would let him grow up. "Monsters, huh."

He nodded solemnly. "Yep. Monsters."

"What did they do to her, Rudy?"

His voice could barely be heard. "Killed her."

"Where did this happen?"

"In your bedroom," he said, a little more confident. "They played Liar's Dice. I only peeked once. It's pretty messy in there."

I sighed. "I'm not kidding, Rudy. All I asked is where's your mother?"

He looked down and I had to lean forward to catch his reply. "Told you."

"Rudy, you told me monsters killed your mother in our bedroom. I want you to tell me the truth."

He made himself smaller, but his stubborn reply could still be heard. "Is the truth."

I forced myself out of the chair and towered over him. "That's enough, son."

"The monsters say you're the liar when you don't believe me," he mumbled.

I stalked off down the hall, speaking over my shoulder. "Okay, Rudy. I'm going to check. If Mommy hasn't been killed by monsters in the bedroom, you're going to get a spanking."

The grotesque enormity of the words I spoke almost made me stop.

When I reached the open bedroom door, I did stop.

My eyes widened and I felt the adrenaline burst into my system as my heart began to beat rapidly.

My mind had begin to scream silently, *NO, NO, NO, NOOOOOOOOOOoooooooooooooooo.*

I forced myself to shut down the panic. There weren't monsters in the bedroom. Genevieve had not been killed by monsters in our bedroom.

I pushed on the door. It squeaked, as if it had been stolen from a cartoon dungeon.

There was blood everywhere.

Genevieve had been ripped or cut to fragments in our bedroom. Her head lay in two halves, brains exposed, eyes wide in permanent terror, the half of her mouth I could see stretched in the rictus of a scream.

I fell to my knees and vomited.

"Should have believed me, Daddy."

The voice sounded strange, as if it came from a vast distance.

"The monsters kill you if you don't believe me."

I shook my head. "Rudy, what in God's name happened here?"

"I told Mommy about the monsters and she said I lied to her. The monsters say you're the liar when you call me a liar. That's when they killed her. They played slice and dice Liar's Dice."

I felt hysteria rising deep inside. "Stop it, Rudy! What happened here? *Don't lie to me!*"

My son shrugged and looked down.

I followed his gaze and saw the little brightly colored monsters marching into the room between his feet. They no longer looked like plastic. They suddenly did not look like toys. They all carried long shiny swordlike weapons.

"You get to play Liar's Dice, Daddy."

The Light of Truth

Benjamin Adams

he millennium was hard approaching, and madness came with it.

In a dark briefing room, two FBI men watched, with mounting horror, the picture from a shaky, hand-held video camera.

"I've seen enough," said Special Agent Kiley. "Turn it off."

The image on the video screen froze and vanished in a rain of static. Losurdo turned to Kiley, his grizzled brow troubled. "I thought I'd seen every kind of millennial nut there was—but I never seen it much worse than this," the native Chicagoan muttered.

"It's supposedly voluntary, isn't it?"

A dark cloud seemed to pass over Special Agent Losurdo's face. "Supposedly. The Cult of Inner Vision is growing daily. I can't go anywhere in town without seeing people blinded in one eye. They're wearing it like some kinda badge of honor. Eyes infected, full of pus—it's revolting. I can't stand thinking about how many of 'em there'll be by New Year's."

Kiley nodded. "And they managed to compromise the last agent we sent in. We haven't heard from Charlie Rizor in over a week—this videotape was the last thing we received from him. So tomorrow, we're going in.

"We'll find out what happened to Charlie."

The Cult of Inner Vision based itself in a dilapidated old Baptist church on the West Side of Chicago. From here, the Cult had spread its word throughout North America.

Kiley and Losurdo wore the simple brown robes favored by the cult, blending in with the group of initiates gathered in the old church's courtyard. Crisp fallen leaves littered the yellowing grass. The initiates moved in a sort of Brownian motion, trying to keep warm in the gray October morning.

A door leading into the church opened, and a lone figure, clad in a white robe, stepped into the courtyard and clapped his hands.

"Initiates! Please! Be still!"

The initiates obediently ceased their milling.

Losurdo nudged Kiley in the ribs.

The man in the white robe had no right eye, merely a grotesquely scabbed-over pit.

He was Charlie Rizor.

"Please form a line behind me," he called, then turned back toward the interior of the building. The initiates meekly formed a single-file line behind him, Kiley and Losurdo bringing up the rear.

Rizor stepped inside the hall and pointed to the left.

"Proceed down the hall until you come to the chapel, and take a seat. I will join you there shortly."

Losurdo's guts ran riot with disgust for what had happened to Rizor. The two of them had been good enough friends, sharing some brews, taking in a few games at Wrigley Field. How could this happen to a regular guy—a fellow FBI agent?

The line of initiates passed Rizor as he stood just inside the hallway. Losurdo and Kiley began walking past the cultist, but he reached out and laid a hand on each man's shoulder.

"No," he said. "Not you."

"I can't see a goddamn thing!" burst Losurdo. "What the hell are you doing, Charlie?"

They were in a pitch-black room off the corridor, away from the chapel and the other initiates. "Once I was as you; I saw only with the eyes with which I was born," Rizor said. "But I have seen the light of truth. And the truth made my inner eye awake, and I no longer needed my outer eye."

"We can get you out of here," said Kiley.

"I don't wish to leave."

"Then let us go," Kiley said reasonably.

"No. You will endanger the movement. We must prepare the path for the millennium. So—you must see what I have seen.

"You must also see the light of truth."

There was a rustle of movement, and then the light went on—

Kiley was never seen again.

Losurdo spent several days in restraints—under observation—at Northwestern Memorial Hospital. When he became sufficiently lucid, his superiors from the FBI questioned him about Kiley and Rizor.

The fragments of information Losurdo offered were vague and frustrating. Still, two months later, on December 27, a series of government raids took place on each of the regional headquarters of the Cult of Inner Vision: Seattle, San Francisco, Des Moines, Atlanta, New York, and Chicago.

But the cult's leaders had vanished, leaving behind thousands of delirious, half-blinded followers.

On December 31, the clock turned over to the new millennium.

And on January 1, at approximately 12:03 A.M. (Central Standard Time), former FBI Special Agent Losurdo removed his right eye with a dirty teaspoon from his kitchen sink.

He'd seen the light of truth.

And oh, how it shone.

Like a Charm

David Niall Wilson

Lucky was feeling anything but as he exited the bar: a red-neck nightmare, complete with pointed boots, toothless women, and hats that would hold half a keg. Not the place for intelligent conversation, that was certain. Also no place for a transient piece of scooter trash to be hangin' out on a Saturday night.

He saw the two hicks as soon as he hit the door. A second later, he saw the old man. They were beating the poor man senseless, chuckling and yee-hawin' to beat the band, like it was great sport or something. Closer examination (Lucky took about three steps nearer) brought the realization that the old man was either a drunk or a bum. Neither was Lucky's business. He started toward his bike with a shrug, then he stopped.

"Damn," he muttered to himself, "here we go again."

His decision made for him by an overactive conscience, Lucky turned with a growl and dived low at the closer country boy, knocking him to the ground. Leaping free, he leveled a kick at the boy's face, planting his steel-toed boot firmly in the boy's nose.

One down, he thought grimly. The second boy was so drunk that Lucky's fist was headed for his face before he caught on that the fun was over. He went down in a heap beside the old man, and Lucky hurried to extricate the man, dragging him away from the prone, moaning bodies of the two drugstore cowboys.

"You get on outta here, old man," he growled. "Damned if I'm helpin' you anymore!"

The old man's eyes glinted with surprising energy and intelligence. Without a word, the old man slipped a leather thong over his head, dropped it in place around Lucky's neck, and melted into the night. Not a thank-you, not a word.

Lucky glanced down at the pendant. A dark crystal bird. Pretty cool, but there was no time to study it just yet. He could already hear more of Billy-Bob and company pouring out the doors of the bar to see what the noise was. He leaped onto his bike, revved it up, and hit the road, sending a shower of stones in his wake.

They saw him. "Damn," he repeated, gunning the Harley and lowering his head against the wind.

It took them only a moment to be on his trail, 4X4 trucks with NRA stickers and rebel flags, hopped-up Camaros and Mustangs—a hillbilly nightmare. He almost expected to see the General Lee pull up beside him.

His bike was faster than most of what they had, but they knew the roads, and it wasn't long before they began to pull nearer. Ahead, he could see a bridge materializing through the early evening fog. *Swell,* he thought. *Just what I had in mind for a night on the town.*

It was then that he saw him. The old man was suddenly there, standing beside the road with his wide, toothless grin. No way that old man got there ahead of him, but there he was. He felt a heat near his chest, where the pendant dangled, but he ignored it, hitting the gas a bit harder and praying there was no curve beyond the bridge.

As he roared across the metal surface, he glanced into his rearview mirror. A dark shadow had blotted the moon suddenly, and huge taloned claws had appeared, diving from the clouds toward the lead pickup. He ripped his gaze away, heart hammering, and returned it to the road ahead, just in time to avoid running off into a field.

Behind him, there was a rending of metal and a shrill, piercing cry that burst through the night with explosive volume. He did not look again. As he turned onto the main road, hitting the throttle hard and aiming for the open road, he heard laughter, cackling through the night. The moon smiled down on him with a toothless grin, and the sounds of pursuit died in the stillness of the night.

Maybe Lucky was the right name, after all. Just maybe.

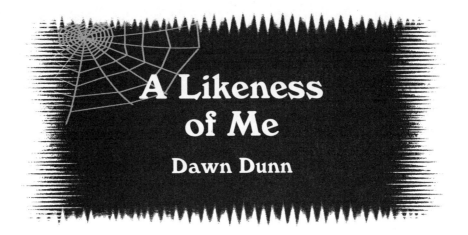

A Likeness of Me

Dawn Dunn

How would you like to see my paintings?"

It was the oldest line in the world, one that probably originated with Michelangelo, but this time the words dripped like southern honey from the lips of the most intriguing redhead I'd ever met. She sat across from me in a smoke-filled bar in downtown Denver. We'd been shouting over the noise of the band for an hour.

She arched her eyebrow, a cute trick, and smiled provocatively, as though her invitation was a dare.

What was the worst that could happen? I could get slapped in the face? She stood only five foot six and weighed about a hundred twenty pounds. I know there are female sociopaths, but the odds were significantly higher of me being one than her.

We drove her red Camaro down Colfax. She lived in the historic district, among a row of crumbling brick Victorian two-stories with woodwork that resembled the painted ladies of San Francisco.

"Nice house," I said, then followed her inside.

I blanched unmistakably at the contents. Books and stacks of three-dimensional art filled every corner. Most of the towering mounds were draped with cobwebs and thick with layers of dust. Paintings adorned every inch of the walls.

"I'm a collector," she said.

But there didn't seem to be any purpose to her collection. The pieces weren't displayed in a way that they could be seen or appreciated, merely piled in heaps like old, discarded newspapers. On closer examination, I saw that they all depicted some grotesque object or action, what an aficionado might've termed horror. I reconsidered the possibility of her being a serial killer.

She started upstairs, where I supposed her bedroom to be. "The best is up here," she promised.

I watched her hips sway and caught a glimpse of the black camisole underneath her blouse, then cast aside my fear of homicidal mania. As I reached the landing, I felt a strange sense of déjà vu, though I was certain I had never been here before.

The second floor had its share of books and magazines pertaining to the horror field, but most riveting of all were the paintings—her paintings.

"They're wonderful," I said, as impressed as I was appalled. So many hideous forms of obsession and depravity. "Where did you study?"

"I didn't," she said, leading me further into the maze of rooms that formed her studio, which was lit now only by moonlight and streetlamps. "Painting comes naturally to me. I've been doing it since the day I was born."

I knew she was kidding, though there was nothing remotely humorous about her or her work. "Why won't you tell me the truth?"

"I am," she insisted. "Come further inside."

Her voice had become disturbingly familiar. "Where do I know you from?" I said.

"Don't you remember, John? Think hard."

She'd disappeared amid the labyrinth of gruesome yet fascinating portraits. Then I noticed that some of the faces, rendered in such agony and pain, were *mine*. "You know me," I said, baffled, and touched my terrified visage in one of the vile paintings. My arm sank into the canvas up to my elbow. I felt colder than I'd ever felt in my life and yanked it back out.

I heard a disembodied laugh. "Don't be afraid, John."

I stood in the final room. I'd reached the outer wall of her chamber of horrors and saw new sketches of myself, ones where I was only partially formed. Suddenly remembering, I shouted and grabbed my head in an attempt to remove every memory she'd placed there.

In front of the window, another painting stood drying. On the floor beneath it, I saw myself as I'd been a few weeks ago, curled in a fetal position, like a life-sized lump of unbaked clay, naked and covered in the red oil of my birth. But this wasn't me, nor was the face in the picture mine.

"Your turn is over, John. It's time for another."

Her gift was not painting at all, but a wholly different type of creation. I was but an idea of her befouled mind, given a brief chance for life and breath, to be discarded like the dust-covered objects in the lower level. Though the window was closed, I felt a huge, cold wind sucking me through the glass, into the air, into the night, into the nothingness of her imagination.

The Little Black Dog

Linda J. Dunn

I 'm worried about Blackie. We were on our way to Grandma's when we stopped for Daddy to make a quick repair. Someone let Blackie out and he ran away.

I cried and wanted to stay until we found Blackie, but Daddy said he would be fine and we couldn't stay.

I hope Blackie finds a good home.

Dear Elaine:

The weirdest thing happened when Gary and I took that short delayed honeymoon to Florida. We stayed in the camper at Uncle Herb's house, just like we'd planned, and had a great time. But a couple of days after we arrived, this little mutt showed up. He couldn't have been any bigger than a chihuahua and was pure black. This had to be someone's pet once. Gary was cooking something on the grill and the little guy wandered over and sat up, begging for food. He looked really cute. Reminded me of an old cartoon about martial arts animals. His one paw was extended oddly while the other criss-crossed in a way I just can't describe.

We fed him a couple of hot dogs and he stuck around after that—didn't want to leave.

I wanted to take him home with us. He's so little and cute. Gary said no. The apartment's small and he doesn't want to mess with walking a dog and all that.

Can you imagine my surprise when we got home and found the dog in the back of the camper? Gary swears he didn't let him in and we're still fighting because he won't believe I didn't do it.

But the dog's here for now. Even as I'm writing this, he's sitting up begging for food.

I think I'll give him a piece of my hot dog.

Dear Elaine:

You're Melanie's best friend and she was writing a letter to you when she disappeared. The police have searched everywhere and can't find any evidence of her existence except some bloodstains on the floor that, for some crazy reason, they think had something to do with the fight she mentioned. Can you talk to them? Make them understand? I loved Elaine and I'd never do anything to hurt her. Sure, I was upset when she dragged that damn mutt home but I kept it, didn't I?

It's still here, sitting at my feet. It's probably hungry. I'm going to feed it before mailing this letter.

Mrs. Elaine Gormley:

The enclosures are the notes I mentioned in our earlier telephone call. Both Gary and Melanie Emerson have disappeared without a trace. Although we've found no evidence of foul play, we have found some fresh bloodstains that appear to match Mr. Emerson's blood type. Any assistance you can provide would be appreciated.

Thank you for expressing concern about the dog. It's being held at the local humane shelter. If you're interested, I'm sure they can make arrangements for you to adopt it.

The animal would, of course, have to be neutered first.

I've got a new pet now. His name is Brownie and he's a Petrie that Daddy got from a pet store when he was on a business trip to the Third Quadron in the East Galaxy. I still miss Blackie but Daddy reminded me how upset the neighbors were when he ate their son, Rikkie, and they had to have him regrown from cloned cells.

I still say it was Rikkie's fault. Blackie was part-Shelton and they get real mad if you feed them anything smaller than, for example, a side of that strange four-legged animal with horns that we saw when Daddy stopped to fix our ship on that little backwoods planet called Earth.

I really hope Blackie found a good home with people who feed her right. Blackie was pregnant.

Little Man

Scott M. Brents

The small boy was looking at his feet. He kicked absently at a pebble. His sneakers were very worn.

"What did you say?" Jim asked the child.

"I saw an alien in the woods. Behind the house." Raymond pointed.

"How old are you, Raymond?"

"I'm eight, almost nine. My birthday is on the Ides of March. Mom says so. March fifteenth." Raymond had quit with the pebble and was looking off into the distance, like a dog listening to a sound no one else could hear.

This kid is a riot, Jim thought. Guess I have to teach him a lesson. Hate to do it. Sure I do. But next thing you know, little Raymond will be old enough to walk down the street with an old rusty nail, scratching up the paint jobs on the neighborhood cars. Not my car. Not if I can help it.

"Well, Raymond," Jim said, his voice dropping down an octave to convey the sincerity in his words. "Do you know what happens to little boys who tell lies? Hmmmm? Do you?"

"Mom says, that if you . . ." Raymond started.

"Forget what your mom says, kid. What are you, a *momma's boy?* Listen up. Liars go to hell. Straight down like a rock to the bottom of the sea. Then they burn there forever and ever in the lake of fire."

Raymond's eyes had widened, his lips became white as he held them tightly together.

"But I *swear*, in the woods, behind the house, there was a little man, shorter than me. He had this metal thing in his hand. I tried to talk to him, but he wouldn't listen, he just kept bouncing around the trees so fast I could hardly see him."

"Son, I wasn't born yesterday. I don't understand why you want me to believe such a pile of turkey droppings. I used to think you were a bit of a grandson figure to me. But no grandson of mine would try to lie to me like that," Jim said, lifting his eyebrows.

Raymond wasn't listening to him. The boy's head was still turned halfway around, looking at the woods where the alien was supposed to be. He was crying.

"I don't want to go to hell," he blubbered.

I screwed up, Jim thought.

"You don't have to go to hell, Ray-Gun."

Jim called Raymond by that nickname only when everything was A-OK, or cut-and-dried. Raymond sniffled, looking at him. The Arkansas sky was turning gold as the sun went down.

"I don't? I'm not talking about lying; I'm talking about something else," Raymond said, wiping his nose.

"Hell, no. Hell doesn't even exist, except in some parts of East Drexell." Jim laughed loud and hard but then he got quiet.

"I'm sorry, Ray-Gun. I was just trying to scare you; forgive me."

Jim didn't know why he suddenly decided to be honest with the boy. Maybe it was the fact that a person can only be meaner than spit for so long before it gets to be silly. Especially being mean to a small boy.

"Tell me more about your alien, son."

Raymond's face brightened, and he began to describe the greenish little man who had crawled out of a silver can, and how the teeth on the stranger were sharp and scary, and how it fanned out its wings like a bat. More disturbing was the description Raymond gave of the loud buzzing noise the creature made as it leapt from tree to tree, swooping down via its leathery wings, trying to grab Raymond with its metal pincers that served as its feet.

The boy finished the story by describing how he had destroyed the beast, and then dug a hole, giving it a proper burial.

"When I killed it, I didn't think it was like killing a human. I thought it was like killing a bug. You don't think I'll go to hell for killing it, do you?"

"Of course not. And I told you already that there ain't no hell. Just people feeling vengeful or guilty. Remember that, Raymond."

Raymond nodded, but he was still looking at the woods.

Lopez

Benjamin Adams

It started with another call for Lopez.

"No, you have the wrong number," she told the caller, and then blearily looked at the digital clock on the bedstand. 5:30 A.M.

"Lopez again?" her husband muttered from his half of the bed. "When the hell are they going to figure out that Lopez doesn't have this number anymore?"

"I just want to know who the hell this guy is," she said, shutting off the alarm, her last half hour of sleep stolen. "Why no one ever calls for him at a civilized hour."

Her husband moaned noncommittally, burying his face in his pillow.

Wearily, she rose from bed and began her morning routine.

The rest of the day followed suit. Somehow she made it through and finally emerged from the office tower, blinking up at the steely gray sky like she'd never seen it before. She felt cold and clammy in spite of the ferocious August heat.

Alone in her Saab she enjoyed a few blissful moments of silence. *This day,* she thought, *has been hell. There's no possible way it could get any worse.*

She picked up the GE cell phone from the slot just under the indash Blaupunkt and punched the memory key for her home number. If her husband was there, she could tell him to get dinner started; spaghetti, maybe. She wondered if the tomato sauce would sit heavy on her stomach after a day like this.

She heard her home phone ring five . . . ten . . . fifteen times. "Where *are* you?" she hissed, and punched the button again.

Still no answer. Not even the answering machine was on.

Frowning, she replaced the cell phone and started the Saab's engine.

The iron-gray clouds promised rain. At every intersection she was caught in a seething, honking morass of cars and trucks, moving just a few feet at a time. Sweating, pale faces swam behind glass at the periphery of her vision, other drivers caught in the rush-hour maze.

She tried calling home again. The unanswered ringing was gone. Instead there was the quick, insistent beeping of a disconnected phone.

A plain white moving van took up most of the street in front of her building, and she barely managed to squeeze past, into the parking lot.

For once, the building's elevator worked on the first try. She found herself sharing the ride to the fourth floor with a large man wearing dirty white overalls. One of the movers, she figured.

The brief ride passed in silence, and they both exited on the same floor.

She blinked and pulled up short as he kept walking.

Wait, she thought. *Did I get off on the wrong floor?*

Because this should be—

She ran to the open door the man from the elevator had just entered.

"This is my apartment!" she screamed.

The place had been stripped bare. There were only a couple of boxes left in the center of the living room floor. A second, slighter man in matching white overalls was sealing the boxes with clear packing tape.

"What the hell are you doing here?" she demanded hysterically. "What did you do with our stuff? Where's my husband?"

"Mrs. Lopez," the slight man said soothingly.

"What? What?" she sobbed.

"Mrs. Lopez, calm down—"

"No! I'm not Lopez! You've made a mistake." She turned from one to the other. "This has got to be a mistake. Lopez used to have our phone number, you see? That's all! *He used to have our phone number!*"

The slight man nodded, concern evident on his face. "Of course. It's always a mistake. But we didn't make it—Mrs. Lopez."

She heard a puff behind her, and felt a sting in her right thigh.

She turned and saw a small pistol in the hand of the larger man, who shrugged nonchalantly.

"What—what the hell—"

"Tranquilizer," the slighter man explained as the room began to spin. She stumbled but was easily caught by the large man before her legs gave way completely.

He swung her over his shoulder and grabbed one of the boxes with his free arm. The slighter man followed with the last box.

They moved down the hall quickly toward the elevator; from where she swung upside down, she saw her neighbors' pale, sweating faces peering from their doorways.

One by one, their doors slammed shut.

"Think it's gonna rain," said the man from the elevator.

"Yeah," said the slight man.

After loading the boxes, they carefully placed her on an overstuffed burgundy couch in the back of the truck. Her husband was already there, propped up like a rag doll.

A little drool rolled from the corner of his mouth as his eyes registered her.

The rolling door slammed shut.

In the humid darkness she tried to speak, to spit the word, to scream it:

Lopez!

But there was only the sound of the first fat drops of rain on the roof of the truck.

Lost Pao

Jessica Amanda Salmonson

Hu'ang Pao wandered from his home when he was four. Many days and many nights, his entire family searched everywhere. The people living in the neighborhood joined the sad quest. No boy was found. No one had any idea what happened to him. But years later, a handsome stranger came to Hu'ang Pao's old neighborhood. "Look at that young man," a woman whispered; and her friend replied, "Haven't we seen him before?"

"Aunties," said the stranger to the district. "I am looking for the house of Hu'ang."

"What would you bother them for, young man?" asked one of the two women.

"I knew the way but have forgotten," said the stranger.

The women failed to realize this answer was evasive, but pointed him along the route. When he was gone, the first one said, "You are right; we have seen him before. Surely that is little Pao grown tall, finding his way home at last."

The house of Hu'ang received the stranger for an interview. Little by little, the family members began to feel they recognized the cryptic youth. The elderly mother said, "Aren't you my lost son Pao?" A sister said, "Aren't you my baby brother?" A grandfather said, "Didn't I bounce you on my knee when you were small?" And so on until everyone had tried in their various ways to make him confess his identity. He never would confess it. Finally the father said, "He was only four when he was lost; probably he doesn't remember any of us. Son, tell us where you have lived all this while."

"I have lived among black lotus. I have wandered in thick clouds of incense. I have searched in dark ashes. I have eaten the soul of Hu'ang Pao."

In an instant, the stranger transformed himself into a monster with a horrendous visage. The house of Hu'ang was in turmoil, fetching weapons and battling the beast. At last he was killed and, when he had fallen in the garden, was restored to a handsome young man.

"Was he our little Pao after all?" the family wondered. They put him in the family tomb as though he were.

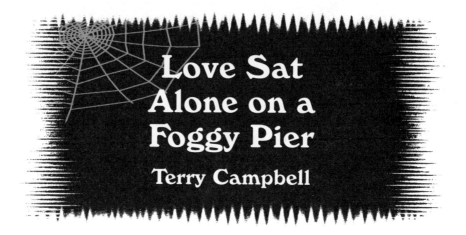

Love Sat Alone on a Foggy Pier

Terry Campbell

It was so foggy on the pier that night, I was afraid I might walk off the end and drop right into the middle of White Rock Lake. *Damned fog.* I would never see the Lady of the Lake in this mess. I kept walking slowly, but the gentle tickle of the low clouds on my face and the rhythmic lapping of the water against the pier supports produced a hypnotic effect, and I found it difficult to pay attention to what I was doing. In fact, I didn't see the girl sitting at the end of the pier until I was right on her.

It really startled me, and I think I may have grabbed her to keep myself from tripping over her and doing some night swimming. But she didn't even look up.

"I'm sorry," I said. "This damned fog. I almost didn't see you there."

She nodded her head, almost imperceptibly. She continued to stare across the lake, seemingly at nothing in particular. I happened a sideways glance at her.

"Are you here to see the Lady of the Lake?"

"Lady of the Lake?" she asked. Her voice was smooth, like liquid.

"You know. The old legend. The woman who drowned in this lake." She didn't react. I didn't know if she was unfamiliar with the story, or just wasn't listening to me. "They say you can see her on a foggy night." She didn't look at me. I gazed out across the water at the fog. "Not gonna see her in this mess, though."

"Do you often look for ghosts?" she asked.

Finally, I thought. "Oh, it's just a whim."

She nodded. "I stopped looking for ghosts a long time ago."

"You did?" I started to say something else, but then she turned to look at me for the first time, and all grasp of intelligible speech fled my brain, replaced by only one consuming thought: beauty.

She was beautiful. Her eyes were dark and piercing, and I imagined she could cut the fog with her gaze. Her hair was long, dark, and slightly damp from the moisture in the air. She didn't crack a smile, and for some reason, that made me love her even more.

"Ghosts are things of the past," she said. She turned her attention back to the lake. "There's no point in looking for the past."

Somewhere across the water, a lake loon wailed. It was a disturbing sound, especially in the dense fog. I wished it wasn't so foggy.

"Why are you afraid of the past?"

"I'm not afraid of it," she answered. "I just can't go there."

"What about your future?"

"It's foggy," she said.

I looked around, couldn't see much, could barely see *her*.

"Yeah, I hate this weather."

She looked at me again, and I thought I saw a tiny crack of a smile, but it was gone quickly. Instead, she leaned over and gave me a soft kiss. Her lips were cold from the night air; I wondered how long she'd sat out there. "I have to go," she said. "The fog will be lifting soon."

She stood and started to walk away. "Wait, you didn't even tell me your name," I called out.

She turned and faced me. That almost-smile again. "Call me Fog," she said, and walked away, disappearing into the foggy night after only a few steps.

I never saw her again. I often walk or ride my bike around the lake at all hours of the day and night, hoping to catch a glimpse of her. But I never do.

The thing that bothers me is the way she left that night. I've gone back to that pier many times. At least, I think it's the same pier. There are so many on the lake, it's hard to tell. I situate myself on the pier, try to reenact where we stood that night, and I keep coming up with the same problem.

Where she walked away into the fog, there is no pier. Only the murky depths of White Rock Lake.

At least, I think it's the same pier. I can't be sure.

I never think about trying to find the Lady of the Lake anymore. I just keep coming back, especially on foggy nights, hoping to see my own special lady of the lake again.

Lovelocks

Brian McNaughton

Caleb Hopkins would have kissed the devil's backside to win Abishag Barebones, but she laughed.

"The devil, Goodman Hopkins? This is 1690. In London, they scoff at talk of witchcraft."

"This is Massachusetts."

She sighed. "If I doubted that, one look at you would disabuse me." She scraped the mud from her boots at her door. "Oh to be in England, now that April's there!"

"Did you just make that up?"

"No, it hasn't been written yet."

He flung himself to his knees. "You *are* a witch! Admit me to your coven, take me to your debaucheries in the woods where you dance naked with demons!"

The door opened to disclose Preserved Barebones, Abishag's horrible father. "The tongue is an unruly evil, and no man can tame it," he intoned. "However—" he kicked Caleb in the face and sent him sprawling—"one must try. Such talk is dangerous, Goodman Hopkins."

Pain devoured the world, but Abishag destroyed it by shielding him with her voluptuous body. He felt her warmth, smelled her breath. The pressure of her breasts stopped his heart. "Caleb's not dangerous, father! He's merely a ninny."

"If you believe anything is more dangerous than a ninny, child, then your two centuries—I mean decades, of course, your two *decades* on earth have been wasted! Come inside and leave that malodorous refuse to the hogs."

Her lips! They were inches from his face; her attention was diverted. He mashed his mouth to hers. Like a lonesome leech, he had found his one true place, and all thought evaporated as he sucked. Preserved plied his vengeful foot once more, this time most intimately.

Caleb shrieked, gabbled for air, gripped something that tore. Abishag wrenched herself free. Somewhere in a world where happy people anticipated more than a moment of life, a door slammed.

He came to himself clutching a fistful of black hairs that he had torn from the head of his beloved. He'd show her! He had harkened to Old Zuvembie, the Adamses' slave, and he knew something about witchcraft. He would bind her to his will.

He hobbled home and pried up the loose floorboard behind his bed. Beneath it lay female figurines that he molded from clay to help him court naughty thoughts. The latest had been formed on his notion of Abishag, although they suffered from his woeful inexperience. He sat down at a table by the fire with the likeliest figurine and pasted the hair on with spit. He was ignorant of devilish details, but he hoped his intention would satisfy the Prince of Darkness.

Two hairs, three—but where were the rest? He'd treasured a handful against his breast on the way home. A draft must have blown them from the table.

He knelt to examine the floor. Dust kittens deluded him. The firelight made strange shadows dance. "Have pity, Satan," he prayed.

It worked! He spotted a black clump. But when he crawled forward, the mass unraveled into separate strands that wriggled every which way. He tore his nails in his haste to gather as many as he could.

He must have picked up a splinter. He was afraid to open his hand and examine it lest the lively hairs escape, but he could stand the pain no longer. He opened his hand and screamed when he saw a strand boring voraciously beneath the nail of his index finger.

He could still grip the end, perhaps, and pull it out, but his left hand wouldn't work. He screamed again, for the hairs in that hand were winding around his fingers to bind them. He forgot the pain under his fingernail as they tightened and bit into his flesh like wires.

The hairs writhed all over the floor now, but they converged on him with purpose. He stamped furiously, but this had no effect as they crawled onto his boots and squirmed up his legs. When he opened his mouth to scream for help, they slipped loathsomely into his mouth to bind his tongue and stop his throat. He ran, smashing his way through the door, when the hairs at last scaled his legs to penetrate his private parts.

"I saw him bumping down the street on his hindquarters like a dog with worms last night," Preserved Barebones said when Caleb's strangely riddled body was discovered. "I let him be, assuming he was enjoying a religious ecstasy. He was a good man."

Everyone said amen to that, except Abishag, who was home nursing a headache.

Magpie

Brian McNaughton

After burying Marcia's handbag in the trash, Dwight washed his hands like a satisfied craftsman. Not even the fluorescent candor of the men's room mirror could spoil his pleasure.

Upstairs, she had discovered the theft. Male admirers swarmed around her. Winded by his climb from the basement, he gasped his excuses as he squeezed through.

"What's wrong?"

"My bag."

"She had it slung over her chair," the bartender said. "You can't do that here."

Dwight had hoped he would say that, but he pounded the bar and shouted, "What kind of place is this?"

The bartender bought them a round. The manager seated them at his best table. But these things happened. Even Marcia knew that.

"She couldn't help herself, I guess."

Dwight was inattentive. His veal cutlet was underdone.

"I needed a new one anyway," she said.

"I'll buy you one. I brought you here."

"She could have been anywhere. She didn't need it; that's my point."

He saw no point. Her mind was poorly organized, but that was part of her youthful charm. He refilled her wineglass. "Why do you say *she*?"

"I understand her. Women steal things on impulse, like shoplifting."

"You know who stole your bag? Any one of a hundred guys who stroll through bars on Friday night are looking for loose stuff."

"There are people like that?"

"They're called thieves."

"He sure picked the wrong person. I had a twenty. And personal things."

"He would ditch the bag. Sometimes people find them and mail the stuff back."

"My pictures! It makes me sick."

Her pain almost melted him. He could play detective and find it. Better play it safe. If his conscience bothered him later, he could call the restaurant anonymously and tell them where to look.

"Credit cards?" he asked.

She grimaced. "An unemployed dancer?"

"ID?"

"Sure."

"He knows where you live."

Dwight turned his full attention to the waitress. He let Marcia chew on his remark while he ordered coffee and cognac.

"You aren't suggesting he'd go to my place?"

"Probably not."

"Wouldn't he just take the money?"

"Probably. Were your keys in it?"

"Oh, shit!"

His face felt warm, perhaps due to the cognac or the steep climb from the men's room. It could be nerves. He was now on her ten-yard line.

"You'd better stay at my place and call a locksmith in the morning."

"Sure." Her look was wry.

"Suit yourself."

He talked about the play they'd seen. When he paused, she said, "The super could let me in, but . . ."

"Look, I can sleep on my couch."

She smiled ruefully. "All right."

In the cab, she snuggled into the arm he draped around her shoulders. She said, "I can't help feeling it was a woman."

"Maybe."

"Why are so many kleptomaniacs women? There must be some reason."

"I guess."

A shrink might have something to say about his own game. It was as much fun as the object. Maybe it was his way of getting even in advance for rejection. Before he saw a shrink, though, he would see an internist. You know you're getting old when you take a beautiful girl home and look forward to Gelusil.

"Like what?" she asked.

"Hm?"

"Like what would be the reason a woman steals things as opposed to a man?"

"Some maternal instinct. Feathering the nest."

She moved closer. He might have breathed more easily if she hadn't.

"I always thought it was because of some secret desire to be punished—"

"I'm sorry," he interrupted. "Make him stop the cab."

"What?"

"Indigestion, it's nothing. The bouncing—"

"Stop! Pull over, okay?"

"I don't feel well."

The driver stared ahead. Dwight could read his mind: Don't let the geezer croak in my cab.

He could no longer blame his position for the pain in his left arm. It had spread to his chest and become a clutching hand. He fumbled in his right topcoat pocket for his nitroglycerin pills, but the pocket was empty.

"Left pocket. Pills. Please."

He read in Marcia's stare the horror of youth for age and illness, and he couldn't blame her, but he wished she would overcome it and help him. "Pills. Pocket."

"I couldn't help myself! I didn't think they were important. I never steal anything important."

She wrenched the door open. What was she doing? "My pills," he gasped. "Where are they?"

"They were in my bag. I'm sorry!"

"Don't dump him on me, lady!" the cabby shouted after Marcia as she flew recklessly through traffic.

Making It Right

Bob Stein

I t took a moment for the boy to register on Charlie's alcohol-soaked brain. His leather-wrapped flask flew off the seat and slammed into the dash as he hit the brakes, shattering in a spray of Jack Daniel's and glass with a crack that punctuated a soft thud from the front of the car.

The Buick pitched and swerved on crumbling blacktop, skidding sideways to a stop more than a hundred feet past. He gripped the steering wheel with white knuckles, instantly sobered by fear. "Ohmygodohmygodohmygodohmygod."

Throwing open the door, he staggered out and ran back down the country road. Charlie almost cried in relief when he saw the kid kneeling over a shaggy form. He'd hit a dog, not the kid!

The impact had nearly torn the beast in two, yet the big mutt was still trying to lick the child's hand, and its tail thumped feebly. Blood ran from the dog's mouth, guts rolling out of a ragged tear on one side. The kid, a towheaded boy no more than six or seven, gave Charlie a sad look.

"You hurt him."

Oh, shit. No longer faced with the prospect of manslaughter, Charlie tried some damage control. "Uh, look kid. I'm real sorry. Musta jumped in front of me. Shoulda been on a leash, shouldn't he?" He talked fast, hoping to confuse the boy. There was no license in his wallet, thanks to an earlier DUI conviction. That was the main reason he'd been using this backwater road. If the police got involved, he could get locked up.

Fumbling out his billfold, he pulled out the two twenties inside and held them out in a shaking hand. "He'll be fine, kid. Take him to a vet or something. Here!" The bills floated down to lie on the road, unnoticed.

"You hurt him." The boy looked directly at him now, displaying large ice-blue eyes. "You was going way too fast, and you was drinking. I can smell it. So you gotta make it right."

Was the little shit actually trying to shake him down? Charlie opened the worn billfold to display the insides. "Nothin' left, kid." Of course, he had a couple hundred stashed in the trunk, but the kid didn't have to know that. "Tell you what. I'll go get a doctor, and bring him back so he can fix your doggy up, OK?"

The boy kept staring at him with those damned strange eyes. There was no anger, only deep sadness behind that gaze. And Charlie had the weirdest feeling that the sadness was directed at him. The dog shuddered again, and the kid shook his head. "Too late for that. You gotta make it right."

Shit! Charlie looked around in panic. No houses, no other cars or people in sight. The Buick was too far up the road for the kid to read the license plate. He spun and ran back to the car. No way he was going to jail for killing some damned dog.

His legs gave out under him before he was halfway there, and he sprawled heavily on the pavement. Dazed, he struggled to rise, but his body wouldn't obey. He could see the kid, still stroking the dying animal as he stared in Charlie's direction. The dog seemed to shudder, and Charlie screamed as pain washed over him. Then there was numbness.

Vision blurred, but he saw the boy stand and snap his fingers. The dog scrambled to its feet, tail wagging. They approached him, the mutt sniffing at the spreading pool of blood and entrails that pushed out from Charlie's shirt. He tried to speak, but found that there was no air left. As darkness closed in, he saw the boy squat down beside him. The two twenties fell next to his head, unnoticed.

Mall of the Dead

Del Stone Jr.

When Beverly came out of the department store fitting room, she found the sales associate sprawled in the aisle, a mannequin knocked over and a colorful heap of sweaters lying around her.

The lady was dead.

Beverly gulped a solid lump of breath and backed away, staggering to the cash register kiosk.

The associate there was dead, too.

A madman, Beverly thought, and almost simultaneously she realized that if a madman were on a killing spree, she might become his next victim. She ducked below the sales tables and crawled for the entrance to the mall center court.

As she made her way she spotted more bodies—women and men—blocking the aisles, every one of them frozen in rigid postures of stark terror. *Impossible,* she thought. *No man could have done this alone. It must have been a gang.* Mannequins lay amid the chaos, their wigs knocked off, staring with blank eyes at the ceiling tiles. What had they seen, she wondered, and if they could speak, what would they tell her?

She reached the store front. The mall spread out before her, a fresco of corpses, scattered packages and smashed windowfronts.

A clot of bodies lay by the counter at Morrow's, surrounded by scatterings of candy-coated peanuts that still trickled from the broken display case. Packages and articles of clothing lay in a confused jumble. Even mannequins from stores two or three windows down the concourse lay by the counter. Beverly guessed that whatever had killed these people had blown through with the suddenness and violence of a tornado.

She darted across the concourse and held up at a pillar that separated Morrow's from a tuxedo rental shop. She could see the mall entrance, and there, piled by the doors, was a huge mound of bodies. The glass in the doors had been shattered. Outside, she could see the blue strobe of police lights. She thought she saw movement—huddled figures training guns on the doors.

She began edging along the front of the tuxedo rental shop. The windows there had been broken too, the silk-clad mannequins leaning in well-dressed apposition to the chaos and death that surrounded them. As she stepped closer to the slaughter at the front door, she heard a voice shouting through a bullhorn:

"This is the police. If you can hear me, you must leave the mall at once."

No shit, Sherlock, she thought morosely.

"If anybody inside can hear me, this is the police . . ." the voice boomed.

She glanced at the shadowy figures outside and saw them point to her. They began waving to her, motioning for her to run. Several of them scurried toward the mall entrance.

At that moment, something touched Beverly on the shoulder.

The knobs of her spine glazed over with a sudden coating of ice, and she stopped, willing every molecule of her body into absolute stillness. She peeked at her shoulder. . . .

She had bumped into the tuxedo-clad mannequin.

The breath hiccuped out of her in a sob, and she felt her knees going weak with relief. That was when she noticed that the jumble of bodies at the door consisted partly of human beings. The rest were mannequins.

And some of them had their plastic hands around people's throats.

Beverly stopped breathing. She turned, and the mannequin in the tuxedo was staring at her.

The scream that had been simmering at the back of her throat boiled out now, and she jerked away and ran madly for the doors as a stampede sound of plastic feet against carpeting and tiles arose behind her, and the piles of bodies at the door began to stir sluggishly. She threw herself onto the pile and began to scramble for the top, stepping in the soft, pliant faces of people, and the hard, shifting torsos of dummies. Something grabbed her ankle and she screamed again and kicked as a shot blew just past her ear and something behind her exploded into plastic shrapnel. The grip on her ankle tightened, and she could feel its remorseless strength and knew she would never be able to pull herself free, that she would be drawn into that pile and strangled and—

A hand grabbed her and hauled her over the top—the cop, the cop, thank God it was the cop, and other cops were shooting through the entrance to the mall as the officer dragged her through the broken glass and into the blessed dark, where men in flak vests swarmed around her and helped her to her feet as the shooting rose to a roar—

"It's happening all over!" one of the cops screamed at her, but all she could think of was: *Get it off, get it off me*—

The plastic hand around her ankle, trailing a broken connecting rod, still squeezing, squeezing—

—as the war continued. . . .

Many Happy Returns

Brian McNaughton

Returning late to my new home, I spied a stranger in the alley. "May I help you?"

He ignored me. He needed no help to trespass.

The gate to the alley was locked. I entered my front door, grabbed a flashlight and a ring of household keys, and hurried through to the garden.

Lights from tall buildings around me revealed no lurkers. I unlocked the gate from the garden to the alley. Except for trash cans and litter, it was empty.

The house next door was a classic Federal house like mine, but divided into apartments. The stranger must belong there. But where had he gone?

I soon found an answer. A door into the neighboring house was blocked by old packing crates, but a man could squeeze through. The door looked unused, though. The knob was missing.

I examined the windows. They were above the level of my head, and securely barred. Lights shone in a few of them, and I glimpsed motion. I realized that I wouldn't have to call the police if I kept prowling like this.

Hurrying back to my garden, I saw a depression in the wall of my home. It had once been a door, but it was bricked over.

My home was the sort that Susan would have liked. She had enjoyed entertaining, and she had collected too many antiques for our East Side apartment.

"Why on earth did you buy a house?" my sister, Janice, had asked. "You should have moved to a *smaller* place when . . ."

"I can afford it."

"If you can afford an elephant, should you buy one?"

"It feels like home."

"It feels like a museum." Her disapproving gaze stopped at the urn on the mantel. "Or a tomb."

I was awakened that night by footsteps. They must have come from the house on the other side, which shared a wall with mine, although I had never heard untoward noise from those neighbors.

The next night I saw a woman in the alley, who vanished as neatly as her male counterpart. I went to the house across the alley and buzzed the super, but he affected to speak no English.

That night I heard two sets of footsteps and voices, as if the female stranger had moved into my walls, too. The conversation seemed pleasant, but I couldn't make out a word.

"You never get out, do you?" Janice scolded. "You're coming to my place for New Year's."

"No, I had planned . . ."

I couldn't continue. I had planned nothing. Susan's New Year's Eve parties had become a tradition. This would be the first year without one.

"Why don't we have my party here?" Janice said. "I always go to yours, anyway. You must have the list."

Going through the list was a ghoulish exercise. So many names had been crossed off, and still more had to be. Life is like the trenches in the First World War. Instead of five minutes, it takes sixty years or so to lose your friends, but you lose them.

Frank Capra takes over New York City when it snows at the holidays. The buildings are scaled down by the black sky; bright lights glorify sifting snow. The derelicts are replaced by charming character actors. "Hello, *Lion's Head!*" I called. "Hello, General Sheridan!" People smiled at me and I wished them all a happy new year as I hurried home, somewhat tipsily, with last-minute party supplies.

This would never do: the gate to the alley stood open. Trying to pull it closed with my arms loaded, I slipped on the ice and tumbled painfully down the steps.

Someone helped, but he guided me deeper into the alley. That bricked-over door was open. Light poured out.

"Now, wait—"

"What you need is a drink," my helper said. By God, it was *Roy!* Where had he been keeping himself all these years?

Inside the house I found that just about everybody had gathered. I hadn't seen Claire since . . . since she slashed her wrists. She didn't look any the worse for it.

"I think the mice are having a party," she said, one ear pressed to the wall.

"Acoustics," explained Paul, still the professor, although he had choked to death at a restaurant ten years ago. "The party's really here."

That should have been my cue to dash for the real entrance to my home. But I knew beyond all doubt as I walked into the next room that Susan was waiting for me.

Memory

Mollie L. Burleson

She couldn't stand it any longer. The tedium, the repetition, the sameness. Even the damned air conditioner blowing directly on her head, making her sinuses throb.

She'd been at this same job for longer than she could remember. And *what* a job! Chained to a desk, with a boss who harassed her constantly and coworkers who whispered behind her back all day long. She could do better than this. Why, washing dishes would be better. Anything would.

Carol was lonely and tired and unhappy. She felt she deserved something better out of life. She remembered something she had read once about how one should be grateful for what one has and should make the best of any situation. Right! As if one could be grateful for working here. Oh, sure, things *could* be worse, she supposed, but everyone had their own bugaboos. What bothered one person did not bother another. This place bothered her.

There was something else she couldn't quite remember, something she had heard or read, something that fled the minute she tried to grasp it. Hell, what difference did it make? Every moment spent in this dump was misery. Sometimes she wondered just what she had done to deserve this. But that, of course, was her religious upbringing. If bad things happened to you, it was because you deserved them. Well, what had *she* done? Nothing. Alone in life, no family, no friends, nothing but this damned rotten job.

She made some entries into the computer, wrapping her sweater tighter about her neck. Her head pounded, her sinuses ached, her eyes watered from the glare of the screen. She reached for a journal, and her back went out, sending screaming pains down her spine.

Groaning, Sarah gripped the small of her back. That's it, she told herself. She'd had it. She was out of here. She'd complained loud and long enough. Today she was going to do something about it.

She threw down her pen, switched off her terminal, gathered up her few belongings, and left her cubicle. Walking down the hall, she passed people, people who looked away from her or down at the carpet, never *at* her. People who always seemed to be smiling knowingly to themselves, and after she passed, tittered behind her back. So what! You can rot here for all I care, she thought.

Nearing the exit, she paused to look back, gloating over her decision to finally leave. That's when *he* put his hand on her shoulder. "Go back to your desk," he said. The smell of something like burnt matches filled the air. His nails clawed into her flesh, and in one horrible instant she remembered everything. She had come close to it earlier when she was thinking about how things could be worse and how certain things bothered some people and others not at all, and how tedium had always bothered her, and air conditioning.

She remembered now where she was and why. The terrible thing about the memory wasn't that she was in her own private hell and suffering her own kind of torture—it was that she had forgotten about it yesterday, and now, as the hand touched her, she remembered anew. And she would continue to forget and have to remember each day, every day for all time.

The Midwife's Temptation

Michael L. McComas

Not for Mary Brendan those childish games of Salem; for her I had a different plan. A bit of evil and mayhem to play upon her Puritan ethics, for is the evil not sweeter when done with only the best of intentions?

"Goodwife Brendan, I will give you a gift," I said, appearing to her in a form more beautiful than an angel's, my marks of shame hidden under one velvet-downed wing. "Will you accept it?"

"Oh, my lord, yes," said she, falling to her knees on the wooden floor by her hearth, and ashes smeared her skirts. She wept for joy as she asked, "Tell me, what is this gift?"

"Do you believe in predestination, that every soul's place in the Book of Life is written at birth? This is the doctrine of your Church?" I asked, though I knew it was.

"Yes, my lord," she said, and prostrated herself in the dust. I bent low over her and whispered into her ear.

"This, then, is your gift," I said, raising her face to mine with one long-nailed finger. "When a child is delivered into your hands, midwife, you shall know its fate, whether it be saved or damned."

"But how shall I use this gift?" she cried.

"Wisely," I said, for I knew with certainty she would not.

That very Sabbath, Mary Brendan was called from church to birth the Tewsbury's child. She hurried to their farm under a sky threatening snow, and no thought of her gift entered her mind until she finally held Goodwife Tewsbury's pale and writhing son in her hands, covered in his amniotic gore.

This one is surely damned, she thought, and I could taste her bitter dilemma. What to say, or to say nothing. To act, or to take no action. The indecision tore her soul to bits, as I knew it surely would.

She stuffed his infant maw with linen and severed the mother's cord. " 'Tis stillborn," she told the mother, and that was all. She took the bundle and hurried from the house as the stricken mother wailed to break the steel-gray sky.

"Would it not be kinder, Goodwife Brendan," I said, appearing to her in the twilight shadows by the barn. I took the meaty parcel from her and held it to my breast. "Would it not be kinder to speed the saved ones on to God, and let the damned tarry here while they may?"

"But the evil they will do?" she asked. "Should I not spare us all from that?"

"If you kill the saved, Mary Brendan," I said with a smile, "then only the condemned will remain, and evil done unto evil matters not to God." I left her then, standing in the brittle autumn air, her breath like smoke clouding her vision.

Goodwife Brendan set about her task with zeal then, to speed the righteous children of Chelham on to their place in the heavenly choir. She choked them and smothered them, dropped them and drowned them in buckets, until the blood on her hands was thick as paint and the whispers of the townsfolk erupted into shouts like fire from banked embers. "She's a witch. Mary Brendan is a witch!"

They came for her on a winter's day so cold none dared stir from beside their hearths, save those who burned with the witch hunter's zeal. Mary Brendan saw them coming, the parson and Elder Fenwycke and Sheriff Clarke. She barred the door as they came, the childless fathers gathering in the square behind them. Mary Brendan called on me, crying, "Angel, angel, come and help me!"

"Angel?" I asked from my perch in the shadows of the rafters.

"You must save me," she cried as the first knocks came at the door. "You must tell them of the gift you gave me. Please! Show yourself to them!"

"Gift, you old crone?" I asked, and showed her my true form. The bar across the door cracked under the sheriff's battering. "You have no gift, midwife. I lied."

Mirroring

Tim Waggoner

Greg knew that the man in the mirror wasn't his reflection; the problem was how to prove it.

He stood at the bathroom sink, hands gripping the counter, glaring into the eyes of the man behind the glassy surface of the medicine-chest mirror. The man glared right back.

Greg cocked his head slowly to the left, then to the right. As usual, the man in the mirror matched each motion precisely. Greg never ceased to be amazed at the man's skill at duplicating his movements so exactly. Then with a swift motion, Greg drew back his lips, baring his yellowed teeth and red-pink gums. The man beneath the glass was not caught off guard. His lips pulled back, his teeth and gums were exposed in unison with Greg's. Greg thought he detected the slightest twinkle in his double's eye, as if he were saying, *You ought to know better by now.*

True. How many times since becoming aware that his reflection had vanished—or been stolen—and replaced by this . . . person had Greg stood like this, making faces, wiggling his fingers, turning his head and body this way and that, going through all manner of contortions in an attempt to trick his duplicate? But no matter how he moved, the man in the mirror kept right up with him. In fact, sometimes Greg had the sense his double was actually a fraction of a second *ahead* of him.

Greg had tried everything he could think of to expose his duplicate's charade. He had gone into his bedroom, changed clothes, then returned to the bathroom, only to find the man in the mirror wearing exactly the same outfit. Greg had even tried mixing and matching his clothes in order to make the most outlandish combinations, wearing his pants on his arms, his underwear on his head, sweater over his legs. But regardless of how strangely Greg garbed himself, his duplicate was always dressed the same.

Then Greg had gone downstairs, taken a felt-tip marker out of the junk drawer, and drawn a smiley face on his stomach, using his belly button for the right eye. But when he stood before the medicine-chest mirror and lifted his shirt—the man in the mirror matching this procedure precisely, of course—Greg saw that the man had drawn a smiley face on his stomach, too. Though his belly button formed the face's left eye. Clever.

Greg had wondered if perhaps the medicine chest itself had something to do with it. He opened it, but there was nothing inside other than what could be expected, various medicines and toiletries. He closed the door. He considered for a time, his duplicate appearing to think right along with him. Perhaps it wasn't the medicine chest itself so much as its location. Greg hurried to the garage, got a screwdriver from his toolbox, returned to the bathroom, and removed the mirror.

He carried the mirror all around the house, even took it outside. He held it before him at different angles as he walked, but it didn't matter. The man was still there, still copying him movement by movement. Since the mirror's location obviously didn't matter, Greg put it back in the bathroom where it belonged.

He then tried to trip up his nemesis by reciting song lyrics, watching the other's lips closely for a slip, but his duplicate made none. Greg then babbled nonsense syllables, but still the man was able to copy him.

Now, here before the mirror once again, Greg realized he had no choice. He went into the garage, retrieved a hammer, and came back to the mirror. He was not a violent man by nature, would rather catch a spider or a fly and take it outside than kill it, but the man in the mirror had driven him to desperate measures.

As he lifted the hammer to strike, an expression of triumph crossed his double's face, an expression Greg knew was mirrored on his own face. And then he brought the hammer against the glass with all this strength, and the sound of shattering sliced the air.

Greg's world fell away and he found himself falling, tumbling, spinning, and then crashing to the floor in a thousand jagged shards.

The bathroom was still for a moment, and then from the surface of the unbroken mirror slowly emerged a hand.

Miss Courtney's Beau

Michael Mardis

Beatrice Courtney was a proper woman, a woman who believed that things should be done a *certain* way. Her father had taught her that long ago. It was advice that the silver-haired octogenarian still took to heart.

She reflected on this as the doorbell chimed incessantly in the background. What would Father say about her present suitor? She pursed her thin lips in distaste. He would tell her that this man was just another gigolo, a gold digger like all the rest.

Slowly, she made her way toward the doorway. It wouldn't do to hurry; Father always said that an eager woman makes a late bride. Even so, there had been many suitors over the years, and Beatrice was convinced that this latest would not be the last.

The doorbell chimed again and she tried to suppress her irritation at the man's impatience. A man *that* impatient would probably be anxious to take liberties, Beatrice thought warily, Father had warned her about that. Still, a slight shiver of forbidden anticipation coursed up her spine, and her hand was moist as it closed on the tarnished brass knob.

Pulling the heavy walnut door open with a flourish, Beatrice examined the gentleman who was standing on the porch. He was holding a clipboard in his large hands, and his fingers were drumming an impatient beat on its hard metal backing.

"Mrs. Courtney?"

"It's *Miss* Courtney, young man, and don't tell me you didn't know that already," she replied coyly. "We don't have to play games, not at our age."

The man, who was in his early thirties, raised his eyebrows slightly but recovered nicely.

"Er, of course not, Miss Courtney. As you probably know, I'm here about the bill. Union Electric doesn't want to be unfair, but . . ."

"Posh! I said that you could quit pretending!" Her eyes glittered in the afternoon light, and her lips turned up in a wrinkled smile.

"Yes, ma'am. But if you could just write me a check, I'll be on my way."

The twinkle died in her eyes, and the smile faded. So this was the way it was going to be, just like every other time! Another gigolo, interested only in her money!

Her voice was noticeably cool as she stepped back into the vestibule.

"I never handle monetary affairs; it isn't ladylike! Father would never forgive me!" She examined the young man closely, noting his uniform. Obviously he was a tradesman. She was quite glad that she had found out his intentions early.

"Lady, I don't want to be hard-nosed about this, but if I don't get a check, I'll have to turn off the power."

"You dare to threaten me?" She asked in shocked disbelief. "I've never had a suitor actually threaten me before!"

The man's eyes widened in shocked disbelief. "Suitor?" He took a step back from the open door. "I must've come at a bad time. How about if I try later when someone else is at home?"

Beatrice sniffed. "No one lives here except Father and myself. If you must discuss business, I suggest you take it up with him."

"Your *father* is still? . . ." Quickly, he reconsidered what he was about to say. "I'll be happy to speak to your father."

"Good," Beatrice sniffed. "I'm sure he'll have this unpleasantness straightened out in no time at all." She made a quick gesture with a deeply veined hand. "You'll have to come with me; he doesn't get out much these days."

"I'll just bet he doesn't," the man muttered softly, as he followed Beatrice into the dimly lit house.

She led him to a small door at the rear of the house, frowning at the way his heavy boots thumped on the carefully waxed floors.

"Right this way." She opened the door, revealing a rectangle of darkness.

"Don't you have a light?"

Beatrice smiled sweetly. "I'm trying to save on the electric bill, remember?"

The man gave a weak grin and took a tentative step forward. The grin changed to an openmouthed grimace of terror as he began to fall, and his scream reverberated through the house, abruptly punctuated by the thud of his body on the packed earth ten feet below.

Beatrice smiled. "Father will take care of you, my love. And if you're still alive, perhaps he can teach you a few manners!"

She closed the door slowly, and just for good measure, turned the knob on the lock. Father always said that it never hurt to be careful.

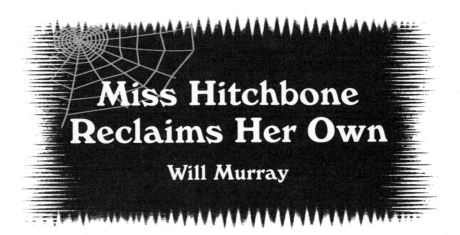

Miss Hitchbone Reclaims Her Own
Will Murray

I waited with my apartment door half-open for the tenant in 4-C to return, Chinatown neon painting my living room with garish splashes. I didn't hear the damned scratching. But it was early yet.

Somewhere in the eleventh hour the dull clumping of footsteps trudged up the worn oak stairs. I stepped out to meet him.

"Mr. Queet?"

"Yeah." His voice was as empty as his expression.

"I need to talk to you about your cat."

His loose fleshy face jumped, gray eyes turning evasive.

"He's kept me awake scratching at your door the last three nights," I explained. "What are you going to do about it?"

"You hear it tonight?" he asked guardedly.

"Not yet. Bring it in now so I can get some shuteye. Okay?"

Reaching the landing, Queet took hold of the banister post and peered up through the shadows to the scarred door at the end of the hall. His door. Meeting mine, his eyes were penitent.

"Her name was Eldreth Hitchbone," he croaked.

"Your cat?"

"I don't have a cat," Queet muttered.

"I keep hearing a cat scratching at your door, Queet."

"She died back in '99. Almost a century ago."

"Can we stay on the subject? Please?"

Queet chewed his lip. "Trade you a beer for the story. What say?"

It seemed like a fair deal. Queet shut my door behind him, rattling it to make sure the lock tongue had caught.

I popped him a cold Sam Adams while he dropped into a chair. Queet took it with a grunt. I decided to stay on my feet.

"I wouldn't have gone down into her tomb, but it was already open, see? Stone slab flat on the grass and stone steps leading down. So I went. Why not? Hundred-year-old tomb. I like old burying grounds. And Copp's Hill's one of Boston's best. They got old Cotton Mather buried there, you know."

He took a sip. A long guggling one. I thought I heard a scratching down the hall. Queet didn't react. He went on.

"There was trash at the bottom. From kids drinking. Coffin was still there though. Just planks, all fallen in with the dry bones scattered like dice. I really wanted her skull. But it was gone. So I settled for two fistfuls of spine bone. God, I should've left the damn things there. Souvenirs, hah!"

Between sips, his voice got progressively lower.

"The scratching started the very next night. Thought it was a cat myself. At first."

"Sounded like a cat," I said. "Footpads scraping along the hall."

"That's her bare-boned feet you hear," Queet said harshly. "Ever peek out?"

I shook my head no. "Allergic."

"I looked the first night. Never again. It was *her.*"

"Eldreth?" I was humoring him.

He finished the can. "Wanted her bones back, but I wouldn't let her in for 'em. She hasn't the strength to bust in, fortunately."

"Why not give them back?" I asked casually.

He crushed the can in his heavy fist. "Can't. Dumped 'em in the trash next morning. Guess she don't know that. Won't give up."

Disgusted, I was about to show Queet out, when the scratching came again. Distinctly. This time low on my door.

Queet came out of the chair, face shuddering. "It's her! My voice musta carried. Goddamn!"

"I'll get it," I said, reaching the door before Queet. "Always wanted to meet a ghost," I added dryly.

My chuckle died in my throat as I flung open the door, while Queet's wretched voice screamed, "That's her damn fingerbone scratching, you idiot! And I've no bone to give her!"

A short brown skeleton floated there, skull staring sightlessly at my belt buckle. I laughed, swiping the air over its head for supporting wires, expecting the bones to jiggle.

Instead, the grinding skull rotated on its spinal column. The empty sockets came to rest on trembling Queet. Gathering itself, it brushed past me, clicking like an old pocket watch.

That's when I ran from the building.

They found poor dead Queet with his back gouged open, spine exposed, the lumbar vertebrae missing. They never found the missing bones, or the killer. Once the nightmares stopped, I went to Eldreth Hitchbone's tomb and found it sealed. I hope forever.

It was her fleshless skull in my doorway that night. Trust me, I know. For the stunted deformity of bone that clicked by me walked with the lower points of its shoulderblades scraping the pelvic saddle.

You see, the spinal column designed to hold them apart was painfully, disturbingly, *truncated*.

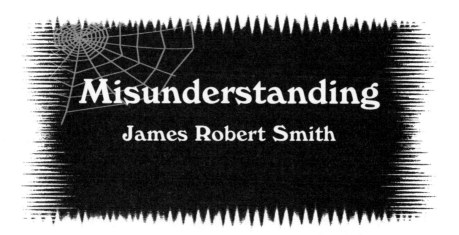

Misunderstanding

James Robert Smith

Leo peered up the walkway. This was the place. There was a kid sitting on the porch, playing with two GI Joe dolls, making screaming sounds as one doll shot another. *No, kid. You got it wrong. That ain't how a guy sounds when you plug him.*

He hated jobs that should have been finished. Spike, Leo's partner, should have taken care of this fish, but the leg-breaker hadn't reported, so here was Leo. He was going to miss his daughter's piano recital and was miffed about it. He didn't know who to be angrier at: the fish or Spike.

Adjusting his tie, Leo put his foot on the step leading up to the yard, cleared his throat. The kid ceased the feigned screaming and looked.

"Hey, kid," said Leo.

"Hi," said the kid.

"Are you Nick Berger's kid?"

"Yeah."

Leo took another step, up to the yard, sidewalk behind. The kid looked at him funny, and Leo was wondering if the Berger creep didn't have the kid as a lookout. He'd known guys to do lowdown stuff like that: putting their kids in harm's way.

"Your dad around?"

"Nope." The kid was looking at Leo's feet.

"What about your mom? You're not *alone?*" In this day and age, only a scumbag would leave a six-year-old alone. A guy like Leo might come along.

"They ain't here."

"I'm huntin' for your dad."

"So was that other guy. Before I went to school."

"What guy?" Leo took another step, his size thirteen coming to rest on the lawn.

"He looked like you," the kid said. "He said his name was Spike. But he didn't listen when I warned him what my dad said."

"Spike was here?" Leo reached into his coat and patted his nine millimeter.

"Yeah. And you ought not stand there on the grass. Put your foot on the paving stones. Safer."

"Huh?" Leo shrugged and stood on the stone. There were a lot of them leading to the steps where the kid was, and around the house. Nice setup.

"Where's Spike now?"

"He wouldn't listen. My dad warned me about the shark and Spike didn't listen. He's dead."

"What?" Leo raced across the yard and stopped at the kid, looking down from his six and a half feet. "What do you mean *he's dead?* Nobody ever got the drop on Spike Finazzo. And Spike ain't no shark." That was their boss.

"Don't get mad, mister. I told him but he wouldn't listen and now he's dead. Just like that movie."

Leo reached and pulled the kid by the wrist, arm like a dry twig in his big fist. "Show me where. Show me or so help me . . ."

"Ow! You're hurting!" Leo lifted the kid and glanced to see if anyone was looking. No neighbors were around.

"Where?"

"In the back! He was walking on the lawn in the back! I told him not to!"

Leo, the kid in his left arm, went around the house. The kid was staring at Leo's feet. "The rocks. Make sure you walk on the rocks!" The kid was bug-eyed.

"Where's Spike?" They were in the back.

"Put me down. I'll show you."

As soon as Leo put him down, the kid jumped on the walkway like his life depended on it. Then he pointed to a dark spot in the grass. "He was right there when it happened."

Looking, Leo recognized the dark stain in the lawn. Blood. He should know. In the center of the splotch was something else he recognized: Spike's right hand. His pistol was still in it, the one with all the notches in the handle.

"You lousy dirtbags. Your dirtbag dad killed my best pal." Leo reached for his piece. Ten grand owed to his loan-shark boss was a leg-breaking offense. The killing of his best pal could be paid only in blood. The kid would have to go.

Before he could draw a bead there was a movement in that grass. Standing in the yard, the nearest stone about eight feet away, Leo watched the fin rise, slicing grass as if it were a plane of water. He tried to aim when the rest of the thing rose and most of Leo vanished in a gout of blood. Spike's right hand had a mate and then everything was still.

"Lawn sharks," the kid muttered as he hopped from stone to stone. "Daddy said to watch out for the lawn sharks."

The Monster Within

S. Darnbrook Colson

His eyes stare up at me, the question Why? stitched across his baby blue orbs.

But just as I know why, he knows why. Why my hands are around his throat, my thumb pressing slowly and continuously, just below the cartilage of his Adam's apple, against the soft, giving windpipe, cutting off the breath of life. For eternity.

Yes, he knows why. He knows what happens when the moon is full—that men like him transform themselves, descending into the night to tear, rend, and kill. He knows what happens when the sun fades below the horizon—that men like him ascend into the night to sustain themselves on the blood of others. He knows what happens when the clouds blanket the light of the moon—so that men like him creep into the dark and eat the flesh of the dead.

I can feel the life force draining from him, his eyes no longer questioning, only gazing into the darkness in a hollow, inanimate, fixed look—staring into oblivion. I release him and he slumps to the floor, a lifeless slab of inert meat.

There are others. Many others. And they are so easy to find. They are everywhere: long-haired ones, ones with broad, flat, animal-like noses, ones with tongues that are foreign to my ears, and, like this one, ones with earrings piercing their earlobes.

Yes, they're different from me, and they're everywhere. And when the rage fills my soul, I will find another one.

Monsters
Richard T. Chizmar

Did you hear it *this* time?"

Manning leaned forward in the driver's seat and cocked his head to the side, a movement designed to show that he was *really* listening this time. He shrugged his shoulders. "Just the crickets, baby. And the wind."

Baby shook her head and shivered and felt an army of goosebumps march across her forearms. The night air was unseasonably cool, but not *that* cool. Her eyes searched the darkness, found only tall trees dancing in the summer breeze beneath a fingernail moon, shadow partners following their rhythmic lead.

Her name was Mary Beth and she hated being called "baby" almost as much as "darling" or "gorgeous," but now was *not* the time and this was *not* the place to start an argument. It was downright spooky out there in the middle of nowhere and she just wanted to get it over with and get back to the motel to a big glass of iced tea and the clean, cool sheets of her bed.

"Don't worry, little darling, I'm right here to take care of you." Manning put his arm around her and pulled her closer. He smelled of sour whiskey and cheap aftershave. His Trans-Am had designer bucket seats—leather, of course—but with a blanket stuffed down into the space between the seats, it allowed for comfortable cuddling. He'd learned that trick many years ago.

"What would you do if something came out of the woods?" she asked, looking nervously out his side window. Her window was closed tight, but his was rolled more than halfway down. "A monster or something?"

He laughed loud and harsh and mean. "A monster? You mean like the Mummy or Frankenstein?" He shook his head, arched his eyebrows. "Shee-it! I ain't never seen no monster before, but you can bet I'd jump on out and go right to ass-kicking if I did."

Mary Beth almost laughed and was glad she didn't. Manning was a lot of things, she knew, but an ass-kicker wasn't one of them. She had played the dumb redhead role perfectly when they'd met earlier at the bar, but the facts were all committed to memory. Peyton Manning. Twenty-nine years old. Ran his father's furniture factory over on Elf and 14th. Spent money like it was paper. Local playboy, especially with the teeny-boppers. And—this was her favorite—he still lived at home, with his folks, in an attic-converted apartment.

"You mean you wouldn't be scared?" she said.

"Hell no."

"Why not?" She made her eyes wide and fascinated.

"First of all, because there ain't no such thing as monsters." His chest was swelled out now and his heavy breathing filled the car with the flavor of cinnamon chewing gum. Again she swallowed a giggle. "Second of all, because I'm Peyton Manning and I'm not afraid of anything."

"So you'd protect me?" she purred, leaning in a little closer and kissing his earlobe, flicking it with her tongue.

"You're damn right I would. What kind of a man do you think I am?"

And then, with the frantic grace of a fourteen-year-old in a dark movie theater balcony, Manning made his move. He rolled his bulk onto her, his chest pinning her tight against the seat, and then his tongue was inside her mouth like a fat, sloppy slug. His fingers found the three buttons at the top of her blouse and roughly pulled them open.

Christ, she thought, this was Mr. Playboy's idea of romance and seduction in the moonlight. Ten minutes on a deserted dirt road, a little sweet-talking, and right to the good stuff. She sure could pick 'em.

He paused to catch his breath and she took advantage of the break. "How 'bout we go outside, big boy? Take a blanket and have some fun underneath the stars." It was still creepy as hell out there, but she no longer felt she had the advantage inside the cramped front seat. She wanted out.

"Uh-uh," he said. "Ain't no stars out. How 'bout we get that shirt off instead." He yanked the bottom of her blouse out from her jeans and began to pull it over her head. He let out a whistle when he caught a glimpse of her breasts.

Instinctively, her arms came up to stop him . . . and she panicked. With one swift movement, she pushed him off her and raked at his face with her left hand.

He shrieked and reacted with a backhand slap to her face. "You bitch. You stupid, stupid bitch." He started the car, and the engine was painfully loud, the stereo still louder.

"Get out," he screamed above the music.

Mary Beth slowly reached over and unlocked the door, ignoring her stinging cheek. She knew exactly what would happen next: she would swing a leg out the car door and just before she got out, she'd turn back to him, lips pouting, and apologize and promise to make it up to him . . . and then later she'd show him what a monster *really* looked like—and felt like—up close and personal.

She pushed open the door, held it slightly ajar, so that the inside light flashed on. Manning's face was flushed red, and thin railroad tracks of blood crossed his forehead. Mary Beth opened her mouth—

—and he surprised her.

He gave her a hard two-hand shove and slammed his foot on the gas pedal. The Trans-Am swerved wide, tires spinning, sending her tumbling out into the night, screaming like he had never, ever heard a human scream before.

Manning sped home in silence, windows rolled down, the air cool and soothing on his ravaged face. You sure can pick 'em, he thought. Crazy, crazy bitch. That's the last time I pick up a stranger. Acting all hot and bothered at first, then all scared, then friggin' crazy as a mountain man. And all that screamin' and hollerin', like she was back there dying or something. Christ, all she had to do was pick her skinny ass up off that dirt road and hike a few miles into town. Not like I abandoned her in the middle of nowhere.

He pulled to the curb in front of his parents' split-level house and switched off the ignition. It felt damn good to be home again. He was halfway up the driveway—no one *ever* walked on the grass, not even the mailman—when he smelled rain in the night air and turned back. Both car windows were still open.

He yanked open the passenger door and screamed.

An upstairs light clicked on inside the house.

He screamed louder.

The front door opened and he heard his daddy's voice behind him, tired and clearly agitated. "What the hell's going on, boy?"

Manning dropped to his knees and lost his club sandwich and bourbon dinner on the neatly clipped grass.

When Daddy reached his side, Manning motioned inside the car . . . to the gleaming metal hook which was swaying gently on the *inside* door handle, a bloody stump of flesh dripping red and black onto the leather seat.

Manning's final thought before he fainted at his daddy's feet was of the woman's tortured screams echoing in the wind-blown summer night.

Moth

Joe Meno

Goddamn bugs," Dick frowned, placing the poison green liquid tablets in the damp, musty basement corner. "I hate goddamn bugs. That's why I became an exterminator." He paused. "But you know, insects were one of the first forms of life? Even before the dinosaurs." He took a drag on his cigarette, smiling.

"Isn't that stuff flammable?" Ms. Miniko, the landlady, whispered, eyeing Dick's smoke.

"I'm a walking time bomb, lady," Dick grinned. "I face death every day."

"That's thrilling." Ms. Miniko rolled her eyes.

"But this is the cleanest apartment building I've been in. Usually the whole boiler room is crawling with bugs."

"I told you on the phone we didn't have a bug problem. It's those awful bats."

Dick shone his big black flashlight in the basement corner. Hanging from a steel beam, four or five bats, huddled together, squeaked suddenly; their black eyes flashed menacingly. "Well, these tablets should take care of them. Have you seen the bats anywhere else in the complex?"

"They're everywhere," Ms. Miniko frowned. "Everywhere."

She led Dick through each apartment, through each floor; and in every dark, pungent closet, there were bats. Four or five in each apartment, they hung from rotten holes. Their shiny claws and teeth glittered with saliva; they screeched nervously with rabid pink tongues as Dick slipped a tiny dish of pellets into each closet and quickly shut the door. He had never seen anything like it before, hundreds of bats, fat and healthy, plump and right at home in their closets. Dick realized why there were no bugs. The bats had been eating them all.

Ms. Miniko let Dick into the last apartment. He entered quietly, quickly stepping past a decrepit elderly lady who sat much too close to her television; her wrinkled face was lit with the blue light. Dick marched into her front closet and slipped the green pellets in a corner. Suddenly, the cigarette fell from his mouth and rolled across the beige-carpeted floor. The bats squeaked above nervously; as Dick reached for his cigarette, he flinched, knocking over a box of old clothing. He grabbed his smoke and shoved the clothes back into the box, then noticed the large tear marks in each garment. The clothes looked like they had been partly eaten. Beside the tear marks were thick white patches of oily residue that shone with grease and stuck to his fingers. He shuddered, stuffing the box back into place.

Dick nervously backed out of the closet as the old lady began to mumble something. She screamed out suddenly as Dick turned to face her; her browned skin began to bubble and swell, cracking open. Dick shook his head in utter confusion as something white and powdery pushed its way through the old woman's skin. Dick ran for the door as the creature tore through, stepping out of the old woman's shell; its round, red eyes glared above a furry white neck, and its seamless white body glimmered as a long black tongue darted between two large mandibles. It looked human, and yet altogether inhuman. Tiny white wings flapped from her shoulder blades. Dick backed out the door, and was stopped by Ms. Miniko.

"You don't understand," she whispered. Her long black tongue slipped over her lips; her eyes shimmered red. "We were here first. Even before the dinosaurs. We just wanted you to get rid of the bats. We loathe bats," she whispered in a metallic voice. From behind the landlady, other moth-people began to appear, fluttering from their apartments on powdery wings they had concealed.

"We can't let you leave now." She frowned. She placed her cold, scaly hand to Dick's cheek. "Now we can punish you for all the sins you've committed against our brethren."

Dick smiled; he dropped some green tablets to the floor, then crushed them with his foot, and flicked his cigarette into the green mess. Immediately the toxin burst into flame; giant red tongues of fire leapt in the air. The moths screamed, their eyes lighting with the fire's brilliance. In one primal, irrational thought, the landlady threw herself into the flames. The others followed; their powdery white skin bubbled and churned as the fire spread throughout the hall.

Dick ran out to his truck, slammed the door, and tore away; he swatted at himself nervously as the fire raged on behind. Hundreds of bats took to the sky, flapping their wings, their mouths full of charred meat. Dick saluted them.

"Damn all bugs."

Mother Lode

Öjvind Bernander

Missa Fim."

Finn's hangover lay over his temples like a block of concrete.

"Missa. Eskuse me." The voice came from outside the open window.

Finn groaned. It was Prakong, his Thai gardener. No matter how vehemently Finn cursed, the man was always impeccably polite—but insistent.

"Wha . . ." Finn's voice cracked. He cleared his throat of mucus, swallowed. He rose, walked stooped to the window, head hammering.

"What the fuck is this?" A large hole gaped in his lawn, brown with wet earth, at least five feet deep.

"Is a hole. Missa say 'dig till say stop.'"

Finn sneezed in the bright California sun. Shockwaves spread inside his skull. He had said that? He probably had, last night when he came reeling home. Prakong, the idiot, had kept digging all night.

"Well, fill it in again!" Finn growled. "Just plant the fucking rosebush."

Prakong didn't move. "Found this," he said. "In hole."

Finn squinted at the gardener's outstretched hands. They held an egg, glistening like metal in yellow and blistering white.

"Huh?" Finn took the egg. It was heavy and hard. Some oriental antique? "Well, get your ass back to work!"

He got a beer from the fridge. Then he put the egg on the kitchen table, sat down and stared at it. The surface was smooth and colored in a patchy mosaic of gold and silver. Could be valuable. He knocked on it with his beer can. The egg clanged hollowly and rolled an inch. Then it clanged again—by itself!—trembled in place, and clanged a third time.

Finn took another swig of beer and poked the egg. It responded so vigorously it almost rolled off the table, like some giant Mexican jumping bean. He looked from his beer can and back to the egg, where cracks had formed across the mosaic and were spreading like lightning in a summer sky.

A head poked out: large eyes, a sharp beak of metal, and a tuft of golden filaments crowning the otherwise bald head. "Rah!" it cawed.

Finn stared for a moment, then, careful to keep his fingers clear of the beak, helped the thing crack its shell. The rest of the bird was no bird: it had hind legs and a tail like a lion. There was a word for these creatures, Finn seemed to remember. Griffin?

"Zah!" Its caw was almost a hiss. It looked so weak and helpless Finn got up to look for milk in the fridge. He found none and so poured some beer on a saucer. The griffin pecked once at it, shuddered, and turned away.

"Wah! Wah!"

"All right, all right. I'll try and find some cereal."

By the time he got back with a box of corn flakes, the griffin had torn the beer can to shreds. Not, it was clear, to have a drink, but to gobble down the aluminum. Finn stared in wonder as the little creature finished the can and proceeded to attack a glass, shattering it and swallowing the shards.

Finally, it came to rest, lifted a leg, shivered, and dumped a handful of pebbles that glittered like gold.

"Missa!"

Gold. Finn was sober now. The alcohol in his system evaporated through the pores of his skin. His brain was still heavy, but the thoughts clear as glass.

He'd be rich: feed the bird junk metal, sell the pebbles on the exchanges of the world. He'd get another gardener, one who spoke English and had a brain. He'd . . .

"Missa! Missa Fim!"

Finn frowned. A new gardener would be a high priority.

Something came flying through the window, lobbed through the air, and landed in the kitchen sink.

A bucket? The rosebush? Was Prakong having a little mutiny after all?

He went to the sink and grabbed the object: Prakong's head, torn from the neck and dripping blood.

"Ma!" The griffin skittered on the table with excitement.

A shadow blocked out the sun. A windowpane shattered as something large squeezed through. For a millisecond, Finn felt the claws sink into his flesh. Then, mercifully, he felt nothing more.

Mr. Bauble's Bag
Scott David Aniolowski

The carpetbag was old and worn, with a small rip in one side. The bag's once garish stripes and polka dots were pale and vague, and the MR. BAUBLE had nearly faded away. But it was still durable enough to hold everything it needed to: floppy shoes, crimson hair, a round red nose, an oversized sequined tuxedo coat, baggy paisley pants, a few tricks. Everything Mr. Bauble needed—everything Mr. Bauble owned.

No one came to the circus anymore. Parents were too busy, too absent. And children just didn't care: it was all video games and action figures these days. Most of the troupe had left the small circus for bigger and better things—the big traveling shows. Some of Mr. Bauble's old friends had even made it to TV. He was envious, but he couldn't leave of course. This little circus was Mr. Bauble's home, his life. But it was getting harder and harder to survive as business dropped off. So few people anymore, so few children.

Mr. Bauble's fat white-faced reflection stared back from the dressing room mirror. He sighed. Half of the lightbulbs were blown out or missing. But Mr. Bauble still had enough light to put his happy face on each day. First he'd put on the baggy paisley pants, then the red and green sequined tuxedo coat, then the big floppy shoes. Then on went his white gloves and his squirting flower. The face was always last: the wide smile, the fat cheeks and double chins, the tufts of crimson hair that stuck up like wings on either side of his head, the big red nose.

And at night everything came apart in reverse. First the big red nose. Mr. Bauble's white-gloved hand gently dropped the rubber nose into the bag. There was a dark empty spot in the grinning reflection.

Tonight there had only been a couple dozen children in the audience. Only the little fat boy had been afraid, but Mr. Bauble did what he could with him.

The crimson wig came off next. Mr. Bauble stroked the fake hair as if it were a kitten and then dropped it into the bag.

Mr. Bauble had nestled next to the scared little boy, pushing the other tittering children away, his red and blue smile cracking wide.

Next went the fat cheeks and the double chins—all soft white rubber. Mr. Bauble squeezed the rubber bits between his gloved fingers before they went into the old bag. More of the grinning reflection darkened.

Mr. Bauble had honked his horn and had made a purple balloon-dog for the boy, but he still cried and tried to crawl into his mother's coat. Fear. Such a strange emotion to evoke, when clowns were supposed to bring joy and laughter. Could it be the cadaverously white face? The enormous mouth? The exaggerated size? Mr. Bauble still didn't know exactly what induced the fear, even after all these years. But Mr. Bauble always went to the scared children.

Piece by piece, Mr. Bauble took himself apart, carefully storing everything away in his faded bag until the next show. He sighed again. *Old clowns never die, they just . . .* Mr. Bauble gazed at his faceless reflection in the darkened mirror. *Old clowns just never die.*

Finally, Mr. Bauble had performed his special trick to quiet the little fat boy. It worked, as it always did, and it was just enough for Mr. Bauble—enough to get him through another day.

When everything was packed away in the old carpetbag, Mr. Bauble zipped it up and hefted it to the dressing table. Dust spun in the air, drifting like snowflakes around the few bare bulbs. He reached over and clicked off the mirror lights. Something rustled in the blackness of the musty little room. Some dry thing: a diaphanous, shadowless apparition of dust and cobwebs. The dry, dusty thing sighed deep and hollow. *Old clowns never die.* And then the dusty thing seeped down through the floorboards of the tiny dressing room. There it would rest and wait—wait for the next show and the chance to put on Mr. Bauble's happy face again.

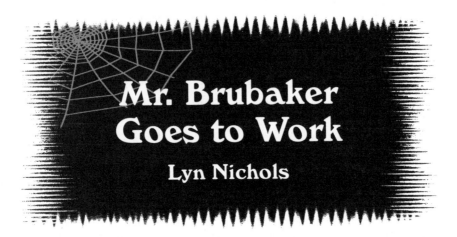

Mr. Brubaker Goes to Work

Lyn Nichols

Brubaker dressed carefully. His Woolworth's suit was threadbare but clean and his worn shoes were freshly shined. His white cotton shirt was dingy from too many washings, but all the tears had been painstakingly sewn with small, precise stitches. He shrugged into his suit coat, looked into the faded mirror, adjusted his tie and smiled.

ONE CANNOT BUT SUCCEED WHEN ONE DRESSES FOR SUCCESS.

The little sign hanging above the mirror was a constant reminder to Brubaker, one he firmly believed. He picked up his briefcase and retrieved his hat from its hook, placing it carefully on his still damp, neatly combed hair. A last quick glance assured him that all was as it should be. He opened the front door and descended the cracked steps into a brand-new day.

Brubaker walked along the crumbling sidewalks, his keen gaze busily searching the strewn rubble, probing into the shadows of half-hollowed buildings. He whistled as he walked, a jaunty tune that echoed the spring in his cautious step. Wouldn't do to turn an ankle or fall, he reasoned.

Somewhere up ahead a dog barked. Brubaker paused, listening, his tune dying in the still, dank air. A smile split his weathered face, and his step became more determined as he adjusted his course to follow the dog's yammering.

"Yes," he murmured as he passed the listing shell of a two-story building and turned a corner. In the open area beyond, a young man knelt just beyond the reach of a tethered, yapping dog. The man held something toward the dog, dropping it and snatching his hand away as the small beast lunged at him. The dog grabbed the scrap and swallowed, then lunged once more at the man, barking furiously.

"Easy, fella," Brubaker heard the man say. "Here's more for you. Gentle now, gentle."

Brubaker set his briefcase down on a shattered piece of concrete wall and opened it up. He rummaged a bit, selecting a few items and setting them off to the side, discarding a few others. For a moment he paused, studying the young man so intent on taming a dog. Not one to succeed, Brubaker decided, noting the torn, dirty jeans and the ragged sleeveless shirt the man wore. The observation made Brubaker smile.

Taking up the one item he felt he needed, Brubaker approached the man, coming up behind him. The dog whined at his approach and barked once, then backed away, no longer interested in the scraps the young man offered. The man, still totally engrossed in making a friend of an enemy, called out: "C'mon, boy. It's all right. Here, boy."

"It won't work, you know," Brubaker said when he stood right behind the man.

Startled, the man turned, scrambling to his feet. Brubaker steadied him with one hand and plunged his knife deep within the man's chest, just below the sternum. He stepped to the side as he twisted the blade, not wanting to have the man's blood splatter on his suit or shoes.

The young man struggled for only a moment before sagging to the ground, guided by Brubaker's capable hands. For a moment, Brubaker merely observed as the young man gasped and floundered in his dying. Satisfied that the death was proceeding well, he walked back to the low damaged wall where his briefcase and the other instruments of his trade waited. He took the small hand towel and wiped blood from his hands. He removed his coat and carefully folded it, setting it neatly beside the briefcase. He rolled up his sleeves and donned heavy yellow rubber gloves. A glance over his shoulder assured him it was time. He picked up his scissors and carving knife with one hand and the carefully folded bundle of plastic bags with the other.

It was time to work.

Brubaker whistled as he worked: a steady, deliberate tune that matched his concentration. Doing one's work well was of paramount importance. Brubaker enjoyed doing his work well, and knew he was exceedingly good at it. Dressing out a carcass is very exacting work. He lifted the steak he carved from the young man's body and wrapped it in plastic, tossing a few scraps of sinew and gristle to the waiting, hungry dog.

"Yes," he told the begging mutt, "one cannot but succeed if one dresses for success."

Much More Than You Know

Brian A. Hopkins

Vincent van Gogh, so the story goes, cut off his ear for the woman he loved. Wrapped it in a silken hanky and placed it in her hands. "This is how much I love you," I imagine him saying on that insane December day in 1888, "enough that I would mutilate myself to prove it, dear lady."

I went out and read everything I could find on van Gogh. Biographies. Character studies. Psychological profiles prepared by other men seeking the same answers. I studied his art. I read the letters he wrote to his brother, Theo. I wanted to understand the passion, the drive, the absolute heartache that could bring a man to such an act of desperation. I wanted to understand because I was on the verge of performing something equally destructive on myself.

I daydreamed of knives carving great glistening red crenulations across the breadth of my chest, up and down my arms, across my face. The crimson demarcations would part and the blood would flow, symbol of all the pain pent within me. It was as if I wanted you to see some outward proof that you had hurt me, as if visible physical torture could mirror the inner torment. It was as if some token piece of myself, given like chocolates or roses, could serve as irrefutable evidence that I loved you, loved you enough to part with something as personal and precious as an ounce of flesh.

But van Gogh was a madman. Nothing more. There's nothing romantic about the truth behind the misconception. In a fit of manic depression van Gogh came at his friend Paul Gauguin with a razor. When Gauguin demanded to know what van Gogh was up to, Vincent came to his senses. When he realized what he'd been about to do, he cut himself instead, running about the village of Arles, copious amounts of blood streaming from his head. He happened upon a peasant woman whom he hardly knew. It's to her that he gave the ear.

Van Gogh failed me. There were no answers there.

The Bible says thou shalt not covet thy neighbor's wife. What it should say is thou shalt not *fall in love with* thy neighbor's wife. Covet her, lust after her, sleep with her if you must, but never, ever fall in love with the wife of another. Therein lies ruin.

Therein lies a sticky piece of heartache especially made for three.

At the end of it, I had this terrifying thought that subconsciously our every action in life is designed to bring about our eventual defeat, that what we are doing and what we think we are doing are two diametrically opposed truths. If so, if trapped within me is this demon determined to bring about my demise, then the road to ruin is planned and plotted and I've merely to walk it. It's a road, I think, which has been traveled before.

Perhaps what van Gogh was really after was simplification. An excised piece of himself which, discarded, would bring him that much closer to his soul. A paring down to the essential truths that fueled his art. Art and love are the only truths in this world. Peel back the layers that intervene, the barriers that link us to—as much as shield us from—reality, and turning within you'll always find . . . truth . . . art . . . love.

So, perhaps Vincent did, after all, cut off his ear for love.

But he had it all wrong. I can't give you something of myself as proof of just how far I'd go for you. You already declined the whole of me. What good, a piece? What I must give you, then, is something you had already, but could never in your wildest dreams have imagined I would go so far as to take.

But I have. And now I return it with the hopes that it will set you free.

You see, I do love you.

Much more than you know.

Much more than he ever could.

As you hold his heart in your hands, you will see this is true.

Mud

Juleen Brantingham

Bitch!" Jason yelled, shoving the girl out of his pickup and slamming the door.

The girl, whose name he couldn't remember, stumbled back from the truck, sobbing. He drove off. Served her right, being left out here in the rain. She had some nerve, letting him spring for a movie and popcorn, waste gas driving out here, then telling him she didn't *do* that. With looks like hers, why else would anyone take her out?

His buddies must know her, must have figured something like this would happen. They'd made a point of telling him to bring his date out here tonight. And the funny looks they gave him, especially Wes. They must be laughing their asses off right now. Bayou Betaille Road. A track in the swamp. He wondered what Betaille meant.

He caught a glimpse of the girl in his rearview mirror as he drove away. Her hair and clothes were soaked, her blouse ripped off one shoulder from when she'd pulled away from him too suddenly. *Wet bow-wow*, he thought, laughing.

The pickup fishtailed. Rain rattled on the roof. The black waters of the bayou gleamed off to his left, higher than he'd ever seen before. His buddies didn't know that he'd already discovered this spot, a great place to bring a girl, nice and secluded. Something about being far from town, with the water sliding by, made girls more agreeable. Usually.

He didn't *like* having to hit them.

The pickup didn't feel right, like he'd caught a branch underneath. He wasn't nuts about the idea of getting out in the rain, but a guy with any sense took care of his truck, like a cowboy took care of his horse. He got out, leaving the headlights on.

He stepped down into water that was over the tops of his boots. Damn!

Feeling a twinge of pity for the girl, he thought about going back but, nah, she wasn't sugar. She wouldn't melt.

There was a raw, wet smell in the air. Jason knelt, cursing the water that soaked his knees, and peered under the pickup.

And damn near had a heart attack.

Something under there. He couldn't quite make it out. Human-shaped, glistening with mud. At first he thought it was the girl, that he'd somehow run over her. But no, he'd seen her reflection in the mirror. It couldn't be her unless—

He laughed at the thought of that bow-wow throwing herself under his truck just to give him a bad time. He reached for the muddy mass, had to get it off or it might damage something.

It was warm, like flesh.

It moved.

He scrambled backward, spitting curses. He suddenly remembered the last girl he'd brought here, Wes's cousin. When he turned down Bayou Betaille Road, she'd started chattering about her family once owning this land. Who'd want to own a swamp?

That was one he'd had to hit.

Could Wes—nah, around here everyone was related somehow to everyone else. Didn't mean anything.

The thing from under the truck crawled out. Its eyes were red. Panic took Jason's breath away. The only sound was the rain and the thudding of his heart.

A creature made of mud? Too crazy.

Red eyes glared.

Jason could barely move. He looked down. Mud was piled several inches deep on the road. He looked at the creature and found it smaller than before.

The rain was melting it.

His breath whooshed out in a sound of relief. This was nothing but a big clot of mud. After the rain finished with it, there wouldn't be anything left. He started to get up.

His only warning was a blast of putrid breath. The mud creature loomed over him, its maw gaping. The mud came down over his head and swallowed him, filling his eyes, his nose, his mouth. He forgot the girl, forgot everything except trying to catch his breath.

His former buddy Wes found him a week later, baked in a crust of mud. Wes's lips curled in a humorless smile as he thought about people who belonged to the land, cared for it, loved it—land that, perhaps, loved them back.

The Music Box

Lisa Lepovetsky

Julia sits on the bed, the day after her mother's funeral, and holds the music box in her hand. An inlaid rose twists on its lid, deeply grained, dark as Mama's promises, red as the polish on Julia's manicured nails. The wooden stem curls itself tighter and tighter around her heart, until she can barely breathe. She follows the thorns with one trembling fingertip.

She whispers, "I love you, Mama. You promised you'd never leave." But the stillness of her mother's room is her only answer. It's been years since Julia's been home, years since she's heard her mother's voice. Too late now, she thinks, she'll never hear it again.

She brings the box close to her face, inhales the polished wood smell. She remembers aching to touch the music box as a child. She lay in the dark for hours, tangled in Mama's arms, listening to the lonely words, feeling hungry tears dampen her shirt. And always, always yearning to lift that hinged lid, reveal the rose's secrets.

"What do you want the most, my darling?" Mama would ask in a sing-song voice before kissing Julia and tucking her in every night. Julia would answer without hesitation: "I want you with me forever, Mama."

"I'll always be there. I promise."

One afternoon, while Mama was out, little Julia had tiptoed into her room and crossed to the high oak dresser, where the box lay. She'd reached one small hand over her head and grasped it. Suddenly, a slap sent her sprawling into a corner. Mama stood over Julia, her face dark crimson, and her eyes narrow with fury.

"Don't ever touch that box again," Mama rasped. "Your father made that box. He gave it to me the day he died. It's not to be opened until . . . well, until you need it."

"Need it for what, Mama?"

"Never you mind. You'll know when the time comes."

It was the only time Mama ever struck her. And the only time she ever spoke of Julia's father, no matter how Julia begged.

"Your father was special," was all she'd say, "very special. Someday you'll understand."

Julia had drifted away from her mother as she grew, away from the strange woman who muttered to herself and kept the lights burning all night. But she'd never touched the box again. Until now.

Almost thirty years later, she thinks that time has come. She holds her breath as she lifts the lid of the box, ecstatic and terrified to see what lies locked in its sacred darkness.

At first, there's only a dull click, like a bubble caught in the throat of someone unused to speaking. Then, while the late-afternoon light creeps into the small room, tiny bells wander around a shard of Bach. The music seems lost somewhere under the frayed crimson velvet and the broken mirror on the bottom.

A huge wave of disappointment washes over Julia. She hadn't cried at the funeral, was only dimly aware of her hollowness. But now grief burns her gut like a raw, red patch of need, too deep for tears to reach.

She grinds her teeth. "It's only a music box, after all," she mutters. "Only a damned music box." She looks into the empty air and cries, "You said you'd always be there. You promised."

The only treasure the box holds is a shriveled brownish object, like a dried tadpole, curled in on itself like the rose on the lid.

Reaching for it, Julia cuts herself on a ragged splinter hidden somewhere among the thorns on the lid. The pain makes her eyes water. A single tear and a drop of blood spatter on the small dried brown object resting on the glass. It squirms.

Suddenly, the tinkling music swells to a carillon, and the room grows brighter, too bright. Julia clenches her eyes closed and crouches back in the corner where her mother's slap sent her so many years ago. When she opens them again, something is growing in the middle of the room. Something wet and red that looks a lot like Mama.

My Evil Twin

Brian Craig

My mother and father worked out terms of their own separation. They split everything right down the middle, including us. I always knew I had a brother, of course, but I never knew whether he was an identical twin or a fraternal one. My mother wasn't sure. All she was sure of was that he "took after my father" and was a "right little bugger"—unlike me. Needless to say, I took after her.

I resolved that even if my twin and I had been identical, I would ensure that my life did not mirror his. I knew this would be difficult, given that I had no idea where he was or what he was doing—my father never contacted us again once he had gone off with his "filthy floozy"—but it was quite straightforward. If he had been a fraternal twin the problem would never arise; the calculus of probability would ensure that his actions and mine would be uncorrelated. The danger lay in the possibility that we were identical, in which case our inner natures would be forever tempting us to seize similar opportunities and make similar mistakes. But if this were the case, I had only to make certain that I didn't follow the promptings of my inner nature. All I had to do in order to break the invisible bonds which might or might not be tying my destiny to his was to attend carefully to my every spontaneous impulse, and then do something completely different.

It wasn't long before I realised that my twin must be a very nasty person indeed. Whenever I was under pressure I was constantly assailed by the most hideously violent impulses. I couldn't walk along a busy street without wanting to stab the people who accidentally strayed into my path. I learned to drive long before the notion of "road rage" became fashionable, but I never had a moment's peace from its angry promptings. In my work as a bank clerk—and later as a manager—I was continually tormented by the urge to steal huge sums of money. When I married, it was only by exercising the utmost restraint that I was able to refrain from wife-battering and uxoricide.

Every time I saw the report of a violent incident in the newspaper I thought: "I bet my twin had a hand in that!" Every time the disappearance of a young girl was reported I said, silently: "She's dead—and my brother is responsible." In the end, I could bear these complex stresses and strains no longer—I set out to find my evil twin.

It wasn't easy. Fortunately, I had always kept a tight rein on my spendthrift instincts, and was therefore able to hire a private detective to assist me. Had it not been for his undoubted wisdom and honesty I might have doubted our eventual findings. We found that my brother was the vicar of an inner-city parish; he was famed for his kindness, his charity and his tirelessness. I would have concluded that we must have been fraternal twins after all, but for the fact that photographs taken by the detective testified that we were as alike as two peas in a pod.

It was obvious what had happened. Like me, he must have been haunted by the idea that he had a twin somewhere, and like me he had decided to distance himself from that twin by making sure that he defied the promptings of his own inner nature. The only difference between us was that he had gone to a much further extreme.

I wondered whether I should go to him and reveal myself, in order to explain how we had become what we were—but I decided against it. It wasn't that I was ashamed to admit to him that I had not succeeded as well as he, but that I was afraid of the effect the revelation might have on him. Once he knew the truth, might he not cease to suppress his violent and wicked urges, and cease to be the admirable man he was? I couldn't be responsible for that. I stayed away. Unfortunately, I forgot about the possibility that he might have come looking for me, and found a disillusionment even deeper than mine.

Anyhow, whatever your witnesses say and whatever your forensic evidence indicates, it really wasn't me who murdered those girls. It must have been him. It *must*.

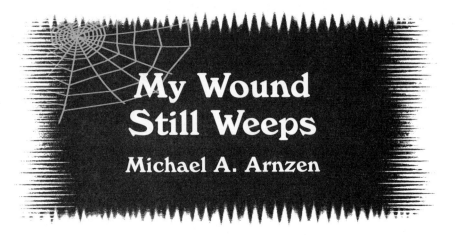

My Wound Still Weeps

Michael A. Arnzen

They try to tell me I'm here because I have an eating disorder, but that's not it at all: it is not my stomach but my wound that is perpetually empty.

It's on my left arm, a circular hole, wet and wide open, waiting for pink skin to sponge inside and fill it all up. It's right in the crook of my elbow—the spot where nurses draw blood—and that's why they've said it won't heal: because I don't hold my arm still. Especially when I'm eating—too much, too fast—so they've tried to change my habits, making me eat with a fork in my right hand or strapping my wrist to my thigh instead. But that doesn't work at all. My wound still weeps. And I still eat to fill it up.

My wound is like a mutant eye—an eye that never shuts because the lids aren't long enough. And it cries. My wound weeps dark yellow tears that trickle warm down my forearm like the splash of spilled coffee.

It's been crying for years: outliving even Dad and his damned cigars. Sure, the cigars killed him, but that doesn't change what he did to me. He's dead of cancer, but he didn't *lose* anything: cancer is something that filled him up. It occupied him, flooded him up with black phlegm. Those cigars may have suffocated him, but he died full. Full of himself.

But me: my wound is on the outside, my hole won't ever fill. I can't feel it anymore—there's nothing there to feel. All I feel is perpetual leaking. And I've been losing a tiny bit of myself ever since.

So I eat.

Otherwise, the only thing I have to hold on to is that last moment—right before I started losing myself, drop by drop. I was being a brat, not finishing supper, and Dad was so mad at me because he had made the dinner himself with his very last dime. I don't remember what he cooked. But I do remember that it tasted horrible and that I couldn't swallow any more. When he said I had to, it was all we could afford, I asked him how he paid for his cigars. I can still feel the pain from when Dad slammed my wrist down on the kitchen table and gently rested his hot heavy cigar on the soft white underside of my elbow, the fat roll of tobacco stoking on my arm as if in a ceramic ashtray. What got me worse than the bright red pain was the smell of his cigar smoke, somehow made more potent with the catalyst of my flesh to smolder. I cried, I begged him to put the cigar out, and after I finally promised to finish my dinner, he did, lifting my wrist up to my shoulder, squelching the hot coal between the chub of my forearm and biceps. I think it was then that I dropped the fork I had been squeezing for my life. And when he let go of me, I kept my arm bent, holding the cigar in place like the gauze the nurse gives you after taking blood: grasping the pain like a plug in your elbow—flexing your muscles so you won't empty out through the puncture.

But that's all I've been doing for years. Emptying out.

I know I eat too much, more than my stomach can hold, but I never gain weight: I just keep on leaking. My wound sometimes closes, but it never stays shut—always stretching itself open to spill more coffee tears, always widening just a little bit further, always peeling its eyelids back when I sleep. Sometimes the white fibers of tendon peek out from their sticky blanket of yellow, crusted like eyes waking up in the morning beside me.

It won't fill me up, but still I keep eating.

Because when I don't, sometimes I catch it out of the corner of my eye: a tiny tuft of gray smoke, rising up from my elbow.

Peeling the scabs with my teeth, I'm really just trying to feed it itself. That's what they don't understand. There's a chance that if I keep eating, my wound might stop weeping. I know what it's like when smoke gets in your eyes. Crying over dinner. Tasting tears. But I won't break my promise: yes, Dad, I will finish.

A New Life

William Rotsler

They buried me at midmorning with an appropriately low-key funeral. After everyone left, Cardiff came back and spat on my grave, muttered a few things, and left. The gravediggers tapped down the loose earth and laid one of those turf mats of real grass, and watered it in the late afternoon. Nothing much else happened until moonrise.

Then I arose.

It's not easy these days—steel coffin, six feet of earth (even freshly spaded), groggy condition. But then I always am groggy when I revitalize. I've done it enough this last century.

It used to be so easy. People didn't travel much. Go three, four, five days away and you were unlikely to run into anyone who knew you. If you wanted to go back, years later, for whatever reason, like property or just because you liked the place, you went back as your own son or grandson.

Or you could just wander off into the forest, leave a bloody cloak to be found, a torn boot. "Gone to America" was a handy rumor years later. In America, you'd "go west." It was easier then. No ID, retinal photos, fingerprints, paperwork. It kept you on your toes, planning ahead, doing your homework.

Each of us works out our standbys. Lost at sea. Gone to war. Unrecognizably burned body. Explosion. Faked kidnapping. Unexplained disappearance. We all have ways.

As usual these years, I'd planted the rumor of being buried with considerable personal jewelry. That explained the ruptured grave, though it didn't really explain the absence of a body. But after a couple of days people usually stop looking.

Now I can start a new life. Just as soon as I settle this thing with Cardiff.

New Oldies

John B. Rosenman

T oo bad there are no new oldies," Sam said, finishing another beer.

I frowned. "That's an odd thing to say."

He shrugged, glanced about his living room. "Fred, you know I knew most of them, don't you? Elvis, Fabian, Darin . . ."

"Sure, and you managed some too. Though not the really big ones."

He gave me a strange smile, like at some private joke. "Rock 'n' roll was king, and we knew it would never die."

I lowered my beer. "Okay, Sam, what is it?"

He sighed, a man in his sixties going to seed just like me. "Fred, did I ever tell you what my big dream was?"

"Nope."

"Well, would it surprise you that what I wanted more than anything else was to manage a *star?* Not just an opening act, but a bona fide *headliner?*"

"Like Elvis?"

"Or Fabian or Darin or Avalon. But somehow the wheeler-dealers always sliced me out of the picture. The few chances I got—like with Paul Anka—they cut me dead. And if I'd only been given the chance to manage one of the star's careers, I would have been *good!*"

I squirmed. After several beers, Sam could get maudlin, but self-pity was something new. "Well, hey," I finally said, "it wasn't the end of the world, was it?"

He blinked, his wrinkled face twitching. "For *me*, it was. You see, I used to dream about seeing *my* client on the *Ed Sullivan Show* or the cover of *Variety* and *Time*, of being there when the cameras flashed, of advising him on his movie contracts and tour schedules."

"But it didn't happen."

"No." He smiled again. "But one day, I finally found a way to make things right."

" 'Right?' "

"Yeah. It was in '66. The kid walked right into my office, green as they come but with one basic thing going for him."

"And what was that?"

He winked. "Talent, Fred. The greatest pure talent I'd ever seen. More than Elvis, more than Darin, more than any three of them put together. Plus, I might add, he was better looking and far sexier."

"You're joking."

He shook his head. "No joke. I've even got a few demos we made. Fred, I could tell this kid couldn't miss, that he would go straight to the top."

"High as Elvis?"

He sneered. "He would have made Elvis look like Tiny Tim. You see, Roy Grant was what they all *tried* to be. He was not only the soul of rock but a master crooner too. If he'd had his chance, he would have been the brightest star of them all."

I gaped. "What happened?"

He rose, wheezing. "Come on."

Puzzled, I followed him to the cellar door, watched him switch on a light.

"Sam . . ."

"Shh. Just follow me."

I followed him down, thinking we were two drunk old men and I should leave. But something in his voice held me.

It was cold in the cellar, so cold our breath fogged. Shivering, I followed him to a corner where he stopped before a worn curtain. He pressed another switch.

"No one else has ever seen this," he said.

I shivered, though this time not from the cold. "What are you—"

"I'm talking about justice, Fred," he said, his face completely sober. "You see, if I'd let others know about Roy, I never would have had a chance. The sharks would have converged in a feeding frenzy." His eyes moistened. "So, *on this night exactly thirty years ago*, I did it. 'Cause I had no choice."

I licked my lips. Gazed at the old, faded curtain.

"The greatest of the great." Sam grinned. "And he's mine, all mine. *Forever!* This one they'll *never* take away from me."

He parted the curtain and for a long moment I gazed at the skeleton that stood mounted on a small stage in the bright glare of spotlights. Over six feet tall, it wore a black leather jacket and carried a gleaming guitar in its bony fingers.

Its bare white skull grinned right at me, one of its smashed empty eye sockets seeming to wink.

Sam pressed another switch, and an old, scratchy soundtrack came on. Despite its poor quality, I could tell the singer's voice was very beautiful and that he sang about eternal love.

We listened for a moment, then Sam turned. "Fred," he said, grinning with proud possession, "I'd like you to meet Roy Grant."

Night Chase

Sara Simmons

He was following very slowly but still I could not escape. I looked over my shoulder again, at the little old man a dozen paces behind. He looked clean, like he'd been scrubbed for his funeral. His suit was baggy and grey. He walked with his head bent, and shuffled, almost limped along, at a pace with no hurry in it. When I'd first noticed him he'd been further back. Against all reason, he was gaining.

I couldn't stand it anymore. At the next corner I turned sharply and ran, twisting through the dark streets—left, right, right again. I wanted to run forever, but there was no breath left in my lungs. I slowed to a walk and looked back. He was still there, a very little closer, but then I no longer believed he might be gone.

Once I had. Once, in some oh-so-distant time, I had not noticed him at all. It had been slightly later than I usually liked to be walking in the city, but I had managed to keep any fear tucked away. Then, in the middle of a long, deserted block, something made me look back. That must have been the trap. He was so ordinary, moving at half my speed. *He'll be out of sight by the corner.* I thought. But he wasn't. He never would be.

Every store I passed was shut. No one else was in the streets now. I was left with glass and steel and concrete and the occasional car, swishing by with no one inside. Each pair of headlights lit the street for an instant, then passed, leaving darkness which made even the safe places dangerous.

I saw faces which did not belong to the city. These new ones appeared reflected in windows, pale faces superimposed on displays of clothes or electronics. They were dressed in formless robes the same colour as the glass. Their faces were masks made of white moulded paper, the ragged edges extending to either side. Trickles of blood ran from the eyes.

For a long time I did not look back. My feet hurt and I wanted nothing more than to rest. I made myself count steps. A thousand. More. I couldn't hear him behind me. Perhaps he was gone. I turned.

He was only a few paces behind. The masks had come out of the glass and followed him, his army, surging behind us in a loose pack. He was too close. I could feel him now. As we passed beneath a streetlight I could watch our shadows moving together and I thought I could see how he did it, how he took one step for every one of mine and how he made his slow shuffle equal the same space as a running stride.

Step by step through the endless streets his shadow crept up on mine. My pace slowed until it matched his. I kept expecting to feel his touch on my back.

Then I came out unexpectedly into a square, an open space in the heart of the city. I almost stopped—only the pressure of the little man's presence kept me going across the huge expanse of paving. On the other side, waiting, were the dark mouths of the streets.

In the centre of the square was a fountain, dry, no water moving in the half-light. I thought that I had been here once before, in daylight, but there was no such thing as day, only night and the chase.

On the far side of the square I saw a row of white spots. Not a row but a circle, a circle of masks, extending behind me. I was trapped, but I was too tired to think, too tired for anything but fear. In the shadows beneath the fountain I stopped. At least the hunt was over.

The masks drew in from the edges of the square until they were within arm's reach of each other. The little man had caught up at last and stood beside me. I waited to see what he would do.

He gestured towards the masks and two of them stepped apart. Between them I could see the dark slash of a street, leading back into the city.

"There is still plenty of the night left," he said. "Run!"

I ran. At the edge of the square I looked back and saw he was following. Slowly.

The Night Club

Scott David Aniolowski

he old hearse rumbled along the snow-crusted back road, thick black smoke trailing from its rusted, dangling tailpipe. Brittle icy trees stooped along the roadside, bare branches moaning in the bitter January wind. A razor-sharp sickle moon hung in the clear night sky, shrouding the snowy fields with cold blue light.

"So, what's the name of this nightclub?" Jimmy asked above the melodic lamenting of the car radio. Like the others, he dressed head to foot in black. Silver skulls and crosses decorated his ears, fingers, and neck—just like the others. Jimmy had a mane of long, thick black hair and a scruffy goatee. His newfound friends preferred the clean-shaven, bald look.

"You'll love it," laughed Hyena, a waif-thin, doglike boy of probably eighteen.

"We only take certain people," mumbled Leviathan, an enormous pale bulk about the same age as Hyena. "But we like the looks of you." He put his arm around Jimmy's shoulder and squeezed.

"Yeah," grinned Jimmy, sandwiched between Hyena and Leviathan in the hearse's back seat. "This is awesome." He nodded toward the old brass-decorated coffin in the back.

"Goes with the look," the girl in the front seat hissed. She was just plump, with a pretty round face and black lips. She, like her male companions, was also bald. They called her Phobia, and she was Parasite's girlfriend.

Parasite sat silently behind the wheel, watching the headlights dance across the icy road. He was tall and muscular and wore dark glasses day and night. In the few weeks since Jimmy had met them, it had become obvious that Parasite was the group leader, even though he never spoke. He was older than the rest. He also owned the hearse.

"This place is sort of out of the way, isn't it?" Jimmy said after several minutes. Empty, desolate fields roll by. The hearse rumbled and coughed along the twisting country road, bouncing roughly through potholes.

"Yeah, it's far out." Phobia adjusted her black makeup in the rearview mirror. Jimmy met her gaze in the mirror and she winked at him. He looked away nervously.

"So, Jimmy, you never did tell us how long you're planning on staying with us," Phobia finally said after another long lull in the conversation.

"Yeah." Hyena giggled and patted him on the knee.

"I don't know. Depends, I guess." The goateed boy shrugged. "Hey, I think I need a cool nickname."

"How about Goat?" Leviathan tugged at the boy's facial hair. Hyena cackled. Phobia tittered. Parasite was silent.

"Nah." Jimmy wrinkled his nose.

"So, you want to be in the gang, do you?" Phobia asked.

"Yeah," replied Jimmy.

"Yeah?" The plump, round-faced girl turned around and reached over the seat. A knife sparkled in the cold blue moonlight.

"Hey!" Jimmy dodged. Leviathan caught him in a viselike grip, held his arms tightly behind his back. Hyena giggled in his ear, so close he could feel the breath on his neck. Parasite kept his eyes on the road and just drove.

"Come on, baby, I thought you wanted to be in the gang." Phobia grabbed the goatee and slid the blade along Jimmy's cheek.

"Uh, come on." He swallowed. He didn't know which was colder—the knife or the girl's hand. Tiny glistening gems of sweat rolled down his face. His heart raced, his arms ached.

The car suddenly lurched to a stop, sliding several yards on ice. Parasite clicked off the lights, turned off the engine, and stared silently into the dark, empty field.

"This is it," laughed Hyena.

"Where?" Jimmy wriggled in Leviathan's arms. "There's no nightclub. We're out in the middle of nowhere."

"Hm, I guess you misunderstood. *We're* the Night Club." Phobia smiled a black smile at him.

Hyena, drooling and cackling, unzipped Jimmy's leather jacket.

"Hey, what the . . ." He tried to kick out at the dog-faced youth.

"And tonight you're our guest," Phobia giggled. Jimmy squeezed his eyes closed as she hooked the knife under his chin. Slowly, she cut down the front of his T-shirt, exposing the damp, trembling flesh beneath. "Nice." She licked her black lips.

They dragged Jimmy kicking and screaming from the car, ripped off his clothes, and held him down on the hard cold ground. Then they hungrily tore into his flesh. After several minutes Jimmy's screams stopped and he moved only a little.

"I can't wait for spring when the ground thaws," growled Parasite, his mouth red. "I'm tired of eating this fresh stuff."

Night Eyes

Tim Waggoner

In the darkness at the foot of Jerome's bed, two glowing eyes hovered. Yellow eyes, hungry eyes. Eyes that swayed hypnotically back and forth as they inched slowly forward.

Jerome pressed back against the headboard, as if he might somehow push himself through it and the wall behind, push himself to safety. But the headboard and wall held. No escape that way.

And then the sound began. A cicadalike drone, but deeper and slower, as if someone had recorded the noise made by the summer insects and then played the tape back at a far slower speed. Or perhaps it was more like the staccato vibration of a rattle, thick and heavy, growing forth from the scaly smooth tip of a snake's tail.

The eyes swayed as if they might belong to a huge serpent, but they were a solid sour amber. Nothing at all like snake eyes.

The eyes, and presumably the unseen head to which they were attached, continued swaying forward.

Jerome clutched the sweat-sodden bedsheet to his chest, fingers digging into the damp fabric. His pulse beat a trip-hammer counterpoint to the creature's drone, but his lungs had seized up in his chest and refused to work. He wanted nothing more than to fling the sheet at the eyes, to snuff out their baleful glow, and then spring off the bed and make a dash for the light switch. Instinct told him that whatever this apparition was, it couldn't stand the light. And if his instinct was false, then at least he would be able to see the thing. Seeing would make the creature solid, would define it, force it to be real. And what was real could be dealt with. But this—glowing orbs and nerve-jangling drone—how could this be fought?

But no matter how hard Jerome willed his limbs to work, they refused to obey him. He could only lie there, body rigid and pouring sweat, as the eyes came ever nearer. As a child, he had once looked at a book about snakes. He recalled one picture of a sparrow standing helplessly in the grass, frozen by the mesmeric gaze of a snake as it approached to devour the tiny bird. The picture had been meant to illustrate one of the many myths about snakes, but Jerome knew it was no mere fable, for he was the sparrow now.

The eyes reached his feet, then swayed and bobbed past ankles, calves.

What was this thing? Why was it here? He had never been especially afraid of snakes, had never harmed any, had never seen any close-up outside of the reptile house at the zoo, for godsakes. There was no reason for this thing to be here—past his knees, thighs, crotch, sliding through the air above his belly—no reason. And that frightened him infinitely more than the eyes set into the darkness, more than the rattling drone that filled the air: that this might very well be happening for no reason whatsoever.

Then the logical part of his mind broke free of the fear and spoke up. This couldn't possibly be real. From the position of the eyes, if there were a snake, he should be able to feel its coils upon his legs and stomach. But he felt nothing. Therefore, it was just a dream, or at worst a hallucination. All in his head. How could it be anything else?

Moving across his chest, closing in on his face, the drone rising in pitch and volume, nearly deafening now.

Still, Jerome felt no weight on his body, sensed no movement of the air caused by the swaying of a large serpent head.

The eyes drew nearer, their glow completely filling his vision.

And then they were gone, their light extinguished; the rattle-drone ended, the room fell silent.

Jerome lay there for a long moment, before finally drawing in a relieved breath. *Just a dream*, he thought gratefully. A dream that was now over.

His throat was bone dry and he had to go to the bathroom something fierce. He got out of bed—his limbs no longer frozen now that the dream was over—and padded across the floor, wearing only a sweaty pair of pajama bottoms.

In the bathroom, he turned on the tap and then looked into the mirror. He saw a pair of glowing yellow eyes staring back at him, heard the rattling erupt in his skull. And he realized with a cold stab of horror that he had been right.

It *was* all in his head.

Night Terrors

Blythe Ayne

Tracy and Tim had been married a mere two months when Tim woke up with a start and a muffled yell.

"Wha-what's wrong?" Tracy pulled the sheets up under her chin, inexplicably frightened.

"I . . . I . . . don't know. Eugh, what a terrible dream."

"Tell me about it," Tracy urged, not entirely sure she meant it.

"Maybe in the morning. I don't want to think about it now."

The next morning Tracy asked Tim if he could remember his nightmare.

"Heavens, I'd almost forgotten it—there was this beautiful woman seducing me. . . ."

"Not me?" Tracy said, hurt.

"No, Hon, not you. Next thing I know, we're going at it. . . ."

"We've been married two months, and already you're dreaming about having sex with another woman?"

"It's a nightmare, Trace, and here's where it gets creepy—she turns into this frightening, powerful thing, sucking out my human energy." A sheen of sweat broke out on Tim's brow.

Tracy was quiet and angry.

"It was a terrible nightmare like I've never had in my life," Tim said. "Seems like you could show a little sympathy."

"I don't know what to think, you dreaming about having sex with someone else."

Tim sighed a deep sigh and left the subject alone.

But the nightmares became more frightening, and as the dreams augmented in frequency and horror, Tracy became more distant. Finally Tim suggested they visit his doctor, hoping he would prescribe something to make the creature lurking in his nights go away.

In Dr. Kauf's office Tim poured out a description of his experiences, and the monster that instigated them. "At first she's supernaturally beautiful, her skin glistens, and there's a kind of light in her eyes that you can't look away from." Tim saw Tracy's neatly crossed little foot start to twitch angrily. "But then, when she . . . she's had her way with me, she turns into this horrible thing. Her flesh becomes like a toad and she smells putrid, like rotten vegetables or something. I wake up, or I think I wake up, and it's like she's still there."

Dr. Kauf nodded, nodded, nodded. "It sounds like a succubus." He chuckled like the wise old doctor he was, having seen many vagaries of the human experience in fifty years of practice.

Consternation ruffled Tracy's features. "Is it contagious?"

Dr. Kauf laughed out loud. "No, dear. A succubus is a mythical demon who seduces a man during sleep. Her male counterpart is the incubus."

"We come to you with a serious problem, and you make fun?" Tracy was seething.

"I apologize, Tracy. I was just trying to relieve some of the anxiety I see in both your faces." Dr. Kauf put on a serious, professional look. "You've gone through a lot of major life changes lately, Tim, and you have new responsibilities. It can be a tough adjustment. I'll prescribe a mild sleeping tablet which I suggest you take with a glass of warm milk. Let's see if that doesn't take care of the problem."

Tracy was mollified when the doctor put on his professional face, and was delighted when Tim slept like a baby that night. In fact, she had to wake him the next morning when the alarm failed to rouse him.

The next night she spooned up next to Tim, who had again fallen asleep almost before saying good night. She watched the shadows of leaves on the wall and drifted into a peaceful, safe sleep, happy that the nuisance dreams were gone.

Suddenly, she couldn't breathe. Her eyes flew open. Above her, pinning her to the sheets, was a beautiful man who was not like a man at all, glowing golden brown, with gorgeously defined pectorals—not one of Tim's strong points, she found herself thinking. Something stirred in her that she had never known was possible. But as she felt herself giving way to the beauty and power of him, he began to transmogrify. His eyes sank under a frightening brow, his pectorals deteriorated into a scaly, gray, oozing putrescence, and a foul odor surrounded her.

"My sister was furious at your intervention," the monster sputtered. "Your husband was such a delight! But the good fortune comes to me. You and I, we'll have wonderful nights." The fistules on his body became open sores that dripped on Tracy's beautiful young flesh with a searing, acid pain. Still, she could not yell or move, she could not wake up, nor even go back into her sleep.

416

Night Train

Bob Morrish

Achorus of crickets, invisible among yellow grasses and flowing cattails, punctuates the stillness of an August evening. A small fire crackles, its yellow flames peaking beneath a starry sky. At the fire's edge sits a small, weathered man, arthritic knees tucked stiffly beneath him, staring contentedly into the bright embers. The odor of cooking meat wafts through the air. His stomach grumbles; his tired eyes squint and almost water in the rising smoke. His face, in shadows, is occasionally caught and briefly held by flickers of light; his dark brown skin lies in folds and wrinkles like creased leather. Ragged jacket, soiled shirt, baggy trousers—their true colors rendered mute by the darkness—hang loosely from his sparse frame, like material draped upon a tailor's clotheshorse.

Too much clothing, it would seem, for such a humid night, but years of exposure to the elements have numbed the old man to all but the most extreme conditions. He nods, rocks minutely on slight haunches, hums snatches of partially remembered songs. From far off comes the insistent whistle of an approaching train, reduced by distance to a drawn-out moan.

William Amos Jefferson, he was christened long ago; he is vague about his exact age. "Call me Willie," he says to those he meets up and down the rail lines. "Just call me Willie," his introduction delivered through a mouth possessing significantly less than its original complement of teeth.

Hobo, many would call him, a rider of the rails, a few saying so with envy in their voice, envy of his travels, his freedom. Only Willie, and his dwindling group of widely scattered colleagues, know how misplaced that envy is. Through years of drafty boxcars and endless wanderings, Willie has known hard times. He would not trade his life with many, but neither would he recommend it.

On this particular night he feels fortunate. Earlier, he managed to avoid confrontation with a yard boss in Baton Rouge, a large, angry man who had tangled with Willie in the past. Because of him, Willie seldom travels this far south on the lines anymore. But a change of scenery seemed in order, even if it meant venturing deeper into the summer's heat. The drab flow of Illinois cornfields had begun to depress Willie; it had been good to feel the rumbling tracks beneath him again, the exhilarating rush of an empty freighter returning for new cargo.

A solitary bead of sweat formed high on his brow and trailed a meandering pattern down his cheek and through the stubble that lay below. Lazily fanning himself with a section of the *Gulfport Times*, he reminisced of days long past. The train's cry intruded upon his thoughts. He cocked his head to one side, pondering. According to the schedule, there shouldn't be anything coming through for at least another hour. But then again, he hadn't been down this way in a long time. The schedules must have changed.

It was no matter; he had already decided to spend the night right where he was, in a small hollow about thirty yards from a culvert beneath the elevated tracks. He almost always camped this close to the tracks; the late night freights had ceased to wake him years ago, and there was something strangely reassuring about staying so near to his livelihood. Willows rustled around him as a cloying wind briefly caressed the weeping branches. Willie closed his eyes as the unexpected breeze swept over him, thankful for the touch of respite. He felt the ground begin to vibrate beneath him as the train approached.

Although the sky was clear, the moon was but a crescent; its weak glow lit only a corner of the night ceiling. Through the darkness, beyond the curtain of trees, Willie heard the hum and throb of the locomotive engine at work. The whoosh of the cars cutting through the vapid air conveyed an impression of great speed, but the train was not yet in sight. Not that Willie would have seen it if it were. His eyes were still closed, his lips slightly parted. He was lost inside himself.

Vibrations coarsed up from the ground and through his body; he was held in a rumbling grip. Willie had a moment to think, to realize, that he had never felt this way before, then the emanations flooded him, carrying him away on waves of darkness. He gave in weakly to the sensations that swept over him.

The train cried out again, its shrillness almost disturbing him from his rapture. The whistle pierced the night, resounding like the cry of a thousand lost souls. Willie's eyelids fluttered, but then the harsh noise melted into a comforting symphony, one that lulled him even further, entwining itself in his dreams.

Willie knew he was dreaming. He looked up and saw the train

standing before him now, silent save for a solitary hiss from the air brakes. He had heard no screech from those brakes, had seen no shower of sparks, yet there it sat.

Patient. Waiting.

And the cars . . . they were of all types: a coal tender for an ancient steam engine; an oddly ornate dining car—the likes of which Willie had not seen since the forties; a tri-level automobile car, occupied by gleaming new coupes dating from the mid-sixties; and, pulling this strange assortment, a sleek, modern diesel engine. Willie gazed upon all this and knew he must be dreaming.

He smiled slightly as he felt the train calling to him, beckoning him to climb aboard. A gentle pull, an alluring whisper. Lost in the spell of the rails, Willie rose and walked slowly toward the train.

Climbing the steps, Willie heard a hoarse voice whisper "All aboard," and dimly realized that he might be a passenger on this train for a very long time.

The train moved on, its screams seeking through the night.

Nightmares

Linda J. Dunn

Jenny looked over at the psychologist and shrugged. "I'm losing my grip on reality. I keep having the same nightmare over and over again every night. Or maybe I should say I have the same kind of nightmare. The dreams are always different, but it's the same old plot."

"And what do you dream?" he asked.

Jenny took a deep breath. "I dream that I wake up and everything that's happened the last few years has been a dream. I'm still married to my abusive ex-husband and I spend the rest of the dream trying to find a way to leave him without getting killed. What do you think this means?"

The psychologist smiled and laid down his pen. "What do *you* think it means?"

"I don't know. You're the shrink. You're the one who's supposed to give me the answers."

"I can't give you the answers. Only you can provide those."

"Then what are you supposed to be doing for this outrageous fee?"

"I'm guiding you by asking the right questions."

Jenny stared into the psychologist's eyes. *Why did I ever think this would work?*

"Thank you. I think I can handle this now."

"You don't want to make another appointment?"

"No."

"I really suggest—"

Jenny stood up and opened the door. "I'm quite capable of asking my own questions now, thank you."

And maybe even finding the answers.

Jenny stopped at the local gun store on the way home, determined to put an end to this hell. It was a long shot, but what did she have to lose?

Jenny tossed and turned in her sleep, knowing that she was dreaming but still unable to change anything. She woke up, and Dave was there, waiting for her, as always.

"You had the same nightmare again?" her husband asked.

"Yes." Jenny shivered and sat up. "It's the same dream every time. We're divorced and I'm seeing a psychologist."

Jenny bit her tongue, not mentioning the wonderful second husband and the lovely house and car.

The only thing that's bad about that dream is going to sleep every night and waking up here: married to an unemployed, abusive alcoholic who'll kill me if I leave.

She reached under the pillow, and her fingers closed upon the gun she'd bought in that dream world. Evidently, it *was* possible to bring something back if you just held on to it when you fell asleep.

"Get me a beer," he said. "And you better hurry if you don't want to be late at the factory. You know how long it takes to make breakfast the way I like it."

Jenny nodded and waited for him to turn away before releasing the safety.

She didn't know anymore which world was real and which was a dream. But she was about to find out.

Nikola, Moonstruck

Lisa Morton

It was nearly lunchtime when Nikola found the severed hand in the ditch.

He had been repairing a broken irrigation pipe at the edge of one of his fields. The rest of the body was a few yards off, floating facedown in the shallow water. He recognized his friend Milan, even from the back.

And yet what he felt wasn't grief or fear—it was rage. This was the sixth murder to occur near the village on a full moon night. The pattern was obvious to Nikola, and yet the rest refused to believe, said this was the modern Romania, not old Transylvania.

But the evidence all pointed to a werewolf.

Even his wife, Lena, scoffed. "Nikola, for the love of God, grow up," she'd hissed, "this is 1995. We have serial killers and junkies and war criminals to worry about, not werewolves."

Lena had refused to discuss it further and had shut the door to her bedroom. Nikola and his wife hadn't shared a bed in nearly a year.

The other villagers had scorned him as well. "A wolfman, Nikola . . . you know, I hear Lena's got her own bed now. If anybody around here's got hair on their palms, it's you."

That'd been Milan two months ago. Now he was dead, torn apart.

The police were called in, from Sebes, twenty miles away. Two officers and a coroner came, looked at the body, declared Milan a victim of animal attack and left, promising help. Nikola's friends listened to those bland assurances, but ignored his suggestions of melting down silver for bullets, or having all the men gather by the light of the next full moon so they could catch the beast in midtransformation.

Three weeks passed, and the full moon was one night off. Nikola tried again.

One man told him he thought it was a Serb fanatic, who had crossed borders and was in hiding, still committing his atrocities. Several brought up drugs and kids on the lam from Bucharest.

Lena tried to reason with her husband. "Nik, you've made me the laughingstock of my friends—"

"And will your friends still laugh when one of their husbands becomes a wolf tomorrow night? Or it could be that new doctor, the one from Tusla . . ."

Lena looked away, bitterly. "Don't you see where this is leading? We suspect all the new ones, we look to blame the ones we don't know. You're living in the nineteenth century. I *like* the twentieth century, Nik. I *want* to live here . . ."

Nikola went to his cold bed that night and dreamt of men with fur-lined capes and armor who became fearsome beasts and tore through lines of their enemies.

It was the day of the full moon. There was an undeniable tension in the air; the few of his neighbors whom Nikola passed barely gave him a nod, then hurried on their own way.

Nikola spent his day at a silversmith's in Sebes. There wasn't much he could spare out of the bank accounts, but he managed enough to buy three silver bullets. Now moonrise was only an hour off, and he was cleaning his gun. Lena watched him for a while, then finally came forward and knelt gently before him.

"Come away, Nik. Come away from this."

He stared at her in disbelief. She reached up, took his face in her hands and kissed him, sweetly. "Please, Nik. Men don't turn into wolves. I don't want you to hurt anyone tonight. Come with me . . ."

He resisted at first, then let himself be led down the hall, to her bedroom. He hadn't seen the room in a year.

She opened the curtains, letting the night in. "We'll watch the moon rise together, Nik."

Lena took him into the bed, and held him tight as the first faint luminescence appeared outside. When the moon shone full on them, she grasped him tighter. Too tight. Nik felt something turn over in his stomach.

"Lena . . ."

Her face was turned away from his, and she made a strange noise in her throat.

Like a wolf growl.

When she turned back to him, her face had lengthened, grown hirsute, feral. He tried to pull away, but now there were claws digging into his back.

"You were looking for a wolf*man*, Nik . . ."

She laughed then, a hideous sound that ended in a snarl and one last taunt: "Welcome to the twentieth century, darling."

Then she tore his throat out.

No Pain

Lyn Nichols

L onny absently picked at the scab on his forearm. He worked a fingernail under the edge of it and lifted. The blackish brown cracked into an ugly gray-white as it pulled away from his skin. He pulled a little more.

It hurt! A drop of blood welled up from the edge of the scab. Still fresh, he thought. Hell. Where'd that come from?

His head still felt muggy and hollow, short-circuited. Crash-burn. Goddamn crash-burn followed a good high no matter what you dropped.

He fingered his shirt pocket, caressed the tiny folded paper that could make things right. He should just pop the hit and be done with the crash-burn. He'd sure as hell feel better.

Lonny pulled the folded paper from his pocket and looked at it. He'd gotten lucky. His regular dealer had been busted, put away. Finding this other guy, this stranger, was a piece of luck.

"Good stuff, this," the guy had said. "No pain. Kick your ass and blow you away, but hey . . . no pain."

Lonny couldn't remember much of the first trip on this stuff. Yesterday was just a vague blur, filled with some wickedly real hallucinations—scary, but controllable. No sweat stuff, no pain—and a case of the giggles that would not quit. He smiled and unfolded the paper.

"No pain," he whispered.

Inside, a small, flat, brown square of . . . stuff . . . waited. It looked like someone had clipped it off an audio cassette tape. Windowpane. No pain.

Carefully, he lifted the small piece of celluloid and touched it to the corner of his eye, let it slip under the lower lid. He blinked back the sudden tears and slight sting.

"No pain, man. No pain."

In minutes, Lonny's perspective of the world was changing. The room brightened, edges grew sharp and clear, colors were vibrant. He reached for a cigarette and was transfixed by the rainbow of colored hands that followed his.

The light from the window sparkled with flecks of flying gold. Lonny pushed up from the chair and looked outside. Beautiful day.

Time ceased to matter. Lonny found a field overgrown with grasses and flowers. Butterflies flitted, and left streaming trails of color behind them. Flowers nodded and Lonny had to laugh and nod back at the smiling faces. He walked out into the field and sat down.

"Yeah, man," he told the world. "No pain. Fuckin' no pain at all."

Little black specks in the grass caught his attention.

"Shit!"

Ants surrounded him. They were everywhere. Lonny started to stand, then collapsed, laughing. Not ants, he realized. Not ants at all.

"Shadows," he giggled. "The fuckin' shadows of the grass. Just looking like ants. It's cool." He lay back in the grass, still chuckling at the sudden fright. "Fuckin' wimp. Scared of a fuckin' shadow."

Something tickled his bare legs and he looked down. The shadows were covering him. He laughed and watched them move up his legs toward his crotch. He lifted his arm. Shadows moved in random patterns between the hairs. He giggled at the crawly tingly sensations the shadows caused.

When they swarmed up over his face, he closed his eyes and gave in to the sensations. No pain, he smiled. No pain at all.

"Tiger, come here!" Bill Sawyer shouted after his Labrador as it bounded into the field. Tiger didn't listen. Instead the dog stopped, backed away from something, barked.

"Come here, Tiger," he called. "C'mon, boy."

Tiger looked at him and then back at something hidden in the grass. Bill could hear his whine.

"Damn dog."

Bill stomped through the high grass. Obviously Tiger wasn't going to leave whatever it was unless he was dragged away. He reached the dog's side and looked.

424

And immediately backed away, bile choking him. He stumbled a few feet, fell to his knees and vomited. Tiger whined and huddled against his side. After a few minutes, he stood, taking several deep breaths.

"Stay, Tiger," he ordered the dog, then steeled himself for another look. He needed to see, needed to be sure before he called the cops.

It was all he could do not to puke again as he looked down at the ant-covered corpse. The insects had eaten the skin off the body and were exploring every visible opening. Bill shuddered and started to turn away, then froze.

"No pain," he heard the ant-covered body whisper. And then it giggled.

No Strings Attached

David Niall Wilson

A small ocean of tiny faces were turned up to meet her gaze, and Miss Lily smiled out at them brightly. She could be stern, and she could be haughty, as all queens are wont, but today she was cheerful.

At the door to the tent, Adolph the dwarf stood stoically by, collecting the dollars and the change, handing out tickets and escorting the children to their seats.

Adolph leaned in close whenever he saw a familiar face enter, whispering secrets to the children and handing out sweets.

"She's in rare good spirits tonight, my boy," he'd chuckle, winking and sneaking a gumdrop into a chubby palm. "Hurry to your seat now, you know how she can get."

And many of them did know. She was unmercifully cruel to the small man, demeaning him, slapping him in front of her audiences, ordering him about like a trained lap dog. Her anger was almost theatrical, like an odd part of the act. Nobody liked that part of her show, but Miss Lily's puppets were magical. Adolph wanted to hang around and get mistreated, that was sad—but not sad enough to keep them away.

Miss Lily bowed off the stage, disappearing through the red velvet curtains in preparation for the show. The show was on!

Bright marionettes of all sorts frolicked for the next hour, calling to one another in musical voices, performing skits and comedy routines, smacking one another around playfully. Adolph watched from the door of the tent, counting the money. His shadow lengthened as the show went on, sliding slowly across the floor of the tiny enclosure until it loomed huge and ghastly, threatening to engulf the back rows of spectators in its ebony talons. When the seats were full, it followed Lily backstage.

He found her seated, her face in her hands, tears streaming down both cheeks as she sobbed quietly but uncontrollably.

"Pull yourself together, my pet," he crooned. She glanced up at the sound of his voice, her eyes brimming with terror.

"I . . ."

"No excuses. Clean up and get your drink—you have to go and bring them back in in a few minutes, and Miss Lily can't be showing up on stage with tearstains on her face, can she?"

Lily shook her head and gazed at the floor, rising docilely. She moved to the small counter in the back of the tent and pulled down a bottle, filling a small wineglass with pinkish liqueur.

"That's better," Adolph grinned, hopping from one foot to the other. "Drink up, drink up . . . time to get them back here and caged up. Time to put the little toys away. Maybe you'd like me to pull those two little cherubs from the third row to join us?"

"Oh, no!" Lily cried, gulping the contents of the glass in a rush and moving back toward the stage. "Not that . . . not again."

Adolph's cackling voice followed her out. "Hurry then, my pet . . . bring the little ones in. They, too, must drink, to feed your strength . . . then you will stay with me, always."

It was all Lily could do to keep the tears from her eyes, but somehow she managed. She brought the puppets in, one after the other, removed their strings and stood them in a row before Adolph, who brought each of the small figures a smaller version of the drink she herself had finished moments earlier. Tiny hands reached eagerly for the glasses, tiny mouths opened greedily and the liquid disappeared down minuscule throats. Their tiny features solidified noticeably as she watched, and the shame nearly drove her to her knees—she had no experience controlling human emotions. She had been created to be controlled.

Lily herded them carefully into separate little cages and lowered the lids into place. By the next show they would be one step closer to the puppets they mimicked. Soon she would have to begin manipulating them herself, pulling their strings. Somewhere their families still cried in the night. She would be stronger, but the price was too great . . . too much to bear.

After the crowds dispersed, Adolph came up behind her and laid his hands on her shoulders, sliding her dress downward. As she shuddered, trying not to flinch at his touch, he caressed the reddened, healing sores on her shoulders and back—where once the strings had made her dance. As the tears welled in her eyes once more, the crowds began to gather outside.

Novice

A. M. Dellamonica

Requiem Chaos was a dead bar.

The house band, Scream Phoenix, drove their van off a bridge in the seventies. Tag Naguchi and the Roman vampire played chess there on midsummer evenings, and werewolves dropped in when the moon was sinking and the hunt had ended for another month. Jasmine Spencer Lord could be found there, carving monstrosities into the banisters and windowsills. The waitresses had the pallor of maidens set to rest, not in warm beds but in the close comfort of the tomb.

The bartender at the Req was a zombie from the old Irish school. He could draw a pint of ye olde ale with the best of them, but his regulars' tastes ran to concoctions like the Red Cross Special and Abattoir Brew. Danny was fond of saying the Req was the only pub in town that spent more money bribing the health inspector than buying liquor.

The bar drew a crowd of warm-blooded thrillseekers every Hallowe'en, and if it had been any other holiday, many of the regulars would have stayed away. But All Hallows was a night that often brought someone new to their community. They came, in spite of the gawkers. The band could handle mere tourists.

Onstage, Fyodor was enjoying himself. He had been doing arsenic shooters since nightfall, and he was in fine voice. The living, half terrified, were transfixed by the sound of the Scream, and the dead rejoiced in their confusion. Some of those innocent souls would be waking up with nightmares beside them in the morning. Scream Phoenix played a siren song to the dead, a clarion to let them know Requiem Chaos was open for business. You have a place, Fyodor was telling them. You're welcome here.

The kid came in at midnight.

His head was nearly severed, balanced on his neck by strands of hair matted to the skin like stitches. He clutched at Angelina and didn't notice when his hand passed through her. She swept doubloons off the table into her apron and gave him the look: arms folded, eyebrow raised over an empty socket. The look had driven men to tears, to sickness, to fainting. Fyodor found it irresistibly erotic.

"You've got to help me," the kid told her.

A faint murmur, good-humored, from the regulars. Under the blood, the kid's clothes were circa 1950 and through the shreds of his shirt they could see his internal organs, dried and green.

"Take a break," Fyodor told the band. He cut through the crowd to the young man's side. Angelina went back to wiping down the table like nothing had happened. Her locket swung back and forth over the ashtray as she bent over the black wood. The kid's eyes followed its silver arc as if hypnotized.

Fyodor nudged him. "Fell asleep in the guillotine again, did we?"

Blue eyes searched his face. "We were fighting, in the car. Me and my girlfriend."

"Driving and fighting at the same time?" That brought back memories. Fyodor glanced at Phil, who'd frozen at the backstage door, gripping his drumsticks. Remembrance impaled Fyodor: his best friend's hand on his throat, Floyd and Freddie screaming, the taste of blood rolling over his tongue as they plummeted toward water so black and clear you could see the stars in it.

Impact. Drowning.

"I need a drink," Fyodor said. Phil disappeared through the door.

"I wasn't watching the road," the kid said.

"I can just imagine what you hit." Fyodor towed him to the bar and dusted off two seats in front of Danny.

"It was my fault. My girlfriend . . . I killed her."

"We'll compare notes sometime," Fyodor said. "I'm a vehicular homicide myself."

"I've got to go back," the kid said. "Turn myself in."

"Drink one," Fyodor said. "Maybe she'll turn up. You can apologize."

The kid stared at him. "She's dead."

Fyodor saluted him with a glass. He'd get the idea eventually.

The kid's jaw opened and closed as he worked through his confusion, revealing worms ringing the meat at the back of his throat. Finally he dipped the decaying tip of his little finger into the glass and swirled it in the red fluid before bringing it to his tongue for a taste. He sighed and sank onto the stool.

Fyodor knocked back his drink and ordered another. He could just hear the footsteps coming up the road, clattering and uneven, the steps of a woman walking in only one high heel.

The Number You Have Reached

Brian McNaughton

I had just started weeding the garden when the telephone rang. "Hannah! The tel—"

I caught myself, not quite in time. No neighbors in sight. They were all inside, laughing about the old coot who wanted his dead wife to answer the phone.

I ran inside, picked it up. "Hello?"

"Who is this?"

"I give up," I said. "Who?"

"Huh?"

No fun jerking a moron around. I hung up.

I figured I would have a short wait. I reached for a cigarette before I remembered that Hannah had made me give them up.

Ring.

"Hello?"

"Who is this?"

"Wow, I get another guess?" I said. "Rumpelstiltskin."

He still didn't know what I meant. He vented the frustration stupid people must feel in obscene abuse. I hung up.

Hell, I had cigarettes in my desk. I lit one, staring at the answering machine while I coughed my damn lungs out. Answering machines always break. This one broke, unbeknownst to me, the night they tried to get me from the hospital to say Hannah had no more time. I never did get to say good-bye.

I hadn't got around to ripping it out by the roots and slinging it at the wall. I did now. "You're next," I told the telephone.

I returned to weeding the garden. The phone rang all morning. Sometimes I reached it in time. No, this isn't Irving's Bakery. There's no Linda here. Sorry, I don't speak Farsi.

"You *are* next," I told the phone.

Ring, ring. "Hello?"

"Good morning, Mr. Wainwright! If you hold a major credit card, it's my pleasure to tell you that you've won an all-expenses paid cruise to Aruba. What's your reaction?"

My *reaction?* Good God, she was marking time with this scam while waiting for a job on the evening news: "What was your reaction, Mrs. Jones, when little Johnny got squashed by the snowplow?"

"How's this for a reaction?" I hung up.

It rang almost immediately. "Take me off your sucker list, you crook!"

"Huh? Is Linda there?"

"Yes, but I just finished cutting her up with my chainsaw. *Muahahahaha!*"

I turned off the ringer and went back to work.

When did all this crap with telephones start? When I was a kid we had operators who kept nitwits from dialing so many wrong numbers.

Around lunchtime I got sick of wondering if one of the kids might try to call me and turned the phone on.

Ring, ring. "Hello?"

"Who is this?"

"If you believe that's how to start a conversation, pal, you have the wrong number. You force your way into my home and demand—"

He hung up. Smarter than the other one.

Fog rolled in while I was eating lunch. No more gardening. I decided to give Jack Daniels some overtime, and he helped me get through the second cigarette without coughing. Much.

Phone kept ringing. Half the callers hung up before I reached it. The others wanted Irving or Linda or greeted me by gabbling, "Etaoin shrdlu!"

The fog was incredible; it looked like the house was packed in cotton. I wanted to open the back door for a better look, but it was stuck. That happened in damp weather. I went to the front door and that was stuck. That never happened. I wrestled with it for a good fifteen minutes before I gave up and went—yeah, funny—to the telephone. Hanson, the guy next door, fancied himself a handyman, and I'd never hear the end of it if he had to rescue me, but—

"Hi, this is Linda. I'm not home now—"

What the *hell?* I checked the listing and dialed again.

"Irving's Bakery, please hold."

Maybe Irving could help me, but after ten minutes of Tony Bennett on hold, I hung up and tried again.

"Hello?"

I began: "Oh, hey, Hanson, this is—"

"Wrong number, bozo. Next time get your mommy to dial."

Click.

I tried a window, but the lock was jammed. And did I really want to open it on that fog? Less like cotton, it now looked like something old and nasty and curdled. In the corner of my eye, never directly, parts of it writhed. I stepped back, watching it, all the way to the telephone. As I put my hand on it, it rang.

"Hello?" The line was silent but not dead. "Hello, don't hang up, this is—"

"No," said the telephone in its flat, inhuman voice. "*You're* next."

Odd Jobs

Jason A. Tanner

T he elevator climbed silently, prowling from floor to floor unattended. On the eleventh floor the passenger compartment
was empty. Same on the twelfth. Typical of tall buildings, the
thirteenth floor was a phantom. When the doors crawled open on the
fourteenth floor a man stepped out.

A slight wobble marred his progress and he steadied himself with a
hand against the wall. He took a deep breath. The hall smelled of
pine and disinfectant as though the tile floors had just been mopped.
The dim lighting created ghostly swirling shadows. His vision hadn't
quite adjusted and the world rippled like a reflection on lake water.
It would pass soon enough.

Being inside skin again felt so strange . . .

He moved cautiously down the hall.

This flesh seemed tight, constricting, like fifty pounds of needles
stuffed in a twenty-five-pound bag.

The doors had numbers on them. A hotel then? No, by the look of
it an office building. After hours, most likely, with the low lighting
and lack of foot traffic. Things started coming back to him. His
name: Chris. His job . . .

He dug through his coat pockets, found a crumpled scrap of paper. In handwriting he didn't recognize: 1420C MELISSA CARTER.

He followed the ascending numbers. Light shone under the bottom
edge of door 1420C. He heard shuffling papers and a voice singing
quietly out of tune.

Chris turned the knob and swung the door open. Inside, sitting on
top of a large oak desk cluttered with scattered paper and Post-it
notes, sat a young woman, reading. Amid the mess, she sat Indian-
style, her shoes off, her hair pulled back in what appeared to be an
impromptu ponytail. The way she sat hiked her skirt a bit too high
and made Chris remember suddenly that he was a man this time.

She still hadn't noticed him. "Melissa Carter?"

She started—looked for a second like a child caught searching for Christmas presents. She tugged the headphones from her ears and said, "Excuse me?"

"Melissa Carter?"

"Yes." She slid off the desk, pulled her skirt down to its proper position. "I think better that way," she said, tossing a thumb over her shoulder and cracking a nervous half-smile. "We're, uh, closed. Can I help you with something?"

Chris closed the door behind him. "I'm afraid so." He pulled gloves from a coat pocket, stretched them over his hands, pressing between fingers to get them snug. "Sometimes you just don't have a choice in the matter. You ever feel that way Melissa?"

"I, I guess so." She backed away, stumbling over her shoes. She glanced toward the phone on her desk.

"You'll be dead before you hit the last digit. And don't even *think* about running. Sit down."

She sat.

Chris moved over to the window, studied the concrete and steel highrises across the street, the snow falling lightly in the intervening space. A chill pierced the window and he shivered. "Not a half bad view. This is New York, isn't it?"

"Yes." She paused, then asked quietly, "Are you going to murder me?"

"Execute, actually. But why worry about semantics." He breathed on the window and drew simple little faces in the mist. "I'm not too thrilled about it either. I should have done it by now."

"You're joking, right?"

They *always* thought that.

"No joke."

"Why me?" Her voice cracked. "I've never done anything to anybody."

"You killed an entire family. Husband, wife, two children, both girls, one only three years old. Maybe not intentionally, but they're dead all the same. Authority doesn't care much for details."

Her face went pale. "My God. How could I have done something like that and not remember? There must be some kind of mistake."

"No mistake. 1863. South Carolina. During the American Civil War. You led a group of slaves in an escape and you set a fire as a diversion. It engulfed the entire manor, killing Reginald Cutter and his family."

Melissa stood up. "But I wasn't even born until 1961!"

"In that body," Chris said.

She slumped back into her seat. "You mean, you are going to kill me for something you think I did in some sort, some sort of, past life?"

"The wheels of justice turn slowly."

Chris wrapped a length of piano wire around his gloved hands and pulled it taut until it bit at his skin.

"It's, it's crazy!" she said.

"I agree and I'm sorry. I don't make the laws. I only enforce them."

The Odor of Sanctity

William Marden

irector, come quick. All hell's breaking loose."

The tall man in the trendy Nehru jacket and bellbottoms threw himself toward the smartwall which irised open an extra six inches to allow him to follow his secretary into her office.

"Castro and Milošević," he swore colorfully, "what a day to have problems arise."

The shorter, sandy-haired man who followed him out of the irishole asked, "Why can't you put off the official resurrection ceremony, Jamal? Everybody's been waiting fifty years to see them rise, another day can't hurt."

As the director of Immortality, Inc., disappeared down a gravity chute, he called back up, "Because the entire world web is primed for this. And there's no reason why everything shouldn't have gone smoothly. All the technical bugs were worked out months ago."

Dropping down the tube behind Jamal Polverino, board of directors member Israel Cohen felt more than his stomach dropping. He had awakened this morning with a bad feeling, the sense that something was about to hit the fan. He *hated* it when his premonitions proved prescient.

The two men were whisked onto a rolling transmat and past cryonic units to the chamber where popsicles, as those frozen cryogenically in the late twentieth and early twenty-first centuries were known, would be revived for the first time ever.

Had been brought out, Cohen reminded himself hours earlier to ensure that when the first images went out on the webs there would be no unpleasant surprises.

Right now both men were looking at a very unpleasant surprise as techs and security men wrestled down to the floor a screaming naked man whose body was covered with raw red scars and burns and who foamed at the mouth.

Estrellita Muñoz, head of the technical corps, was shaking in a combination of rage, fear and frustration, her white tunic smeared with blood.

"What is going on, for God's sake, Stell?" Polverino asked. "Do you realize we're supposed to have six billion eyes observing a healthy pop . . . freezee wake up smiling in a little under an hour?"

"I'd go male again—and God knows I hated packing balls—if I could tell you," Muñoz said, watching security men inject the screaming man with enough tranquilizers to sedate a raging bull elephant. He finally collapsed in midscream.

"Everything went fine during resuscitation," she said. "Brain wave scans showed normal awakening. Then—there was something, we haven't pinned it down yet—a flicker on brain scan, and he turned into this raving animal you see."

Staring at the mass of bloody bruises and burns that mottled the unconscious man's body, Cohen asked, "How did he wind up like that? He looks like he's been tortured for six months."

"I know we didn't inflict them," Muñoz said. "I watched them as they just—appeared. My best guess is that they're psychosomatic. There are cases on record, though they're rare. If the body is under enough stress, it can produce such lesions."

"But what kind of stress?" Polverino said. "The poor bastard has been unconscious, dreaming at worst, for the past sixty-one years."

Another tech ran up to Muñoz and whispered to her. She looked at him incredulously, then said, "Come on. We've got something weird in the second resusci-chamber."

The trio were stopped in their tracks as they entered the second chamber, observing a young girl who had been frozen at the age of nineteen with a then-incurable brain tumor. She lay on the resuscitable clad only in a white sheet.

It wasn't the sight that stopped them in their tracks, but the scent that filled their nostrils and their bodies, their beings. For an instant, time ceased and pain and worry left their bodies and they couldn't help smiling at each other.

There was no way to put that feeling into words, but Cohen remembered days at the synagogue in his youth and recognized the odor of sanctity that the rabbis had spoken of. Recognized it, and knew in that instant where this young girl and the man terrified out of his mind had been before being recalled to their physical bodies.

And was not surprised to hear the wail of loss that rang out from the young girl as she opened her eyes, the cry of a heart that has lost something infinitely sweet, the cry of a soul cast out of paradise.

On Spending the Night Alone in a Haunted House
A User's Guide
Bruce Boston

1. Avoid eating solid food for six hours before entering. Drink water in sufficient quantities to prevent dehydration. Do *not* drink wine or other spirits, particularly brandy.

2. Wear no jewelry or metal of any kind. Most of all, no gold. Be forewarned that even the fillings in your teeth can serve as foci for etheric discharges.

3. Cut your hair as short as possible. Wear a thick woolen cap or a wig that can be pulled from the head if grabbed from behind. Choose clothing that fits snugly but does not impede your movement. Leave no openings. Pockets should be zippered (plastic) or buttoned.

4. You may take reading material to pass the time, but avoid works of fiction unless they are of a morally uplifting tone. For illumination, use candles made from beeswax.

5. Carry no weapons, since they would be useless and only serve to irritate whatever presences appear.

6. Enter the house at the instant of sunset, as the last rays of failing light touch the doorstep, front or back. Choose a down-

stairs room with as little furniture as possible. If you explore other rooms, move loudly, cough, and shuffle your feet. Make your presence known at all times.

7. If you must sleep, do so sitting up, in the downstairs room you have chosen. Do not remove your clothing or shoes.

8. When strange noises—whispers, mumblings, moans, the rattling of chains—begin to sound, act as if nothing untoward is happening. Do not attempt to transcribe the goings on with cameras or tape recorders. If you must make some record of the proceedings, use a small notebook that can be concealed on your person and a crayon made from beeswax.

9. When the walls begin to undulate, when the ceiling seems as if it is lowering upon you, do not panic. These are illusions and cannot harm you.

10. When the apparitions begin to appear, do not attempt to converse, touch, or hinder the movements of ghostly figures in any way. Do not call out or look at them directly. If they come toward you, move out of the way. If they call your name, do not answer. Particularly avoid responding to dead relatives, dead friends, dead pets, and headless horsemen.

11. If slavering beasts surround you; if growls, screams, and cries for help rise to an infernal din; if all the creatures from the pits of hell arise . . . sprouting scabs and running sores and grotesques pustules, eyes dangling from their sockets, brains spilling down their cheeks, strips of raw flesh trailing from their arms and naked torsos; . . . if all of this reaches a feverish pitch, clasp your hands over your head and pray aloud to the Lord who made you.

12. No matter what you experience, do not attempt to leave before the first rays of the rising sun touch the front or back steps. Flight can be fatal. Most often a heart attack is the cause, but in certain documented cases, individuals have been torn limb from limb.

13. When you survive the night intact only to discover that you are paralyzed with fright, your throat so raw that all you can manage is a croaking whisper, your mind overflowing with the horrors that have transpired, then you must wait until they come to get you.

14. When they carry you out, when they slip a straitjacket over your suddenly writhing form, when they force you down upon a metal table and plunge a needle of sleep into your veins and incarcerate you in a padded cell, never admit for a second that you are now as mad as the midnight sun. Don't give them the satisfaction.

15. Yes, these images will lodge forever in the chambers of your mind. Their screams will echo and resound for you without respite. They will fill your waking and sleeping consciousness with horripilating visions from beyond the veil, with cold chills and sizzling flanges of pain that will set you trembling at any hour of the day or night.

16. But you can do it! I know you can! All you have to do is follow my instructions to the last bloody letter. You can be the first on your block to spend the night alone in a haunted house!

On the Panecraft Train

Tom Piccirilli

High-pitched laughter and pleas for aluminum foil spin through the night from within the walls of Panecraft psychiatric hospital. Topaz somehow got out again this afternoon, and now I'm hip-deep in the thickets behind the asylum as I hunt for my dog in the dusk. He's got a nose for this area that keeps him whining all night, haunted, something bringing him back here all the time. My brother once told me that after the war, behind the hundreds of rows of cube windows above, the faces of the mad would press against the bars like bearded skulls, staring out over the town and peering into our bedrooms.

Topaz enjoys running in the fields surrounding Panecraft, where illegally dumped garbage, dead leaves, husks of stripped cars, and frost cover the forgotten potter's field and the abandoned train station. Tracks run up to the razor-wire–topped fence as if seeking access, ending sharply. The state used to route the shell-shocked, homeless, retarded, and eccentric immigrants right in off the boats and from the bowels of Manhattan.

Holding my breath, I squeeze through a thatch of willow and diseased oak branches, leaving scratches against my shoulders that well blood. It's getting cold as night approaches, a half-moon nailed to the dwindling blue of the sky. In the clearing beyond I can make out the crumbled remains of poorly constructed markers and crumbling tombstones: there are no names or dates, only fractured numbers assigned the dead. Here are the aborted, the miscarried, the ill-advised. Papers whirl in the wind, catching on roots and broken brick. I've a nearly overwhelming urge to start cleaning the place, to give these remaining damned a fraction of respect, but first I've got to find my dog.

A series of poorly prepared wooden crosses dip and sway in the breeze, clacking loudly together. My God. A man in their midst, dressed in torn and soiled patient garb, is feeding Topaz from a plastic container, the kind that tranquilizers are given in. I shout, "Topaz, no!" and rush forward in a clumsy arc, unsure of what to do now, pinwheeling across the graves, but the stupid dog loves eating too much, accepting anything from anyone, and never listens to me.

Thick eyebrows arched in a demonic glare, the edges of his hideous smile nearly reaching the corner of his eyes, he shows me his yellow teeth. Long, shaggy hair swirls about like striking asps. His voice is gentler than expected. "This isn't a dog," the man says, "you fool, it's a rat."

"Okay," I say. "Just stay calm."

"Not 'okay,' you patronizing nut. It's a rat."

Topaz comes to me squeaking, nose twitching as I bend and hold out my hand and he scurries into my palm. I put him in my jacket pocket and shrug. "So I've been wrong. He's a rat."

I scan the crosses and notice my own handwriting, the block letters spelling out the names of my parents, uncles, cousins. My brother and I recognize each other in the same instant, and his smile, if possible, grows even wider. I reach up and feel my face, and realize my own grin is as hideous as his.

"Uhm . . ." I say.

"Come on."

We walk the train tracks leading toward the asylum; we try for balance, and separately stumble along, until each of us holds out a hand to help the other stand upright on his track; it's been a while, but I feel like I'm coming back into my own. Topaz nibbles at my side and I bark laughter. Beams of flashlights abound around us in the fields. In the distance we hear police sirens, frenzied shrieks of patients, more calls for aluminum foil, and the beginnings of another neighborhood crusade that will again try to close down the hospital. Laughing like children we scamper once more onto this train that will take us back home to the safety of our insanity, riding into the soothing warmth of the loving, open arms of Panecraft.

One for the Road
Judith Post

Cold drizzle. Slick pavement. Dense gloom. The neon sign over SAMMY'S shone like a lonely beacon in a sea of black asphalt. My steering wheel turned as we reached our destination.

The bar sat at the edge of town. A cluster of thrown-together, pre-fab houses huddled across the highway—unglamorous shelters for people enduring unglamorous lives.

My Camaro's door opened—its signal for me to get out. It was the damn anniversary—the seventeenth. Eight years down, an eternity to go.

Only a few patrons were sprinkled here and there when I drifted inside. I took a seat at the back, tucked into a shadow where the overhead light didn't reach.

The place had a shabby hominess about it—the kind of bar I used to love—the wooden tables nicked and scarred, water stains forming pale circles across their tops. A pool table nestled in the corner, and a jukebox hugged the far wall. A haze of smoke blanketed the air.

For half an hour, there were no other customers. I was beginning to think my old Camaro had made a mistake, when a husband and wife hurried through the door. Wind and rain whipped behind them.

They shook the water off their coats, then took the booth next to mine.

"Awfully cold in this corner, isn't it?" the wife asked her husband. They headed to a table near the center of the room.

Putting out her cigarette, the waitress slid off her barstool to greet them. "What brings you out on a night like this?"

"It's our twenty-third anniversary." The wife's face was lined with creases. She'd waved her shoulder-length hair and dressed in her best jeans.

The husband grinned. "Almost a quarter of a century." He patted his wife's work-roughened hand.

They ordered the day's special—open-faced sandwiches with gravy and mashed potatoes—and two beers.

A wave of nostalgia swept over me. My parents would be about those people's ages now. They'd always been pinching their pennies, too. Working to provide a good home for my brother and me. I'd heard they hadn't gotten over it yet, but I hoped what everyone said was true, that time heals a broken heart. I hated to think of them as suffering, but I'd been too selfish to care about it at the time.

A few long-haired kids came in next, sat at the table by the juke-box and began pumping quarters into it. Not one of them, I begged. They were all so young. It didn't take long to spot the main candidate though. He had the right look. They all get it after a while. He hadn't touched a speck of food and was best friends with the waitress before his words began to slur. A beer later, he was telling his life story to anyone who'd listen.

The waitress tried to switch him to coffee. His eyes were two red holes of need—a look I remembered from my mirror.

When the bartender refused to serve him, he wobbled to his feet, staggering from the building. It took him a while to find his car, but once he did, he heaved himself behind the wheel and started the engine.

Damn you to hell! I seethed, then immediately regretted it. It just might happen.

The Camaro's engine purred to life. It had been a Friday like this—bleak and wet—when I'd had my accident, when I'd swerved across the median and crashed into another car. The man I'd hit had a family, two kids and a wife. A wife who loved him, who hated me for taking him from her. Hated me enough to curse my name, to spit on my closed coffin, to wail that no other wife should suffer her fate . . .

As the guy wove back and forth on the slippery pavement, the Camaro closed in behind him. When the road curved, it rammed into him and didn't let go. A celestial bumper leaves no dents, but a tree and a ditch do mortal damage. As his car rolled and burst into flames, the Camaro idled, forced me to watch. One more drunk gone to his Maker. A chance I didn't get . . .

When the flames died down, the Camaro turned toward the east, and my mind drifted. Another month, another anniversary. But until then, I slept. The sleep of the dead but not yet departed.

One Romantic Evening . . .

Greg McElhatton

S o, you're a vampire," Kate said, sipping her Diet Coke.

The gaunt man across the table from her nodded slowly. "That is correct." His Diet Coke sat in front of him, untouched. "I have been a vampire for fifteen decades."

"Wow," Kate said. "That's a long time." She started to count on her fingers. "1896, 1796, 1696, 1596 . . ."

"Decades, child, decades," the man snapped. "Those are centuries."

"Oh," Kate pouted. "I always get those two backwards. 1986, 1976 . . ."

"I came into this existence," he snapped, "on December eleventh, 1843."

"It's rude to interrupt," Kate said, frowning. "I don't like people who interrupt me."

"Ah," he smiled. "But I am not a person. I am a vampire."

"Right, right," she nodded. She looked around. "That waiter is horrible. I'm getting hungry." She opened her purse and pulled out a compact mirror and a tube of lipstick. "So, tell me more," she added before tracing her lips carefully.

"I was born Count Fyodor Rasputin," he said. "My friends called me Fyodor, my enemies things far fouler."

"I dunno," Kate said, snapping the compact shut and setting it back into her purse. "Fyodor's not such a great name either. Have you thought about changing it? Maybe Fred. That way, your friends could call you Freddy or something."

Fyodor cleared his throat. "It was snowing, and I dwelt unhappily in my family estate. Alone in hundreds of acres with nothing to do . . ."

Kate snorted. "Nothing to do with hundreds of acres? Oh, please. You could go sledding. Or if there aren't any hills, cross-country skiing." She peered at Fyodor carefully. "I thought you said in your personal ad that you liked to do things that sent the blood racing. No offense, but you've been pretty boring so far."

Fyodor half-rose from his chair, but then slowly sat back down. "As I was saying, I was alone and lonely. Then, a dark stranger came to me, seducing me with words of darkness and bloodlust. I agreed to his wishes, and that night . . ."

"Excuse me," Kate said, "but if you're going to sit here talking about your gay lovers, I'm leaving. I'm not into kinky stuff, and I think I know where this is leading."

Fyodor gripped his napkin tightly. "Perhaps I should tell a different part of my story," he said finally. "I arrived in your United States in the year 1929. Work was scarce with your Great Depression, and there were many people on the streets who would not be missed if they . . . vanished."

Kate looked around the restaurant helplessly, trying to signal for a waiter to come to their table.

"And so," Fyodor said, "I gained my sustenance. Hot, glorious blood. The bubbling liquid filling my mouth, rushing through my body . . ." Fyodor was shredding his napkin as he spoke, his eyes fixed on Kate. "The hunger . . . it was so great . . . the need . . ."

Kate tilted her head back and yawned. The expanse of neck was too much. The next thing Kate knew, Fyodor was on top of the table, hands reaching for her neck.

"Get off me, you pig!" Kate gasped, swinging her purse at Fyodor's head.

Fyodor shrugged off the blow. "Your sweet blood," he snarled, Diet Coke all over the table. "I must have it! I must!" His mouth opened wide, and his lips touched her neck . . .

. . . and began to sizzle and burn. "Gaahhh!" Fyodor cried, recoiling as his lips burst into flame.

"Creep!" Kate cried. "Get away!" She grabbed a small container out of her purse angrily. "Eat mace, jerk!" She pointed the aerosol container and squirted away.

Fyodor, in a shriek of pain and terror, exploded in a ball of flame.

As waiters ran over with fire extinguishers, Kate looked at the container in her hand. "Oops," she murmured. "I could have sworn that was mace, not perfume. Oh well!" As Fyodor's body disintegrated into ashes, she vowed never to answer a personal ad again, and put her new bottle of True Faith back into her purse.

One Way

Hugh B. Cave

Say this for Arthur A. Arnheim: He was about the most handsome feller ever set foot in our mountain town. Which is saying a good deal, because some of our young lumberjacks are no slouches in the Department of Manly Good Looks.

Say this also for Arthur A.: He was the most obnoxious, conceited, arrogant man who ever came to "solve" our mystery. But he had the money to pay what Joe Hinson and I asked for guiding him, so at six o'clock one nippy Sunday morning the three of us set out for Morgan Peak.

"Now then," says Arnheim, "suppose while we hike up there you fellows fill me in on this 'point of no return' I've been hearing about. Just exactly what is it?"

"I guess you could call it a doorway of sorts," I said. My name is Cliff Case, and it was my cousin Charlie Bickford who first disappeared.

"A doorway to what?"

"That's what we don't know."

"The stories I've heard," says he, "focus on a cave near the top of a mountain. Are you saying the doorway is in this cave?"

"Yes, sir," says Joe.

"And that's where you're taking me now? To the cave?"

"That's where we're taking you," says I, mentally adding, "you and your camera, so's you can take pictures that'll most likely wind up in that supermarket tabloid you work for."

He asked a heap more questions and then we got to the cave.

"Would one of you take a photo of me standing here at the entrance?" Arnheim says then, fiddling with his camera.

I said I would, and he handed me the camera and went to pose, standing so you could see who he was even though he seemed to be peering into the mouth of our mystery cave. He had a kind of sneer on his face, and after I snapped the picture he said, "You understand, I hope, that I don't believe a word of this crazy story. I may be here to give it national exposure, but if you think I'm just another sucker to be taken in by it, you're out of your minds."

Joe and I looked at each other, said nothing, took flashlights out of our backpacks, and went on in.

Now I'm no expert on caves but, believe me, that one near the top of our mountain is spooky. The first passage is all twists and turns, with a ceiling so low in places you have to go down on your hands and knees. Then comes a big, high-ceilinged chamber some two hundred feet across, and in the far wall of that are three more openings. We walked Arthur A. Arnheim to the middle one.

"Here it is," says I. "This is where my cousin Charlie and those other two disappeared."

"What's in there?" Arnheim asks, fiddling with his camera again. "You've investigated, of course."

"Investigated?"

"Well, you went in there to look for them, didn't you?"

"We done that," says Joe. "Fifty yards in, the tunnel ends in a rock wall."

"You mean the three men who went in there just vanished?"

"They just vanished."

"I'll bet," says Arnheim in a voice that dripped sarcasm.

"Well," says I, "some of us have been in far enough for our light-beams to hit the wall, and that's all there is—the wall. No pit to fall into. No bodies. A professor at the college thinks there could be some sort of time change in there, like a doorway to the past or future. Anyway, here we are. You do what you like."

He thought about it awhile, then said he guessed he had enough for his story without going in there. Then he said, "Oh hell, why should I be another sucker?" and did go in.

Joe and I waited four hours for him to come out, but he didn't. We yelled ourselves hoarse, and got no answer. Finally we went in with our lights, just far enough to make sure he hadn't tripped on something and knocked himself out.

The tunnel was empty, so we went home.

"If we ever do this again," Joe said to me on the way down, "we better ask for our pay in advance, don't you think? I hate to work this hard for nothin'."

Only Death, Sir

Peter Atkins

When the King of all the lands that were fair asked for berries, berries were brought. When his thirst sought sweet water, sweet water was found. So when he asked for wisdom, it was not long before his courtiers brought to him a man of whom no question had been asked for which he had not found an answer.

And the King made the man his servant and bade him walk with him all his days so that wisdom was ever at hand.

And the Servant showed him all the pleasures of the world and how to partake wisely thereof.

And many years passed and the King, grown old with wandering, spoke again to his Servant.

"And after this, what then? After flesh and fruit and song—what more remains?"

And the Servant made him an answer and the answer was not kind.

And the King, who by now was not himself unwise, accepted the answer but, seeking consolation, went to his window and looked out at his people below.

"That sweet girl who runs eagerly, summer on her cheek, to find a faithful lover—who will receive her embrace?"

And the Servant made him an answer and the answer was the same.

"And that young man whose heart seeks glory, be he poet or soldier—what will he find?"

And the Servant made him an answer and the answer was the same.

"And those trees, those flowers—to what end do they blossom? Those birds—to what end do they sing?"

And the Servant made him an answer and the answer was the same.

And the King looked at his servant and saw him for the first time and his heart was heavy in his chest and all his joys were ash. And he gave to his servant one more question.

"And who are you, o most faithful servant, who has shown me all these wonders, who has walked always beside me, thy footsteps planted next to mine down all my days e'en like those of my own shadow?"

The Servant smiled. And he made him an answer and the answer was the same.

Parasite
Greg McElhatton

The first time Marissa felt the parasite was in November.

It was a crowded Thanksgiving, and Marissa remembered eating several platefuls of white meat, candied yams, and corn bread. She'd drunk at least two glasses of wine, and felt a slight buzz forming.

She'd made it over to one of the armchairs and wrestled it away from a giggling niece who'd rather play with the dogs anyway. Sinking into the cushions, she felt herself relaxing as the chaos sank over her. Relatives were talking, children running through the house. She'd almost dozed off when it was there.

It felt almost as if something were moving inside her stomach—but it wasn't her stomach. She pressed her hand to it, wondering if she had indigestion. Then it started to move again, tentatively extending into her stomach, pushing inward. And then, she could feel the food start to drain out . . . Marissa's cousin found her throwing up into the toilet twenty minutes later, shuddering and gasping.

By December, Marissa had almost forgotten about Thanksgiving. It was the busiest time of the year for retail, and Marissa needed to focus on staying one step ahead of the customers. Getting sale items in, moving out markdowns, setting up displays, and starting all over again . . . It was utter exhaustion that made Marissa decide to sit in the store after it closed one night, to try and catch her breath.

When Marissa sleepily opened her eyes and pushed the hair out of her face, she realized that she'd dozed off. Still, she told herself, she needed the sleep. She was almost standing when she felt it. A probing sensation in the back of her head, where it met her neck. She tentatively reached back, expecting some disgusting bug, but felt nothing. And still the probing continued.

She could feel its long tendrils pushing upward, sinking deep into tissue and worming its way through. She stood up and shook her head, but it was getting worse. The room swam in front of her eyes, and she staggered forward. "Oh God," she gasped. "Oh God." Grasping the counter, she fumbled for the phone, while the tendrils pushed their way into her skull, spreading and branching until she couldn't stop from screaming and screaming.

Marissa's terrified roommate banged on the door of the store for almost ten minutes before Marissa pulled her head off the counter. She looked around in a daze, not understanding. The phone was off the hook, beeping incessantly at her. Marissa slowly stumbled forward to let her roommate in. The probing was gone, and Marissa found herself feeling more and more foolish by the minute. "A nightmare," she babbled. "A horrible nightmare."

By January, Marissa was laughing about her vivid nightmare. Thanksgiving was wiped out of her memory entirely. She'd even lost some weight and felt wonderful. And so she was in a dressing room, looking at herself. Yes, she told herself. She was definitely slimmer. She didn't have the energy she used to, but Christmas always did that to her. She pulled the sweater on and stared at it for several minutes from different angles before deciding that it didn't look as good once it was on.

As she tugged on the sweater, she felt it catch. Frowning, she pulled harder, and it tore free of the black needle sticking out of her stomach. Marissa's eyes grew wide, and she began to gasp uncontrollably. And then it began to extend, waving tentatively around and moving further into the air. Marissa tried to scream, but her throat refused to obey. Her hands flew to her face in terror—and long, thin, black needles began to tear out of her arms. Marissa managed to gurgle a single cry, staggering toward the door. First one step, then two . . . but when the needle legs tore through her legs and protruded from under her skirt, it was simply too much.

The doctor smiled at Marissa's roommate. "She'll be just fine," he told her. "She's just undergoing some changes from her pregnancy. It's several months along now—are you sure she didn't know?" He frowned as if to say otherwise.

Marissa's roommate shook her head. "She never told me." She looked at Marissa's smooth complexion, her chest rising up and down. "Some people get all the luck." A minute later, a look of curiosity came over her face.

"I wonder what it'll be?"

The Park

Phyllis Eisenstein

Don't cut through the park at night, her mother had said, so of course here she was, in the park, on a night so overcast that even the full autumn moon was just a faint pale patch overhead. Everyone who lived west of the Youth Center cut through the park to get home after a game; going around added fifteen minutes and almost an extra mile to the trip.

Too many trees in the park, her mother had said. *Too many places for muggers to hide*. Sandy had laughed at that, calling her mother a worrywart. But always before, she had crossed the park in a group, a dozen at least. No one would bother twelve tall, well-muscled basketball players, even if they were all female.

But tonight she had stayed late to help clean up the gym, a chore few players or spectators cared for, and everyone but the coach was gone by the time she was done. He had offered to drive her home, but she'd just waved and said she'd be fine.

She didn't feel so fine now, nearly halfway along the concrete walk that bisected the park in a series of lazy curves. There were eight streetlights along the walk, old-fashioned ones like slender chess pieces, each lamp topped by a queen's crown. She had counted four of them so far, and though she knew they were equally spaced, the stretches between seemed to be getting longer and longer. And the deeper she got into the park, the more trees there seemed to be, their trunks like the huge thick legs of massed prehistoric animals, their leafless branches tangling together overhead and waving in the cool night breeze, waving at the near-invisible moon like maniacs' arms. Sandy shivered, though her coat was heavy enough.

She felt like someone was following her.

She couldn't see anyone when she looked over her shoulder. She couldn't hear anyone. Still, there was a feeling in her spine, a prickling at the back of her neck, as if some subliminal cue were nibbling at her mind.

She walked faster.

In the dimness between streetlights, a branch swiped her face. The shock of it made her stumble, but she caught herself before she fell. She clapped a hand to her stinging cheek and felt something wet. Dampness from the branch, she thought, and then she peered at her fingers and saw something dark. Blood? She felt her cheek again, and the pain was too sharp for a surface scratch. She pressed at it with the sleeve of her jacket. Why did the park authority let the branches hang so low over the walk? She could see the stain on her sleeve. *God, I might need stitches.*

Leaves rustled behind her, and she looked back sharply. The path was empty. But anyone could be hiding among the tree trunks, where the leaves were thick underfoot.

She turned toward home and began to trot.

The next streetlight was up ahead, finally. Number five. Three more and then the end of the park. She was tired from the game, and her legs ached, and the steady drip of blood down her cheek stung and tickled at the same time. She reached the light, touching it with the tips of her fingers as she passed, and kept going.

The rustling was still behind her, but now it seemed to come from both her left and her right, as if two runners were pacing her, each half a dozen steps back. But when she glanced back, she couldn't see anything. Was it an animal? Two animals? She ran faster, her mouth wide open, sucking air. Light number six seemed a mile away, down the empty concrete walkway. *Impossible*, she thought, *just my imagination*, and she looked back again, just a quick glance, toward the rustling. Nothing.

And then she slammed into a bough set like a roadblock across the path, a bough nearly as thick as any prehistoric behemoth's leg, and she would have somersaulted over it except that another bough smashed into her back, pinning her against the first. Then another bough swiped at her face, and there was much more blood this time, much more, though Sandy didn't care anymore.

The rustling leaves caught up with her then, and swirled and skittered about her like excited dogs, while the trees of the park crowded close and divided her up among themselves until there was nothing but blood left, and the leaves took care of that.

Parlor Games

Lawrence Schimel

Peter Hearne operated the only licensed funeral parlor in all of Baltimore proper. Sure there were black-market outfits that offered similar services, but who could really be sure that the bodies stayed dead once they disappeared into those warrens? Bodies sent to those places could be found working fields in the farm belt.

Staying dead was a luxury only the very rich could afford. But anyone who could afford it invariably paid for such services. Peter Hearne's place was costly, but he guaranteed results. And he'd always come through on his word. Until yesterday.

They'd been professional, even to the point of relocking the crypt after they'd taken the body. But that night, the electronic surveillance checks had registered the crypt as empty. It had to have been Roger Blackwood, Peter thought. Only he could have afforded someone that good. And only he would have the desire to do so, as the major black-market competitor to his parlor.

If word leaked out that he'd lost a body, the surviving kin of all his customers would pull their dearly beloved from his crypts, wiping him clean. He'd go bankrupt paying back all the fees, probably lose his license as well. And, of course, Roger would be there to pick up all his customers as they went looking for somewhere else to store their dead.

Unless Peter got that body back.

He would do it, of course. After all, he guaranteed results. But Roger had struck too low this time.

Watch out, Roger, he thought, we're playing no holds barred now.

Word did leak out; how could it not? Sergeant Lovell showed up two days later for the investigation. Peter calmly led him down the passageway to the crypts, letting him check anything that took his fancy and maintaining a running narrative as he answered the sergeant's questions in great depth.

"I wasn't aware that you used reanimates in your establishment," the sergeant said when they reached the door to the crypts. "I thought they went against everything you stood for."

Peter put his arm around the reanimate in question. "To answer your unasked question: No, this isn't the body that was supposedly stolen. That one had been female. I keep Roger for customers as an example of what they're preventing by storing their dead here. I know it must seem ironic. But it works. And he makes a good watchdog."

"I see," the sergeant said, looking closely at Roger as they walked past him into the crypts. The investigation found the rumors false and Peter found himself receiving an influx of customers now that one of his black-market competitors had mysteriously dropped off the scene. Peter guaranteed results, and he always came through on his word.

Patient Fate

Tom Piccirilli

She's been on that corner lot near the underpass, standing in the shadows of the abandoned prison, since I can remember. The fences have been torn down by teenagers ripping across the empty prison grounds in trucks, weeds layered in brick and barbed wire, median littered with busted bottles, illegally dumped sacks of garbage, smashed box springs. Still, she strikes the familiar pose on the side of the road—curly black hair splayed over the shoulder, hands low at her sides but not quite on the hips. Ugly ropes of silver necklaces and peace sign pendants clink lightly as she moves forward a step, wearing a frayed black halter top, torn jean vest and skirt, and boots that have come, gone, and come back again into style. A huge leather bag dangles from her shoulder. She spots me with the same borderline grimace as all the times before.

Billy used to tell me I was imagining things as I paged through comic books in the backseat of the Mustang, even when I pointed and questioned over the heady volume of The Who, and spotted the fear rolling into his eyes like storms coming off the bay. His adolescent manhood pressed him to drive this lost strip of highway even when taking me to the movies in Evansville, heading in the opposite direction.

There are fates that cannot wait and those more patient. I slowly roll to a stop beside her and unlock the passenger door; she scans my face, the Mustang, the prison in the distance. "Can you give me a ride?" she asks.

"That's why I'm here."

She hops in, a hint of a smile tugging her narrow lips apart, showing off the red, ruddy spaces in her mouth, the mauled tongue. "Not going too far." Her bag has most everything I expect, as she opens it and lays aside the contents: my Springsteen cassettes, the Mustang's gas cap and side mirror, a burned floor mat. Tokens, I think; me-

453

mentos, clues, or simply facts of life. She stares at me as if curious to know just how high a ransom I'll pay for them.

"It wasn't me," I say.

"It was you, all right; don't bother denying it." Resolve enters her voice, thickening it. "I remember you, and this car."

"It wasn't me, or my brother Billy, either. You've been here much longer than that. You've got to stop."

She slumps back in the seat and kicks her heels up onto the dash. Even in the boots I can see her feet are horribly twisted. Thin trails of blood slowly leak the length of her legs. "Where is he?"

"In a nursing home."

"He'll come again," she says, the sliced black tongue unfurling. "One of these days."

I really don't doubt it; after moving up to a Buick Regal, he'd passed the Mustang on to me, with a rabbit's foot keychain and a free month's insurance, but not nearly enough warning. I could just see Billy, a low-functioning paraplegic for a decade since wiping out against the underpass, stealing one of the handicapped vans and heading out here for one last shot at some notion of redemption. To save me, or her, or simply himself.

I reach over and part her hair, and see the hideous gaping wounds hidden beneath those curls, splintered skull and wet viscera extending from her neck.

"You've got to start listening to me. I did research years ago, checked the papers and the police. You were hit by a guy named Leonard Franks, driving a '66 Chevy. He's dead; you got him in '78. You can forget it."

"It was you," she says, unable to meet my eyes. "I remember."

"Listen to me . . ."

"Let me out."

I pull back into the vacant lot and she repacks the bag and jumps out, drifting once more into that exact same pose. I check and realize my own wounds have opened, the thrust of shattered clavicle protruding from beneath my t-shirt, crushed ribs poking through. In the rearview I see a long line of other cars behind me, even a '66 Chevy back there, patiently awaiting their fate: to stop, argue, perhaps even beg, but always to roll on again.

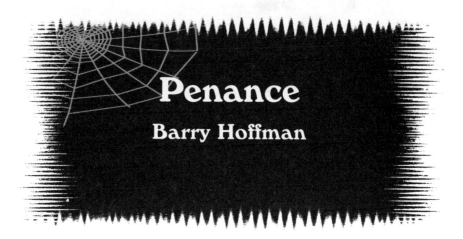

Penance

Barry Hoffman

She looked at the old nurse—familiar, yet changed beyond recognition—seated in the hospital nursery, her lips moving imperceptibly as she sought to soothe the frantic wailing of the newborn nestled in her arms.

The crack baby, abandoned by its mother, attempted to push itself away from the thin wisp of a woman. Its arms flailed up and down like a penguin's wings, and she could see the woman next to her feared the nurse might drop the infant.

The young nurse could almost read the woman's thoughts as she gazed at the child. *Her child,* if the woman desired. A child she could adopt if she had the fortitude and patience to deal with the multitude of problems she would encounter from a baby who'd spent seven and a half months floating in a womb-sea of self-inflicted chemical poison.

"Is the baby safe in there?" the woman asked the young nurse, who stood by her side.

The nurse looked at her quizzically.

"I mean she's so *old*. Mightn't she drop my . . . I mean, the baby? . . ."

Her voice trailed off as they both witnessed the transformation taking place within the nursery.

The nurse inside had wrapped her gnarled, arthritic fingers around the infant's body and cradled it to her bosom. Within seconds, the child's seizures had abated, then its crying ceased and it lay contentedly in the old woman's arms. The nurse's face seemed etched with excruciating pain. She closed her eyes, breathed deeply, then sighed. Soon both appeared asleep.

"Shana's only twenty-four," the nurse standing next to the woman said, breaking the silence.

"That's impossible. She looks eighty if she's a day."

"She's absorbed so much pain, it's taken its toll. That child—*your* child, if you wish—won't go through the agony of withdrawal. Shana will. Penance."

"I don't understand," the woman said. "Her hair is not only white, but its lost the luster of youth. And her face—wrinkles upon wrinkles. And just look at her fingers, like branches of a tree, so twisted and deformed. She looks so fragile, a good gust of wind could bowl her over."

"Yes," the nurse said, shaking her head in agreement. "But though I'm new here, I'm told two years ago she looked as young and vibrant as you or I."

The woman looked at her incredulously.

"She came to us from a sanitarium for the criminally insane. She'd smothered her three-month-old son, a child she'd had as a teen. Five years later, she was considered cured—for want of a better word—trained as a nurse, and came here to atone for what she'd done. The child she holds is just one of hundreds on the brink of death she has given herself to—literally. She drinks in their pain, torment, and physical afflictions so they can be at peace and start anew. As you see, it's taken its toll on her. The crack cocaine, coursing through the blood of that baby, now resides in her. She will go through withdrawal, as she has dozens of times before."

"Penance, you say?" the woman asked.

"She can never undo what she did to her child, no matter how many others she saves. Her work here is almost done, though. She's not strong enough to take much more."

She looked at the young woman sternly. "If you adopt this child, I only hope you are willing to sacrifice yourself as Shana has."

The woman smiled weakly. "I can. I *will*. I wasn't sure I wanted the responsibility of a crack baby. Now I am."

She made her way down the hall to where her husband was filling out a maze of bureaucratic forms.

The young nurse went into the nursery and gently took the sleeping baby from Shana's arms, placed it in a crib, then gently roused the old woman.

"Your work is done, Shana," the nurse said. "You may die in peace. I've been sent to take your place."

Shana merely nodded, then closed her eyes.

The young nurse picked up another baby, whose shrieking chilled her to the bone, wailing so much like her one-year-old, the daughter she'd killed in a fit of rage and despair.

She held the child close: a crack baby, like the other. Soon the infant relaxed in her arms. She was wracked with pain, the drug snaking its way through her body and soul. She withstood it willingly.

It hurt so much.

It felt so good.

Her penance had begun.

The Perfect Baby

Linda J. Dunn

Jenny smiled at the woman sitting across from her at the airport. "Your first trip?"

She shook her head. "Just the first time for Amy." The woman nodded toward the stroller parked in front of her.

"She's certainly a good baby," Jennifer said. "I haven't heard her cry once the whole time we've been here."

The woman nodded. "She's always been a good baby. Amy doesn't even wake up at night."

Jennifer smiled politely, feeling her fingers itch in anticipation. She'd never even thought about stealing a baby from an airport before. Security was too tight.

But this was too good to pass up. Scott paid top dollar for healthy white babies.

Jenny turned around, noting the destination and time of the next departure. "I'm Jennifer Dubois and I'm going to Orlando to see my parents. Will we be on the same plane?"

The woman nodded, her eyes widening. "I'm Nancy Whitman. I'm flying out to surprise Nick. He's the baby's father and he left for Orlando as soon as he learned I was pregnant. I'm sure he'll change his mind about everything as soon as he sees Amy." Nancy leaned backward slightly and smiled down at her baby.

"My parents don't think it's a good idea. What do you think?"

"Sometimes guys panic," Jenny said. "Does she look like her daddy? Men love it when they see themselves in their kids."

Nancy nodded. "She's got his red hair. He can't deny Amy. Not with hair like that."

Yes! Jenny kept her face blank, trying to present the image of a matronly woman who would never present even the slightest danger to a baby. A healthy Caucasian baby was worth the price of a new Ferrari.

"I'm glad you're here to wait with me," Jenny said. "It seems sort of spooky this late at night with so few people around."

Nancy nodded and looked around. "The place is kind of deserted."

Jenny bit back a smile. *Yes. It is.*

"May I hold Amy?"

Nancy hesitated. "I don't know. You seem okay but—"

Jenny smiled. "I understand perfectly. You can never be too careful nowadays."

Nancy hesitated a moment. "I do need to go to the bathroom though. I hate taking Amy inside. They're so dirty and it's hard to hold her while I—you know."

Jenny nodded, feeling her face growing hot in anticipation. *I've got her. Just a little more.*

"Would you feel better if I gave you something of mine?"

Nancy sighed deeply. "That would make me feel so much safer."

Jenny pulled off her diamond ring and handed it to Nancy. *With what Scott will pay me, I can get a dozen of these.*

Nancy stared at it, admiring its beauty beneath the lights. "It's gorgeous. Is it real?"

Jenny laughed. "Absolutely."

Nancy hesitated a moment. "Do you mind if I wear it while I'm—"

"Just don't lose it down the drain."

"Thanks." Nancy tugged the comforter tight and pushed the stroller beside Jenny. It took every strength of will to sit quietly and not grab the baby and run. As soon as Nancy entered the restroom, Jenny picked up her carry-on luggage and pushed the stroller toward the nearest door.

Jenny hailed a taxi immediately and gave him the name of a local hotel. She'd call Scott from the lobby and make arrangements to drop off the baby with one of his contacts.

Jenny glanced at the pile of blankets in the baby seat and an ugly thought crossed her mind. *I never saw the baby. How do I know she didn't stick me with a blanket-stuffed stroller in exchange for my diamond ring?*

Fingers trembling, Jenny reached out and pulled the blanket away.

There was a baby there. Or something that was a baby at one time.

Jenny stared for a few moments, remembering Nancy's remarks. Amy was a good baby. Amy never woke up during the night.

Jenny swallowed hard, staring at the shriveled skin and the empty eyesockets before covering the remains and tapping the cab driver on the shoulder.

"Can you stop at a drug store, please? I need some more diapers."

"The meter will keep running."

"That's fine," Jenny said. She hesitated and, with just the right edge of concern, asked, "Is it safe to leave Amy in the car with you for just a few minutes?"

A Perfect Lady

David Niall Wilson

They say that to the old fishermen, the ones who've lived their lives from swell to swell and dragged their nets along the reefs since men have lived near the blue-green seas, a boat grows closer than any lover. They say that the harmony of motion and grace that flows from gnarled, weathered hands to billowing sails and sweeping nets is a form of lovemaking akin to that of the angels. If you ask the fishermen, that is what they say.

Eric had sailed so long on *Old Mary* that he felt himself an extension of the wood. Each trick of light or waves, each nuance of weather or glint of stars had a single effect on boat and man. Eric was a married man these past fifteen years, but even his Jenny knew who came first. *Old Mary* had carried his father, had been built by his father's father, bringing in haul after haul of fresh fish to the markets, withstanding all that time and Father Neptune could throw at her.

If Eric were hung over, he could come to *Old Mary*'s decks and be gently rocked. If he lost his night's fun over the side, *Mary* didn't complain, but remained steady. If he wanted only to be alone, she was silent, and yet he felt her presence always, shielding him from the endless depths, protecting him like no earth-bound companion could hope to.

This night he'd taken her out to be alone. His wife's normally soothing voice had grown caustic; his children had driven their nonsense into him like iron spikes, time and again, grating on his patience. He'd taken a bottle, and he'd taken his leave. Now he and *Old Mary* plowed through the choppy surf, heading toward the reef.

He wanted to skim around to the bay and enter where there would be no one around but himself. Then he could toss a line over to occupy his thoughts and let the world drift away in the endless motion of the waves.

No stars were in evidence, and there was a stiff, cool breeze from the north. Eric paid no attention to this, his thoughts centering closely around the contents of the bottle and the wind in the sails. He was making good time, and he had already passed the reef when the first brilliant streaks of lightning reminded him that the ocean was no place for the inattentive.

The storm was running in fast. He could hear it, could make out the larger swells and the encroaching sheet of water that seemed to fly across the waves, losing sight of it each time the lightning flash faded, only to catch it again moments later and miles closer.

He turned *Old Mary*'s prow toward shore, but he knew in his heart he wasn't going to make it. Thoughts of Jenny and the children flooded his mind. He'd come here to flee them, but now the lack of them was an ache in his chest that would not release his tensed muscles.

He felt it just before it hit, felt the sting of the salt spray driven by the force of the winds, felt the oppressive weight of the water, rising high above him, the wave that would be his last, that would part him—dying—from his first love. The ocean was a jealous lover as well, it seemed. He'd brought the troubles of his life to her, and she'd reacted as Jenny would have had he come home with another affair of the heart.

He felt *Old Mary* being lifted high, felt the world disappear from beneath them, then a splintering crash brought blessed darkness, and he released himself to his fate. As the waves washed in to swallow him, he sent a message from his heart to his family, an apology for his life. Then it was dark.

They gathered around the odd bit of wreckage, first in curiosity, then in awe. All that remained of *Old Mary* was a flat bit of decking, somehow warped with such power that it seemed to have folded in upon itself. It was like an odd seedpod of wood, brine soaked and weathered.

When the first gasping breath broke free—when they looked close enough to see what was held tightly in the cold, wooden grasp, many crossed themselves. Then, consigning their souls to the savior, they pulled Eric free and warmed him by the fire.

Phone Tag

John R. Platt

Hi, this is Ted and Julia. Sorry we can't come to the phone. You know what to do."

Beep.

"Mommy . . . Mommy? Are you there? Mommy? You were supposed to pick me up at school after my half day . . . Mommy? . . . (sigh) . . . It's okay. I've got my key. I'll walk . . ."

Beep.

"Hey, Julia, it's Carol. Sorry I missed you at the school yard. Guess I'm missing you again, huh? So was that your new Olds I saw Stephie getting into as I pulled up? I thought you guys were gonna go for the Lexus . . . Oh well, talk to ya later . . ."

Beep.

". . . uh . . . damn machines . . ."

Beep.

"Mr. and Mrs. Anderson. You don't know me, but I know you. I got your daughter, Mr. and Mrs. Anderson. She looks real pretty in that pink dress you had her wear today. I think you know what I want. I hope you'll be there when I call back . . ."

Beep.

"M-Mommy? . . . Daddy? . . . P-please?"

"Didn't believe me? Does it sound more serious to you now? I want a hundred thousand dollars by the time the banks close tonight or

I'm going to have to hurt your little Stephie. I'll call back to let you know where to send the money . . ."

Beep.

". . . damn it . . ."

Beep.

"Mrs. Anderson, this is Doctor Roberts' office. You missed your appointment this morning. Please give us a call to reschedule."

Beep.

"Damn. I just got a busy signal, I figured you were home . . .

"Time's running out, Ted and Julia. I don't have all day . . ."

Beep.

"Tick tick tick tick tick ti—"

Beep.

"Damn you people! You think I won't do it? Listen to this!"

"Mommy! Daddy! Please, do what he says! He's hurting me! Mommy plea—"

Beep.

"Listen to me, you rich bastards! I don't know what your game is, but my price isn't going down. What did you do, bring the cops in? You can't trace these calls; I'm moving around. No two calls from the same place. Too smart for ya, aren't I?

"You've got one more chance, Andersons. Then I hang up more than just the phone."

Beep.

"Hey, honey; hey, sweetie, it's Daddy. The Fox account fell apart on us, so I have to fly out to L.A. and do some damage control. I picked up my suit at the cleaners so I've got some extra clothes. I'll call you as soon as I get to the hotel. Hope you guys are enjoying your afternoon together! Love you!"

Beep.

"Mr. Anderson?. . . This is Doctor Novello down at County General . . . I'm sorry to leave this message on your machine, but I've been trying to reach you for a couple of hours now. I'm afraid your wife was in a very serious accident this morning. She's in stable condition, but I really think you should get down here right away. Again, I'm sorry."

Beep.

Picnic Under the Sky

Greg van Eekhout

We lie on the shimmering grass and watch clouds sail across the endless blue.

"They're so beautiful," she says, her hand in mine. "So big and white."

"Cumulus," I say. "What do you see?"

I'm pleased when she doesn't utter something stupid, like I see cotton candy, or I see a big, rolling puffy castle. As if a castle could be puffy.

"I see a ship cutting through the waves," she says.

The clouds don't look anything at all like that to me. But that's okay. She's a person who can see her way to her own truths. She's wrong about the clouds, of course, but at least her interpretation is plausible.

"Your turn," she says.

I close my eyes to clear my mind, then, once prepared, gaze at the sky. At first there's something that might be a horse, the stormy sort with flames shooting through flared nostrils and lightning playing through its wild mane. But the image dissipates before fully resolving. It would have been too easy anyway, a false vision designed to placate and distract from actuality.

My father operated a candy store in Pasadena. The store earned him a modest living. It was never robbed. It never caught fire or got flooded by a broken pipe. No one ever broke the windows, spray-painted graffiti on the old red bricks, or drove a car through the front entrance. Only once did a famous person walk through the door, way back in the sixties, and it was just some actor from a sitcom whom my father recognized but whose name he could never remember.

My father's father was a bookkeeper at a feed company, and his father before him sold shoe polish wholesale.

All the men in my family are cloud readers.

I look more closely at the sky. I think it's trying to hide something, so I probe deeper, patient and unblinking.

I see a comet streaking through the dark.

I see men and women with telescopes and computers and pages upon pages of numbers.

I see a man in an oval room with beautiful wood furniture surrounded by dozens of people in suits and military uniforms.

I see rockets lifting majestically off the ground, leaving behind great plumes of flame as men and women watch and calculate and pray.

And I see those men and women pale as ghosts, some crying, some unable to speak, some even laughing, but all of them deathly white as the rockets explode far away from their intended target.

Then I see a great flash, and nothing more.

"Well?" she says. "Aren't you going to tell me?"

I look at her, and she's beautiful, and I don't love her, but later, I will tell her I do, because I know it will make her very happy.

"I see a big, rolling puffy castle."

She's disappointed with my answer, and I have to laugh.

Picture This

Scott Edelman

Someone should have warned me that it would end like this. Looking back at the photos taken of me as I grew, I can see the problem growing with me, rotting my soul like a piece of fruit left too long in a forgotten fruitbowl. In those photos, it is the eyes that tell.

They must have known. They could have prevented this.

Nothing seems out of the ordinary in the earliest surviving photos of me. I seem a normal, happy child.

I am alone. My young neck cranes upward from the flowered bed-spread. I might as well have been presenting that neck for a guillo-tine. I have long wondered who was on the other side of that shutter. Mom? Or was it Dad? A wild thought strikes me, and I get a magnify-ing glass to see if one of their reflections might be found frozen by the flash within the pupil of an eye. Nothing. Why didn't they try to tell me what the camera would bring? In our last conversation I wanted to find out which one of them had snapped the picture, but neither could remember.

Or if either had remembered, would not admit it.

The earliest of these photos is in my hand now. I keep coming back to this photo, the first of many. Too many. And I keep looking into my own soulful, trusting eyes, and think: How could they have clicked the shutter?

I see what has occurred. They must have known that I would someday see. Did they think that by the time I noticed, by the time I figured it out, I would no longer care?

I put the picture down and pick up another. Years have passed.

We are at the beach. I am not alone this time. Mom and Dad are both in the picture with me. I hold a mud pie toward them, but they do not look. Did some passing stranger commit the sin this time? My eyes are starting to die as my soul begins to seep out of me, into the camera.

Other photos follow.

Third grade. A certificate of merit on the refrigerator door. I stand before the award, smiling oddly. The eyes are less alive, dim as cloudy marbles.

High school graduation. Freddie took that one. My eyes glow red. Freddie claimed it was from the flash. But I know better.

Marrying Gina. Her pushing the cake into my cheek as I turned my face to escape it. My eyes were partially closed, but even had they been fully opened, they would have shown no more life than if they already had pennies on them.

I arrange the stills chronologically, and see the eyes slightly deader with every frozen moment. They could not have been ignorant! How could they have kept on taking the pictures knowing the process I was undergoing?

I did not come to realize this myself until Gina left. As I sat in our apartment flipping through photo albums, I saw the changes for the first time, and began to suspect our marriage failed because I no longer had a soul left for her to love, and I was filled with anger.

I rushed here and confronted my parents. I was calm at first, un-til I had all their photos out on this table alongside my own.

Then, it all came together.

When I accused them of their murderous crime, they did not deny it.

Instead, when they realized how serious I was, they laughed. They always laughed.

They laugh no more.

The fact that I did not cry when I did what I had to do shows that the camera has done its work. What final evidence could be needed?

I look at the last photo of me, the one I made Dad take with the instant camera. A bloody thumbprint marks where he pulled the tab with trembling hand. I have studied those eyes for hours.

There may still be hope. I have tried to light a match, and finally the flame catches. The photos in a pile in front of me smell of gasoline, and the rest of their home reeks as well. That final photo sits atop the mound. I look into my eyes. Inside, I think I can still see the final flickering of a soul, struggling to burst back to life. If I can only destroy all of these, maybe I can have my soul back.

And then, maybe then, everything will be all right. Maybe I'll be able to feel again.

Or maybe not.

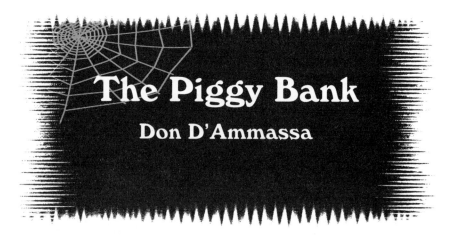

The Piggy Bank

Don D'Ammassa

Buster brushed aside the shrunken heads hanging in the window and climbed into Old Man Crenshaw's house. He'd waited until Crenshaw was gone, watching from the bushes as the ancient Ford backed slowly from the driveway and turned toward the center of town.

It was shadowy inside and he waited a full minute for his eyes to adjust to the dim light. Crenshaw never let anyone into his house, kept to himself except for regular shopping trips like this one, every Monday afternoon. He'd lived on this lonely side road in northern

Managansett for longer than anyone remembered, and about the only thing people knew about him was that he had lots of money, and didn't keep it in a bank.

Once a week he came into town with two crisp hundred-dollar bills and did his shopping.

Buster figured it was time to liberate some of that cash.

The house was crowded with furniture, most of it covered with dust. There were four rooms on the ground floor, and a narrow staircase leading upstairs.

"All right, old man, where do you keep it?" Buster made a cursory search, found piles of books about magic and ghosts and things like that, but nothing resembling cash. He hoped to do this clean, get away with the money before Crenshaw returned. But if he couldn't find it, he had a folding knife in his pocket that he figured would persuade the old geezer to be forthcoming about his wealth.

The second floor was every bit as dark as the first. One bedroom, a full bath, another room full of junk, and the last with a locked door.

"Gotcha!"

It wasn't much of a lock; Buster used the blade of his knife to pop it and entered.

An enormous glass sculpture dominated the room, a vaguely piggish body resting on its haunches, with two batwings raised like a cowl above the head. The face was so ugly Buster involuntarily retreated a step: blunt snout, narrow eyes, oversized jaw stretched wide revealing needle-sharp teeth of shiny glass. The entire statue was transparent, so Buster had no difficulty seeing the large pile of hundred-dollar bills resting within, as though the creature had swallowed them whole.

"Jackpot!" Once over his initial surprise, Buster wasn't shy about approaching the statue. He used one hand to test its weight, discovered that it was massive enough he wouldn't be able to move it. It might be possible to break the glass if he could find something heavy, but that would cause more noise than he cared to make. The Wilsons next door might not be friendly with Crenshaw, but they were close enough to hear and report any disturbance.

"The old man gets the money out, so I oughta be able to do it."

The jaws were opened wide, but the teeth were so long that there wasn't much clearance. Still, as long as he was careful . . .

Buster cautiously raised his hand and stuck it down the statue's throat.

Although he brushed the tips of the teeth more than once, he found the task easier than he'd expected. The cash was just at the limit of his reach; he wouldn't be able to get more than half of it this way. But that's all he needed. No reason to be a pig about it; let Crenshaw keep enough to live on.

His fingers closed on a packet of bills and he started to withdraw. Something stabbed him in the upper arm.

"Damn!" He'd been careless. One of the glass teeth had torn through his shirt and drawn blood. Buster eased away and winced as teeth from the lower jaw penetrated his flesh.

"What the hell?" For some reason, there didn't seem to be as much clearance as before. It was almost as if the jaws were slowly closing. Closing on his arm.

Blood was trickling from his shirt. Buster tried to withdraw at a different angle, and the sudden serrating pain caused him to jump, which only made things worse. He dropped the wad of bills and concentrated on escaping the trap.

It took almost half an hour and another score of cuts before Buster's arm was free and he collapsed against the opposite wall, weak from shock and loss of blood.

"Hope I left a bad taste in your mouth, you bastard," he said softly.

Then the statue slowly turned in his direction, jaws opening again, and Buster realized he'd only made it hungry.

Pine Supine

Robert Devereaux

'Twas that hazy indeterminate time betwixt dusk and nightfall. My new acquaintance tarried when he ought to have known such behindhandedness foolhardy. The evening's balm, not a hint of chill in the autumn air, did nothing to assuage my impatience with him.

His was the task, after all, to bring bonesaw, stake and mallet, crucifix, garlic—all the froufrouesquerie he claimed would make a difference. I insisted it wouldn't, that animal strength and cunning were required to triumph over such monsters; clever beasts they were, and swift in the kill, or so I'd heard.

"What a peculiar man of the cloth you are," he had yesternight exclaimed, ferreting me with those cold, dark, penetrant eyes. "Trust me," he said, "who have hunted and undone countless of their number."

I had seen such zealots before. Churchyards breed them. No doubt he had murdered mislabeled victims of his own delusions. The look he pierced me with gave me pause, made me wonder if he might, in his imbalance, suspect *me* of being monstrous.

In any case, I knew where the coffin lay, had seen it, touched it. Had I opened it? No, I told him. But I could guide him there. This particular sector of the city had suffered a recent rash of enfeeblings, of neck wounds, of sepulchral pallors bleaching the faces of distraught and then missing victims. Rumblings about the undead had blanketed the countryside, had brought Herr Scheuter—if that was indeed his name—into town, where he'd been sure his expertise was bruited about.

A figure popped up beside me. Unnaturally swift and silent, the hunter gave me a fright. "Father," said he abruptly, "good even to you." A burlap bag hung at one shoulder, malevolence upon his face.

"Herr Scheuter," I muttered, squelching impatience. He would not want any delay in our maraud, nor did I. If by some miracle we both survived the night, the time for castigation would arrive.

Spurning delay, I led him to the gate, slipped in my passkey, quickened my steps, heard him follow suit behind. When I halted, the gravel fell silent.

"There." I pointed.

The mausoleum seemed larger by dusklight. Hillocked, it overlooked a greying expanse of headstones.

Herr Scheuter glanced with distrust upon me, doubting perhaps that the coffin I had spoken of would be found in so obvious a place.

I pressed on, pretending that exposing my back to him made me nervous not in the least. The wrought-iron gate glided open without protest at the press of my palm, which took me aback. I could not recall this absence of sound in my last passage through the gate.

Boldly, upon the marble floor, stood the plain pine box. "Open it," said Herr Scheuter.

I managed a shudder. "Not I."

He scrutinized me. We were near enough in the fading daylight to read one another's faces. I wondered if this hadn't been a mistake.

But I concealed my misgivings lest not to do so prove fatal. Thank heaven the hunter yielded first, deciding I was trustworthy.

Kneeling, he loosened the burlap mouth, allowed iron to sprout. His fingertips tested the lid. "Unsecured." I sensed fear in his hesitation. Would the beast spring out? he must be wondering. Would it clamp a hand on his wrist? Crush him? Wrestle him inside?

Steeling himself, he swiftly raised the lid. Velvet plush, and a tang of death, an aroma I knew well; nothing inside but indentation, dark oily hints of wear that old instrument cases sometimes exhibit.

In that moment, when surprise jarred his perception, I sprang upon him. Too late he understood. Had his bag been closer, his tools out, he might have bested me. We have no superhuman strength, contrary to popular belief; no need to shun daylight, garlic, crosses.

But we do have speed. We have misdirection, when we can get it. In twisting away, he exposed what he tried to protect. I latched on to the jugular, and the vacuum inside me did the rest. There need be no slow feasting among us, no languor, especially in the heat of battle. His life capillaried out at once, a sizzling rush, filling me quite content, lightening my enemy's head and arresting his heart.

A welcome prize.

Scheuter smelled of rats and the killing of my kind.

To separate head from body proved, in his case, pure pine-scented pleasure.

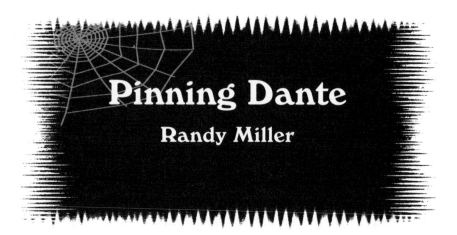

Pinning Dante

Randy Miller

Grandma never believed the astronauts reached the moon. That was only Hollywood fakery. But she never doubted Main Event Wrestling.

She'd sit on the edge of the sofa every Saturday in her nightgown with a tumbler of Coca-Cola and a pack of Pall Malls to watch her ninety minutes of wrestling, taped at Fort Worth's North Side Coliseum.

Every week, she'd cheer when the hero made his inevitable rally and began pummeling the assorted thugs. She loved to see the bad guys get their just deserts.

One July night, a villain named Dante debuted. He dressed in red leggings and a black singlet (always a sign of treachery; the heroes stuck to black or blue trunks) and a matching mask that depicted a demon.

She watched as Dante flew about the ring and destroyed his hapless opponent. In those days, wrestling was mostly headlocks and chokeholds and punches. You didn't see too much athleticism, aside from an occasional dropkick. But Dante leaped from ring ropes and turnbuckles and attacked his fallen foe as the stretcher carriers bore him to the locker room.

"Spawn of the devil," she said, which I thought was a little much.

Next month, Grandma insisted on attending a Monday taping down at the coliseum. I wasn't excited about driving my '65 Mustang to an uncooled auditorium in a dangerous neighborhood.

But what are grandsons for?

We ate grease-drenched french fries and cheered the heroes. Until Dante stormed down the aisle. He was larger than he looked on television and he demolished a popular cowboy in short order. The crowd was unusually subdued, save for a few shrill voices in the back.

He finished his assault and marched up the aisle, right past Grandma. That's when she stabbed his thigh with a hatpin. She was wiry strong, having worked on the farm for years. That pin must have hurt, but Dante only turned to meet her eyes for a second—and in that second, I felt something primordial and evil in his glare under that shiny mask. He went up the aisle wordlessly.

Grandma began seeing Dante everywhere, particularly in her dreams. We learned this when we found a hatpin embedded in her bed's headboard.

Every night, she whispered to me, Dante comes to seek vengeance. She must fend him off or die, she said. I merely thought she was scared by that seething stare and, besides, I was more worried about whether I'd start as cornerback for the Eastern Hills Highlanders.

It got worse, of course. Dante was delivering our mail. Dry-cleaning our clothes. Working at the beauty shop. Washing lettuce in the grocery store.

Grandma clutched her hatpins all through the day and used them to ward off Dante at night.

The situation became irreversible when she poked Mr. Tuthill, the scrawniest usher at the neighborhood Baptist church. He was remarkably Christian about it, though he did yelp a sincere plea to his savior. However, he bore utterly no resemblance to Dante. Don Knotts, maybe.

So Grandma had to be placed in a nursing home. She couldn't go on like this, Mom said.

Dante, of course, worked at the home. Grandma told me on my weekly visits, but she had a hatpin or two hidden.

I called her the afternoon of our first football game.

"Mrs. Atchley's room."

"This is her grandson, Brian. Where is she?"

"I'm here. Is this Brian?" Her voice dropped. "He's coming tonight, Brian. They took my protection."

"I could bring some from your box after the game."

"Thank you, dear. I'd love to jab him right in his satanic butt."

She wished me luck that wasn't delivered. Some sprinter from Arlington High burned me for two touchdowns, but worse, I heard the PA system call for Mom during the fourth quarter. And I knew, somehow, that Grandma was dead.

The doctor was apologetic, but pleased that she'd gone peacefully before her mind completely deteriorated. As we left her room though, I glanced under her bed and saw a bent hatpin and a swatch of black-and-red fabric.

The next wrestling telecast featured Dante facing Chief Wahoo in a live loser-leave-town battle for that gaudy Texas Championship belt.

Dante dominated the match with chokeholds, cheap shots, and eye-gouges that left the Chief prone and helpless.

Dante climbed atop the turnbuckles to finish him, when he suddenly grasped his buttocks and toppled headfirst to the concrete floor. This time, Dante rode the stretcher.

It was as if he'd been stabbed with an invisible hatpin.

Plant Kingdom

Scott M. Brents

Cirus McDaniels dropped the cucumber seed into the small dimple in the dirt. The soil was moist and rich, almost alive at his touch.

He covered the hole.

"Please grow for me," the thirty-three-year-old pleaded.

He went to the next hole and dropped in another seed, repeating his statement after he covered the hole.

Cirus did this for the entire row he was planting, then when finished, pushed a small wooden stick into the ground. On the stick was a picture of two healthy specimens of cucumbers.

"Please grow for me," he said to the whole row.

Time would tell.

"Biggest damned cucumbers you ever did see," someone said.

"Big as a whale," someone else would agree.

"Too bad Cirus is such a simpleton."

"Yeah, that *is* too bad. I wonder what else he grows?"

Cirus took his stick and made a small hole in the ground. Poke and then twist. He stepped a few inches to the left and jabbed the earth again. He did this until he had finished ten rows with twenty-five holes in each.

With each poke, he imagined his father was right behind him, telling him what to do. With each small twist of the wrist, he thought about his mom in her red and white apron, making him his lunch. The same lunch he had every day.

Cucumber sandwiches.

"It ain't normal, keeping a boy like that at home. Hell, he is a grown man. He should be in a special school for the mentally handicapped," someone would say.

"Yeah, he might be happier that way," someone else would agree.

"*Of course* he would be happier. Don't be such a Cirus McDaniels, Walt. There is no 'might' about it."

"Well, you got me there. You're right. *Of course* he would be happier at a school. Hey, do you think he can grow turnips?"

The stick had served well as a seed drill, but today Cirus was feeling grown-up and wanted to try the shovel, although he would stay away from the rake.

Cirus retrieved the shovel from the shed. The silver blade shone like chrome. It had never been used before. He had always used the pokin' stick his father had made for him. His father had used the stick on many occasions too, to discipline Cirus.

He stepped gingerly through the cucumber patch, careful not to step on his prized plants. (His father had once knocked him unconscious after Cirus had stepped on a seedling.) He finally made his way to a back corner lot, next to an ancient oak tree.

He began to dig.

Later when he took a break, he remembered that the oak tree was where his pokin' stick had come from.

"I went out there today, to the McDaniels place," someone said.

"What did you get, Bill? Did they have anything besides cucumbers?" Walt asked.

"I got sick to my stomach, that's what I got. I saw Mr. McDaniels beating the living hell out of Cirus. I'm thinking about calling the authorities."

Walt nodded his head in agreement, but inside wondered where in the world they were going to get such nice cucumbers if Cirus was taken away.

The two rows beneath the oak tree were finished. The shovel was put away, safe and sound; his father had not even missed it.

Cirus stuck a small wooden stick on each end of the rows.

The first stick had a picture of his mother, wearing the red and white apron. The second stick was a photograph of his father, sporting his faded overalls and straw hat. In his father's hand was the pokin' stick.

"Please grow for me," Cirus said to the freshly turned dirt.

Time would tell.

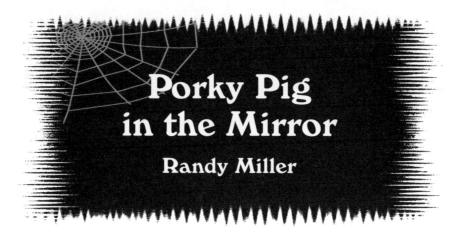

Porky Pig in the Mirror

Randy Miller

I'm Porky Pig.

Coach Nelson called me that after I botched my dismount from the balance beam today.

It's after hours here in the boarders' suite. The others sleep. I stare at the bathroom mirror with a towel jammed in the doorway so they won't wake and see the light.

I am fat. A blimp. A pregnant buffalo. That's what Coach Nelson says whenever I mess up.

I study the mirror closely. I don't want to grow breasts. Gymnasts can't have them. We can't do our routines. We can't please Coach Nelson.

Coach Nelson told us that we could resist having older bodies if we had a strong enough will. He's seen others—Eastern Europeans, Chinese, and Americans—stay beautiful and agile.

Coach Eskenazi, his assistant, gives us some pills to help our will.

Coach Nelson has a will stronger than Superman's chest. He can make us Olympians if we listen and learn. He's the best coach in the world. When I complete a difficult move, he hugs me and I know I'm doing things the right way. And when I finished second at last year's Nationals, he told me that I was going to be the one to win Olympic gold.

He called me a good girl.

I must vomit to stay thin. Seventy-six pounds are too many. I must weigh seventy by the Olympic trials. Maybe even sixty-six. Then I won't be too fat to hit that dismount.

The younger girls need to put a finger down their throats, but I can work my stomach muscles and up comes dinner. I think Coach Eskenazi knows, but he hasn't said anything.

I look again to see if my breasts are larger.

Mom and Dad and Sydney came to visit. Mom and Dad were so

proud when Coach Nelson told them I should make the Olympics. I've never seen Dad smile so hard.

Sydney was worried about my weight, but she's fat. My sister's three years older and must weigh 115, 120 pounds, but she thinks I'm too thin. She says thirteen-year-olds shouldn't be so tiny.

Still, Sydney can afford to be a blimp. She isn't training to be a gymnast. She can have boyfriends and pizza parties, but she can't be a gold medalist. She tried to sneak me a couple of candy bars, but I gave them away to some of the other girls.

They had to go back to Chattanooga. I miss them, but I don't really miss them, you know. I haven't lived there for five years.

When they left, so did Patty Rinelli. Her family couldn't afford the tuition, and besides, Coach Nelson told her she was too chubby to make the Olympic cut. No wonder, she's practically a woman at seventeen.

Coach Nelson doesn't like it when you become a woman. He says you can't perform as well. You don't take instruction as well.

I must check my breasts again. I want to stay a good girl. I want Coach Nelson to like me. Otherwise, he'll think I'm a hippo.

I will go to bed soon. Tomorrow we're going to the mall, and the coaches will let us shop and watch a movie. But they will keep us away from the food court and the snack bar. Seriously. One of them will stand guard by the popcorn machine while we sit in the theater. As if.

I have a plan. I will break away from the group long enough to go to the cutlery shop. Mom gave me plenty of walking-around money.

When I buy the knife, I will sneak it into a hidden pocket in my bag. Then I will tape it underneath my dresser drawer until I need it.

For the time I will become a woman.

The Predator

Don D'Ammassa

The last thing Daniel Ryan wanted was a pair of nutty Russians who thought they could "help" him. But that's what was sitting in his office.

"Look, Mr. . . . ?"

"Borzhoi, Detective Ryan. Alexei Borzhoi. And this is my sister, Tania."

"Right." Ryan tried to smile. He'd been pulling double shifts ever since the string of mutilation killings had begun, and his inadequate sleep was haunted by images of horribly mangled bodies with missing parts.

"We believe we can be of assistance in this matter of what your news media call the Predator."

Ryan studied the couple thoughtfully. They both had long, oval faces, a nearly identical mass of chalk white hair, shoulder length. Well over six feet tall but slender, both exuded an aura of strength and competence.

"We appreciate your good intentions, but unless you have some concrete evidence . . . ."

It was Tania who replied. "We appreciate your situation, Detective Ryan. Please assure yourself we have no desire to interfere. We simply wish to offer our expertise. We're associated with a private organization which concerns itself with crimes of this nature."

"That's all quite interesting, folks, but in this country, amateurs don't get involved in official investigations." He pushed his chair back and rose, glancing meaningfully toward the door.

They left with obvious reluctance, insisting that Ryan note the address at which they were staying. When they were gone, Ryan sighed, cleared the paperwork off his desk, then called for a progress report on the stakeout.

"O'Herlihy says the subject hasn't left the house all day."

Ryan drove across Managansett to the surveillance area, arriving just before midnight. The murders were confined to a limited area, and the only new resident was a recluse named Fenton. There was no hard evidence, but most of the pets in the neighborhood had been slaughtered shortly after he moved in, and neighbors had reported mysterious comings and goings.

The surveillance team was set up in an empty house across the street.

"What's up?"

Tim Caulfield shrugged. "He's been pacing back and forth like a wild animal."

"Are we ready to move?"

"I called in the cavalry. We have cars and foot soldiers everywhere." He gave a quick summary.

Satisfied, Ryan sat down to wait.

Ten minutes later, Caulfield whispered, "He's on the move."

An indistinct human shape reached the street and started away.

"Let's go!"

They followed him carefully as Fenton crossed Main Street, unexpectedly slipped through a break in the privet hedge, and entered the grounds of the Sheffield library.

Ryan cursed softly, realizing their quarry was out of sight, and reluctantly ordered everyone to converge immediately.

They found Fenton crouched behind a dumpster, an eviscerated body at his feet. Ryan assumed it was Fenton wearing an elaborate costume. The face was right, but the unnatural shape of the torso looked more animal than human.

Two uniformed officers advanced and Fenton snarled, then seemed to flow across the ground. One man was thrown against the side of the dumpster with such force that it boomed with the impact, and the other collapsed with blood welling from deep cuts in his abdomen.

Then it came for Ryan.

Stunned, Ryan waited for death. Fenton ran on all fours, not like a man pretending to be an animal, but more like an animal pretending to be a man. At the last moment, there was a flash of white and Fenton spun away.

Ryan turned as well, saw Fenton recoil from a second white shape. Both newcomers ran on four legs, but where Fenton's body was lumpy, dark, and filled with menace, these were graceful, sleek, and well groomed.

Fenton's head turned from side to side, snapping at his tormentors. One darted in, sank teeth into the scruff of Fenton's neck, while the other secured a similar hold from the other side.

By the time Ryan reached them, they had already torn Fenton's throat out.

"He's dead, isn't he?" Ryan recognized his rescuers despite their partial transformation: Alexei and Tania.

They were silent, but Tania nodded her head.

Already the body was starting to revert, the hair growing shorter, the unnatural turns of bone and tissue straightening, reassuming human form.

Fenton's killers turned and ran off into the darkness. It made sense, he supposed. If werewolves were real, it made ecological sense that another entity existed to keep their population growth in check. If he could accept werewolves, why not werewolfhounds?

Prime Crime
William Marden

He could sense rather than see the figure sitting in the chair behind the desk in the dark, vacant office in a building two streets down from New Day Broadcasting Channel headquarters.

"Sit down," the figure said in a raspy voice.

"I . . . I don't think that's necessary," George Elmont whispered. "I've brought your money. Now you—you . . . can fulfill your part of the bargain."

"There's a chair in front of you. Sit."

Elmont found the chair and sat. He just wanted to get this over and get home to Elaine. She'd been out, probably shopping, when he'd called, but he knew she'd be there when he got home.

"We don't have anything to talk about," Elmont said, wanting to get this over with as quickly as possible. "You'll get your money . . . and . . . you'll keep up your end of the deal."

"Oh, I'll keep up my end of the deal," the voice said, with a hint of amusement in it. "But I was a little curious to learn why a respected network executive—even if it is a piddling little network like NDBC—would make such a deal."

"You know why. That's why you called me."

"Ah yes, the exigencies of network life," the voice said. "Live by the ratings, die by the ratings. What are you at now, about a point four compared to NBC's fourteen or even UPN's four? Not much life left in the corpse, is there, unless I give you an infusion."

"We might make it," Elmont said, unable to believe his own words. "But a videotape of an actual murder to be broadcast on our Prime Crime special . . ."

"What did the Miami Beach murder videotape do for Fox? Didn't they draw an audience of thirty million people the night they broadcast the tape of the butchering of the Maranza couple?"

"Thirty-two million," Elmont said. "Even with all the court battles, even minus the goriest segments, they still beat NBC, CBS, ABC, everybody. Nobody would admit watching it the next day, but everybody did. Thirty-two million people . . ."

"That's why I called you. I figured you were the neediest outfit around, and that a deal would be good for both of us. I get rich and you guys get a continuing series of exclusives. You know this could make your network, don't you?"

"Yeah, I know," Elmont said, remembering afresh the emotions that had raged within him after taking the phone call from someone claiming to be the Bayside Head Hunter. Disgust and panic and fear, and for the first time in a very long time, hope.

"But still I wonder," the voice asked, "how do you sleep at night? I know what I am, why I do what I do. But you're a respectable, law-abiding citizen."

"Because I know a sick bastard like you would be killing people whether anybody pays you for the videotapes or not," Elmont said. "And if I didn't pay for the videotapes, somebody else would."

"You're right about that, partner," the voice said, clicking a switch and flooding the office with light. When his sight returned, Elmont stared at the short, balding man sitting across the table from him.

The Head Hunter pointed to a tape recorder which sat running on the desk and the video camera sitting on a tripod behind him, focused on the chair in which Elmont sat.

"Now give me the money, which I'll capture on tape, and I'll know that I can trust *you*, partner. Then I'll show you how good I treat my partners."

Elmont handed the bag containing the ten thousand dollars to the

Head Hunter, who put it to one side, saying, "I won't count it. I know I can trust you."

"Now," he said, pushing the large paper bag in front of him toward Elmont, "here's my gift to you. When you start showing these videotapes, you and NDBC would come under a lot of suspicion from the cops. But I've fixed it so you'll never be a suspect."

As Elmont looked inside the bag and recognized its contents, he knew that the doors to hell had been flung wide open and he was sliding down through them. He could only whisper her name in disbelief and utter a plea for forgiveness that he knew would never be granted, while the Head Hunter clasped him on the shoulder, smiling and saying, "Don't thank me. That's what partners are for."

The Proof in the Picture

Lisa Morton

A *possessed kid . . . what next . . .*
Derek laughed as he pulled up before the address they'd given him. It looked like any other brownstone, not exactly the haunted houses and morgues he was used to.

He pulled his camera bag from the car, already imagining how he'd retouch the photos. *Possession . . . glowing eyes, levitation, maybe add blood like I did to those victim photos . . .*

It was all part of the job. Derek had always been a practical joker; now he got to pull the wool over the eyes of millions of tabloid readers who bought whatever lie he fed them, be it Satan's face in a tortilla or Dracula reincarnated as a rabbit.

Sure, some of the assignments had proven to be eerily realistic. The remains left by the latest serial killer had made him queasy.

But today he expected nothing more than a sad, sick kid.

The boy's mother, haggard from weeks of worry, met him at the door. She led him down a hall, explaining that the priests had already left today. The exorcism had been going on for weeks.

She indicated a door and waited. Derek mentally assigned her performance a B and entered.

The room was dark, the smell bad, but hardly demonic. He let his eyes adjust, then looked down.

The fourteen-year-old was asleep on the bed. He was pale, emaciated. His arms and legs were strapped down.

Poor little shit, Derek allowed himself as he pulled out his camera and attached a flash. He was setting his meter when the voice startled him.

"Are you here to take pictures?"

It sounded like a boy's voice. Derek turned, ready to capture something diabolical. "Yes. Do you mind?"

"No. Tell me what you want. If I opened my mouth, you could airbrush in a forked tongue or projectile vomit."

Derek hadn't anticipated that. A fourteen-year-old who knew more about tabloids than most adult readers. "I was hoping for something I wouldn't have to retouch."

"Now, Derek, did you think it would be that easy?"

Big deal, so they told the kid my name . . .

Derek snapped a shot, and the boy blinked. "That should be good. My eyes'll look red and glowy."

That'd been Derek's thought exactly. "C'mon, do something special."

"Real evil doesn't work that way. Surely even *you* must have realized by now that it's subtler."

"Subtle doesn't sell."

The boy chuckled, then replied, "Don't worry, I'll give you something that'll sell."

Derek snapped more shots. "Like what?"

"That's enough pictures. Go home and develop them."

Derek tried to snap again, but the shutter wouldn't release.

"I told you to go home, Derek."

The boy went back to sleep.

Derek fiddled in vain with the camera, then shrugged and packed it away. He knew the shots he had were good enough to sell papers.

He developed the pictures that night. The photos of the boy were blurry. But the photo on the end of the roll was crystal clear.

The photo of Derek crucified in the kitchen doorway of his apartment, his neck slit.

He blew the photo up as big as he could. There was a newspaper propped at his feet. It had tomorrow's date on it.

Derek stared at it for a long time. It was impossible.

I'll give you something that'll sell . . .

No. There were no demons, only airbrushes and retouched pictures . . .

That was it. Somehow the roll had been tampered with. Maybe someone not too pleased with Derek's past work. *That* was certainly not impossible.

Fine. He'd stay in a hotel for the next week.

He left immediately. Drove until he saw a vacancy sign.

He noticed the man behind him in the lobby, but didn't want to seem paranoid. He got a first-floor room. He found it, unlocked the door, was about to lock it again when another hand slammed against his chest, sent him reeling into the room. It was the man from the lobby. He hit Derek and tied him and told him he didn't like the way he'd added more blood to the photos of his victims. Then he told Derek he'd followed him all the way from his apartment, and they were going back there now.

He crucified Derek in the kitchen doorway and slit his throat.

After they found Derek, the photo was front page news. His own paper made millions on that issue.

They didn't even have to retouch.

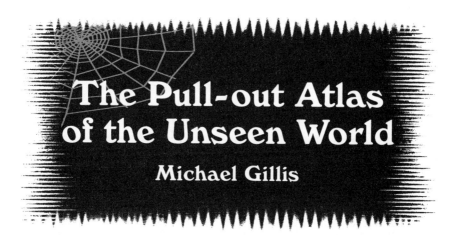

The Pull-out Atlas of the Unseen World

Michael Gillis

Outside were twenty-thousand believers. There were Shiites and Sunnis; Maronites, Druze, and Roman Catholics; a smattering of Baha'is and even Zoroastrians. Beirut was not lacking dangerous comminglings.

But outside Jack's ailing apartment of pocked stucco and cracked windows, they sang. Not in competition of faith, but together. A twelfth-century Sufi ballad had threaded its way through the crowd as if by its own volition.

"Shit," was Jack's response as he watched from his bedroom. From the shrine.

Marwan looked away from the wall. "I no paint it over. They kill me."

"Right," Jack said abstractly. "Probably not a swell idea."

"No swell," Marwan said.

Jack paced. He cursed the day he ever rented the place. "I've spent my last franc. I can't afford to protect it anymore," he said. "Or myself."

"What we do?" Marwan asked.

Jack walked over to the sacred wall, elevated from a commonplace of barely adequate protection to lofty esoteric significance. He gently tugged the triangular swath of wallpaper, exposing the detailed water stains underneath.

"We no mess it up, Jack," Marwan said, lost in the wallpaper's richness.

Jack had to tell him. He had no choice. It had gone too far. Dangerously far.

"It's not real, Marwan," he said. Marwan turned slowly to look at him. "I was tired one night—delirious almost—and the idea came to me. Like a fever. The next thing I know I'm writing a book, copying the patterns under the wallpaper."

Marwan said nothing. A gradual expression of defeat turned quickly to horror. "They kill us for this."

How easy it had been, Jack thought, to promote belief. He had first described the "atlas" in a short Associated Press release: something about old Phoenician patterns and sketches discovered under wallpaper in Beirut. That, of course, had been the easy part. He had worked for the Press then. Before he could stop himself, though, he was penning books about the atlas under the wallpaper. It was pure fabrication which he peppered generously with the mystical quirks of myriad religions and occult sciences. When the first among the curious arrived at his apartment, he was cautious. How far could he take them? After all, L. Ron Hubbard had initiated his own religion. Why couldn't he? He explained the atlas under his wallpaper in ellipses, saying that it dispensed secrets like soap.

It was all so easy.

"Most have you books," Marwan said. "They waving them at guards."

"It's got to stop," Jack said. He walked to the window, almost tripping up on his nerves. He lifted the window and yelled down to the pilgrims. "Listen to me," he repeated until they were still. They stared at the discoverer. "There is something you have to know." He paused to smooth his resolve. He regretted that his creation would cease, but it wasn't safe any longer.

"I have something to confess." They looked into him. "The atlas of the unseen world, in the room behind me, is not what you think. It's . . ."

They glowered at him, their eyes narrowing with rage. He had almost said "a fraud." What would that have done? he wondered. He had to be resourceful.

"The atlas is, in fact . . ." What to say? ". . . something altogether different. It is . . ." They were drawing him out with their eyes. "It *is* an atlas of the unseen world, yes, but not what I thought." He heard Marwan gasp behind him.

"It is unseen *worlds*. Evil worlds. Gulfs and pits stewed with horrors. They wanted us to seek them out. To bring them here. That's why they left a map." He couldn't stop himself. Creation was so easy, he thought. They believed everything he said. They had all read his books, pored over his impressions of the atlas; some had been privileged enough to see it. They trusted him.

Now they were taken with fear, terrified of what he was saying. He went on.

"They are passing through. We have . . . inadvertently opened it up." He drew upon everything he knew: forgotten names, gibberish, old spells in Latin and Arabic. He even mouthed a few in French, which ultimately set them running. Most important, though, they believed.

Watching them scatter, he connived the future. He could continue to nurture his religion, fine-tuning it with trifling, more archaic gnosis.

"Did you see them run, Marwan?"

Marwan did not respond.

Jack turned, but it was too late. Already they had spilled out from the black stains that had moments before been brown.

His last thought before their impossible maws closed around him and the apartment was how easy it had been.

Pullover

Robert Devereaux

It's bleak outside. Blizzard winds bleed around the imperfect seal of his condo door. Frazell would prefer to stay in, but commitments have been made. Besides, he can forehear laughter beneath cozy blankets at evening's end. His mind lingers over hands at play, upon dives made into dark depths to sample hidden delights.

In his bottom dresser drawer, sweaters lie tossed or folded. Several are ancient, stretching back to college: musty, hole-bit by larvae although cedar blocks have kept the munching minimal. He'll never toss them, never wear them. Ah. The purple one. Old reliable. He pulls it out. It flops open in his hands.

Thrusting his arms halfway into its sleeves, he raises the collapsed, toothless, eel mouth above his head and jams the sweater down. Straitjacket. A ski mask's slide upon his forehead and over the jut of his nose. His arms go further, are caught in an awkward embrace, the sort of sweater hug one needs always to wangle free of. To regain control, as much a triumph over inert wool as the initial knitting was for its maker, will offer simple satisfaction.

It's slow in coming, the regathered mastery of body, ergo soul. An obnoxious nuisance. Were anyone to spy him fumbling thus, he'd be branded nerd. Cabled wool presses at his lids. His lashes brush oddly up, like dead idle legs of a swatted mosquito. Pinpoint interstices of light torment him. He can't make out a thing, of course. The weave is far too close for that. Sufficient light exists, though, to imagine stray corkscrews of frayed yarn.

He begins to tire. His voice huffs. "Come *on*," he says aloud, twisting and turning, body bent forward at the waist, arms held up like trapped elephant trunks. If he isn't careful, he'll smack his wool-wrapped hands on dresser edges, on a doorjamb or wall. Abruptly, he halts the wild whirl.

At his crown, his combed-over bald spot, the air feels cooler than inside. The pouting head hole's without a doubt more constricted than at first. Absurd. If anything, it should have stretched from his exertions.

He'll sit.

He does.

Slowly, he lowers himself.

The mattress presses upon his lumbar. Six inches of Sealy, a comfort. He decides, if he can't get the damned thing on, he'll try to peel it off. He attempts mightily to bend his arms, to grapple with the neckline at his crown and tug upward. But his hands are trapped in the sleeves, firmly clutched and bound, as though they were wrapped in drying papier-mâché. In any case, his fingers won't quite reach, no matter how strenuously he calipers with his elbows.

It's hot and close in here. The air is weak, oxygen poor, after its quick filtering through tight weave. He can no longer make out light, no interstices at all.

Nonsense.

He stops.

Takes stock.

Torso's as close bound as Chinese fingercuffs. Chest, constricted. Arms, virtually in traction. Top hair, out and sprawling (it'll need several runs of the comb) where a taut circle of sweater refuses to yield. The yarn's lower limit, at his belly . . .

But wait. That's not where it ought to be. It ought surely to be barrel-staved about his chest, where it stuck eons ago.

It *can't* have budged since then.

Suddenly everything's too cramped, cribbed, confined. He's got to escape. Once, on a scuba trip, guided into an underwater cave, he suffered a panic attack, breathing wrong, afraid he'd pass out, die down there.

He flails and whimpers. No air at his crown. None. The circle has irised shut. Ribbed bottom yarn claims his waist, lazing downward, a slow, hot, heavy, black sludge.

Cocoon.

Time unravels.

Gradually, he loses all sense of confinement. The odor of wool is gone, the warmth. The absence of light is so complete that *black* no longer bears meaning; the light is a vacant nullity. He exercises his lungs, but the sounds dwindle, are dampened, and die even as he makes them. Then there are only feelings of effort made by jaw, ribs, lungs.

At last, even that effort—as though an anesthetic has taken swift hold—can no longer be felt, exists no more. There's nothing to hold on to.

Nothing holds on to nothing, clings to it, moves into the undifferentiated void.

Quality Time

Gary Jonas

Dennis Pratchett couldn't wait to get down to see his children. A year ago his wife, Elizabeth, filed for divorce and took them away from him. He missed them terribly. But today was Friday and the workday was almost over. He'd have the entire weekend to spend with Jimmy and Suzy.

He finished up his last few reports and e-mailed them to the corporate office, then signed off the computer for the day. He adjusted his tie, donned his jacket, and left his office.

"Leaving early, sir?" Olga, his secretary, asked.

"Yes," Dennis said. "I get to go see my kids."

"Have a good time. Oh, Mr. White wants to see you in his office before you go."

"Thanks, Olga."

Dennis didn't want to see Mr. White. Mike was the supervisor over all the projects in the firm and it seemed to have gone to his head. Dennis should have had that position. Of course, when the position came up, Dennis wasn't doing so hot since his wife had just left him, taking Jimmy and Suzy away, too. He put on his professional smile and went over to Mr. White's office.

White's secretary, Heather, smiled when Dennis entered the outer office. "Mike's expecting you, Mr. Pratchett."

"Dennis."

Heather's eyes sparkled. "Dennis," she said as if trying it out. "Go on in."

Dennis thanked her and went into his supervisor's office wondering if he should ask Heather out. She was a bit young for him, but . . .

"Ah, Dennis. Good to see you. I just wanted to go over a couple of things with you. You aren't busy, are you?"

"Actually, I was just on my way out the door."

"Really?"

"Yeah, I get Jimmy and Suzy this weekend. I hope Elizabeth has them ready to go. I was hoping to take them to the IMAX tonight and to the zoo tomorrow. They love the zoo."

"It's good to see you're bouncing back from the whole divorce thing, Dennis. Tell you what, none of this is all that important. It'll keep for the weekend. You go see your kids. Buy them an ice cream or something."

"Thanks, Mike. I'll catch you first thing Monday morning."

"Sounds good. Oh, and Dennis?"

Dennis turned back to face him. "Yes?"

"Your work has really improved lately. I just want to say thanks. I appreciate it."

"Just doing my job."

Dennis felt good as he drove home. He was glad they knew he was doing a good job. That meant that when promotion time rolled around again, he'd be a shoo-in.

He pulled into the garage and entered his house. He could hardly contain his happiness as he changed clothes. Soon he'd be with his kids. Get to spend some quality time with them at last.

Unable to keep the smile from his face, he went to the basement door and opened it. He carried his dirty clothes down the stairs and dropped them by the washing machine, then moved toward the old basement bedroom.

He entered the room, still grinning. "God, I've missed you," he said, and rushed over to embrace the two small skeletons placed just so in their chairs, while a third, larger skeleton looked on.

The Quimby House Ghost

Dan Perez

The old Quimby house sat, in stately, Gothic Revival neglect, on a ridge overlooking the neighborhood. It was haunted, everyone said.

Even a practical man like Horace Weller thought so. He had researched the history of the house and found the requisite familial intrigues and murders, and, to a self-trained parapsychologist like Horace, all the ingredients were there. The thing to do, he decided matter-of-factly, was to observe the ghost or ghosts in their natural, or (Horace smiled at the thought) supernatural environment.

He had dipped into his savings after retiring as county postmaster, tracked down the owners of the Quimby house, and secured a year's lease. He moved in under cover of darkness: no need for publicity seekers from the neighborhood lurking about, spoiling his observations. He converted a small, windowless room on the ground floor to a headquarters, so he would have a comfortable place to sleep and take his meals. His plan was to sleep during the day and stand watch for ghostly manifestations by night, for however long it took.

Oh, the excitement of that first night! It was too soon to expect any phenomena, of course; the fragile para-ecology of the house had been disturbed by his presence. But soon things would settle, and then Horace would see indeed.

The weeks wore on with little sign of ghostly phenomena. Oh, to be sure, there were noises, but all had been investigated and found to have mundane causes: a loose shutter here, mice in the attic there. Horace was not deterred. Contrary to popular belief, many ghosts are shy and retiring, avoiding contact with the living. One had to allow these hesitant spirits time to adjust to the vibrations of a corporeal person, and given time, they, too, would betray their presence.

As the weeks passed, and Horace reviewed his notes, he came to realize that it was Lily Quimby he hoped most to encounter. A beautiful, frail teenager in the photographs he had seen, Lily had been drowned in an upstairs bathtub by her sister, Mavis, in a jealous rage over a suitor. Mavis had then hanged herself in a coat closet. There had been other deaths, even other murders, in the troubled Quimby household, but Lily was the first to die in the house. And Horace, who had never married and never had children, fancied a sort of spiritual link to the poor, doomed Lily.

Horace was near despair at the six-month mark. None of the Quimby ghosts had shown any sign of their presence, yet he felt that Lily, at least, must still be trapped in the house.

A sign finally came two weeks later. Horace was reading by penlight in the upstairs hall, as he usually did, when a distinct, loud *bang* came from the bathroom at the end of the hall. He knew all the Quimby house's mundane sounds by heart now, and this was distinctly different. Horace crept down the hall and shined his penlight into the bathroom, toward the bathtub where Lily had drowned. A haze of dust motes filled the air and he thought he heard a child's muted shriek. Horace shuddered with excitement and satisfaction.

Just before dawn broke, Horace scribbled in his notebook: *Breakthrough. Believe I have finally made contact with L. Quimby.* He could barely get to sleep that morning.

A week later there were two sharp raps in the bathroom, and Horace, who had set up his chair just outside, savored his startlement. There was an odd familiarity to the sounds. He heard no voices this time, but he believed in his heart that Lily was acknowledging him now, perhaps even trying to communicate.

A few days later, there was a clatter of sharp impacts and a shattering of glass. Horace leapt from his chair and ran into the bathroom. Cool air filtered in through the dust-filmed window above the bathtub. One pane was broken, and he saw a large rock amid the shards of glass on the bottom of the tub. Horace hurried to the broken pane and peered through it. Below, a handful of neighborhood kids saw him, screamed, and ran off.

Horace sighed bitterly. He shined his penlight at the bathroom mirror and caught sight of his haggard, milk-pale reflection. He went in utter defeat to his notebook and began his final entry. *Have finally come face-to-face with the ghost of Quimby house . . .*

Rain Brujah

Jessica Reisman

Uncle Sy's umbrella always hung from the coat tree in the front hall. The handle, tines, and tip had all been carved and fitted from the same pale yellow-brown material. Its panel sections were some fine beige fabric, from which the rain rolled in silver drops, so that the umbrella appeared to repel water, and never needed to be shaken or left in the hall to dry. Jonathan had been told never to touch Uncle Sy's umbrella. Sometimes, when he walked past it, he smelled a strange perfume, not at all like the one his Aunt Rachel wore, and thought he heard someone breathing.

One Saturday in November a fine rain needled down from the sky, thick as stitching in a heavy brocade. Jonathan had to go to the drugstore to get his aunt's bromides. He'd left his own umbrella, which was black and too small and coming off its tines in three places, at school. Uncle Sy was at work at his candy store, but his umbrella hung in its usual place. Jonathan stood looking up at it, listening: he heard no breathing but his own. He sniffed experimentally: nothing but the musty pipe tobacco and wood oil smell of the hallway. He reached up and wrapped a hand around the umbrella, lifted it down. It felt curiously warm in his hand, and the fabric had an ever so slight fuzziness, like the skin of a peach. For the barest moment he imagined it shivered against his skin, but he knew that he was just imagining things. He took the umbrella.

Outside, the umbrella not only kept him wonderfully dry, but seemed to create a bubble of warm air, too. As he walked, however, the umbrella grew heavier and heavier, and the perfume scent coalesced, and the breathing began to pulse through the air, in and out, faint at first, but growing stronger, until warm breath tickled his ear and blew over his collar.

He walked faster, as if he could somehow escape. He lowered his arm and tried to fling the umbrella from him. Cold rain immediately stung him, and pain shot up into his arm from his hand. He looked down and saw that the handle of the umbrella had become a skeletal hand gripped hard about his, finger bones woven tight with his fingers. The hand gripped so hard that the bones poked into Jonathan's hand and blood welled, slicked his skin, and ran along the bones, down along the umbrella handle.

Jonathan screamed and shook his arm, clawing at the skeletal hand. But the hand gripped tighter and tighter, grinding the bones in Jonathan's hand harder. He slipped to his knees in a puddle, drenched in the rain, breath heaving. He looked about wildly for help, but the streets were empty in such weather; there were only a few cars, far away through the heavy rain. As his blood slicked down the umbrella shaft, the shaft began to change, too, becoming the bones of an arm. When spots and drippings of his now copiously flowing blood hit the pale fabric of the umbrella, it too began to change. The blood burned briefly, absorbing into the fabric, sinking into it, fading, leaving traceries of blue. The fabric seemed to engorge on each new sprinkling.

Jonathan heard his heart, pumping his blood, beat louder and louder as he grew weaker and weaker. He watched in fascination as the umbrella continued to transform.

Uncle Sy came home late that evening. He found his wife, Rachel, in her housedress, sitting on the hall steps, staring up at the coat tree. Sy looked and saw the umbrella was gone.

"Jonathan, he never came home," Rachel said. "I sent him for my bromides."

Rain drummed cozily on the roof, on all the roofs, all through the city.

The Ramp on Trumbull Street

Wayne Allen Sallee

The wife of the guy who lived at 7822 South Trumbull Street got cancer back in April. The family's name was Nefti. Hugh and Nadine Nefti. I knew this because I occasionally do voter canvassing for the precinct captain, Sheridan, who lives past the viaduct. Hugh, who works for Commonwealth Edison, kept a tight reign on Nadine and their two kids. Keith was three, Alyssa four.

Throughout the summer, I heard stories from the Neftis' neighbors, who rode the bus downtown to work, same as I. How the chemo wasn't helping. I listened with the proper grim smile. The cancer spread, and Nadine Nefti died just before her thirty-sixth birthday, six months after the initial diagnosis.

In August, a wooden wheelchair ramp was installed over the front steps of the Neftis' bungalow. I saw two of the neighbor men sliding it into place as I walked to the 79th Street bus stop. It was painted reddish brown, like the color of a picnic table. The ramp covered the three cement steps at a gentle angle so that it stopped just short of the front crosswalk.

I never saw Nadine being wheeled from the house at all. By Labor Day, the stories I heard at the bus stop involved Hugh not really giving a damn about his wife's health. I even heard tell that when Nefti saw her wearing a wig Mrs. Peterson had given her, he burned it.

And he was yelling at the kids all the time.

Nefti wasn't even at the hospital when his wife died.

Mrs. Peterson whispered conspiratorially that Hugh's elderly mother had broken her hip after falling down the stairs. This was back when the Neftis were newlyweds, according to Mrs. P., and they had been living with the mother on Pope John Paul II Drive. Point being, evidently, that Hugh could care less about anybody's health.

Weeks passed and the ramp remained, which I thought strange, because Hugh was hardly sentimental. Just before Halloween, I noticed that the ramp had been moved to the north side of the porch. When I passed on the opposite side of the street, the ramp was now obscured by the big maple tree that dominated our block.

And Nefti continued yelling at his kids.

I had spent Halloween night in Bucktown, in the house of a girl I knew from college, up near the old Humboldt Park neighborhood where I grew up. We had an argument over something stupid, and I ended up taking the Western Avenue bus home and walking down 79th.

When I reached Trumbull, I stopped, noticing a shadow on Nefti's porch. Wanting to take my mind off the evening's failure, I shuffled closer to see what melodrama I could.

You ever have second thoughts?

Hugh Nefti had his wife's wheelchair at the edge of the porch. He was holding Keith, still asleep, in one arm. He had a bottle of vodka in his free hand.

He gently set the bottle on the railing, and just as carefully put his son into the chair. He pushed the chair down the ramp, and when it hit the sidewalk, Keith was tossed against the maple tree.

Hugh walked down the stairs, picked Keith up, and brushed chips of bark out of his hair, then went back inside. I thought about how Nefti's mother really broke her hip.

He came out again—I thought he had seen me—and took a moment to set the wheelchair back in place. He went back inside.

When the door opened again, and I saw his sleeping daughter in his arms, that was when I screamed.

Rattle Them Bones

John B. Rosenman

There were two out in the fifth inning when Sloan noticed he was pitching to a skeleton.

He froze, then rubbed his eyes. Nope, no mistake. The batter had a bare white skull, and from the mound, Sloan could see right through his rib cage.

He sucked in his breath. He'd known, of course, that he drank too much, but he'd never actually seen things before, certainly not a live skeleton who didn't even have the courtesy to wear a uniform.

Cautiously he glanced about. Thank God, everybody else looked normal, though Carter, the catcher, seemed bothered by his long delay. He'd better start throwing before his teammate came out to question him.

Numbly, he wound up and delivered a slider that hung in the air like a fat grapefruit. To his relief the bone man managed only a weak fly.

Back in the dugout, Sloan collapsed on the bench. It must be his imag—

"Sloan, you all right?"

He jumped, seeing the team's manager.

"Uh, yeah."

"You sure?"

"Yes, I . . ."

He stopped. As he watched, the manager's face dissolved. In seconds it became a mere skull with vacant eye sockets. The uniform was gone too, and unless he was mistaken, he heard the wind whistle through the man's pelvis.

"Sloan, are you *sure* you're all right?"

A bony hand squeezed his shoulder, and he forced himself to smile even though the man had spoken without lips or lungs. "N-never better. It's just a t-t-touch of indigestion."

"Good!" The manager nodded and clacked off.

Trembling, Sloan glanced up and down the bench. A touch of indigestion? But that didn't explain why half the team now resembled a boneyard that rattled when it moved.

Closing his eyes, he whispered a prayer. By the sacred grave of Ty Cobb, he'd never take another drink again.

But good intentions had no effect, for by the time he returned to the mound, every player, plus thirty thousand fans, looked like they needed an undertaker. Everywhere Sloan glanced he saw gleaming bones and hollow skulls.

Nuts. He was going stark raving nuts.

Wait a minute. Was it possible the booze was actually making him see more clearly, perceive the reality beneath the surface?

Struggling for calm, he turned and gazed out at center field. Never had the distant bleachers looked so clear and detailed. In fact, he felt as if *all* his senses were razor sharp.

Could his drinking have somehow improved him? Now that he thought of it, he'd chugged down a particularly potent drink the night before, one in which he'd thrown in everything from bourbon to brandy. Had he accidently created just the right mix, a concoction that had marvelously transformed his system?

Gripping the ball, Sloan toed the rubber, wound up, and let fly.

Strike one!

The ball went so fast that both batter and umpire stood stunned. The catcher, who wore only a glove, shrieked and did a weird dance of pain, his arm and leg bones cracking.

Exulting, Sloan waited until the catcher recovered. Shaking off one sign, he nodded at the next and went into his windup.

Strike two!

Why, the ball must have curved *three* feet! He saw it carom off the catcher's clavicle and strike the batter's skull.

When Sloan finally got the ball back, he hefted it gaily. This time he'd really rattle them bones. By the spirit of Satchel Paige, he'd throw the greatest pitch of all time.

Triumphant, he raised the ball.

His fingers.

He gasped as they grew long, red, gleaming nails. As if that weren't enough, his hand thickened and sprouted a thick mat of green fur.

Dimly, as the players gaped, he heard the beginning of screams from the stands.

Sloan reached up and touched his head, finding it was now twice its normal size and crowned with what felt like pointed horns. Worse still, razored tusks jutted from his mouth.

The stadium rocked with shrieks and screams. Dazed, he realized that while everyone might not be aware of their change, they certainly were aware of his.

Moments later, when the players from both teams started to converge upon him, Sloan found that he needed a drink very badly. For they all moved with precision teamwork, with skulls that seemed to be grinning.

And each and every one of them carried a bat.

Reading the Cards
Lisa Lepovetsky

Lay 'em down, honey. Just you cut away and lay 'em down in a cross. Position's important, how they lay. Now face 'em over, one by one. No, you gotta do it, I'm just an old woman with hands crippled up, and the cards want your touch.

See there, the Fool's reversed. Name's Innocence, and his head's in my lap. It's usual that way, don't worry none. Fool and I made our peace a long time ago.

Time was, younguns come runnin' in here to have me tell 'em how to live or where gold's to be found. Or love. They's always lookin' for love. They don't come 'round so often now winter's headin' in and the trees are weepin' for their leaves.

Ah, the Tower's upright. You see them fiery bolts tumblin' the walls, and them folks screamin' as they fall to their deaths in the rocks and sea? Some say disaster's ahead, some enlightenment. Me, I buy disaster.

Look there, the Lovers' hands almost touch. But their fingers never quite cross that last inch, eyes eatin' right through each other. No, honey, I can't force 'em neither. I been flippin' these cards for a lifetime and their fingers never make it. A damn shame.

Speakin' of love, you look a gal who's had someone leave you to wither on the branch, like summer's last apple. Now, nothin's ever helped by tears. For a dyin' of the heart I've found there's cures don't hurt as much as love and cost less. Let's see what card's next— that card on top, closest to your breast.

Don't fret so over the Reaper, darlin'. A skeleton, yes, but all in finery, see? Smooth leather boots, ostrich plumes. And clutched in his fingers that bloody blade gleams, waitin' one final thrust. Hear him singin' his love song? Music old as these hills, and darker than a moonless autumn night. That's right, stroke him gently, daughter—a true lover at last. He'll be waitin' for you down by the crossroads tonight, to take you with him. It's a long and wild ride to his home, so you better dress warm.

The last card—turn it over and look. A blackened, goat-faced devil points to me? Don't mean nothin'. Now cross this old palm with your gold, lass, and you be on your way. I have others waitin' for comfort.

Revelations

Gerard Daniel Houarner

When I was young," Richard said, pouring the wine he had brought the night before, "I used to steal money from my mother's purse after she beat me, and buy so much candy I got sick eating it."

Carmen laughed, bowed her head in thanks for the wine, and took a sip. "When I was a young girl," she said, ladling aromatic stew on two plates of rice she had brought out from the kitchen with the stew pot, "I stole a Barbie sequined gown from my cousin, who my Mom thought was the perfect child, just so her doll wouldn't look as nice as mine."

Richard smiled. He tasted the meal she had prepared and rolled his eyes in mock ecstasy. "When I was in junior high school, I set a small fire in the chemistry lab once when I didn't have my lab reports done on time."

Carmen broke off a piece of bread and sopped up gravy. "When I was in junior high school, I told the principal that my English teacher asked me to sit on his lap after class when all he actually did was give my book report on *Wuthering Heights* a D."

They ate quickly, swallowing chunks of meat and vegetables, draining glass after glass of wine. They finished his bottle and two she kept in a rack on the kitchen counter. The stew pot was empty when they finally stopped eating, sat back, looked at each other. Richard burped loudly. Carmen put her napkin to her mouth and turned her head to the side.

"In high school," he said at last, toying with the bread knife, "I killed a girl's dog when she wouldn't go out on a date with me, and I planted the knife in her ex-boyfriend's locker."

Carmen stood and went to the window. She hugged herself, as if chilled. "In high school, I worked for a man who arranged for older men to see me after school. He arranged for the abortions, as well. That's why I told you I couldn't have children anymore."

Richard went to the stereo and put on a CD of salsa music. Horns blared, voices cried out, intricate percussive rhythms laced the air.

"About the scar on my chest you asked about last night," he said, hips swaying as he danced his way to her. "That was from the first one I killed. She carried a razor in her purse and slashed me through my jacket. I've been much more careful since then."

Carmen turned. Her gaze traveled smoothly from the steps of his dance to the swaying hand holding the bread knife to the subtle, steady smile on his lips. "You never told me you could dance," she said.

He shrugged his shoulders, drawing nearer.

"I always wanted a dancer. My first said he could dance, but when we went to the club he made us both look ridiculous. What I took from the hospital where I worked as a nursing intern gave him a fatal heart attack and could not be detected without specialized tests. Since his family had a history of heart problems, no one bothered to look for anything else."

Richard pressed his body against hers, pushing Carmen back against the wall.

"I'm so glad you wanted us to get to know each other," he whispered in her ear. He put the serrated edge of the bread knife to her throat. "Sharing our pasts as well as our bodies makes our time together so much more satisfying."

"It's not every man who opens himself up to a woman," she replied, staring into his eyes, hands splayed against the wall.

Richard stabbed her once, expertly, in the carotid artery and threw her to the ground. "I'll stay a little while longer," he said, crouching beside her as she lay pumping blood on the floor. "So you're not alone as you die."

"Thank you," she croaked, a halo of blood surrounding her head, "but you don't have to."

Richard winced, dropped the bread knife, passed a hand over his stomach.

Carmen caressed his pale face with bloody fingertips. "I drank all the antidote before dinner."

Revival Meeting at the Breakfast Bar

Gary Jonas

The old woman was hungry.

She moved along the sidewalk with her walker. How long had it been since she'd had a decent meal? Even she could not remember. Up ahead, she saw an all-you-can-eat breakfast bar. A church bus was parked in the lot. The banner on the side of the bus read: ATLANTA REVIVAL TABERNACLE.

The old woman entered the restaurant. It was filled to capacity. People crowded in the lobby waiting to be seated. The old woman moved up to the hostess.

"Excuse me, dear," she said in a shaky voice. "I need to use the little girl's room."

The hostess smiled and pointed to the back of the restaurant. "Through the double doors on the left, ma'am. Would you like some help?"

"I've been doing this myself since before your parents were born, dear. But thank you for offering."

She placed the walker in front of her and began the long trek through the restaurant. Halfway through, she saw the table with the church youth group. A large group of dashing young men, all studying to be preachers, no doubt. And they had an empty chair at their table.

She was hungry, so she moved toward them.

"Pardon me, young man, but I'm so very hungry. Would it be all right if I sat here with you so I don't have to wait?"

The eldest of the young men was barely old enough to drink. He rose and smiled. "Why certainly, ma'am. We'd be honored to have you eat with us. Have you accepted Jesus Christ as your personal lord and savior?"

"No, dear. I haven't."

"Do you mind if we tell you about Him?"

"Not at all, dear." She folded her walker and sat down.

One of the young men went to the food bar and brought her a plate filled with eggs, sausage, hash browns, pancakes, and a blueberry muffin. Another poured her a glass of orange juice from a pitcher. She smiled at them, pleased to have the attention of such handsome young men.

The young man beside her reached for the salt.

The old woman took a breath.

They started telling her about Christ. She listened attentively.

The young man returned the salt shaker to its holder and slowly reached for the pepper. He sprinkled some on his eggs and when he returned it to its place, his hand shook. The man smiled at her and tasted his food.

The old woman took another breath, deeper this time.

The man on her other side reached a shaky hand for his orange juice. He took a sip and slowly set the glass down.

The woman smiled, breathing easier.

The men continued to tell her about the god they worshipped and why she should accept him into her heart. She nodded, asking them to tell her more, which they happily did.

She closed her eyes, feigning fatigue, and took a much deeper breath.

The old man beside her lifted a piece of toast with a decrepit motion. He thought better of it and let it drop to the plate.

The old men forgot what they were saying about their god, and their breathing grew weak.

The woman took one more deep breath.

The vibrant young woman rose from the table. She didn't touch any of the withered old men seated there for fear that they would crumble to dust. "Thank you," she said. "You were all so very sweet."

She left the restaurant to begin her new life.

The Riddle of the Sphinx

Brian Stableford

I don't believe in destiny. I don't even believe in luck. Nothing is mapped out for us, and there's no mysterious force outside of us which touches us with fortune or blights our lives according to its whim. Life isn't a riddle which has to be solved—life just *is*. It doesn't even have to make sense.

Other people called me lucky, of course—and sounded like they were spitting acid when they did it. I was just nineteen years old when I won the National Lottery. I'd only been out of council care for eighteen months, and I'd never had a job. Sure, I bought the lottery ticket with the proceeds of a crime—but it was still *my* ticket, *my* numbers. It was my seven million pounds.

I think it was the first time somebody homeless had won the jackpot. I was the first instant millionaire who'd been sleeping in a cardboard box the night before and watched the draw through the window of a TV showroom. That's why the media took such an interest in me, in my *story*. From friendless orphan to toast of the town; from *nothing* to *everything*. I don't think there'd been any transformation quite as dramatic as that since the days when fairy tales were true.

I was utterly and absolutely helpless. It sounds crazy, doesn't it, to say that I had no idea at all how to spend money, but I hadn't. I'd never had a bank account, never owned any significant possession. I had no idea at all what to do with my money, or with myself. There was no shortage of people wanting to take me in hand, of course—but how was I to choose between them? It wasn't that I wanted to find one who wasn't after my money—I just wanted to find one who would do what I needed him or her to do.

Belinda wasn't the first I latched on to; she was just the one who seemed to be the best. The fact that she had millions herself only mattered because she knew what to do with money: how to use it, how to live with it. Maybe I didn't have to marry her, but I wanted to. The age difference didn't matter to me at all. In this day and age, a woman can look as good at thirty-eight as she did at twenty, if she has enough money.

It wasn't me who started digging into my background. I didn't give a damn about that. It was the *Sun* and the *Mirror*. They were just looking for one more story about the rags-to-riches wonder boy. I didn't encourage them at all. They got into a kind of race with one another, and they wouldn't give up. The winners must have thought they'd hit a bigger jackpot than I had. Belinda had no idea, of course—never an atom of suspicion. I think she'd blanked out the memory that she'd ever had a child. All that stuff about her subconsciously seeking the offspring she'd given up for adoption and me subconsciously seeking the mother who'd given me up, and the fatal attraction that sprang out of our mutual subconscious recognition is just so much psychoanalytic garbage. Anyway, this is the twentieth century. So I accidentally married my mother—so what? What do you want me to do—pluck my eyes out?

Personally, I think the digging should stop now. Incest is one thing, but I think the hints they're dropping now are plumbing new depths of malevolence. It was as much a surprise to Belinda as to everyone else when she found out that my father had been murdered the day before I won the prize—she hadn't seen or heard from him in nearly twenty years. And maybe I don't have what you'd call an alibi, given that I was sleeping rough—but nor do half the population of London. I didn't murder a man to get the money to buy that ticket—it was a different crime entirely. It's all just coincidence, and it's quite bizarre enough already, without trying to add anything more to the pattern. The mystery of how that bastard got stabbed and who did it is just one of those riddles that never will be solved. Why on earth should anyone think that I might know the answer? I don't.

I truly don't.

And I've got seven million pounds which says that no one will ever prove otherwise.

Road Story

Benjamin Adams

As they neared Sioux Falls, the sky turned green and heavy. "Maybe we should think about finding a motel," Mona muttered, staring out the passenger window of their rented Chrysler.

Harry coughed in response, his hands tight on the steering wheel.

The tinny sound of the AM radio hissed through the car; the distant commentator's voice filtered through occasional bursts of static. Grain prices were up. Scam artists from Oklahoma were doing shoddy roofing work. An escaped serial killer from Minneapolis was suspected in the kidnapping of a waitress from the downstate burg of Albert Lea. And every few minutes the far-away voice repeated the information that a tornado warning was in effect for the Sioux Falls area.

"I'm gonna push on," said Harry. "I want to get out of Minnesota for the evening."

"But the radio says—" began Mona.

"Screw the radio." He stabbed out a beefy finger and punched the "Off" button. "There."

Silence, except for the rhythmic thrum of the Chrysler's wheels on the hard concrete of Interstate 90.

"We could pull over in Luverne," offered Mona. "It's not that far—"

"God*damn* it, I'm not stoppin'!" The cars approaching from the west now had their headlights on. A few drops of rain spattered on the windshield. "Besides, this isn't so bad," Harry said optimistically.

Abruptly the windshield was awash with rain, coming down in blinding sheets.

"I can't see a goddamn thing," cursed Harry. He toggled the windshield wiper switch frantically.

They raised up, flicking water out of their way, then fell back down—and stayed down, hanging limply despite the growling of the wiper motors.

He jiggled the switch again.

Nothing happened. The wipers didn't budge.

"What's wrong? Why don't they work?" she asked, her voice becoming agitated.

"I don't know!" he gasped through clenched teeth, squinting his eyes. Through the blurry windshield he thought he could just make out the center divider, and tried to align the car with it as best he could.

"You should pull over!"

"The shoulder's too narrow—I can't. *Why aren't these damn wipers working?*"

A green road sign came up, too blurry to make out anything except one word:

EXIT

Harry took the turn.

After a while, the rain let up somewhat, and Harry uncomfortably climbed out of the Chrysler.

The exit had led to a stretch of country road with a nice, wide gravel shoulder. While they waited, Mona had fallen asleep, so he didn't have to hear her kvetching anymore.

The passenger side wiper was gone completely, having flipped off in the storm.

Fortunately, the driver's side wiper still hung on, barely. Its lug nut was almost completely off the shaft; he'd have to tighten it up with a wrench.

Harry checked the trunk. No tools.

"Goddamn rental," Harry cursed, tightening the nut down with his fingers. The light rain that now fell soaked right through his shirt. "I thought they were supposed to check these things out."

There was a sudden noise on the rain-slicked asphalt, and then a crunching sound on the gravel shoulder; Harry looked up sharply.

A Minnesota State Trooper's jeep had pulled up behind the Chrysler. Inside the jeep, the trooper spoke into his radio handset. Harry couldn't make any of it out. Maybe the trooper was checking in or something.

Harry smiled and waved.

Finally the trooper got out of the jeep. "Please step away from the vehicle, sir," he requested.

"Good afternoon, Officer—" Harry squinted at the man's badge. "—Tompkins. Do you have a lug wrench I could borrow?"

"Sir, please step away from the vehicle," Trooper Tompkins reiterated. His hand moved menacingly toward the butt of his gun. "Place your hands behind your head and lay down on the ground."

Harry stepped away from the Chrysler. "Gravel's gonna hurt."

"*Do it!*" ordered Tompkins.

Never losing his smile, Harry did as the trooper said.

Tompkins stepped toward the Chrysler and peered inside. "That's her, isn't it? The waitress from Albert Lea."

"She's sleeping. Leave her alone," said Harry.

Tompkins reached out and prodded Mona. She rolled toward him, exposing the ragged gash on her throat where it had been slit. "Oh, dear God—"

Before he drew another breath, Harry was on him.

"On to Sioux Falls," Harry said merrily. He slammed his foot down on the accelerator as they hit Interstate 90 again.

"Maybe you shouldn't go so fast," Mona said nervously.

"No problem, honey. If we get pulled over, Tompkins can fix it."

In the back seat, Tompkins smiled grimly and patted his gun.

"No problem," Tompkins said. "No problem at all."

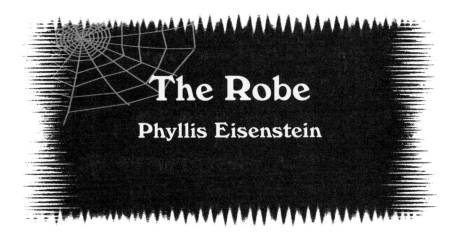

The Robe

Phyllis Eisenstein

Allison found the robe at the thrift shop. It was hanging on the rack in front, the place reserved for new arrivals in the best condition; Allison always looked there first, every Monday. Her husband didn't like her buying clothes at the thrift shop. Somebody else's sweat, he called them, somebody else's ringworm or body lice. Allison would just smile at his protests. He knew perfectly well that people with ringworm or body lice weren't likely to donate clothes to the Salvation Army, and a thorough washing would get rid of anything else. He just didn't like the idea of secondhand goods. He wouldn't even buy a used car.

Allison doubted the robe had ever even been worn. It looked new, not a stain or a rip anywhere. Full-sleeved and floor-length, draping softly as silk, it had an elegant Thirties appeal to it—Allison could imagine Jean Harlow wearing this kind of robe. How could she pass it up? The thrift shop charged ten dollars for it, and she paid gladly.

It wasn't silk, of course. The tag, nestled unobtrusively in a side seam, called it 100 percent acrylic, machine washable, and so Allison washed it and wore it, and her husband finally decided it wasn't so bad, in spite of its questionable origins. It was a robe that felt good, inside and out, good against her bare skin and good to his caressing hands. Allison wondered, sometimes, why anyone would have given it away. Too small, she supposed, or too large, or too long.

The answer came to her two Mondays later at the thrift shop. The cashiers all knew Allison, of course, and would chat if business was slow. This day, the one who had taken her payment for the robe had some gossip to pass on.

"That robe," she said, "you know, the one you bought. I wouldn't tell this to just anybody, but . . ." She lowered her voice to a whisper. "Someone was murdered in it."

"Oh my," said Allison.

"Strangled."

"Oh my," said Allison again.

"So, if you want to bring it back . . ."

Allison shook her head. She wasn't superstitious. She knew death was one of the common reasons things showed up at the thrift shop. She had donated some of her own grandmother's size forty blouses to the Salvation Army after the funeral. "That's all right," she said. "I'll keep it."

But she decided not to tell her husband.

That night, the robe was just as comfortable, just as sensuous, just as elegant as before. And for many months, it remained Allison's favorite lounging garment. Over time, though, it gradually lost its newness, as all garments do. It acquired numerous coffee and jelly stains that would not wash out. The elbows began to wear thin, the cuffs to fray. The hem came down from being stepped on too many times, and Allison, never much of a seamstress, could only tack it up awkwardly. Finally, one night when her husband was out of town on business, and Allison was all alone in their apartment, the left sleeve caught on a drawer handle and ripped through.

Allison surveyed the damage in her bedroom mirror. The robe, comfortable as it still was, looked pretty bad. Time to retire it, she thought, tear it up for rags or just throw it away. She sighed and took a sweat suit out of the closet—not nearly as elegant as the robe, but serviceable for now. She tossed it on the bed and reached for the sash that was tied in a snug bow at her waist.

The sash wouldn't untie.

Silly, she thought; somehow she must have double-knotted it. She peered at the knot. It didn't seem more complicated than usual. She picked at it with her fingernails. It wouldn't budge. The sash itself even tightened as she worked on the knot. When it was uncomfortably tight, she found a pair of scissors and just snipped through it. She was going to throw it away, after all.

The sash lay limp in her hand for a moment, and then the silky length of synthetic fabric turned like an eyeless, mouthless snake and slid up her arm to her shoulder, to her neck, encircled her neck, and began to squeeze.

Her husband found her when he came back from his business trip, two days later. She looked pretty bad by then. But the robe looked as new as the day Allison had bought it, not a stain or a rip anywhere, not even on the sash.

Romance for Violin and Knife, Op. 1

Trey R. Barker

"Carmine," Ana had pleaded, "your dream is absurd."

"It isn't, my love," he'd answered. "I've the skill for any of the world's great orchestras; I lack only the perfect sound."

"You can't find a sound that isn't inside you."

Ah, but listen now! On the new strings, played with the new bow, his music soared. He played the *Scheherazade* cadenza with a passion built around the gentle warmth of his new sound. The high G was perfectly in tune. He grinned in exaltation and tripped over her head. "Perhaps not in me, but in you, Ana!"

The absolute sound. Perfection was not modern innovations: synthetic hair on the bow, synthetic strings on the instrument. Perfection was the past: genuine hair, genuine gut.

Her doubt had infuriated him and now the knife lay near her torso, the blood long since dried rusty brown. He'd left her remains while he wove her hair onto his bow, dried and wound her entrails into strings.

And now she was his elusive sound, the tones of perfection. Her doubt had given him perfection.

Carmine frowned as the tuning slipped. He spotted a tiny crack in the bridge. The strings, still a bit damp, were drying and shrinking slightly, exerting too much pressure on the bridge.

"A new bridge," he said to Ana's hairless head, putting down the violin and reaching for the knife.

A bridge of bone, he thought, carving skin away from her skull; more than strong enough for the pressure of the strings.

"My lovely Ana. You will help me to play perfectly."

Romany

Janet Berliner

Around dawn, J.J. wandered onto the Santa Cruz Boardwalk. He owned it at that hour, like Coney in the off-season.

The smell of candy apples mingled with the steam of freshly brewed coffee. The glaze would stick to his bridgework and the coffee wouldn't taste half as good as its aroma, but he bought one of each and walked toward the railing that faced the Atlantic. An old beachcomber waved. J.J. waved back, spilling a few drops of coffee onto the sand below.

"I smell death."

J.J. looked around. The only other person in sight was a ponderous woman whose dyed titian hair escaped in wisps from a scarf wound around her head.

"I am R-r-r-Romany. I know the future."

The *r* emerged from some visceral point under an embroidered blouse, stretched too tightly over an ample bosom, and tucked itself into a patterned skirt that looked more Aztec than Romanian. Except for her hoop earrings, she looked little like the Gypsies of his imaginings.

The woman stood in the doorway of a small, circular wooden structure, much like one he had seen on Brighton Pier during World War II.

Picking sugar off his molar, J.J. walked around the building, reading the faded clippings on its outside wall.

Romany aids police in finding psychopath.

Gypsy predicts quake.

"Come in, come in."

"I don't think so," J.J. said, tossing his apple core onto the beach. He liked to think of himself as a confirmed psychic agnostic, though as a "prop"—a professional house player for a local card room—his life was infused by superstitious rituals which he did not entirely eschew. Stack your chips this way or that, and you'll be lucky tonight . . . or unlucky. Use your right hand to pick up the cards, your left to toss them out. Wear this shirt, that hat.

"Come in," the woman repeated.

He peered inside at a room crowded with memorabilia: faded, framed photographs; more clippings; a few dusty plastic flowers; a silk parakeet in a rusted brass cage; a Lucite Tiffany-style lamp.

"I can spare two dollars," he said. His bankroll had shrunk. He'd broken a twenty for the candy apple and coffee, and he still had to buy lunch and gas.

Businesslike now, she removed a pair of bifocals from her skirt pocket and put them on. "If I tell you things you no want to hear, you no blame me."

Some world, J.J. thought, fingering eight quarters. Now even Gypsies play CYA.

Everything in the card room depressed J.J.: the windows, encrusted with salt and dirt; the room itself, dense with smokers' fumes; the bums and businessmen who read *Card Player* while taking his money.

He felt his blood pressure going out of control.

"*I see only pain and blood and death,*" Romany had said.

Bullshit, he thought, as he collapsed across the green felt of a short-handed Lo-Ball game. A waste of money.

Next he was in an ambulance. It careened sideways and he heard the squeal of brakes, muffled screams, sirens that seemed to be coming from the end of a long tunnel.

He thought he saw uniforms, hell's policemen come to take him to judgment.

Short of a hold-'em hell, he figured he was through worrying about his bankroll.

To J.J.'s disappointment, he wasn't dead. Less than a week later he was signed out of the hospital, along with instructions to take better care of himself. On his way home, he detoured via the boardwalk. He wanted to tell Romany that she was wrong. He wanted another candy apple to celebrate life.

The round structure looked less dilapidated than he remembered. It had a window in it now, and the clippings had been removed from the outside walls. Behind the window, a Limey in a white apron offered fish and chips.

"Where's the Gypsy?" J.J. asked.

The man shrugged. "You want fortunes, eat Chinese."

J.J. bought a serving of fish and chips, wrapped in old newspaper and sprinkled with vinegar—the way he remembered it in London. A grease-stained headline caught his attention:

BOARDWALK ROMANY KILLED BY AMBULANCE

The ambulance ride. The sirens. The policemen. Her voice: *"I see pain and blood and death."*

She had smelled death that day, all right, J.J. thought.

He smiled as happily as if he had been dealt four aces against the Gypsy's four kings.

"That was a bad beat, R-r-r-Romany," he said, rolling his *r*'s. "A real bad beat."

Romeo and Juliet

Jessica Amanda Salmonson

Now Romeo, unaware that his beloved is merely in a curious state and still alive, drinks poison, and so falls upon her breast. Juliet awakens and—tearful lass!—sticks herself with a dagger in order to rejoin Romeo. Ah, but chance has confused apothecary jars. Romeo, too, awakens from false poison, saddened and chagrined. From Juliet's hand he reclaims the knife and stabs himself beside the heart, to fall again on little Juliet. She, far sturdier than frail appearance says, revives beneath the corpse of Romeo, her self-inflicted cuts well clotted. Lament! Lament! She bashes her head upon the floor of the horrid crypt, breaking skull and nose, then lies unconscious, appearing surely dead when Romeo's eyes flutter. He draws the knife from out of his chest and wails terribly while storming about the tomb, cursing and making blasphemous signs with his fingers, leaving a track of blood with every step. Then with Juliet's scarf he contrives to strangle himself, his face rendered a vivid blue and puffy. How frightful he looks to Juliet, who some minutes later rises to hands and knees, confused and disoriented on account of the damage to her brain. Tears mingle with the blood of her battered face as, with piteous dawning, she crawls to her dear love. There, she bites through the veins and tendons of her own pale wrist and collapses. Romeo's purple face lightens. He coughs, sits up, and sees gory Juliet in a new attitude of wrongful death, and he smothers himself, face pressed to her raw wounds. So both have tasted blood of a virgin and become vampires. On dark nights their voices can be heard: "Ass!" "Ass!" "Ass!" "You're the ass!" "You." "Ass," thus—forever.

The Root of the Matter!

William Marden

The receptionist pushed the frosted glass panel back and looked out at the middle-aged woman sitting nervously in the waiting room.

"Dr. Miller will see you now, Mrs. Simon," the receptionist said.

As she stepped into the hallway behind the receptionist, Diana Simon gagged at the sickening sweet smell of the antiseptic solution always found in dental offices. She shuddered at the whir of a high speed drill. There was no torture she could ever begin to imagine like the whirring sound of the high speed drill.

Actually there was something worse and she trembled as she heard the rocky *brrrrrr* of the slower drill as Dr. Miller leaned into a patient, forcing the head of the drill further and further into the soft pulp in the center of a tooth.

Everybody said Miller was good, but there was always at least one time in each visit when he'd hit a nerve with one of the damned drills.

The sound of the drill stopped, and a moment later he was out of the cubicle.

"Diana, how are you today? What's the problem?"

"No problem, Doctor. Your office said it was time for my semiannual checkup."

"Well, let's get you back into Cubicle 2 and I'll take the X-rays."

That personal attention was one of the things that people loved about Dr. Miller. He came back nearly fifteen minutes later with a concerned look on his face.

"I'm sorry, Diana. I know you hate this, but the X-rays show two new cavities. One is under a crown and could be abscessed. We may have to do a root canal."

"I knew it!" Diana said, sitting up straight in the dental chair.

"Knew what?"

"I knew there was something funny about you," she whispered, feeling the sort of dread you experience in a nightmare when you want to speak but can't. "I went to Dr. Abraham and had a complete checkup yesterday. He said my teeth were perfect."

Miller stepped back, looking from her to the X-rays.

"I don't understand. It's possible for two dentists to read an X-ray differently. But why would you go to another dentist before you came here to see me?"

She slid out of the dental chair to face him, still unable to raise her voice above a whisper.

"Because I've been suspicious of you for years. Every time I come in with no symptoms, you find cavities. And do your root canals and crowns and the rest of your money-making schemes. How many people have you done the same thing to?"

"You're mistaken," he said, stepping between her and the exit.

"I'm going to go to the State Attorney's Office," she whispered. "I know what you've done is a crime, and they're going to put you away, or at least take away your dental license."

She pushed past him when he caught her. She started to scream, but a stinking cloth was over her mouth and nose . . .

She was staring at the light directly above the dental chair. She realized she was tied down into the dental chair, her mouth gagged. Distantly she could hear Miller saying, "Go ahead, Melissa. I can take care of Mrs. Simon myself."

Then he was in the room and taking the gag off her.

"What are you doing?" she whispered.

"I had a nice thing here," he said, taking out a pair of dental pliers. "Now, because of you, it's all over. I'll have to move on."

"Why? Why did you do it, Doctor? You could have made a good living honestly."

Bending over, he clamped the pliers on one of her front teeth and yanked hard, ripped the tooth partially out of her mouth.

She was writhing so hard, the pain shooting through the top of her head in colored streamers, that he had to practically climb on top of her, but he succeeded in immobilizing her head in his left arm and snapped the tooth completely out.

Holding the bloody piece of enamel and stringy flesh in the pliers, he smiled at the moaning, gasping woman in the dental chair and said, "Oh, I didn't do it for the money!"

Throwing the tooth down to the floor, he grabbed her head in one hand to immobilize it again, and as he reached in with the pliers said, "Only thirty-one to go, but we've got all night."

Rosa Two-Coins

Billie Sue Mosiman

In the moist twilight land of New Orleans, Rosa Two-Coins wandered the streets like a wreath of fog, insubstantial. Some who saw her say she was a flower peddler, holding out nosegays for the tourists to buy. "Just two coins," she was heard to call. "For your ladylove, sir, just two coins."

Some say she wore a nun's habit, and when she paused on the sidewalk near the haunts dealing in sickly sweet liquors, she would bless the people who came and went, holding up her rosary in one hand against the sky like a talisman and in the other a tin cup for offerings.

Some called her demon. Some called her saint.

They all knew Rosa was not of this world and, depending on what they believed, either shunned her or sought her out.

On this night of summer mists and sudden showers, when the streets shined like wrinkled foil with reflections of lamplight, Bartholomew wove his way through the French Quarter in search of the mystical Rosa.

Two coins were all he had to his name, having been luckless at the game of chance in this dreadful Crescent City, but he believed firmly that if he found Rosa and paid her the last he owned, his luck would return.

Rosa found him, rather than he finding her. She stepped out from between two cedars near the church steps and said sweetly, "Young mister, for two coins I will return you your fortune."

Bartholomew withdrew from her, afraid for his life. No one had told him that Rosa was a hag with many decades of bitterness written in dark scrawls across her aged face. "I . . . I need luck, Rosa. I need my luck back or I'll be homeless by morning."

He lay the two coins in her extended palm and saw them disappear. He followed her as she turned. They walked for blocks, past warehouses and closed fruit stands, walked on through the cold rainy night. Finally Rosa ducked into an alley and he rushed after her, not to be cheated of his money. There in the alley was a black door, and behind it he found Rosa squatting before a low hearth of embers.

"Please," he said, "won't you help me? I've paid what you asked."

"When you win, betting on credit, will you return to me here and pay me two thousand coins?"

He almost choked. "Two thousand!"

"It will be as nothing to a rich man like you come morning."

He agreed quickly, but jumped when she stood abruptly and handed him a chunk of coal.

"This is dead earth, cold and old, and for you, perhaps lucky. Keep it in your pocket and win your fortune, young mister."

Bartholomew hurried away, drew credit on his good name, and played through the night. Rains came to flood the streets and still he played, amassing more and more winnings.

When morning came he had won so much that he could not carry it all and had to have it put into a leather bag with a shoulder strap. His ship was sailing at noon and he must hurry, having business up-river. He forgot all about his promise to Rosa until he had boarded and the ship left shore. He sighed, then smiled craftily. Two thousand! The old hag was mad.

Before the ship docked again, Bartholomew had said too much about his luck, bragged too often.

The thieves found him asleep in his cot and bludgeoned him until his face was pulp. When the captain found the body, he set into the first landing and called for the authorities.

A day later in New Orleans, Rosa sold bouquets of violets on Desire Street. The sun was out once more, causing Rosa to shield her face with black lace so as not to scare off her customers.

Two men came to her and dropped two thousand coins into her bucket, smiled, and bowed.

"And the bit of coal?" she asked.

"In his gullet, Rosa, to keep him warm in hell."

Rosa Two-Coins cackled madly, covering her mouth with her hands. When she was done with mirth, she sobered, for she had a living to make. Her eerie voice bawled into the street, "Violets for your ladylove, sir! Just two coins, two coins only for your pretty one, two coins . . ."

Rosner's Hat

Yvonne Navarro

Oh, man—look at this!" Rosner snatched something off the ground, then beat it against his leg—*whap whap*—to get the dirt out.

Louie tried to see in the lousy light. "Whazzit?"

"It's a *hat*, man. Don't you have eyes? It's just *too* cool."

Further down the alley, Louie finally got a glimpse of the thing Rosner was bragging about. "Sure it is," he sneered immediately. "Looks just like the one my grandpa's wearing in his old photos."

"That's why it's *cool*, you idiot." Rosner crammed the thing on his head, then grinned. "What do you think?"

Louie opened his mouth to say something sarcastic, then closed it. He had to admit that the hat, although filthy and misshapen, did something for Rosner. But what? "It looks . . . okay," he said cautiously. He didn't know why he suddenly felt it was important to give a positive answer; he and Rosner had been hanging out for years and Louie had always been stronger, meaner, fearless. Theirs was a standard inner-city friendship: both were gangbangers, one was a badass, one was a little smarter. Now Louie felt as though something unseen had switched their positions, moved his simple world into a new scheme. He didn't like it, but instinct kept his mouth shut, as one avoids fast moves around a loose dog suddenly gone mean.

Rosner's grin got wider, his teeth glinting yellow under the streetlights, and Louie resisted the urge to backstep. What the hell was going on here?

Aloud, he heard himself ask, "I wonder who it belonged to?" A stupid question.

To Louie's surprise, Rosner's answer was thoughtful rather than sharp. "I dunno." His fingers reached to caress the brim of the worn, stained felt. "But he's a part of me now."

For some reason, those words absolutely terrified Louie.

*   *   *

"Hey, Ros, I found out something about that alley where you found your hat." Louie kept his voice carefully casual; in the weeks since he'd found that ugly fedora, Rosner had rocketed to the top of the gang hierarchy. Louie could only watch and wish it were him while marveling at the audacity of the smaller man, the viciousness of his moves in the 'hood, the incredible strategy that was oddly natural to a guy formerly too stupid to know which bus went downtown. But Louie was sure it wouldn't last; there were levels involved of which he and Rosner knew nothing, the kind of money, power, and crime depicted only in the occasional national federal indictments on television.

"What's that." Not even a question, Rosner had so little interest.

"Rumor has it that over twenty people have died there in the past two years. The cops call it the gangway of death or some shit."

Rosner grinned unpleasantly. "Yeah. I know."

What could Louie say to that? He shrugged and turned to glance in the store window they were passing, saw the swift change in his reflection as Rosner's hand snaked out and slammed him against the glass with a speed and strength Louie would never have guessed existed in the smaller man. All he could think was *Please, God, don't let the glass break,* and how pissed off his girlfriend, Juanita, would be if he got his face messed up. "Hey, man," he managed to squeak, "what the hell's your problem?"

"How'd you find that info, Louie?" Rosner's voice was soft and dark in his ear, like Juanita's in the middle of the night, but with all the wrong intent.

Too late, Louie realized his fatal mistake in letting the other man know he'd made a call or two to the precinct house—from a payphone, but it was still a question raised, a warning flag sent to the copshop. The kind of moronic thing he'd always thought would make some senior gangbanger eventually take Ros out. They hadn't spent time together since that damned hat had come into the picture, but apparently it didn't take much. A day or two hanging around and the other person started doing all the asinine crap that Rosner used to do, while Ros himself just kind of . . . picked up the wits and strength of his target. "I-I just heard—"

"You asked a little too much, old *buddy.*"

Louie felt steel shoved against the fabric of his cheap shirt before the gun went off, had time to think about just how far Rosner could go in the world—

Now that he had that hat.

Rubber-Face

Brian McNaughton

How had Lucien and I grown so different? We had romped together as infants, been mistaken for brothers at the *lycée*, courted the same woman. . . .

Isabel. Three years in hell had changed her, too. She had blossomed with tropical excess into a vision of Venus. With her blonde hair unpinned and her loose garments scarcely masking her sweaty charms, she would have been unwelcome at a staid dinner in Brussels. But no guest would ever have forgotten her.

I had won her, and Lucien applied himself to his work with demonic energy: in fact with all the qualities of a demon.

And now this demon I had once called brother announced that my career with the king's company and my life were ended.

"You can't blame me for a poor harvest, my friend. If—"

"Ah, but I do! All along the upper Congo, they ship twenty times more rubber than you. Richard, you are too soft-hearted to drive these devils."

"I have not stinted to use the cane."

I looked to Isabel for confirmation. Defying my orders, she never failed to witness punishments. But she lowered her eyes to the table.

"The *cane?* Richard, you poor fool, there is only one cure for idle hands."

He tossed something onto the table. It was the old Lucien, scaring me with a snake or, in this case, enormous black spiders, and I cried out unmanfully.

Isabel merely stared at the display, her face flushed, her eyes bright. I looked again.

I stood up, kicking my chair over. "You are not merely a criminal, Lucien, you are a ghoul."

"I do what I must, Richard. Since you cannot—"

"I shall prove to you that my time has not been wasted. I must go to the village."

"What you must do is pack. My men will escort you downriver in the morning." After a pause, he added: "And madame, of course."

The idiots! Feeding the demand for bicycle tires and raincoats with human blood while ignoring a treasure that might transform the world! I had not planned a demonstration, but I would do more than demonstrate.

I found my way to Malinga's dark hut, she who had told me of the tree whose sap God used to make the first man. I had seen it work wonders that I will not even hint at until my claims can be supported by more painstaking research.

In the meantime I would use it to rid the world of the demon, and then Lucien "himself" would order his troops back to Leopoldville, leaving me free to do my work until I could present its fruits to His Majesty.

I overrode Malinga's warnings and ordered her to apply the resin, an uncomfortable process that became far worse as the paste seared through to my skull. And rearranged it. After a time I recovered sufficiently to demand a mirror.

"You stupid hag! That agony for nothing? This is my *own* face."

"Monsieur Duroc—"

"You dare mock me?" I sent the witch flying with the back of my fist. "I am who I was, Lucien Civin."

I trudged through the darkness and hivelike murmuring, striking aside any who strayed across my path. Why had I gone among these savages in the first place, wasting my time on Richard's fantasies? I would pay him back. Thank God, *everything* is permitted here.

I had meant to send him downriver in irons. Isabel would stay. But when I burst into their bedroom and beheld them embracing, I went mad. I tore him loose and shot him five times.

"No, Richard, please!" she screamed.

What, her too? I was tempted to use my last round on the sarcastic bitch, but I flung her back and took her as I had dreamed so long of doing.

"Oh, Richard," she sighed. "If only you had been like this before . . ."

I was terribly confused, but I knew now that I was Richard Duroc. The body on the floor belonged to the demon, Lucien Civin. But when I stumbled to the mirror, it was the face of Civin, created by Malinga's magic, that returned my horrified stare.

I tried to tear it off, hooking my fingers into the nostrils. I was a bloody mess by the time Civin's men restrained me.

Now I am in irons on my way to judgment, but they don't know I have concealed a spoon.

While they sleep, I will scrape this hateful face down to the bone and set everything right.

Rude Awakenings
Tim Waggoner

On Monday morning, Stephen's clock radio started blaring at 6:15. But before he could roll over to turn it off, a giant green lizard with huge rubies for eyes did it for him.

Stephen sighed and rubbed the sleep out of his own eyes. The lizard, all seven feet of it, glared down at him, rubies glittering.

"So are you going to get up, or do you plan on sleeping the whole day away?"

Stephen didn't reply. His head throbbed something fierce. He chided himself for going out and drinking so much on a Sunday night.

In the bathroom he discovered a large spider with the head of his Uncle Maurie perched on the toilet.

"Hey! Do you mind?" it said.

"Yes, I mind very much. Get the hell off!"

"First come, first served, pal!"

Stephen didn't feel like arguing. He turned around and headed for the kitchen, where he found a naked woman covered with quivering leeches making herself a bowl of cereal.

"Good morning," she said brightly as she moved past him and into the living room.

Stephen started the coffee. He'd make a full pot. He knew they would just complain if he didn't.

When the coffee was done he poured himself a cup and went into the living room. The leech woman was sitting on the floor, a pile of her black glistening friends around her. A couple had fallen into her bowl, but she didn't notice. She spooned one of them up and popped it in her mouth and started chewing.

She had turned on *Headline News*, which was fine with Stephen since he couldn't read his paper: a rotted corpse with an equally rotted vulture's head was sitting in his easy chair, perusing the paper and leaving bits of itself smeared on the pages.

The ruby-eyed lizard stomped into the kitchen, followed by the human-headed spider. They ransacked the freezer and then began arguing over who was going to get to eat the last Eggo.

Stephen glanced at the wall clock. Six-thirty. Usually his dreams went away after about fifteen minutes, but all these were still quite solid. He sighed. It looked like it was going to be one of those days.

He got up without a word and headed straight for the bathroom. He locked the door, used the toilet (he was disgusted—the spider had forgotten to flush), and hopped in the shower. But before he was finished soaping up, the door splintered apart and the giant lizard burst in, the others right behind him.

"You better not have used up all the hot water!"

After fighting over the towels, the hair dryer, the toothpaste, and the deodorant, they rifled through the contents of his closet until they found clothes that fit—or in the case of the lizard, clothes that could be stretched and torn until they were at least draped more or less over the body. The leech woman was disappointed he didn't have any dresses, and the spider with his uncle's head had to settle on wearing an old hat. They were all still depressingly solid.

"Well, off to work!" the spider-thing said cheerfully.

"I hope you four don't think you're riding with me," Stephen said. "There's not enough room in my Escort."

The lizard interlocked its fingers and cracked its knuckles. It grinned, ruby eyes twinkling. "There will be."

The spider scurried down the hall toward the front door. "I get dibs on the front seat!"

The other three dream-figures hurried after, shouting protests.

Stephen plopped down on his bed and massaged his aching temples.

God, he hated Mondays.

Runaway

Don Herron

The angel rocked gently in the moonlight, as Joe drove the crowbar deeper under its base. He yanked the bar violently from side to side, breaking the concrete seal, then threw all his weight onto it. The shadow of a wing fell across his face as the statue toppled.

"Yeeeeeehhhaaaaaaaa!" Joe screamed. "Yes! *Yes!*"

Slowly at first, reverently, the angel bowed toward the earth. *Slo-mo,* Joe thought. *Cool.* But in an instant gravity seized it, bringing it savagely down on the adjacent tombstone, like a starving animal falling upon a carcass. Half a wing snapped clear off the statue, and the head rolled thumping across the grass. *Cool!*

Joe felt the earth jar suddenly under his feet. *Heavy mother, too.*

"Hey, Tony, did you catch that, dude?"

"Sure did, man. Took it *down!*" Tony slid around the tombstone, dropping onto his knees next to the angel. He shook his can of spray paint in his right fist before turning it on the stump of the neck. In the moonlight the glistening layer of fresh paint looked much like blood.

"*The* artistic touch, dude. You *are* the genius going to make this place rock."

Hopping on bent knees over to the pedestal, Tony deftly swept his tag over the chiseled name SKOOG.

"A dumb ass name anyhow, huh, Joe?"

"Stupid *and* weird. What a place."

Joe looked out over the cemetery: acres of headstones and statuary rolling away down the hill and climbing up the next. Hardly a normal-sounding name in the lot. Salbok. Drkula. But prime, virgin territory. On the way in, looking for a good observation post, he had not spotted a single tag or maimed form.

They had set up lookout in the shadowed doorway of a crypt. The Kroll family vaults. Couldn't get the heavy metal doors open, even with the bar. A good enough spot to kill the six-packs, though, make some noise, see if anybody was going to show up. *Not a soul.*

And now it was time to get down to serious fun.

The dirt under his feet heaved gently.

"Yo, Tone, do you get earthquakes around here? Little ones, maybe?"

"What are you talking—"

Water suddenly flooded the air around them. Joe couldn't hear Tagger Tony for the hissing, hissing like angry snakes.

Sprinklers! Man, really wailing sprinklers! Laughing, he grabbed Tony by the arm, dragged him stumbling down the hill, out of the thick spray. His clothes felt like weights. He dripped water as if he had fallen in a pool.

"Whoa! Must be on automatic cycle, Tone . . . Really nailed us."

"Joe—I can't get my breath—can't—"

"We're out of it. You'll be okay," Joe said, then the hissing sound swept around them again. He inhaled water, began to strangle. Blinded, he staggered backward, arm across his face. Came out into the air. *Air!*

He couldn't see Tony, only spouts of water gushing, splashing off the gravestones, coming closer.

Closer?

Turning, Joe started to run. *Forget Tone, man. Run!*

Just before noon the following day, the body of Anthony White was discovered by the edge of the ornamental lake near the center of the cemetery. Death by misadventure was finally declared in his case. His lungs were filled with water, and something, some kind of wildlife, had been at the exposed flesh of his face and hands.

Not long after, White's friend Joseph West was reported missing, and was presumed by authorities to be a runaway.

But in the hollow earth deep under the Kroll vaults, Joe did not feel like a runaway. His torso was pinned under a mound of dirt, his head hanging down from one side, wrapped in some kind of moldy sack or something. He couldn't feel his arms anymore. But his legs were free, and the things were back to gnawing slowly at them with their long, loose teeth. In the darkness, Joe felt another toe tugged off by a tongueless mouth.

No, he just hadn't run away fast enough.

Rural Legend

Nancy Kilpatrick

At twilight, Old Mother Rainey's cypress cane stabbed the dry earth, then her dust-covered sandals shuffled forward down the dirt road. She'd travelled this route her long life, the highway to the left, the Okeefenokee Swamp on the right. The swamp bred life, all kinds, and death. Of course, so did the highway. The swamp had always been here, but the highway hadn't; now that it was, things were easier.

As she reached the curve in the road, her stomach growled. The bog in the swamp came into view. She sighed, squinted her aged eyes to focus better and ran a skinny hand through her hair as if she still had a lush head of it.

Nearer the bog's edge, the air changed. Hot and humid to chilly. Insects stopped scuttling. A fake coral paused, suddenly comatose on the road. Others might be put off, she thought. And she was hungry. She knocked the snake into the slimy water with her cane.

The fallen log stretched out into the green water. A terrible stench rose up through the static air. Old Mother Rainey gingerly stepped onto the wobbly log.

Once she'd gotten her balance, she poised there, stock-still, cane in one hand wedged into the bark, nearby cypress branch clutched in the other.

Good thing it wasn't long before a car pulled onto the shoulder. Something about how the light hit this curve and bounced off the trees blinded the driver. And then, of course, they'd caught a glimpse of her. . . .

Pennsylvania plates. Figures. The driver got out, young fella, city type. The woman stayed inside. "Hi!" he called.

Old Mother Rainey just stared at him.

The woman, still seated, said something, then got out of the car, as women do. "You all right?" she called.

The sky darkened suddenly. Often did this time of day. It took the glint off the curve, which was fine. Wasn't needed now.

The old woman was as feeble as Janice's grandmother, as her mother was becoming, as she herself would be one day. As her daughter would end up. The dismal thought caused her to lay a protective hand on her swollen stomach. Bill was too suspicious. If people couldn't help one another, well, they weren't worth much.

Janice walked to the dirt path, Bill following. "We just stopped to make sure you're okay," she smiled. "Do you . . . live around here?"

"I am from Cthulhu," the old woman said. Her voice creaked, like the boughs of a tree bending in the wind.

"Ca . . . *who* loo?" Bill asked?

Janice ignored him.

The old lady didn't answer.

In the eerie gloom, the old lady seemed to blend with the cypress trees. Each time a car passed, both she and the trees glowed silver. It was as though she were not flesh, not even bone. . . .

"Come on, Janice—" Bill began.

"It's okay," she told him. Just an optical illusion. What else could it be?

Suddenly the old woman's arm moved, the one holding on to the branch. She lowered it and pointed to her stomach as another set of headlights flashed. In that moment, Janice saw a hollow cavity. Within the emptiness, something moved, like a fetus. . . .

Before she could stop herself, Janice hurried forward.

"Don't!" Bill yelled, but it was too late.

"Why, it's a . . . ," Janice said, reaching inside that eternal womb.

The cord slithered up her arm. Around her body. Strangling her. Slipping behind her to Bill's body. Finally reaching the living fetus within her belly. . . .

"Nothing mysterious at all," the stocky cop said to her new partner, hiking up her slacks as they got out of the cruiser. "Light draws 'em. They step onto that log, and wham! Weight sinks 'em. Then the gators come."

"What about her?" the skinny one said.

"Who?"

"That old woman . . ."

The chunky cop laughed. "Old Lady Rainey. The old woman who eats babies before they're born. My ma told me, and her mamma told her, and I tell my kid. Don't make her real."

"Well, she *was* there."

"Still is." The cop walked out onto the wobbly log and pointed to a cypress directly across the bog. The tree did resemble a skinny old woman, balding on top, stick arms, and a big gap with a knot in the middle where her stomach, or her womb, would be.

Sarcophagus

Stephen Dedman

Hubbert handled the coal-brown skull gingerly, rather like a nervous actor auditioning for *Hamlet*. The glint of gold was unmistakable. "You're sure?"

Finn shrugged. "It's beyond reasonable doubt. The skull's too distorted for a facial reconstruction, but most of the teeth are still intact, and all the gold is . . . well, you must have suspected before now, Hub. Where did you find it?"

"Early Cretaceous," said Hubbert, glumly. "We found the skeletons of a whole pack of *Utahraptor,* some of them beautifully preserved. We were excavating the largest, and Carol found this in the stomach. We thought it had to be a hoax at first, something some creationist had planted . . . but all the tests confirmed that it was the same age as the rest of the bones, about one hundred twenty million years." He stared at it, and smiled sourly, showing his gold teeth. "I didn't know I was that old; I don't feel a day over forty. A few weeks later, one of the volunteers found a Teflon pad—the same sort I had put in after that jeep accident last summer—a few yards away. It looks like the raptor had its stomach ripped open by one of the others—they were only about eight feet tall, but they had ripping claws about fifteen inches long, real killing machines . . ."

"Have you spoken to Sarah?"

"Sure," replied Hubbert, grimly. "Three years ago. She phoned during the wedding reception to scream abuse at Carol and me. I tried phoning her last year, to congratulate her, but she never re-

528

turned my calls." Sarah, Hubbert's first wife, had won the Nobel Prize for Physics for her proof that time travel was possible. She had accepted the money without smiling and had told no-one what she planned to do with it, though it had long been rumoured that she was building a time machine.

Finn had known Hubbert long enough to accept that some of Sarah's vindictiveness was justified. "Maybe we're misinterpreting this," he said, cautiously. "Maybe she's forgiven you—she can afford to be magnanimous—maybe she sends you back as a research project, and something goes wrong . . ."

Hubbert snarled metallically at him. "Is there anything we can do? Legally, I mean?"

"I doubt it. Even if you could convince someone that this is manslaughter—which is difficult when you're obviously still *alive*—what proof do you have that she was responsible?" He shrugged. "Look on the bright side: you're going to get to see live dinosaurs. There must be worse ways for a paleontologist to die."

Hubbert swore. "Just between you and me, Rich, I prefer my dinosaurs dead. I *hate* reptiles, and Sarah knows it." He shuddered. "I just hope it's quick."

"I'm sure it will be," Finn assured him. He sat down and stared at the skull for several minutes after Hubbert had left, then jumped as the phone rang. "Richard Finn."

"Is Professor Hubbert there?"

"You just missed him," replied Finn.

"Blast. Can you take a message? I'm one of his students—we just found another piece of gold. It looks a lot like a wedding ring, but it's been pretty badly mangled. It was in the stomach of one of the raptors—not the one that ate the skull, another one. We've found what look like toe bones in two other skulls, too, and there's lots of scars on most of the skeletons. It looks like there was a real feeding frenzy going on. Anyway, do you know when he's coming back?"

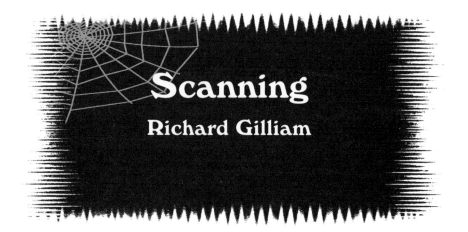

Scanning

Richard Gilliam

Because Marvin Duran was busy at his computer altering grocery prices so that key items scanned significantly higher than advertised, and because he wasn't really expecting any employee to bring a semiautomatic rifle to work, and particularly because he would have thought meek little Jimmy Harris with the very pregnant wife to be the least likely of employees he had cheated out of a profit bonus to go postal and shoot up the place, Marvin Duran was greatly surprised when a spray of bullets pierced his upper torso and even more surprised at how clearly he could think of these things within the scant seconds before he lost consciousness and died.

The first thing Marvin noticed when he awoke were the signs on the doors. The doors marked LOUNGE and REST ROOMS interested him less than the doors marked PARADISE and SHORTCUT TO PARADISE. The door marked OBLIVION interested him not at all.

The door marked SHORTCUT TO PARADISE had pictures of fine homes and people in luxurious surroundings, so Marvin opened it, stepped through the portal, and proceeded down the hallway.

The first indication something was amiss came when Marvin smelled the odor of burning coal and heard what sounded like a train approaching. There was a platform, much like a railway platform, and a person dressed in a conductor's suit beckoning Marvin forward.

"Is this the train to Paradise?" asked Marvin.

"This is Earth return," said the conductor. "Please stand back. The train will be here in a moment."

"Earth return? The sign said 'Shortcut to Paradise.'"

"I'm sorry, sir, that's last week's sign. We just haven't taken it down yet."

"The sign said 'Shortcut to Paradise,' " insisted Marvin. "I don't want to return to Earth."

"There's nothing I can do, sir," said the conductor. "I just work here. You'll have to take the train back to Earth. The Paradise door will be available to you again after your new lifetime."

"New lifetime!" Marvin exclaimed.

"There's no need to shout at me, sir. You can't expect every door in infinity to be labeled correctly all the time, can you? Signs aren't my job. I can't help what the sign manager does."

"Can I speak to the sign manager?" asked Marvin, trying to remain calm.

"Afraid not, sir. The sign manager doesn't show himself around here much. Not many of us employees like him. He cut our transit bonuses so he could get kickbacks for routing passengers onto higher-cost lines. You'll have to contact Transit Central, not that they'll do much."

Marvin grimaced. "Okay, how do I get to Transit Central?"

"Oh, that's easy, sir. They have an office in the lounge. When you get back to the station room after your new lifetime, just take the lounge door."

"I'll walk back to the station room."

"I wouldn't recommend that, sir. You'd likely wander into oblivion. They say that everyone gets brought back from oblivion eventually, but you'd probably wait more than a lifetime for the rescue party."

Marvin sighed. "Another lifetime? Since this is your sign manager's fault, the least you can do is send me back handsome and rich."

"I wouldn't know, sir. Won't see the manifest until the train arrives. The train just moves you between the stations anyway. The choices are pretty much yours. Could be that how well you make choices during your lifetime affects how well you make choices later, but I couldn't tell for sure. Like I said, I just work here."

The screech of metal on metal startled Marvin as the train began to brake. It was a large train, longer than Marvin could see. There were cars of all descriptions, some of which looked like chariots and some of which looked like imperial carriages. There were elegant coaches and ordinary coaches; farmers' wagons, snow sleds, and factory trucks; and a few that bore no inscription and others that were entirely black.

When the train stopped, Marvin looked at the car in front of him and shuddered.

"This is your car, sir," said the conductor. "Please step aboard quickly. Others are waiting."

"A grocery delivery truck," said Marvin, trying to chuckle inwardly. "A lousy grocery delivery truck."

"May you have a better trip this time," said the conductor, his voice deep and his face solemn. "The manifest says that you'll be an orphan, that your mother will die when you're born prematurely after your father kills himself and his employer. . . ."

Scarecrow's Discovery

Jeff Strand

Completely shredded. Arms and legs torn from the body, leaves scattered everywhere, the burlap head impaled on a wooden stake—the scarecrow had been mangled beyond repair. Ray stared at the mess for a moment and sighed.

"Guess some crows were kinda peeved." Hank grinned. He was his best friend, though Ray had no idea why.

"Shaddup." Ray shook his head in frustration. "Lousy kids. No respect for a man's property. Third one this week."

"What kids? Haven't seen any kids around here since your Charlie started serving his five-to-ten."

"Shaddup." Ray bent down and yanked the scarecrow's head off the stake. "Look at this twisted stuff they did. Like one of them pagan ritual sacrifices or something."

"Those can be a problem."

Ray tossed the head back on the ground. "It's not losing the scarecrows that bugs me, it's that these kids need to learn respect. Between the ages of twelve and seventeen, might as well just lock them in the basement."

"I know. Darn kids."

"They need punishment."

"I know. Darn kids. So how're you planning to teach these whippersnapper rapscallions a lesson?"

"Charlotte's got an unstuffed scarecrow inside that she made to replace the first one. Tonight I'm gonna wear it like a costume and just wait out here. Once those kids show up, I'll jump out at 'em and scare the livin' pee out of their rotten little disrespectful bladders. They won't be back."

Hank chuckled. "You're actually going to stand out here all night?"

"If that's what it takes."

"What if they go after one of the other scarecrows?"

"I'm takin' the others down first."

Hank shook his head in mock sadness. "Ray, I hate to be the one to tell you this, what with us being best friends and all, but you're an idiot."

"Shaddup. Now take your lazy butt over to the barn and help me finish up our work."

After three hours, Ray was starting to get really sick of waiting. The scarecrow costume was itchy and uncomfortable, his back was getting sore from leaning against the wooden post, and he was falling asleep. Since he had a perfect view of the road from here, there was no need for him to be completely motionless, but nevertheless his muscles were starting to stiffen.

But it would all be worth it if those kids showed up.

He estimated it was around midnight once they finally did. He saw them off in the distance, two figures, probably young children, both carrying flashlights. As they got close enough to be illuminated by the streetlight, he saw that they *were* children—a boy and a girl, no older than six or seven. Far too young to be doing stuff like this. If this was the future, society could kiss itself good-bye.

They headed right for him, the boy carrying a small grocery bag. They stopped about five feet in front of him, and the girl wrung her hands together in excitement.

"Give me the electric knife," she said.

"You got the 'lectric knife last time," whined the boy. "It's my turn."

"Fine, be a big baby. Give me the cleaver, then."

The boy took a large, shiny meat cleaver out of the bag and handed it to her. She grinned, then took a step toward Ray.

He suddenly lurched forward, arms outstretched, and let out a horrific moan. *"Leave me aloooooooooooone!"*

Their first reaction, terrified shrieks, was exactly what he had expected. Their second reaction, the girl slashing his leg with the meat cleaver, was not. Ray dropped to the ground, gritting his teeth in pain but forcing himself not to cry out. He quickly pulled off the scarecrow mask.

"Wait!" he winced. "It was just a joke. Just a mask, see?"

The children stood there, staring at him as if unsure whether to run or not. Ray tried to stand up but the pain in his leg was too great.

"I need you to do me a favor," he said. "Go over to my house and knock on the door—get my wife, okay?"

The children were silent.

"C'mon, hurry up! I'm really bleeding!"

Finally, the girl's face broke into a wide grin. "This is great! Tonight we don't have to practice on those stupid scarecrows! We can do it with a real-live person, just like Mommy and Daddy showed us! Won't they be *proud?*"

The boy nodded, the electric carving knife started to whirr, and Ray began to scream.

Screamer
Gordon R. Ross

Screaming at funerals can be unnerving. Not that it doesn't happen often. Too often.

Being a mortician, you'd think you'd get used to it, wouldn't you, Sam? But when the shrieks come from the coffin?

There you stand, Sam Hutchins . . . a thin, bent figure in threadbare black suit and worn, black loafers. Alone in the rain. Alone, above the hole the grave diggers dug.

You're waiting for them to return and fill in the space above the box and the vault. They better return soon, Sam, or you'll catch your death. But the moans!

After all, Gerald was a ventriloquist. Not a very big one, either. He is certainly dead. You drained him . . . personally. Even though he hadn't a lot of blood left to let, after . . . You watched it thin as the water flushed it, pushing it out through not-yet-collapsed arteries. Pinkish streams spilling from slashes in wrists, ankles, and other places, flowing out and down the indented gutters of the tilted stainless steel table.

You pumped Gerald's stomach, flushed the thin little midget's bowels, introduced formaldehyde into veins and organs, sewed up cuts, packed orifices, and stapled lips shut. You bathed, shaved, covered bruises and wounds, and clothed him.

Then, Sam, you placed Gerald, doll-like, in his tiny coffin. Just like someone was going to be there to see him planted.

But Gerald had no one, did he? No one but you, Sam, and his blasted dummy, Gerry. Gerald's carved wooden alter ego was almost as wooden as Gerald himself, wasn't he, Sam? And Gerry lost all life when Gerald went, right? In fact, right now Gerald's exact likeness is having his own cremation . . . in the mortuary fireplace.

The act wasn't much even when Gerald was alive. "Wooden" pretty well defined both of them. Now, at least, Gerry could be "warming up the audience" back at the mortuary . . . if anyone drops by. Kind of fitting, isn't it? Sort of adds to Gerald's send-off out here in the cold and damp, waiting for the grave diggers, and the dark.

Gerald hadn't had a booking in three years. Even the folks at the rest home where Gerald vegetated grew tired of him. It got so bad, he used to drop around your depressing funeral home, two doors down, to visit you, just for company.

He died there Tuesday. So you, Sam, being elected coroner and knowing a corpse when you see one, even one as hard to judge live or dead as Gerald; you, Sam, took care of the official pronouncement and paperwork. As executor of Gerald's will as well as sole beneficiary, you knew how much was to be spent on the funeral and how much was not. You followed that request to the letter, didn't you, Sam?

But the screaming? The shrieks from the open grave? You can still hear them, can't you? Are you certain Gerald is really dead?

Maybe somebody substituted Elixir Number Four for embalming fluid. No. That's just a joke, Sam. A *joke!*

Maybe the moans are the wind. The wind through the bare branches of the scrub oak, the naked bushes, the iron fences, and the carved stones. Maybe. Maybe not.

Can ventriloquists delay their replies . . . throw their voices so far away it takes hours, days for the sound to come back? Can they, Sam? Delay their cries, their screams, as they are being killed?

Oh, oh. Here comes company. You thought you might have to finish the job yourself, didn't you?

The back loader sure beats shovel work, doesn't it? They'll be done in minutes and maybe then the screaming will stop. It's hard to hear over the sound of the motor, anyway.

Quiet now, isn't it, Sam? Rerolling the sod and placing the stone puts a finish to it. Time to crawl into that nice, comfortable old Cadillac hearse. Oh, I'm sorry, "crawling" into a hearse sounds so morbid. Forgive me. Time to get back to the office and tend the fire, Sam.

Golly. Looks like you've got a crowd at the door, Sam. Most of the folks from the nursing home. Did you get the time of Gerald's funeral wrong? Of course not. And none of them cared about Gerald, either, did they?

But why is the sheriff's car here? Could it be the smell? The smell of burning flesh?

The smell coming from the fireplace?

Are you certain which one was the dummy?

Is it *you*, Sam?

The Second Time Around

Adam-Troy Castro

Now!" the doctor shouted.

Igor turned the crank, lowering the mad doctor's second creation from the lightning storm that raged above the castle. They had both spent years preparing for this moment: the moment that would erase the tragedies of the past, redeem the once-honorable family name, and immortalize Victor Von Frankenstein in the annals of science.

The slab hit the laboratory floor with a thud that echoed hollowly through the ancestral keep. The creature began to sit up. He was almost as tall as the first one, but not even remotely as grotesque: The general reception given its predecessor had taught the mad doctor a few lessons about the importance of good public relations. Not only did this creature look entirely human, it also had the face of a nobleman and the bearing of a saint.

Would it be a poet? A scholar? A great scientist like its creator? Or perhaps the ultimate ambassador, capable of ushering humankind into a new era of world peace? The possibilities were endless! But so were the dangers . . . "Igor, are you sure you didn't get this brain from the same place . . . ?"

"Of course not," the hunchback assured him. "I got this one from the lab next door. The jar was labeled NORMAL."

"Oh. That's all right, then." Frankenstein faced his creature and spoke with a voice of complete authority. "You there! Look at me!"

The creature cocked its head to one side.

"Come here!"

It hopped off the slab, barked, and ran on all fours to lick its astonished master's face.

The Second Vial

Lawrence Schimel

Doctor Mornay came back into the examining room and said, "We're going to have to run some blood tests. Lucy will be in in just a moment."

"Is anything wrong?" Wendy asked.

"I don't think so. This is just routine stuff. But we have to be absolutely sure you're in good health before we can give you the insurance." The doctor smiled at her. "Don't worry, it's just a prick of the finger."

Yeah, right, Wendy thought as the doctor left. *Just a prick of the finger. They'll probably take two vials of blood like doctors always do.*

Little goosebumps broke out on her skin when she thought about the injection. Wendy shivered, suddenly very cold in just the light hospital gown. She looked toward the door, wishing Lucy would hurry up. It was always best to get these things over with as quickly as possible, so she wouldn't regret her decision.

At last the nurse came in, carrying a tray with swabs and syringes. Sure enough, she drew two vials of blood. The entire time, Wendy stared at the nurse's name tag, repeating the letters of it over and over again so she wouldn't look down and see the needle sticking out of her flesh: LUCYLUCYLUCYLUC—

"You can put your clothes on and wait outside," Lucy said as she put the Band-Aid on Wendy's arm. "We'll be ready for you in just a moment."

Wendy got dressed, rolling her sleeves down to cover the Band-Aid on her arm. She went into the waiting room and stood in front of the window until the receptionist noticed her. She signed some more health-related forms, then the receptionist asked her to take a seat until they were ready.

Wendy sat and read through some issues of *People* that were at least two years out of date until she heard her name.

"Ms. Circo?" Lucy called. "If you could just sign one more thing, you'll be all set."

Lucy handed her a clipboard with a pen. Wendy scrawled her name on the line. "Hey, this writes in red. Is that OK?"

"Of course it's in red." Lucy smiled at her. "It's only valid if it's in blood."

Wendy glanced down at the sheet she had just signed, skimming the top:

This is a contract between Lucifer (hereinafter to be referred to as the Insurer) and Wendy Circo (hereinafter to be referred to as the Insuree) for the possession of the Insuree's immortal soul (hereinafter to be . . .

Wendy looked at the pen in her hand, twisted it open. Inside was a vial of blood, sticking out of the nib like an ordinary cartridge.

Lucy smiled at her again, showing a lot of teeth, and said, "What did you think the second vial was for?"

The Secret of Bees

Tim Waggoner

David Bell was an avid hiker, but in all his years of trekking through woods and up and down mountains, he had never encountered anything like the monstrosity that crouched snuffling before him.

It looked something like a cross between a bear and a boar, huge, covered with black fur shot through with gray. It had six tree trunk limbs, and a tail like a possum's, except green and scaly.

Whatever it was, the creature was right in the middle of the trail, regarding David with mean little pig eyes, its breathing hot and labored like an old furnace that might blow at any time.

Now, anyone else who encountered a monster like this in the wilds of southern Ohio would have done one of two things: run like hell or freeze, petrified.

But not David Bell. For he knew the secret of bees.

David had been five when his father taught him the secret.

He'd been sitting on the front lawn of his parents' house, playing with a handful of army men, when a bee flew up and stung him. He jumped as if he'd been shot and ran inside, into the comforting arms of his father.

His father took him into the bathroom and rummaged around in the medicine cabinet for something to put on the sting.

"I hate bees," David said sullenly, fighting tears.

"No reason for that," his father said as he searched. "They do a lot of good. They make honey and pollinate flowers."

"Why do they have to sting people though? I wasn't doing nothing."

"Anything," his dad automatically corrected. He found what he was looking for, a bottle of some clear liquid which David didn't recognize. David closed his eyes while his dad dabbed some of the medicine on his sting with a cotton ball.

"Bees go after people because people scare them," his dad said. "You probably disturbed it while you were playing."

"But if they're scared, why don't they just fly away?"

His dad finished and tossed the cotton ball in the waste basket. "Because it's not their nature, I suppose. But it's pretty easy to avoid getting stung if you know the secret."

"Really?" David said skeptically.

His dad knelt down before him. "Sure. The first thing you have to do is not run away. When you run away, they'll just come after you and sting you. And the second thing is harder, but it's even more important. You have to try real hard not to be afraid. Animals sense fear. Even bees. And if they sense fear, they'll attack you. But if you can keep from being afraid, they'll leave you alone." His dad stood up and smiled. "Okay?"

David nodded. His sting hardly hurt at all now, and David gazed up at his father as though he were the wisest man in the world.

So David didn't run from the monster. And he did his very best to keep from feeling—or at least showing—any fear. He stood still and concentrated on keeping his breathing even and his pulse steady.

The creature cocked its head, as if it were puzzled. Then it lumbered toward him.

Stay calm, stay calm. Remember the secret of bees. David repeated it mentally to himself, like a mantra. *The secret of bees, the secret of bees.*

The monster came up to David and sniffed him, first one leg, then the other, its thick black snout bumping into David's crotch at one point.

The beast backed up a step, as if completely confused over what to do next.

David allowed himself a tiny smile. It was working! By God, it was . . .

Then the monster seemed to shrug. It stepped forward, fastened its jaws around David's leg, and bit down.

David realized something as the eternal darkness rushed to claim him: his dad was an idiot.

Serial Killers

Stephen Woodworth

The driver turned up the volume on the radio, and the news-reader's deadpan voice swelled inside the bus. Janet didn't want to hear it but listened anyway, as did everyone around her.

". . . residents discovered another victim of the so-called Sunday Slasher this morning in the dumpster of an apartment building on Rosemont Boulevard. Like the previous victims, the body of Mrs. E. L. Lester had been ritualistically mutilated. Police still have no clue to the identity of the killer who has claimed the lives of five men and seven women in the city . . ."

His curiosity satisfied, the bus driver turned the radio down. The passengers relaxed into contented detachment again, their hunger for headlines sated. *Like vultures*, Janet thought cynically.

No, not vultures, she decided. Like people in a doctor's office, waiting for their names to be called. Not morbid. Expectant.

The bus turned, jostling her against a middle-aged man in a business suit. She renewed her grip on the overhead handrail, and scanned the faces of the passengers around her. The old man with the quavering jaw. The young housewife silently absorbed in her paperback romance. The gum-chewing teenager slouched in evident boredom. Strangers. All avoiding even the most casual interaction. In the dim light of the bus's interior, Janet fancied she could see the cold auras that isolated each of them from the others. It was hard to believe one of them might be a murderer . . . or even a victim.

As she looked around, Janet inadvertently met the gaze of a handsome but morose-looking young man in the rear of the bus. His eyes were watery and red-rimmed, as if he had cried recently.

Janet flashed a brief but cheerful smile at him, then focused her attention on her feet. She shifted her weight to try to relieve the dull ache in her left arch, and wished her boss understood that waitressing required functional footwear. She shut her eyes and wondered what to do with her evening. Maybe she would call David.

The bus jarred her eyes open again, and she realized that the next stop was hers. She pulled on the wire above her to notify the driver. A bell rang. The bus swung over to the curb beside a weather-faded bench and a bright blue sign. Janet nudged her way through the crowd and stepped out into the night.

A small group of passengers disembarked at the stop, then drifted apart in their separate directions. With her tired feet, Janet didn't want to walk all the way around the block to get to her apartment, so she cut across the parking lot of the supermarket on the corner and turned down the alley that ran behind her building. She felt exhausted; maybe she wouldn't call David after all.

A shadow suddenly blocked her way. She looked up from the ground, and her brow furrowed as she tried to distinguish the figure before her. "Oh . . . hello," she said hesitantly, recognizing the young man from the bus. Those eyes. "Live around here?"

The man merely stared at her, trembling, on the verge of tears. "*Please*," he rasped. And with a flick the blade sprung, glittering, from his fist.

Janet screamed and bolted back the way she had come. But the man was quick. He caught her around the waist, knocking the wind out of her, then threw her up against one of the dumpsters that lined the alley.

"*Please*," he repeated, desperation in his voice. He held the knife up for her inspection.

Squirming from his grasp, she thrust her knee in his groin. He doubled over, and she took off down the alley, stumbling as she kicked off her high heels to run faster. With superhuman effort, the man lunged after her and caught her in a running tackle. They dropped onto the asphalt, his weight grating Janet against the rough pavement, skinning her arms, her legs, her cheek.

He turned her over on her back and sat on her, straddling her waist. Sobbing, she saw his pained face through the strands of her tousled hair. "*No!*" she screamed, and struggled to free herself.

"*Please*," he begged. Then pressed the cold steel of the knife's handle into her palm.

Her sobs quieted as she saw the knife in her grasp. She looked into the yawning blackness of his pleading eyes, plumbing the depth of the despair. She recognized it now, had seen it in the eyes of everyone on the bus, everyone on the street. It ran like a polluted river through their lives, sweeping their consuming loneliness and accumulated misery along on its ebony tide. Her eyes dilated to receive the rush.

And her fingers closed around the knife's handle.

The man showed her how to make the incisions.

Hours later, Janet languidly rose from her bed and went to her apartment's sole window. Black stains spotted the pillow where her mascara had run, and tell-tale streaks had dried on her face. Other stains covered her dress. She felt hollow, worthless, saturated with grief. But most of all, she felt alone.

And the only consolation she had as she scanned the blinking black nothing of the city was that, somewhere in the darkness, she, too, would find her savior.

Shades of Gray

Sue Storm

Under the night, the sky is wide and gray and full of water. The water falls down and pats the earth.

Gently.

Like a blind child searching for earthworms.

Drenched, Janey's flannel jammies stick to her skin. She opens her eyes and sees the world's colors reduced to shades of gray. Even the clowns on her jammies sport gray noses.

Not cold. She thinks about earthworms, thinks about chopping them up, putting them in her baby sister's chocolate pudding. Janey smiles. Her fingers curl, making ten crescent moons. Under her bare feet, the ground shifts and gurgles, spits out worms.

"I could, you know." Holding absolutely still as worms slip through her toes. "I could."

Janey hates her baby sister.

Above, the black shape of her mother moves behind the curtain in the baby's room, back and forth, back and forth. The baby cries from gas, or colic, or maybe a new tooth. Janey doesn't care. What matters is her mother's arms around the baby, not her.

Not Janey.

She wants to go inside. But then she'll hear it, her mother singing: "Oh, la, oh lala, la lollie-oh."

It is *her* song, not the baby's song. Her mother steals it for the baby, everything for *the baby*—the little beast taking her place.

Janey stamps her foot in the mud, lifts her head to the sky. It's not even her house anymore. It's the baby's house. Baby powder in the bathroom. Baby clothes in the washroom. Baby toys all over the floor. Her mother never let Janey leave toys all over.

"It's not fair!" Janey wants to scream it, but rain pours in through her open mouth and runs down her throat, choking off her words. *Not fair.*

She clicks her teeth. *Look Ma, no cavities.* Her mother never looks anymore. *I got an A today. I made two baskets in gym. Look at the picture I drew. Look, look!* No one looks. *I hit the boy next to me, the one wearing the silly dark suit and the tie.* Gray tie. Stupid gray tie. *Look. I hit him and blood spilled out everywhere.* Not red. Not blood then, not really, but something, *something bad. I'm bad, Ma. I hit him, and he never even moved.*

Look, Mommy.

Please, look.

Nothing happens. Nothing ever happens, only the baby crying and her mother singing. Her father—why won't he do something? Big hairy arms, sweet smell of pipe tobacco. Used to rock her on his knee, tickle her till she screamed.

Tell her goofy jokes.

"What do you get when you cross a hippopotamus with an elephant?"

"What, Daddy? Tell me, tell me?"

"An elephantoplotamus, that's what!"

Tickle hands and screaming. Big, fuzzy hugs. So warm. So very warm.

Not cold.

Not really.

Water streams down. Everything looks gray. Even her hair, gray hair slicked against a gray head. Like a seal bobbing in the sea. She wants to shriek at the night.

Go away!

But it stays, of course.

Janey almost makes it to the door before a dark and mottled hand pulls her back.

"Oh-la, la-la-la, lollie-oh, sweet, sweet baby-oh."

The woman murmurs to the child against her shoulder. "Sweet, sweet, baby-oh." She breathes in the baby's smell, all innocence and powder, the yeasty scent of unformed dough. Her fingers twitch on the baby's blanket.

Twitch, twitch.

"Claire?" He stands in the doorway, his voice soft and full of pain. She ignores him.

"See," she tells the baby, stopping in front of a shelf filled with pictures. "See, that's your sister." Little girl, maybe six, in a swing high against a bright blue sky. Blonde pigtails, freckles.

"Your sister, Janey."

One tooth missing in a wide, bright smile that loves the camera.

"She's—she's gone. Away." The woman's voice catches, then rushes on. "But we won't forget, will we? Never. We'll sing her song and look at her pictures and never, ever—"

The man's arms encircle his wife and daughter. Her tears soak his sleeve. "Let it go, Claire," he whispers.

"Let her go."

Under the night, the sky is wide and gray and full of water. The water falls down and pats the earth.

Gently.

Like a blind child searching for earthworms.

Janey turns over and hugs the boy with the gray tie.

Shadrach

Adam Niswander

Galen Thomas loved fire.

The dancing of red, orange, blue, and yellow flame mesmerized him, sent him to a place where life was right, where time stopped moving, where he could control the world.

The building on the corner of Fourth and Main—the former Temple of the Hours—had been abandoned by the sect five years before. For some curious reason, no one had purchased it in the interim. As a result, the strange, old, gothic monolith stood untenanted and falling into decay.

Twisted gargoyles and demonic figures leered down from the edge of the high gabled roof, and mosaics of weird alien creatures capered and gamboled in an endless pattern, circling the upper levels.

Galen could already picture it as a blackened stone shell.

And that is why, at midnight on Friday, he entered the narrow alley beside the five-story structure with his bag of tricks: flashlight, gasoline, paraffin, fuses, and a lighter.

The old wooden door off the alley gave him no trouble.

Once inside, he secured the entry and stood in the darkness. He clicked on his flashlight to examine the walls, then broke into a wide grin.

Wood . . . everywhere—wainscoting, paneling, huge frescoes carved out of ebony and teak hung on every available wall. And large tapestries, faded and worn, but intricately woven.

A thick carpet of dust overlay everything, but the interior was in remarkably good condition. Other than being dusty and bereft of furniture, it appeared ready for the next occupant.

Why did the Templars leave? he wondered.

A wide, banistered staircase led upward from the far corner of the room. Galen made his way to it carefully.

Floor by floor, he explored the building. Each level seemed more promising than the one before. Dozens of rooms, alcoves, and chambers boasted ever more intricate decoration. Sconces, paintings, intricately carved panels—the place was a treasure-house for curio dealers.

Why hasn't it been stripped? he asked himself silently.

There was no security. The alley door had been easy to pry open. Why had the local vagrants not ripped the building to shreds, taking its obviously valuable assets to pawnshops and antique dealers?

When he reached the fifth floor, however, he stopped. An unwilling sigh of wonder escaped his lips.

In the middle of the room, like a centerpiece, stood a large wooden altar, and above it, stretching upward to the peak of the dome, rose a sculpture of the Phoenix.

This would be his masterpiece.

Kneeling, he opened his bag and began his work.

He packed the base of the altar with wads of paraffin, then ran a trail of gasoline to the four corners of the room.

Backing down the stairs, he continued floor by floor until he reached the bottom of the stairs. Midway, he took a surgical mask from his pocket and donned it, as protection against the fumes.

Just as he was about to step onto the ground floor, however, he heard a sudden stirring of activity. Footsteps clattered on the floor. He sensed, rather than saw, shadowy figures moving toward him.

A strange chanting began, echoing in the emptiness.

Galen retreated back up the stairs.

Behind him, the harsh sound of strangely clad feet rattled on the stairway.

Finally, breathless, Galen crouched behind the altar, quaking.

Could some of the Templars still be alive?

Desperately, he searched his memory for anything having to do with the Temple of the Hours.

To his horror, he did remember.

The manner of their deaths had stirred his imagination.

They had been found in a forest . . . in a clearing . . . dead of self-immolation.

Just then, the chanting stopped.

Trembling, he stood and clicked on his flashlight.

He was surrounded by loosely robed figures. When he directed the beam of his flash and focused on the nearest, he could not suppress a gasp.

Within the robe, the light revealed a charred skeleton holding a candle and a wooden match.

Galen opened his mouth to scream just as the fleshless fingers struck the match.

* * *

The Temple of the Hours did, indeed, burn brightly that night, and Galen Thomas found his heaven in the fires of hell.

Shattering the Sonata

Devon Monk

Leona knew she should wear a stiff black concert gown when she faced him—that's how he liked it. She chewed on her bottom lip and straightened her sweatshirt. Her jeans were faded and had holes in both knees, and she wondered why she hadn't thought of changing.

But today was only practice. If he didn't approve of how she dressed, she would—Leona paused. What would she do? Lock him in the closet maybe, or throw him out the French windows. She smiled at the thought and opened the door.

The room was dwarfed by a huge grand piano. It squatted, glossy and black, like a poisonous spider in its web. The windows were curtained with lace, allowing thin gray light to bleed through, stringing patterns across the floor. Leona felt the room close around her like a damp blanket as she walked across the smooth, cold marble. She tried not to look at him, tried not to make eye contact. But he was staring at her, angry, deaf, dead.

Her eyes flicked to the top of the piano. Less than half a man, the sculpture of Beethoven sat above the keys, a master, a tyrant, even in his death. Pupilless eyes bored into her forehead as she sat on the hard bench.

Hadn't she turned the statue around the last time she practiced? She shuddered. Someone had turned him back to face her—glaring, hating.

After tomorrow, she would tell her parents. No more practices, no more sweaty palms and sleepless nights. And no more of Beethoven's burrowing anger.

She set the metronome to fifty-two. Her fingers shook as the tempo ticked out the pace of her torment. She lifted the lid and touched the keys. She knew the piece—*Moonlight Sonata*—had memorized it for tomorrow's concert. But a spot about halfway through was giving her trouble.

Beethoven glared down as she began. Softly, softly, the music slipped out from under her fingertips. She could feel his heavy gaze, almost hear his anger as she slaughtered the next stanza. Her hands trembled as if it were a real performance, as if life or death hung on the outcome. She glanced up, met his scowl, and realized she was breathing hard, her fingers curled into fists as if expecting a slap across the knuckles.

The statue hated her, hated how she played his music. His anger was a heat in the still gray room. Leona bit her bottom lip and began again. Her teeth pressed harder and harder together, as her fingers convulsed across the keys. Blood trickled down her chin and she scowled, matching Beethoven's furious concentration, trying to be perfect, trying to become the music.

Breathing came in rhythm to the metronome. Her foot pumped the sustain pedal like the bellows of a forge, feeding the music with her fear. Now was the hard part, where B natural turned sharp. She flew into it, trying to go beyond her fear, beyond her own clumsiness. She felt as though she were on the edge of a slippery cliff, running to stay balanced, or to move fast enough before the cliff ended and she fell.

I'd give anything to get through this, she said silently.

The music built, steadied. Her fingers suddenly took position, stroking the keys of their own accord. *Moonlight Sonata* filled her with its quiet séance quality, until she felt lifted, an observer of her body as she played and played.

Athletes feel this way, she had once read, when they perform for medals. She watched as her body rocked with the music, arms bent, then extended, eyes closed, and music pouring out an emotion more powerful than passion.

Then the music stopped.

Everything was wrong. Leona watched as her body rose and glared down at her. Her brown eyes were hard, angry, her forehead creased with disapproval.

Leona felt a shock of heat as fingers contacted plaster. She looked up at her own face and realized she was no longer in her body.

Frozen in plaster, she tried to scream, but she was only a statue with no air, no lungs, no heart.

"The lesson is over, student," her voice, no, Beethoven's voice said.

She was lifted, tipped, thrown. For a moment, the gray ceiling came closer, then pulled rapidly away as she fell. She hit the marble floor in silent agony and shattered into dust.

Sherri Goes to the Office

Yvonne Navarro

My mouth dropped open when I walked into work and saw Sherri sitting at her desk.

"Charlene, may I see you in my office?" Her boss's voice was strained and subdued at the same time, infinitely preferable to his normal high-volume hollering. Pat and Debbie were sitting at their desks staring at Sherri, faces blank and quiet. They were lucky; *I* was going to be the buffer zone—my desk was between theirs and Sherri's.

"Close the door, please."

I did as he asked and stood there, waiting. This ought to be good.

Bryan cleared his throat. "I-I guess you saw Sh-Sherri out there."

"Little hard to miss."

"I thought she was . . . what I mean is, Human Resources sent me a memo. . . ." His voice faded and he looked helpless. I liked that.

"She's dead."

"Well," he said brightly. "There you go!"

"What?"

Bryan shuffled papers around on his desk, succeeded only in making more of a mess. "I want you to go and tell her that."

My eyes widened. "Excuse me? I don't *think* so. You're her boss—you do it. Better yet, call that dorky guy from H.R. 'I'm sorry, Sherri, but you can't work here anymore,' " I mimicked. " 'You died in a boating accident two weeks ago. We all went to your funeral.' " I shook my head for emphasis. "I just push paper, Bryan. No way." I strode to the door, pulled it open, and stepped out, then stuck my head back through the opening. "But you'd better be careful," I pointed out smugly. "Couldn't firing someone just because she's dead be considered discrimination?"

Word got out, of course, but the managing partner of the firm clamped the place tight before the news made it out of the office— God knows we didn't want any publicity. People from five floors drifted by in steady numbers, their expressions going through a predictable routine—curiosity, horror, disgust—before they fled. A few rude fools gagged but shut up at the scowls on our faces. Okay, so Sherri looked a little drippy, but what did they expect from someone who'd spent three days trapped underwater in a wrecked speedboat in Lake Michigan? Try giving *that* problem to the shampoo commercials. Her skin was a fetching combination of green and purple, more suited to Halloween than the coming Easter holiday—speaking of which, maybe that whole resurrection thing had something to do with it. If Jesus moved a stone out of the way when he wanted out, who was to say Sherri couldn't have dug her way out of the ground at St. Mary's Cemetery?

Everybody else was too chicken, so around three o'clock, after sitting next to her all day—did I mention she smelled kind of like an open can of sardines left on a radiator?—I decided to talk to her. Bryan, the big coward, had hidden in his office since morning, and the dork from Human Resources had come around the corner, taken one look, and ran for the bathroom. Wimps, one and all.

"Hey, Sherri," I said casually. I tried not to sound like I was holding my nose. "Can you, uh . . . talk?"

"Whadda wan'?" Her voice sounded like her tongue and vocal cords had gone through a cheese grater; mercifully, she'd ignored the phones all day in favor of going through her filing, a massive pile of papers that had come out of Bryan's office the Friday before her accident.

"Well, you know," I said carefully, "there's a . . . little problem here."

Sherri glared at me despite one foggy eyeball that tilted toward the direction of the ceiling. "Wha'?"

"Well," I said again. "You're not really supposed to be . . . uh, at work. You're kind of . . . well, *dead*."

She rolled her eyes, a horrifying thing to see. "I *know* tha'. I'm nod s'oopid." She sniffed as though she had a bad cold and I flinched, suddenly afraid water was going to start dribbling out of her nose. "Bud I'm nod goin' an'where undil ma filin' id done."

"Ah." I sat back. "You know, I could do that for you."

The look she tossed me was more dreadful than the first. "Forge' id. Id's ma responsibili'y, an' I'll hannel id. An' I won'd leab undil id's all done."

"Oh." I glanced at my other coworkers; they looked pained, but what could we do?

"On'y pro'lem id," Sherri continued, painstakingly sorting the papers on her desk. "Ah can'd seem da 'member da damned albabet."

She Waits . . .

Kay Reynolds

I was running up Plume Street with Manolito Wu, leaving a trail of broken glass and petals. Raiding florists is not my idea of a fun midnight excursion, but when a guy like Mano enlists your aid, you change your plans. Mano's awfully good with knives, you see. And very persuasive.

We piled into the car. Mano floored it and said: "Have another drink. You're looking mighty white."

No joke. I'm not keen on graveyards, day or night. Mostly, I don't think about them at all. But Carcosa Hills is all Manolito Wu cares about. That and Lela. That's our destination—Lela Butler's grave. I swallow another drink. And another.

We pile out deep inside the cemetery, back in the section reserved for charity cases. Next we unload our floral heist and tromp over to Lela's marker. There's still a lot of stuff strewn over the ground which strikes me as odd. Especially when I see what it is—garlic braids and wild roses. Mano's been here before.

Manolito does most of the work. Afterward, he just stands there. I wanted to say something but can only come up with, "It looks nice." Mano stays quiet. So I follow up with, "Lela liked flowers, did she?"

"Lela liked me," Mano says. "She was my family."

I nod like I understand but that's not true. The gene pool that makes up Manolito Wu and the one that went into Lela Butler were oceans apart and on different planets.

"We were both wards of the state," he said. "Both raised in foster homes. Do you know what that's like?"

No, I don't. All I can do is shake my head.

"Nobody wanted us." There's no bitterness in his voice, only an acceptance which chills me through.

I thought about what I'd heard . . . dangerous games about how the two hustled together. One would bait the fish while the other waited. Instant shark attack. Usually, nobody got seriously hurt. Mano and Lela were after money, not blood. Then one night, they picked the wrong mark—or, more likely, the mark picked them, set them up. When it was done, Lela was dead and Mano was messed up. Bad. When she was buried, he was still in the hospital. The cops are still clueless. It was less embarrassing to let Mano go.

Ankle-deep in garlic and roses, Mano said: "I knew he was wrong. When it went bad, I couldn't stop him. He messed me up, Bracey. Then he hurt her. And I had to watch."

I started to say, "I'm sorry," but we weren't alone any longer. A tall gent had strolled up on us, very well dressed, handsome in a *GQ* kind of way. He smelled like old money and something else. . . . I was thinking that if we're not supposed to be here this late, then neither is he . . . except he looks like he belongs.

"You simpleton," GQ says. He kicks at the garlic with the toe of an immaculate boot. "Do you really think this will stop me? That it will stop her?"

"I don't care about stopping her," Mano says back. "All I want is to stop you."

He's so fast. Something flashes from his hand and hits the guy's chest dead on. I hit the ground, rolling into a heap of floral shit. Tangled, I slide down right into this guy . . . who is suddenly smelling *really* bad. His head rolls back. There's blood on his mouth where's he's bitten himself with exceptionally interesting teeth. But he's looking surprised, too. Right. I'd be surprised to find a wooden dart sticking out of my heart. Almost anyone would.

Mano stalks over. There are metal blades in his hands now. "We've never used a pimp, bloodsucker, and we won't be using one now." He spits on this guy, although GQ—dissolved like he is—is past caring. Mano looks disappointed. "I thought it would take longer," he says, "like it does in the movies. I thought he would suffer more."

This is not the sort of conversation I'm really comfortable with. The booze is burning holes in my stomach. What I'd really like now is to throw up. "I've got to go," I say.

Mano nods, waving me on. Heading back to Lela's grave. I can guess who's waiting for him there.

Hysteria grabs my upper hand, the words almost come out: "Give my best to Lela. Be seeing you!"

But I don't think I want to see Manolito Wu ever again.

Shift

David Annandale

Neilson's first thought was that the lens was cracked.

He'd bought the telescope at an estate sale. He liked the look and feel of it: a long brass tube, heavy with age. He wasn't sure how well it would work, but it was too gorgeous to pass up.

He set it up in his backyard, aimed it at the moon, and bent down to look. The focus was all off, but he was surprised to see he'd sighted the moon properly on the first try. Undefined white light filled the view. But there was also a splayed collection of lines. Neilson grimaced, disappointed. He hadn't noticed the cracks when he'd looked the telescope over earlier. He reached out to focus.

And the cracks moved. A wavering twitch, awakening, like the first electric charge of life.

Neilson stood up. *Cobwebs?* he wondered. He walked around to the front of the tube and blew on the lens. Then he went back and looked through again. Still there, still twitching, but not like threads in a breeze. He adjusted the focus, and the lines disappeared.

So did the moon.

Neilson blinked. "Um," he said. He straightened up. No, the moon was still there, still round. He must have jiggled the telescope. He bent down, tried again, and this time the moon appeared, huge and detailed. No cracks.

This was great. Neilson felt his face break into a little-kid grin. He hadn't expected such a clear image with this museum piece. He felt a surge of warmth towards the cold metal, nostalgia for a period five generations back.

He looked at the moon for a few minutes more. Then, curious, he deliberately put the moon out of focus.

When it came back, he realized that the light he had seen before wasn't the moon's. It was too pale: faded, white becoming grey, and dying. The lines were there too, writhing now. They jerked, spasmed, and twisted, a Dali spider on speed. Neilson suddenly had the impression of looking not through a telescope, but down a tunnel, where something huge waved in the light at the other end.

The lines lunged at him.

Neilson reared back, knocking the telescope into a spin. He was sure he'd seen jagged ropes shoot down the tube for his eye. He shook his head, trying to think, *No, don't be silly,* but failing. He left the telescope where it was and marched into the house, where light was bright, electric, and measured in watts.

Only it wasn't.

There are shifts of paradigm, of Doppler, and of focus. Shifts of state and shifts of feeling. And there are shifts that are all of these, bigger than tectonic, but as easy to get into as a glance gone wrong, and irrevocable beyond the laws of any god. Neilson had looked awry, and had shifted. This was the gift of knowledge, a terminal epiphany that was given to him as he stepped into a house now empty except for the pale limbo light. He had a good three seconds to savour the privilege of the gift before fear, a reflex delayed by shock, overtook him.

He heard a sound behind him. Uncoiling, moisture and steel, tentacles and teeth, the sound of the cracks in reality's lens springing for him. He didn't want to turn, didn't want to see, but he did, and in his last second received one more gift:

A fear so huge his old universe could not have held it.

Shooting Evil

Lawrence C. Connolly

Firist they made love. Then he shot her—thirty-six times as she writhed and contorted atop the rumpled sheets of his bed. And then, together, they entered his darkroom and developed the film.

She stood behind him while he slipped the sheet of photographic paper into the developing tray. Overhead, a vent hummed, sucking the fumes from the tiny room while a red bulb bathed their naked skin in bloody light. Neither one of them had bothered to dress. His skin tingled as she brushed against him in the ruddy darkness.

"I've heard that black-and-white film contains silver," she said as she watched the paper sink into the bath of developer.

"Yes," he said, tilting the tray, eagerly watching the paper as it darkened. "Silver is the basis of black-and-white photography." He pointed to a shelf stacked high with plastic jugs, aluminum trays, and spent film. "There's a silver recycling company that comes around once a month to buy my used chemicals and—"

"Do you know the legend of silver?" she asked.

"Legend?" There was something wrong with the picture that was slowly taking shape in the tray. He leaned forward, taking a closer look.

"There's a legend," she said, "that silver has the power to repel evil. That's why you can't see vampires in silver-backed mirrors. That's why silver bullets kill werewolves."

Something definitely *was* wrong with the photograph in the tray. The photograph showed the rumpled sheets of his bed, but the woman wasn't in the shot at all.

She laughed. The sound seemed to come from deep in her throat. "This is great!" she said. "I've always wanted to reveal myself this way."

He felt her grip tightening on his shoulders.

"In the old days," she said, "I used to reveal myself to my lovers by standing in front of mirrors. But silver-backed mirrors are so rare these days, and usually I have to reveal myself by simply flashing my teeth. But this way is so much better than either of those. I'm so glad I've finally got to meet a photographer."

His hand trembled as he pulled the fully developed print from the developing tray. She definitely wasn't in the photograph, and now his mind was reeling, scrambling to come up with a logical explanation. Surely she couldn't be a vampire. That was crazy. Wasn't it?

She set her mouth on his neck. She kissed his skin. Her lips felt warm. He dropped the photograph and turned toward her. She smiled at him in the red light. Her incisors grew, folding down like the protractible fangs of a snake. Her jaw clicked as it came unhinged. And then, in a red blur, she was on him.

They stumbled backward, falling, slamming into shelves and tumbling to the floor while aluminum trays and plastic jugs rained spent developer over their naked bodies. He felt her teeth push against his neck. He felt the sting of her teeth breaking his skin, and then she was screaming in his ear—bellowing words that he did not recognize. She arched her back, rearing away from him while her face erupted into rivers of yellow pus. He pushed her away. His hands went through her, ripping her skin and shattering her bones.

The red-lit darkroom filled with his screams as he scrambled away from her decomposing body. He stood, stumbling toward the door as his bare feet slipped in puddles of developer and decomposing flesh. It dawned on him then. The developer contained silver! The same silver that had repelled her image was now eating away at her flesh.

He found the door. He threw himself against it. He stumbled into the adjoining room—his bedroom, where the unmade bed accosted him with memories of what he had done. He had made love to a vampire! His gorge rose, and then he saw the blood trickling across his chest. She had bitten him. He touched his neck. His hand came away red. Her teeth had drawn blood! Did that mean he was a vampire, too? He felt the developer beginning to burn his skin. He ran into the bathroom and showered. Then he got out and looked at himself in the mirror. His reflection was there, but hadn't she said that mirrors no longer contained silver?

There was only one thing to do.

He was going to have to shoot himself.

Shutter

Gordon Linzner

Click.
  Leaving her brownstone.
  Click.
Crossing Columbus Avenue.
Click.
Waiting for a crosstown bus.
Click.
Boarding.
Click.
Getting off.
Click.
Entering an office building.

Annette Masters sat at her desk, not seeing the ledger before her. Her staff had left. She reached for the raven wig Jeanine bought her on her lunch hour . . . while Annette ate in the company cafeteria.

Delaying longer would only make her more obvious. She just hoped the wig and reversible raincoat would throw him.

Who was he? She only recognized his clothes: plaid, high-collared overcoat; green scarf; shapeless, wide-brimmed hat. And the camera, always hiding his face, always aimed at her.

Three days ago she had noticed him outside her home, following her to work, dogging her on the way back. He never came near or spoke. Confronted, he ran, but was soon back, clicking away. She should call the police, but for what? Taking pictures?

She put on wig and raincoat, rode the elevator down, joined a crush through the revolving door. If she could elude him today, she would feel in control. Maybe failure would discourage him.

He sat on a fountain rim, gadget bag at his side. She tried not to look at him.

Maybe she walked too fast, kept her head too low, moved too stiffly. A low, brittle, too familiar sound echoed above the traffic roar.

Click.

She ran. He did not follow. She knew, though, he would soon be behind her, or waiting up ahead. He was clever.

There was no bus in sight. She glanced at the sky. The sun set early in mid-October, but there was light enough to walk through Central Park. She could be home in twenty minutes.

Annette realized too late she had taken a wrong path. Three teenagers were discussing the contents of a brown bag. No one else was around.

Show no fear or interest. Walk swiftly. Don't look like a victim. But anxiety shone in her eyes, contorted her face. They moved in. Two had knives.

"We don't want trouble, do we, lady?"

Annette shook her head.

"Just give us the purse."

"Hey, she's a fox. We gonna settle for a purse?"

The first teenager looked around, nodded at a dark tunnel. "All right. Let's take a walk, lady."

Annette shook her head. If she held her ground, they might decide she wasn't worth the effort.

Or they might kill her.

A hand tugged her forward. She went with it. Maybe she could use her attacker's momentum to pull free.

Another hand caught her shoulder. "I know that trick. Just come along and enjoy it."

Click.

"Come on!"

"You're being watched," she said.

Her captor looked back. "He don't want trouble, either."

Click.

"Help!" Annette called.

"Shut up, lady."

Click.

"Are you just going to take pictures of me being killed?"

"Hey! He's got a camera."

"Not for long."

Clop, clop.

The muggers melted away. A mounted patrolman appeared at the other end of the path. "You okay, miss?"

"Yes, thank you."

"I radioed for a patrol car. I'd chase them, but you shouldn't be alone."

"I appreciate that."

"Can you describe them?"

"I don't know. They looked ordinary."

Click.

Annette spun. "That man in the plaid coat. He's got a camera. He took pictures."

"Did he? He's not leaving. Here's my backup."

The photographer said nothing to the police, his eyes fixed on Annette. They confiscated the camera. One of the officers knew at once something was wrong.

"There's no film in here."

"What?"

He opened the camera over his partner's protest. Empty.

"Maybe he hasn't reloaded. Check the gadget bag."

"No film, new or used. No equipment. Just old newspaper."

"We'll get a statement, anyway. You, too, Miss."

Annette nodded. Her pursuer's eyes said that whatever he'd been up to was over. He would not wait outside her brownstone again.

She got home late, too keyed up to eat. She locked the door, stripped to bra and panties, turned on the shower, closed the bathroom door, finished undressing, stepped under the warm spray. After a minute, she felt a draft. She shivered, not from cold, then grinned at herself. *The bathroom door didn't shut all the way, that's all.*

She threw back the shower curtain to push the door closed.

Click.

Sibling Rivalry

Brian Hodge

While waiting for the siren, they had between them gone through the expected stages at an accelerated pace: disbelief and shock and anger, with no time like the present for deciding whom to blame.

"It's your fault. If you hadn't bought that thing, treated it the way you did," he told her. "It was unnatural."

"I bought it because I felt so empty inside." She glared, ashen, looking ten years older than when they had gone to bed the night before. "What would've been the harm of you *talking* to me once in a while, after I was in the hospital? I still had things I needed to let out of my system, and you shut me out!"

He shook his head, didn't want to listen to reminders of last year's ectopic pregnancy, the egg that lodged in her fallopian tube and nearly killed her.

"I'm shutting off that damned TV," he said. "Those cartoons, they sound obscene now."

"Don't you dare. Maybe, somehow . . . Tommy can still see them."

He shook his head again, now with disgust. "That's how all this happened—you not living in the real world. Had to buy that creepy thing and treat it like it was real. Like it was alive!"

"We could've adopted. *I* wanted to adopt. *You* didn't. Like if a child hasn't come from your own loins, it isn't worth raising."

He looked across the living room where Tommy lay out of view, blocked by the sofa. Glad he couldn't see that small blue face or the creepy thing on the sofa next to the boy.

"What kind of parents would we have been, anyway?" he moaned. "Couldn't even keep our nephew safe for a week. What'll we ever be able to tell them?"

For a few wonderful days while his brother and sister-in-law were off on the honeymoon they'd been unable to afford five years ago, having Tommy under their roof had been almost like having a son of their own. The arrangement felt consummately right. The boy loved Wiffle ball and cartoons, chocolate chip cookies, and being read to, and the two of them were happy to indulge him. So happy, in fact, she had mostly forgotten about the store-bought surrogate.

"Tell you what I *do* know," he went on. "You're burning that creepy thing. I'll watch you burn it with your own two hands."

She ignored him, or hadn't heard. Wrapping both arms around herself, she began to tremble, staring at the back of the sofa as though she could see through it, where Tommy lay with his eyes crimped shut, blocking out something he hadn't wanted to see. She'd been the one to find him, to frantically dig clots of half-chewed cookie from his mouth. They had gone all the way in, past the reach of fingers. A quick Heimlich had freed the rest, but too late. Too late.

"Tommy can't be gone," she whispered, rocking herself. "It was only last night we read *The Velveteen Rabbit*, and . . . and . . ."

She had been unaware, but he'd been listening from the hall at the boy's bedtime, listening to her read the entire story. He had smiled at Tommy's acceptance as perfectly natural the notion that toys are not alive until they are well and truly loved. Then the smile had wilted from his face as images of velveteen rabbits gave way to realities beneath his own roof.

There was never any telling where he would find it, that creepy thing she'd bought. Underfoot sometimes; at others, positioned in a chair, motionless but seemingly aware of his intense hatred of it. Its freckled face, its blue saucer eyes, its tousled ruff of too-red hair. And that insane grin, greedy for all the love she had intended to lavish on a child of her own and now never would. She'd named the thing Annabel Lee, and each bedtime tucked it into a tiny cradle that he swore he'd more than once heard rocking in the dead of night.

Let her grieve in her own manner, said the psychologist he'd consulted. She'll put the doll away when she's ready.

And if the doll didn't want to go?

It had come with its own adoption papers, and a manufacturer's claim that each was unique in its own special way.

Evidently so.

"You're burning that thing," he said again, in impotence and fear, knowing she would *have* to be the one, because he would never be able to touch it.

Not while it sat with plastic skin so like flesh you were almost tempted to believe.

Not while it perched so brightly on the sofa, its unblinking eyes on cartoons, and crumbs filling its pink, plump hands.

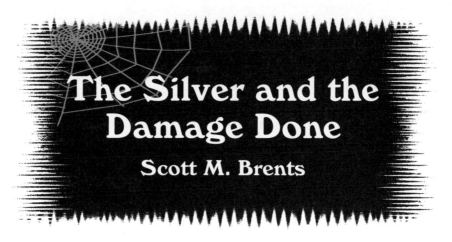

The Silver and the Damage Done

Scott M. Brents

The peasant girl didn't see him crouched in the shadows near the pile of firewood. She had no idea of the evil about to be done to her body.

She wore a long skirt, which was stirring up dust in the yellowish lamplight. She set the lamp down. . . .

She bent over. . . .

And Walter sprang out from the dark and landed on her back, making a swiping gash on the small of her neck with his claws. If anyone came out of the cottage, Walter would kill them too. He was a werewolf, and nothing short of magic would stop him.

He bent down and fed eagerly on the body. He was ravenous and unstoppable.

When sated, he looked up at the stars which were barely visible due to the glare of the moon. There came a commotion from the cottage.

Men were shouting, women were screaming.

Walter smiled, baring his fangs.

The people erupted from the small dwelling, bearing guns, crosses, and torches.

Walter snarled at them all, saliva and blood spewing forth in a spray. He would kill every one of them before they knew what was happening. They were fools, thinking they could stop him.

A lone shot was fired. It echoed through the night like a dying wraith. A bullet—made of a melted-down silver crucifix—ripped through Walter's heart and sent his barbaric soul to hell. . . .

The peasant girl didn't see him crouched in the shadows near the pile of firewood. She had no idea of the evil about to be done to her body.

She wore a long skirt, which was stirring up dust in the yellowish lamplight. She set the lamp down. . . .

She bent over. . . . And Walter sprang . . .

. . . and sent his barbaric soul to hell . . .

The peasant girl didn't see him . . . the evil about to be done to her body. She bent over. . . .

. . . and sent his barbaric soul to hell.

"Man, oh mighty, that stinks. We better tell the coroner to bring the black baggies," Harris said.

Officer Harris had seen a lot of bizarre stuff, but this was damned near ridiculous. They were in the basement of a wealthy individual named Walter Pindowell.

Harris stepped away from the machine in which the corpse sat. On the side of the cabinet, painted in bold red letters blazoned across a full white moon, were the words SILVER DEATH. Harris remembered the old commercial: "The virtual werewolf game, so real that it should be illegal."

And it was. It had been outlawed back in 2003. It swept the country's arcades like a plague and made the machine's developer (Nrutigliqua, Inc.) millions of dollars, but not before interfering with the everyday lives of thousands of people.

The VR properties were so strong that it was impossible to break out of game mode; only when the game was over did the machine release its electromagnetic tendrils from the mind of the player.

Harris couldn't figure out why Pindowell rigged up the machine to play indefinitely. He should have known he would die from thirst and exhaustion.

Detective William Ward had opened the machine, oblivious to the stench of the body. Harris didn't see how he could do it without losing his lunch.

"Here's the problem," Ward said. He handed a coin to Harris. "This fifty-cent piece was lodged on the credit switch." It had the year 1943 on it.

"This virtual werewolf was killed by a solid silver fifty-cent piece. The machine was designed to take newer half-dollars, of a different weight." Ward smiled.

Harris looked at the monochrome blue light that leaked from the visor of the playing helmet onto the visible white cheekbones and blackened gums of Walter Pindowell.

Inexplicably, Officer Harris dropped the coin into his own pocket.

Silver Futures

Stephen Dedman

The ship was still accelerating towards the jump point when the door to the cargo bay opened. Ferris peeked into the corridor, to see Tyrell leaning nonchalantly against the opposite wall, next to the intercom. "Peter Ferris?"

The werewolf froze, and stared. "You're under arrest, Ferris," said Tyrell, not unkindly. "You have the right to remain—"

The naked man pointed at the tiny gauss pistol. "Silver needles?"

"Of course," lied Tyrell. The werewolf sniffed, and then grinned. Tyrell tried to maintain his poker face, without much success; the needler used electromagnets to propel steel darts, and he hadn't had the time or facilities to electroplate any. Could werewolves smell silver—or the absence of silver—even in their human form? "I suppose it's a waste of time trying to handcuff you," the cop replied, hoping Ferris wasn't about to call his bluff. "Do you mind going back in with the wolves until we get back to Earth? Why were you going to Odin anyway? I thought werewolves never left Earth."

Ferris shrugged. "We don't, but how much choice do I have? I was the General's bodyguard; with him dead, there's nowhere on Earth that's safe for me. I was going to hide in the reserve on Odin and not worry anyone." A smile slowly spread across his bearded face. "If you forget you've seen me, I won't have to kill you. You know you've bitten off more than you can chew."

"Sorry." Tyrell reached for the intercom with his left hand, and Ferris changed and leapt. Tyrell fired, but the burst of needles passed over the wolf's head, through where the man's chest had been an instant before. The werewolf's jaws closed around Tyrell's left hand before it hit the com button, and crunched down on his fingers.

Tyrell screamed with pain, then slid an antique silver steak-knife from his right sleeve. Ferris released the mangled remains of Tyrell's left hand, changed back to human form, and rammed his knee into the cop's groin. Tyrell groaned, doubled up, and then simultaneously smashed his elbow into the back of Ferris's head and his knee into his nose. The two men collapsed to the floor and lay there groaning for a few seconds.

"Not bad," wheezed Ferris, scrambling unsteadily to his feet and breathing through his mouth as blood trickled from his nose. He aimed a kick at Tyrell's head; Tyrell grabbed his foot and twisted, but Ferris changed before hitting the ground, slipped out of his grasp, landed softly on his paws, and pirouetted to face him again.

Tyrell stared him down, feinting with the silver knife. Ferris changed yet again, and, from his crouching position, head-butted Tyrell in the nose. Tyrell glanced at the watch on his finger, then kicked up and out with both his feet, throwing Ferris across the corridor. He stood, and reached for the intercom again, but the werewolf was quicker; he changed back into wolf form and leapt. Instinctively, Tyrell tried to parry with his right forearm, but the wolf closed his jaws around his hand and wrist, his teeth grating against the pistol. Tyrell screamed with the agony of the small bones of his hand crunching, stared into the werewolf's amber eyes for a second, and then everything went black.

For a moment, he thought he was dead, and then he realised that it was only the instant of discontinuity as the ship jumped out of real-space. He opened his eyes and saw Ferris, in human form, crouching before him, his cheeks and throat distended by the fist and pistol that filled his mouth. He made only the feeblest gurgling sounds, but Tyrell could feel the scream travelling up the bones of his arm to the bones of his skull. Through his agony, Tyrell realised that the ship was now an unimaginable distance from the moon, and that Ferris— the first werewolf ever to leave Earth—had lost the source of power that enabled him to change shape.

He tried to pull his mangled hand out from Ferris's mouth, without success. "*Now* who's bitten off more than he can chew?" muttered Tyrell grimly, and drew a deep breath. "I guess you're coming with me after all, Ferris. You have the right to remain silent . . ."

Six Deaths More

Judith Post

The nightmares were leading somewhere, she knew. They'd started several months ago with a single recurring dream, but it had been followed by others, each spiraling her farther and farther backward in history.

The first takes her to the Roaring Twenties. Teresa slides into Mario's Duesenberg. His dark eyes tell her he likes what he sees—the new short skirt, rolled silk stockings, and raccoon coat. People stop dancing as they enter the speakeasy. The band plays "Happy Birthday" and two waiters roll a huge, three-layered cake across the floor. Candles sputter, champagne flows as the top of the cake slides open. A machine gun fires, and bullets splatter Mario's head and chest. Teresa tries to pull away, but bullets drill into her abdomen. Her blood oozes from the holes, smearing the floor, mingling with the scarlet pool around Mario before forming a crimson background for her next dream of death.

Her second dream begins with the scent of magnolias and the rustle of weeping willows, sweeping leafy fingers across the lawn. Acres of cotton march to the horizon. In her mouth, there is the taste of fear. Teresa wraps another bundle of silver and hands it to Eliza Mae. All of the other slaves are gone. Teresa's wrapping the tea set when Eliza spies them. "The Yankees, they're comin', ma'am." Teresa's lost everything else: her husband and two sons. "You go," she says. "The Yankees won't hurt you. They're here to free your kind." Eliza sobs as Teresa bolts the door behind her, then goes to the window. "We've got no quarrel with you, ma'am," the soldier begins, but the Yankees' reputation precedes them. She fires her rifle, aware her mission is suicide. Bullets buzz around her, thicker than mosquitoes, until pain sears her chest. Her gun falls from her hands, and she sags against the window ledge. The Yankees won't have her, by God. No Yankee will ever take her. . . .

The blackness that swallows her swims into shape—a face with big, dark eyes. Tituba finishes another story of witchcraft and voodoo, and Teresa shivers with pleasure. She's young enough to enjoy a good scare. In bed, though, she cries in her sleep. Wax dolls dance around a voodoo priest, and zombies rise from her floorboards. "I've had two other cases like this," the doctor tells her father. "The devil is knocking at these girls' souls, trying to make them his own." Her father shakes his head. "A witch is among us." In the morning, Tituba is summoned, along with Teresa and her two young friends. The girls embellish Tituba's stories, throwing themselves on the floor and giggling. The crowd grabs Tituba and two other black slaves from the West Indies. They drag them from the townhall. Judge Sewall orders the girls restrained. By the time Teresa breaks free, Tituba's body dangles from a stout rope, her dark eyes bulging and her tongue thick and swollen. Teresa's nightmares worsen, only this time, instead of voodoo dolls and zombies, Tituba points an accusing finger. The townspeople search for more witches, and before the purge is over, five more lives are taken.

On the couch, she yawns. Coffee can't keep her awake. She slouches onto the cushions and drifts into a new dream: She's late for work. The sky, the scenery, all are swirling mists of gray. She hurries to the subway, racing down the stairs. The legs of a man slumped against the cement wall block her way. He looks up at her, his face unwashed and ashen, his hair a greasy snarl of salt and pepper, his eyes the color of dried dun. Drab rags of clothing hang from him, blending with the gray walls and stairs, the pewter sky, her mounting fright. As he reaches for her with filthy hands, he pulls a coil of rope from the folds of his jacket. The prickly hemp bites into her neck as she struggles, but she cannot breathe. Her lungs burn; her eyes bulge; her tongue protrudes. As she slides into blackness, she sees a face, black and distorted. Tituba's face. And she knows. Eight innocent victims. Her fault. She's paid for her sins twice. And she will again soon. She has only six more deaths to go. . . .

Skeptic

Tim Waggoner

On the glowing television screen a fist flashes and a kneeling, sweaty man stomps the canvas in pain.

"Geez! Did you see that? That had to be the lamest move I ever saw! The purple guy's fist was at least a foot away from the other guy's face!"

"The Raider."

"Huh?"

"The 'purple guy' is called the Raider. And his opponent is Big Mike Martin. Now would you please be quiet? I'm trying to watch."

"*Big* Mike? I think he needs to swallow a few crateloads of Wheaties before he deserves to be called Big Mike."

The Raider grabs Mike by the hair, pulls back his head, and slams it into his kneecap. Mike's entire body quivers with agony.

"No way! Big Mike started acting like he'd been hurt before the Raider even got halfway through his move. It's bad enough that this stuff's fake, but don't these guys even practice?"

The Raider steps away and raises his hands over his head. He turns his back on Mike and struts arrogantly around the ring, drinking in the boos and hisses of the crowd. They clearly favor Big Mike, who has staggered to his feet and is standing woozily beneath the harsh, bright lights.

"Now that's acting. Big Mike really looks like he's in a daze. Then again, maybe that's his normal expression."

"Look, you don't have to watch, okay? Why don't you just go do something else until the match is over?"

"What's wrong? Don't tell me you actually believe this stuff is real."

Big Mike shakes off the effects of the Raider's blow and, teeth gritting, determination burning in his eyes, he runs toward the Raider, whose back is still turned as he shouts taunts to the spectators. The audience roars with excitement as Mike plows into the Raider and knocks him into the ropes. The Raider bounces off and comes running toward Mike, who's ready with an outstretched arm. The Raider goes down hard and just lies there.

"Yeah, but how can you believe in this farce? If this is real, then why didn't the Raider turn around when he heard the crowd cheering as Big Mike attacked? And how come he ran right into Mike's arm? Couldn't he just duck? Or is that too complex a maneuver for these guys?"

The crowd cheers wildly as Mike climbs up on the ropes and launches himself into the air. He lands atop the Raider, who starts spasming as if his nervous system has just short-circuited.

"Did you see how the Raider had his arms up to catch Mike as he landed? This has got to be the most ineptly executed script in wrestling history!"

The TV screen flickers and goes black.

"Hey, why'd you turn it off?"

"Because you spoiled it for me, that's why. You know what your problem is? You've got no imagination."

"I don't think that people should act like something is real when it isn't, that's all."

"Let's just drop it, all right?"

"I mean . . ."

"I said, let's drop it!"

"Okay, okay, it's dropped. Look, you want to go get a bite to eat? It's Saturday night. Should be some teenagers drinking down by the lake."

"All right. But I have to sharpen my claws first."

Slips of Pink Paper

Cindie Geddes

No, it's true," Rich yells. "Really, c'mon! I swear to God!'"

"You seen it happen?"

"Well, no, not personally." Then more quickly before anyone can interrupt: "But my brother did. He comes here all the time. Best food in Reno, he swears. It was last month, corner booth." He motions to the red Naugahyde surrounding them. "Right here. And he was with Tony Rosto, y'know, that guy." His eyes beseech first Larry, then Mark and Stan in turn. They are finally quiet, the name of Rosto stopping them at last.

"So they get the bill and the fortune cookies, and my brother's says his lover will be true to him. Well, no shit. Everyone knows how Diane is. Loyal as a pitbull. And about as likable."

The Scotch-soaked men nod and Rich continues. "Well, you know how it's been on the news and all, about Rosto's divorce and how he was about an ass-hair away from losing *everything?*"

"Yeah?"

"And?"

"The cookie said, 'Your financial worries will disappear like smoke.' "

"Damn, thank God for the life insurance, huh?"

"I read about that," Larry says. "The fire. Shit, did you guys see the pictures of her? I can't believe they can print that kind of thing."

Larry wishes he hadn't had so much Scotch. His head is swimming in it. His stomach is beginning to turn around the image of Rosto's wife's burned body. He thinks he may throw up before the fortune cookies come, but then the waiter sets them down.

Stan and Mark laugh nervously.

"The moment of truth," Rich says, snapping his cookie open and extricating the slip of pink paper. " 'A gamble will pay off in the near future,' " he reads.

"Ah, bullshit," Mark says. "In Reno?"

"Yeah, but I've lived here my whole life," Rich says, "and I've never won more than five dollars."

"Well, go on then," Larry says, handing him a couple quarters. "There's a Quartermania machine by the door."

Rich hesitates, but Mark grabs his arm and pulls him out of the booth and toward the slot machine.

"Open yours," Larry tells Stan.

Stan smiles and slams his fist down. Bits of cookie scatter across the table and the patched red Naugahyde. He picks the pink slip out from the mess.

There's yelling from the doorway as Larry grabs the paper.

"Oh shit!" Mark is repeating as he runs to the table. "That son-of-a-bitch won seventeen thousand dollars! He's collecting right now." He sits down beside Larry and eagerly picks up his own fortune cookie. "Dinner is definitely on Rich tonight!"

Before Mark can break open his cookie, Larry hands him Stan's fortune.

" 'There's no such thing as a free lunch, but never pass up a free dinner.' "

"Shit," Mark says reverently as he breaks his cookie neatly in half. He pulls out the pink slip and reads with obvious disappointment. " 'Sunny skies will smile upon you.' "

"Oh my God," Stan says in mock horror. "Sunny skies! In the desert? In June?"

Larry laughs, but he's still nervous. He wishes he were sober. He wishes he were home.

"C'mon, Larry," Stan urges. "Did we save the best for last?"

Larry smiles weakly and closes his fist around the cookie. When he opens it, the pink slip is amid a bunch of crumbs. He holds it up. Nothing. He flips it over.

It is blank.

"Aw, shit," Stan says. "You got rooked."

The men laugh and Larry decides it is time to go. The Scotch has been too much and he knows, if he is going to avoid a hangover, he needs to get it out of his stomach. And he prefers to throw up at home.

When Rich comes back and pays the bill, grinning and talking a mile a minute, Larry says his good-byes and walks to his car, the blank fortune still clutched in his closed fist.

He decides to take the freeway. Fewer cars, just go the speed limit.

He concentrates on the straight, wide road, checking his rearview often for signs of cops. The fortune pokes at his palm. How could he not have a fortune?

He holds it up in front of his eyes, the light in front of him shining all the way through, highlighting even the grain of the cheap paper.

The light in front of him?

A horn sounds.

He lowers his blank fortune.

Just in time to see the truck's shiny silver grille fill his world.

Smell

Brian McNaughton

Wilbur never noticed how people smelled until he got knocked on the head.

He woke up to an earthy scent that put him in mind of heat and energy.

"That cologne," he said. "What is it?"

"No, man, you s'pose to say, 'Where am I?' "

"Oh. Yeah. That, too."

"On the way to St. Vincent's. You'll make it, don't worry."

Wilbur wasn't worried, except about the smell. It wasn't unpleasant, but it cut through even the odor of disinfectant, and it was connected with the black man in the white coverall. He was still pondering this when he passed out.

Sniffing cautiously and asking discreet questions while hospitalized, he learned that he could determine the ancestry of nearly anyone by scent alone. He could also amaze the staff by "guessing" whether a given person lived in Manhattan, Brooklyn, or Queens. He resisted telling them what they'd eaten recently, or who was sleeping with whom, although he could have.

He didn't dare confess his queer ability. All his standard tests looked fine, and he wanted to get back to work.

First he had to identify the man who'd mugged him.

"See anybody you know?" the detective asked.

"No, I didn't—" Wilbur almost admitted he hadn't seen his attacker clearly. He said, "I'm nearsighted. I have to be on the other side of the glass."

"That's not how it works," the cop said. "They'd throw your ID out of court. Oh, what the hell."

Walking down the line of swarthy men on the dais, Wilbur knew that the first was Puerto Rican, the second Lebanese, and the third . . . The third man smelled a little like Wilbur himself.

"That's him," he declared firmly.

It turned out that the suspect was still carrying Wilbur's wallet.

Wilbur was a sales rep for an airline. Shortly after returning to the job, he had to persuade a Japanese industrialist named Fukunaga that his executives could be happy and productive only by flying South Wind. Others had tried, but this businessman had elevated sales resistance to a martial art.

On his way out the door, hoping to catch Fukunaga at his hotel, Wilbur grabbed a raincoat belonging to Jack Ishimasa, a computer tech. He knew whose it was instantly, but he had no time to correct the mistake.

When Wilbur caught his target checking out at the desk, the industrialist actually looked at him when he introduced himself. Fukunaga didn't smile, but his corpselike rigor moderated. More important, he took the contract Wilbur had prepared and promised to get back to him.

Jack Ishimasa couldn't understand why Wilbur wanted to buy one of his suits. It wouldn't fit. But the price was irresistible, and Wilbur had been acting funny lately. Nobody cared how funny he acted after he landed the Fukunaga contract.

He concluded that everyone shared his talent and that it influenced momentous decisions, but that few, if any, were aware of it.

He had long lusted after a neighbor in his building named Heather, but she had the power to make "Hi there" sound like a command to melt through a crack in the floor.

He stole a handkerchief from Tommy LoBianco, the corporate Casanova. When he carried it next day, Heather said, "Hi . . . there," and suggested something that would be more fun than going to work.

After he accidentally sent the handkerchief to the laundry, she ditched him.

Once he had got someone to isolate the omnipotent pheromones and patented them, he would be sitting—not on a goldmine, on the throne of God Almighty. Meanwhile he had business to take care of, and it took him to London. He cleverly filched a Harris tweed jacket that smelled British from a pub on the eve of his meeting with Lord Cummerbund.

He was returning from the pub when the sky fell on him. When someone kicked him back to consciousness, he was lying in an alley.

"You want to take it standing up, you sodding Prod bastard?" an Irish voice demanded.

"What the hell! Take what? If you want my wallet—"

"He's a Yank, Liam," another man said. "Leave him be."

"Yes! I'm an American. I'm wearing—" Wilbur screamed. His keen nose told him that the gun had been made in Sweden and shipped by way of Libya before it shredded his insides.

"Sure and he sounded like a Yank, Liam."

"Bloody black Protestant Belfast murtherer," Liam said. "Been watching fooking *Simpsons* on telly, that's all. I can smell his lot a mile away."

Smother Love

Nancy Kilpatrick

Shall I send her away, Timothy?"

"I . . . I don't know, Mother."

"It's probably for the best, dear, don't you agree?"

"I guess so, Mother. Whatever you say."

"Why, Timothy, you're not a child. Surely it's not a question of what I say, is it? If you want to see that girl, it's entirely up to you. Why should I care one way or the other, although I must admit, I don't really see the point. You two have nothing in common. But it's your life, dear."

The doorbell chimed again. He imagined Marcie waiting outside. The bright moonlight would highlight the strands of her golden hair and add just a touch of glow to her soft, tanned skin. Marcie's large, gentle, inquisitive brown eyes would seek him out—*Tim, it's been so long. I was afraid you'd forgotten me. Why did you leave so suddenly, without a word? . . .*

"Well, Timothy? What will you do?" His mother's voice startled him. "Having visitors tonight may not be a very good idea. You need your rest, dear. But if you insist on making yourself ill again, that's up to you. You'd better decide soon, though, because I don't want that girl hovering out there."

Timothy closed his eyes. His eyelids were like shades, blocking everything from view. "Send her away, Mother." He heard a voice whisper that sounded much like his own.

By the time he reached the window and peered out from a crack in the heavy curtain into the dazzling white night, Marcie was walking away. He watched her long after his photo-sensitive eyes could tolerate this indirect light, until she disappeared. Outside, the bleak winter landscape framed an image of his own pale, ghostly form reflected in the window's glass—empty eyes, sunken chest, and vague lingerings of the elusive shadow of who he might have been. And then his mother's bloated image loomed behind his own. Tall. Strong. Devouring.

The Snow Globes
Benjamin Adams

What's the name of this place again, Tully?" Brian Sanders asked. He took off his cashmere greatcoat and folded it over his left arm.

She looked up absently from a set of 1962 World's Fair glasses. " 'That's Atomic!' " she murmured. "Here, what do you make of these?"

Her husband picked up one of the glasses and made a show of inspecting it, tracing the outline of Seattle's Space Needle with his right index finger. "I don't know. Color's gone all faded and funny."

"That's a mint set," the man at the counter suddenly announced, his voice like paving stones. Both Tully and Brian jumped; the shop-keeper hadn't even appeared to be paying them any mind.

"Come on, now," argued Brian. "This can't be mint. Look how the lead's come to the color surface. There's no gloss left."

The counterman laid beefy hands atop his vintage cash register. "That design only ever came in a matte finish; the color's s'posed to be like that."

"I rather like the set," Tully said, taking the glass from Brian's hand.

The two Londoners had been in Seattle for a week, hunting down vintage Americana for Tully's East End boutique. This was their last stop prior to leaving for SeaTac Airport and the long trip home to England. They must have passed the tiny shop, hidden away on Olive Way East, a hundred times over the last several days, only to suddenly have "That's Atomic!" jump out at them on their way back from breakfast on Capitol Hill.

"Oh, I *do* like these," Tully exclaimed in a voice full of wonder.

She stood before a shelf of ten crystal snow globes, each finely polished and resting on a cherrywood base. Inside every globe stood a highly detailed miniature figurine of a person.

"They almost look alive!"

Tully picked up one of the globes and gently shook it, watching the fine snowflakes drift down on the figurine inside.

"Hey, careful there," warned the shopkeeper.

"How much are they?" asked Brian, joining Tully's side, shifting the greatcoat folded over his arms.

"Two hundred dollars for the set," enunciated the counterman.

"No," Brian said, "I meant individually."

"I won't break up a matched set."

"Oh, come now—"

"Wait, I'm sorry—I meant *three* hundred, not two."

Brian stepped away from the case as if he'd been slapped. "That's . . . that's outrageous!" he sputtered.

The shopkeeper shrugged. "Each one of them globes is handmade, one of a kind."

"I *don't* think we're interested, darling," Brian said to Tully.

Dejectedly, she replaced the snow globe on its shelf.

"That man was fairly rude, wouldn't you say?" Brian suddenly asked Tully.

They sat on hard plastic seats at SeaTac airport, waiting for their connecting flight to New York.

"I don't know," she mused. "I've found most vintage dealers are like that. I managed to talk him down on those lovely fringed leather jackets. Oh, and those cups shaped like Easter Island statues—"

"No, no—when he told you to be careful with that snow globe. I found him quite rude. And that price—just absurd. As if anyone's going to be interested in an entire *set* of snow globes."

Tully considered this for a moment. "Well, it wasn't as if I truly needed it, you know."

Brian smiled slyly then. "Are you sure?"

He reached into the pocket of the cashmere greatcoat folded across his knee, and produced the snow globe with a flourish.

Tully gasped with shock and pleasure. "You bought it for me?"

Brian's smile jerked sideways. "Well—"

"No! You *nicked* it?!"

"While you were settling the bill."

Tully leaned toward him and kissed his cheek. "My scandalous husband," she murmured, stroking his thigh with her fingertip.

Abruptly Brian squirmed in his seat, away from her. "Damn," he said, "I'm feeling funny." He loosened his collar. His normally florid face suddenly drained of all color.

"Brian!" Tully said in alarm. "Brian, are you all right?"

As if in response, Brian Sanders staggered to his feet, then pitched forward in a heap on the rust-colored rug of the International Terminal.

The snow globe flew from his hand and landed a few feet away, on the hard linoleum walkway, where it shattered into a million crystal shards.

The shopkeeper gave the new snow globe a final polish, holding it by the cherrywood base as he removed any trace of fingerprints from its fine crystal surface.

The exquisitely detailed figure inside bore more than a passing resemblance to Brian Sanders.

"They'll never learn," the counterman grated softly to himself.

Gently, he set the snow globe where it belonged, with the others.

"I absolutely *refuse* to break up a matched set."

Snowman

Donald R. Burleson

The night sky was ghastly gray-white with falling snow. Looking out his front window, though, Roland saw that the flakes were getting large and fluffy, and big wet flakes meant that the snow was probably about to stop. What was it the fellow on the radio had said—snow tapering to flurries before midnight? Well, the storm was indeed nearly over, and that meant it was time to go shovel out the entrance to the driveway.

He hated shoveling snow, hated the filthy stuff itself. When Alice was alive she would have told him he was too old to shovel snow, even then, seven years earlier. And he especially disliked shoveling at night. Maybe he could let it go till morning. But no, he would need to get the car out early, wouldn't have much extra time in the morning, better go out and do it now.

He switched the front porch light on and glanced out the window again while he was pulling on his overcoat and boots. Struggling against the dark, the illumination from the porch reached nearly to the street, far enough to show him the piled-up snow at the end of the drive and, a few yards to the right, the snowman, standing just within the yard like some strange sentry on duty there.

The Dudley kids. He'd almost forgotten about them. Buttoning up his coat and wrapping a wool scarf around his throat, he remembered now, looking out through the storm that afternoon and seeing them out there, Tommy and Lucy and Matt, in his yard out by the street, rolling snow up into fat white globes and stacking them to make a snowman. The nerve of them, playing on his property. He had stuck his head out the door and yelled, "Hey, you kids—" but his voice had been caught up in the howling wind and scattered like drifting snow, dispersed, lost. Out by the half-formed snowman, Mrs. Dudley's odd, gnomelike children had merely glanced up, undaunted, and proceeded to set the bulbous snow head in place. They appeared then to be playing some kind of frolicking game, dancing around their creation, but Roland couldn't see too clearly through the blowing snow, and he retreated inside.

Now, grabbing his shovel from the porch and padding off down the steps and down the vaguely outlined path to the driveway, Roland eyed the snowman, a distant form barely visible out there, snow against snow, eyed the thing with renewed annoyance. By the time he had half shoveled away the mess that the snowplow had left on his driveway, he could no longer resist the urge to have a closer look at those Dudley brats' presumptuous work. He trudged across the yard, sinking knee-deep, and stood facing the snowman, whose details were only dimly discernible in the light from the porch.

There was something, something unsettling about the thing. Fat, squat, somehow unpleasant-looking, the snowman seemed to eye him back, seemed to contemplate him with snow eyes, seemed to think its own snow thoughts about him. This was crazy, of course—but then again, what were these odd markings in the snow around the thing, markings nearly filled back in again with new snow? The Dudley children always *were* weird, nearly as weird as their mother. Those marks—was that a circle around the snowman, or something with corners?

But he had scarcely formed the thought, when something happened. It seemed to happen on the instant, between snowflakes, between heartbeats. What had happened? He was still staring through the gloom, but now he was looking not at a snowman but at himself, or someone who looked like him. He watched this overcoated figure grin a self-satisfied grin and shoulder its shovel and walk back toward the bright warmth of the house, moving out of the line of his vision. And he gradually realized that he was standing frozen in the snow, or would have been standing there, if he had had real feet. The snow wasn't stopping after all, and insistent flakes were pelting down upon him, snow upon snow. He had wondered once, as a child, if snowmen could feel the cold.

And now he knew.

Solstice

Lisa Jean Bothell

Megan lay ramrod straight in her narrow bed, barely breathing as the babysitter flicked off the overhead light. As darkness settled, her body twitched in uncomfortable anticipation.

She hated it here already.

It was their first night in the new house, in *her* house. *Grandmother's.*

Grandmother. Who'd seemed all too eager to envelope Megan in mounds of flabby, powdery-smelling flesh, impaling her with beady, too intense eyes. Who'd died a week ago, leaving them her house on Whidby Island.

Megan stiffened as a branch scraped across the windowpane. It was still too dark to see anything. She was accustomed to her tiny bedroom in their West Seattle apartment, with close walls and plenty of light filtered from the supermarket next door.

Right, she thought to herself. Local papers would read: "Girl Smothers in Total Blackness." *Right*.

Megan stared at the window. She regretted insisting that the babysitter not close the flowery curtains. Not even a moon. Only the black-upon-black oak branch waving and scraping. It reminded her of the creature-under-the-bed tales grandmother had told her.

Great! She would have to think of that now, here on her first night in this ghastly, huge, creaky room. What a pisser!

Sorry God, she muttered silently, hitching the covers higher. *I'll never curse again. Just don't let anything get me. Thank you, Lord.*

Megan didn't believe in those tales. Not in the bright, nouveau apartment. But now . . .

Grandmother had always gotten such a kick out of scaring her. "The monster won't get you if you keep covered up, Meggie," she'd said. "Don't stick your foot out, or . . ."

"Stop scaring her, Martha," Mom had admonished.

"And don't call me *Meggie!*" Megan had muttered under her breath.

When Mom's back was turned, Grandmother had continued in her harsh whisper. "Even if you let your arm drape over the edge of the bed, it might reach up for you. Then, when it grabs you . . ."

Megan's heart thudded almost painfully and she shuddered. Stop it, Megan, she whispered to herself. *Just stop it right now!*

"Girl Dies of Overactive Imagination," reads the *Inquisitor*, the small article buried between "Mother Eats Own Fetus" and "Men from Mars Impregnated My Grandmother."

She suppressed a giggle. Maybe *Grandmother* had been a Martian. Her giggle broke off, sounding tinny and far away.

Megan turned over on her side impatiently, then stiffened as she heard a . . . scuffle.

"It came from beneath my bed," young girl says earnestly to reporter of the *Seattle Times*. "And it ate my babysitter."

Megan shuddered. There was nothing there! There were *no* monsters, no matter how many Freddy movies she had seen. The only monsters were perverts, and they couldn't be under her bed!

To be sure, Megan hitched the covers up to her armpits, but she was already hot. It was summer solstice, for chrissake—*Sorry God, I'm really trying. Thanks.*

"One of the special days when windows to other, stranger worlds open up, *Meggie*," Grandmother had assured her conspiratorially.

She heard it again—something furtive, hidden. No use taking chances; she immediately stuck her hands under the covers. *To sleep, to sleep* . . . Summer school tomorrow. She was allergic to sheep (wool anyway), but she started counting them. One sheep, jumping and baaaing over her bed. Two sheep . . . Baaaaa . . .

"Girl Remains Awake All Night, Falls Asleep in Lunch Tray." "I didn't mean to do it," she protests as hall monitors lead her away.

She'd begun drifting off when a sudden thought struck, sending a sliver of ice into her heart.

"Of course, Meggie, if they can't reach your hands or legs, they might grab your hair," Grandmother had added. "They'll go for anything they can."

Oh, *damn!* She wriggled carefully, trying to shake her blonde hair under the covers without pulling her hands out. *Sorry, God, I meant darn.*

It wasn't working, so she abruptly flipped the covers up and over her head, covering up entirely. *I can't breathe.*

"Girl Dies of Asphyxiation and B.O." reads the coroner's report.

She cautiously rearranged the blankets so her nose poked out. Better. Slowly, lassitude overcame her.

Misty tendrils of ectoplasmic tentacles undulated beneath the single bed. They crept up the side, searching for limbs: none. They probed for hair: none. Then one of them gently pasted itself over the dozing child's nose.

It shuddered in orgasmic pleasure as the terrified figure began struggling for air.

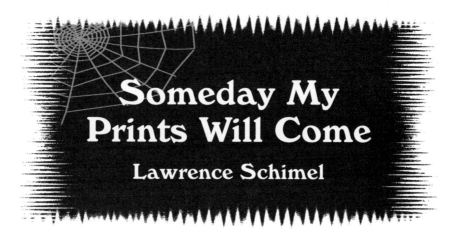

Someday My Prints Will Come

Lawrence Schimel

People bought millions of copies of romance novels because of the covers Eleanor Sassano painted for them. Year after year, she was voted the best cover artist in the industry. But still she was not happy. She was in love.

For a series of covers for superbestseller Wendy Bond, Eleanor had begun dreaming of one particular man. She had never met him—he wasn't a model of hers—but she knew him somehow. He was a good seven inches taller than she, had jet-black hair, and the most beautiful, sparkling green eyes. His skin had that natural tan look to it, the kind where there's a pink glow underneath simply radiating health. His face was sharply defined, almost roughly cut, but with a softness to it as well that made him absolutely gorgeous.

Even after the series had been published, she continued to paint this man, hanging the painting around her bedroom, next to the cover flats of Wendy's books, and dreaming about him as he watched over her at night.

She made love to him as she painted, running the brush slowly up his bare leg. She was jealous of the women she painted on the covers with him, who got to hold him in their arms, to make love to him, while all she could do was watch helplessly. For the paintings she did of him at home, strictly for herself, she always painted him alone, pining away with love and lust for her. In the privacy of her home she could control him however she wished.

One day Eleanor decided to paint herself into a picture with him. She closed her eyes and looked into that imaginary world inside her head where she could always find him; today, he wore a small crown of silver upon his head. Eleanor smiled and began to paint him on one side of the canvas, astride a tall white stallion. He was smiling, reaching out his hand for her. Eleanor had decided against painting herself directly into his arms. They would have a courtship first; it would be so romantic.

A wave of dizziness washed over her unexpectedly as she finished painting herself. When she opened her eyes she nearly fainted; she was actually there, standing in front of her prince! He leapt, in a graceful arc, from his horse's back to the grass in front of her. He came forward, all poise, reached for her, and tore the front of her blouse.

Eleanor slapped him. "What was that for?" she yelled. He grabbed her head in his big strong hands and violently kissed her. Eleanor tried to struggle but he was too strong for her. He tore the rest of her blouse away and ran his fingers over her breasts. He tumbled her to the ground, using her body to cushion his fall, and began to unfasten his pants. Eleanor tried to struggle away, but he was too strong and too determined. She could not prevent him—

The canvas tore under Eleanor's hands, paint smearing her fingers and clothes as she stumbled and fell with the easel. She lay still for a while, as she pulled herself together. Her blouse was torn off. She looked down at the canvas under her, and could see only his face, looking confused.

She should have known he'd be like that. The proof was in all the paintings she had done of him: In every one he was tearing some woman's bodice or raping her. Eleanor was disgusted with herself for having fallen in love with him.

But she knew how she could get her revenge. She smiled again as she looked around the room once more. She stood up and let her skirt drop to the floor, then went into the bathroom and washed away all traces of him from her body.

The next day Eleanor called all her regular art directors and quit. She then called the art directors for every line of horror books she could find. On the basis of her reputation, she was assigned work immediately and began her first horror cover that night, closing her eyes to find him as she stood before her easel. She began to paint him, starting with his little finger off in a corner of the painting, opposite the rest of his body, where the ghouls had thrown it and forgotten about it as they tore him limb from limb.

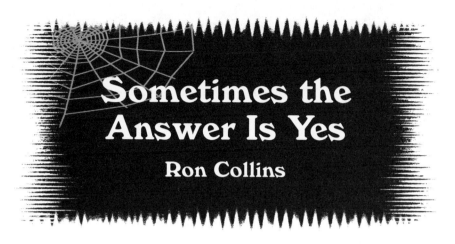

Sometimes the Answer Is Yes

Ron Collins

Johnny Lane struggled in hooded darkness as the ocean closed over his head. Sinking, he held his breath, his lungs bursting, his mind struggling, coming to grips with death. He slowly exhaled, extending the time before he would suck water.

Oh, sweet Jesus! I'll do anything, God. Anything! Just give me a chance to get even with the bitch!

I'm not God, came the reply. *But perhaps I can be of assistance.*

Over a hundred feet of ocean covered Johnny Lane's body. Worse than that, a thick coating of mud and the slimy writhings of sea snakes against his cold skin made him shudder.

Of course, death has a way of making these things seem insignificant. Especially when you're in that condition only because your half-crazed girlfriend decided your life was worth less than a c-note of cocaine. Oddly, Johnny took his condition in stride, seemingly unaffected. Yes, he was cold, and he thought he had broken a rib or two in the current. And yes, he truly missed the unconscious feel of his chest rising with each breath. But, to Johnny, revenge would be sweeter than honey—he could live with these inconveniences for the time being.

The currents ripped away the blanket that had covered him, leaving his hands free. He struggled out of the bottom sludge, lifting first one arm, then the other. He shook the silt off as best he could, then rubbed his eyes.

Once his eyes adjusted to the darkness, Johnny peered at his feet. They were tied by a cord, tightly wound around both ankles and twined upward to bind his legs at midthigh. Superman couldn't have gotten out of this tangle. Enrico "The Stiff" Torcelli obviously took no quarter from people who try to skip out on a twenty-eight-grand IOU.

After a short search, Johnny found a sharp rock and began working at the cord. It took a while, but time was one thing he had plenty of. His efforts stirred the bottom's sediment, and he stopped often while the current carried the muck away. Finally free of the coils, he stood up, stretched his muscles, and exercised his stiff joints.

The current was strong at this depth. It would be a long walk home.

She would die horribly, Johnny decided as he stepped onto a midnight beach, trailing seaweed from his pants leg. He would slip into her house—she always kept a key behind the mailbox—and he would stalk her, showing himself only at the last instant. Her face would twist, and she would scream in recognition.

These thoughts churned as he slipped through shadows, walking between houses, leaving a dribbling trail of saltwater. With each step came a new tactic. With each of the breaths he would have taken were he actually alive came a new torture.

Finally, he made it to her place.

The key was right where he expected it. It slid into the lock and turned easily.

Music blared, and the house smelled sweet, a mixture of incense and cannabis—cannabis bought with *his* money. Thin light shone from the back. Johnny slunk through the living room and down the corridor before stopping to peer into her bedroom.

She sat on the bed, swaying to the music with her eyes shut, her head back, and her jaw hanging slack. Tears flowed down her face.

Damned bitch! Doesn't even have the courtesy to be straight when I kill her!

He strode quickly toward her, his dead hands ice-cold and stretched out, ready to wrap themselves around her throat.

Selia sat on her bed, visions of bats and snakes and flying lizards twisting through her brain. The creatures snapped at her as they flew, baring fangs dripping venom. Her heart pounded. Her breath ripped her throat. Every inch of skin prickled.

For a lucid moment, Selia knew the stuff had been laced. For that same lucid moment, she saw her life for the wasteland it was. Senseless nights, vacant days, nothing to show for being alive. Tears came, streaking her cheeks.

Dear God! I'll do anything. Anything at all! Just help me beat this stuff once and for all!

I'm not God, came the reply. *But perhaps I can be of assistance.*

The Sound

Lawrence Greenberg

You're not exactly sure, but you think someone is in the house. It's 2:10 A.M., and you've just heard something that's awakened you. A sound of something falling. Something heavy. You always keep your windows open to air out the place, but tonight there's no wind. Not even a breeze. Then how could something fall on its own?

You reach out. Even in the dark, you know exactly where your night-light is. You turn it on, then open the top drawer of the small night table. Inside there's a flashlight, a small one, and a gun. They're always there. Where you keep them. You take both out. Carefully, silently, you get out of bed, trying not to make any noise. You slide your feet into the slippers, always at the side of the bed you sleep on. You throw on the bathrobe you always keep folded at the foot of the bed. Then you leave the bedroom, flipping on the flashlight, pointing it down at your feet.

The sound came from upstairs. Maybe the attic. As quietly as you can, you move up the carpeted stairs. You don't hear a thing. Even the chirping insects outside have disappeared. Maybe it's too quiet. You're not sure. As you move up the stairs, something doesn't feel right. But you don't know exactly what it is.

Then suddenly, you hear the sound again. Much closer. Much louder. It *is* from the attic. And it *is* heavy. When you reach the upper landing, you see the attic door is open. Slightly. It shouldn't be. You always keep it closed. The light's on—the small 40-watt bulb that gives off just enough light to let someone see the attic's contents. No more, no less. The light should be off. You take the gun out of your pocket.

You're not sure if you should open the door silently, or try surprising the intruder with a sudden movement. Finally, you don't know why, you choose the latter approach. You bang open the door, gun pointed straight out in front of you. Nothing's there. But the strange feeling you had moving up the stairs is much stronger now.

The air feels clammy. Stuffy. More than usual in the attic. As though something settled there for a while and moved on, only after the air had absorbed the essence of whatever it was. There's no evidence to show what made the sound. Still, it feels as though something's there with you. But you can't see it.

Then you hear it again. Downstairs. Where you just came from. Your bedroom. The same sound. Something heavy. You don't know what the hell's going on. *Downstairs*, you think. By now, it's probably too late; you know you won't see anything when you get there. But you have to go. You have to.

This time when you move downstairs, you're not as quiet. What for? The thing, whatever it is, is playing with you. Like it knows where you are. Like it knows where it has to go to make you worry. To unnerve you. Your teeth clench. Almost as though it knows what it has to do to keep you right on the edge of being scared.

When you get to the bedroom, the air has the same stuffy quality as the attic, in spite of the windows being open. And just as up in the attic, you don't see anything. Only the same familiar surroundings. The same day-in, day-out trappings of your regular, structured life. But this stuffy feeling—that's different. That's not part of your life. Something's changed.

But you don't know what it is. Maybe if you listen closely you can hear this thing, whatever it is, moving on its fast, silent feet, or haunches, or whatever it moves on. But there's nothing to hear. Strain as you will, the house is deathly quiet. And then, without warning, it happens again. The sound. This time it's even louder. Even closer. Your walk-in closet. Right there in the bedroom.

Sweat begins to coat your hands. Your face. Your heart pounds faster in your chest. Your knees feel wobbly. But you have to see what's in the closet. You have to. You approach the closet door, and the gun is shaking in your hand. Your mouth feels as though someone's stuck a sponge in it and soaked up every last bit of moisture. The closet door is slightly open. It's not supposed to be. You always keep it closed. This time, you're going to open it very slowly, very quietly. Even though you know this thing knows where you are, maybe you can surprise it anyway. Maybe you can get the drop on it and kill it once and for all. So it will be out of your life. For good.

You nudge the door easily. Now there's just enough room for you to enter. But nothing's inside. Nothing more than your clothes on hangers, your shoes, and those miscellaneous boxes on the top shelves. The air inside is so stuffy, so clammy, that you feel like you almost can't breathe. Then you yank the pullchain for the closet's light and turn to the mirror on the other side of the closet door.

What you see in the mirror is very bad. You look terrible. Pale.

Wan. Thinner, somehow. There are dark circles under your eyes. You tell yourself that all of this is from having to get up in the middle of the night; more than that, having to get up and look for an intruder in the middle of the night. But you know better. It's not that at all. You begin a scream, but it's abruptly cut off when your chest tightens. Like it's in a giant vise. And the vise tightens even more.

And that's when you know exactly why the air is so stuffy, so clammy. It's the air of death. And when you realize this, you also know what the sound is. Why it's following you. Everything in your life up until now has been so predictable. So matter-of-fact, so everyday, so humdrum. But now something's happened. Something so different that it's trying, through some part of you, to let you know in advance. But that doesn't do any good, does it? Because you're so used to knowing where everything is and how to perform every little detail of your life, you couldn't possibly figure out what this new thing was. Could you?

And as the heart attack claims you, you fall to the floor, knowing this will be the last time in your life you will hear the sound.

Special Interests

Lillian Csernica
and Kevin Andrew Murphy

October 25, 1995

Dearest Sebastian O—

I received your compatibility analysis, as well as your photograph. If you don't think it too forward, I have to say, you're just my type.

All the little bubbles we filled in were the same. Even the personalized bit at the end—"What three things do you find most important in a relationship?"—was so very familiar: knives, duct tape, and large breasts.

You can see the attraction. My answers were almost the same: kitchen utensils, duct tape, and chest hair.

I know you know what the duct tape is for, but I plan to surprise you with the kitchen utensils. Preferably alone, at night.

Please send me a picture of you with your shirt off. I've enclosed one of my own. Do you like them?

Kisses and duct tape,
Sharisse

October 26, 1995

My darling Sharisse,

Here's the photo. I thought you might like a shot of me in my "workshop." Please excuse the mess. You know how it gets at the end of a long day. All you want to do is relax, but you just have to hose down the floor.

Kitchen utensils? You hussy! A colleague told me he scorns knives as being too obvious. What can I say? I'm just a traditional guy, into the classics. A clever woman like you must appreciate the need to avoid falling into accidental patterns.

Lovely photo. They're marvelous. Where did you find someone willing to do that particular tattoo? It's certainly provocative. When can I take a closer look?

Love and whetstones,
Sebastian

October 28, 1995

Dearest Sebastian,

I'm sorry for the extra day it took to respond, but as you can see from this morning's headlines, I've been busy—HAPPY HOMEMAKER STRIKES TWICE!

Where do they get these ridiculous names? Honestly, when I started this hobby, I intended to make a name for myself—and I envy you yours, the Red Slasher is so romantic—but then what can I expect when I send them the organs neatly sealed in plastic containers?

I suppose it could be worse. They might have dubbed me the Tupperware Lady.

Since you admired my pair so much, I've sent you last night's in a matched set of lettuce crispers. The tattoos aren't as provocative, but then I'm still rather attached to mine. But it's the sentiment that counts, isn't it?

I've also enclosed my favorite bread knife. It has a lovely serrated edge I know you'll appreciate.

A kiss lasts forever, if you seal it properly,
Sharisse

P.S. I absolutely adore the photograph. You look so virile and creative. But you must have me over so I can show you how well—and quickly—you can clean up with a shop vac.

More kisses for an adorable bachelor,

S.

October 29, 1995

My darling Sharisse,

You do know how to handle leftovers, don't you? I'd have preferred something more elegant than the Red Slasher, but it's better if they name us. Choose your own name and they read so much into it, most just plain silly. As if I actually hated my mother. She was a saint. My sister, on the other hand . . .

I can't ask you over just to show me how to clean house. That's no way to thank you for your thoughtfulness. Instead, I hope you'll accept these roses. White felt right, but that seemed too plain for such an exotic lady. A splash of red here and there added just the right touch.

How about meeting me on neutral ground for a little Halloween fun? We'll start off with a shopping spree in your favorite housewares department, then find some charming neighborhood with plenty of noisy children and a few dark streets.

Let's put the "trick" back into "trick or treat."

Your creature of the night,

Sebastian

October 29, 1995

Dearest Sebastian,

What a lovely suggestion! Though honestly, I'm the last woman who needs a housewares spree. Just bring a selection of your knives and meet me at the cemetery gates. I'll dress as a witch. You dress as Jack the Ripper. (Isn't that an easy costume?)

I know a street where we can pick up any number of precious little pumpkins. After we finish cutting and hollowing them out, we can light them up for all the neighbors to see. But safe and sane, Sebastian. I insist. We'll use glow sticks and watertight flashlights. Candles are dangerous, and blood tends to put out the wicks. I'll hold the pumpkins while you hold the knife, then we'll take out the guts together. Won't that be fun?

Your Black Magic Woman,

Sharisse

Speed

T. W. Kriner

The day after losing his second Boston Marathon to Reignbos, Marasigan visited Robin Goodfellow, manager of Gehenna Bioengineering. Goodfellow reached over an onyx desktop to shake hands. "How can we help you, Mr. Marasigan?"

Marasigan sat down and blurted, "I want my face redesigned."

"You're already handsome."

Marasigan blushed. "With this flat mug and these ears sticking out like sails? Come on—you've seen prettier chimps. But who cares about looks? I want *speed*."

"Speed?"

"I'm a top marathon runner, but I don't have the body to win big races. I train maniacally, but it doesn't make up for my short stride. I can run all day, but not fast enough to beat Reignbos."

"Rainbows?"

"Jason Reignbos. He beat me in college, then bumped me off the Olympic squad. Two years now he's won at Boston. I'd do *anything* to beat him."

Goodfellow smiled. "I understand."

"I need a design I can take to a plastic surgeon. Maybe pin back these ears somehow, chisel the bones and push everything forward—a hatchet face to lessen wind resistance. Anything to cut my time."

"Winning means that much?"

"No. Beating Reignbos does."

Goodfellow tapped his computer keyboard; a printer at his elbow spat out several sheets of paper. "Would you like to beat Reignbos's best time to date on any course?"

Marasigan's jaw dropped. "With a *face-lift?*"

"No." Goodfellow laughed. "More than that. You'll have your hatchet face *and* longer legs. Maybe a little something to increase efficiency. Old Harry downstairs has eons of experience; he'll redesign you. Our contract surgeons and therapists will see that the operations and recuperation go smoothly. Our attorneys will make certain no modification violates race rules. The organizers will seek injunctions to prevent you from racing, naturally, but the attorneys will—"

"Excuse me," Marasigan interrupted, "but *Michael Jackson* couldn't afford this. I've got only ninety grand."

"We don't want money."

"What then?"

Goodfellow fished the papers from the printer and handed them to Marasigan.

Marasigan read them quickly and grinned. "You're kidding, right? My *soul?*"

"Think about it, Mr. Marasigan," Goodfellow said pleasantly. "The contract describes the procedures in exacting detail, from bone splicing to relocating musculature. Who else could have anticipated your needs and prepared a contract so speedily?"

Marasigan reread the contract. "*I* beat Reignbos. *You* get my soul. No *cash?*" He chuckled. "Gimme a pen."

Goodfellow obliged him. "We guarantee you'll beat Reignbos's best time to date."

"Where I come from, that spells victory." Marasigan scribbled his name. Then a puzzled look crossed his face. "What's this about *wings* on the last page?"

"They'll reduce drag and dissipate heat."

"I'll look like a hood ornament!"

"You'll be efficient, fast, and *devilishly* handsome."

Marasigan had an arrowhead profile and flat, pointed ears. The transplantation of four-inch sections of his humeri to his femurs made him look like a thalidomide nightmare. Fused thoracic vertebrae canted his torso in mantislike fashion, but assured the optimum angle of attack into resisting air. The wings had been seeded with Marasigan's own tissue at a Massachusetts lab, then grown over polymer scaffoldings mounted on an immunosuppressed pig. Red surgical scars webbed his body.

He looked like a bat out of hell.

Marathon officials lost the court battle, as Goodfellow promised, but the judge directed that he start dead last in the pack—despite his second-place finish the previous year.

On race day they made him await the starting gun in a tent. When the race began an official lifted the canvas flap. Marasigan emerged. Spectators shrieked as he flexed his wings and began to run.

The pack fell before him like rioters before rubber bullets. Runners looking over their shoulders gaped in horror and bolted from his path. Panicked men and women ran in all directions, screaming and stumbling.

An hour after he cleared the pack, Marasigan began to pass strong runners. Some gave him bewildered, startled looks. Others seemed blasé. All tried to keep pace with him, to no avail. An hour later he passed a cluster of world-class competitors. Ahead of them was a solitary runner.

Reignbos.

Marasigan closed quickly, at a pace well ahead of Reignbos's best time ever. As he pulled within several strides of him Marasigan bellowed, *"Reignbos!"*

Reignbos looked back. His face contorted into an expression of abject terror. Instantly he turned and sped toward the finish line faster than Marasigan or anyone else had ever seen him run—as though the devil himself were chasing him.

Speed Demon

Jay R. Bonansinga

Dickie Pelham spotted the shepherd at dusk. The sun had trickled down the drain off the southwestern horizon, and the vehicle had appeared like a gunmetal mirage off the interstate's distant heatwaves.

Late Kansas summers were like that. Solitary sedans would materialize out of nowhere, metal-flake ghosts hugging the shoulder, getting in Dickie's way, just like those teenagers who had gotten in Dickie's way back in '79. The pathetic little farm boy and his freckled waif of a girlfriend. They'd been crawling along the shoulder in their whiskey-bumped Jimmy, weaving directly into Dickie's blind spot. Dickie had barely gotten a chance to apply the brakes before gobbling up the Jimmy's right rear quarter panel, sending the Bobbsey Twins down an embankment and into concrete oblivion. The subsequent litigation and myriad death claims had kept Dickie off the roads for nearly six months. And for a senior account executive at the nation's leading manufacturer of lightbulb socket collars, being off-road meant stasis, and stasis meant lost income, and Dickie Pelham wasn't about to lose income. That's why he always kept his eyes peeled for shepherds.

Dickie goosed the foot-feed.

A quarter mile away, the shepherd's tail-end coalesced, a liquid mercury shadow metamorphosing into a raven black El Camino, and Dickie pushed his little four-cylinder Eurasian go-cart as fast as it would go. In the closing distance, the El Camino kept screaming along, inhaling the pavement, clocking at something near three digits. *Hot damn*, Dickie thought to himself, *a gear head*. Gear heads were the best shepherds.

Dickie had discovered the process back in the seventies, around the advent of the double-nickel speed limit. Hard-wired on truck-stop java, juiced up on cheap methedrine and impossible schedules, Dickie started latching onto errant hot-rodders tooling along at ninety miles per. Ducking into the slipstream behind the speed demon's bumper, always staying a couple car lengths loose, Dickie could tag along for miles without fearing reprisals from the local County Mounties. The hot-rodder became Dickie's shepherd into the promised land of higher productivity, more accounts, and very few speeding tickets. And no goddamn dead farm kids—no matter how innocent or freckled they might have been—were going to haunt Dickie's memories. Haunted memories only slowed a person down, and slowing down meant . . . well, you get the idea.

Dickie glanced at the speedometer and felt his stomach lurch. The needle was pinned, for Christ's sake. *Pinned*. One hundred and twenty miles per hour. Impossible. The little Japanese crate had never broken ninety-five, and now the landscape was streaming past his windows, a khaki-green blur, the high-line wires pulsing like a flat-line cardiogram, the wind buffeting the hood, engine bellowing, tires singing high opera, and Dickie started squinting, because the last gleam of the dying sun was glinting off the El Camino's chrome molding, a rhythmic beacon, flickering like a mesmerist's watch, flickering, flickering, and Dickie clutched the wheel with sweaty hands, heart racing, mouth as dry and cold as metal shavings.

In the final moments, he wanted to pull away. He wanted to let up on the gas, fall back, give up, give up, give up on setting this insane land speed record, but something about that flicker off the El Camino's bumper kept him glued to the speed demon's rear end, a poison pinhole in Dickie's brain sending magnesium-bright tendrils of revelation into the dark recesses of his mind, his guilt, his shame.

He didn't realize that the El Camino had drifted several feet toward the shoulder until it was too late. The speed demon swerved suddenly, back onto the road, revealing the overpass directly in Dickie's path, and all that Dickie could do was open his mouth to shriek—a shriek that would never come—as his little car hurled into the massive concrete rampart.

For Dickie, the impact was like a light switch being flipped off.

He was killed instantly, and never got a chance to feel the colossal pressure instantly collapsing the entire frame and chassis of the tiny sedan around him, or to hear the volcanic explosion in his ears, or to experience the searing tidal wave of heat engulfing his shattered body.

Or to see the pale ghosts of two skinny farm kids, tooling off in their new El Camino, vanishing in the dying light.

Spring

Joe Meno

They kissed, pressing their lips together in one immutable embrace; the lust inside burned between them like fire. Brody slipped his hand through Sheila's hair, then slowly maneuvered it down to her bra strap.

"I'm not ready," she whispered, with a frown.

"What? What the hell are you talking about? We drove three and a half hours up to my parents' cottage just to be alone and you tell me you aren't ready?" Brody shook his head with anger.

"I thought we could just be together," Sheila whispered.

"Just be together? We can do that at home!"

Sheila began to cry; her blue eyes began to fill with tears. "Don't talk to me like that!" she shouted, and stormed toward the thick wooden door. She swung it open, then stepped into the chilly spring night.

"Sheila!" He threw a can of beer at the door as it slammed shut.

She just needed some time to cool off. She'd be right back. Brody leaned back in the sofa, staring at the bright orange flames in the gray fireplace as the door flew open again.

"That was quick. Did you change your mind so soon?"

Brody turned to smile at her, then felt his blood turn cold; his heart wobbled in his chest. A naked man stood in the doorway, with long, greasy black hair; his arms and face were caked in red blood; his skin glistened with sweat. He stumbled inside, then swung the door closed, then slammed the brace over the door. Brody swallowed hard, unable to breathe.

"It's too late," the naked man mumbled, cowering in a dark corner of the room. He licked his wounds. "Spring is here."

Brody eyed the large shotgun above the fireplace as the naked man pulled his knees to his chest. "Too tired to keep moving," he gasped; his pallid chest heaved. "Have to make a stand here." He buried his face between his knees, avoiding the moonlight.

Brody lunged for the shotgun, gripping it nervously; he pointed it at the naked man. "Don't move," Brody murmured. "Don't move."

The naked man smiled.

"That's not gonna do any good."

Brody's entire body trembled as he tried to steady the shotgun. "You just sit still while I call the cops."

"Sure, kid." The naked man grinned. In one terrific move, the naked man bounded across the wooden floor and tore the gun from Brody's hands. He smacked Brody in the jaw, sending him reeling across the room. Brody lay still on the floor as the naked man stood above him, lowering the rifle to his head.

Suddenly, a lonely wolf bayed at the moon. The man turned toward the call with a look of terror; his eyes filled with blackness.

"No," he gasped, taking aim at the door. "It's my goddamn scent. That's what it is. My goddamn scent."

Something pounded on the door. Bang-bang-bang.

The naked man cocked the shotgun.

"No," Brody whimpered. "It's my girlfriend! Don't shoot! It's my girlfriend." He ran in front of the door.

"The hell it is, boy," the man growled, baring his teeth as the pounding grew louder. "Move aside!"

The pounding at the door continued. *Bang-bang-bang!*

Brody unbarred the door and flung it open. "Sheila?!"

There was no one there. The naked man stood poised, staring out into the night. Brody turned as something huge, something covered in gray fur, tore past him. A wolf. A giant gray wolf.

"*Noooo!*" the naked man screamed, opening fire. The thing was upon him now, knocking the rifle from his hands and pinning him to the ground. The thing clamped its huge jaws into the man's neck, and slowly began to transform. Soon enough, the giant gray wolf became a dark-haired woman; her naked skin glistened with sweat as she dragged the naked man outside, she growled forcing her partner in a kiss. He struggled, gnashing his teeth, hissing, pulling her to the wet ground, returning the kiss. As the silver moon struck them, they changed again, gripping one another with sharp fangs and claws, dripping blood and saliva. As they both finally surrendered, their howls slowly became one.

Brody slammed the door shut and collapsed on the floor, shivering with confusion and terror. Within a few moments, Sheila returned. She smiled, sitting beside him.

"I'm ready," she whispered, kissing him gently. She bit his ear playfully. He flinched.

"No, that's OK. Maybe you're right. Maybe we should wait."

St. Louis #2

Michael Grisi

"They do what?"

"The ground is so wet, they have to bury everyone in mausoleums. The people that can't afford one of their own are put in these things called oven vaults. It's a wall that lines the perimeter of the graveyard. These vaults are stacked about five high. The people that are real poor are put in disintegratable coffins, and after a year and a day they can put someone else in the same vault. They push whatever is left in there to the back."

"And where does it go?"

"The back is hollow and it just falls off the edge."

"And the bodies just pile up in this hollow wall?"

"You've got it."

"That's the grossest thing I've ever heard."

"Gross, but true."

"You're bullshitting me."

"Would you like to see it for yourself?"

"Now?"

"Why not?"

"It's eleven o'clock at night. We can't go skulking around some cemetery at this hour."

"It'll be fun."

"No way, man."

"What's the matter, little baby, scared?"

"No. It's just not right. It's sacrilegious."

"Where's your sense of adventure?"

Larry North didn't like the idea, but he knew Jim Morgan, his roommate at the University of New Orleans, would not quit until he relented.

"We'll grab a few flashlights and check it out."

Against his better judgment, Larry agreed. They left the building on Canal Street and walked up to North Claiborne. There, they made a right and walked down to St. Louis #2 Cemetery.

It was no surprise to Larry that the gate was locked. Lining the perimeter was the wall of oven vaults that Jim had described. The thought of what was inside turned Larry's stomach. It was hard to believe that people considered this a suitable means of burial. No one back in New York would ever go for this.

"I'll hop over first and you follow," said Jim.

"No, we've taken this far enough."

Jim stared at Larry to intimidate him. "I'll meet you on the other side, chickenshit." He put his flashlight in his back pocket and climbed over.

Larry hesitated.

"Well?" Jim said, then Larry reluctantly climbed over.

When he turned from the fence, Jim was gone. All he could see were rows and rows of mausoleums in the shadowy moonlit graveyard.

"Where are you?" No answer. "Quit fucking around, man."

"Over here."

Larry heard the whisper coming from behind one of the mausoleums. With each step, he wondered what the hell he was doing. How did he let himself get talked into doing something so dumb? He couldn't help thinking about movies like *Night of the Living Dead*, and wondering when the zombies would come and get him.

"Where are you?"

"Up here," said Jim.

He was hanging out of a fifth-level vault that apparently had been broken open by vandals. Larry shined his light at Jim.

"What are you doing up there? You're going to get us in trouble."

"You're such a pussy."

Jim got on his hands and knees in the vault as if he were about to climb down, but then it appeared as if something pulled his legs from behind. He landed flat on his stomach. The expression of fear on his face was almost comical, as whatever it was that had him pulled him further into the vault.

Larry wasn't sure how Jim was pulling off his illusion, but it was convincing. Jim desperately tried to cling to the outside of the vault, but the unseen force pulled him until he was consumed by the darkness.

Larry applauded. "Wonderful. Academy Award caliber. Can we go now?"

No answer.

"Enough is enough. This isn't funny anymore."

Still no response.

Larry inched his way toward the open vault.

"Let's get out of here. This place is giving me the creeps."

Larry reached up, intending to help Jim get down, but a hand came out of the vault, latched on to Larry, and pulled him off the ground. The decaying hand that had emerged from the vault had a death grip on him.

He could not escape. As he was pulled into the vault, he couldn't help thinking that if he hadn't doubted Jim's word, they wouldn't be in this mess right now.

When he fell into the hollow pit behind the oven vault, he landed on the pile of decomposing bodies. With his dying breath, the last thought that crossed his mind was that he was right.

The way they bury people in New Orleans is pretty damn gross.

Stains

Lawrence Person

It won't wash off."

Flavius looked up from the table, setting his golden hook aside.

"That's impossible. We have drained all his essences, washed every inch of his body three times. We saw his hands after the last time. There are no wounds. He must be clean."

His young assistant sighed. "I know. But still, they *are* stained. Look."

Flavius walked over to the slab, embalming fluids running down his arms. And saw yet again the blood they had thrice washed away, beading in red droplets on the corpse's hands.

Flavius shook his head. "Then cover him. After tomorrow, it won't matter anyway."

His assistant shrugged, then, with a slight shiver, pulled the sheet up over Pilate's face.

Stakeout

Don D'Ammassa

It was bitterly ironic that Carter failed to lock his car door that late afternoon when he finally caught up to Kaszlow. Like most of Kaszlow's lairs, this was a crumbling tract house in a low-income project, windows shuttered, postage stamp lawn littered with fast food wrappers and other debris, paint cracked and flaking.

The front door was likely to be boobytrapped. Kaszlow was overconfident but not stupid. Carter walked around the house, and found a window that seemed safe, mounted over the kitchen sink.

He returned to the rusting Pinto for his equipment and discovered his mistake. The zipper bag and its contents were missing.

There was no sign of the thief. Carter glanced at his watch. "Damn!" Less than an hour before darkness, certainly no time for a round trip to his motel room. He'd have to improvise.

With a rag wrapped around his hand, Carter smashed the kitchen window, cleared away the shattered glass, and climbed into the house.

The rooms were all poorly furnished and filthy. Kaszlow selected for privacy, not for the amenities. The basement door was in the hall, under the staircase. Carter tried the lightswitch and was pleasantly surprised to discover that it worked, although the small bulb did little more than disperse the shadows crowding around the foot of the staircase.

He descended carefully.

Kaszlow's coffin lay behind the water heater, under a small slit window covered with black felt. Carter approached cautiously. During the three years he'd been pursuing Kaszlow, he had found seven coffins, each untenanted.

The lid was well oiled and failed to creak melodramatically when he lifted it. Carter froze as he stared down into the motionless face of Nils Kaszlow, vampire.

He lowered the lid carefully, silently, even though Kaszlow would not wake before his time even if the house exploded. It was growing dark rapidly. Carter would have to move quickly.

Upstairs, he searched desperately for something he could fashion into the tool he needed. The couch and chairs were modern, plastic and fabric on an aluminum frame, unsuitable for his purposes. But the dining room table was a chintzy imitation mahogany, with legs designed to be removed easily.

It wasn't as sharp as he would have liked, but the end of one leg was reasonably pointed and it would have to do. From the living room window, he could see the sun, an orange globe, dipping toward the horizon.

This time he threw back the coffin lid with a flourish, so that it bounced against its stays and remained upright. His work was going to be awkward without a sledgehammer, but the memory of his dead family was enough to overcome Carter's uncertainties. He raised his makeshift stake high into the air with both hands, and then slammed it down into Kaszlow's chest.

Carter was a strong man, empowered by years of anguish and hatred. The table leg stopped only when it reached the lower surface of the casket.

The deed done, his adrenaline rush rapidly dissipating, Carter staggered up out of the musty basement and threw himself onto the couch, exhausted physically and emotionally. Now that the long quest for revenge was complete, he felt a sudden uncertainty. With his family and job gone, his very sanity tottering, Carter was confused and frightened about the future.

His agitation hadn't diminished appreciably when Kaszlow walked into the room.

"My God!" Carter turned to face his nemesis, but lacked the strength to rise. "How can you be alive?" Or animate anyway. Kaszlow hadn't been alive for at least a century.

The vampire's deeply lined face twisted into what might have been a smile. "You're wondering about this?" He was holding the table leg in his right hand, as though offering it to Carter.

"How could I have missed? It should have gone straight through your heart, you son of a bitch!" Could he have misjudged the angle, stupidly failed on the brink of success?

"Why, no, as a matter of fact." Kaszlow's English was quite good, but there was still the faintest trace of an accent. "A trifle off center perhaps, but remarkably accurate considering the crudity of your attack."

"Then how . . . ?"

"Modern technology," Kaszlow answered pleasantly, moving to

stand directly above Carter. "The small amount of actual wood pulp mixed into this synthetic paste won't even give me heartburn."

Carter was still laughing when the fangs bit into his throat.

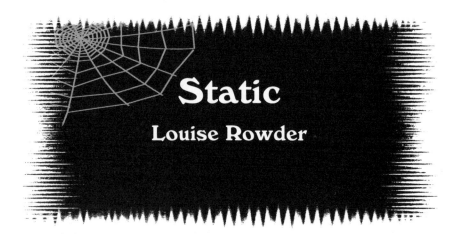

Static

Louise Rowder

Bladrej surreptitiously recorded the small human, Lark, as she continued to energetically kick and yell at the disabled transport. Most of the words filtered through the translator were little more than cloudy static. Perhaps this ceremony was related to the Yelling at Equipment ritual he'd seen mechanics perform. Understanding humans was tough—especially with all their forbidden religious references.

Lark threw a final handful of dirt at the shattered, scarred transport before collapsing in its shade.

"It's hot as h——!" Lark wiped dust from her face.

Bladrej shrugged his photosynthesizing collar and wobbled his eyestalks noncommittally. It was a pleasant day for a walk, but she wasn't showing the bones in her mouth to express pleasure.

"The transport and its radio are shot. We should be able to set up an MB-link when we reach your home. D——!" Lark removed a small yellow bug from her arm. "It's dead; didn't like my coppery blood."

"It's only a few more kilometers." Bladrej tried to be helpful, and pointed toward the shimmering hills and began walking. His large, splayed feet only lightly stirred the sand.

The only sound following them on their walk was the whisper of wind over sand and the steady breathing of the human. The silence was all the sweeter to Bladrej, who knew that soon Lark would feel compelled to shatter it.

As they topped a low rise, Lark pointed toward the hillside fortress. "What are those things outside Kamaiti? They look like trees."

Bladrej had an instinctive dislike for lying, but his orders had been clear: *Record her unprepared reaction.* The golden hills would soon shutter the view. Bladrej tried to turn her attention away from their shadowed tribute.

"Why do humans like noise?" asked Bladrej.

"We're sociable. You're *so* quiet. Except for your religious celebrations, then you sound like you're skinning live cats."

"Cats? What are cats?" Bladrej checked his translator.

"Never mind. Your curiosity is worse than theirs."

Bladrej felt his collar relax and soften across his shoulders. She didn't suspect. He offered up a quick prayer to the gods who made humans so easy to distract.

As they cleared the final rise, the Kamaiti's tribute to the God on a Stick stood revealed.

Lark was obviously impressed—she danced and screamed as she pointed at the two desiccated humans hanging from the creeper-branch crosses—their arms and legs stretched out in a welcoming gesture, a pile of dead insects at their feet.

Despite the fading light, anyone could see that the faces of the aliens—missionaries, Lark called them when her words made sense—were filled with joy. They'd certainly been loud in their worship; Bladrej hadn't known their mouths could open so wide.

Bladrej knew his people did the right thing for those two humans hanging above them. Bladrej worked hard with his people to imitate the pictures and small medallions the missionaries carried. Lark continued to scream and point enthusiastically.

Perhaps Lark wanted help to worship, too? He looked at her.

Bladrej believed in being helpful; it was a cornerstone of his faith.

Stone Face

Blythe Ayne

Alesia stood at her old, bubbly-glassed office window, mesmerized by the black storm pouring out torrents and wind and sheer lonely darkness from a roiling sky above the canyon of office buildings. Lightning tore at the blackening sky with a blinding intensity, followed by shock waves of thunder felt beneath her flesh and deep into her bone.

Her attention was taken by the row of gargoyles on the facing building, at the edge between this dimension, a world of office buildings and boring work, and that other reality—animate wind, wild electricity, crashing clouds, pelting water. The gargoyles hunched and leered at the elements that beat upon them from above and the creatures who made them, scurrying below. They were made to scoff at everything, everyone, including themselves, as water gushed from their mouths. Except the one at the end with a furrowed brow and deep, deep-set eyes, so deep-set—as if what he knew would be too much for any mortal. He had a thin-lipped grimace under high cheekbones and long, protruding, pointed ears; the muscles in his contorted limbs strained as he held up the corner of the building. No water gushed from his mouth.

The image of him fairly bursting from containment of the deluge haunted Alesia, and the gargoyle's deep, bony stare fixed on her as she attempted to return to her work. She decided an early lunch would release the thought. However, after putting on her dark gray trenchcoat she crossed the street, took the elevator to the top floor, walked down the empty hall to where a sign read TO ROOF—NO ADMITTANCE, and opened the door to the gravelly roof.

Her coat whipped like a ship's sail, threatening to take her into the tempestuous sky. Soaking, she struggled to the edge of the building and peered through pointed stone spires. The gutter was jammed with debris—twigs, leaves, and a burbling mud chanting, "Shed blood, shed blood."

Flustered with fear, she reached through the stone spires, grabbing at the twigs and leaves and muck, farther into the back of the creature's throat, grabbing and thrusting, until suddenly a great inhalation of wind flung her backward onto the roof. She landed, sprawling, fingers cut, blood mixing with the downpour and running onto the gravelly roof. She watched the blood flow, amazed that she could do such a thing to herself.

There was a thud beside her. She looked through the sheet of rain into deep, impossibly deep-set eyes.

"You gave me life!" The gargoyle danced stiffly around her. "You not only gave me back my stone life . . . I can't tell you how long my windpipe has been stuck, years and years . . . but you gave me *blood!* You gave me breathing *life!* Oh, those looks we've shared across the distance . . . I knew you cared, but I didn't know you'd give me blood!"

Alesia attempted to sit more ladylike, if such a thing were possible on a roof in a gale storm. "Ahm, well . . . I, uh, I didn't mean to, ah, give you life." The old sadness returned to his eyes, and her heart crumbled into weakness. "I mean, I *felt* something for you, but I had no idea you'd . . . you'd come to life."

He touched her hand and it stopped bleeding, then he sat cross-legged in front of her, looking serious. "You don't want me?"

"Want you?"

"Of course—my life is yours."

"What would I do with you?"

"Anything you please. I'm yours to do with as you please."

"Really?"

"Absolutely."

"It pleases me to see you on the corner of this building, just as you were, except now, you know, able to spout water."

A hundred-year-old melancholy fell on his features, and his sadness touched Alesia profoundly.

After Alesia came down from the roof, she went shopping for pillows, of all things. Then she spent some little while in the ladies' room, attempting damage control to her hair, makeup, and nails. She stuffed the two huge pillows into one of the bags, leaving the other free, then returned to her desk, only a few minutes late.

"What an awful day to go shopping!" her cubicle-mate commented. "What'd you get?" Before Alesia could stop her, she peeked into the bags. "Pillows and . . . a gargoyle? Hmm . . . kind of peculiar, but what great eyes! Looks like it cost a fortune."

Alesia shrugged. "Oh, only a few days' blood."

Straight to the Heart

David Niall Wilson

Hiram stared at the old tree, a slow grin playing across the weathered features of his face. It had been years since he'd seen it, and it could still push the old buttons. He imagined for just a second that he saw faces pressing outward from the bark, calling to him, begging him. Shaking his head to clear it, he hefted the chain saw and moved closer.

The tree bordered his own land and that of Joshua Bagwell; it had stood there for years—too many years. Not a night went by that Hiram didn't see it in his dreams, didn't see the bark chipping and flipping into the darkness, didn't see the trail of sap oozing down the tree where the bullet had struck home. That bullet had missed him. Barely.

His own aim had been better, and all for the love of a woman. That was exactly it, too—her love, not his own. Hiram had been filled with the lust of the moment, but that was all. Amy had wanted him, but she was engaged to Sid Bagwell, Joshua's brother. Hiram hadn't minded a quick roll in the meadow, but there was no way he would ever have tied himself to a woman who'd cheat on her fiancé. She hadn't been able to see past his smile to realize this, and it was under this very tree that they'd been meeting the night Sid found them.

Love is a funny thing. Sid saw Hiram, and then he saw Amy. He smiled at Amy, all tenderlike, and for Hiram his eyes were ice. He was blind to the truth, and though he'd made a half-assed attempt at explaining the truth of the matter, Hiram had known Sid would never listen. They never did, not when they were in love.

Sid had suspected all along what was going to happen that night, so he'd come prepared. He had his pistol, an old one that had belonged to his father, gripped tightly in one white-knuckled hand. Hiram was also no fool. Amy was a beauty, and she wanted him all right, but she was another man's woman. Hiram had his own weapon, tucked beneath his belt, which, thankfully, he'd not yet removed.

He remembered the sharp retort of the old pistol, the puff of smoke, and that barrel, as big around as a train tunnel, staring him down. He remembered the feel of the bark chips embedding themselves in his neck, the certainty that he was a dead man, and the sudden realization he was not. Then his own gun had leaped to his hand—pure instinct, and it was over.

Amy told the truth on the witness stand, and Hiram was left a free man. When he wanted nothing more to do with her, she hanged herself. Here. Right from the lowest limb of this damnable tree that would support her weight.

It had to end. He lit the chain saw off and advanced on the tree, letting the blade swing slowly at the bark, bringing it in at a careful angle. He felt it grip, felt it dig in and rip away the wood.

What happened next was sudden. He heard a sharp sound, like a stone being kicked up by a passing car's tires. The chain saw jerked nearly from his hands, falling to one side, and there was something . . . something wrong with his chest. He fell backward to a sitting position and stared down at his hands. They were already coated in fresh red blood, and more was pouring out of the wound just over his heart.

"The bullet," he muttered, staring at his hands in incredulity, "the damned bullet." He turned to the tree, tried to calculate the angle, but it was too much. His sight was fogging over, and everything was cold . . . very cold.

The last thing to meet his gaze was the tree, looming above him like an avenging angel. In the bark and among the leaves, faces stared back at him, familiar faces. He thought, just for a moment, that Sid smiled.

The Stranger's Tomb

Terry Campbell

We're sure obliged to you for visitin' our humble burial ground, Mr. Farber," the overall-clad yokel said. "And we hope you can find room for us in yer book."

Wylie Farber met the man's hopeful gaze, then studied the rest of the entourage that had gathered at Chapel Hill Cemetery. The locals were much what Wylie had expected when he chose to make Ladonia, Texas, one of the stops in his quest for photographic material for his book, *Memories in Stone—Rural Graveyards of the South*. The people reflected the atmosphere exuded by the town itself—aged and crumbling and near death.

"Well, I hope I can make that a reality," Wylie said.

"Let's show you what ya came to see then."

The cemetery was rather large for a small town in such a state of decay, and very well maintained. Birds chirped, horseflies buzzed, the smell of daffodils lingered in the air. Wylie could detect a clinking noise, the sound of someone toiling in the distance.

"Tell me about the stranger's tomb."

"All anybody knows is from legend," the denizen said. "Back in 1857, a stranger came through these parts. He stayed fer the night at the hotel. He musta been sick, 'cause he died the next day. Nobody knowed his name, nobody knowed where he come from. Seemed only fittin' to give him a proper burial here in our own cemetery." The man stopped in front of a white granite marker that read: THE STRANGER'S TOMB. "And here he lies."

Something about the stone struck Wylie as odd. Then he realized what it was: the tombstone looked new.

"So what do you think?" the townspeople asked.

"To be honest, I was hoping for something a little more photogenic," Wylie said. "Maybe if I looked around, I could find something else I could use."

The group's leader looked insulted. "You don't like the stranger's tomb?"

"It's not that I don't like it . . . ," Wylie said, his words trailing off. "Maybe if I looked around?"

"I don't think that's possible," the man said, suddenly gripping a shovel. Wylie hadn't noticed it, but many of the townspeople were carrying shovels and picks.

"Why not?" Wylie said, glancing down the rows and rows of simple granite markers.

That's when he noticed them. The tombstones. They all bore the same words: THE STRANGER'S TOMB. As far as the eye could see.

Wylie looked back at the first tombstone, and realized what it was that looked so unnatural. The earth around the grave was not flat. There was a noticeable hump with only a scattering of grass growing atop it. Definitely not one hundred fifty years of dirt settling.

"There's a little more to the story of the stranger's tomb." Wylie was only dimly aware that some of the others had begun digging. "The stranger was from New Orleans, and he was some kinda voodoo witch or something. When he was found dead that morning, there was candles and weird books and things that reeked o' Satan hisself."

Wylie looked around nervously. The sun had almost completely disappeared behind the surrounding woods. He suddenly heard a squeaking sound, then realized the distant clinking had stopped. He turned to see a wheelbarrow being rolled into the graveyard, a large chunk of white granite in tow.

"You see, our grandfathers buried that stranger," the farmer said, "but the dangdest thing is, he came back. As a matter of fact, they *all* come back. The first full moon of autumn, they come back."

The squeaking wheelbarrow stopped near the hole that was nearly completed. Wylie realized the cemetery was now well lit by the full, round moon. "I got the stone finished," the new arrival announced.

"We always bury the strangers, Mr. Farber, but they don't stay buried. And it wouldn't be proper to say that we got a stranger's tomb in our cemetery, and not really have a stranger in it. So we got no choice but to replace 'em. You understand, don't you?" The town leader looked around and shivered. "A bit nippy for late September, wouldn't you say?"

Wylie looked down. The dirt around the stranger's tomb was being pushed upward, and a chalky, skeletal hand emerged.

"Right on time," the yokel said. "I'm really sorry you won't be using the stranger's tomb in yer book, Mr. Farber. But maybe we can talk about it again. Say, same time next year?"

Suds

Adam-Troy Castro

It was only after a full afternoon of soaking in the tub that Lydia gave some serious thought to getting up and perhaps spending what was left of her long-awaited day off maybe doing something or other.

Naaaah. More hot water.

She sent her toes the message to emerge from beneath the bubble bath and manipulate the tap.

Nothing happened.

She furrowed her brow, and sent another message racing down her spine. *Come on, toes.*

No go.

Too groggy to be alarmed, Lydia surveyed the surface of Lake Tub. The water was covered with an opaque film of melted soap. The only sign that it contained anything at all were the four small islands formed by her knees and breasts.

Oddly, they did seem to be lying a bit low in the water. And their positions seemed a bit off. It was probably just a trick of perspective, but it nagged at her. She decided to flex her legs so they looked right.

Her legs didn't move.

The cords in her neck tightened just enough to create ripples in the surface of Lake Tub. The ripples traveled in a wide semicircle from the place where the curve of her shoulders disappeared below the surface of the water. Her breasts bobbed up and down like things with no substance of their own. Her knees capsized entirely, revealing what lay underneath: a soft spongy whiteness the consistency of melted soap.

She tried to scream, but couldn't muster the breath.

The water lapped over the tops of her shoulders, melting them like sugar beneath a warm spring rain. Her neck and head slid down the porcelain backrest and met the surface of the water. The splash sent a fresh pattern of ripples against the four small islands of flesh bobbing at the far end of the tub. All four rode much lower in the water after the ripples crashed against their shores.

The ripples hit the far wall of the tub and returned. They lapped gently against her neck and lower jaw. She instantly lost all sensation in both. Her head slid the rest of the way down, hit the water, and began to drift.

Screaming was no longer possible. She could only open her eyes and focus on the only parts of her body that still remained solid: essentially, two wafer-thin slivers of cheek, an upper lip, and a nose that now cut the surface of the water exactly like the dorsal fin of a shark.

Somewhere far away, the front door of the apartment slammed. "Hello?" her husband called. "Lydia? You home?"

In here! she breathed. *Please!*

A ripple washed over her upper lip. Good-bye, upper lip. More water washed over her cheeks, and then they were gone too.

She heard Harold turn on the lights in the bedroom. She heard the springs on the mattress bounce as he put down his briefcase. Then she heard him approaching the bathroom.

She heard all this while her eyes sank beneath the surface, and her view of the ceiling blurred behind a translucent curtain of soapy water.

Hurry!

The doorknob clicked.

"Oh, damn," he muttered. "Lydia, did you spend the whole day in there again?"

Her nose was going down now, pointing straight up in the air, like the *Titanic* in its final death throes, and slowly but majestically sinking, while in her by now thoroughly deranged panic she thought she heard a heavenly choir singing "Nearer, My God, to Thee."

Harold rapped on the door. "Lydia?"

He went away, came back with the key, and unlocked the door.

Then he walked over to the bathtub and looked down.

All he saw was a tub of soapy water, discolored by an oily, gelatinous cloud just below the surface. He thought it was undissolved bubble bath. He couldn't know that it was alive, and terrified, and aware of every move he made.

He *tsk*ed disgustedly, said, "Come on, at least empty the damn thing," reached down, and pulled the plug.

Then, still muttering his annoyance, he put away her soap, her towel, her bathrobe . . .

. . . and her bottle of extra-strength skin moisturizer.

Summer Retreat

Kevin Shadle

It wasn't easy for Basil: being head of the Copse household, perennially sneaking around, fabricating stories, taking risks to meet his family's needs.

Still, life was normal most of the time. They lived in a nice brick house, out in the sticks. He was an elder at church. Holly, his wife, always kept herself spruced up. Their son, Laurel, was very popular. Little Poppy was truly the apple of everyone's eye; she'd be five months old on the vernal equinox.

He got out of the car, shut off the lights, and took the full trash bag from the trunk. Willow, the cat, watched curiously. Basil hated stealing from the morgue—doing so really mushroomed the risks—but it hadn't been a fruitful winter.

Bark! Bark! Barkbarkbarkbarkbark! Buckeye greeted him. He planted a kiss on Holly's two lips and tousled Laurel's bushy hair. "Poppy killed a mouse today," Holly said as they sat down to dinner.

"Great! I told you putting my seed in her formula would do the trick! You kept the mouse, didn't you?"

Holly nodded. Laurel complained about the leafy vegetables.

"Now, son," Basil said, "we need plant foods in the winter, just like we need meat in the summer."

"Go figure."

It wasn't easy, being a Copse.

Barkbarkbarkbark.

The next day, Basil and Holly went out to their shed and began opening the forty other bags.

"Oh, whew!" said Holly, "this is the part I hate." She stepped outside to puke, then returned to find Basil elbow-deep in the bags. "That smell!"

Basil stood, his arm slimy with blood. "It just means the flesh is decomposing, my honeysuckle, and that's good." He grabbed a rag and wiped most of the slippery human remains off.

"Hello there, neighbors." They both jumped at the voice. "Preparing for your summer retreat? Basil—your palm!"

"Huh? Oh, I must have cut myself."

"Yes, we're getting ready," Holly said, going to the door to escort the neighbor away.

When she returned, Basil said, "Now *that's* the part *I* hate. I'm going to go dig."

"Need any help?"

"No, you make sure ol' Lonely Neighbor doesn't come back."

He crept out to the clearing in the forest and raked away the leaves they had dropped there last fall. He had barely dug the largest hole, eight feet wide and five feet deep, when Laurel came running to him.

"Dad, Dad, Mom just got some fresh food!"

"Fresh? Okay, let's go help her. Hurry!"

They found her trying to push the wheelbarrow while keeping the neighbor's limp body in it. She had shoved a garden stake through his iris, into his brain.

"Good job, Mom!"

"Good job, my rosebud. We'll harvest him first."

"Hey, Buckeye! Quit peeing on my leg!"

"The time is near, isn't it, son? Hey, do you want to help."

Would he? He was plumb tickled to.

Laurel took the knife and began pruning the flesh from the neighbor's limbs, dropping it in the holes. It was fun, and Laurel was glad he was finally old enough to help with this family chore.

It took all day for them to dig five more holes of varying sizes and scrape the meat into them. Holly lovingly put the mouse Poppy had killed into one of the smaller holes. When they finally topped off the holes with dirt, they were left with a bag of bones which Basil took to the quarry for disposal.

That evening they vegetated, watching some sappy sitcoms in front of the fire made from the neighbor's clothes.

Three days later Laurel balanced an egg on the kitchen table before they undressed and solemnly walked out to the clearing. Holly laid Poppy on the circle of ground where the mouse was buried. She looked at a wound on Basil's thigh, the one in the shape of a heart with four letters in it. "Young love," she said, and gingerly kissed the year-old scar tissue.

Each stood in the middle of a circle, arms outspread, and looked up toward the life-giving sun. Within minutes they felt their legs elongate and sink into the earth. Their faces began to dissolve; their skin began to harden. As their heads rose toward the sky, their body hair began to change, becoming thick and lush.

At least they were all together—Elder, Spruce, Poplar, Apple, Dogwood, and Pussy Willow.

It wasn't easy, even for the Copse family, being were-trees.

Swamp Flowers
David C. Woomer

The flat-bottomed skiff cuts cleanly and silently through the black water. It is late afternoon, and the sunlight struggles to penetrate the thick vegetation. Cypress trees crowd in close around me, and from somewhere a loon lets out an unearthly cry—I cannot tell direction or distance because the trees damp and reflect the sound so thoroughly. The heat is oppressive and the air so thick I can hardly draw a breath. Nonetheless, I stop paddling to shudder and wrap my bare arms around my body. I glance at the newspaper-wrapped bundle in the bottom of the skiff and feel strangely comforted. August third, our anniversary, and I do not want to miss her. In the twenty years since it happened, I have never missed her. Lynette.

What on earth had possessed us to spend even a small part of our honeymoon in the Great Dismal Swamp? Going out at night was stupid, but we were young and invincible, were we not?

I shake the thoughts out of my head and concentrate on finding the spot. I check my compass again, and then I see it: the scarred, dead cypress tree. A quick mind flash before I can stop it: Lynette striking the trunk head first, the crack of skull on wood like that of a ball player getting all of a high fastball and sending it far into the stands. Lynette slumping into the black water, probably already dead, taking our dreams with her. Me, diving in after her, scraping my chest and sides on submerged roots. Floundering and splashing all around, screaming her name, not finding her.

Her body was never recovered. I still have nightmares about a swamp-going scavenger dining on her remains. Her eyes are always open in the dreams.

I gently lower the cinder block into the still water to anchor the skiff. I pick up the bundle and peel layers of newspaper carefully away to avoid damaging the delicate contents.

A dozen roses, long-stemmed, flawlessly red. Lynette's favorite. The scent of the roses unleashes a flood of memories and I am helpless to stop them: our first kiss; the lovely, musky scent of her skin the first time we made love; our wedding. As often as the memories come, they never seem to lose their clarity. Nor does the pain they cause ever lessen. I whisper her name.

The ritual begins again.

With a low grunt, I slap the first rose against the base of the tree trunk, scattering petals on the water. "Lynette!" I scream, trying to make my voice match the way it sounded twenty years ago. The voice is older and rougher, but the sound of pain and horror is very nearly the same. With a thorn from the next rose, I trace lines of blood across my chest and sides, unmindful of possible infections. The shallow grooves in my skin do not bleed nearly as much as the wounds I incurred by diving recklessly into the water in my aborted rescue attempt, but they bleed enough.

I take the remaining ten roses and tuck them stem first under my arm, trying not to damage them as I lean against the tree trunk with the other arm for balance. With great care, I lower myself into the murky water.

I take the roses in one hand and I thrash around wildly, screaming her name again and again just as I did twenty years ago. Each time I call out to her, I toss a rose into the air and watch it arc into the water. I repeat this until I'm holding the last rose in my hand.

Holding the flower out in front of me, I become still. I feel the movement of the water on my partially submerged forearm before I see anything. My breath catches in my throat.

Slowly, a hand rises from the water. She still wears the one-carat marquise-cut diamond with matching wedding band. "Lynette." My voice is hardly a whisper. The hand moves forward, reaching for the rose. Barely brushing my skin, the hand takes the offered flower, and both rose and hand disappear from the surface in a trail of silvery bubbles.

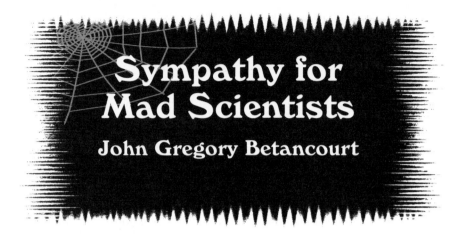

Sympathy for Mad Scientists

John Gregory Betancourt

Dear Dr. Schmidt:

It is with great pleasure that I received your invitation to address the Hammelberg Conference. That you deem my research of interest gives me great encouragement. Yes, yes, a thousand times yes! I shall be happy to attend.

Yours in science,
Baron Victor Frankenstein

Dear Dr. Schmidt:

The train tickets have arrived. I am, however, forced to return one set to you. My assistant, Igor, has suffered an unfortunate accident. Until the pitchfork punctures and torch burns are healed, I have forbidden him to travel.

I anticipate no change in my own schedule, however. Indeed, I find myself keenly anticipating the company of open-minded scientists such as yourself. Here in the lowlands, one is forced to suffer the boorish pranks and pryings of those who would suppress the sciences.

I remain,
Your humble & obedient servant,
Victor

Dear Heinrich:

Pardon my boldness in addressing you by your Christian name, but I feel that I have grown to know you through our correspondence as a friend—as a brother. Your letters offer such support that, at times, I feel they are all that keeps me going.

My assistant, Igor, remains quite ill. I plan to operate on him tonight; perhaps some small part can be saved. Do not worry; nothing will prevent me from attending your conference!

Yours in science,
Victor

Dear Heinrich:

Thank you for asking about poor Igor. Alas, despite my best efforts, all I managed to save was his brain. He will be accompanying me after all, but in freight, as one of the displays for my lecture. (Although a crippled hunchback, he had a good mind. I find his disposition much improved now that he no longer suffers the constant physical agony his old body caused.)

You will understand fully when I unveil my exhibits.

Yours,
Victor

Dear Heinrich:

Pay no attention to rumors spread by rabble such as Dr. Andersen. Although he was my professor some years ago, I have long outstripped his teachings. Rather than blacken the good name of Frankenstein, he should look to *me* for leadership and guidance. I would not scorn him, despite how he persists in treating me. If I have learned one thing from my research here, it is that the quest for knowledge must never be blocked. I am sure you agree.

There are peasants at the castle gates again. I have prepared a cauldron of a particularly noxious-smelling liquid to pour on them from the ramparts. I have had enough of them, and so has Igor!

If only Andersen could be dealt with so easily. I note from the program you enclosed that I am scheduled to follow his paper on brain chemistry. Thank you for that favor, my friend. I shall show him up for the fool he is.

Yours in science,
Victor

Heinrich:

I am bewildered. How can you revoke my invitation to speak at the conference? The program has been printed! Can Dr. Andersen be the cause? Has he spread such vile lies about me that you fear to invite me lest I be assaulted? I can assure you that Igor makes a fine bodyguard. He is somewhat over seven feet tall, with the strength of any ten men. *That* is the extent of my genius. You will understand when you see him.

Andersen is such a *small* man.

Still, I return my train ticket herewith, as requested.

I hear the peasants again. Pray that my wrath does not extend beyond them to your conference and its attendees.

Yours,
Baron Victor Frankenstein

Dear Heinrich:

It seems Igor overheard me reading my last letter to you aloud, and he has run off. His disappointment at not being able to visit your noble city—how eloquently I spoke of its gardens and architecture!—knew no bounds.

Another feather in the cap of Dr. Andersen. Had I wished to attend your conference now, I would not be able to—my chief exhibit has fled.

Yours,
Victor

Dear Heinrich:

I was saddened to hear of the death of Dr. Andersen. A beast tore him apart? How odd! I cannot imagine how such a thing could happen in this day and age. However, I am pleased to accept your apology. I will attend the conference.

More good news: Igor has returned. Perhaps he just needed some time alone.

I look forward to finally meeting you.

Yours,
Victor

Sympathy for Mummies

John Gregory Betancourt

I brushed dust from my eyes, then zippered the tent's flap shut. The wind was coming up again, sighing through our camp. It was a sound I had grown used to over the last two months.

"Everything locked up?" asked Linda, my wife.

"Yep," I said. As director of the excavation, I had to make sure everything was put away before I turned in. Stretching sore muscles, I peeled off my dust-and-sweat–impregnated shirt, then washed up in a basin. "We're getting close," I said.

We were excavating the tomb of Atenkham, a court official in Egypt's Valley of the Kings. Tomorrow we would reach his burial chamber. There was little chance of riches; Atenkham hadn't been a king. But artifacts were gold, metaphorically, to archaeologists.

"Still not worried about the curse?" Linda asked.

"What Egyptian tomb doesn't carry a curse?" I asked with a laugh. I toweled off, then leaned over and planted a kiss on her full red lips. "Besides, curses only apply to big rich tombs when the moon is full and you haven't said your prayers by night."

"Mmm."

"So I get my movies mixed up." I crawled into my sleeping bag, exhausted. It was nearly midnight. I'd be up in five hours.

"Besides," I muttered, "what kind of curse could a bureaucrat muster?"

At dawn the next morning, I was ready for work. Although this was my seventh tomb, I still felt a mounting sense of excitement.

I had dreamed of Atenkham's mummy. I saw priests removing his organs and preserving them in jars. I saw them filling his veins with embalming fluids and carefully wrapping his body in layers of white cotton swathing. But mostly I had seen papyrus scrolls, thousands of them, the lifework of this ancient Egyptian bureaucrat. Those scrolls were the sort of treasure I sought.

Now I would see what truth lay in my dream.

My grad students were sitting at our breakfast table with someone. I sighed when I recognized Mr. Abdul from the Department of Antiquity. He was in charge of excavation permits.

"Mr. Abdul," I said to him, "what brings you here?"

"Paperwork, Mr. Jones," he said in his precise British accent. He passed me a sheaf of papers.

"What's this?"

"New regulations go into effect this morning," he said. "First of the month. I told you last week, as you may recall."

"Yes, yes," I said. He had mentioned something of the sort.

"If you would fill it out, please."

I stared at the forms. None were in English, of course.

"This will take me hours," I said. I glanced over at the tomb. We were so close—

"Paperwork," he said, "must be done properly. I shall leave you to it." He crossed to his jeep, got in, and drove off in a cloud of dust.

"Shall we start anyway, Professor?" Neal Jameson asked me. He was a young, eager, promising grad student.

"No," I said, imaginary bandages tightening around my chest and throat. "Mr. Abdul doesn't like me. If we begin without the paper-work, we'll be shut down."

"He can't—"

"He *can*," I said.

My Arabic was lousy, and making sense of the application was a dense process, even with an interpreter. *This*, I thought at one point, *is the curse of Atenkham: buried alive in paperwork.*

I kept thinking of his mummy, swathed in hundreds of yards of cloth, surrounded by scrolls, laughing at me.

Picketers arrived at two o'clock. They stood outside our camp waving signs: EGYPTIAN TOMBS FOR EGYPTIAN ARCHAEOLOGISTS and NO FOREIGN DIGS! It was an old dispute. Foreigners received more excavation permits than Egyptian archaeologists.

Promptly at three o'clock, Mr. Abdul returned. He had two uni-formed men in his jeep. When Abdul gave the picketers a nod, I felt Atenkham's door slam shut in my face.

"Your papers," I said numbly.

He barely glanced at them. "Permit denied," he said. He stamped the documents in red ink.

"Why?" I asked.

"Improperly filled out. And an objection has been raised."

"Them?" I gestured at the picketers. "You sent them here!"

"Me, Professor?" He raised his eyebrows, feigning indignation. A cheer went up from the picketers as the guards took positions near the tomb entrance.

"And so," I whispered bitterly, "the curse is made true."

"That's it?" Neal Jameson demanded, looking from Abdul to me, shock and outrage on his face.

"Afraid so," I said. "The curse wins out."

"He can't—"

"He did," I said.

Mr. Abdul smiled.

Atenkham must have been like him, I thought to myself.

I knew, suddenly, why pharaohs buried their bureaucrats.

Sympathy for Psychos

John Gregory Betancourt

The spiders were coming for him again. John Crane could hear their footsteps all around him, and he cowered lower in the open grave he'd been digging, his fingers pressing deep into the cold, hard soil.

The footsteps stopped just over his head.

"Hey, Charlie—take a look at this! There's somebody here!"

"What's he doin' there?"

"Crying, looks like." The voice softened, but Crane knew it was a trick. "Hey, buddy, come on out. Nobody's gonna hurt you."

They could only get him if he looked. *Mesmerize with their eyes.* It was their weakness. *Never meet their gaze and you're safe.* If he ever did look, one would jump on his face, stick pincers into his ears, and take control of his mind.

Quickly he began scrabbling at the loose earth and stones, pulling them over himself, trying to somehow disappear from their view. Spiders didn't have long-term memory. He'd escaped from them often enough to know. If they couldn't see him clearly, he wasn't there.

"What's he doing?" he heard the first spider say.

"Forget him," the second said. "Some homeless creep."

Crane lay still, hardly daring to breathe. Slowly he counted to a hundred. They seemed to be gone. He was safe.

After crawling out of the open grave, he paused for a moment, looking this way and that. Spiders could be crafty; this might be a trick. But no, not this afternoon—the old graveyard was deserted as usual.

He picked up the shovel he'd used to dig the grave, turned, and hurried back to the cottage where he lived. Once the place had belonged to the cemetery's caretaker—a strange old fellow named James Wicke—but James had died in the spiders' first attack. That had been almost six months ago. Crane had been lucky. He'd escaped.

The cottage was off the path the spiders usually took. Crane hadn't had much trouble with them until this afternoon, when they'd snuck up on him without warning. As he locked himself inside for the night, he began to shiver uncontrollably.

Tomorrow, he promised himself, he'd spring the trap.

Before dawn he heard them. They came marching through the headstones and monuments and mausoleums like they owned the place. Their legs click-clacked, click-clacked on the marble, and several wailed some weird crooning sound.

Crane peered between shutter slats, out across the tangled vines and waist-high shrubs surrounding the cottage. They were massing around the grave he'd dug . . . six humans, all with spiders on their heads. He knew they were trying to pick up his scent.

He had dug tunnels all through the graveyard as a precaution. Now he knew what to do. First he took Wicke's old pistol from its velvet-lined case, checked it over, and made sure it held six bullets from his precious small supply. Then he tucked it into his belt and took a deep breath. This was always the hardest part. But it was necessary. Pulling up the trapdoor in the center of the floor, he lowered himself through, then carefully, navigating by touch alone, he moved forward through darkness. A wet, earthy smell rose all around him.

Then, finally, he was in position. He paused, straining to hear. From overhead came the muted sound of voices . . . the spiders talking among themselves.

". . . to ashes, dust to dust, we return . . ."

". . . a nice fellow, never deserved . . ."

". . . can't wait till it's over . . ."

He ignored the hypnotic power of their words. Their voices could dull his senses. Spiders were crafty, but he was craftier. He was directly below them. He had measured carefully.

Tensing, he gripped his pistol more tightly. Then with a savage cry he broke through the side wall, into the grave, into the sunlight, out, and on top of something hard and made of wood.

The spiders gaped down at him, all pressing closer to get a better look, preparing to pounce—

Crane whirled, squeezing off six shots in quick succession. The spiders were collapsing with inhuman screams. He pulled himself back into his tunnel, crawling like his life depended on it.

He emerged on the far side of the graveyard, through a secret opening at the base of the statue of an angel. Cautiously he circled around to see the spiders and their hosts.

All of the humans were dead. He'd hit each of them once in the forehead. He felt no emotion at their deaths though. They'd been brainless slugs, controlled utterly by their inhuman riders. But the spiders he'd seen on them . . . they were gone now. *Crawled away in the grass*, he thought uneasily, looking around. He'd been so sure he'd hit at least *one* this time.

Not this time, though. Next time he'd get them. He knew it.

He'd been telling himself that for the last six months, ever since he shot Wicke to save him from the spider on his head.

He began pushing bodies into the grave he'd dug. He'd bury them before more spiders came. If they saw human corpses, they'd get suspicious, and that wouldn't do. As it was, he'd have to get rid of the cars they'd brought. But there was a lake at the back of the cemetery, and he thought it still had a little room left, deep at the bottom.

Then he heard a small sound behind him. His stomach became ice. He touched the pistol at his belt, but he knew it was empty. The hairs on the back of his neck began to prickle with their nearness.

At last a hard pincer touched the small of his back.

"Don't move," the spider said. "You're under arrest."

He gave a shudder, then whirled suddenly, trying to grapple with the creature. But it fired on him, and as pain bit into his belly and chest, as he felt himself falling and the world closing in, he heard the creatures laughing, a chorus of them, and finally he knew the truth.

The spiders had him all along.

Sympathy for Vampires

John Gregory Betancourt

Shelly," a low voice called. "Shelly, my love."

The curtains billowed, even though there was no breeze, and suddenly he was floating there: Fred Davis, my next-door neighbor. For the last week, he'd been visiting my bedroom window each night and trying to get in. I wondered if his wife knew.

I held out a silver crucifix with a hand that trembled more from annoyance than fear. He hissed and averted his gaze.

"You may not come in," I said firmly.

"An invitation to visit cannot be revoked," he said.

"Well, I'm revoking it anyway," I said. "That invitation was made before your death. Or undeath. Or whatever you call it."

"Rebirth," he whispered.

"Begone!" I cried, and I shut the window.

He floated outside for fifteen minutes, calling my name, but I ignored him. Finally he left.

Enough was enough. The next morning, I went over to Fred's house. His wife answered my knock, opening the door a few inches and peering out. She had a doleful expression. Dark circles lined her eyes.

"Good morning, Shelly," she said.

"Good morning, Mindy," I said. "I hate to bother you . . . but I'm having trouble with Fred."

"What kind of trouble?"

"He's been outside my window every night this week, calling my name and trying to get in."

"He's going through a difficult period . . ."

"I'm sure he is," I said firmly, "but I need my sleep. If it happens again, I'm going to call the police."

"I'll talk to him," she promised.

I didn't see Fred for a few days. But then on Friday night, as I was returning late from the supermarket, I spotted him hovering over my house.

"Shelly, my love . . ." he called softly.

I felt my stomach tighten with barely concealed rage. Neighbor or not, he wasn't going to harass *me*.

"Shelly . . ."

I opened the garage door with the remote control and drove in. By the time I turned off the engine and got out of my car, he was waiting. He wore a long black cape with a red lining. He held out a single black rose for me.

"Here," I said, thrusting bags of groceries into his arms. "You win. I'm yours."

"I *vant* to *suck* your *blood!*" he said in a Bela Lugosi voice.

"Yes, well, there'll be time for that later, after chores." I pulled out two more bags. "Into the kitchen!"

"But—"

"Move it!"

He took a step back and tried staring me down. He arched his eyebrows.

I frowned. "Look, Fred, if you're going to leave Mindy for me, we're going to need some ground rules. First, no evil-eye tricks. You're giving me a headache. Second, no biting till after chores are done, and not at all on work nights. And third, all this skulking about stops tonight."

"Skulking?" he asked.

"You know, going out every evening. I want you inside at eight o'clock sharp. I have a schedule, you know."

"Schedule?"

"You'll be a big help," I continued, getting into it. "Friday is bathroom cleaning night. I've always wanted a man around for the hard work—you know, scrubbing the toilets and the shower stalls, then mopping down the tile. It won't take more than an hour or two. After that we can start on the kitchen. And I want to rearrange the bedroom furniture. And then—"

Abruptly I found myself talking to a dense gray fog. My bags of groceries settled onto the car's trunk. Then the fog evaporated.

I snorted. Cleaning toilets wasn't part of the romance of being a vampire, I supposed.

For the next few weeks, I made a show of looking for Fred. I left my bedroom windows open. I called to him whenever he flew overhead, as I used to hear Mindy call when he first became a vampire. He never answered.

That was two months ago. I don't keep garlic and holy water close at hand anymore, though I still wear my crucifix.

Fred's been spotted by daylight now and again, so perhaps he's turning back into a dutiful husband. I hope so. Still, I can't help feeling sorry for him . . . for them both. And sometimes I wonder if that's why I haven't married. What sort of beast would I bring out in a man . . . and what sort of beast would he bring out in me?

Sympathy for Wolves

John Gregory Betancourt

I could hear wolves scratching like dogs at my door again. It was a full moon, or close to it, and I still felt a stirring deep in my soul, a longing to join them for the hunt, just as they longed to join me. I fought it, as I always did, and those wolfish instincts subsided for a time.

As I pulled back the shade and peered out, I marveled at the crystalline perfection of a crisp Montana night. It was January, and a coating of frost had silvered the land, etching a light pattern of crystals around the windowpanes.

I couldn't help myself. I opened the window and leaned out, sniffing the air, letting my senses heighten and expand well beyond the human norm.

Six gray wolves stood on the ridge behind my house, noses up, smelling the air this way and that, letting loose yips and soft communicative growls. Their leader, who called himself Bear-Hunter, was an old male with a long white scar down the left side of his haunches. He'd gotten it years ago in a brief fight with a bear (he lost). Bear-Hunter glanced at me and gave a plaintive cry.

"Not tonight," I whispered. "It's too cold. I'm human."

I leaned back and shut the window. Suddenly I shivered uncontrollably. It was bitterly cold out there. I didn't envy them their freedom. On nights like this, I knew I'd made the right choice in trying to remain a man. If I'd given in to my wolf instincts and let myself go, given in to my desires to *be* a wolf, I'd be suffering like them. No, I was better off holed up in my house with its oil heat and its thermal windows and its wood-burning stove, a human safe and secure and, if not entirely happy, at least warm.

The wolves began to bay, calling to one another, pack to pack, and other wolf howls answered through the still night air. There were at least thirty separate voices, probably more, and as I listened to the rich timbral sounds, I began to identify one and another and another. Rabbit-Hunter, Silverpaw, Snowfoot, all the rest, coming down from the hills to see me.

They knew I had a soft heart. And finally, as they encircled my house, crying, I could resist their calls no longer.

I strode to my door, threw it open, and one by one they slunk into my living room. Old Bear-Hunter came last, gazing up into my face with his piercing yellow eyes, as if searching for some trace of my lost wolfhood. I met his gaze for a second, then looked away, submissive. He could be leader; I didn't want the responsibility.

And on that cold, cold, bitterly cold night, as I stretched out on my sofa before the crackling fire, I could hear the soft lapping of water from my toilet bowl, hear the soft rustling of paws prying open the refrigerator door and rummaging through the meat bin for coldcuts and steaks, hear the squeaking of springs as heavy feet circled three times on my bed before lying down.

And, as often happened on these cold and lonely nights, all these wolves who had once been men joined me for a brief time in my humanity, and I joined them in their wolfishness, laying my head upon my paws and pulling my tail around my nose for the night with a reluctant yet somehow happy sigh, and the pack was whole.

Teacher's Pets

Hugh B. Cave

I discovered the footprints on a Sunday morning when I went to get the newspaper out of our roadside box. The first snow of the season had fallen during the night.

Something with bare feet had walked up our driveway. I say some-*thing* because the prints were too wide and blunt to have been made by human feet. Halfway up the driveway they turned off into the woods, toward the home of our nearest neighbor, Professor Langendorf.

The professor lived alone with several strange-looking dogs that we had never been able to identify because he let them out only at night. Before retiring to our rural community, he had taught biology at a university I'd better not name, because folks say he was dismissed for working on experiments his superiors didn't approve of. Something to do with gene transplants.

Langendorf was something of a recluse, so after showing my wife those strange footprints that Sunday morning, I said to her, "Ellen, we better go over there." I was a police officer before I retired. Without even thinking, I took along my old thirty-eight.

We walked down the road together and rang the professor's front doorbell. No one answered. A little surprised, we went around to the back and found the back door wide open.

In the snow on the wooden stoop were two more footprints like the ones in our driveway. Turning, I saw where the creature had come out of the woods and walked to the house.

"Hey, Professor!" I called, but got no answer, so we took a chance and went on in.

Professor Langendorf was dead in a lake of blood on the pale gray carpet in his living room. Slashed to death, apparently, by some kind of animal with long, sharp claws.

While Ellen used his phone to call our local police, I looked around and found a notebook lying open on a desk in the prof's study. We gave it to the police when they arrived, but I remember some of the entries. They went about like this, with dates three or four months apart:

> Every breed of dog has its defects, but I think by mixing genes I may be able to produce something superior.
> Success at last, but only in a limited way.

And the last entry:

> Still only partial success. What would happen, I wonder, if I used a human gene?

A shout from Ellen in the living room interrupted my reading. "Joe! Come here! Quick!" Rushing back there, I found my wife staring at the carpet again. "Look!" she said, grabbing my arm to steady herself.

We hadn't noticed it before because it was at the edge of the big bloodstain and almost blended with it . . . Almost but not quite. There, apparently written by some kind of animal paw dipped in the blood, was the following message:

DAMN YOU, LANGENDORF, I DON'T APPRECIATE BEING PUT INTO THE BODY OF A DOG!

Side by side we stood there, staring at it until suddenly, without warning, a door crashed open behind us. We spun around.

On two legs, like an angry bear, the thing rushed at us. When I saw the claws on its outstretched hands, or paws, I knew this was the thing that had killed Langendorf and left the message. I did what any sensible man would have done in such a situation. Snatching my weapon from its holster, I squeezed the trigger until the gun was empty. That stopped the creature.

I won't try to describe it. I'm not that good with words, and, for that matter, the police never really described it either. I can tell you this much, though. As it lay sprawled on its back on the carpet, looking up at us in death, there was an expression of relief, even gratitude, on its doglike face. A look of peace.

There was no sign of the professor's other pets anywhere in that old house, so even though the place is boarded up now, we wonder, Ellen and I, what else may be out there in the woods, and what other kind of footprints we may discover someday on our driveway.

It's a thing we think about a lot.

Temperance
Stephen Mark Rainey

I met her in a little dive bar off Rush Street, where most of the clientele looked like they'd been swept in the door by a passing street cleaner. She was beautiful; tall, with raven hair, wide green eyes, narrow lips. Long muscular legs.

She was devastating in a slinky black catsuit, with leather boots and a gold chain around her waist, and as out of place here as a queen among peasants. My curiosity, among other things, became aroused.

She noticed me almost immediately. Not to brag, but I hardly look like the refuse that teetered on these barstools slurping cheap beer at repulsive volume. I also wore black: silk shirt, jeans, leather boots, and duster. One seldom dresses to impress when visiting dive bars, but I had stopped in here because I've often found the most interesting things in shadowy grottos. Eventually, I would make my way toward some of Chicago's more exclusive night spots.

She spared me the trouble of making the first move, because, before I knew it, she had sauntered up and placed a gin martini in my hand.

"I'm Lysette," she purred softly. "And who might you be?"

"Sean. You drink martinis too?"

"Sometimes. You look like a man who likes things . . . strong."

Dozens of murky eyes ogled Lysette, and if she noticed, I'm sure she enjoyed it. But for the moment, her attention was focused solely on me.

"I appreciate a woman with the self-confidence to indulge her, shall we say, exhibitionist tendencies?"

Her eyes sparkled. "I'm . . . hunting."

"I see."

She slid close to me and wrapped herself in my free arm. "I think I've found what I'm looking for."

I nodded. "I should say so."

She leaned over and kissed me gently on the neck. One of the nearby "patrons" chuckled and muttered, "Kissy, kissy. Ain't that sweet."

Lysette looked at him: an old wrinkly thing who should have stopped drinking in 1970. "That was no kiss," she said, then turned and locked her lips to mine, working her tongue deep into my mouth. I responded ardently, but she quickly withdrew and turned back to the tippler. "One day," she whispered seductively, "if you're a lucky, lucky boy, maybe you'll get a real kiss too."

The old man hissed embarrassment and disgust, and turned back to the more rewarding prospect of a glass of Old Style.

Lysette said to me, "Shall we get some fresh air?"

"Yeah," I said, downing my martini quickly. "It's stifling in here."

We stepped into the chilly night, and I pulled Lysette close, wrapping her in my duster. We kissed again, and her taste, her scent was exquisite. She had an animalistic aura that I found enthralling. Perhaps I might forget about any further social venues this evening.

Just then, I heard a nearby yammer of voices—Spanish, by the sound of them. Something hard smashed into the back of my head, sending me reeling to the sidewalk. Through a red-tinged mist, I made out a trio of figures swarming around Lysette, who crouched defensively, vainly attempting to reach me.

"Snag his wallet, quick!" one of the youths yelled in English.

I felt a hand rifling my duster—but suddenly a harsh, guttural roar came from nearby, and something hot and wet showered over me.

The questing hand fell to the sidewalk, severed at the wrist. I rolled onto my back, saw a flash of something large and black. I heard screaming from all quarters now—and a shrill wail as a second assailant fell beneath the ripping claws of a sleek jaguar. Blood spewed as fangs tore through flesh. And in a moment, the surviving attacker had fled into the night, leaving the cat to almost playfully shred his two unfortunate companions.

I rose, and the jaguar gazed at me with cool green eyes, which quickly became Lysette's. She hurried to me, touched my cheek with worried fingers.

"Are you all right? I'm sorry. . . ."

I swatted her across the face and she fell onto her backside. *Damn it,* I swore. She was skillful; she had masked her true nature incredibly well.

My claws had ripped a furrow in her cheek. I saw tears welling in her eyes, and she shouted, "Get the hell away from me! Now!"

Happy to oblige, I broke into a furious run down the deserted street, raising my voice in a long, piercing howl. I couldn't believe I had been fooled; a werewolf's senses *are* extraordinarily keen.

It wouldn't have been so bad, except that I've always hated cats.

Terminal Intensity

Joel S. Ross

Morgan ripped off his earplug. "Trouble," he said. "We go in now!"

"Wait," said Lucy Medina. "He hasn't made the buy yet."

"Big deal." Morgan checked his revolver. "They've made him."

"What if . . . ?"

He pushed himself out. "And what if it were you alone in there, surrounded by pushers? You coming?"

Morgan was just like her ex-husband, except Morgan didn't end his condescending remarks with "poor kid."

Lucy fumbled for the radio. "Officers need assistance, a Hundred Sixty-Fourth and Third. Backup!"

Morgan was gone, already in the Bronx tenement, probably through the front door. A middle-aged cowboy, fighting male menopause, he'd take the direct, dangerous approach. The Book said cover the rear.

Lucy slipped around back, greeted by silence, except for vague, soft sounds. Her penlight beam revealed only battered garbage cans overflowing with stench, and the discards of the unwanted.

By the numbers. Revolver drawn, breath in, out, don't blast at shadows.

If something was going down, there should be shouts, shots, something.

With only six months on narcotics stakeout, she didn't know all the tricks and could only go by the Book and trust instincts which hadn't served her well thus far.

Behind her . . .

She froze, heard nothing, but it was there, just the same, like a rash on your back, felt if unseen.

She inched toward the door, her sweat-slicked finger caressing the grooved trigger, and peeked around the corner and ducked back.

Nothing. Spanish music drifted across the alley as . . .

Clanging behind her. She whirled. A rat the size of a cat stood on hind legs by the tipped trash, teeth glinting, challenging her for the feast of scattered discards.

A dull boom. Then another, followed by a crisper, louder bang.

Yelling—in Spanish and English.

Doors banging open and slamming shut.

She crouched against the cooling brick and sighted down the barrel. Two men dashed past, one clutching glassine bags filled with white, the other a shotgun.

"Police! Freeze!"

They spun. She fired twice, the muzzle blast blinding and deafening her. She blinked away the flash's afterimage. The shotgun toter lay dead, a glistening rose blossoming across his chest.

Footsteps down the alley.

Check on her partners or chase?

She sprinted after the cocaine holder.

The alley ended in a T. Left or right? There was no telltale sound of clopping feet. Quick, or she'd lose him.

Left.

Soggy refrigerator cartons rested against one corner, offering no cover but some concealment. She sidestepped against the wall, her revolver probing the dark.

An angry squeal from a rat larger than the one behind her.

Out of the corner of her eye she saw a lighter shadow within the darker one.

She pivoted and fired.

A hot punch slammed into her chest, knocking the wind from her lungs, the legs out from under her. Flattened now, she saw the dealer scoot away.

Her gun . . . but her fingers refused to obey. Nothing moved, hands, feet, head. She stared at the cracked wall, wondering if she'd hear the sirens wail before she bled to death.

Gut shot, her life spurted away through punctured arteries.

The Book said stuff the wound and roll onto her stomach to slow the bleeding, but the only thing she still controlled was her eyelids.

She only had minutes, unless help came at once.

Few windows looked down on the alley, and no lights came on. In the ghetto—with shots and screams part of the landscape—no one would help, or even call.

She shivered, a reflex independent of conscious movement. *Guys, the backup call was five minutes ago!*

In her case, the rest of a lifetime.

Claws scrabbled behind her.

Rats.

Peering down her leg, she saw her jeans jerk as they gnawed her still-warm meat. She screamed, but made only a throttled gasp. She coughed out a half-congealed glob of blood and tried again, making a mewling sound.

Sirens now, but probably too late. Her hemorrhaging increased as the rodents feasted on her.

Dimness . . . blackness. Up ahead—as she cartwheeled through a tunnel—a pinpoint of brilliance became the size of a dime at arm's length, then a nickel, a quarter.

"Medina, hang on! Fight with us!" The voice came from her old lifetime. "Don't die, Lucy!"

She paused, contemplating her inaction.

Should she return to her inert body, to life as a quadriplegic, with machines breathing for her, living for her, or pack it in?

The siren grew louder and the light shrank back to dime size.

"Hang on, Lucy! Poor kid."

She coasted toward the light, now big as a half-dollar.

The Book couldn't advise her this time.

She did nothing, and thus decided.

The next life at the tunnel's end might be better.

She accelerated toward the brilliance, bursting through placental fluid toward delivery room lights.

An obstetrician held her up. "A girl . . . Something's wrong . . ."

"Spinal cord damage! She'll never walk. Poor kid."

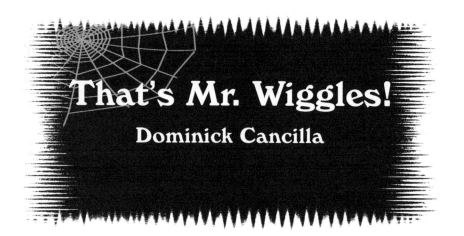

That's Mr. Wiggles!

Dominick Cancilla

Elvira Tugalug was an aging nutcase, but when she called the All Volunteer Fire Brigade they came running just as they would for anyone else.

Not that they didn't gossip about her a bit on the way.

"They say she fancies herself a witch," Billy-Ray Knolls yelled over the blare of the siren.

"I hear she tries to call down hail on the PTA picnic every year," Geordie Gallagher shouted back.

"My boy's afraid she'll turn him into a frog," Marvin Barbatson yelled over his shoulder. The others told him to concentrate on traffic.

They got to Elvira's house—a rickety gray thing with a gabled roof and dead lawn—in record time. To a man, they were disappointed that no smoke was visible, but Elvira Tugalug, running back and forth along the sidewalk in panic, seemed to have enough fire in her to keep them busy.

As soon as the old woman's eyes caught the bright red engine, she began jumping about in place and pointing to the huge fir tree that dominated her front yard.

"Uh-oh," said Marvin, shutting off the siren.

"What?" asked Geordie.

Marvin sighed. "She's pointing to a tree."

"Oh, drat," said Billy-Ray. "A cat."

If there was one thing the Fire Brigade hated, it was treed cats. Rescuing pets seemed a horrible waste of their one-weekend-a-month training.

Geordie hopped down from the cab just as the engine was pulling to a stop. "Did you call us, ma'am?" he asked as he quickly stepped over to the frantic woman.

"It's Mr. Wiggles," Elvira said, waving both arms at the tree. "He won't come down! I should never have let him out!" The hem of her black sack dress and the rim of her pointed witch's hat bounced with each hop, making her look like something fresh out of a jack-in-the-box. To Geordie, she smelled like an egg farm.

"Don't worry, ma'am, we'll take care of Mr. Wiggles," he said, and turned to address his companions. "Get the ladder."

As the three men struggled to get their largest extension ladder off the back of the truck, people gathered along the sidewalk at either end of Elvira's property, drawn by the fire engine and, perhaps, the hope that their odd neighbor's house was in danger of burning down.

"Thank you, gentlemen, thank you!" Elvira gushed when the men walked past her with the ladder. "I'll bless you all! You'll be wealthy! Famous! Fertile beyond your wildest dreams!"

Billy-Ray, whose wife had just delivered their fourth, rolled his eyes. "Just what I need," he mumbled under his breath.

At the base of the huge tree they set the ladder down. None of them could spot the cat through the thick needles.

"How high up is he?" Geordie called to Elvira, who was once again running up and down the sidewalk.

Elvira interrupted her cry of "Woe is me, woe is me!" with "He's at the tippy-top. Poor Mr. Wiggles!" and resumed her bizarre fit of panic.

"I'll go up," Billy-Ray said. "Geordie can hold the ladder, and Marv, you can stand by with the big hose to melt the witch if she tries to zap me."

"Very funny," said Marvin.

They separated, put the ladder in place, and extended it as far up the tree as it would go. Billy-Ray started to climb.

"Be careful," Elvira shouted as he started up the ladder. "Mr. Wiggles isn't used to firemen. I just conjured him up this morning!"

There were giggles from the growing crowd.

Almost a minute passed and Geordie was starting to get nervous. "Billy-Ray?" he called up the ladder.

His answer was an inhuman cry, sharply cut off. Before anyone could react, Billy-Ray's flayed corpse was ejected from the tree with enough force to carry it across the street, followed closely by his bundled clothes and then his skin, folded like a new shirt. People in the crowd started to scream, faint, and wet themselves all at once.

The cry had sent Geordie rushing up the ladder, but the horrific sight stopped him in his tracks. He turned to Elvira and yelled, "My God! What kind of cat is it!"

Elvira stopped, looking surprised. "Who said anything about a cat?" she asked above the commotion. "That's Mr. Wiggles!"

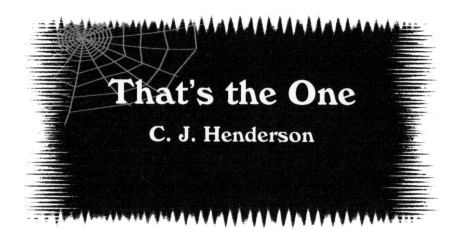

That's the One

C. J. Henderson

"That's the one!"

The two officers continued to move in on the young blonde girl as the tiny bottle kept screaming, "That's her! She won't drink me. I keep flashing my tag at her; she picks me up, reads it, sniffs, and then she just puts me back down. Over and over and *over!*"

"We'll handle this," interrupted the senior officer. Turning toward the somewhat frightened girl, he asked, "All right then, what's the story, Alice?"

"Please, sir," she answered, "I'm afraid."

"Afraid of what?"

"The fall down the rabbit hole was so awfully terrifying. I don't want to go on any further. I just want to go back home."

The junior of the two enforcers had already positioned himself behind the girl. Holding the indignant bottle in his hand, the older of the pair said, "Alice, you *have* to go on into Wonderland. You can't just go back home. That's not the way the story goes. You can't just go back the way you came—no one can. One must always struggle forward against the world no matter how absurd it seems." The senior officer sniffed absently at the air, then added: "My dear, you have literary precepts to reinforce."

"I don't care," wailed the crying girl. "I want to go *home!*"

The older man with the bottle nodded. His partner grabbed Alice, holding her firmly. Quickly they pried her jaws apart and forced most of the bottle's contents down her throat.

Mike closed the magazine at that point. "Too bizarre," was his only comment on the story he had been reading as he put it aside.

Besides, he thought, *I'm just stalling.*

Mike picked up the gun again. He had bought it two days after she had left. It had gotten to the point where he could no longer remember how many times he had taken it from its box, cleaned it, loaded it, placed it in his mouth . . . and then backed down. The wastebasket was overflowing with crumpled suicide notes.

The newest one, fresh from his printer, lay on his desk looking up at him. Staring at the letter, he fumblingly picked up the revolver once more. Closing his eyes, he slipped the barrel between his lips and began tightening his finger around the trigger—and then, once more, he set the heavy piece of metal back down on the table and walked away from it.

But this time he did it for a different reason.

Suddenly, he realized, he was being more than foolish—he was acting childishly and just plain stupid.

No matter how definite it had seemed that his only course of action was to take his own life, that feeling had passed. He knew now he would not kill himself. When the door to his apartment started to open, he was smiling. By the time the squeaking hinge caused him to look toward the door, the officers were already inside.

"That's the one!" screamed the revolver, huffing with indignation. "That's him!"

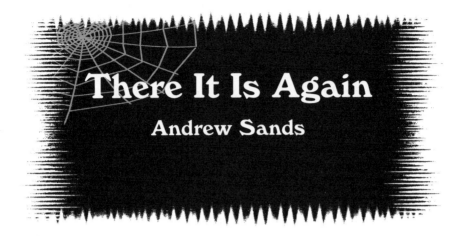

There It Is Again

Andrew Sands

Vivian heard something.

She was in bed with her husband, her mind perched precariously between being fully awake and drifting blissfully back to sleep, when a brief dull sound floated up from someplace downstairs and tipped that internal scale in her head to the side of wakefulness. Aside from opening her eyes, she didn't move. The house was unnaturally silent. The electric clock on the nightstand by her head hummed almost imperceptibly. Outside and far away, a dog barked. Other than that: a thick, blanketing stillness.

There it is again.

She shifted in bed and jabbed her husband in the small of his back. When she leaned over to whisper in his ear, she realized she had been holding her breath.

"I heard something," she said, and when he didn't respond, she raised her voice half a notch. "I think someone's downstairs."

All she got back was a slight *humph?* more breath than response. She prodded him again and not so much tipped as yanked his internal scale to the side of consciousness.

"Christ . . ." he mumbled. "What? . . ."

"I heard something."

He rolled over onto his back, and she saw that his eyes were still closed.

"Yeah, you heard me getting a good night's sleep for once."

Vivian leaned in closer, and when she spoke, the surface of her lips tickled against the rim of his earlobe.

"Shhh. Listen." She held her breath. "There it is again."

He moved his head away from her face, opened one eye.

"There *what* is again?" His voice was loud against the prevailing silence.

"Eric, sshhhh. Quiet." and she jabbed him hard in the stomach. "I heard a noise. Downstairs. Someone's downstairs."

"Christ, Viv, it's . . . dammit, it's three thirteen in the morning." He said that as he rubbed the spot above his navel where she had poked him, but he said it in a hushed voice.

"Listen." She slowly sat up, cocked her head to one side, turned to look at him. "Something's moving around downstairs."

Eric propped himself upright. He forced open his other eye.

"Viv, I don't hear anything."

"Go down and take a look."

He yawned. "You heard something, you go down."

She poked him again, her index finger like a bullet between his ribs.

"Oww! Dammit!"

"You go."

"Fine. Fine, dammit, I'll go." He had stopped whispering as he whipped the covers away. He grabbed his bathrobe off the chair in the corner and slipped it on as he bent down next to the bed. When he stood, he had lifted a long, thick Little League bat from the floor.

On the way to the door he shook the bat and said, "I should use this on you; then maybe I'll get some sleep." He was whispering again, and as he walked out of the room, Vivian noticed that he walked on tiptoe.

She let herself slide down flat onto the bed and dragged all of the covers over her like a shell. She was going to say *be careful* but was afraid to make even the smallest sound.

Vivian was jolted awake when he crawled back into bed. Her eyes snapped open, twin holes exploding on her face. The clock read three fifty-four, and it took her a second to make sense of those glowing numbers. He commandeered most of the covers; as he settled himself in next to her, he twisted them around him, wrapping himself from head to toe.

Her first reaction was to lie there unmoving and listen for a repeat of the noises from below, but when she realized that was what she was doing, she immediately stopped and rolled over toward her husband. "Well. . . ." she asked, "What was it?"

He shifted inside the jumble of covers. She didn't know whether his back was to her or his chest was facing her. She moved closer to him and started tugging at the comforter.

"Eric?"

Except for the illumination from the clock, the room was dark. She noticed the baseball bat resting at a haphazard angle in the corner by the chair. The dim red light of the clock made the bat's rough, dented surface look wet.

"Eric?" and her voice, while still a whisper, grew louder. "Hey."

She primed her best finger, took aim, and jabbed it at what she hoped was his kidney. What she struck was hard and disappointingly unflinching.

"Hello. Earth to Eric."

He stirred a little, then reached out to grab her. One arm slithered under her back, his hand curling up onto her chest like the head of a wandering snake. His other hand grabbed at her from a gap in the bunched covers. Each of his hands rested on the outside edge of one of her breasts.

"Hey, what was it banging around down there?" Vivian asked.

He pulled her closer and she slid herself toward him to cuddle. "Eric?"

He pressed her against him, and she began to feel his large, solid outline beneath the cushion of blankets.

"Eric, what was making that noise?"

His grip tightened; the cold tip of each finger applied uncomfortable pressure.

Vivian was having trouble breathing.

"Eric!"

In an unbelievably deep and unfamiliar voice, the man under the covers said to her: "I'm not Eric."

The Thing in the Dark

Del Stone Jr.

Danny scrunched his eyes shut and pulled the covers over his head, entombing himself in darkness and silence.

On this night he would see nothing. He would hear nothing. He would spend the night in his bedroom without once screaming for his mother, his voice climbing the panicky octaves until even the sound of his own shouts frightened him.

Nothing would breathe beneath his bed. Nothing would growl behind the closet door. Nothing would scratch the window behind the curtains. It was all in his imagination, he told himself, reciting the mantra that had been drilled into him by his exasperated mother. How many nights had she staggered into his bedroom, her breath sickly sweet with bourbon, to dump herself on the edge of the mattress and yank back the covers and blabber at him drunkenly about his foolish, childish fear of the dark? How many times had she come into the room angry, then seen the look of stark terror in his eyes and tried to salve her anger with sloppy kisses and stern but gentle insistences that he look under the bed, or in the closet, or through the part in the curtains?

Always, he had checked. And always, nothing was there.

But it was the light that chased them away, he told her, and then her anger would return and she'd stalk from the room, slamming the door behind her, and he'd try to sleep with the light on until sometime later when she'd snatch the door open—a loud rasping that always sent his heart jumping into his throat—and flick it off.

The terror would begin anew.

But tonight he would put it out of his mind. That scrabbling sound beneath the bed—that was the floorboards vibrating from a passing truck. The shudder from the closet door was not the furtive movement of the runner within the track as a clawed hand slowly drew the door ajar. And he did not hear a soft thumping at the window as something out there tested the glass for a way to get inside. These things were all perfectly normal occurrences that the darkness transformed into mysteries, things that would go totally unnoticed in the blessed light of day. In fact, if he peeked at the closet door, he would see it was shut, as he'd left it. If he yanked back the covers and hung his head over the edge of the mattress, he would see a jumble of toys beneath the bed and nothing more. From the window, he would see the soft glow of lights brightening the neighborhood windows.

If he peeked—if he peeked—he would see that it was all in his imagination, and that he had nothing to be afraid of. If he peeked.

He slitted an eye and eased the covers back.

The closet door was open.

The mattress shimmied ever so slightly, and the pressure of the bedspread on his legs decreased as something lifted the corner and began to probe softly for something to—*something to grab and haul beneath the bed: an ankle, a calf, the arm of a trembling nine-year-old boy—*

Bobby hurled himself from the bed and hit the light switch.

Nothing there. Closet door, closed. Toys, beneath the bed.

And then he heard it. A tapping at the window.

He tiptoed across the carpet and paused at the curtains, knowing with dread certainty that if he dared look out, something horrible would look *in*—

"Bobby! Let me in!" The whisper snaked through the glass.

It sounded like his mother.

"Bobby? Are you there? Let me in! I heard a noise outside. I went to check and—and I locked myself out! Let me in!"

It really did sound like his mother. But Bobby hesitated.

"Let me in, dammit," the voice whispered. "I think there's someone out here!"

What if it weren't his mother?

"Bobby, there's someone out here—I hear them!"

What if it were something using his mother's voice to trick him into opening the window?

"Open the goddamn window!" the voice said, louder this time, a tremble of fear wiggling through the words. "Bobby, *please!*"

And if he opened the window, it would reach in with its claws and grab him around the throat—

"Bobby—oh, Bobby—" the voice wailed.

—and the blood would splatter the walls and the bedspread and the closet door—

He heard a scream and a low-throated growl, and then a thrashing sound, as if some kind of struggle were being waged outside.

He stepped away from the curtains. He padded back to the bed and slithered beneath the covers. He could hear his heart pounding. It might have been a monster's heart pounding.

But he would get through this night without calling his mother. Because it was all in his imagination.

This Is a Test
John C. Bunnell

A black metallic teardrop hovered silently in the night sky, almost invisible against the stars above and the rugged landscape below. Within it, in an elliptical chamber, two human forms lay silently on cool platforms of some faintly iridescent material.

A slender gray figure entered the chamber and addressed another of its kind. "Technant: report."

The second figure looked up from its work. "Administrant: both subjects were tested and modified according to appropriate parameters."

"Specify."

The Technant motioned with a shiny-skinned, six-fingered hand toward one of the sleeping humans. "Subject One was found suitable for alpha modification. Standard alpha abduction/examination memories were imprinted, nonphysical memory blocks placed, and a corresponding delayed-action virus programmed to remove the blocks over an appropriate period."

The Administrant inclined its head slightly. "The subject's identity profile has been recorded?"

"Yes," said the Technant. "Local-species information exchange media will be monitored, and data concerning the subject collected. No variance from successful camouflage effect is expected."

"The subject is ready for return?"

The Technant inclined its own head. "Administrant: yes."

The Administrant studied the unmoving female form with lidless green eyes. "Acceptable. And the other?"

The Technant moved to the other platform, the glow of its own eyes bright in the shadowed work chamber, and made a hand motion. A tangled web of multicolored light appeared over the subject's head. "Subject Two was found suitable for theta modification. Relevant behavioral inhibitors were removed, a suitable pattern of fixation was imprinted, and appropriate instinct centers were boosted."

The Administrant studied the light pattern. "Acceptable. Theta modifications are confirmed; primary mission goal is achieved. Program subject for fifty repetitions before self-destruct."

"Administrant: acknowledged," the Technant said, tapping a finger against a metallic band on its wrist. "Programmed. This subject is now ready for return."

"Technant: return the subjects."

The Technant stepped to each platform in turn, drawing a finger along the edge of the iridescent surface. The air around both subjects rippled in response, giving off a lightless flicker as the transfer effect took first one and then the other.

The Administrant turned and left the elliptical chamber. The black teardrop hung in the sky for a long moment, then shot soundlessly upward and was gone.

A half hour's drive east of Seattle, Washington, in an old red Volvo sedan parked on a lonely stretch of state highway, a young dark-haired woman opened her eyes and looked at her watch.

"Three in the morning!" she said, surprised. "Wow, I didn't think I was that tired."

In a well-appointed downtown Seattle hotel room, a man wearing black boxer shorts sat up in bed, rubbing his eyes. Silent, he gazed intently into space for a moment. The image in his dream had been unusually vivid, and he would need to remember it—such an attractive girl, so vulnerable, so delicate. And how well she'd responded to stimulation. . . .

He would need to shop in the morning. Soft rope, a small rubber ball, a new cigarette lighter—and a knife. A long, sharp knife.

Three Dark Doors

Richard Gilliam

Once there was a gentleman whose family had lived in its fine home for many generations. How many not even the gentleman could say, for years ago the local courthouse had burned and all records of the county had been lost. The gentleman had been well blessed with a family that he dearly loved and with a great prosperity in his many business dealings. Indeed, local tradition claimed that all generations of the gentleman's family had been similarly blessed.

Unknown to the townspeople, there was an unusual matter that disturbed the gentleman, keeping him awake nights while he vexed and fretted. At the end of a long corridor in the basement of the mansion there were three dark doors, which all persons were forbidden to open. Legend held that two of the doors could be opened safely, but that the third contained the ruin of whoever exposed what waited inside.

One summer night while pacing in his study the gentleman inadvertently kicked the iron grating of the fireplace so that it came crashing down with a great noise that awoke his wife.

"Husband," said his wife, "you told me of the three doors before we married and I accept that they are a fact of our life. Our life together has been rewarding in all ways save my inability to console your curiosity for these three doors. Please, allow me to open them and put behind us this singular thing that separates us each night."

"I would not be so much the knave as to place you at risk, dearest," replied the gentleman. "I know not why these doors disturb me so. Surely it would be better for me to end this curse and open them tonight."

As it would happen, there was a drummer traveling through the area who heard the crash. The noise was from the direction ahead of him, so when he came to the mansion and saw its lights, he stopped.

In quick order he was admitted to the house, advised of the circumstances, and offered an opportunity.

"Let me understand," said the drummer. "I may keep any and all riches I find and may abandon anything that I do not want. My only obligation is to open the three doors and then to leave. Is this correct?"

"Truly it is, sir," said the gentleman. "A great favor you would do our household. I have endeavored to inform you truthfully and honestly to the extent of my knowledge."

And so it came that the drummer agreed. The three of them proceeded to the cellar, where the gentleman lit a torch. The corridor was much longer than the gentleman remembered, it having been many years since his father had revealed to him the secret of the house. At the end of the passageway was a small room, and on the far wall of that room were the three doors.

There was no hesitation in the drummer as he stepped forward and opened the left most of the doors, pulling mightily to free hinges that had long ago rusted. The gentleman poked the torch forward, but there was nothing behind the door except a small, closet-sized room, which was empty.

The middle door opened more easily but likewise proved bare. Only the third door remained.

"You do not have to do this," said the gentleman. "Please, allow me to give you a generous gift for your time and to release you from our agreement."

But the drummer stepped toward the third door and said, "For years I have passed by this house, making my rounds and offering my wares in the nearby towns. I have always wished there might be something that I had that you in all your riches did not." With those words he flung open the third door, exposing a room that was as barren and as dark as either of the first two. While the faces of the gentleman and his wife were still agape, the little drummer stepped into the darkness of the third room and disappeared, never to be seen again.

Many nights have passed. The gentleman lived but another year then died, his wife soon following from a winter chill she took at the funeral. The manor is now occupied by their eldest son. At each sundown he begins to pace, never sleeping, thinking of the corridor in the cellar and wondering what dismal fate would befall him were the three dark doors to be closed.

'Til Death Do Us Part

Michael Mardis

I'm cold, Harry! Cold as ice, and it's your fault! You'd think that once, just once in your life, you'd do something right!"

Harry Wilson shook his head sadly, his deeply lined face showing the scars of a marital battle that had been raging for twenty years. He flexed his large, work-callused hands on the red gingham tablecloth, trying desperately to keep his voice even and calm.

"It wasn't my fault, Mabel. I had no idea that . . ."

"You've never had an idea in your life, at least not a good one!" Her voice had risen to an ear-splitting screech. "Do you always screw up everything, Harry Wilson? For once in your miserable life, can't you think of my feelings first?"

Harry sighed and briefly closed his eyes. "You're right, dear. It's probably my fault."

"No probably about it, Harry Wilson! It's definitely your fault!" Her voice became shrill and insistent. "I want to know what you're going to do about it!"

Harry shrugged. "I don't know what I can do, dear. Things have gotten a bit out of hand. Even you have to admit that."

Her voice rose to the edge of hysteria. "I'll admit no such thing! If things have gotten out of hand, I think we know whose fault it is! My mother always said that you were worthless, but I didn't listen. I believed in you, Harry Wilson, and look where it's got me!"

He looked across the table with pleading brown eyes. "I'm sorry that you're cold, dear. It's just that I don't know exactly what you want me to do about it."

"For starters, you can bring me my sweater, the yellow one. It's in the top drawer of my bureau. Make sure that you get the yellow one; it's my favorite."

Harry rose slowly, his joints aching with the effort. "I'll get it, dear, anything to make you happy."

"Anything to make me shut up is what you really mean!"

Harry trudged slowly into the bedroom and retrieved the sweater, which smelled of mothballs and cheap perfume. Returning to the kitchen, he placed the garment gently on the tabletop.

Mabel released a disgusted snort. "I'm hardly in any condition to put it on myself, Harry! You're going to have to do it."

His eyes widened in disbelief. "But it's so late! And I'm tired, Mabel, really I am!"

"You should have thought of that earlier, Harry Wilson! You've never done anything right in your entire miserable life! Now you put that sweater on me, or I'll see to it that you never get another moment's peace in this life or the next!"

"If I do it, will you please leave me alone?" His voice was soft and pleading.

"We'll see. I doubt that I'll let you off this easy, but I'll think about it."

Harry nodded his head in defeat. Tucking the woolen sweater under his arm, he stepped out into the cold night air and gingerly made his way to the tool shed. The shovel was hanging neatly on its peg, right where he'd left it only a few days earlier. He examined the metal head of the tool closely and shook his head in satisfaction when he could find no traces of blood. Digging the grave had cleaned it well.

"Harry! Hurry up! I'm freezing, damn you!"

Harry sighed. "I'm coming, dear. Don't be so impatient." Slinging the shovel across his shoulder, he began the long walk into the woods. Perhaps he'd dig it a bit deeper this time. Mabel was correct about one thing; he rarely did anything right, at least the first time.

Time

James Robert Smith

Alan woke, leaning forward in a sturdy chair as he strained against the ropes that bound him to it. He lifted his head, wincing at the light glaring down. The last he remembered he'd been in his office and he'd heard a sound and turned to see.

"Rob."

"I'm here," Rob said from the catwalk above.

"Where's Billy?" Alan asked.

"Over there." Alan saw Rob pointing to an open door across the room. Now that the pain in his head was fading, he saw that they were in an old warehouse. Through that door was Billy, his gigantic bodyguard, sitting in a somewhat larger chair, similarly bound.

Billy noticed Alan looking at him and shrugged. *Things happen.* From across the room, Alan could hear the ropes creak as Billy shrugged. The man was inhumanly strong, like some Neanderthal, and Alan knew that given time Billy could break those ropes and shatter that chair like kindling. They just needed time.

Alan looked at Rob, who looked down from the catwalk. The other man's hands were gripped about the railing. He was wearing jeans and flannel, dressed for dirty work. There was a pistol on his hip. It looked like Billy's Glock. "Why?" Alan said.

"Shut up, Alan," Rob yelled, and Alan knew that they were far from help. Rob didn't care how loud he yelled. "You know well why you're here. You ripped me off. You screwed me out of everything, you weasel. And you will *not* leave this place alive. I wanted you to know that. That's the only reason you're not dead already."

Alan took a deep breath. It wasn't over. Billy could break free. Alan *believed.* He'd seen the guy do things you wouldn't have thought possible. His hands were like clubs, fingers like crowbars. "What about Billy?" Alan yelled, head throbbing. Rob had always liked Billy.

"Billy's problems are Billy's problems," Rob told him. "You need to worry about Alan's problems. Which will shortly be at an end."

Alan looked up. Rob had the pistol unholstered; he truly feared this was it. But his erstwhile partner turned and went across the catwalk to a door up there. His feet clanked atop the rusting iron.

Time. Time. Through the opened door, he could see Billy straining, his huge arms tugging, his shirt all but bursting with the effort. Sweat was trickling down Billy's grizzled jaw. Even from this distance, Alan noticed that Billy's ropes were loosening. His eyes met Billy's. *You can do it, Billy.* Billy seemed to smile.

And then Alan saw Rob in that room with Billy. He saw the gun leveled at Billy's face. Rob backed to the door and slammed it shut. Through the steel barrier Alan could hear Rob's voice, raised, yelling, but could make out none of the words. *Time!* He strained at his own bonds, but only succeeded in chafing his wrists and elbows.

Bam! A single shot.

Alan struggled, ignoring the ropes that dug into his joints, cutting soft flesh. He felt blood soaking into his new shirt, felt it trickling down. Alan, wide-eyed, panicked.

The other door squeaked open; light from the bulb in there silhouetted the figure in the threshold.

Billy!

"Man! I *knew* you could do it, Bill!" Alan relaxed and let himself feel the burning ache of the ropes, even his knotted skull. Billy shrugged off the ropes that clung to his blocky frame; the chair was in splinters now. Alan couldn't see Rob's body, but knew he was in that room. Maybe the sucker was unconscious. It might be fun to make him squirm before he killed him.

Billy came out of the other room and moved slowly across the dingy floor. "Get me out of this thing, Bill. Did you kill him?"

"No. He didn't kill me." The voice was Rob's, and it came from the catwalk.

Alan stared up at Rob.

"I always liked Billy. A family man, like myself. I know he'd like to see his little boy grow up, just like I'm going to see *my* little boy grow up. So I let him bust free of those ropes, but he's not leaving here alive until you're dead, Alan."

"What?" Alan's voice was a squeak.

"I've never killed a man, Alan. But Billy's got natural ability. And I'd really like to watch."

Alan felt Billy's crowbar fingers ratchet down on his shoulders, felt his collarbone go to pieces.

"Slowly," he heard Rob say. "We have *time*."

And they did.

Time Capsule

Martin Mundt

I almost missed an entire civilization. If the wind hadn't died, the red dust settling from the air; if I hadn't watched the sunrise; if I hadn't examined the ground as always, searching for what didn't belong. If, if, if. I saw the fingertip; that's what mattered.

I packed away rumors of bone fields farther west in order to dig here, now. The caravan stayed camped. My curiosity was still virgin; that is, I have never been the first to find anything. I've met tribesmen in Takla Makan and Java, natives bizarre and isolated, nearly megalithic, but normal as rain after a few days; common as neighbors, no matter how much sand or sea insulated them. Indeed, I have been the oddity, digging in the earth for bones and pots.

I dug around the fingertip. I worked through the day, uncovering the entire statue. He was white marble, with white skin so smooth the dust dropped off his polished surface as if the marble were frictionless. He had white hair and white eyes, wide set, almost on the sides of his head. He smiled with black teeth and tongue.

He wasn't eroded or broken or chipped, nor was he connected to anything deeper in the sand. He stood alone, an unearthly David, ages older than any merely human artist, because he clearly wasn't human. He was no centaur or minotaur either, parts dreamt together into an unconvincing whole. He was a living being, carved from life, surpassing Polycleitus or Michelangelo or Rodin.

He offered no explanation of himself, no inscriptions or chisel marks or ruins, no context of bones, buildings, or even a simple plinth, as though he had been alive but turned to stone.

He tilted his face to the sky. He reached right-handed into empty air, like Abraham for the knife, or Cain for envy. He was the find of my lifetime, a Troy or Knossos, but more. He was something unremembered, unrumored, from before men named the world.

The more I watched him, the more I glimpsed cathedrals in him,

653

all eerie glory, the Great Pyramid of his culture. His limbs were elongated with grace, a snapshot symmetry of motion and ease, more serene than any saint's vision.

That night I dreamt a city. I dreamt spires beneath a blue, blue sky, and innumerable stairs circling up the spires, worn from endless climbing. I dreamt stars shifting slightly from my own comfortable night skies. I dreamt a new moon.

When I woke, the campsite was covered in sand. Dunes sagged against my tent, filled in the footpaths, buried the fires. The caravan was gone, men, horses, and wagons. I was alone with the statue. I didn't care. I watched.

He glowed brilliant white in moonrise, and I touched his bright fingertips with my own. A storm of faces with wide-set eyes, singing unknown songs or prayers, hailed against my eyes and ears. My hand went numb, as though frostbitten. My arm went numb, then the rest of me.

The statue closed his white eyes and lowered his hand. I hardened to stone; he lived. He brought his eyes close to mine, cocked his head, squinted. He smiled a black smile. Then he disappeared behind me, and I couldn't turn to watch.

Sand filled the excavation to my waist, then my neck, then my lips and nose. I expected to suffocate, but stone doesn't breathe. My eyes didn't blink against the rising sand. The sand was warm, reddening with sunrise, finally deepening to black.

I dreamt a wide, white staircase rising in a tremendous half arch, ending in midstep five hundred feet high, held aloft by ocher and gold spires. He balanced at the edge, like a white statue made flesh, watching nothing but moonlit air. He reached out into empty space with an elegant hand and touched . . .

Me.

I don't know how. He had watched me, waited for me. I looked back for my history; he looked forward for his.

Now I dream the thing that will come and touch me, ages in the future, coiling along my fallen body, crawling across my face. No, I should say I have a nightmare, because it will be dark, with no moon or stars, and I'll see only blind white eyes before it turns to stone, and I to flesh, both of us still buried, I don't know how deep.

Time Flies
Scott M. Brents

The clock rang out, forlorn and cold, its chimes signaling death and destruction. A catch released and a spring engaged. A small door opened, revealing a dime-sized hole just below the center of the clock face. A red metallic fly with yellow eyes crawled out. It rubbed its diseased feet together several times, and on glistening green translucent wings, it took off.

There came another, just as mean as the first, and just as hungry.

The time was 7:58 P.M. By 8:03, nearly one hundred flies had emerged. At precisely 8:10 P.M., the small door quickly shut, severing the head of a fly unfortunate enough to be perched at the entrance. Had it taken off in time, it would have been the six hundred and sixty-seventh fly.

Its head careened downward, passing the intricate woodwork of the fireplace, down to the limestone hearth. It bounced three times (like a dead jet pilot's helmet) and rolled off the stone surface. The fly head came to rest on the wooden floor of the shop. The mandibles clicked open and clacked shut, while the antennae waved furiously.

A static-electric voice emerged from the fly, a voice so small that a machine of considerable sensitivity would have been required to hear it. A large healthy cat by the name of Terrance sat at a nearby window.

Terrance heard the fly, but did not understand what it said.

"Bbbbbbzzzz (click) . . . zzzzzzzzz . . . bubbbbbbb (clack) . . . bbelllll . . . zzzzbub (click) . . ."

The cat promptly trotted over to the fireplace and lapped up the head, swallowing it, ignoring the flies that congregated on the ceiling, which formed a strange and plutonic image: a symbol known to have driven some men mad.

"How much is the clock?" Anna asked.

"The clock isn't for sale," Joseph Dark-Cloud replied.

"Surely you must have *some* price in mind," she continued.

The proprietor shook his head in the negative.

Stupid and backward, Anna thought. *If he had half a brain, he'd realize I'd pay a lot of money to have that clock. Why is it that the best items are not for sale?* She fidgeted.

"I got more clocks in the back though, if you want to take a look," Joseph said.

Anna released a long, melodramatic sigh.

"Sir, I assure you, I have no intention of leaving *this* store without *this* clock. I don't care if I have to steal it from right under your nose, I intend to take it." Anna followed this remark with a laugh, to indicate she was joking, although she was really quite serious.

The Indian didn't reply. Instead, he shook his head from side to side again, indicating he couldn't believe how stubborn she was being. He turned and left the room.

Anna stood there, checkbook in hand, for ten minutes before realizing she was being ignored.

"Well, I will just pick my own price," she said to herself. Anna quickly filled out a check for two hundred and twenty-five dollars. She lifted the clock from its hook on the wall and placed the check on the mantel.

As she quickly walked out of Dark-Cloud's Souvenir Shop, she kept thinking he was going to come out and try to stop her. But he didn't.

As she drove away, she could have sworn she saw him standing in the window, appearing very calm. Obviously, the amount of the check had impressed him enough to ignore her stubborn acquisitiveness.

She left the hillbilly town of Drexell like a bat out of hell, happy as could be. After a few hours of driving, she became hungry and looked for a place to stop.

According to her watch, it was 7:58 P.M.

She heard the first fly almost immediately, could actually feel the buzzing inside her ear. She waved at it with her hand, then noticed several others swarming around her head. She looked down in horror as red flies virtually poured from a hole in the clock face. The flies gathered together on the windshield, forming a living, undulating pentagram.

"Beelllllllllll . . . zzzzzzzzzzzz . . . bubbbbbbbbbbb . . . ," they cried in unison as her car drove straight off the mountain road, headed for certain death.

She knew the clock would somehow survive without a scratch.

The Tooth Fairy

Del Stone Jr.

A pack of cigarettes. That's all Jimmy wanted. A pack of cigarettes, and the safety of his townhouse, and sleep.

But sleep brought the Tooth Fairy, and that was no good. The Tooth Fairy . . . a monstrous vision of teeth clicking and snapping at him from his nightmares, set within a face as pale as moonlight on dead flesh, surrounded by a field of black, as if Jimmy's fear of the world had taken on a predatory life of its own.

So Jimmy couldn't sleep, and after reaching for the pack of Marlboros on the nightstand and coming up empty, he climbed into his blue jeans and sweatshirt and drove to the twenty-four-hour Food World across town, a careful visit to the grocery store, a foray into a realm he tried to avoid. The world was full of horrors, yes: murderers and thieves and liars. But it was the little deaths that nibbled at his soul: the petty indifferences and incessant sales pitches and the all-consuming, voracious demand for his attention that warped him and transformed him into something unnatural, so that his time away from home became a gauntlet of senseless noise and chaos, and his time at home took on the quality of a siege. What lay between had become one thing:

The Tooth Fairy.

But if he remained awake all night he might eventually collapse into that merciful land of exhausted unconsciousness that lay beneath fearful dreams. So.

The supermarket was electric and weird this time of night, the lights as bright and the aisles as quiet as an oncology ward. They kept the cigarettes up front where the store manager could watch for shoplifters. But nobody was there. Jimmy yanked a pack from the kiosk and walked straight to the express lane.

Another customer was already there, dressed in a broad gray duster that brushed the linoleum floor. He was unloading groceries onto the conveyor belt in front of the register, and the teenage cashier was running them across the scanner: big cuts of meat, bloody and shiny in the preternatural light.

Jimmy sighed and scanned the racks of tabloids. Famous actor is really a vampire. Woman gives birth to seventeen babies. Rendering of Mr. Spock found in Egyptian tomb. Jimmy shook his head. Nothing shocked or amazed him anymore. It was all a blizzard of images and sounds.

The scanner beeped: steaks and flanks trimmed in opaque fat. The man certainly liked his meat, Jimmy thought, watching him stoop over the shopping cart and extract packages and set them down on the belt. The girl whipped them across the scanner, and as Jimmy studied her, he noticed she would not look up, not even once. A fellow sojourner, he decided. Probably waiting to start her weekend.

The man slapped down dripping packages. Jimmy peered around the sweep of the man's duster and saw heaps of meat still in the cart, cuts of meat he'd never seen before. The man dropped a shrink-wrapped package on the belt, and the scanner bleated. The girl waved it across the laser three more times, and each time the scanner refused to ring up the price. She gazed at the bar code with an exasperated look. Then her face went white.

She dropped the package. She snatched her fingers away and wiped them on her apron. She glanced up at the man then, and her lips trembled, as if a scream were forming behind them but refused to come out.

The package contained an assortment of jawbones.

Jawbones studded with perfectly normal incisors and canines and molars. One of them had a gold filling.

Jimmy felt a part of his brain go numb, like a pot roast that had thawed on the outside but remained frozen on the inside, and a tiny gasp escaped him so that the man turned and looked down at him, and Jimmy recognized the bloodless pallor of that face and the picket fence of teeth that sank into his sleep, and he knew this time he would not awaken in his bed, the sheets drenched with sweat, to wonder how he might keep the world at bay another day.

"Hurry home," the man whispered in a tissue-soft, dreamlike voice. "Hurry home and go to sleep. I'm hungry."

The cigarettes slipped from Jimmy's fingers and went bumping down the belt, where they joined the man's other possessions.

The world sank its teeth in, and would not let go.

Trigger Moment

Yvonne Navarro

Halloween was next week, and Ellen rented a horror movie to get into the spirit of the party she was throwing tomorrow night, a gala event complete with costumes, munchies, and plenty of beer. Everything was ready, and now she badly needed some brain-dead time. Her movie featured the traditional scarred psychopath hacking up stupid, stumbling teenagers. It wasn't frightening, but there were a few good "trigger moments"—ones where you're so primed for the next scare that you unwittingly jump right out of your skin when it comes. You *knew* the killer was around the corner, and you *knew* he was going to jump out and grab the dull-witted blonde. None of that mattered. At each appropriate moment, predictable as clockwork, Ellen gave a little scream of surprise; once she nearly upended the bowl of popcorn; thus the movie, despite the clichéd plot, was damned good fun.

When the movie ended and the snack dishes were washed, Ellen went to bed.

And dreamed:

She was running down a long, silent hallway. It was dark and washed in gray tones, the way turn-of-the-century schools look when everyone's gone home and all the lights except the EXIT signs are turned off. Like the empty-headed teens in the movie she'd watched—and yes, she was very aware of the similarities—Ellen was running from something unseen and dreadful; unlike the fools in the movie, she neither fell nor screamed. In *this* movie dream, whatever was chasing her was completely and utterly bent on destroying her.

The hallway ended abruptly in a door. She could feel but not see the creature behind her, monstrous and hot, an animal of death that the makers of movies had never imagined. In the way that dreams were, the door she faced was locked but not all that tall; she could just reach her fingers above it and feel a ledge that was more than adequate to provide her with a grip. Above it was another ledge, then another, and she began to pull herself up, hand over hand, as though the ledges were a rope with knots conveniently placed for climbing.

Too late; the creature was there, invisible and vicious, and for the first time since the dream's start, Ellen cried out, screamed in panic and desperation, to the only person who had provided her comfort most of her life—

"*Mama!*"

But the word was only in her mind; no sound echoed through the dull, unlit hallway. Even the monster she sensed below but still couldn't see was mute in its hunt; she could hear only the roar of her own heartbeat as blood rushed through her arteries. Another crucial ledge and Ellen reached for it, fingers finding strong purchase and starting to pull upward and, finally, out of the beast's range. Almost there—

—and she felt claws, cruel and sharp, slide up her sides and hook around the top of each hipbone. The pain was immense and shockingly real, and now she *could* see something . . . the claws themselves, yellow, curving, deadly as old ivory knives. The beast's weight settled into its grasp and began to pull her inexorably back, and all Ellen could do was hold on and scream again.

"*Ma-a-a-ama!*"—

She woke sweating in the murky dawn, fingers scrabbling for unseen ledges before they relaxed amid the crumpled sheets. She managed to toss and turn for another hour, then gave up and dove into the final party preparations. The first guests started arriving at eight, and by ten the place was in full chaos. The dozen or so run of mummies, witches, and ghosts milled among a generous turnout of truly unique monsters and space aliens, plus the expected showing of rubber celebrity masks. As expected, people went in and out, and Ellen kept an eye out for her mom, who'd promised to come by with an "eligible" young man she'd met and was anxious to introduce to Ellen. When the doorbell rang at 9:30 and Ellen saw her mother's smiling face, she hurried to greet her and the handsome dark-haired man she had in tow.

"Ellen, this is Frank, the person I told you about."

Ellen gave him her best smile and offered her hand. Frank grinned in return. "I'll shake, but careful of the claws. I had them done especially for tonight and they're really, *really* sharp."

When his long, curving, yellow claws curled comfortably around her flesh, Ellen began to scream.

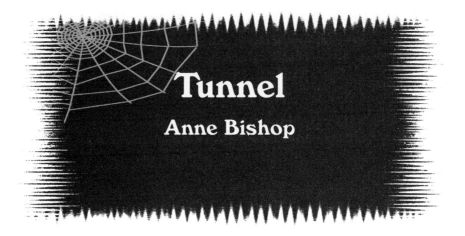

Tunnel

Anne Bishop

Her hand slipped on the sweat-greased steering wheel as she groped for the headlight switch. Her last thought was that it looked like a giant's open mouth displaying large stone teeth and an endless asphalt tongue.

Then the tunnel swallowed her.

Black. Silent except for the hum of rubber on asphalt. Full of savage red eyes in front of her, round white eyes in back. The car directly in front of her was an old model, the taillights, cat-eye slits in the fins, staring at her above a gleaming bumper grin. The Cheshire cat gone mad.

She concentrated on the lights, on the movement, grateful to be surrounded by cars on three sides. To her left there was only the darkness, the unforgiving stone. She wiped her hands on her jeans, one at a time, and concentrated on that still unseen pinprick of light at the far, far end. Concentrated on the promise of fresh air, daylight, a world expanding outward. Hope.

Chasing the cat-eyes, her hands tight on the wheel, she remembered a drawing class she'd once taken, remembered horizon lines and vanishing points. A trick of the eye. A matter of perception.

She flicked a glance to her right and suppressed a whimper. Only half a lane there, empty of cars. Empty of everything except encroaching stone. She took blind comfort in the glaring headlights behind her as she stepped on the accelerator, trying to close the distance between herself and the cat-eyed car in front. But the Cheshire cat sped along the asphalt thread until, with a last glowing wink of its eyes, it disappeared.

Only one pair of headlights behind her now. One where there had been so many.

There! For a moment she saw it, the pinprick of light up ahead. Hope surged through too tense muscles, and she smiled just before a flash of light made her squeeze her eyes shut for a second. Nothing behind her now except the unrelenting dark.

She swerved to the right as stone scraped on metal, slowed a little to retain control, straddled a solid white line that divided nothing.

Stone scraped metal again, this time to the right. She slowed a little more, a little more, making fine adjustments with the steering wheel, her eyes steady, determined, fixed on the unwavering pinprick up ahead.

She slowed to a crawl, refusing to stop, while the stone scraped one side and then the other. Finally, when she heard both sides scrape, she stopped and tried to reverse . . . but the walls had narrowed. The scream of metal twisted by stone ended any thought of going back.

Her labored breathing filled the car as she opened the glove box and her hand closed on the small flashlight. She flicked it on for a moment, comforted by the weak yellow circle. Slipping her head and one arm through the long strap of her purse, she put the flashlight inside the purse, rolled down the window, and squeezed through the narrow opening. She slid across the car's hood, finally resting against the grille, safe in the fading circle of the dying headlights.

Still ahead was the pinprick, the promise.

She took one step toward it and was surrounded by the dark. Reaching back, she couldn't feel the car, not even a trace of heat. She dug in her purse until she found the flashlight. Flicking the switch, she wasn't surprised to watch the glow fade a minute later. Still, it represented safety, so she held on to it as she took step by cautious step toward the pinprick of light.

Twelve All Hallows

Lou Kemp

The bleat of a foghorn pierced the dawn, sounding like a wounded animal's cry as it carried across shrouded fields of yellowed grasses. The fog advanced—diffracted, thick, and gray—over the land.

The smell of salt and brine permeated the air, mixing with the smells of the village sty and the burning wood of morning fires.

In front of the abbey, rows of peat houses leaned into each other. The River Green circled the village, and ran swift and cold to the sea.

The City is a half-day's journey away, down rutted roads and across many bridges. On market day, sacks of grain thud into carts before dawn touches the sky.

"Leave the rest!" Seth issued the command. A skinny dog ran underfoot as the wheels of the cart creaked under the weight, turning slowly in the mud, gathering speed.

Noisy and dirty, the village came alive. Drab-colored women herded scrawny chickens and sickly children. A few, their breath like smoke, cheeks a ripe red in the morning cold, hoisted bundles of soiled clothes in readiness to trudge to the river. It is All Hallows' Eve; nothing has changed.

Margaret, her gold curls framing her face, waited by the south path. She clutched a bag of sweets from the village shop.

The fog covered and uncovered her, shifting in swirls. She was there; she was gone. Into the stillness, the foghorn moaned again. Margaret saw me.

"You came back—" she cried. Her face was no longer forlorn; her voice was high and innocent. "Look, I've brought Poppy."

Cradled in her arm, ugly and beloved, was her doll. Clothed in a coarse dress, it was eyeless and had horsehair on its head.

We walked the path toward the river. The willows bowed overhead, their long graceful arms whispering in the dawn. Margaret skipped beside me, chattering.

A voice called: "Margaret!"

Her eyes grew fearful.

"Margaret!" It was Seth's voice, black and sure.

"Yes, Father." Margaret answered with obedience, without love.

He loomed behind us on the path, a large cruel man holding a switch of birch.

"So." In one word, menace and power covered the ground between us.

Margaret trembled as his heavy steps approached.

Seth had grown to be a bitter man, a lonely man who had driven everyone away. Had Margaret's mother lived, she too would have feared him. Too weak to leave, she would have cowered under his rages.

"Who were you talking to?" Seth peered into the velvet grayness, seeing nothing.

"No one, Father." She backed up, slipping in the mud.

"Don't lie!"

"Glenna." Margaret whispered: an unwise answer.

"*What did you say?*" Seth's face mottled.

In her innocence, Margaret didn't understand. Twelve summers and twelve All Hallows had passed since Seth spoke my name.

"Her name is Glenna." Margaret smiled at me. "She looks like me."

Margaret knew nothing of how Seth threw my doll into the river, followed me in, and held me under in a jealous rage. Through the murky water, I saw his bulging eyes and contorted face as he screamed my name over and over again. My brother Seth, who held me under until I struggled no more, then let my body bob in the current, floating down river to the sea.

"Father?" Margaret whimpered. She held my hand. "Glenna is here."

"She is *not* here!" Madness, like the fog, faded in and out of his eyes, twisting guilt with cruelty.

Margaret dropped the candy and tried to hide behind me.

"Glenna? Where did you find the name?" Seth suspected one of the women in the village of telling old stories.

"Glenna is my friend—"

Margaret gasped as her father raised the switch high.

"I'll drive the name from your lips. You'll never speak it again—"

Swirls of thick fog came between us as Seth brought the switch down. The fog parted; we disappeared.

* * *

Like a mad bull, Seth stormed through the woods, breaking branches, shuffling through tall grasses, calling Margaret's name. Desperation overcame rage, his bellows pleading Margaret's name.

Seth stepped into the mud of the River Green, sloshing toward us.

Margaret nodded, and I placed Poppy into the shallow water, pushing the doll into the current. It bobbed in the murky water until it reached Seth's feet.

"*Margaret!*" My brother plunged into the water, wailing his daughter's name, grabbing for the doll as it floated away from him.

The bleat of the foghorn pierced the grayness like a wounded animal's call.

Twelve summers, and twelve All Hallows.

Margaret placed her hand in mine, and we walked to the sea.

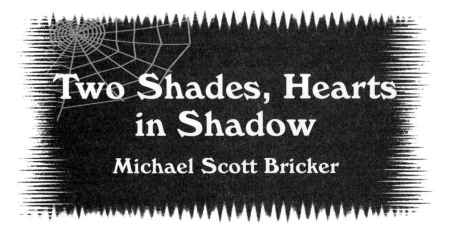

Two Shades, Hearts in Shadow

Michael Scott Bricker

The sun never set in the Valley of the Shadow, nor did it rise. Hooves peppered with moon dust as gray as the cool, dead gray of the land, pressed shallow bone-prints into the sand. *Ride, boldly ride . . .*

The pilgrim shadow had ridden with the knight in his thoughts during the time when he could reason, and rode with him in his dry marrow after his thoughts, like his flesh, had powdered away. There may once have been life here, but the knight doubted it, imagining that the fossils in the dry riverbed, the dusk-bleached shells, and the upturned blocks of limestone were as eternal and unchanging as his quest for Eldorado.

Ride, boldly ride . . .

A man up ahead stood on the shore, his black greatcoat oddly interrupting the dreary grayness. The knight, questioning his own sanity, stopped and dismounted. "Who are you? What are you?" *Why?*

"Eldorado." Eternal shadows played within the hollows of the man's eyes, and over his tired face and mustache. He reached for the knight, his hand brushing dry bone. "Shades. Both of us."

"Perhaps." The knight's armor crumbled as he moved, as his finger bones brushed his sockets, wiping away dusty tears. "Eldorado? Here?"

"Of course. Forgive me."

"I don't understand."

"I created this, created *you*." The man stared, his eyes glassy, distant, black as his coat. "I'm damned. There is no way out."

The knight stood, held his horse's reins. "My quest has created me." He paused, looked at the ancient mountains surrounding the valley, wondered where to go. "This is not Eldorado."

The man reached out again, collapsed on the shore, held his head in misery. "My name is Poe. Don't you see? *My name is Poe.*"

The knight climbed back upon his horse, began to ride away. "Means nothing to me."

"Wait. Please."

"I seek for Eldorado. I have no time." *Ride, boldly ride . . .*

Poe ran, took the reins, stopped the horse. "Take me with you."

"Why?"

"I know the way. There *must* be a way."

"Is there a way? Do you really know?"

"Perhaps not. Perhaps . . ."

"Join me then, before I change my mind."

They rode, silent save for the clicking sounds of bone on bone, and then the knight asked his question. "Where can it be? . . ."

"This land of Eldorado?"

"Of course."

"Ride, boldly ride," Poe replied.

Forevermore . . .

Unfinished Journey

Hugh B. Cave

The trouble, Henry said, was that he kept waking up before the dream ended. Henry Jorgens was our next-door neighbor, seventy years old, a retired carpenter, widowed, and living alone.

"I've been having this crazy dream for weeks now," he told us last Thursday, "and it's always the same one. I'm walking down a god-awful slum street in some strange city, and there are doorways on both sides. Dark doorways, with even darker shapes standing in them, staring out at me."

"Human shapes, you mean?" Beryl asked.

"Yes, sort of, but with weird red eyes, like in a horror movie about vampires or such. You believe in vampires?"

"Lord knows there's been enough books written about them," Beryl hedged. My wife is a great reader.

I only shrugged. When it comes to things like vampires, werewolves, and zombies, I never know what to believe. I'm just an ordinary Joe selling real estate.

"So it's like I'm in this street of vampires," Henry went on, "and I'm trying to get out of there without actually running, because if I start running, these things may think I'm trying to escape and grab me. And I can't ever get to the end of that god-awful street, because I wake up too soon. It's driving me crazy."

"It's only a dream," I said.

"But it's the *same* dream night after night! And I wake up soaked in sweat, scared half to death."

"Why not talk to Doc Zengler, the psychiatrist?" I said. "I'll go with you if you like. I know him."

Doc is my age, forty-five, and has a fine reputation. We went to see him the next afternoon.

Doc listened to Henry's story and told him his dreams could be real. "Not real like your house or car," he said, "but when dreaming, you could be living a real other life in another dimension. Who knows how many parallel dimensions there may be out there? When it comes to that kind of knowledge, we're all in kindergarten."

"Well, if the dream puts me in some different dimension," Henry sort of wailed, "how in God's name do I get out of there?"

"I'll give you a prescription to make you sleep longer," Doc told him. "That should give you time enough to finish your nightmare journey and leave the whole thing behind you." He wrote something on a pad. "Get this filled and take it tomorrow night. It should make you sleep through the night and most of Sunday."

We got the prescription filled at a drugstore on our way home.

The next evening, Saturday, Beryl and I invited Harry over for dinner and he told us he'd be taking Doc Zengler's medication when he went to bed.

"Call us when you wake up," I said.

He left about 9:30, and we saw his lights go out just after the eleven o'clock news. Sunday there was no sign of him. Sunday evening I phoned him and got no answer, and figured he must still be asleep. When he didn't call Monday morning, I went over there and rang the bell.

Nothing.

I could get in, all right. I had a key he'd given us so we could check his house when he was away on trips.

He was in bed with his eyes wide open, staring at the ceiling. There were half a dozen deep fang-marks in his neck, but no blood, and no color in his face. No color at all—as if all the blood had been drained out of him.

I called 911. An ambulance came and the medics pronounced him dead. When I asked, "Dead of what?" they only shook their heads.

Beryl and I have talked about it a lot since that awful morning. What we think is, Henry never got out of that dream street of his like he was supposed to. On the other hand, Doc Zengler's prescription kept him dreaming long enough for those shadow-shapes in the doorways to make up their minds. When I asked Doc about it later, he didn't say he disagreed with me. All he said was, "I'm sorry. But the truth is, we know very little about the real nature of dreams."

Until the Next Train

Benjamin Adams

That was the night Jourgensen met the new gods of the city.

The last glimmers of dying twilight flickered through the scratched windows of Jourgensen's Shoe Palace. He squinted at the meager amount of cash in the register drawer. "Son-of-a-*bitch*," he muttered under his breath.

A deep rumble shook the shop. Just the el train, passing by on the tracks out back.

Maybe, he thought, it was time to hang things up.

The neighborhood had changed. The good families had gone, moved out to the suburbs, where they could buy their shoes at the big chain stores like Chernin's or Payless Shoe Source. The barrio had encircled his shop, and he didn't have the capital to move into the kinds of shoes these tough new kids wanted.

No one cared about sensible shoes anymore. Good, practical shoes, for wearing to church or earning an honest living.

Bitterly, he went around the business of closing the shop for the evening. Maybe for good.

He didn't know yet.

The name MALO stood in five-foot-high white letters painted on the rear outside wall of Jourgensen's shop.

The bastard, thought Jourgensen, feeling his chest tighten at the sight.

The mayor's office claimed that if shopkeepers kept washing the walls, soon the graffiti taggers would give up and move to new spots.

Not Malo. No sooner did he clean the wall than Malo tagged it again.

For nearly a year now Jourgensen had battled with this unseen enemy. Once the shopkeeper had even stayed outside all night, intending to catch the tagger in the act. Instead, Jourgensen had fallen asleep in the front seat of his car, and in the morning he discovered that Malo had struck again.

This was something over which the old shopkeeper had no control. To him it signaled a loss of civilization in the heart of the city, a breakdown of the distinction between rational thought and animal behavior.

Malo can't be human, Jourgensen thought. It just wasn't human to ruin one's environment that way.

Maybe it had something to do with worship of new and strange gods, unknown to him. The shopkeeper felt like a dinosaur, watching the passing of his era.

He stepped forward and touched the paint, as if by force of will he could make the graffito fade away.

The paint was still damp.

He's still here, Jourgensen thought, his heart jumping in his chest.

He slowly turned and faced the el superstructure.

The maze of iron girders supporting the track confronted him. The kid could be anywhere in there, he thought. Probably knew it like the back of his hand.

A rustling came from within the structure.

Jourgensen stepped toward the shadowy mass of girders and glimpsed a smudge of dark movement.

"All right!" he called. "I know you're in there, you son-of-a-bitch!"

The fuzzy outline of a head regarded him silently from behind a girder.

"Yeah, you!" Jourgensen burst. "*Malo,* or whatever the hell your name is! I've got a few things I want to tell you!"

The head dipped in a nod.

"Okay!" called Jourgensen. "I'm sick and tired of seeing your graffiti everywhere I look! Why the hell don't you get a job or go to school and do something productive like a *normal* person?"

He paused for breath. He had been holding this in for so long that he felt as if he might cry.

"You bastards ruin the city for the rest of us!" he yelled.

There was silence for a long while. Jourgensen fidgeted nervously as he waited for a response from the figure.

Jourgensen began sweating. Why the hell didn't the kid say something?

Suddenly the figure emitted a high, thin whistle, a harsh, sibilant sound that made Jourgensen's blood turn to ice water. He turned to run—

Several slender, dark figures had gathered behind him. They had moved in silence and blocked his escape.

He had thought of them as not being human. He had been correct all along. There were openings where eyes and a mouth should have been, but out of them wriggled dozens of tiny black tubes. More of the tubes wiggled at the end of their long arms instead of hands, and he saw with horror what looked like—paint—dripping from the tube openings, different hues from each hole.

A creaking sound overhead made him look up. In the dim light he could make out maybe twenty more of the creatures clinging to the underside of the tracks.

It came to him then. There was no telling how long they'd been living there. Under the tracks, in the subway and other dark places of the city, making their strange art, announcing—*We Are Here.*

Graffito by graffito—*We Are Here.* And not just here, but in New York, Los Angeles—around the world, perhaps. Jourgensen fought the urge to giggle. Soon, maybe on the wall of a Chernin's or Payless Shoe Source in the suburbs—

We Are Here.

The new gods of the city regarded Jourgensen, and for a time there was silence under the el tracks. Until the next train.

Up Our Block

Benjamin Adams

Hey, this is how it is up our block.

Over here, we got the White family. Real nice sorts. They just got themselves a real nice girl, name of Jenny. Let's pop on in for a visit:

Jenny opens her eyes to the sight of the ceiling fan spinning lazily overhead. It looms in her vision, its brown latticework blades swooping around and around. Oh no, she thinks. I'm alive again.

Laughter and the clanking and tinking of cutlery against plates reaches her ears, and she turns her head to the right. Framed against the lacy white curtains in the breakfast nook, the afternoon sun making them little more than silhouettes, the family is eating. Father, pepper-haired and lantern jawed. Mother, blonde, bedecked with pearls even at this hour. Older brother, flat-topped and cruel-eyed. And Junior, all pug-nosed and shifty as only a nine-year-old can be.

Under her back she feels the hard, fabric-covered surface of the ironing board.

Junior looks her way as she slowly sits up and swings her legs over the edge of the board. He points a fork, laden with something red and unidentifiable, at her. "She's back," he announces brightly.

"Ah. When's that washing going to be done, then?" Father asks, patting his lower lip with a bright white napkin.

Jenny gains her feet, wobbling slightly. Her head aches and part of her sense of balance seems gone. She feels around to the back of her skull. Her probing fingers gingerly probe the jagged edge of a deep indentation. Blunt trauma, she thinks, fighting the urge to laugh, to scream.

"The laundry?" gently reminds Father.

She nods, picking up the wicker basket. "Yesss, sirrr," she slurs.

(Part of her speech center had been damaged in an earlier death, not long after the family first acquired her. The problem comes and goes.)

Making her way down the basement stairs to the washing machine, Jenny wants to cry, but somewhere along the line she's forgotten how to do that, too.

Jenny's a sweet gal, no doubt about it.

The Whites don't know it, but she's gone and got herself a suitor. They won't be too pleased when they find out, but they might as well try and stop the rain from fallin', that's what I always say.

What I mean is, these things happen.

In the basement, with its damp earthen walls, there exists a kind of solitude. The dark coolness envelops Jenny, embraces her with the welcome air of the grave.

Loading the family's laundry into the large open-front machine (so huge, so enormous, if she wants she can climb inside the washer drum and curl up, like a fetus), she puts her lips together and whistles briefly.

The notes come out flat, off-key. She stops whistling.

But after a moment the notes continue, echoing out of the large drain set in the center of the basement floor. Reverberating true and clear.

Jenny turns toward the slimy grate. "Kevin? Is that you?"

The grate rattles. "Yes," hisses a dry, raspy voice. "Who else do you know who lives in the friggin' sewer?"

She smiles and places another handful of clothes in the washer. At least here she isn't alone. She doesn't think the family knows about Kevin.

Kevin is a snake-boy.

He hasn't always been that way, of course; it's his life in the sewer that's changed him. Since Jenny has known him, Kevin says his back legs have almost completely shriveled away, and his skin's gotten rough and scaly. She's never seen him though—only spoken to him through the drain—so she doesn't know if Kevin speaks truly or not.

Even with these physiological changes, Kevin says he's happier in the sewer than with his family. And Jenny knows how he feels. If she could escape into the sewer and join him, she'd do it in an eyeblink.

"You haven't been down here in a while," Kevin rasps. "Were they beating you again?"

"Worse than that. Kevin," she whispers after a long moment, "do you remember? What it was like, before?"

"Sometimes," rasps his voice from the drain. "I remember incidents, visions. . . ."

"I think . . . I think I was a nurse. Sometimes words come to me—"

—*blunt trauma*—

"—and I can't think why else I'd know them."

Through the grille covering the drain, two shining eyes stare upward. A pair of scaly fingers grasp through the grille, and Jenny reaches down and links hers with Kevin's.

"We were something else once, weren't we? I know we were something else."

No more words are spoken. Sometimes survivors don't need them.

Those two, they just darn near tear out my heart.

What, why don't I do somethin' about it? You got lots to learn about the way things are 'round these parts.

Nope, we like things just fine the way they are, right on up our block.

I think you're gonna be happy here.

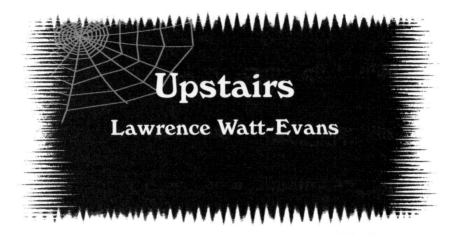

Upstairs

Lawrence Watt-Evans

They're so damn loud up there. Yelling and fighting, and then that thumping—I guess it must be folk dances or something. They could show a little consideration, couldn't they?

And then there was the time they left the water running and it leaked through the bathroom ceiling and damn near flooded the place, and of course it was the weekend and we couldn't get hold of the landlord until Monday—no, Tuesday, it was a long weekend! And there was wet plaster falling all over the sink and the floor. And stains everywhere.

I tell you, if we could find a decent apartment, we'd have been out of this rathole years ago.

And they won't talk to us when we see them in the halls; when I shout at them, they just walk right on by like they didn't even hear me. I went up there once to complain, but they wouldn't answer the door.

Maybe they were busy; I think their refrigerator must have broken down or something, because even with the door closed I could smell something rotten.

They can't be very clean.

Anyway, tonight was the last straw, more yelling, and singing this awful high-pitched song, like something the Arabs sing in one of those old movies, and then thumping about, and I swear I heard the furniture breaking.

"I've had enough," Jack said, and I agreed and said he should call the cops, and he said no, he'd settle it himself, and he went up there.

There was more yelling then, and banging, but then it stopped. I guess he talked some sense into them.

I wish he'd get back though. There's something dripping through the ceiling again.

It's not water though; it must be paint.

It's bright red.

The Valley of the Shadow

Francis Amery

Do you know the Dearne Valley in Yorkshire? It lies between York and Sheffield—the railway line goes straight through it. In the old days, the coal from its open-cast mines and the steel from its ironworks used to be shipped out by rail, so it still has a vast network of derelict sidings. It was a prosperous place once—when Sheffield Steel was legendary and the coal stripped from the hillsides was the cheapest in the north. There was talk once of reclaiming the exhausted mines and greening the slagheaps, but it never came to anything. The landscape is utterly black now, and the pall of polluted air that used to hang over the place when all the chimneys were belching away still casts its shadow, even though the chimneys have all been blown to smithereens.

That's where I had my moment of revelation; that's where the God of Industry showed himself to me and turned my life around. You probably think of that kind of landscape as hellish, but that's a mistake. When Blake wrote about "dark Satanic mills" in *Jerusalem,* the Industrial Revolution had hardly begun; the "mills" were metaphorical—they were the universities which had begun to secularize education. The factories of the Industrial North were the proverbial Mills of God—the ones which grind slowly but grind exceedingly small. That's what happened to the Dearne Valley: it was slowly ground down into black dust, which will never go away.

That's what human beings are *for:* that's the purpose of our existence, the reason why God chose us. Man is a tool-making animal, as your very own Ben Franklin once said; machinery is the very essence of his identity, the tangible expression of his soul.

The worship of Nature is essentially pagan, essentially pantheistic. The One True God isn't interested in Nature; He's interested in *work* and transformation. He's interested in the release of energy: in furnaces, in crucibles, in steam-engines, in nuclear power-stations. He is, above all else, the God of Fire.

Even the Greeks knew that, in their way: the fire which Prometheus stole from Heaven in order to make—to *manufacture*—mankind wasn't any kind of metaphorical fire, it was *fire itself*. You might think that we worship God and pay Him our dues in church, but that's only a tiny part of it. We worship God every time we set a light to wood or coal or oil, and we worship Him most effectively of all when we liberate the power locked within uranium and plutonium.

You have to understand that, if you want to understand what I did. It's all in the Bible, clear as day, if you'll only take the trouble to learn it. It's there at the very beginning, in Genesis. The proper worship of God involves *sacrifice*, and the best form of sacrifice involves *burning*. So many people have misread that, thinking that what mattered to God was *what was burnt*, but that's just a silly mistake. What matters to God is the burning itself. Fire is the ultimate worship. Didn't God show Himself, at the very beginning of things, as a burning bush? Didn't the leader of his angelic army set forth to fight the good fight in a Chariot of Fire? It's as plain as plain can be, for anyone who can read with a modicum of intelligence.

The point is, you see, that you have hold of the wrong end of the stick. You're calling what I did an act of mass murder, but it wasn't. The people you call my "victims" don't really figure in the equation at all. It wasn't *them* I was sacrificing—they were incidental. The explosion itself was the act, the sacrifice, the prayer. Ashes to ashes, dust to dust: the whole purpose of human life. Why should you complain about it, when you're no different at all? Aren't you, in your own more patient way, remaking the entire planet in the image of the Dearne Valley? Why should you think that you're the truer Mills of God just because you grind so exceedingly slow?

All I ever wanted to do was to be nearer to Him—to bring us *all* nearer to Him. Even if you're right to say that I hurried things along, you can't possibly have any complaint about the smallness of the particles my act of worship left behind—and the hottest will burn for a hundred thousand years to come.

Vampire Nation
Thomas M. Sipos

You accept that your . . . *ancestral castle* is now the property of the people of Romania?"

"With your doctors' kindness, I understand . . ." What was this century's proper honorific? "*Comrade* Colonel."

Colonel Popiescu snorted, skimmed the report. "Farkas. You are Hungarian?"

"My ancestors . . ." Count Farkas waved the subject aside with the delicate hand of an aristocrat, pulled his hand away from the pale sunlight spilling through the grimy window, illuminating air heavy with dust. He stared at the dour, sluggish soldier. Peasant. In spite of the bright red stars piercing his drab brown uniform, Colonel Popiescu was still just a slothful, anemic peasant. Weak blood nourished on potatoes and vodka.

"You also understand, Transylvania has been liberated by the Romanian People's Army from Hungarian fascist occupation?"

Count Farkas smiled with thin red lips. "I am happy to hear it." The dusty calendar on the wall read 1977. Until he awoke a month ago, it had been a hundred and twenty years since he walked the earth. Luckily, he knew Romanian, now apparently the dominant language in this portion of the old Hapsburg Empire.

Colonel Popiescu set the report aside, pressed a button. "Of course, the Constitution of the People's Democratic Socialist Republic of Romania guarantees equal treatment to every citizen, regardless of ethnicity. Did you not find this to be true at our state psychiatric hospital?"

Count Farkas eyed the Colonel's medical certificates hanging beside portraits of pasty-faced bureaucrats. An office without vitality, aside from that blood-red flag. A nation of cattle patiently awaiting slaughter. As soon as Farkas established himself . . . "The doctors are very . . . agreeable."

Popiescu nodded, pressed the button. "The people considered

prosecuting you for criminal assault, but the people's psychiatrists diagnosed you as mentally ill." Popiescu pressed the button, slammed it, bellowed toward his door, "Nurse! Water!" He turned to Farkas. "The report states, *Count*, you no longer believe your delusion of aristocracy."

The Count winced on cue. "Please, Comrade Colonel, refer to me only as Comrade Farkas."

Popiescu grunted, satisfied.

A fat woman with thick ankles shuffled into the office, carrying an aluminum tray, glasses, bottles of mineral water. She set the tray atop Popiescu's papers, wiped her sweaty brow with her stained apron. She found a bottle opener, wiped a glass with the apron, opened a bottle, poured its water into the spotted glass.

Count Farkas narrowed his red eyes, snatched a bottle, saw a dead fly and bits of insect debris floating atop the water.

The woman took the bottle from him, glanced at it, saw the fly. Expressionless, she opened the bottle, poured the fly and debris onto Popiescu's floor, poured the remaining water into another spotted glass, handed it to Farkas.

Popiescu watched this incident with glazed eyes, limply held his own glass in a dirty hand.

The woman shuffled out of the room, gray hair spilling from her babushka. Farkas espied one of her hairs stuck to his glass.

Popiescu drank before continuing, dribbling onto his soiled tunic. "It is good, Comrade Farkas, you no longer suffer from these delusions. The people require clear-headed workers, uncontaminated by ancient superstitions."

Farkas leered. This was the best news upon awakening. "The doctors cured me of all such superstitions. I no more believe in aristocracy than in Christ, heaven, or . . . vampires."

Popiescu nodded sleepily. "Comrade General Secretary Ceausescu is correct in stating that once atheism is firmly anchored in the class consciousness of the proletariat, then revolutionary Marxism-Leninism shall enter a new stage of dialectic materialism in which scientific socialism . . ."

Count Farkas let the Colonel drone on. This was better than Monsieur Voltaire's influence in France. If the vampire's strength is that no one believes in him, what more could he ask than to awaken in a nation of atheists?

Farkas exited his apartment, shuffled along Brasov's broken sidewalks, seeking quarry. He squinted against an overcast sky. Still enough sun to burn him. Shrugging, he scratched a lesion, wiped the pus against his trousers.

Peasants and laborers, faces blackened by nearby refineries, slumped against empty store windows, clutching liquor bottles. A soft breeze stank of benzene. A slovenly group of soldiers, red patches upon shabby uniforms, bantered beneath a large bleacher; one of them urinated in public.

Farkas squinted at the empty and dilapidated bleacher. Its sole vitality derived from massive blood-red banners hung beside colossal portraits of bureaucrats. Everywhere scarlet banners draped buildings, lampposts, monuments, bleeding the nation.

Comrade Farkas browsed for prey. Everyone was too distant, or too unruly, or too much trouble. Shrugging, he shambled back to his state-owned apartment.

The Vampire's Burden

Tippi N. Blevins

Teddy liked New York. No one ever noticed the winter-white skin of the vampire who walked among them. He could go to parties and chatter with future kills, or meander through art galleries looking every bit the pretentious, black-garbed human. Teddy was safe in New York.

Hungry, Teddy wandered into one of the city's numerous clubs. Everyone was vampires within. Eyelids dark as oiled leather fluttered up at him, exposing glassy hematite eyes beneath. Black lips blew him kisses, white bone-hands reached out to touch. Disgusted, he wanted to leave. They were all so thin, so gaunt with empty desire, that they would hardly have been worth the effort.

But there was one girl different from all the others.

He bumped into her just as he turned to leave and caught her plump little arms in his hands. Her gray eyes looked like the backs of antique silver spoons. Her lips were juicy raspberries just hidden beneath the thick, oily lipstick.

"I'm a vampire," she said to him.

"Are you really?" She wasn't, of course. The flesh against his palms was warm, soft. She was all too human.

She smiled and showed her acrylic teeth. As far as fake canines went, they didn't look too bad. "My name is Miranda. I'm three hundred years old."

"I'm Teddy," he said, kissing her hand. He brushed his teeth against her flesh. "I'm only *two* hundred."

Her eyes widened. "Oh, Teddy! I've been waiting so long to meet another vampire like me!"

"Is that so?"

She pointed at the crowd. "They're all pretenders. Not like us." Her eyes glittered. She was a child.

"Then shall we go?"

She put her arm through his.

As the night went on, she chattered about how she had been born in France and made into a vampire at the age of seventeen. It was lonely, she said, and so very dreary being immortal.

He stopped walking. "Dreary? But I love being a vampire."

She pulled on his arm and he followed her. They found their way to an old house in the inner city. The brick crumbled to powder beneath his hands. All but one of the windows was boarded up. The sign on the door—which Miranda ignored as she opened it and led him inside—proclaimed the house condemned. Inside, it smelled like burnt wood.

"I hate being a vampire," she said. Tears glossed her eyes. "I want to kill, but it makes me feel so guilty."

He laughed. "You've been reading too many books, Miranda. Only story-vampires feel guilty. I kill because I *want* to. No law applies to me. No hands can touch me, save those of the others of my kind." Her mouth fell open. He smiled gently. "*Our* kind, I mean."

She looked down. "We can sleep here for the day." Her voice sounded quiet, rough. "I'll bring someone back. You must be starving."

She left. Teddy watched her go, listening to her sobs, her footfalls on the predawn pavement. He was surprised at how easily he fell asleep.

"Wake up, Teddy. The sun's coming up."

Opening his eyes, he writhed against the floor and heard the rattle of chains. He jerked his arms but found his hands bound tight. Looking down the length of his body, he saw his legs enchained as well.

Miranda knelt beside him. "Vampires like you are dangerous, Teddy. We have to be beautiful and sad—just like in books. Otherwise, why would anyone want to be a vampire?"

"Miranda, don't do this. I can change!"

She shook her head. "That's what all the others said, Teddy. But they lied, so I had to teach them a lesson."

As the sun began angling in through the one open window, Teddy realized with horror that it hadn't been burnt wood he had smelled.

"Wait, Miranda! I can make you into a vampire—a *real* vampire. Just let me go."

Standing, Miranda blew him a kiss and wiped away her beautiful vampire's tears. "But, Teddy," she said sadly, "I *am* a real vampire."

No! he wanted to scream, but the sun had already begun to paralyze him. *Just real enough.*

The Vampire's Caravan

Ilona Ouspenskaya

It was on the night of the summer solstice of my sixteenth year that I saw seven wagons of the Vampire's Caravan.

The first wagon was driven by the Master of the Trail, his headless horses pulling a hearse made of darkened gold. In the coach sat the Vampire King, enigmatic and regal; the handsomeness of his glory is still bright within my mind. He looked my way and waved, but I did not fear. I trembled less, I think, than if I had been in the presence of a mortal king.

In the second wagon lay his treasure: riches taken from the places of the dead. I saw jeweled swords and gleaming crowns, some with skulls still inside. The tombs of the once mighty, plundered from their trove.

So fine a treasure must have an appropriate guard. The third wagon bore the ghouls whose existence it was to attend the riches they had stolen. I have heard it said that a true ghoul will not disturb the unburied dead. I have no desire to know the truth of this firsthand.

There were goblins in the fourth wagon, their craggy hands filled with tools and devices of strange origin. In their cart they repaired a giant wheel, and I knew it to be from the legendary Mill of Souls, destroyed eons past when giants yet walked this earth.

Of the retainers in the fifth wagon, I recall little that distinguished them from the nobles at our castle. They were courtly and mannered, though false in the dignity they presumed. Only the pall of their faces marked them as undead. I looked for fangs and saw none. Perhaps they were not yet among the converted.

The sixth wagon bore the vampire horde. Many taunted the retainers, while others practiced changing their shape: some into wolves and some into falcons, and yes, even some into bats. A few vampires preened in their current form, far more stylish and imposing than the retainers who preceded them. Perhaps I gazed too long, for one of the bats circled and landed on the shoulder of the driver of the seventh wagon.

"Come, pretty one," said the driver, a man more handsome than any I had ever known. "I carry the living who serve our king. Is our king not majestic and grand? And are my passengers not well dressed and cared for, so much better than those who serve mortal kings? Come, pretty one, and join our play. Come, and I shall give you a gown of silk to replace your dress so tattered and gray. The time is yours, young maiden, if you take it now. Come, before we're on our way. Give to us your happy vow."

I looked to the head of the caravan, but the King's carriage had already crested the nearby hill. The golden glow grew dimmer, and I knew that my decision must be made quickly. The treasure, the guard, the goblins, the retainers, and the vampires were far beyond me now. Even the living began to pass into the night. Behind them came seven horses ridden by seven skeletons, the last of which stopped to speak.

"The shortest night brings the longest decision. Choose as you will. None will force you to take our path." And with that he was away, riding quickly to rejoin the caravan as it vanished into the night.

So much did I want to leave the fields where I grew old each day. Which fate to take? The allure of the caravan or the assured demise of a mortal life?

Alas, I chose that life I knew. Much time has passed. The husband I took in my eighteenth year died fighting a war in another land. We had one child. She will be sixteen this summer. On the night of the solstice I shall watch and hope. Perhaps again I will find the Vampire's Caravan.

Vengeance Is Me

Tom Piccirilli

Implications and accusations abound in the silence.

Each gesture, as she turns in her sleep, is a calculation of murder. By dawn, she'll have killed me a dozen more times in her nightmares: broken fingernails *scritch* upon the sheets, scratching with a passion as if it were my skin, my eyes. She blames me.

The shower stall drips in rhythmic precision with the rain that pounds the bedroom windows. Her brow is feverish and twisted, ears extremely red in the heat, and a soft wheezing noise escapes her chest. The constant reminder of water—around us, all the time—causes her to drop her face further into the pillow. I see her tongue dart out to taste the corner, to bite and hold; it is my jugular or carotid, so much sweeter now, my blood to be washed away in the rain.

She blames me. For exactly what, at any given moment, I'm uncertain. There are so many possibilities to choose from. Any one betrays hope for redemption. I've failed, and that is, as always, enough. The dead daughter has giggled in the darkness for two years now. The unborn child, son or daughter, twice as dead for having never been alive, fell from our world only three weeks ago.

Scritch, scritch. She's patted the faint stretch marks on her belly with a washcloth, like a soldier shining medals.

She turns again now to face me in her sleep, eyelids slightly raised as she sighs, lips damp and partially open, permanent screams in her eyes. Occasionally, she cries out with grunts of pain or ecstasy, after a particularly brutal and satisfying murder of me.

The daughter, born dead, and also wet, prances into the room chasing a beachball, her feet making loud squishy sounds on the carpet. Her long blonde hair is wrapped around her neck like a garrote, sand and seaweed from the surf cling to her cheeks and chin. Her forehead is badly sunburned.

Once she had a name, but now it vanishes whenever I try to remember. She comes to the bed and holds the ball out to me. "Daddy? Play?"

Misery is a catchword, no better or worse than Purgatory. My unborn child, son or daughter, twice as dead for three weeks, hobbles and hops in the shadows, mewling. It comes closer to the bed and slaps a hand against the crumpled sheets at my feet, as if wanting to climb between us.

Her eyes flutter, caught in dream, and my deaths begin again. She has no doubt imagined everything from a quick violent slashing to slow, lengthy torture. There are methods that take two nights for preparation, another four or five nights to complete. My daughter, born dead, cartwheels across the floor and nearly slams into the closet door, seaweed flinging against the lampshade. The unborn child, son or daughter, twice as dead, harrumphs a slick chuckle, clapping its sticky hands.

Rain struggles to grip me, the shower stall attacking from within. Seaweed slips to the headboard. My daughter, born dead, has grown older in the minutes she's now played in the bedroom. A stolid but not quite reproaching look flattens her features. "I don't blame you, Dad. We were having fun there on the beach. It's not your fault you were talking to the lady in the bikini." She cocks a thumb at her sibling-thing. "And this certainly doesn't hold you responsible for anything. I mean, it's not like you pushed Mommy down a flight of steps." In the shadows, my unborn child, twice as dead, flops and waddles, brushing against my desk, knocking papers down against its slippery face.

At dawn she awakens, and shows me her teeth. The light flickers in her eyes, fading and burning, as if she were almost puzzled to find me still alive after dying so often during the night. Her hand reaches out to my cheek as she tries to decide which method of murder would prove most applicable this morning. We get up and share the bathroom. There are small clumps of sand between my toes.

In the kitchen, at the table, she raises the butter knife in one petite, nearly fragile hand, a piece of especially burned toast in the other, deciding whether to cut into the stick of butter or my throat. Choosing to prolong my agony, she slowly butters the toast and—with no attempt at gilding the utter contempt in her voice, hissing with treacle and bitterness and death—says, "Do you want coffee?"

Vocabulary

Adam-Troy Castro

There is a word on the tip of my tongue. I've been trying to remember it for weeks now. So have you.

You know how that is. You know a word, you've used it a thousand times, but the one time you need it because no other word will do, it dangles just outside your reach, behind a fuzzy cloud that forever refuses to disperse for you. You concentrate on the word, and for a fraction of a second it seems to come into focus, but then the fog rolls in, and again you lose it. I hate when that happens. So do you.

If I could define the word I wouldn't need it so badly. If I could come up with a workable synonym we wouldn't even be here. No. It needs to be that word, and no other: no pale clumsy approximation will do. Remembering it will be like an orgasm. Or, for you, a release.

We will both feel better when one of us speaks it out loud.

But you can't speak anymore, can you? None of you can. You can moan, you can writhe, you can even make guttural subhuman noises . . . but you can't speak a single coherent word. You can't even speak the word. If one of you suddenly remembered the word I'm talking about, and wanted to tell me about it, you wouldn't have any way to say it. You would probably find that very frustrating. You have pens though. And most of you can reach some paper.

So let's start again.

It's a very common word that should be very familiar to anybody reasonably literate.

It has to do with the redemptive nature of pain. It begins with either an M or an H, and it perfectly invokes a point I wanted to make in an argument just before I brought you here. Forget what and when. I think that if I knew the word, I would have won the argument and I wouldn't have had to hurt anybody. Maybe if I remember it today, I won't have to hurt anybody else.

You know the word I'm talking about. I know you do.

But it wasn't on the tip of your tongues either.

None of you were very articulate at all. Most of the sentences you spoke contained the words *please* or *no*. None of them contained the word I'm looking for. None of them even came close.

Now, you can't talk anymore.

I'm sorry about that. But I've had all I can take of please and no. Everybody says please and no. My mother said please and no. I said please and no. Nobody listens to please and no.

They're two pointless words: the vocabulary of victims.

I don't speak them anymore unless I'm quoting you.

But since you can't talk anymore, I guess I won't be quoting you anymore either.

Unless you come up with the word. Then I'll let you go.

So let's try again. It's a simple word. One you use every day. One you know. One that will seem incredibly obvious once you finally manage to think of it. One that probably seems just barely out of reach. If you reach for it hard enough, then maybe you'll find it, and the nightmare will be over for all of us.

It begins with an M. Or an H. One of those.

Unless.

Hmmm. I'm not sure.

No. I'm definitely on to something.

I think it starts with a Y.

Voices in the Dark
Steve Rasnic Tem

In the cartoons, all kinds of things talked: trees, flowers, dogs, cats, birds, even toasters.

In the dark, all kinds of things talked, too. Only more softly. *Where is it? Why is it? What is it? Who is it?*

Brian listened to the clock. To the clocks. There was the electric alarm clock in his bedroom that made strange noises like hums and purrs, especially when he had it sitting on the bare wood of the dresser top. And there was also the old-fashioned grandfather clock that stood in the hallway just outside his bedroom door. The one that ticked, clanged, chimed, and gonged so loudly that sometimes he thought it was the loudest sound in the world, beating into his brain.

When his mom asked him why he didn't sleep at night, he always told her it was because of the two clocks: the hum and purr of the bedroom clock and the tick, and the clang, and the chime, and gong of the grandfather clock going on and on like they were arguing. But she only laughed and told him he had a "vivid" imagination.

Where is it? Why is it? What is it? Who is it?

Maybe she was right. Because after a while Brian found he could hear other voices in the dark, too. The window whined as if it had no friends, even when he had been sure there wasn't much wind outside. The floor creaked and cracked when there wasn't anyone walking on it, as if it were complaining in its sleep about how people walked on it all day.

Where is it? Why is it? What is it? Who is it?

"Go away," Brian ordered. "Leave me alone. Let me sleep."

Then the voices would stop for a while, as if they were actually considering leaving him alone. Or they would change tone, as if they were confused that Brian had decided to talk to them at last.

I don't know. Do you know? I don't know. Do you know?

Sometimes, maybe, Brian would fall asleep. He would dream about shining a flashlight on the window, shining a flashlight on his electric clock, shining a flashlight on the floor. Everywhere he pointed his flashlight, he would find a mouth, talking to him.

And then he would wake up. And they *would* be talking to him.

Where is it? Why is it? What is it? Who is it?

Brian had heard these voices in his room, at night, for years. He was getting older and older, and when he became a teenager he found that he was embarrassed by the voices in his room. He was too old to be hearing voices.

Where is it? Why is it? What is it? Who is it? the voices cried again one night, and Brian was sick and tired of the whole thing.

"Leave me alone!" he cried.

Where is it?

"I don't know! Just leave me alone!" He climbed out of bed and started looking at the floor, the window, picking up things and throwing them around. Because he was looking for the mouths that were saying these things.

Why is it?

"How should I know? Shut up! Just shut up!" Brian turned on the light in his room, and he was shocked to find that he could still hear the voices, even when it wasn't dark in the room.

What is it?

"*You* tell *me!* I can't find it! I can't find it anywhere!" Brian ran to his bedroom door and threw it open, thinking that he could outrun the voices, thinking that he could swallow his pride and tell his mom and dad about it and they would explain to him exactly what he was hearing; they would explain it all away and then he would never hear the voices again.

Who is it? a soft voice said behind him.

Brian turned around and looked at the figure sleeping in the bed, talking to himself. He walked over for a closer look. The figure in his bed looked exactly like him.

Who is it? said the figure in the bed. *Who is it?*

Brian looked down at his own sleeping face and whispered carefully so as not to awaken himself, "It's me."

Waiting Up for Father

Greg van Eekhout

I hunker in a corner of the castle and watch rain come in through the ceiling, watch it loosen flakes of blood on the stone floor. Rust-colored water runs down the iron grates. It is my blood, given to me by Father, spilled by Father.

I try to sleep on my bed of straw, but the straw is wet and smells of rot, and the smell of rot gives me nightmares. I dream of many graves, from the elaborate marble tombs of dukes and barons to the unhallowed trenches where they plant thieves. All graves are the same. They are cold and lonely places, where greedy worms take sustenance.

Fat drops of water break apart on my flesh, and I rise to find someplace warm, someplace dry. My heart pounds within its vast cavity as I enter Father's bedroom. I am forbidden here. Hundreds of candles radiate shadow-cleansing light like an army of God's angels. I feel heat from the flames and am afraid.

Father's curtained bed is massive, white, silken, brilliant as a sunlit cloud. What might it be like to sleep here, I wonder. What dreams might I have? Dreams like Father's? Dreams of creation? Before I succumb to the temptation to lie down, I turn away and flee the room, plod down darkened halls, return to my dripping straw.

Wet. Stinking. Hard.

That is what I am.

Sometimes Father tests me.

I can read, and he gives me books, and I read them, and he tests me.

"Science. Who was Luigi Galvani?"

The Italian scientist who discovered that electricity can be produced by chemical action.

"Poetry. Name the source. 'Ingrate, he had of me all he could have. I made him just and right, sufficient to have stood, though free to fall.' "

Paradise Lost.

"Anatomy. Name the components of the hindbrain."

Cerebellum. Pons. Metencephalon. Middle cerebellar peduncles . . . I start to say something else, falter, pause.

He arches his eyebrows and waits.

My breathing grows labored. There is something else. I know there is something else!

"You forgot the fourth ventricle," he says.

"I'm sorry, Father," I say.

Showing no emotion, he shakes his head. "I am not your father."

"I'm sorry, Master."

But Father isn't interested in "sorry."

Father is interested only in perfection.

He picks up his knife, ignoring my cries as he cuts open my head.

Breath held in check, I tread through Father's workroom. Here he keeps his knives and saws, his needle and thread. Here he spends days and nights and years, toiling, tinkering, honing; howling his failures and triumphs aloud to no one but himself.

Jars line shelves like delicacies in a shop.

Hands clutch brown water.

Eyes and ears and tongues bob lazily in their containers.

I have seen these things many times in many ways.

But then I find new things in new, clean jars, and I cannot look away. I see hands that are much smaller than mine.

I see smooth, slender arms.

I see a delicate jaw.

I see breasts.

There's more. I find a table on which lies a form under a sheet, and for a while, I contemplate its gentle contours, struck dumb by the shrouded curves and dips and swells.

Trembling, I pinch the corner of the sheet as gently as I can between thumb and forefinger.

If Father finds out I've been here, he will hurt me. He will tear me with his knives. He will rend me with his saws. He will punch holes in my flesh and drain the blood from my body. He will sever my hands, pull out my teeth and eyes. He will put my brain in a jar.

I pull back the sheet.

My flesh is coarse, like rawhide.

Her flesh is white and perfect.

My hair is like unruly wire.

Hers, golden curls of silk.

I am an unworthy son, and Father has replaced me.

It takes Father decades to construct his children.

It takes a mere second to become a monster.

I hunker in a corner of the castle and watch rain come in through the ceiling to wash skin and glass, blood and formaldehyde from my sticky hands. Lightning rips open the sky, and I flinch from the light and noise. Jove is a mean, angry god.

Father is coming home.

And I have been bad.

Wall Art

Shikhar Dixit

Our kind live in the walls. We reside in the lightly textured sheetrock of the interiors of modern houses and drink up the darkness. Others walk between our walls and cast flat planes of darkness on our skins; they sweep away the dirt and wipe the dust from the furniture that has sat too long against our sides. We wait.

In the languorous darkness of late night and early morning, we part from the drywall, the brick or stucco or wallpaper that is our bed, and we live. We make markings on the surface of space and set our decorations precariously on the creaky floorboards so that the others, the day people, the ones just like you, can knock them to the ground when the lights come back on. And that is how we make our art.

You bounced down the stairs that morning, smiling. You had finished loving your spouse and returned to the kitchen to make breakfast, and you knocked over one of our creations. It tumbled like the building blocks your son loves to pile high until they can no longer balance. It stained you. You frowned. The walls around you seemed to squirm with delight. You shrugged in dismissal and returned to your task.

That night we did not come down from the walls, but rather, we waited and shifted like frozen masses in the northern seas. You made love. You laughed. You slept. From the walls, we watched.

The next morning you padded down the carpeted stairs. Your eyes did not shine. No smile graced your features. The walls around you seemed to wriggle in anticipation. You shuddered.

That night we did not come down from the walls, but rather, we watched and raced like sleighs pulled by a dozen huskies across a frozen tundra. You argued gently. You turned away from your spouse. You slept. From the walls, we watched.

The next morning you stomped down the stairs. Your eyes narrowed. The walls around you seemed to bulge malignantly. You covered your face with your hands, whining.

That night we did not come down from the walls, but rather, we watched, and you saw us watching. You screamed. You raged. You slept downstairs. From the walls, we watched.

The next morning you rose from the couch. You smiled once more. You smiled at us. We smiled back.

That night we did not come down from the walls, but rather, we watched. You smiled. You chased. You killed. From the walls, we watched.

The next morning you prowled from the kitchen and into the brisk dawn. You buried the knife. You buried your spouse and son. You spoke to us. We spoke back.

That night we did not come down from the walls, but rather, we talked. You pressed a .38 revolver into your mouth. You pulled the trigger. Then you were among us.

Tonight a new couple arrives. When the darkness comes, we will live. We will again make markings on the surface of space.

Welcome Home

Juleen Brantingham

I rang the doorbell and turned to look down the street, which had changed little in fifteen years. The same overgrown shrubbery concealed shabby old houses. Same potholed street.

No answer. I rang the bell again.

It was my second day back home. I'd only had time to pay Mother's electric bill, get an overdue haircut, and pick up some groceries. Determined to make it as a freelance writer while I cared for my ailing mother, I'd made out a list of topics I might write articles about. It was Mother who suggested the one that caught my interest: an interview with a local woman who collected dolls to give to poor children at Christmas.

The woman's name was Clara Daniels.

Was that a footstep? The woman must be getting on in years, I reminded myself, trying to restrain my impatience.

Clara Daniels was an ugly woman, scarcely larger than a child herself. My friends and I had taunted her, calling her a witch. How cruel children can be. She had sounded so pleased when I phoned to set up this appointment. Seeing that she received recognition for her charity work would be my way of making up for childhood cruelty.

Still no answer. Deciding that the bell must be out of order, I rapped on the door. It swung open at my touch.

"Miss Daniels?" I stepped inside.

The watery light of a gray November day showed a room filled with dolls. They crowded every chair, table, and windowsill; they were lined up on the mantel and the bookcase; there were baby dolls, boy dolls, bride dolls; there were dolls that walk, talk, wet, and spit up.

I had the feeling when I closed the door that all the dolls turned their eyes to look at me.

"I'm back here, dear. Come right on in."

Her voice touched a chord inside me and I shuddered. She had been the bogeyman of my childhood, but always someone viewed from a distance, around a corner, down the street. Had I ever heard her speak before? Might she have come to the house to talk to my parents that time I stuffed a dead cat in her mailbox?

I moved through the front room toward the arch at the back. Beyond it was a dining room table and chairs. Clara Daniels sat in front of the window, the top of her head barely rising above the back of the chair.

My steps slowed. Those rows of frozen doll smiles and blank, icy doll eyes. I shuddered again. Surely the smiles were nasty rather than sweet, those eyes shadowed with malice.

I had been here before.

I broke into a sweat, remembering. After the dead cat incident, after my punishment, I decided to pay back Clara Daniels for getting me into trouble. One day when she was out I'd sneaked in here—

Hours later the police found me wandering the street, dazed, with no idea where I'd been or what had happened.

Whispering. Behind me. I whipped around. The dolls were all in their places, except one. A bride doll I'd brushed against in passing had fallen over. The rustle of her skirts must have been the whisper I'd heard.

"Please step into the light. My eyes aren't what they used to be and I'd like to get a good look at you."

She was sitting at the head of the table, looking the same as the last time I'd seen her—in this very house, terrified out of my wits. She was so short her feet didn't touch the floor; her iron-gray hair was skinned back in a bun; her glasses were so thick I could barely see her eyes; she had short fingers like sausages. In her hands she held bits of what looked like human hair. She was tying knots in it.

Hair the same color as mine.

"Miss Daniels, my name is—"

She gave me a wicked smile. "I know very well who you are, my dear."

Why was she tying knots in my shorn-off hair?

I felt myself shrinking.

Raising her voice, Clara Daniels called out, "Children, come and welcome your new sister."

Behind me I heard whispers and giggles and the sound of hundreds of hard little doll feet scampering across the floor.

Shrinking.

I couldn't move, even to shudder.

The Well

Adam-Troy Castro

On the very last day of a long and prosperous life, as you watch TV beside your wife of fifty years, you suddenly remember the boy you threw down an abandoned well when you were twelve.

It's the only murder you've ever committed, and though the precise details have faded with each passing decade, the memory has a way of peeking out at you at odd moments, like when you're in line at the post office, or filling out forms at the bank. Sometimes you've gone months without thinking of it; other times, like when you're in your big old house surrounded by the laughing figures of your grandchildren, the barriers between you and that one crime disappear. At such moments, sixty years melt away like the last of the winter snow, and you find yourself vividly reliving those last heartbeats at the edge of the well, when your best friend, Jackie, was hanging on for dear life, screaming at you for having pushed him, and you, rather than reach down to pull him up, instead stomped hard on his pathetically clutching fingers.

You still don't know what drove you to it. It was an impulse. A whim. And though it filled you with a savage, unmitigated pleasure that startles you to this very day, it hasn't stopped you from living all the rest of your life as a gentle, loving, law-abiding man.

You think of that, with no small amount of self-satisfaction, and then you drop dead, your heart simply giving out between one beat and the next.

The pit of hell opens up beneath you.

You feel the heat of the open flames, hotter by far than anything you've ever endured: hot enough to instantly burn away all the contentment you've known in your lifetime. You scream and clutch blindly for something to hold on to, something that will prevent you from falling into that terrible place.

You find a handhold: the edge of the pit. Your legs, dangling beneath you, blacken and blister, but they're a thousand miles away. They're not important. What's important is holding on and preventing that inferno from swallowing you whole.

What's important is the dimly glimpsed shape that stirs in the darkness above you. One of your grandchildren, maybe. You scream out: "Please! Please! For God's sake, help me!"

And the child kneels and looks down at you.

It's Jackie.

Who smiles angelically, and says the two words that let you know that you are forever beyond rescue, beyond hope.

"My turn."

Western Moves

Michael Scott Bricker

His father sits motionless in the car seat beside him, while Ricky checks his war paint in the mirror. The makeup is running down Ricky's cheeks, and he wonders how hot the desert is today (certainly above one hundred degrees) and whether his father is still alive.

The Indian stares from a distance. His body catches the sunlight, glows from within.

Ricky wears a gun, a cast-iron Lone Ranger cap pistol with marbled grips. He removes it from the holster, pokes his father with the muzzle.

The Indian moves closer.

It has been hours since the car moved off the road and hit the boulder, and Ricky wonders why nobody has driven by, why the cavalry has not arrived. Dad said that the Chrysler is a good car, that it would take care of them. Ricky liked to watch his father as he pushed buttons on the dashboard, shifting into drive or reverse. It is the Pushbutton Powerflight, one of the modern advances for the new 1956 Chryslers. Ricky wishes that Dad had gotten a high-fidelity long-playing record player for the car, but Dad said that it was an expensive option that didn't work very well. It would have been nice if Ricky could have played his Stan Freberg record on the way to his grandfather's trailer. The ride through the Arizona desert was long and boring. Ricky might have played his Davy Crockett record as well. What would Davy Crockett do if he were stuck in the desert?

The Indian vanishes, then takes shape once again from the heat and dust. He stands in front of the car, tomahawk in hand, staring, waiting.

Cowboys do not put on war paint. Indians rarely carry guns. Before leaving for Grandfather's trailer, Ricky could not decide whether to be a cowboy or an Indian. Cowboys are good shots, but Indians can ride horses better. Ricky knows that he is a bad shot. He wishes he knew how to use a bow and arrow. Guns can go off so easily. Using a bow and arrow takes skill.

The Indian sits on the hood, looks through the windshield.

Ricky opens the door, gets out, walks around the car. The heat is making him dizzy. The wind kicks up sand, blinds him. He coughs. His tongue is swollen. Ricky wipes his eyes, drops his gun. He opens the driver's door, but it is difficult because his hands hurt so bad.

The Indian sneaks up behind Ricky, raises his tomahawk.

Blood is never red in the movies. It is on the door, the seat, the window. Ricky wishes that he had never seen the gun, that he had not taken it from Dad's desk, slipped it under his jacket. Sunlight reflects from Dad's gun. It is still on the car seat where it has fallen. Ricky's Lone Ranger gun is a good one, but Dad's is better. It is so big and heavy, so real. Dad did not pay attention to Ricky as he took the big gun from beneath his jacket as they drove. He talked about the last family picnic as Ricky held the gun with both hands, as he played with the hammer, as he pulled the trigger with two fingers. When the explosion came, everything changed.

Ricky does not want to be a cowboy; he wishes Dad had kept his big gun locked up like Mom had told him to. He unbuckles his gun belt, drops it on the sand by his Lone Ranger gun. The heat makes him so weak that he falls to his knees. He feels the burning sun on the back of his neck, then everything begins to grow dark.

The Indian puts his hand on Ricky's shoulder, brings down the tomahawk . . .

White Beauty

Cynthia Ward

I smell the blood of a virgin, nothing so pure and fine in all the world. I advance through the forest, my horn parting branches; soft oak and prickling pine leaves caress my white flanks. I scent men, their rank, anxious sweat, but still I advance, to the shadowed edge of a glade. I see an image such as men celebrate in art: a beautiful girl seated beneath a leaf-crowned oak, her golden hair loose as befits an unwed lass. She is clad with maidenly modesty, in a brightly colored wool kirtle that hides her legs to the crossed ankles; her lap invites. Though I cannot see them, I know the men wait in the oak boughs above her, holding a net.

These mortals think me a base animal, no wiser than their slave horses. I am supernatural, white, and beautiful; they know I am as much a creature of Heaven as the angels, though angels live not upon the earth. Yet I am nothing more than prey in the eyes of men, a brute beast to be slain and robbed of my horn.

I step into the glade, and my pricked ears catch the sharply drawn breaths of the hidden men, the frightened gasp of the waiting virgin. But she settles herself with determination. She knows I will not harm her. I am helpless with devotion.

I advance on cloven hooves of purest white, and lower my head to her lap. She cries out in alarm that gives way to a sharp, possessive pleasure, and reaches up to embrace the perfect arch of my neck.

Her cry rises and shatters as my horn enters her gut.

The men scream with disbelief and horror, struck motionless by the witness of their eyes. I have time to feed, my horn blushing pink, the color deepening quickly to heart's-blood red.

The men release the net. Fools! I have done the unthinkable, yet still they believe me a stupid beast. My sharp hooves and horn slice hemp strands as easily as damascene steel parts silk thread. But the men have not waited to see whether their net would hold me; already they leap from their boughs. With a toss of my head I slice one man open in midplummet and trample the others beneath my hooves. They fight to survive, and their crude knives and spears break on my beautiful hide. Why do they never realize a supernatural being is not a cow to be led to slaughter? In their terror they shriek blasphemies, and I slow the pace of my hooves that they may not be silenced too soon.

No mortals have ever captured a unicorn, yet they refuse to understand. They look upon my white beauty and think of heaven. They fantasize that my horn must be a pure ivory spiral which, when powdered, will create fantastic medicines and effect miraculous cures; they never dream it is a blade keener than any Damascus sword; it is a hollow serpent-fang to draw forth the maiden's blood that sustains me.

One man screams, "Satanspawn!" before my hoof crushes his skull. This crude peasant comes closer than most, but does not realize that my Lord has not yet sired His Son. Though not an angel, I am one of those immortals who Fell with my Lord in the age before Adam.

Men know the unicorn did not ride upon the waters in Noah's Ark; they never wonder how I could have survived if I were naught but a beast.

The men are all dead now, their souls stained by their blasphemous last words—and the girl still lives. I have done my work well. I return my horn to the virgin's belly, entering through the same wound, and finish drawing her blood and life into myself. Those chaste maidens who resist my Lord's temptations to debauchery are my prey. Those mortal females who emulate the Mother of our enemy are righteously slain, pierced through the virgin womb.

The White Lady of the I-70 Overpass

Linda J. Dunn

Tina stood near the bridge, watching and waiting. It would be soon now, very soon. She could already hear their voices as they carried their ammunition to the overpass.

Gary said, "I don't think we should do this, Bob."

"What's the matter?" Bob asked. "Scared?"

Gary shrugged. "No—yes. I'm afraid we might hurt somebody."

"Don't worry," Bob said. "We're not dropping ten-pound rocks on the cars. We're just going to sprinkle a little gravel on the windshields. Ain't nobody gonna get killed. We'll just spook 'em. That's all. Come on. It'll be fun."

"I don't know. I think—" Whatever Gary thought was left unsaid as the fog cleared and Tina stepped forward. The moon was full tonight and she smiled as she walked toward them. Everything would be all right now.

The boys looked up and their faces turned deathly white before they screamed and ran away.

Tina looked below as a new blue station wagon drove under the overpass.

My mother's car.

Tina felt her body shimmer and fade away. The haunting was over. She was free.

Gary sat up in bed, sweat running down his forehead as he choked back a scream.

"Are you all right?" Tina asked.

He nodded. "That same nightmare again."

"I really wish you'd tell me about it."

Gary sighed and lay down again. "It's weird. I just keep dreaming about something that happened years ago. Only different. Horribly different."

"Can you describe it?"

Gary shivered as the moonlight cast pale shadows in the bedroom.

"I dreamed I went to the overpass on Halloween with Bob. We were going to throw gravel off the overpass on cars driving under it."

"Gary! That's a terrible thing to do. People—"

"I know. Relax. We didn't do it." He paused and took a deep breath. "I told you the road near here is haunted. Remember? That there's a white lady—?"

Tina laughed. "Every place seems to have a legend of a female ghost dressed in white. You'd think the ghosts would have a little more variety in their clothing. Why not red or blue—?"

"It's not a joke." Gary shook his head. "Bob and I both saw it that night and we ran. Neither one of us ever went there at night again."

"It was probably a patch of fog or some trick of light."

"No." He hesitated a moment before adding: "We both saw her. This ghost was real."

Gary turned toward her. "In the dream, Bob and I go to the bridge but the ghost never shows up. Instead, we throw some gravel off at the first set of headlights we see approaching."

He paused and sighed. "The driver loses control and crashes into a ditch. A woman staggers out of the car a few moments later, covered with blood and crying. Her little girl's dead."

Tears rolled down his cheeks and his voice shook as he added, "And then I see the girl's face for the first time." He stared at Tina for a long moment before adding: "It's you."

Tina closed her eyes and remembered. It all came flooding back like it happened yesterday. Gary's dream was the way it really happened.

She wasn't here. She hadn't lived long enough to be here.

Tina held Gary tightly in her arms until he fell asleep again, then she got out of bed and walked to the window. The security light illuminated the old station wagon she'd bought from her parents. How was it in one piece now? It had crashed. She had died. How could she and the car both be here when she should be cold in a grave and the car in some junk yard?

Tina turned and looked toward the road. That lonely strip and overpass near their house had always haunted her. Now she knew why and she knew what she had to do.

She slipped on her robe and tennis shoes and walked out the door. As light fog closed around her, she walked up the hill toward the overpass.

Tina stood near the bridge, watching and waiting. It would be soon now, very soon. She could already hear their voices as they carried their ammunition to the overpass.

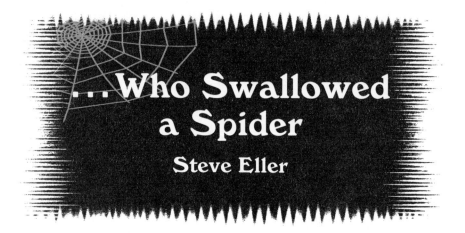

...Who Swallowed a Spider

Steve Eller

Nana set her cross-stitching down and rubbed her throbbing knuckles. The orange thread of the grinning jack-o'-lantern gleamed in the dreary morning light. She ate another spoonful of Cheerios.

She smiled, gazing at the dark spiderwebs stitched around the pumpkin. Her model was the fragile web spanning her windowpanes. She glanced up at the delicate whorls, the shimmering light tangled in the silver strands. But the spider was gone.

"Oh my."

Nana brushed the curtains back, searching for the creature. Nowhere. Her fingers twisted the tattered fringe of her apron as her eyes skittered around the room.

Absently, she ate more cereal. As she swallowed, it dawned on her. She'd eaten the spider. Her stomach fluttered like a moth against a screen door. She dropped the spoon, wringing her hands.

"Oh dear. I don't know how this could've happened. Muffin's supposed to keep the bugs out. Muffin! Come here, you lazy cat!"

Muffin remained where she was, silent beneath a faded wooden cross in the backyard.

Nana pushed the bowl away and lifted the cross-stitch hoop. She scowled, concentrating on back-stitching the pumpkin's single tooth. Her mind wandered, and she started humming a tune. Softly, the words rose to her lips.

". . . who swallowed a spider . . . wriggled and jiggled and tickled inside her . . ."

The material tumbled from her gnarled hands. A spider was in her belly! Her heart hammered beneath the stained gingham of her dress.

"Tom will know what to do. Tom! Just like a man! Probably off sneaking a drink when I need him."

On the mantel, Tom's smile raised crinkles at the edges of his eyes, half-shaded beneath his hat brim. The frame around his face was tarnished. The picture had been taken only days before he'd died in a trench near Somme.

Nana dumped her cereal into the sink. The spigot whistled, and water swirled down the drain. She searched for a drowned body among the tiny tan rings. Nothing.

The screen door slammed as she stepped out onto the porch. Flakes of paint fell to the faded floorboards, a miniature snowstorm. She lowered herself into a chair and began to rock.

Nana felt a tickle. Down there. It was the spider. Alive. Creeping. She laid a trembling hand across her middle, feeling for the movement, as she had done when she was with child.

"Where is that young 'un? Off playing somewhere, and me needing help."

Nana didn't sleep the night her baby was conceived. Come morning, Tom would be off to the war. She lay awake, holding her snoring man in her arms.

The child came too early. She cried in hollow pain, her mind far away at the end. She never saw her womenfolk bundle the still, silent body in bloody sheets and take it away. She never knew where it was buried.

The sun was setting. Nana felt the cool evening breeze against her cheeks. She rose from the creaking chair and went into the house. After changing into her nightshirt, she splashed water on her face. But she felt no urge to use the toilet. The spider was working, she realized. Spinning webs inside her, catching her food for itself.

The spider couldn't stay! But how to make it leave? Drink a lot of milk in the hopes that it would be washed away? But spiders have sticky feet and can hold fast. Eat a whole kettle of oatmeal and push it out? It would just spin more webs, and the food would bloat her like a balloon. But she couldn't leave it in there! What if it lived a long time? What if it laid eggs in her belly?

She felt the creature crawling inside her, its feet flowing like fingertips tapping a tabletop. Panic scurried in her chest like a raccoon in a trash can. Her vision blurred. She grew light-headed and tumbled to the floor.

The wood was cool against her cheek. She tried to lift herself but couldn't. All she could do was roll to one side and curl up like a baby. The spider had sapped her strength.

She saw the wicker basket beneath the sink. She had woven it herself, to hold her crochet things. She pulled it closer.

"Why are you never here when I need you, Tom?"

The spider had to go. Now. She lifted the scissors from the basket.

And a slender silver needle, trailing black thread. Nana opened the
scissors, and pressed one point against the pale skin of her stomach.

Why We Fear the Dark

Brian McNaughton

Eep?" I repeated.

"Ypres," Dogman said, and spelled it. "The Brits called it
Wipers in the First War. Most of them probably got killed then."

"The cats?"

"No, the cultists. The people who. . . . You ever read Blackwood's
Ancient Sorceries?"

"Yeah, I think so." Keep the perp talking, first rule of police procedure.

"It was based on the history of Ypres," Dogman said. "In the Middle Ages, the people were accused of cat-worship, so one day a year
they flung cats off the cathedral. Only it was probably still worship.
Ritual sacrifice of a god."

Moog stood on the brake. I grabbed his arm before he could unclip
the shotgun under the dashboard.

"Give me a minute alone with this guy, Sarge. Please."

"You and him and the shotgun?"

"That's the idea." I never noticed what a nasty smile Trooper
Moog had. Great. Alone at midnight in the pine barrens with *two*
loonies.

I said, "They were *cats*, Trooper. It was nothing you wouldn't see
in a slaughterhouse. If we ate cats."

No. It was worse. Probably the most sadistic mess I'd ever walked
into. But you had to keep your sense of perspective.

"If he hadn't taken a shot at us," I said, "he would be looking at
minor misdemeanors."

"He took a shot at *me*," Moog said.

"I missed," Dogman said.

"I won't," Moog said.

"Drive, Trooper." On a sudden hunch I asked Dogman, "Why'd you shoot at Moog? You think he's a cat-worshipper?"

"The gun went off."

"You got any other cat-worshippers buried in your basement?"

"They change," Dogman said. "If you dig up my yard, you'll only find cats."

Hoo boy. Mental note: dig up his yard. "That's interesting. When they kill a werewolf in the movies, it changes to a person."

"That's just superstition," said Dogman, the supreme rationalist. "If there is a reason, it's because a werewolf is supposedly a person to start with. Cat-people are the opposite."

"So . . . all those cats in your house, they were *people* when you killed them?"

"Sometimes it's hard to tell. Did you know we all come from Africa?"

"I'm Flemish," Moog spat.

"Way back, I mean. And in the same place where humans evolved, at the same time, a special sort of cat evolved. Scientists believe it developed the way it did to prey on us."

It was hard to keep a straight face while flashing on Sylvester Pussycat chasing Raquel Welch, cavegirl. I said, "A killer kitty-cat?"

"I mean *cat*, generically. Big. And *specialized*, the ideal man-killer. It's why we still fear the dark, when it could see. Being so specialized, it may have been able to read our minds, hypnotize us, control our thoughts, who knows?"

"Yeah, but we won," I said. "Where is it today?"

"Where, indeed?"

"So you believe—Moog!"

He swerved, and I saw a bright light. No sound, no impact, just a red flash.

I woke up hearing crickets. The burst radiator hissed. Noisy place, when all I wanted was to sleep.

Two shotgun-blasts squelched that idea. I was alone in the car. I figured Dogman had just been shot while trying to escape.

I squeezed out into the ditch and staggered up to the road. I was bleeding, and some parts would hurt like hell later.

I was almost knocked down by the slipstream of a semi. When it passed, I saw a figure with a shotgun across the road.

"Hey, Trooper!" I shouted.

"I don't know where he is," Dogman called back.

"Oh, Jesus!" Before I had my automatic out, Dogman tossed the shotgun to the middle of the road.

With my eyes on the suspect as I crossed, I stepped in something. The truck driver had seen the wreck and was backing up. By his lights I saw the fresh flat remains of an animal. A large cat, maybe.

"How did you fire the shotgun in handcuffs?" I asked Dogman.

"Your friend shot at *me*. I just picked up the gun when it came flying my way."

"You mean, he got hit by the semi?" I called. "Moog!"

Dogman clammed up after that. Since he hadn't killed any people that we knew of, he was committed to a state hospital only briefly. He's out now, probably pursuing his mission.

We never did find Moog's body, but the barrens are vast, full of bogs and quicksand. The case would puzzle me less if, beside the car, I hadn't found his neatly folded uniform.

Wild Animals

Phyllis Eisenstein

The raccoons came to the Keithleys' front porch every night, the whole family, mama, papa, and three little ones. They came right up to the door and scratched at it as if they wanted to get in.

"That's what we get for buying a house in the country," said Jack Keithley. He was looking out the window that faced the porch, and he was smiling. Wild animals on his property, he thought. To a man who had lived in city apartments all his life, it was wonderful.

Amanda pulled three-year-old Jeremy away from the screen door. He was just tall enough to reach the handle, and he obviously wanted to go out and make friends with the raccoons. "No, darling," she said, hoisting him into her arms. "You mustn't play with them. They might bite you." And to Jack: "Maybe we should get a dog. To keep them away."

He shook his head. "A dog might hurt them."

Amanda nudged the inner door shut with her knee. "Then put another latch on the screen. A high one."

Jack did that, and Jeremy stayed inside when the raccoons scratched.

They never came by day. Jack thought they probably slept in the daytime, in a hollow tree or a burrow somewhere. The Franklins across the road said the raccoons had visited them for a couple of weeks before the Keithleys moved in. They suggested that if Jack and his family ignored the animals, they would eventually go away.

Not wanting that to happen, Jack started leaving food for them.

And so mama, papa, and their three raccoon babies would all happily crunch dry dog food for half an hour every evening while Jack and Jeremy sat by the window and watched them. Amanda didn't join the watching, having—she said—better things to do. But she did stick her head through the kitchen door now and then, to check on her men. After the raccoons finished their meal and ambled off, she and Jack would tuck Jeremy into bed and cuddle up together in front of the TV.

That was what they had done, one summer evening, when the windows and the inner front door were open to a cool breeze, and the screen door was firmly latched. They were cuddled up comfortably when, over the sound of the television, they heard a small noise. At first Jack thought it was the raccoons, though two visits in one night was unusual. Then the noise came again and he got up to see what it was.

He found one of the lower corners of the screen slit raggedly and rolled back, making a space just big enough for a three-year-old to slip through.

He half turned toward the boy's room. "Jeremy?" he said.

Amanda was already running down the hall.

Jack didn't wait for her scream. He was out the door.

In the spill of light from the house, he could see the boy a dozen yards away, sitting on the grass, surrounded by raccoons. He was laughing.

Jack made himself slow down. He caught Amanda by the arm when she would have rushed past him, and he forced her to walk as slowly as he did. He didn't want to frighten the raccoons into biting his son. "Jeremy," he called softly. "Come to Daddy."

But Jeremy still laughed, and though Jack and Amanda were barely six feet away, the raccoons stood their ground.

And then, as Jack was reaching down for Jeremy, he saw that his arms, his own long muscular arms, were changing, shrinking, sprouting thick fur. He saw the grass loom close and felt his clothing suddenly swamp him. He struggled to free himself from the entangling fabric, and realized Amanda was doing the same, her banded tail twitching frantically.

Five people now stood tall and naked in the grass, a man, a woman, and three children. The woman caught the smallest child up in her arms and ran for the house. The others followed her, and the screen door and the inner door both banged shut behind them.

Jack trotted to the porch and crouched there uncertainly. He looked back at Amanda; she was gently closing her sharp-toothed jaws around the neck of the small furry bundle that was Jeremy. A moment later she carried him off into the night, toward some hollow tree, some burrow, somewhere.

But Jack stayed, scratching at the door again and again.

The next day, the people in the house got a dog.

A Wild Hair

Tim Waggoner

Wayne didn't see the small black hair floating in his beer until it was too late to avoid swallowing it.

He slammed the mug down, gagging.

"What's wrong?" His buddy Ken leaned across the table, his face full of concern.

Wayne waved him away. "I'm fine." He opened and closed his mouth a couple times, then felt around with his tongue, hoping he'd find the hair so he could spit it out. Nothing.

Ken hovered over him, uncertain. "What? Was there something wrong with the beer? You want me to get the waitress?"

Wayne shook his head quickly. The last thing he wanted was to have the waitress come over. He didn't want to look at her hair and picture one of the strands falling from her head, wafting gently through the air, only to make a tiny splash as it landed in his beer.

Forget it, he told himself. *It's nothing. Just a hair. A little extra protein, that's all.*

The itching began later that night when Wayne was trying to get to sleep. It started off as a mild irritation in his stomach, but the feeling intensified until it was almost painful. And then, deep within his gut, came the first tickle. The merest hint of sensation, like being lightly touched with just the tip of a feather. Then again, only a bit stronger.

He slept naked, and when he removed the covers, he made a horrifying discovery. There was a little tuft of black hair just below his belly button.

Wayne, while not especially hirsute, had his fair share of body hair, but nothing like this. This was far blacker than his hair, and it stuck out from his belly a good inch, maybe more. And it seemed to rise from the center of the itching.

He wanted to leap out of bed and rush to the bathroom, grab a pair of scissors, and cut off these . . . these invaders. But a heaviness came over his limbs then and he found his eyes closing. The itching was still there, but it seemed distant now, not quite so irritating. And then he was asleep.

And as he slept, hair continued to sprout.

Wayne awoke with a terrible case of dry mouth. *Probably from the beer last night*, he thought. He was warm, too warm. He threw off the covers. *Must have left the thermostat on too high.*

He wasn't sure what time it was, but it was still dark. He rolled over to check his digital alarm clock, but its gently glowing blue numbers were nowhere to be seen.

Maybe the power had gone out or the damn thing was on the blink. Wayne didn't care. All he cared about was getting a drink of water. His tongue felt like it was covered with . . . fur.

Omigod.

Trembling, he reached a hand to his face and found it covered with thick, shaggy hair. He fought to keep panic at bay as he felt himself all over—chest, arms, legs. He was completely covered, head to toe.

He reached over to his nightstand and, with furry fingers, clicked the light on.

Nothing.

What? Was this broken too? He clicked it a few more times before he realized that the light wasn't broken. He couldn't see.

It's the hair. It's in your eyes, that's all. Just brush it away and everything will be okay.

He tried. He pushed the thick layer of hair over his eyes aside, but the darkness remained.

That's when Wayne realized he didn't have eyes anymore.

He bolted out of bed, trying unsuccessfully to scream through a throat clogged thick with hair.

With hands outstretched to feel his way, he made it through the bedroom door and into the hallway before a massive tremor ran through his body. Wayne fell in on himself and collapsed to the carpet, now nothing more than a huge pile of hair.

The pile remained motionless for a time. And then, when they were strong enough, the hairs inched away, one by one, in search of new hosts.

Windshield
Adam-Troy Castro

The flies and gnats may hit your windshield one at a time, but you never notice the carnage while it's happening: no, that little revelation waits until that special moment, four or five hours into your drive, when your eyes refocus, and you realize you've been viewing the world through a film of shattered bodies.

You must have passed through a swarm, sometime recently; the little black specks dot your windshield by the dozens. They were alive, until they encountered you. Then they died. It was that simple, that clean. In that moment, you offered them no warning, no portent, no opportunity to get out of your way, not even any chance to demonstrate bravery or cowardice or stoic dignity in the face of certain death. You just passed among them, a vast, unstoppable force of nature, hurtling through their tiny world on a mission far beyond their understanding, and wielding enough force to render everything they were entirely irrelevant. To the insects, you were greater than Death, greater than God. You were Armageddon, in the form of a late-model Toyota Corolla. And when you activate the windshield washers, bearing their unrecognizable corpses away from your line of vision, it's like summoning the biblical flood that washes their world clean.

Thirty seconds later, another black spot appears on your windshield. You don't even notice. Why should you? It's an insect. It's nothing. It's beneath your notice. Its death isn't even worth thinking about. After all, it didn't notice either. It didn't even see you coming.

Of course, in the fleeting instant of life still left to all of us, you don't notice much of anything either. Oh, it does get a little darker outside, but not any more than it does whenever the sun passes behind a cloud. And you do feel a certain ominous pressure building in your ears, but that's also common enough. Even if, for some reason, you chose this particular moment to look up at the sky, you might—repeat, might—have enough time to register a blackness deeper than anything you've ever seen, hurtling toward everything on the planet with a force capable of destroying everything we've ever been . . . but it is upon us long before anybody, facing the sky or not, has a chance to truly register what's coming.

The end of the world is too sudden to notice.

Which is, of course, only fair.

And when the rumbles cease, the agent of our destruction has to brush our shattered unmourned residue to one side, so it can still see where it's going . . .

Winter Solstice

L. S. Silverthorne

The longest night of the year had already clawed the pale sun from the sky, and the December moon gleamed bone-white through the evergreens as night prowled the winter solstice. "You should have waited until morning," said Emily, her angry voice misting. Her boots crunched against the hard-packed snow.

"But we didn't," Kyle snapped, and shifted his backpack.

"They told us not to go out without snow chains, but you know better, don't you, Kyle? You always know more than everyone else."

Kyle felt his face flush. He clenched his hands in his stiff, snow-wet gloves. Emily was always right—after something bad happened.

"I would have bought the snow chains for the car if you hadn't insisted on buying that damned ski outfit." She had whined about going on the ski trip, then about not being able to fly, and finally about everything else that had gone wrong over the past five years. When they got married, he told himself she would mellow with age. Like cabernet turning to vinegar.

She wagged a magenta glove at him. "My ski suit has nothing to do with you getting us stuck in the snow. You're always blaming me!"

"It's too damned cold to argue," said Kyle, his voice weary.

"It's too damned cold to be out in the snow," Emily shouted, her voice echoing across the dark wilderness. "And it's too damned cold to walk to Whitefish! We should have stayed with the car."

He hated how shrill her voice got when she was angry.

"We're close enough to walk," he said with a snarl, his boots slamming against the snow. "By morning, we would have frozen to death. This is the longest night of the year, or have you forgotten that?" The crunch of the snow sounded like the crushing of bones.

She whirled around, her magenta glove poking him in the chest. "No, I most certainly have not forgotten that! I haven't forgotten that my feet are frozen and that there's no road for miles! You're going to get me killed, Kyle."

He brushed her hand away. "There's an old cabin somewhere near here—by a pond."

"Oh, good," she sneered. "Maybe I'll go ice skating since it's so warm out."

"We can build a fire and survive the night, unless you'd prefer hypothermia?" He didn't know how that would be possible with all her hot air getting trapped in that expensive snow suit.

Furious, she kicked at the snow and turned back toward the silvery stretch of moonlight leading through the evergreens.

Something screeched behind them. Emily lurched and froze in midstride. Kyle whirled around, scanning the line of trees.

"Kyle," Emily whispered, the syllables sharp and shrill. "What was that?"

"Hell if I know," he muttered.

A loud crash reverberated around them. He felt Emily's hands clutching his sleeve.

"Sounds like heavy snow broke a branch," he said.

"Or a grizzly bear!"

"Run!" he shouted.

Kyle pushed her toward the trees as the sound of crunching snow reverberated behind him. He prodded her forward.

"It could be a grizzly. Don't stop running!"

"I—I can't breathe!" She threw herself against a tree, but he shoved her forward. "I can't run anymore!"

Ahead, moonlight glistened across ice, and a rickety cabin hunkered beside the patch of frozen water. Kyle tripped and plunged into the snow.

Again, something screeched.

"My ankle!" He winced, clutching his leg. "Run!" He motioned her toward the pond. "Hurry!"

"Across the ice?"

"A grizzly won't follow you onto ice. Hurry!"

He had expected her to at least protest leaving him behind, but not Emily. She had to save herself first. If only she had proved him wrong.

Emily turned her back on him, running across the pond. She stopped when the horrible, wrenching sound of cracking ice ripped through the night.

"Kyle, the ice!" she shrieked. "It's breaking! Help me!"

She dropped through the ice and struggled against the frigid water. Her magenta arms flailed against the slick ice until the icy water finally pulled her under.

Kyle stood up as a hawk screeched again. The sound of breaking tree limbs crackled like gunfire around him. A magenta glove floated for a moment and then sank into the dark water.

He started back the way he had come. If she had ever bothered to listen to him (or had grown up here), she would have known that grizzlies hibernate in the winter. Reaching into his backpack, he removed four sets of snow chains. They would get him up to Whitefish by morning.

Wired for Fear

Lawrence C. Connolly

No turning back now, thought Walt as he stood in the light of a cloud-streaked moon and fixed his gaze on the place that Sam Whipple had called the screaming house. Walt turned and glanced back at the rumbling car. A passenger-side window whirred down. Sam Whipple leaned out and said, "Now do you believe?"

Walt believed all right. He believed that Sam had done the right thing by failing to take Eddy Min's $100 bet. Walt, however, wasn't about to admit defeat. He had laughed too loudly at Sam's refusal to accept the $100 challenge, and he had been far too cocky when Min turned and said, "Maybe you want to take the bet. How about it? Are you brave enough to spend a night in the screaming house?"

Walt tried looking nonchalant as he glanced back at the rumbling car. Another window whirred down. Min leaned out and said, "You having second thoughts, brave boy?"

Giving an indifferent shrug, Walt hefted his sleeping bag onto his shoulder and started toward the house.

Eddy Min's car revved and sped away toward the graffiti-covered cliffs of Lookout Hill.

Walt walked toward the house. As he walked, the house began to scream.

Walt froze, cocked an ear, and listened to the muffled screams. *It's only the wind,* he thought.

But there was no wind.

Walt considered running back to the road and hitching a ride to campus. But he couldn't do that. By now, Eddy Min and the others were watching his every move from the crest of Lookout Hill. Walt, not wanting to give them the satisfaction of seeing him run, forced himself to climb the creaking steps that led to the house's front porch. As he reached the door, the screams came again, louder this time, but in the loudness Walt detected something odd. At first he thought it must be his imagination, but as he stepped into the darkened hall beyond the front door, he heard another sound beneath the screams. He heard the faint sound of something *hissing*.

Walt knew the sound!

He ran into the house, following the hissing noise until he found a giant speaker lying hidden in the shadow of the stairs. A wire ran along the base of the wall. The wire led to an old reel-to-reel tape player in the kitchen. Walt hit the off switch. The house fell silent.

Suddenly, Walt understood. Min and Sam had set him up, but tape hiss had foiled their scheme. "Good thing they didn't use a CD player," said Walt.

And then something totally unexpected happened.

The house answered: "CD? What is a CD?" The voice was low. The accent was strange—German with a twist of Russian.

Walt turned. Behind him stood a man in soiled evening clothes. The man's face was a translucent, maggoty white. Dirt clung to the creases of his rumpled jacket.

"Oh my God!" said Walt.

"No," said the man. "I'm no one's god." The man smiled. Thin lips rolled back from tapering fangs. "I installed that machine to keep people away. You see, I travel nights."

Walt tried saying something, but when he opened his mouth, the only sound that came out was a frightened gurgle.

"The tape is on a timer," said the man. "It runs intermittently. Anyone who gets close enough to hear it runs like hell and never comes back. For years it has worked. But now it seems I have a problem."

Walt shook his head. "No," he managed to say. "No problem!" He tried stepping toward the long hall that led to the front door. "I'm out of here."

"But you'll tell your friends about my little secret, and then everyone will come when I'm away."

"No," said Walt. "Trust me. No one'll come. Please, mister!"

But it was too late. The man was no longer a mister. He raised his arms, drew his feet from the floor, and flew toward Walt's neck. The air hissed with the beat of leathery wings, and this time, when the hissing stopped, the screaming continued.

Without Barbara on New Year's Eve

Tom Piccirilli

Without Barbara on New Year's Eve I stand in the ruins of reality, chewing the inside of my cheek until my mouth fills with blood. Her voice is tinny but clear over the receiver lying on the kitchen floor, hissing at me in that husky whisper that once aroused me. "How could you have done this, you son of a bitch? God, I hate you. I hate you!"

The cord is wound tightly four times around Mrs. Grumchek's neck, and her tongue protrudes comically from between her meaty purple lips. Gouts of snow batter the windows. Sweat slides down my collar and bathes my chest. I liked the old woman and used to shovel her driveway after her children—a couple of my high school buddies—moved away. I hope she'll come to my service.

Barbara continues shrieking over the phone. "Kill yourself! Stop it, end it!"

Retreating through the broken back door, I cross Mrs. Grumchek's yard past the snowmen and igloos of her grandchildren, ice spires crackling against the trees. Music is blaring around the neighborhood.

Next door is the Solomons' house, the dainty wife and preacher who used to tip me well when I delivered the Sunday paper. Preacher always took a shine to me at youth Bible studies because I could remember his sermons and helped out with the younger kids. The back door is unlocked, and I knock lightly before stepping inside. Preacher's on the phone talking to his sister, Becky, animatedly swinging to and fro in his rocking chair while his wife crochets a woolen scarf. They each turn to stare calmly at me. I smile kindly and she says, "Yes?"

It feels like blood vessels have broken in my eyes. I grab the phone from his hand and hang it up. It rings immediately. My breath hitches awfully but I find just enough air. "Answer it."

"Answer what?" he asks.

I grab the receiver and listen to Barbara and Mrs. Grumchek arguing loudly. Barbara's voice is shrill and bitter and corkscrews through my stomach. "Who in the hell are you to tell me how I should feel about that schmuck? That maniac?"

"He's a good boy," the blessed Mrs. Grumchek says. I could almost go back and kiss those purple lips. "Give him another chance. You'll be able to work things out this time, trust me."

"Trust you, my ass. He's a nut, anybody can see that! Can't *you?*"

Sadness pervades Mrs. Grumchek's voice. "Ah, it's natural to be foolish when one is so young, but you shouldn't be so cold-hearted, dear."

"Shut the hell up, you freaky broad."

I reach and snatch something off the Solomons' television set: a bowling trophy, I think. Preacher suddenly erupts from his chair, springing forward, struggling ridiculously without truly grabbing or hitting me, saying, "Wha'? Wha'?" His wife continues to sit and watch us, awaiting revelation.

I tell them, "Barbara's left me. You've got to convince her to come back. I need her. Please, you have to help me."

Mrs. Solomon says, "It'll be all right, honey," in a timid voice as Preacher quacks and grunts, trying to get both his trophy and his phone back. The trophy has a nicely balanced weight, a solid oak base. It takes only a minute before we're finished in here. I sit in the warm, wet chair and listen intently to the other end of the line, where I hear doors opening and shutting, dishes being thrown against the wall.

"You've got to be kidding me!" Barbara shrieks.

"You shouldn't have left the boy," Preacher says. "He has a good soul. Sometimes it's hard to forgive our loved ones when they make mistakes. You must not dwell on the sins of the past."

"How can you think that when he's murdered you!"

Mrs. Solomon's knitting needles clack together. "You've hurt him terribly, Barbara."

"Me hurt him? I'm the one with the broken neck!"

More dishes smash. "So young, so young to be so cold," Mrs. Grumchek moans, on the verge of tears.

"All of you get out of here!"

I hang up and grin. Barbara sounds as if she's starting to come around to her senses a little. I leave the Solomon house and find myself wandering the slushy streets of the neighborhood, peering into the homes of those who are my friends or used to be my friends. Revelers are drinking heavily and blowing party horns, their laughter sending twinges through my skull. I head for the nearest house. Barbara is one stubborn woman. I'm going to need a lot more help.

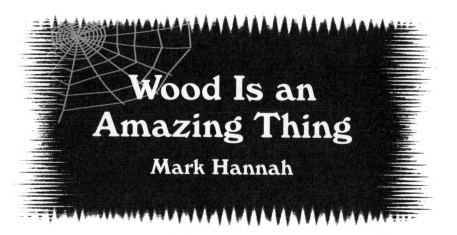

Wood Is an Amazing Thing

Mark Hannah

Wood is an amazing thing.
>*Whack!*
>The fact that it comes from living things.
Whack!
The different colors and grains of the wood. Soft, light maple. Dark, ironlike teak.
Whack!
And so many uses. Houses, furniture, toys.
Whack!
And bedroom doors.
Whack!
Steel is an amazing thing.
Whack!
The fact that something so hard and cold and shiny comes from the earth.
Whack!
And it can be honed to such a sharp edge.
Whack!
Like on an ax.
Whack!
And steel axes have so many uses.
Whack!
Clearing farmland, fighting fires, making campsites.
Whack!
And chopping through bedroom doors.
Whack!
The way the wood splits and splinters and shatters under the force and weight of the razor-sharp edge of the ax.
Whack!

Human flesh and bone is an amazing thing.
Whack!

Worms

Paul Smith and Thomas Smith

I never seen so many worms in my life."

That phrase would have been a cliché in any other circumstance. But not tonight. Worms covered every single inch of ground for ten feet or more in every direction like a carpet of tiny fingers, all pointing and beckoning in a thousand different directions, yet consumed with the same purpose.

"Quit worryin' about the dad-blasted worms," Luke said, "and hold that light still."

Moss Cooper held the flashlight with both hands, but he didn't take his eyes off the worms at his feet. "Look, maybe this don't spook you none, Luke, but I gotta tell you, I'm beginnin' to think this ain't such a hot idea."

Luke Potter, tall and thin with a fringe of greasy black hair around his bald head, stopped working on the lock long enough to punch Moss's shoulder. "Moss, get your mind back on what you're doin', and maybe we can finish up sooner and go home. I ain't exactly havin' a picnic here myself." Luke went back to work on the lock.

One good twist and he felt the big spring move. He pulled the door hard. The mechanism popped, and a minute later the two men were in the Harrell family mausoleum.

"Luke, I don't like this one bit. I'll go back out and watch in case somebody comes through." Moss Cooper had never backed down from a fight in his life, no matter what the odds. But tonight he was scared. And in the dank mausoleum he could feel the worms under his feet. Could feel them become pulp under his work boots.

Luke was not particularly brave, and he had backed down from many fights in his time. But he was greedy. And everybody in town knew old man Harrell and his clan had been buried wearing their best jewelry. The gold rings and diamond necklaces alone were worth a small fortune. And it seemed a shame for them to just sit there year after year going to waste.

"Moss," Luke said, anger edging his voice, "there ain't nobody comin' out here and you know it. We've watched this place every night for three weeks, and there ain't nothin' but corpses out here. Nothin' nor nobody." He turned toward the plate marking A. J. Harrell's final resting place. "Now hand me that ratchet wrench and—"

Moss grabbed Luke's elbow. "Luke, listen."

Luke pulled away. "Listen to what. I don't hear—"

Moss cut him off again. The darkness smelled like mold and . . . something else. "Listen, Luke. Hear that rustlin'?"

Luke cocked his head, turned, and stepped on a fistful of worms. "Yeah, I heard it. Listen." Luke stomped the worms under his feet. Then he grabbed Moss by the shoulders. "We're walkin' in worms, you dunce. Of course you hear noises. You're squashin' worms."

"Yeah, I know," Moss said. "And that's another thing. Where did all them worms come from? Tell me that Luke. Where did all them worms come from?"

Luke shook his head. "It's been rainin' for a day and a half, you dope. The water flushed them out. Now give me a hand with this wrench."

The center bolt which held the bronze plate over the opening of the casket popped and groaned under the pressure of the wrench, the first wrench to touch the bolt since A. J. Harrell was buried there thirty years earlier. Moss and Luke loosened their grip, and the bolt continued to pop and groan.

The center of the plate bulged as the two men stood there, frozen in their tracks. The worms, a living carpet of tiny fingers, waved and beckoned. Each was consumed with a single purpose.

Luke's stomach lurched and rolled an instant before the brass plate exploded into a thousand fragments. His heart stopped a split second after he saw what destroyed the three-hundred-pound marker.

Moss was not so lucky.

The nightmare had no eyes. There were huge bands encircling its body, and the maw that opened not two feet away from Moss was easily three feet across. Moss whimpered once and suffocated when a tidal wave of worms was projected from the toothless mouth.

* * *

I've never seen so many worms in my life," said Chief Arthur Stone as he made his way toward the mausoleum. A uniformed policeman waved him toward the open door.

"Chief, we've got something here you better see."

You Can't Teach an Old Town New Tricks

David Niall Wilson

Timmy and his family had just moved into the neighborhood, and it sucked. Being in a new place on Halloween took all the fun out of it. Timmy had been out combing the neighborhood for hours, collecting here and there, standing on the street corners and watching the other kids and their parents walk by. He didn't know any of them, and seeing them all out having so much fun just thickened the cloud of gloom that had settled over him.

Just as he was reaching the outer limits of the boundaries his parents had set, he saw the house. If there hadn't been a light shining dimly in the downstairs window, he'd have been certain the place was deserted. It was the only street that wasn't clogged with laughing, running kids and their parents—kids he didn't know. What the heck.

He turned down the shadowy lane toward the old house. It was as if he'd entered a new world. The sounds of the holiday unfolding around him died away, and he was swallowed by the huge, brooding shade of the trees and the flickering light that he could now see coming from lit candles within the downstairs window. Now *this* was cool. This was what Halloween was *supposed* to be like.

The front doors loomed high above him. Timmy had never seen a house with one door that large, let alone a pair of them. They were wooden, and in the center of each was a huge brass knocker. Feeling a chill of anticipation, he reached up and grabbed the one on the left, pulling it back and letting it fall forward with a heavy thud.

There was no immediate answer from within, but he felt eyes on the back of his neck, and, turning his eyes upward to the upper-story windows, he just managed to glimpse a curtain being hastily shoved closed. Then the door opened. No one was there, it just creaked open. He couldn't decide whether to pee in his pants or run. He did neither; he went inside.

There were oil lamps lit along a wide hall, and he followed them toward the back of the home. Small clouds of dust rose where he stepped, making his nose itch, but he didn't sneeze. He was beginning to think he didn't want to know who lived there, though he couldn't quite make himself turn back.

He finally exited the hall into a large ballroom. He heard the tinkle of laughter, and wisping shadows slid by just beyond his vision. He turned slowly, scanning the room wildly.

There was no answer, but the laughter increased in volume, and a soft luminescence began to suffuse the air, sharpening the shadows and lining the walls and windows in silver. Timmy's heart was slamming against his chest, and he began to back away slowly, still looking around but seeing nothing. He stopped as he reached the doorway through which he'd entered. He couldn't leave without one last look around, though somehow he knew he'd see nothing.

Suddenly he was not alone. He felt the tickle of something against his cheek. The air was scented with flowers, and the lights were suddenly brighter. He turned in terror, wanting to be home, to be anywhere but where he was, and he staggered back into the hall, out of the now bright lights and away from the haunting strains of music and laughter that filled the air.

He fell to his knees in the dust, choking as it rose to fill his lungs and trying to scrabble back to his feet. There was no light. There was no sound. Only the door, swinging loose on a single hinge, beckoning him back to the streets and home. He started to turn back, to take a final look, then, shuddering, he bolted for the door. He didn't stop until he was nearly on his own front step.

Not really knowing why, he paused beneath the streetlight in front of his house and opened his treat bag. All he could do was stare. On top of the Snickers bars and Reese's cups, an apple sat, wrapped carefully in some sort of cellophane and coated in thick brown caramel. A small tag dangled from where the plastic was tied together with twine, and he grabbed it, reading quickly:

HAPPY ALL HALLOWS' EVE

He turned and looked at the now empty streets, then back at the note, and he smiled. Somehow he felt like he'd been welcomed home.

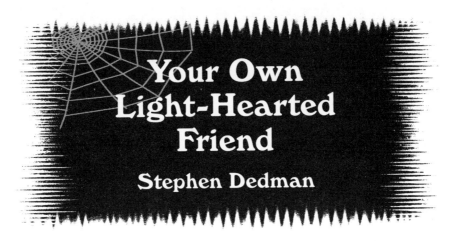

Your Own Light-Hearted Friend

Stephen Dedman

Don't believe everything you may have heard. There wasn't even a hint of fog that night, and hardly a cloud: I could see Mars as clearly as you can see this page, a red pinprick like a first sign of some disease. It was September, and still quite warm; all the usual stenches were nourished by the heat, waiting for rain to wash them into the Thames and poison the rest of the world. A rat was eating a dead cat: His ancestors will rule the world in a thousand years, and welcome to it. What could be worse than this? The garbage, the pubs and abattoirs, the mouldy straw and gin, the brothels and alleys and gutters, all the sin and sickness. Poverty and despair and all the cheap substitutes for life. Music—real music—would be as foreign here as she.

Words failed me, sometimes, even when the music followed me, filling my ears like poison. I call her "she," though she cannot be human, and I doubt that she could be a woman. A machine, maybe—no, *probably*, almost certainly. A machine crafted to look like a woman, as invisible as everyone else in the East End.

London is not my city either, and I would have left these streets to the rats and animals were it not for *her*, were it not for the certainty that *she* will not be satisfied with such refuse. *She* was . . . where is *she* from? Mars? Another planet? The future? Other times, other worlds; let us say another world. Does it matter? *She* can survive here, and learn . . .

I was stared at from dark corners, but not recognised: These people, these children born of children, they have a name for me that they sing in the daylight and in the reeking crowds, as though they were not afraid. They did not see the knife in my sleeve, stolen surgical steel, taken from the bag of a doctor who flees from madness to drunkenness in a squalid surgery nearby, surviving on abortions and stitching up rat-bites and knife-slashes, and who has probably woken on several mornings with bloody hands wondering, How?

Perhaps they thought me a detective—delicious irony; there were many of them here, that September. They are looking for me and they do not know *her;* is *she* amused by their ignorance?

Can *she* laugh? Laughter is for humans.

I am an educated man, perhaps the only one for miles. I have read the works of Poe, and Shelley, and Verne, and Bierce. I have seen van Kempelen's machine. I know what can be done, what horrors the future will bring. I know that the universe does not belong to man, that the world will not be ours forever. I know what must be done; I will save you if I can. I know what *she* . . .

Who sent *her* here (the rats, maybe?), and what will follow *her?* An invading army of pseudo-humans? Fighting machines? Strange new plagues? Scientists? Missionaries?

She was waiting for a man, waiting for me, in the shadows, in a doorway in Mitre Square.

Don't believe everything you may have heard. *She* didn't scream or run: too drunk. All was still cold still cold steel colder still now

but it wasn't *her.* For the second time that night, the fourth time in a month, it wasn't *her,* and I became angry, slashing madly, and

cold steel cold steel steal away now cold she's cold she's still and it still isn't her

The papers, next morning, tell me her name was Eddowes. Before that it was Stride. Chapman. Nicholls. None of them was her, but I didn't stop didn't stop until I was sure I cut I cut until I could see, could be sure, that there weren't any wires.

They have a new name for me, too. Someone with a very strange sense of humour has sent Scotland Yard a letter in red ink, and signed himself Jack the Ripper.

Next time it *will* be her. I'd stake my life on it.

You're Dead

Dawn Dunn

Enveloped in fog, we waited anxiously at the entrance to St. Mary's Bridge for even a glimpse of the woman in white. Both newspapers had run articles about her, despite criticism from a number of local skeptics, who said it was unprofessional for them to give credence to the rumors of a ghost. The critics referred to her as a teenage fantasy, though no less than five city policemen claimed to have seen her.

The air was chilly but not unpleasant. Richard and I crouched near the steps to the hundred-year-old bridge. We held hands, our breaths coming in sharp, excited gasps from laughing and kissing. We were far from teenagers, but the idea of an actual ghost still intrigued us and made us cling to each other with both lust and trepidation.

The newspapers had contacted several parapsychologists, whose theories included the idea that a ghost is the psychic energy of someone who has died tragically but not yet realized he or she is dead. It was Richard's notion that we should be the ones to tell her. We had no real reason for doing it except the excitement of seeing a true ghost, who had now become famous within the city, and because the story struck us as sad. Neither of us had any experience in psychology or dealing with supernatural phenomena, so I suppose it was not only a foolish but a vain enterprise. I almost hoped she wouldn't come.

Most of the sightings had occurred between midnight and three in the morning, so we had arrived promptly at a quarter to midnight. We huddled close to keep warm and soon found ourselves doing more than huddling. The dense fog hid us from any other lurkers, and by two o'clock we felt secure in our solitude.

I was nearly asleep, my face pressed snugly against Richard's neck, both my passion and curiosity waning, when I suddenly felt him tense. "There she is," he whispered. His voice contained an odd, unearthly quality. Then I saw her myself.

She didn't look even remotely alive, but more like a glaring, pulsating mass in the grotesque shape of a woman caught in a perpetual state of melting. Richard seemed drawn to her. I felt him moving away from me. I wanted to pull him back but was too terrified to move. Neither of us uttered the fateful words "You're dead."

Instead, I watched as she pulled him to her, as she took my lover in her arms and kissed him, until I could see her lips shining through the back of his head. The cement all around us grew increasingly warm and turned a deep orange hue. My face reddened with shame, my guts turning to water, as I sat and did nothing. I stared, mesmerized, as they climbed the rail together, their bodies entwined, glowing like fallen meteors, arcing down into the swiftly flowing river, shining like headlights through the murky haze, then abruptly dimming.

I sat shivering, I'll never know how long, before I realized it was over. The cement had long cooled, though my face still felt hot.

Dawn broke over the river as I numbly watched them fish his body, burned and bloated beyond recognition, out of the muddy water. Tears cut a translucent path down my cheeks as my lover's ruined corpse passed near enough for me to touch, but never once did I say, "You're dead."

Acknowledgments

Grateful acknowledgment is made to the following for permission to publish their copyrighted material.